FIVE OF A KIND

OTHER BOOKS BY REX STOUT

Novels

Nero Wolfe Mysteries

Tecumseh Fox Mysteries

Mysteries

REX STOUT

FIVE OF A KIND

The Third Nero Wolfe Omnibus

1961

THE VIKING PRESS

New York

PUBLISHED IN 1961 BY THE VIKING PRESS, INC.
625 MADISON AVENUE, NEW YORK 22, N.Y.

PUBLISHED SIMULTANEOUSLY IN CANADA BY
THE MACMILLAN COMPANY OF CANADA LIMITED

LIBRARY OF CONGRESS CATALOG CARD NUMBER: 61-10444

PRINTED IN THE UNITED STATES OF AMERICA

CONTENTS

THE RUBBER BAND

I

I THREW down the magazine section of the Sunday *Times* and yawned. I looked at Nero Wolfe and yawned again. "Is this bird, S. J. Woolf, any relation of yours?"

Wolfe, letting fly with a dart and getting a king of clubs, paid no attention to me.

I went on. "I suppose not, since he spells it different. The reason I ask, an idea just raced madly into my bean. Why wouldn't it be good for business if this S. J. Woolf did a picture of you and an article for the *Times?* God knows you're full of material." I took time out to grin, considering Wolfe's size in the gross or physical aspect, and left the grin on as Wolfe grunted, stooping to pick up a dart he had dropped.

I resumed. "You couldn't beat it for publicity, and as for class it's Mount Everest. This guy Woolf only hits the high spots. I've been reading his pieces for years, and there's been Einstein and the Prince of Wales and Babe Ruth and three Presidents of the United States (O say, can you see very little in the White House) and the King of Siam and similar grandeur. His idea seems to be, champions only. That seems to let you in, and strange as it may appear, I'm not kidding, I really mean it. Among our extended circle there must be a couple of eminent gazabos that know him and would slip him the notion."

Wolfe still paid no attention to me. As a matter of fact, I didn't expect him to, since he was busy taking exercise. He had recently got the impression that he weighed too much—which was about the same as if the Atlantic Ocean formed the opinion that it was too wet—and so had added a new item to his daily routine. Since he only went outdoors for things like earthquakes and holocausts, he was rarely guilty of movement except when he was up on the roof with Horstmann and the orchids, from nine to eleven in the morning and four to six in the afternoon, and there was no provision there for pole vaulting. Hence the new apparatus for a daily workout, which was a beaut. It was scheduled from 3:45 to 4:00 P.M. There was a board about two feet square, faced with cork, with a large circle marked on it, and twenty-six radii and a smaller inner circle, outlined with fine wire, divided the circle's area into fifty-two sections. Each section had its symbol painted on it, and together they made up a deck of cards; the bull's-eye, a small disk in the center, was the Joker. There was also a supply of darts, cute little things about four inches long and weighing a couple of ounces, made of wood and feathers with a metal needle-point. The idea was to hang the board up on the wall, stand off ten or fifteen feet, hurl five darts at it and make a poker hand, with the Joker wild. Then you went and pulled the darts out, and hurled them over again. Then you went and pulled . . .

Obviously, it was pretty darned exciting. What I mean to convey is, it would have been a swell game for a little girls' kindergarten class; no self-respecting boy over six months of age would have wasted much time with it. Since my only excuse for writing this is to relate the facts of one of Nero Wolfe's cases, and since I take that trouble only where murder was involved, it may be supposed that I tell about that poker-dart game because later on one of the darts was dipped in poison and used to pink a guy with. Nothing doing. No one ever suffered any injury from those darts that I know of, except me. Over a period of two months Nero Wolfe nicked me for a little worse than eighty-five bucks, playing draw with the Joker and deuces wild, at two bits a go. There was no chance of getting any real accuracy with it, it was mostly luck.

Anyhow, when Wolfe decided he weighed too much, that was what he got. He called the darts javelins. When I found my losses were approaching the century point I decided to stop humoring him, and quit the thing cold, telling him that my doctor had warned me against athlete's heart. Wolfe kept on with his exercise, and by now, this Sunday I'm telling about, he had got so he could stick the Joker twice out of five shots.

I said, "It would be a good number. You rate it. You admit yourself that you're a genius. It would get us a lot of new clients. We could take on a permanent staff—"

One of the darts slipped out of Wolfe's handful, dropped to the floor, and rolled to my feet. Wolfe stood and looked at me. I knew what he wanted, I knew he hated to stoop, but stooping was the only really violent part of that game and I figured he needed the exercise. I sat tight.

Wolfe opened his eyes at me. "I have noticed Mr. Woolf's drawings. They are technically excellent."

The son of a gun was trying to bribe me to pick up his dart by pretending to be interested in what I had said. I thought to myself, All right, but you'll pay for it, let's just see how long you'll stand there and stay interested. I picked up the magazine section and opened it to the article, and observed briskly, "This is one of his best. Have you seen it? It's about some Englishman that's over here on a government mission—wait—it tells here—"

I found it and read aloud: "'It is not known whether the Marquis of Clivers is empowered to discuss military and naval arrangements in the Far

East; all that has been disclosed is his intention to make a final disposition of the question of spheres of economic influence. That is why, after a week of conferences in Washington with the Departments of State and Commerce, he has come to New York for an indefinite stay to consult with financial and industrial leaders. More and more clearly it is being realized in government circles that the only satisfactory and permanent basis for peace in the Orient is the removal of the present causes of economic friction.'"

I nodded at Wolfe. "You get it? Spheres of economic influence. The same thing that bothered Al Capone and Dutch Schultz. Look where economic friction landed them."

Wolfe nodded back. "Thank you, Archie. Thank you very much for explaining it to me. Now if you—"

I hurried on. "Wait, it gets lots more interesting than that." I glanced down the page. "In the picture he looks like a ruler of men—you know, like a master barber or a head waiter, you know the type. It goes on to tell how much he knows about spheres and influences, and his record in the war— he commanded a brigade and he got decorated four times—a noble lord and all prettied up with decorations like a store front—I say three cheers and let us drink to the King, gentlemen! You understand, sir, I'm just summarizing."

"Yes, Archie. Thank you."

Wolfe sounded grim. I took a breath. "Don't mention it. But the really interesting part is where it tells about his character and his private life. He's a great gardener. He prunes his own roses! At least it says so, but it's almost too much to swallow. Then it goes on, new paragraph. 'While it would be an exaggeration to call the marquis an eccentric, in many ways he fails to conform to the conventional conception of a British peer, probably due in some measure to the fact that in his younger days—he is now sixty-four—he spent many years, in various activities, in Australia, South America, and the western part of the United States. He is a nephew of the ninth marquis, and succeeded to the title in 1905, when his uncle and two cousins perished in the sinking of the *Rotania* off the African coast. But under any circumstances he would be an extraordinary person, and his idiosyncrasies, as he is pleased to call them, are definitely his own.

" 'He never shoots animals or birds, though he owns some of the best shooting in Scotland—yet he is a famous expert with a pistol and always carries one. Owning a fine stable, he has not been on a horse for fifteen years. He never eats anything between luncheon and dinner, which in England barely misses the aspect of treason. He has never seen a cricket match. Possessing more than a dozen automobiles, he does not know how to drive one. He is an excellent poker player and has popularized the game among a circle of his friends. He is passionately fond of croquet, derides golf as a "corrupter of social decency," and keeps an American cook at the manor of Pokendam for the purpose of making pumpkin pie. On his frequent trips to the Continent he never fails to take with him—'"

There was no point in going on, so I stopped. I had lost my audience. As he stood facing me Wolfe's eyes had gradually narrowed into slits; and of a sudden he opened his hand and turned it palm down to let the remaining darts fall to the floor, where they rolled in all directions; and Wolfe walked from the room without a word. I heard him in the hall, in the elevator, getting in and banging the door to. Of course he had the excuse that it was four o'clock, his regular time for going to the plant rooms.

I could have left the darts for Fritz to pick up later, but there was no sense in me getting childish just because Wolfe did. So I tore off the sheet of the magazine section I had been reading from, with the picture of the Marquis of Clivers in the center, fastened it to the corkboard with a couple of thumbtacks, gathered up the darts, stood off fifteen feet, and let fly. One of the darts got the marquis in the nose, another in his left eye, two of them in his neck, and the last one missed him by an inch. He was well pinned. Pretty good shooting, I thought, as I went for my hat to venture out to a movie, not knowing then that before he left our city the marquis would treat us to an exhibition of much better shooting with a quite different weapon, nor that on that sheet of newspaper which I had pinned to the corkboard was a bit of information that would prove to be fairly useful in Nero Wolfe's professional consideration of a sudden and violent death.

II

FOR THE next day, Monday, October 7, my memo pad showed two appointments. Neither displayed any promise of being either lucrative or exciting. The first one, down for 3:30 in the afternoon, was with a guy named Anthony D. Perry. He was a tycoon, a director of the Metropolitan Trust Company, the bank we did business with, and president of the Seaboard Products Corporation—one of those vague firms occupying six floors of a big skyscraper and selling annually a billion dollars' worth of something nobody ever actually saw, like soy beans or powdered coconut shells or dried llama's hoofs. As I say, Perry was a tycoon; he presided at meetings and was appointed on Mayor's Committees and that kind of hooey. Wolfe had handled a couple of investigations for him in previous years—nothing of any importance. We didn't know what was on his mind this time; he had telephoned for an appointment.

The second appointment was for 6 P.M. It was a funny one, but we often had funny ones. Saturday morning, October 5, a female voice had phoned that she wanted to see Nero Wolfe. I said okay. She said, yes, but she wanted to bring someone with her who would not arrive in New York until Monday morning, and she would be busy all day, so could they come at 5:30. I said, no, but they could come at six, picking up a pencil to put down her name. But she wasn't divulging it; she said she would bring her name along with her, and they would arrive at six sharp, and it was very important. It wasn't much of a date, but I put it on the memo pad and hoped she would turn up, for she had the kind of voice that makes you want to observe it in the flesh.

Anthony D. Perry was there on the dot at 3:30. Fritz answered the door and brought him to the office. Wolfe was at his desk drinking beer. I sat in my corner and scowled at the probability that Perry was going to ask us to follow the scent of some competitor suspected of unfair trade practices, as he had before, and I did not regard that as a treat. But this time he had a different kind of difficulty, though it was nothing to make your blood run cold. He asked after our health, including me because he was democratic, inquired politely regarding the orchids, and then hitched his chair up and smiled at Wolfe as one man of affairs to another.

"I came to see you, Mr. Wolfe, instead of asking you to call on me, for two reasons. First, because I know you refuse to leave your home to call on anyone whatever, and, second, because the errand I want you to undertake is private and confidential."

Wolfe nodded. "Either would have sufficed, sir. And the errand?"

"Is, as I say, confidential." Perry cleared his throat, glancing at me as I opened up my notebook. "I suppose Mr. . . ."

"Goodwin." Wolfe poured a glass of beer. "Mr. Goodwin's discretion reaches to infinity. Anything too confidential for him would find me deaf."

"Very well. I want to engage you for a delicate investigation, one that will require most careful handling. It is in connection with an unfortunate situation that has arisen in our executive offices." Perry cleared his throat again. "I fear that a young woman, one of our employees, is going to suffer an injustice—a victim of circumstances—unless something is done about it."

He paused. Wolfe said, "But, Mr. Perry, surely, as the directing head of your corporation, you are its fount of justice—or its opposite?"

Perry smiled. "Not absolutely. At best, a constitutional monarch. Let me explain. Our executive offices are on the thirty-second floor of our building—the Seaboard Building. We have some thirty private offices on that floor, officers of the corporation, department heads, and so on. Last Friday one of the officers had in his desk a sum of money in currency, a fairly large sum, which disappeared under circumstances which led him to suspect that it had been taken by—by the employee I spoke of. It was not reported to me until Saturday morning. The officer requested immediate action, but I could not bring myself to believe the employee guilty. She has been—that is, she has always seemed to merit the most complete confidence. In spite of appearances . . ."

He halted. Wolfe asked, "And you wish us to learn the truth of the matter?"

"Yes. Of course. That's what I want." Perry cleared his throat. "But I also want you to consider her record of probity and faithful service. And I would like to ask you, in discussing the affair with Mr. Muir, to give him to understand that you have been engaged to handle it as you would any investigation of a similar nature. In addition, I wish your reports to be made to me personally."

"I see." Wolfe's eyes were half closed. "It seems a little complex. I would like to avoid any possibility of misunderstanding. Let us make it clear. You are not asking us to discover an arrangement of evidence that will demonstrate the employee's guilt. Nor are you engaging us to devise satisfactory proof of her innocence. You merely want us to find out the truth."

"Yes," Perry smiled. "But I hope and believe that the truth will be her innocence."

"As it may be. And who is to be our client, you or the Seaboard Products Corporation?"

"Why . . . that hadn't occurred to me. The corporation, I should think. That would be best."

"Good." Wolfe looked at me. "If you please, Archie." He leaned back in his chair, twined his fingers at the peak of his middle mound, and closed his eyes.

I whirled on my swivel, with my notebook. "First the money, Mr. Perry. How much?"

"Thirty thousand dollars. In hundred-dollar bills."

"Egad. Payroll?"

"No." He hesitated. "Well, yes, call it payroll."

"It would be better if we knew about it."

"Is it necessary?"

"Not necessary. Just better. The more we know the less we have to find out."

"Well . . . since it is understood this is strictly confidential . . . you know of course that in connection with our business we need certain privileges in certain foreign countries. In our dealings with the representatives of those countries we sometimes need to employ cash sums."

"Okay. This Mr. Muir you mentioned, he's the paymaster?"

"Mr. Ramsey Muir is the senior vice-president of the corporation. He usually handles such contacts. On this occasion, last Friday, he had a luncheon appointment with a gentleman from Washington. The gentleman missed his train and telephoned that he would come on a later one, arriving at our office at five-thirty. He did so. When the moment arrived for Mr. Muir to open the drawer of his desk, the money was gone. He was of course greatly embarrassed."

"Yeah. When had he put it there?"

An interruption came from Wolfe. He moved to get upright in his chair, then to arise from it. He looked down at Perry. "You will excuse me, sir. It is the hour for my prescribed exercise and, following that, attention to my plants. If it would amuse you, when you have finished with Mr. Goodwin, to come to the roof and look at them, I would be pleased to have you." He moved halfway to the door, and turned. "It would be advisable, I think, for Mr. Goodwin to make a preliminary investigation before we definitely undertake the commission you offer us. It appears to present complexities. Good day, sir." He went on out. The poker-dart board had been moved to his bedroom that morning, it being a business day with appointments.

"A cautious man." Perry smiled at me. "Of course his exceptional ability permits him to afford it."

I saw Perry was sore by the color above his cheekbones. I said, "Yeah. When had he put it there?"

"What? Oh, to be sure. The money had been brought from the bank and placed in Mr. Muir's desk that morning, but he had looked in the drawer when he returned from lunch, around three o'clock, and saw it intact. At five-thirty it was gone."

"Was he there all the time?"

"Oh, no. He was in and out. He was with me in my office for twenty minutes or so. He went once to the toilet. For over half an hour, from four to until about four-forty, he was in the directors' room, conferring with other officers and Mr. Savage, our public relations counsel."

"Was the drawer locked?"

"No."

"Then anyone might have lifted it."

Perry shook his head. "The executive reception clerk is at a desk with a view of the entire corridor; that's her job, to know where everyone is all the time, to facilitate interviews. She knows who went in Muir's room, and when."

"Who did?"

"Five people. An office boy with correspondence, another vice-president of the company, Muir's stenographer, Clara Fox, and myself."

"Let's eliminate. I suppose you didn't take it?"

"No. I almost wish I had. When the office boy was there, Muir was there too. The vice-president, Mr. Arbuthnot, is out of the question. As for Muir's stenographer, she was still there when the loss was discovered—most of the others had gone home—and she insisted that Muir search her belongings. She has a little room next to Muir's, and had not been out of it except to enter his room. Besides, he has had her for eleven years, and trusts her."

"Which leaves Clara Fox."

"Yes." Perry cleared his throat. "Clara Fox is our cable clerk—a most responsible position. She translates and decodes all cables and telegrams. She went to Muir's office around a quarter after four, during his absence, with a decoded message, and waited there while Muir's stenographer went to her own room to type a copy of it."

"Has she been with you long?"

"Three years. A little over."

"Did she know the money was there?"

"She probably knew it was in Muir's office. Two days previously she had handled a cablegram giving instructions for the payment."

"But you think she didn't take it."

Perry opened his mouth and closed it again. I put the eye on him. He didn't look as if he was really undecided; it seemed rather that he was hunting for the right words. I waited and looked him over. He had clever, careful, blue-gray eyes, a good jaw but a little too square for comfort, hair no grayer than it should be considering he must have been over sixty, a high forehead with a mole on the right temple, and a well-kept healthy skin. Not a layout that you would ordinarily regard as hideous, but at that moment I wasn't observing it with great favor, because it seemed likely that there was something phony about the pie he was inviting me to stick my finger into; and I give low marks to a guy that asks you to help him work a puzzle and then holds out one of the pieces on you. I don't mind looking for the fly in a client's ointment, but why throw in a bunch of hornets?

Perry finally spoke. "In spite of appearances, I am personally of the opinion that Clara Fox did not take that money. It would be a great shock to me to know that she did, and the proof would have to be unassailable."

"What does she say about it?"

"She hasn't been asked. Nothing has been said, except to Arbuthnot, Miss Vawter—the executive reception clerk—and Muir's stenographer. I may as well tell you, Muir wanted to send for the police this morning, and I restrained him."

"Maybe Miss Vawter took it."

"She has been with us eighteen years. I would sooner suspect myself. Besides, someone is constantly passing in the corridor. If she left her desk even for a minute it would be noticed."

"How old is Clara Fox?"

"Twenty-six."

"Oh. A bit junior, huh? For such a responsible position. Married?"

"No. She is a remarkably competent person."

"Do you know anything of her habits? Does she collect diamonds or frolic with the geegees?"

Perry stared at me. I said, "Does she bet on horse races?"

He frowned. "Not that I know of. I am not personally intimate with her, and I have not had her spied on."

"How much does she get and how do you suppose she spends it?"

"Her salary is thirty-six hundred. So far as I know, she lives sensibly and respectably. She has a small flat somewhere, I believe, and she has a little car—I have seen her driving it. She—I understand she enjoys the theater."

"Uh-huh." I flipped back a page of my notebook and ran my eye over it. "And this Mr. Muir who leaves his drawer unlocked with thirty grand inside—might he have been caught personally with his financial pants down and made use of the money himself?"

Perry smiled and shook his head. "Muir owns some twenty-eight thousand shares of the stock of our corporation, worth over two million dollars at the present market, besides other properties. It was quite usual for him to leave the drawer unlocked under those circumstances."

I glanced at my notebook again, and lifted my shoulders a shade and let them drop negligently, which meant that I was mildly provoked. The thing looked like a mess, possibly a little nasty, with nothing much to be expected in the way of action or profit. The first step, of course, after what Wolfe had said, was for me to go take a look at the thirty-second floor of the Seaboard Building and enter into conversation. But the clock on the wall said 4:20. At six the attractive telephone voice with her out-of-town friend was expected to arrive; I wanted to be there, and I probably wouldn't be if I once got started chasing that thirty grand.

I said to Perry, "Okay. I suppose you'll be at your office in the morning? I'll be there at nine sharp to look things over. I'll want to see most of—"

"Tomorrow morning?" Perry was frowning. "Why not now?"

"I have another appointment."

"Cancel it." The color topped his cheekbones again. "This is urgent. I am one of Wolfe's oldest clients. I took the trouble to come here personally—"

"Sorry, Mr. Perry. Won't tomorrow do? My appointment can't very well be postponed."

"Send someone else."

"There's no one available who could handle it."

"This is outrageous!" Perry jerked up in his chair. "I insist on seeing Wolfe!"

I shook my head. "You know you can't. You know darned well he's eccentric." But then I thought, after all, I've seen worse guys, and he's a client, and maybe he can't help it if he gets on Mayors' Committees, perhaps they nag him. So I got out of my chair and said, "I'll go upstairs and put it up to Wolfe, he's the boss. If he says—"

The door of the office opened. I turned. Fritz came in, walking formal as he always did to announce a caller. But he didn't get to announce this one. The caller came right along, two steps behind Fritz, and I grinned when I saw he was stepping so soft that Fritz didn't know he was there.

Fritz started, "A gentleman to—"

"Yeah, I see him. Okay."

Fritz turned and saw he had been stalked, blinked, and beat it. I went on observing the caller, because he was a specimen. He was about six feet three inches tall, wearing an old blue serge suit with no vest and the sleeves a mile short, carrying a cream-colored ten-gallon hat, with a face that looked as if it had been left out on the fire escape for over half a century, and walking like a combination of a rodeo cowboy and a panther in the zoo.

He announced in a smooth low voice, "My name's Harlan Scovil." He went up to Anthony D. Perry and stared at him with half-shut eyes. Perry moved in his chair and looked annoyed. The caller said, "Are you Mr. Nero Wolfe?"

I butted in, suavely. "Mr. Wolfe is not here. I'm his assistant. I'm engaged with this gentleman. If you'll excuse us . . ."

The caller nodded, and turned to stare again at Perry. "Then who—you ain't Mike Walsh? Hell no, Mike was a runt." He gave Perry up, and glanced around the room, then looked at me. "What do I do now, sit down and hang my hat on my ear?"

I grinned. "Yeah. Try that leather one over there." He panthered for it, and I started for the door, throwing over my shoulder to Perry, "I won't keep you waiting long."

Upstairs, in the plant rooms on the roof, glazed in, where Wolfe kept his ten thousand orchids, I found him in the middle room turning some off-season Oncidiums that were about to bud, while Horstmann fussed around with a pot of charcoal and osmundine. Wolfe, of course, didn't look at me or halt operations; whenever I interrupted him in the plant rooms he pretended he was Joe Louis in his training camp and I was a boy peeking through the fence.

I said, loud so he couldn't also pretend he didn't hear me, "That millionaire downstairs says I've got to go to his office right now and begin looking under the rugs for his thirty grand, and there's an appointment here for six o'clock. I expressed a preference to go tomorrow morning."

Wolfe said, "And if your pencil fell to the floor and you were presented with the alternative of either picking it up or leaving it there, would you also need to consult me about that?"

"He's exasperated."

"So am I."

"He says it's urgent, I'm outrageous, and he's an old client."

"He is probably correct all around. I like particularly the second of his conclusions. Leave me."

"Very well. Another caller just arrived. Name of Harlan Scovil. A weather-beaten plainsman who stared at Anthony D. Perry and said he wasn't Mike Walsh."

Wolfe looked at me. "You expect, I presume, to draw your salary at the end of the month."

"Okay." I wanted to reach out and tip over one of the Oncidiums, but decided it wouldn't be diplomatic, so I faded.

When I got back downstairs Perry was standing in the door of the office with his hat on and his stick in his hand. I told him, "Sorry to keep you waiting."

"Well?"

"It'll have to be tomorrow, Mr. Perry. The appointment can't be postponed. Anyhow, the day's nearly gone, and I couldn't do much. Mr. Wolfe sincerely regrets—"

"All right," Perry snapped. "At nine o'clock, you said?"

"I'll be there on the dot."

"Come to my office."

"Right."

I went and opened the front door for him.

In the office Harlan Scovil sat in the leather chair over by the bookshelves. As, entering, I lamped him from the door, I saw that his head was drooping and he looked tired and old and all in; but at sound of me he jerked up and I caught the bright points of his eyes. I went over and wheeled my chair around to face him.

"You want to see Nero Wolfe?"

He nodded. "That was my idea. Yes, sir."

"Mr. Wolfe will be engaged until six o'clock, and at that time he has another appointment. My name's Archie Goodwin. I'm Mr. Wolfe's confidential assistant. Maybe I could help you?"

"The hell you are." He certainly had a smooth soft voice for his age and bulk and his used-up face. He had his half-shut eyes on me. "Listen, sonny. What sort of a man is this Nero Wolfe?"

I grinned. "A fat man."

He shook his head in slow impatience. "It ain't to the point to tease a steer. You see the kind of man I am. I'm out of my county." His eyes twinkled a little. "Hell, I'm clear over the mountains. Who was that man that was in here when I came?"

"Just a man. A client of Mr. Wolfe's."

"What kind of a client? Anybody ever give him a name?"

"I expect so. Next time you see him, ask him. Is there anything I can do for you?"

"All right, sonny." He nodded. "Naturally I had my suspicions up, seeing any kind of a man here at this time, but you heard me remark that he wasn't Mike Walsh. And God knows he wasn't Vic Lindquist's daughter. Thanks for leaving my ideas free. Could I have a piece of paper? Any kind."

I handed him a sheet of typewriter bond from my desk. He took it and held it in front of him spread on the palms of his hands, bent his head over it, and opened his mouth, and out popped a chew of tobacco the size of a hen's egg. I'm fairly observant, but I hadn't suspected its existence. He wrapped the paper around it, clumsily but thoroughly, got up and took it to the wastebasket, and came back and sat down again. His eyes twinkled at me.

"There seems to be very little spittin' done east of the Mississippi. A swallower like me don't mind, but if John Orcutt was here he wouldn't tolerate it. But you was asking me if there's anything you can do for me. I wish to God I knew. I wish to God there was a man in this town you could let put your saddle on."

I grinned at him. "If you mean an honest man, Mr. Scovil, you must have got an idea from a movie or something. There's just as many honest men here as the other side of the mountains. And just as few. I'm one. I'm so damn honest I often double-cross myself. Nero Wolfe is almost as bad. Go ahead. You must have come here to spill something besides that chew."

With his eyes still on me, he lifted his right hand and drew the back of it slowly across his nostrils from left to right, and then, after a pause, from right to left. He nodded. "I've traveled over two thousand miles, from Hiller County, Wyoming, to come here on an off chance. I sold thirty calves to get the money to come on, and for me nowadays that's a lot of calves. I didn't know till this morning I was going to see any kind of a man called Nero Wolfe. All that is to me is just a name and address on a piece of paper I've got in my pocket. All I knew was I was going to see Mike Walsh and Vic's daughter and Gil's daughter, and I was supposed to be going to see George Rowley, and by God if I see him and what they say is true I'll be able to fix up some fences this winter and get something besides lizards and coyotes inside of 'em. One thing you can tell me anyhow, did you ever hear of any kind of a man called a Marquis of Clivers?"

I nodded. "I've read in the paper about that kind of a man."

"Good for you. I don't read much. One reason, I'm so damn suspicious I don't believe it even if I do read it, so it don't seem worth the trouble. I'm here now because I'm suspicious. I was supposed to come here at six o'clock with the rest of those others, but I had my time on my hands anyhow, so I thought I might as well ride out and take a look. I want to see this Nero Wolfe man. You don't look to me like a man that goes out at night after lambs, but I want to see him. What really made me suspicious was the two daughters. God knows a man is bad enough when you don't know him, but I doubt if you ever could get to know a woman well enough to leave her loose around you. I never really tried, because it didn't ever seem to be worth the trouble." He stopped, and drew the back of his hand across his nostrils again, back and forth, slowly. His eyes twinkled at me. "Naturally, your opinion is that I talk a good deal. That's the truth. It won't hurt you any, and it may even do you good. Out in Wyoming I've been talking to myself like this for thirty years, and by God if I can stand it you can."

It appeared to me that I was going to stand it whether I wanted to or not, but something interfered. The phone rang. I turned to my desk and plucked the receiver, a female voice asked me to hold the wire, and then another voice came at me.

"Goodwin? Anthony D. Perry. I just got back to my office, and you must come here at once. Any appointments you have, cancel them, if there's any damage I'll pay it. The situation here has developed. A taxi will get you here in five minutes."

I love these guys that think the clock stops every time they sneeze. But by the tone of his voice it was a case either of aye, aye, sir, or a plain go to hell, and by nature I'm a courteous man. So I told him okay.

"You'll come at once?"

"I said okay."

I shoved the phone back and turned to the caller.

"I've got to leave you, Mr. Scovil. Urgent business. But if I heard you right, you've been invited here to the six o'clock party, so I'll see you again. Correct?"

He nodded. "But look here, sonny, I wanted to ask you—"

"Sorry, I've got to run." I was on my way. I looked back from the door. "Don't nurse any suspicions about any kind of a man named Nero Wolfe. He's as straight as he is fat. So long."

I went to the kitchen, where Fritz had about nine kinds of herbs spread out on the shredding board all at once, and told him, "I'm going out. Back at six. Leave the door open so you can see the hall. There's an object in the office waiting for a six-o'clock appointment, and if you have any good deeds to spare like offering a man a drink and a plate of cookies, I assure you he is worthy. If Wolfe comes down before I get back, tell him he's there."

Fritz, nibbling a morsel of tarragon, nodded. I went to the hall and snared my hat and beat it.

III

I DIDN'T fool with a taxi, and it wasn't worth while to take the roadster, which as usual was at the curb, and fight to park it. From Wolfe's house in West 35th Street, not far from the Hudson, where he had lived for over twenty years, and I had slept on the same floor with him for eight, it was only a hop, skip, and jump to the new Seaboard Building, in the twenties, also near the river. I hoofed it, considering meanwhile the oddities of my errand. Why had Anthony D. Perry, president of the Seaboard Products Corporation, taken the trouble to come to our office to tell us about an ordinary good clean theft? As the Tel & Tel say in their ads, why not telephone? And if he felt so confident that Clara Fox hadn't done it, did he suspect she was being framed or what? And so on.

Having been in the Seaboard Building before, and even, if you would believe it, in the office of the president himself, I knew my way around. I remembered what the executive reception clerk on the thirty-second floor looked like, and so was expecting no treat in that quarter, and got none. I now knew also that she was called Miss Vawter, and so addressed her, noting that her ears stuck out at about the same angle as three years previously. She was expecting me, and without bothering to pry her thin lips open she waved me to the end of the corridor.

In Perry's office, which was an enormous room furnished in The Office Beautiful style with four big windows giving a sweeping view of the river, there was a gathering waiting for me. I went in and shut the door behind me and looked them over. Perry was seated at his desk with his back to the windows, frowning at his cigar smoke. A bony-looking medium-sized man, with hair somewhat grayer than Perry's, brown eyes too close together, and pointed ears, sat nearby. A woman something over thirty, with a flat nose, who could have got a job as schoolteacher just on her looks, stood at a corner of Perry's desk. She looked as if she might have been doing some crying. In another chair, out a little, another woman sat with her back to me as I entered. On my way approaching Perry I caught a glimpse of her face as I went by, and saw that additional glimpses probably wouldn't hurt me any.

Perry grunted at me. He spoke to the others. "This is the man. Mr. Goodwin, from Nero Wolfe's office." He indicated with nods, in succession, the woman sitting, the one standing, and the man. "Miss Fox. Miss Barish. Mr. Muir."

I nodded around, and looked at Perry. "You said you've got some developments?"

"Yes." He knocked ashes from his cigar, looked at Muir, and then at me. "You know most of the facts, Goodwin. Let's come to the point. When I returned I found that Mr. Muir had called Miss Fox to his office, had accused her of stealing the money, and was questioning her in the presence of Miss Barish. This was contrary to the instructions I had given. He now insists on calling in the police."

Muir spoke to me, smoothly. "You're in on a family quarrel, Mr. Goodwin." He leveled his eyes at Perry. "As I've said, Perry, I accept your instructions on all business matters. This is more personal than business. The money was taken from my desk. I was responsible for it. I know who stole it, I am prepared to swear out a warrant, and I intend to do so."

Perry stared back at him. "Nonsense. I've told you that my authority extends to all the affairs of this office." His tone could have been used to ice a highball. "You may be ready to swear out a warrant and expose yourself to the risk of being sued for false arrest, but I will not permit a vice-president of this corporation to take that risk. I went to the trouble of engaging the best man in New York City, Nero Wolfe, to investigate this. I even took pains that Miss Fox should not know she was suspected before the investigation. I admit that I do not believe she is a thief. That is my opinion. If evidence is uncovered to prove me wrong, then I'm wrong."

"Evidence?" Muir's jaw had tightened. "Uncovered? A clever man like Nero Wolfe might either cover or uncover. No? Depending on what you paid him for."

Perry smiled a controlled smile. "You're an ass, Muir, to say a thing like that. I'm the president of this company, and you're an ass to suggest I might betray its interests, either the most important or the most trivial. Mr. Goodwin heard my conversation with his employer. He can tell you what I engaged him to do."

"No doubt he could tell me what he has been instructed to tell me."

"I'd go easy, Muir." Perry was still smiling. "The kind of insinuations you're making might run into something serious. You shouldn't bark around without considering the chances of starting a real dogfight, and I shouldn't think you'd want a fight over a triviality like this."

"Triviality?" Muir started to tremble. I saw his hand on the chair arm begin to shake, and he gripped the wood. He turned his eyes from Perry onto Clara Fox, sitting a few feet away, and the look in them made it plain why trivialities were out. Of course I didn't know whether he was hating her because she had lifted the thirty grand or because she had stepped on his toe, but from where I stood it looked like something much fancier than either of those. If looks could kill she would have been at least a darned sick woman.

Then he shifted from her to me, and he had to pinch his voice. "I won't ask you to report the conversation you heard, Mr. Goodwin. But of course you've had instructions and hints from Mr. Perry, so you might as well have some from me." He got up, walked around the desk, and stood in front of me. "I presume that an important part of your investigation will be to follow Miss Fox's movements, to learn if possible what she has done with the money. When you see her entering a theater or an expensive restaurant with Mr. Perry, don't suppose she is squandering the money that way. Mr. Perry will be paying. Or if you see Mr. Perry entering her apartment of an evening, it will not be to help her dispose of the evidence. His visit will be for another purpose."

He turned and left the room, neither slow nor fast. He shut the door behind him, softly. I didn't see him, I heard him; I was looking at the others. Miss Barish stared at Miss Fox and turned pale. Perry's only visible reaction was to drop his dead cigar into the ash tray and push the tray away. The first move came from Miss Fox. She stood up.

The idea occurred to me that on account of active emotions she was probably better looking at that moment than she ordinarily was, but even discounting for that there was plenty to go on. In my detached impersonal way I warmed to her completely at exactly that moment when she stood up and looked at Anthony D. Perry. She had brown hair, neither long nor boyish bob, just a swell lot of careless hair, and her eyes were brown too and you could see at a glance that they would never tell you anything except what she wanted them to.

She spoke. "May I go now, Mr. Perry? It's past five o'clock, and I have an appointment."

Perry looked at her with no surprise. Evidently he knew her. He said, "Mr. Goodwin will want to talk with you."

"I know he will. Will the morning do? Am I to come to work tomorrow?"

"Of course. I refer you to Goodwin. He has charge of this now, and the responsibility is his."

I shook my head. "Excuse me, Mr. Perry. Mr. Wolfe said he would decide whether he'd handle this or not after my preliminary investigation. As far as Miss Fox is concerned, tomorrow will suit me fine." I looked at her. "Nine o'clock?"

She nodded. "Not that I have anything to tell you about that money, except that I didn't take it and never saw it. I have told Mr. Perry and Mr. Muir that. I may go then? Good night."

She was perfectly cool and sweet. From the way she was handling her-

self, no one would have supposed she had any notion that she was standing
on a hot spot. She included all of us in her good-night glance, and turned
and walked out as self-possessed as a young doe not knowing that there's
a gun pointed at it and a finger on the trigger.

When the door was shut Perry turned to me briskly. "Where do you want
to start, Goodwin? Would fingerprints around the drawer of Muir's desk
do any good?"

I grinned at him and shook my head. "Only for practice, and I don't
need any. I'd like to have a chat with Muir. He must know it won't do
to have Miss Fox arrested just because she was in his room. Maybe he
thinks he knows where the money is."

Perry said, "Miss Barish is Mr. Muir's secretary."

"Oh." I looked at the woman with the flat nose still standing there. I
said to her, "It was you that typed the cablegram while Miss Fox waited
in Muir's room. Did you notice—"

Perry horned in. "You can talk with Miss Barish later." He glanced at
the clock on the wall, which said 5:20. "Or, if you prefer, you can talk
with her here, now." He shoved his chair back and got up. "If you need
me, I'll be in the directors' room, at the other end. I'm late now, for a
conference. It won't take long. I'll ask Muir to stay, and Miss Vawter also,
in case you want to see her." He had moved around to the front of his
desk, and halted there. "One thing, Goodwin, about Muir. I advise you to
forget his ridiculous outburst. He's jerky and nervous, and the truth is he's
too old for the strain business puts on a man nowadays. Disregard his
nonsense. Well?"

"Sure." I waved a hand. "Let him rave."

Perry frowned at me, nodded, and left the room.

The best chair in sight was the one Perry had just vacated, so I went
around and took it. Miss Barish stood with her shoulders hanging, squeezing
her handkerchief and looking straight at me. I said, friendly, "Move around
and sit down—there, where Muir was. So you're Muir's secretary."

"Yes, sir." She got onto the edge of the chair.

"Been his secretary eleven years."

"Yes, sir."

"Cut out the sir. Okay? I'm not gray-headed. So Muir looked through
your belongings last Friday and didn't find the money?"

Her eyes darkened. "Certainly he didn't find it."

"Right. Did he make a thorough search of your room?"

"I don't know. I don't care if he did."

"Now don't get sore. I don't care either. After you copied the cablegram
and took the original back to Miss Fox in Muir's room, what was she carrying when she left there?"

"She was carrying the cablegram."

"But where did she have the thirty grand, down her sock? Didn't it show?"

Miss Barish compressed her lips to show that she was putting up with me. "I did not see Miss Fox carrying anything except the cablegram. I have told Mr. Muir and Mr. Perry that I did not see Miss Fox carrying anything except the cablegram."

I grinned at her. "And you are now telling Mr. Goodwin that you did not see Miss Fox carrying anything except the cablegram. Check. Are you a friend of Miss Fox's?"

"No. Not a real friend. I don't like her."

"Egad. Why don't you like her?"

"Because she is extremely attractive, and I am homely. Because she has been here only three years and she could be Mr. Perry's private secretary tomorrow if she wanted to, and that is the job I have wanted ever since I came here. Also because she is cleverer than I am."

I looked at Miss Barish more interested, at all the frankness. Deciding to see how far down the frankness went, I popped at her, "How long has Miss Fox been Perry's mistress?"

She went red as a beet. Her eyes dropped, and she shook her head. Finally she looked up at me again, but didn't say anything.

I tried another one. "Then tell me this. How long has Muir been trying to get her away from Perry?"

Her eyes got dark again, and the color stayed. She stared at me a minute, then all at once rose to her feet and stood there squeezing her handkerchief. Her voice trembled a little, but it didn't seem to bother her.

"I don't know whether that's any of your business, Mr. Goodwin, but it's none of mine. Don't you see . . . don't you see how this is a temptation to me? Couldn't I have said I saw her carrying something out of that room?" She squeezed the handkerchief harder. "Well . . . I didn't say it. Don't I have to keep my self-respect? I'll go out of my way too, I don't know anything about it, but I don't believe Clara Fox has ever been anybody's mistress. She wouldn't have to be, she's too clever. I don't know anything about that money either, but if you want to ask me questions to see if I do, go ahead."

I said, "School's out. Go on home. I may want you again in the morning, but I doubt it."

She turned pale as fast as she had turned red. She certainly was a creature of moods. I got up from Perry's chair and walked all the way across the room to open the door and stand and hold it. She went past, still squeezing the handkerchief and mumbling good night to me, and I shut the door.

Feeling for a cigarette and finding I didn't have any, I went back to the windows and stood surveying the view. As I had suspected, the thing wasn't a good clean theft at all, it was some kind of a mess. From the business standpoint, it was obvious that the thing to do was go back and tell Nero Wolfe it was a case of refusing to let the administrative heads of the Seaboard Products Corporation use our office for a washtub to dump their dirty linen in. But what reined me up on that was my professional curiosity about Clara Fox. If sneak thieves came as cool and sweet as that, it was about time I found it out. And if she wasn't one, my instinctive dislike of a frame-up made me hesitate about leaving her parked against a fireplug. I was fairly well disgusted, and got more disgusted, after gazing out of the window for a while, when I felt in my pockets again for a cigarette with no results.

I wandered around The Office Beautiful a little, sightseeing and cogitating, and then went out to the corridor. It was empty. Of course, it was after office hours. All its spacious width and length, there was no traffic, and it was dimmer than it had been when I entered, for no more lights were turned on and it was getting dark outdoors. There were doors along one side, and at the farther end the double doors, closed, of the directors' room. I heard a cough, and turned, and saw Miss Vawter, the executive reception clerk, sitting in the corner under a light with a magazine.

She said in a vinegar voice, "I'm remaining after hours because Mr. Perry said you might want to speak to me."

She was a pain all around. I said, "Please continue remaining. Which is Muir's room?"

She pointed to one of the doors, and I headed for it. I was reaching out for the knob when she screeched at me, "You can't go in there like that! Mr. Muir is out."

I called to her, "Do tell. If you want to interrupt Mr. Perry in his conference, go to the directors' room and give the alarm. I'm investigating."

I went on in, shut the door, found the wall switch, and turned on the lights. As I did so, a door in another wall opened, and Miss Barish appeared. She stood and looked without saying anything.

I observed, "I thought I told you to go home."

"I can't." Her color wasn't working either way. "When Mr. Muir is here I'm not supposed to go until he dismisses me. He is in conference."

"I see. That your room? May I come in?"

She stepped back and I entered. It was a small neat room with one window and the usual stenographic and filing equipment. I let the eyes rove, and then asked her, "Would you mind leaving me here for a minute with the door shut, while you go to Muir's desk and open and close a couple of drawers? I'd like to see how much din it makes."

She said, "I was typing."

"So you were. All right, forget it. Come and show me which drawer the money was in."

She moved ahead of me, led the way to Muir's desk, and pulled open one of the drawers, the second one from the top on the right. There was nothing in it but a stack of envelopes. I reached out and closed it, then opened and closed it again, grinning as I remembered Perry's suggestion about fingerprints. Then I left the desk and strolled around a little. It was just a vice-president's office, smaller and modester than Perry's but still by no means a pigpen. I noticed one detail, or rather three, a little out of the ordinary. There was no portrait of Abraham Lincoln nor replica of the Declaration of Independence on the walls, but there were three different good-sized photographs of three different good-looking women, hanging framed.

I turned to Miss Barish, who was still standing by the desk. "Who are all the handsome ladies?"

"They are Mr. Muir's wives."

"No! Honest to God? Mostly dead?"

"I don't know. None of them is with him now."

"Too bad. It looks like he's sentimental."

She shook her head. "Mr. Muir is a sensual man."

She was having another frank spell. I glanced at my watch. It was a quarter to six, giving me another five minutes, so I thought I might as well use them on her. I opened up, friendly, but although she seemed to be willing to risk a little more chat with me, I didn't really get any facts. All I learned was what I already knew, that she had no reason to suppose that Clara Fox had lifted the jack, and that if there was a frame-up she wasn't in on it. When the five minutes was up I turned to go, and at that moment the door opened and Muir came in.

Seeing us, he stopped, then came on again, to his desk. "You may go, Miss Barish. If you want to talk with me, Goodwin, sit down."

Miss Barish disappeared into her room. I said, "I won't keep you now, Mr. Muir. I suppose you'll be here in the morning?"

"Where else would I be?"

That kind of childishness never riles me. I grinned at the old goat, said, "Okay," and left him.

Outside in the corridor, down a few paces toward the directors' room, a group of four or five men stood talking. I saw Perry was among them, and approached. He saw me and came to meet me.

I said, "Nothing more tonight, Mr. Perry. Let's let Mr. Muir have a chance to cool off. I'll report to Nero Wolfe."

Perry frowned. "He can phone me at my home any time this evening. It's in the book."

"Thanks. I'll tell him."

As I passed Miss Vawter on my way out, still sitting in the corner with her magazine, I said to her out of the side of my mouth, "See you at the Rainbow Room."

IV

Down on the sidewalk the shades of night were not keeping the metropolitan bipeds from the swift completion of their appointed rounds. Striding north toward 35th Street, I let the brain skip from this to that and back again, and decided that the spot Clara Fox was standing on was probably worse than hot, it was sizzling. Had she lit the fire herself? I left that in unfinished business.

I got home just at six o'clock and, knowing that Wolfe wouldn't be down for a few minutes yet, I went to the office to see if the Wyoming wonder had thought of any new suspicions and if his colleagues had shown up. The office was empty. I went through to the front room to see if he had moved his base there, but it was empty too. I beat it to the kitchen. Fritz was there, sitting with his slippers off, reading that newspaper in French. I asked him, "What did you do with him?"

"*Qui? Ah, le monsieur—*" Fritz giggled. "Excuse me, Archie. You mean the gentleman who was waiting."

"Yeah, him."

"He received a telephone call." Fritz leaned over and began pulling on his slippers. "Time already for Mr. Wolfe!"

"He got a phone call here?"

Fritz nodded. "About half an hour after you left. More maybe. Wait till I look." He went to the stand where the kitchen phone extension was kept, and glanced at his memo pad. "That's right. Five-twenty-six. Twenty-six minutes past five."

"Who was it?"

Fritz's brows went up. "Should I know, Archie." He thought he was using slang. "A gentleman said he wished to speak to Mr. Scovil in case he was here, and I went to the office and asked if it was Mr. Scovil, and he talked from your desk, and then he got up and put on his hat and went out."

"Leave any message?"

"No. I had come back to the kitchen, closing the office door for his privacy but leaving this one open as you said, and he came out and went in a hurry. He said nothing at all."

I lifted the shoulders and let them drop. "He'll be back. He wants to see a kind of a man named Nero Wolfe. What's on the menu?"

Fritz told me, and let me take a sniff at the sauce steaming on the simmer plate; then I heard the elevator and went back to the office. Wolfe entered, crossed to his chair and got himself lowered, rang for beer and took the opener out of the drawer, and then vouchsafed me a glance.

"Pleasant afternoon, Archie?"

"No, sir. Putrid. I went around to Perry's office."

"Indeed. A man of action must expect such vexations. Tell me about it."

"Well, Perry left here just after I came down, but about eight minutes after that he phoned and instructed me to come galloping. Having the best interests of my employer in mind I went."

"Notwithstanding the physical law that the contents can be no larger than the container." Fritz arrived with two bottles of beer; Wolfe opened and poured one, and drank. "Go on."

"Yes, sir. I disregard your wit, because I'd like to show you this picture before the company arrives, and they're already ten minutes late. By the way, the company we already had has departed. He claimed to be part of the six-o'clock appointment and said he would wait, but Fritz says he got a phone call and went in a hurry. Maybe the appointment is off. Anyhow, here's the Perry puzzle. . . ."

I laid it out for him, in the way that he always liked to get a crop of facts, no matter how trivial or how crucial. I told him what everybody looked like, and what they did, and what they said fairly verbatim. He finished the first bottle of beer meanwhile, and had the second well on its way when I got through. I rattled it off and then leaned back and took a sip from a glass of milk I had brought from the kitchen.

Wolfe pinched his nose. "Pfui! Hyenas. And your conclusions?"

"Maybe hyenas. Yeah." I took another sip. "On principle I don't like Perry, but it's possible he's just using all the decency he has left after a life of evil. You have forbidden me to use the word louse, so I would say that Muir is an insect. Clara Fox is the ideal of my dreams, but it wouldn't stun me to know that she lifted the roll, though I'd be surprised."

Wolfe nodded. "You may remember that four years ago Mr. Perry objected to our bill for an investigation of his competitors' trade practices. I presume that now he would like us to shovel the mud from his executive offices for twelve dollars a day. It is not practicable always to sneer at mud; there's too much of it. So it gives the greater pleasure to do so when we can afford it. At present our bank balance is agreeable to contemplate. Pfui!" He lifted his glass and emptied it and wiped his lips with his handkerchief.

"Okay," I agreed. "But there's something else to consider. Perry wants you to phone him this evening. If you take the case on we'll at least get expenses, and if you don't take it on Clara Fox may get five years for grand larceny and I'll have to move to Ossining so as to be near her and take her tidbits on visiting day. Balance the mud-shoveling against the loss of my services—but that sounds like visitors. I'll finish my appeal later."

I had heard the doorbell sending Fritz into the hall and down it to the door. I glanced at the clock: 6:30; they were half an hour late. I remembered the attractive telephone voice, and wondered if we were going to have another nymph, cool and sweet in distress, on our hands.

Fritz came in and shut the door behind him, and announced callers. Wolfe nodded. Fritz went out, and after a second in came a man and two women. The man and the second woman I was barely aware of, because I was busy looking at the one in front. It certainly was a nymph cool and sweet in distress. Evidently she knew enough about Nero Wolfe to recognize him, for with only a swift glance at me she came forward to Wolfe's desk and spoke.

"Mr. Wolfe? I telephoned on Saturday. I'm sorry to be late for the appointment. My name is Clara Fox." She turned. "This is Miss Hilda Lindquist and Mr. Michael Walsh."

Wolfe nodded at her and at them. "It is bulk, not boorishness, that keeps me in my chair." He wiggled a finger at me. "Mr. Archie Goodwin. Chairs, Archie?"

I obliged, while Clara Fox was saying, "I met Mr. Goodwin this afternoon, in Mr. Perry's office." I thought to myself, you did indeed, and for not recognizing your voice I'll let them lock me in the cell next to yours when you go up the river.

"Indeed." Wolfe had his eyes half closed, which meant he was missing nothing. "Mr. Walsh's chair to the right, please. Thank you."

Miss Fox was taking off her gloves. "First I'd like to explain why we're late. I said on the telephone that I couldn't make the appointment before Monday because I was expecting someone from out of town who had to be here. It was a man from out west named Harlan Scovil. He arrived this morning, and I saw him during the lunch hour, and arranged to meet him at a quarter past five, at his hotel, to bring him here. I went for him, but he wasn't there. I waited and . . . well, I tried to make some inquiries. Then I met Miss Lindquist and Mr. Walsh, as agreed, and we went back to Mr. Scovil's hotel again. We waited until a quarter past six, and decided it would be better to come on without him."

"Is his presence essential?"

"I wouldn't say essential. At least not at this moment. We left word, and he may join us here any second. He must see you too, before we can do anything. I should warn you, Mr. Wolfe, I have a very long story to tell."

She hadn't looked at me once. I decided to quit looking at her, and tried her companions. They were just barely people. Of course I remembered Harlan Scovil telling Anthony D. Perry that he wasn't Mike Walsh. Apparently this bird was. He was a scrawny little mick, built wiry, over sixty and maybe even seventy, dressed cheap but clean, sitting only half in his chair and keeping an ear palmed with his right hand. The Lindquist dame, with a good square face and wearing a good brown dress, had size, though I wouldn't have called her massive, first because it would have been only a half-truth, and second because she might have socked me. I guess she was a fine woman, of the kind that would be more apt to be snapping a coffee cup in her fingers than a champagne glass. Remembering Harlan Scovil to boot, it looked to me as if, whatever game Miss Fox was training for, she was picking some odd numbers for her team.

Wolfe had told her that the longer the story the sooner it ought to begin, and she was saying, "It began forty years ago, in Silver City, Nevada. But before I start it, Mr. Wolfe, I ought to tell you something that I hope will make you interested. I've found out all I could about you, and I understand that you have remarkable abilities and an equally remarkable opinion of their cash value to people you do things for."

Wolfe sighed. "Each of us must choose his own brand of banditry, Miss Fox."

"Certainly. That is what I have done. If you agree to help us, and if we are successful, your fee will be one hundred thousand dollars."

Mike Walsh leaned forward and blurted, "Ten per cent! Fair enough?"

Hilda Lindquist frowned at him. Clara Fox paid no attention. Wolfe said, "The fee always depends. You couldn't hire me to hand you the moon."

She laughed at him, and although I had my notebook out I decided to look at her in the pauses. She said, "I won't need it. Is Mr. Goodwin going to take down everything? With the understanding that if you decide not to help us his notes are to be given to me?"

Cagey Clara. The creases of Wolfe's cheeks unfolded a little. "By all means."

"All right." She brushed her hair back. "I said it began forty years ago, but I won't start there. I'll start when I was nine years old, in 1918, the year my father was killed in the war, in France. I don't remember my father much. He was killed in 1918, and he sent my mother a letter which she didn't get until nearly a year later, because instead of trusting it to the army mail he gave it to another soldier to bring home. My mother read it then, but I never knew of it until seven years later, in 1926, when my mother gave it to me on her deathbed. I was seventeen years old. I loved my mother very dearly."

She stopped. It would have been a good spot for a moist film over her eyes or a catch in her voice, but apparently she had just stopped to swallow. She swallowed twice. In the pause I was looking at her. She went on.

"I didn't read the letter until a month later. I knew it was a letter father had written to mother eight years before, and with mother gone it didn't seem to be of any importance to me. But on account of what mother had said, about a month after she died I read it. I have it with me. I'll have to read it to you."

She opened her alligator-skin handbag and took out a folded paper. She jerked it open and glanced at it, and back at Wolfe. "May I?"

"Do I see typewriting?"

She nodded. "This is a copy. The original is put away." She brushed her hair back with a hand up and dipping swift like a bird. "This isn't a complete copy. There is—this is—just the part to read.

"So, dearest Lola, since a man can't tell what is going to happen to him here, or when, I've decided to write you about a little incident that occurred last week, and make arrangements to be sure it gets to you, in case I never get home to tell you about it. I'll have to begin away back.

"I've told you a lot of wild tales about the old days in Nevada. I've told you this one too, but I'll repeat it here briefly. It was at Silver City, in 1895. I was 25 years old, so it was 10 years before I met you. I was broke, and so was the gang of youngsters I'm telling about. They were all youngsters but one. We weren't friends, there was no such thing as a friend around there. Most of the bunch of 2000 or so that inhabited Silver City camp at that time were a good deal older than us, which was how we happened to get together—temporarily. Everything was temporary!

"The ringleader of our gang was a kid we called Rubber on account of the way he bounced back up when he got knocked down. His name was Coleman, but I never knew his first name, or if I did I can't remember it, though I've often tried. Because Rubber was our leader, someone cracked a joke one day that we should call ourselves The Rubber Band, and we did. Pretty soon most of Silver City was calling us that.

"One of the gang, a kid named George Rowley, shot a man and killed him. From what I heard—I didn't see it—he had as good a right to shoot as was usually needed around there, but the trouble was that the one he killed happened to be a member of the Vigilance Committee. It was at night, 24 hours after the shooting, that they decided to hang him. Rowley hadn't had sense enough to make a getaway, so they took him and shut him up in a shanty until daylight, with one of their number for a guard, an Irishman. As Harlan Scovil would say—I'll never forget Harlan—he was a kind of a man named Mike Walsh.

"Rowley went after his guard, Mike Walsh. I mean talking to him. Finally, around midnight, he persuaded Mike to send for Rubber Coleman.

Rubber had a talk with him and Mike. Then there was a lot of conspiring, and Rubber did a lot of dickering with Rowley. We were gathered in the dark in the sagebrush out back of John's Palace, a shack out at the edge of the city—"

Clara Fox looked up. "My father underscored the word city."

Wolfe nodded. "Properly, no doubt."

She went on: *"—and we had been drinking some and were having a swell time. Around two o'clock Rubber showed up again and lit matches to show us a paper George Rowley had signed, with him and Mike Walsh as witnesses. I've told you about it. I can't give it to you word for word, but this is exactly what it said. It said that his real name wasn't George Rowley, and that he wasn't giving his real name in writing, but that he had told it to Rubber Coleman. It said that he was from a wealthy family in England, and that if he got out of Silver City alive he would go back there, and some day he would get a share of the family pile. It said it wouldn't be a major share because he wasn't an oldest son. Then it hereby agreed that whenever and whatever he got out of his family connections, he would give us half of it, provided we got him safe out of Silver City and safe from pursuit, before the time came to hang him.*

"We were young, and thought we were adventurers, and we were half drunk or maybe more. I doubt if any of us had any idea that we would ever get hold of any of the noble English wealth, except possibly Rubber Coleman, but the idea of the night rescue of a member of our gang was all to the good. Rubber had another paper ready too, all written up. It was headed, PLEDGE OF THE RUBBER BAND, and we all signed it. It had already been signed by Mike Walsh. In it we agreed to an equal division of anything coming from George Rowley, no matter who got it or when.

"We were all broke except Vic Lindquist, who had a bag of gold dust. It was Rubber's suggestion that we get Turtle-back in. Turtle-back was an oldtimer who owned the fastest horse in Silver City. He had no use for that kind of a horse; he only happened to own it because he had won it in a poker game a few days before. I went with Rubber down to Turtle-back's shanty. We offered him Vic Lindquist's dust for the horse, but he said it wasn't enough. We had expected that. Then Rubber explained to him what was up, told him the whole story, and offered him an equal share with the rest of us, for the horse, and the dust to boot. Turtle-back was still half asleep. Finally, when he got the idea, he blinked at us, and then all of a sudden he slapped his knee and began to guffaw. He said that by God he always had wanted to own a part of England, and anyway he would probably lose the horse before he got a chance to ride it much. Rubber got out the PLEDGE OF THE RUBBER BAND, but Turtle-back wouldn't have his name added to it, saying he didn't like to have his name written down any-

where. He would trust us to see that he got his share. Rubber scribbled out a bill of sale for the horse, but Turtle-back wouldn't sign that either; he said I was there as a witness, the horse was ours, and that was enough. He put on his boots and took us over to Johnson's corral, and we saddled the horse, a palomino with a white face, and led it around the long way, back of the shacks and tents and along a gully, to where the gang was.

"We rescued George Rowley all right. You've heard me tell about it, how we loosened a couple of boards and then set fire to the shanty where they had him, and how he busted out of the loose place in the excitement, and how Mike Walsh, who was known to be a dead shot, emptied two guns at him without hitting him. Rowley was in the saddle and away before anyone else realized it, and nobody bothered to chase him because they were too busy putting out the fire.

"The story came out later about our buying Turtle-back's horse, but by that time people's minds were on something else, and anyway our chief offense was that we had started the fire and it couldn't be proved we had done that. It might have been different if the man we helped to escape had done something really criminal, like cheating at cards or stealing somebody's dust.

"So far as I know, none of us ever saw Rowley or heard of him since that night. You've heard me mention twenty times, when you and I were having hard going, that I'd like to find him and learn if he owed me anything, but you know I never did and of course I meant it more or less as a joke anyhow. But recently, here in France, two things have come up about it. The first one is a thought that's in my mind all the time, what if I do get mine over here, what kind of a fix am I leaving you and the kid in? My little daughter Clara—God how I'd love to see her. And you. To hell with that stuff when it's no use, but I'd gladly stand up and let the damn Germans shoot me tomorrow morning if I could see you two right this minute. The answer to my question is, a hell of a fix. My life would end more useless than it started, leaving my wife and daughter without a single solitary damn thing.

"The other thing that's come up is that I've seen George Rowley. It was one day last week. I may have told you that the lobe of his right ear was gone—he said he had it hacked off in Australia—but I don't think I really knew him by that. There probably is a mighty good print of his mug in my mind somewhere, and I just simply knew it was him. After twenty-three years! I was out with a survey detail about a mile back of the front trenches, laying out new communication lines, and a big car came along. British. The car stopped. It had four British officers in it, and one of them called to me and I went over and he asked for directions to our division headquarters. I gave them to him, and he looked at my insignia and asked if we Americans let our captains dig ditches. I had seen by his insignia that he was a brigade commander. I grinned at him and said that in our army everybody worked

*but the privates. He looked at me closer and said, 'By Gad, it's Gil Fox!'
I said, 'Yes, sir. General Rowley?' He shook his head and laughed and told
the driver to go on, and the car jumped forward, and he turned to wave his
hand at me.*

"So he's alive, or he was last week, and not in the poorhouse, or whatever
they call it in England. I've made various efforts to find out who he was,
but without success. Maybe I will soon. In the meantime, I'm writing this
down and disposing of it, because, although it may sound far-fetched and
even a little batty, the fact is that this is the only thing resembling a legacy
that I can leave to you and Clara. After all, I did risk my life that night
in Silver City, on the strength of a bargain understood and recorded, and if
that Englishman is rolling in it there's no reason why he shouldn't pay up.
It is my hope and wish that you will make every effort to see that he does,
not only for your sake but for our daughter's sake. That may sound melodramatic, but the things that are going on over here get you that way. As
soon as I find out who he is I'll get this back and add that to it.

"Another thing. If you do find him and get a grubstake out of it, you must
not use it to pay that $26,000 I owe those people out in California. You must
promise me this. You must, dearest Lola. I'm bestowing this legacy on you
and Clara, not them! I say this because I know that you know how much
that debt has worried me for ten years. Though I wasn't really responsible
for that tangle, it's true that it would give me more pleasure to straighten
that out than anything in the world except to see you and Clara, but if I
die that business can die with me. Of course, if you should get such a big
pile of dough that you're embarrassed—but miracles like that don't happen.

"If something should come out of it, it must be split with the rest of the
gang if you can find them. I don't know a thing about any of them except
Harlan Scovil, and I haven't heard from him for several years. The last address I had for him is in the little red book in the drawer of my desk. One
of the difficulties is that you haven't got the paper that George Rowley
signed. Rubber Coleman, by agreement, kept both that and the PLEDGE
OF THE RUBBER BAND. Maybe you can find Coleman. Or maybe Rowley is a decent guy and will pay without any paper. Either sounds highly
improbable. Hell, it's all a daydream. Anyhow, I have every intention of
getting back to you safe and sound, and if I do you'll never see this unless
I bring it along as a souvenir.

"Here are the names of everybody that was in on it: George Rowley.
Rubber Coleman (don't know his first name). Victor Lindquist. Harlan
Scovil (you've met him, go after him first). Mike Walsh (he was a little
older, maybe 32 at the time, not one of the Rubber Band). Turtle-back was
a good deal older, probably dead now, and that's all the name I knew for

him. And last but by no means least, yours truly, and how truly it would take a year to tell, Gilbert Fox, the writer of these presents."

Clara Fox stopped. She ran her eyes over the last sentence again, then placed that sheet at the back, folded them up, and returned them to her handbag. She put her hand up and brushed back her hair, and sat and looked at Wolfe. No one said anything.

Finally Wolfe sighed. He opened his eyes at her. "Well, Miss Fox. It appears to be the moon that you want after all."

She shook her head. "I know who George Rowley is. He is now in New York."

"And this, I presume"—Wolfe nodded—"is Mr. Victor Lindquist's daughter." He nodded again. "And this gentleman is the Mr. Walsh who emptied two guns at Mr. Rowley without hitting him."

Mike Walsh blurted, "I could have hit him!"

"Granted, sir. And you, Miss Fox, would very much like to have twenty-six thousand dollars, no doubt with accrued interest, to discharge debts of your dead father. In other words, you need something a little less than thirty thousand."

She stared at him. She glanced at me, then back at him, and asked coolly, "Am I here as your client, Mr. Wolfe, or as a suspected thief?"

He wiggled a finger at her. "Neither as yet. Please do not be so foolish as to be offended. If I show you my mind, it is only to save time and avoid irrelevancies. Haven't I sat and listened patiently for ten minutes although I dislike being read aloud to?"

"That's irrelevant."

"Indeed. I believe it is. Let us proceed. Tell me about Mr. George Rowley."

But that had to be postponed. I had heard the doorbell, and Fritz going down the hall, and a murmur from outside. Now I shook my head at Clara Fox and showed her my palm to stop her, as the office door opened and Fritz came in and closed it behind him.

"A man to see you, sir. I told him you were engaged."

I bounced up. There were only two kinds of men Fritz didn't announce as gentlemen: one he suspected of wanting to sell something, and a policeman, uniform or not. He could smell one a mile off. So I bounced up and demanded, "A cop?"

"Yes, sir."

I whirled to Wolfe. "Ever since I saw Muir looking at Miss Fox today I've been thinking she ought to have a lightning rod. Would you like to have her pinched in here, or out in the hall?"

Wolfe nodded and snapped, "Very well, Archie."

I crossed quick and got myself against the closed office door, and spoke not too loud to Fritz, pointing to the door that opened into the front room. "Go through that way and lock the door from the front room to the hall." He moved. I turned to the others. "Go in there and sit down, and if you don't talk any it won't disturb us." Walsh and Miss Lindquist stared at me.

Clara Fox said to Wolfe, "I'm not your client yet."

He said, "Nor yet a suspect. Here. Please humor Mr. Goodwin."

She got up and went and the others followed her. Fritz came back and I told him to shut that door and lock it and give me the key. Then I went back to my desk and sat down, while Fritz, at a nod from Wolfe, went to the hall for the visitor.

The cop came in, and I was surprised to see that it was a guy I knew. Surprised, because the last time I had heard of Slim Foltz he had been on the Homicide Squad, detailed to the District Attorney's office.

"Hello, Slim."

"Hi, Goodwin." He had his own clothes on. He came on across with his hat in his hand. "Hello, Mr. Wolfe. I'm Foltz, Homicide Squad."

"Good evening, sir. Be seated."

The dick put his hat on the desk and sat down, and reached in his pocket and pulled out a piece of paper. "There was a man shot down the street an hour or so ago. Shot plenty, five bullets in him. Killed. This piece of paper was in his pocket, with your name and address on it. Along with other names. Do you know anything about him?"

Wolfe shook his head. "Except that he's dead. Not, that is, at this moment. If I knew his name, perhaps . . ."

"Yeah. His name was on a hunting license, also in his pocket. State of Wyoming. Harlan Scovil."

"Indeed. It is possible Mr. Goodwin can help you out. Archie?"

I was thinking to myself, hell, he didn't come for her after all. But I was just as well pleased she wasn't in the room.

V

SLIM FOLTZ was looking at me.

I said, "Harlan Scovil? Sure. He was here this afternoon."

Foltz got in his pocket again and fished out a little black memo book and a pencil stub. "What time?"

"He got here around four-thirty, a little before maybe, and left at five-twenty-six."

"What did he want?"

"He wanted to see Nero Wolfe."

"What about?"

I shook my head regretfully. "There you've got me, mister. I told him he'd have to wait until six o'clock, so he was waiting."

"He must have said something."

"Certainly he said something. He said he wanted to see Nero Wolfe."

"What else did he say?"

"He said there seemed to be very little spittin' done east of the Mississippi River, and he wanted to know if there were any honest men this side of the mountains. He didn't say specifically what he wanted to see Mr. Wolfe about. We'd never seen him or heard of him before. Oh yes, he said he just got to New York this morning, from Wyoming. By the way, just because that license was in his pocket—was he over six feet, around sixty, blue serge suit with sleeves too short and the lapel torn a little on the right side, with a leathery red face and a cowboy hat—"

"That's him," the dick grunted. "What did he come to New York for?"

"To see Nero Wolfe, I guess." I grinned. "That's the kind of a rep we've got. If you mean, did he give any hint as to who might want to bump him off, he didn't."

"Did he see Wolfe?"

"No. I told you, he left at five-twenty-six. Mr. Wolfe never comes down until six o'clock."

"Why didn't he wait?"

"Because he got a phone call."

"He got a phone call here?"

"Right here in this room. I wasn't here. I had gone out, leaving this bird here waiting for six o'clock. The phone was answered by Fritz Brenner, Mr. Wolfe's chef and household pride. Want to see him?"

"Yeah. If you don't mind."

Wolfe rang. Fritz came. Wolfe told him he was to answer the gentleman's questions, and Fritz said "Yes, sir" and stood up straight.

All Foltz got out of Fritz was the same as I had got. He had put down the time of the phone call, 5:26, in accordance with Wolfe's standing instructions for exactness in all details of the household and office. It was a man phoning, and he had not given his name and Fritz had not recognized his voice. Fritz had not overheard any of the conversation. Harlan Scovil had immediately left, without saying anything.

Fritz went back to the kitchen.

The dick frowned at the piece of paper. "I wasn't expecting to draw a blank here. I came here first. There's other names on this paper—Clara Fox, Michael Walsh, Michael spelled wrong, Hilda Lindquist, that's what it looks like, and a Marquis of Clivers. I don't suppose you—"

I horned in, shaking my head. "As I said, when this Harlan Scovil popped in here at half past four today, I had never seen him before. Nor any of those others. Strangers to me. I'm sure Mr. Wolfe hadn't either. Had you, sir?"

"Seen them? No. But I believe I had heard of one of them. Wasn't it the Marquis of Clivers we were discussing yesterday?"

"Discussing? Yes, sir. When you dropped that javelin. That piece in the paper." I looked at Foltz helpfully. "There was an article in the *Times* yesterday, magazine section—"

He nodded. "I know all about that. The sergeant was telling me. This marquis seems to be something like a duke, he's immune by reason of a foreign power or something. It don't even have to be a friendly foreign power. The sergeant says this business might possibly be an international plot. Captain Devore is going to make arrangements to see this marquis and maybe warn him or protect him."

"Splendid." Wolfe nodded approvingly. "The police earn the gratitude of all of us. But for them, Mr. Foltz, we private investigators might sit and wait for clients in vain."

"Yeah." Foltz got up. "Much obliged for the compliment, even if that's all I get. I mean, I haven't got much information. Except that telephone call, that may lead to something. Scovil was shot only four blocks from here, on Thirty-first Street, only nine minutes after he got that phone call, at five-thirty-five. He was walking along the sidewalk and somebody going by in a car reached out and plugged him, filled him full. He was dead right then. It was pretty dark around there, but a man nearby saw the license, and the car's already been found, parked on Ninth Avenue. Nobody saw anyone get out of it."

"Well, that's something." I was hopeful. "That ought to get you somewhere."

"Probably stolen. They usually are." The dick had his hat in his hand. "Gang stuff, it looks like. Much obliged to you folks anyhow."

"Don't mention it, Slim."

I went to the hall with him, and saw him out the front door, and shut it after him and slid the bolt. Before I returned to the office I stopped at the kitchen and told Fritz that I'd answer any doorbells that might ring for the rest of the evening.

I crossed to Wolfe's desk and grinned at him. "Ha-ha. The damn police were here."

Wolfe looked at the clock, which said ten minutes past seven. He reached out and pushed the button, and, when Fritz came, leaned back and sighed.

"Fritz."

"Yes, sir."

"A calamity. We cannot possibly dine at eight as usual. Not dine, that is. We can eat, and I suppose we shall have to. You have filets of beef with sauce Abano."

"Yes, sir."

Wolfe sighed again. "You will have to serve it in morsels, for five persons. By adding some of the fresh stock you can have plenty of soup. Open Hungarian *petits poissons*. You have plenty of fruit? Fill in as you can. It is distressing, but there's no help for it."

"The sauce is a great success, sir. I could give the others canned chicken and mushrooms—"

"Confound it, no! If there are to be hardships, I must share them. That's all. Bring me some beer."

Fritz went, and Wolfe turned to me. "Bring Clara Fox."

I unlocked the door to the front room. Fritz hadn't turned on all the lights, and it was dim. The two women were side by side on the divan, and Mike Walsh was in a chair, blinking at me as if he had been asleep.

I said, "Mr. Wolfe would like to speak to Miss Fox."

Mike Walsh said, "I'm hungry."

Clara Fox said, "To all of us."

"First just you. Please. There'll be some grub pretty soon, Mr. Walsh. If you'll wait in here."

Clara Fox hesitated, then got up and preceded me. I shut the door, and she went back to her chair in front of Wolfe, the one the dick had sat in. Wolfe had emptied a glass and was filling it up again.

"Will you have some beer, Miss Fox?"

She shook her head. "Thank you. But I don't like to discuss this with you alone, Mr. Wolfe. The others are just as much—"

"To be sure. Permit me." He wiggled a finger at her. "They shall join us presently. The fact is, I wish to touch on something else for a moment. Did you take that money from Mr. Muir's desk?"

She looked at him steadily. "We shouldn't let things get confused. Are you acting now as the agent of the Seaboard Products Corporation?"

"I'm asking you a question. You came here to consult me because you thought I had abilities. I have; I'm using them. Either answer my question or find abilities elsewhere. Did you take that money?"

"No."

"Do you know who took it?"

"No."

"Do you know anything about it?"

"No. I have certain suspicions, but nothing specific about the money itself."

"Do you mean suspicions on account of the attitude of Mr. Perry and Mr. Muir toward you personally?"

"Yes. Chiefly Mr. Muir."

"Good. Now this: Did you kill anyone this evening between five and six o'clock?"

She stared at him. "Don't be an idiot."

He drank some beer, wiped his lips, and leaned back in his chair. "Miss Fox. The avoidance of idiocy should be the primary and constant concern of every intelligent person. It is mine. I am sometimes successful. Take, for instance, your statement that you did not steal that money. Do I believe it? As a philosopher, I believe nothing. As a detective, I believe it enough to leave it behind me, but am prepared to glance back over my shoulder. As a man, I believe it utterly. I assure you, my reason for the questions I am asking is not idiotic. For one thing, I am observing your face as you reply to them. Bear with me; we shall be getting somewhere, I think. Did you kill anyone this evening between five and six o'clock?"

"No."

"Did Mr. Walsh or Miss Lindquist do so?"

"Kill anyone?"

"Yes."

She smiled at him. "As a philosopher, I don't know. I'm not a detective. As a woman, they didn't."

"If they did, you have no knowledge of it?"

"No."

"Good. Have you a dollar bill?"

"I suppose I have."

"Give me one."

She shook her head, not in refusal, but in resigned perplexity at senseless antics. She looked in her bag and got out a dollar bill and handed it to Wolfe. He took it and unfolded it and handed it across to me.

"Enter it, please, Archie. Retainer from Miss Clara Fox. And get Mr. Perry on the phone." He turned to her. "You are now my client."

She didn't smile. "With the understanding, I suppose, that I may—"

"May sever the connection?" His creases unfolded. "By all means. Without notice."

I found Perry's number and dialed it. After giving my fingerprints by television to some dumb kluck I finally got him on, and nodded to Wolfe to take it.

Wolfe was suave. "Mr. Perry? This is Nero Wolfe. I have Mr. Goodwin's report of his preliminary investigation. He was inclined to agree with your own attitude regarding the probable innocence of Clara Fox, and he thought we might therefore be able to render some real service to you. But by a curious chance Miss Fox called at our office this evening—she is here now, in fact—and asked us to represent her interests in the matter. . . . No, per-

mit me, please. . . . Well, it seemed to be advisable to accept her retainer.
. . . Really, sir, I see nothing unethical . . ."

Wolfe hated to argue on the telephone. He cut it as short as he could,
and rang off, and washed it down with beer. He turned back to Clara Fox.
"Tell me about your personal relations with Mr. Perry and Mr. Muir."

She didn't answer right away. She was sitting there frowning at him. It
was the first time I had seen her brow wrinkled, and I liked it better
smoothed out. Finally she said, "I supposed you had already taken that case
for Mr. Perry. I had gone to a lot of trouble deciding that you were the
best man for us—Miss Lindquist and Mr. Walsh and Mr. Scovil and me—
and I had already telephoned on Saturday and made the appointment with
you, before I heard anything about the stolen money. I didn't know until
two hours ago that Mr. Perry had engaged you, and since we had the appointment I thought we might as well go through with it. Now you tell
Mr. Perry you're acting for me, not the Seaboard, and you say I've given you
a retainer for that. That's not straight. If you want to call that a retainer,
it's for the business I came to see you about, not that silly rot about the
money. That's nonsense."

Wolfe inquired, "What makes you think it's nonsense?"

"Because it is. I don't know what the truth of it is, but as far as I'm concerned it's nonsense."

Wolfe nodded. "I agree with you. That's what makes it dangerous."

"Dangerous? How? If you mean I'll lose my job, I don't think so. Mr.
Perry is the real boss there, and he knows I'm more than competent, and he
can't possibly believe I took that money. If this other business is successful,
and I believe it will be, I won't want the job anyhow."

"But you will want your freedom." Wolfe sighed. "Really, Miss Fox, we
are wasting time that may be valuable. Tell me, I beg you, about Mr. Perry
and Mr. Muir. Mr. Muir hinted this afternoon that Mr. Perry is enjoying
the usufructs of gallantry. Is that true?"

"Of course not." She frowned, and then smiled. "Calling it that, it doesn't
sound bad at all, does it? But he isn't. I used to go to dinner and the theater
with Mr. Perry fairly frequently, shortly after I started to work for Seaboard.
That was during my adventuress phase. I was going to be an adventuress."

"Did something interrupt?"

"Nothing but my disappointment. I have always been determined to get
somewhere, not anywhere in particular, just somewhere. My father died
when I was nine, and my mother when I was seventeen. She always said
I was like my father. She paid for my schooling by sewing fat women's
dresses. I loved my mother passionately, and hated the humdrum she was
sunk in and couldn't get out of."

"She couldn't find George Rowley."

"She didn't try much. She thought it was fantastic. She wrote once to Harlan Scovil, but the letter was returned. After she died I tried various things, everything from hat-check girl to a stenographic course, and for three years I studied languages in my spare time because I thought I'd want to go all over the world. Finally, by a stroke of luck, I got a good job at the Seaboard three years ago. For the first time I had enough money so I could spend a little trying to find George Rowley and the others mentioned in father's letter—I realized I'd have to find some of the others so there would be someone to recognize George Rowley. I guess mother was right when she said I'm like father; I certainly had fantastic ideas, and I'm terribly confident that I'm a very unusual person. My idea at that time was that I wanted to get money from George Rowley as soon as possible, so I could pay that old debt of my father's in California, and then go to Arabia. The reason I wanted to go to Arabia—"

She broke off abruptly, looked startled, and demanded, "What in the name of heaven started me on that?"

"I don't know." Wolfe looked patient. "You're wasting time again. Perry and Muir?"

"Well." She brushed her hair back. "Not long after I started to work for Seaboard, Mr. Perry began asking me to go to the theater with him. He said that his wife had been sick in bed for eight years and he merely wanted companionship. I knew he was a multi-millionaire, and I thought it over and decided to become an adventuress. If you think that sounds like a loony kid, don't fool yourself. For lots of women it has been a very exciting and satisfactory career. I never really expected to do anything much with Mr. Perry, because there was no stimulation in him, but I thought I could practice with him and at the same time keep my job. I even went riding with him, long after it got to be a bore. I thought I could practice with Mr. Muir, too, but I was soon sorry I had ever aroused his interest."

She drew her shoulders in a little, a shade toward the center of her, and let them out again, in delicate disgust. "It was Mr. Muir that cured me of the idea of being an adventuress, I mean in the classical sense. Of course I knew that to be a successful adventuress you have to deal with men, and they have to be rich, and seeing what Mr. Muir was like made me look around a little, and I realized it would be next to impossible to find a rich man it would be any fun to be adventurous with. Mr. Muir seemed to go practically crazy after he had had dinner with me once or twice. Once he came to my apartment and almost forced his way in, and he had an enormous pearl necklace in his pocket! Of course it was disgusting in a way, but it was even more funny than it was disgusting, because I have never cared for pearls at all. But the worst thing about Mr. Muir is his stubbornness. He's a Scotchman, and apparently if he once gets an idea in his head he can't get it out again—"

Wolfe put in, "Is Mr. Muir a fool?"

"Why . . . yes, I suppose he is."

"I mean as a businessman. A man of affairs. Is he a fool?"

"No. Not that way. In fact, he's very shrewd."

"Well, you are." Wolfe sighed. "You are quite an amazing fool, Miss Fox. You know that Mr. Muir, who is a shrewd man, is prepared to swear out a warrant against you for grand larceny. Do you think that he would consider himself prepared if preparations had not actually been made? Why does he insist on immediate action? So that the preparations may not be interfered with, by design or by mischance. As soon as a warrant is in force against you, the police may search any property of yours, including that item of it where the thirty thousand dollars will be found. Couldn't Mr. Muir have taken it himself from his desk and put it anywhere he wanted to, with due circumspection?"

"Put it . . ." She stared at him. "Oh, no." She shook her head. "That would be too low. A man would have to be a dirty scoundrel to do that."

"Well? Who should know better than you, an ex-adventuress, that the race of dirty scoundrels has not yet been exterminated? By the eternal, Miss Fox, you should be tied in your cradle! Where do you live?"

"But, Mr. Wolfe . . . you could never persuade me . . . "

"I wouldn't waste time trying. Where do you live?"

"I have a little flat on East Sixty-first Street."

"And what other items? We can disregard your desk at the office, that would not be conclusive enough. Do you have a cottage in the country? A trunk in storage? An automobile?"

"I have a little car. Nothing else whatever."

"Did you come here in it?"

"No. It's in a garage on Sixtieth Street."

Wolfe turned to me. "Archie. What two can you get here at once?"

I glanced at the clock. "Saul Panzer in ten minutes. If Fred Durkin's not at the movies, him in twenty minutes. If he is, Orrie Cather in half an hour."

"Get them. Miss Fox will give you the key to her apartment and a note of authority, and also a note to the garage. Saul Panzer will search the apartment thoroughly. Tell him what he's looking for, and if he finds it bring it here. Fred will get the automobile and drive it to our garage, and when he gets it there go through it, and leave it there. This alone will cost us twenty dollars, twenty times the amount of Miss Fox's retainer. Everything we undertake nowadays seems to be a speculation."

I got at the telephone. Wolfe opened his eyes on Clara Fox. "You might learn if Miss Lindquist and Mr. Walsh will care to wash before dinner. It will be ready in five minutes."

She shook her head. "We don't need to eat. Or we can go out for a bite."

"Great hounds and Cerberus!" He was about as close to a tantrum as he ever got. "Don't need to eat! In heaven's name, are you camels, or bears in for the winter?"

She got up and went to the front room to get them.

VI

MY DINNER was interrupted twice. Saul Panzer came before I had finished my soup, and Fred Durkin arrived while we were in the middle of the beef and vegetables. I went to the office both times and gave them their instructions and told them some hurry would do.

Wolfe made it a rule never to talk business at table, but we got a little forward at that, because he steered Hilda Lindquist and Mike Walsh into the talk and we found out things about them. She was the daughter of Victor Lindquist, now nearly eighty years old and in no shape to travel, and she lived with him on their wheat farm in Nebraska. Apparently it wasn't coffee cups she snapped in her fingers, it was threshing machines. Clara Fox had finally found her, or rather her father, through Harlan Scovil, and she had come east for the clean-up on the chance that she might get enough to pay off a few dozen mortgages and perhaps get something extra for a new tractor, or at least a mule.

Walsh had gone through several colors before fading out to his present dim obscurity. He had made three good stakes in Nevada and California and had lost all of them. He had tried his hand as a building contractor in Colorado early in the century, made a pile, and dropped it when a sixty-foot dam had gone down the canyon three days after he had finished it. He had come back east and made a pass at this and that, but apparently had used up all his luck. At present he was night watchman on a constructing job up at 55th and Madison, and he was inclined to be sore on account of the three dollars he was losing by paying a substitute in order to keep this appointment with Clara Fox. She had found him a year ago through an ad in the paper.

Wolfe was the gracious host. He saw that Mike Walsh got two rye highballs and the women a bottle of claret, and like a gentleman he gave Walsh two extra slices of the beef, smothered with sauce, which he would have sold his soul for. But he wouldn't let Walsh light his pipe when the coffee came. He said he had asthma, which was a lie. Pipe smoke didn't bother him much, either. He was just sore at Walsh because he had had to give up the beef, and he took it out on him that way.

We hadn't any more than got back to the office, a little after nine o'clock, and settled into our chairs—the whole company present this time—when the doorbell rang. I went out to the front door and whirled the lock and slid the bolt, and opened it. Fred Durkin stepped in. He looked worried, and I snapped at him, "Didn't you get it?"

"Sure I got it."

"What's the matter?"

"Well, it was funny. Is Wolfe here? Maybe he'd like to hear it too."

I glared at him, fixed the door, and led him to the office. He went across and stood in front of Wolfe's desk.

"I got the car, Mr. Wolfe. It's in the garage. But Archie didn't say anything about bringing a dick along with it, so I pushed him off. He grabbed a taxi and followed me. When I left the car in the garage just now and walked here, he walked too. He's out on the sidewalk across the street."

"Indeed." Wolfe's voice was thin; he disliked after-dinner irritations. "Suppose you introduce us to the dick first. Where did you meet him?"

Fred shifted his hat to his other hand. He never could talk to Wolfe without getting fussed up, but I must admit there was often enough reason for it. Fred Durkin was as honest as sunshine, and as good a tailer as I ever saw, but he wasn't as brilliant as sunshine. Warm and cloudy today and tomorrow. He said, "Well, I went to the garage and showed the note to the guy, and he said all right, wait there and he'd bring it down. He went off and in a couple of minutes a man with a wide mouth came up and asked me if I was going for a ride. I'd never saw him before, but I'd have known he was a city feller if I'd had my eyes shut and just touched him with my finger. I supposed he was working on something and was just looking under stones, so I just answered something friendly. He said if I was going for a ride I'd better get a horse, because the car I came for was going to remain there for the present."

Wolfe murmured, "So you apologized and went to a drug store to telephone here for instructions."

Fred looked startled. "No, sir, I didn't. My instructions was to get that car, and I got it. That dick had no documents or nothing, in fact he didn't have nothing but a wide mouth. I went upstairs with him after me. When the garage guy saw the kind of an argument it might be he just disappeared. I ran the car down on the elevator myself and got into the street and headed east. The dick jumped on the running board, and when I reached around to brush a speck off the windshield I accidentally pushed the dick off. By that time he was at Third Avenue and he hopped a taxi and followed me. When I got to Tenth Avenue, inside your garage, I turned the car inside out, but there was nothing there but tools and an old lead pencil and a busted dog leash and a half a package of Omar cigarettes and—"

Wolfe put up a palm at him. "And the dick is now across the street?"

"Yes, sir. He was when I come in."

"Excellent. I hope he doesn't escape in the dark. Go to the kitchen and tell Fritz to give you a cyanide sandwich."

Fred shifted his hat. "I'm sorry, sir, if I—"

"Go! Any kind of a sandwich. Wait in the kitchen. If we find ourselves getting into difficulties here, we shall need you."

Fred went. Wolfe leaned back in his chair and got his fingers laced on his belly; his lips were moving, out and in, and out and in. At length he opened his eyes enough for Clara Fox to see that he was looking at her.

"Well. We were too late. I told you you were wasting time."

She lifted her brows. "Too late for what?"

"To keep you out of jail. Isn't it obvious? What reason could there be for watching your car except to catch you trying to go somewhere in it? And is it likely they would be laying for you if they had not already found the money?"

"Found it where?"

"I couldn't say. Perhaps in the car itself. I am not a necromancer, Miss Fox. Now, before we—"

The phone rang, and I took it. It was Saul Panzer. I listened and got his story, and then told him to hold the wire and turned to Wolfe.

"Saul. From a pay station at Sixty-second and Madison. There was a dick playing tag with himself in front of Miss Fox's address. Saul went through the apartment and drew a blank. Now he thinks the dick is sticking there, but he's not sure. It's possible he's being followed, and if so should he shake the dick and then come here, or what?"

"Tell him to come here. By no means shake the dick. He may know the one Fred brought, and in that case they might like to have a talk."

I told Saul, and hung up.

Wolfe was still leaning back, with his eyes half closed. Mike Walsh sat with his closed entirely, his head swaying on one side, and his breathing deep and even in the silence. Hilda Lindquist's shoulders sagged, but her face was flushed and her eyes bright. Clara Fox had her lips tight enough to make her look determined.

Wolfe said, "Wake Mr. Walsh. Having attended to urgencies—in vain—we may now at our leisure fill in some gaps. Regarding the fantastic business of the Rubber Band. Mr. Walsh, a sharp blow with your hand at the back of your neck will help. A drink of water? Very well. Did I understand you to say, Miss Fox, that you have found George Rowley?"

She nodded. "Two weeks ago."

"Tell me about it."

"But Mr. Wolfe . . . those detectives . . . "

"To be sure. You remember I told you you should be tied in your cradle? For the present, this house is your cradle. You are safe here. We shall return to that little problem. Tell me about George Rowley."

She drew a breath. "Well . . . we found him. I began a long while ago to do what I could, which wasn't much. Of course I couldn't afford to go to England, or send someone, or anything like that. But I gathered some information. For instance, I learned the names of all the generals who had commanded brigades in the British Army during the war, and as well as I could from this distance I began to eliminate them. There were hundreds and hundreds of them still alive, and of course I didn't know whether the one I wanted was alive or not. I did lots of things, and some of them were pretty bright if I am a fool. I had found Mike Walsh through an advertisement, and I got photographs of scores of them and showed them to him. Of course, the fact that George Rowley had lost the lobe of his right ear was a help. On several occasions, when I learned in the newspapers that a British general or ex-general was in New York, I managed to get a look at him, and sometimes Mike Walsh did too. Two weeks ago another one came, and in a photograph in the paper it looked as if the bottom of his right ear was off. Mike Walsh stood in front of his hotel all one afternoon when he should have been asleep, and saw him, and it was George Rowley."

Wolfe nodded. "That would be the Marquis of Clivers."

"How do you know that?"

"Not by divination. It doesn't matter. Congratulations, Miss Fox."

"Thank you. The Marquis of Clivers was going to Washington the next day, but he was coming back. I tried to see him that very evening, but couldn't get to him. I cabled a connection I had made in London, and learned that the marquis owned big estates and factories and mines and a yacht. I had been communicating with Hilda Lindquist and Harlan Scovil for some time, and I wired them to come on and sent them money for the trip. Mr. Scovil wouldn't take the money. He wrote me that he had never taken any woman-money and wasn't going to start." She smiled at Wolfe and me too. "I guess he was afraid of adventuresses. He said he would sell some calves. Saturday morning I got a telegram that he would get here Monday, so I telephoned your office for an appointment. When I saw him this noon I showed him two pictures of the Marquis of Clivers, and he said it was George Rowley. I had a hard time to keep him from going to the hotel after the marquis right then."

Wolfe wiggled a finger at her. "But what made you think you needed me? I detect no lack of confidence in your operations to date."

"Oh, I always thought we'd have to have a lawyer at the windup. I had read about you and admired you."

"I'm not a lawyer."

"I shouldn't think that would matter. I only know three lawyers, and if you saw them you would know why I chose you."

"You sound like a fool again." Wolfe sighed. "Do you wish me to believe that I was selected for my looks?"

"No, indeed. That would be . . . anyhow, I selected you. When I told you what your fee might be, I wasn't exaggerating. Let's say his estates and mines and so on are worth fifty million—"

"Pounds?"

"Dollars. That's conservative. He agreed to pay half of it. Twenty-five million. But there are two of the men I can't find. I haven't found a trace of Rubber Coleman, the leader, or the man called Turtle-back. I have tried hard to find Rubber Coleman, because he had the papers, but I couldn't. On the twenty-five million take off their share, one-third, and that leaves roughly sixteen million. Make allowances for all kinds of things, anything you could think of—take off, say, just for good measure, fifteen million. That leaves a million dollars. That's what I asked him for a week ago."

"You asked who for? Lord Clivers?"

"Yes."

"You said you were unable to see him."

"That was before he went to Washington. When he came back I tried again. I had made an acquaintance . . . he has some assistants with him on his mission—diplomats and so on—and I had got acquainted with one two weeks ago, and through him I got to the marquis, thinking I might manage it without any help. He was very unpleasant. When he found out what I was getting at, he ordered me out. He claimed he didn't know what I was talking about, and when I wanted to show him the letter my father had written in 1918, he wouldn't look at it. He told the young man whom he called to take me away that I was an adventuress."

She wasn't through. But the doorbell rang, and I went to answer it. I thought it just possible that a pair might rush me, and there was no advantage in a roughhouse, so I left the bolt and chain on until I saw it was Saul Panzer. Then I opened up and let him in, and shut the door and slid the bolt again.

Saul is about the smallest practicing dick, public or private, that I've ever seen, and he has the biggest scope. He can't push over buildings because he simply hasn't got the size, but there's no other kind of a job he wouldn't earn his money on. It's hard to tell what he looks like, because you can't see his face for his nose. He had a big long cardboard box under his arm.

I took him to the office. As he sidled past a chair to get to Wolfe's desk he passed one sharp glance around, and I knew that gave him a print of those three sitting there which would fade out only when he did.

Wolfe greeted him. "Good evening, Saul."

"Good evening, Mr. Wolfe. Of course Archie told you my phone call. There's not much to add. When I arrived the detective was there on the sidewalk. His name is Bill Purvil. I saw him once about four years ago in Brooklyn, when we had that Moschenden case. He didn't recognize me on the sidewalk. But when I went in at that entrance he followed me. I figured it was better to go ahead. There was a phone in the apartment. If I found the package I could phone Archie to come and get into the court from Sixtieth Street, and throw it to him from a back window. When the detective saw I was going into that apartment with a key, he stopped me to ask questions, and I answered what occurred to me. He stayed out in the hall and I locked the door on the inside. I went through the place. The package isn't there. I came out and the detective followed me downstairs to the sidewalk. I phoned from a drug store. I don't think he tried to follow me, but I made sure it didn't work if he did."

Wolfe nodded. "Satisfactory. And your bundle?"

Saul got the box from under his arm and put it on the desk. "I guess it's flowers. It has a name on it, Drummond, the Park Avenue florist. It was on the floor of the hall right at the door of the apartment, apparently been delivered, addressed Miss Clara Fox. My instructions were to search only the apartment, so I hesitated to open this box, because it wasn't in the apartment. But I didn't want to leave it there, because it was barely possible that what you want was in it. So I brought it along."

"Good. Satisfactory again. May we open it, Miss Fox?"

"Certainly."

I got up to help. Saul and I pulled off the fancy gray tape and took the lid off. Standing, we were the only ones who could see in. I said, "It's a thousand roses."

Clara Fox jumped up to look. I reached in the box and picked up an envelope and took a card from the envelope. I squinted at it—it was scrawly writing—and read it out, "Francis Horrocks?"

She nodded. "That's my acquaintance. The man that ejected me for the Marquis of Clivers. He's a young diplomat with a special knowledge of the Far East. Aren't they beautiful? Look, Hilda. Smell. They are *very* nice." She carried them to Wolfe. "Aren't they a beautiful color, Mr. Wolfe? Smell." She looked at Mike Walsh, but he was asleep again, so she put the box back on the desk and sat down.

Wolfe was rubbing his nose which she had tickled with the roses. "Saul. Take those to the kitchen and have Fritz put them in water. Remain there.

You must see my orchids, Miss Fox, but that can wait. Mr. Walsh! Archie, wake him, please."

I reached out and gave Walsh a dig, and he jerked up and glared at me. He protested, "Hey! It's too warm in here. I'm never as warm as this after supper."

Wolfe wiggled a finger at him. "If you please, Mr. Walsh. Miss Fox has been giving us some details, such as your recognition of the Marquis of Clivers. Do you understand what I'm saying?"

"Sure." Walsh pulled the tips of his fingers across his eyes, and stretched his eyes open. "What about it?"

"Did you recognize the Marquis of Clivers as George Rowley?"

"Sure I did. Who says I didn't?"

"As yet, no one. Are you positive it was the same man?"

"Yes. I told you at the table, I'm always positive."

"So you did. Among other things. You told me that through ancient habit, and on your post as a night watchman, you carry a gun. You also told me that you suspected Harlan Scovil of being an Englishman, and that all English blood was bad blood. Do you happen to have your gun with you? Could I see it?"

"I've got a license."

"Of course. Could I see it? Just as a favor?"

Walsh growled something to himself, but after a moment's hesitation he leaned forward and reached to his hip and pulled out a gat. He looked at it, and rubbed his left palm caressingly over the barrel, and then got up and poked the butt at Wolfe. Wolfe took it, glanced at it, and held it out to me. I gave it a mild inspection. It was an old Folwell .44. It was loaded, the cylinder full, and there was no smell of any recent activity around the muzzle. I glanced at Wolfe and caught his little nod, and returned the cannon to Mike Walsh, who caressed it again before he put it back in his pocket.

Clara Fox said, "Who's wasting time now, Mr. Wolfe? You haven't told us yet—"

Wolfe stopped her. "Don't begin again, Miss Fox. Please. Give me a chance to earn my share of that million. Though I must confess that my opinion is that you might all of you sell out for a ten-dollar bill and call it a good bargain. What have you to go on? Really nothing. The paper which George Rowley signed was entrusted to Rubber Coleman, whom you have been unable to find. The only other basis for a legal claim would be a suit by the man called Turtle-back to recover the value of his horse, and since Mr. Walsh has told us that Turtle-back was over fifty years old in 1895, he is in all likelihood dead. There are only two methods by which you can get anything out of the Marquis of Clivers; one is to attempt to establish a legal claim by virtue of contract, for which you would need a lawyer, not a detective. You have yourself already done the detective work, quite thoroughly. The other method is to attempt to scare the marquis into paying you, through threat of public exposure of his past. That is an ancient and often effective method, technically known as blackmail. It is not—"

She interrupted him, cool but positive. "It isn't blackmail to try to collect something from a man that he promised to pay."

Wolfe nodded. "It's a nice point. Morally he owes it. But where's the paper he signed? Anyway, let me finish. I myself am in a quandary. When you first told me the nature of the commission you were offering me, I was prepared to decline it without much discussion. Then another element entered in, of which you are still ignorant, which lent the affair fresh interest. Of course, interest is not enough; before that comes the question, who is going to pay me? I shall expect—"

Mike Walsh squawked, "Ten per cent!"

Clara Fox said, "I told you, Mr. Wolfe—"

"Permit me. I shall expect nothing exorbitant. It happens that my bank account is at present in excellent condition, and therefore my cupidity is comparatively dormant. Still, I have a deep aversion to working without getting paid for it. I have accepted you, Miss Fox, as my client. I may depend on you?"

She nodded impatiently. "Of course you may. What is the other element that entered in of which I am still ignorant?"

"Oh. That." Wolfe's half-closed eyes took in all three faces. "At twenty-five minutes to six this evening, less than five hours ago, on Thirty-first Street near Tenth Avenue, Harlan Scovil was shot and killed."

Mike Walsh jerked up straight in his chair. They all gaped at Wolfe.

Wolfe said, "He was walking along the sidewalk, and someone going by in an automobile shot him five times. He was dead when a passerby reached him. The automobile has been found, empty of course, on Ninth Avenue."

Clara Fox gasped incredulously, "Harlan Scovil!" Hilda Lindquist sat with her fists suddenly clenched and her lower lip pushing her upper lip toward her nose. Mike Walsh was glaring at Wolfe. He exploded suddenly, "Ye're a howling idiot!"

Wolfe's being called an idiot twice in one evening was certainly a record. I made a note to grin when I got time. Clara Fox was saying, "But Mr. Wolfe . . . it can't . . . how can . . ."

Walsh went on exploding, "So you hear of some shooting, and you want to smell my gun? Ye're an idiot! Of all the dirty—" He stopped himself suddenly and leaned on his hands on his knees, and his eyes narrowed. He looked pretty alert and competent for a guy seventy years old. "To hell with that. Where's Harlan? I want to see him."

Wolfe wiggled a finger at him. "Compose yourself, Mr. Walsh. All in time. As you see, Miss Fox, this is quite a complication."

"It's terrible. Why . . . it's awful. He's really *killed?*"

Hilda Lindquist spoke suddenly. "I didn't want to come here. I told you that. I thought it was a wild goose chase. My father made me. I mean, he's old and sick and he wanted me to come because he thought maybe we could get enough to save the farm."

Wolfe nodded. "And now, of course . . ."

Her square chin stuck out. "Now I'm glad I came. I've often heard my father talk about Harlan Scovil. He would have been killed anyway, whether I came or not, and now I'm glad I'm here to help. You folks will have to tell me what to do, because I don't know. But if that marquis thinks he can refuse to talk to us and then shoot us down on the street . . . we'll see."

"I haven't said the marquis shot him, Miss Lindquist."

"Who else did?"

I thought from her tone she was going to tell him not to be an idiot, but she let it go at that and looked at him.

Wolfe said, "I can't tell you. But I have other details for you. This afternoon Harlan Scovil came to this office. He told Mr. Goodwin that he came in advance of the time for the interview to see what kind of a man I was. At twenty-six minutes after five, while he was waiting to see me, he received a telephone call from a man. He left at once. You remember that shortly after you arrived this evening a caller came and you were asked to go to the front room. The caller was a city detective. He informed us of the murder, described the corpse, and said that in his pocket had been found a paper bearing my name and address, and also the names of Clara Fox, Hilda Lindquist, Michael Walsh, and the Marquis of Clivers. Scovil had been shot just nine minutes after he received that phone call here and left the house."

Clara Fox said, "I saw him write those names on the paper. He did it while he was eating lunch with me."

"Just so. Mr. Walsh. Did you telephone Scovil here at five-twenty-six?"

"Of course not. How could I? That's a damn fool question. I didn't know he was here."

"I suppose not. But I thought possibly Scovil had arranged to meet you here. When Scovil arrived it happened that there was another man in the office, one of my clients, and Scovil approached him and told him he wasn't Mike Walsh."

"Well, was he? I'm Mike Walsh, look at me. The only arrangement I had to meet him was at six o'clock, through Miss Fox. Shut up about it. I asked you where Harlan is. I want to see him."

"In time, sir. Miss Fox. Did you telephone Scovil here?"

She shook her head. "No. Oh, no. I thought you said it was a man."

"So it seemed. Fritz might possibly have been mistaken. Was it you who phoned, Miss Lindquist?"

"No. I haven't telephoned anyone in New York except Clara."

"Well." Wolfe sighed. "You see the little difficulty, of course. Whoever telephoned knew that Scovil was in New York and knew he was at this office. Who knew that except you three?"

Hilda Lindquist said, "The Marquis of Clivers knew it."

"How do you know that?"

"I don't know it. I see it. Clara had been to see him and he had threatened to have her arrested for annoying him. He had detectives follow her, and they saw her this noon with Harlan Scovil, and they followed Harlan Scovil here and then notified the Marquis of Clivers. Then he telephoned—"

"Possible, Miss Lindquist. I admit it's possible. If you substitute for the detective a member of the marquis's entourage, even more possible. But granted that we rather like that idea, do you think the police will? A British peer, in this country on a government mission of the highest importance, murdering Harlan Scovil on Thirty-first Street? I have known quite a few policemen, and I am almost certain that idea wouldn't appeal to them."

Mike Walsh said, "To hell with the dumb Irish cops."

Clara Fox asked, "The detective that was here . . . the one that told you about . . . about the shooting. Our names were on that paper. Why didn't he want to see us?"

"He did. Badly. But I observed that there were no addresses on the paper except my own, so he is probably having difficulty. I decided not to mention that all of you happened to be here at the moment, because I wanted a talk with you and I knew he would monopolize your evening."

"The detective at my apartment . . . he may have been there . . . about this . . ."

"No. There had hardly been time enough. Besides, there was one at the garage too."

Clara Fox looked at him, and took a deep breath. "I seem to be in a fix."

"Two fixes, Miss Fox." Wolfe rang for beer. "But it is possible that before we are through we may be able to effect a merger."

VII

I ONLY half heard that funny remark of Wolfe's. Parts of my brain were skipping around from this to that and finding no place to settle down. As a matter of fact I had been getting more uncomfortable all evening, ever since

Slim Foltz had told us the names on that paper and Wolfe had let him go without telling him that the three people he was looking for were sitting in our front room. He was working on a murder, and the fact that the name of a bird like that marquis was on that paper meant that they weren't going to let anything slide. They would find those three people sooner or later, and when they learned where they had been at the time Slim Foltz called on us, they would be vexed. There were already two or three devoted public servants who thought Wolfe was a little tricky, and it looked as if this was apt to give them entirely too much encouragement. I knew pretty well how Wolfe worked, and when he let Foltz go I had supposed he was going to have a little talk with our trio of visitors and then phone someone like Cramer at Headquarters or Dick Morley of the District Attorney's office, and arrange for some interviews. But here it was past ten o'clock, and he was just going on with an interesting conversation. I didn't like it.

I heard his funny remark though, about two fixes and effecting a merger. I got his idea, and that was one of the points my brain skipped to. I saw how there might possibly be a connection between the Rubber Band business and Clara Fox being framed for lifting the thirty grand. She had gone to this British gent and spilled her hand to him, and he had given her the chilly how now and had her put out. But he had been badly annoyed what. You might even say scared if he hadn't been a nobleman. And a few days later the frame-up reared its ugly head. It would be interesting to find out if the Marquis of Clivers was acquainted with Mr. Muir, and if so to what extent. Clara Fox had said Muir was a Scotchman, so you couldn't depend on him any more than you could an Englishman, maybe not as much. As usual, Wolfe was ahead of me, but he hadn't lost me, I was panting along behind.

Meanwhile I had to listen too, for the conversation hadn't stopped. At the end of Wolfe's remark about the merger, Mike Walsh suddenly stood up and announced, "I'll be going."

Wolfe looked at him. "Not just yet, Mr. Walsh. Be seated."

But he stayed on his feet. "I've got to go. I want to see Harlan."

"Mr. Scovil is dead. I beg you, sir. There are one or two points I must still explain."

Walsh muttered, "I don't like this. You see I don't like it?" He glared at Wolfe, handed me the last half of it, and sat down on the edge of his chair.

Wolfe said, "It's getting late. We are confronted by three distinct problems, and each one presents difficulties. First, the matter of the money missing from the office of the Seaboard Products Corporation. So far that appears to be the personal problem of Miss Fox, and I shall discuss it with her later. Second, there is your joint project of collecting a sum of money from the Marquis of Clivers. Third, there is your joint peril resulting from the murder of Harlan Scovil."

"Joint hell." Walsh's eyes were narrowed again. "Say we divide the peril up, mister. Along with the money."

"If you prefer. But let us take the second problem first. I see no reason for abandoning the attack on the Marquis of Clivers because Mr. Scovil has met a violent death. In fact, that should persuade us to prosecute it. My advice would be this—Archie, your notebook. Take a letter to the Marquis of Clivers, to be signed by me. Salute him democratically, 'Dear sir:

" 'I have been engaged by Mr. Victor Lindquist and his daughter, Miss Hilda Lindquist, as their agent to collect an amount which you have owed them since 1895. In that year, in Silver City, Nevada, with your knowledge and consent, Mr. Lindquist purchased a horse from a man known as Turtle-back, and furnished the horse to you for your use in an urgent private emergency. You signed a paper before your departure acknowledging the obligation, but of course your debt would remain a legal obligation without that.

" 'At that time and place good horses were scarce and valuable; furthermore, for reasons peculiar to your situation, that horse was of extraordinary value to you at that moment. Miss Lindquist, representing her father, states that that extraordinary value can be specified as $100,000. That amount is therefore due from you, with accrued interest at six per cent to date.

" 'I trust that you will pay the amount due without delay and without forcing us to the necessity of legal action. I am not an attorney. If you prefer to make the payment through attorneys representing both sides, we shall be glad to make that arrangement.' "

Wolfe leaned back. "All right, Miss Lindquist?"

She was frowning at him. "He can't pay with money for murdering Harlan Scovil."

"Certainly not. But one thing at a time. I should explain that this claim has no legal standing, since it has expired by time, but the marquis might not care to proceed to that defense in open legal proceedings. We are on the fringe of blackmail, but our hearts are pure. I should also explain that at six-per-cent compound interest money doubles itself in something like twelve years, and that the present value of that claim as I have stated it in the letter is something over a million dollars. A high price for a horse, but we are only using it to carry us to a point of vantage. This has your approval, Miss Fox?"

Clara Fox was looking bad. Sitting there with the fingers of one hand curled tight around the fingers of the other, she wasn't nearly as cool and sweet as she had been that afternoon when Muir had declared right in front of her that she was a sneak thief.

"No," she said. "I don't think we want . . . no, Mr. Wolfe. I'm just realizing . . . it's my fault Mr. Scovil was killed. I started all this. Just for that money . . . no! Don't send that letter. Don't do anything."

"Indeed." Wolfe drank some beer, and put the glass down with his usual deliberation. "It would seem that murder is sometimes profitable, after all."

Her fingers tightened. "Profitable?"

"Obviously. If, as seems likely, Harlan Scovil was killed by someone involved in this Rubber Band business, the murderer probably had two ends in view: to remove Scovil and to frighten the rest of you. To scare you off. He appears to have accomplished both purposes. Good for him."

"We're not scared off."

"You're ready to quit."

Hilda Lindquist put in, with her chin up, "Not me. Send that letter."

"Miss Fox?"

She pulled her shoulders in, and out again. "All right. Send it."

"Mr. Walsh?"

"Deal me out. You said you wanted to explain something."

"So I did." Wolfe emptied his glass. "We'll send the letter, then. The third problem remains. I must call your attention to these facts: First, the police are at this moment searching for all three of you—in your case, Miss Fox, two separate assignments of police. Second, the police are capable of concluding that the murderer of Harlan Scovil is someone who knew him or knew of him, and was in this neighborhood this evening. Third, it is probable that there is no one in New York who ever heard of Harlan Scovil except you three and Clivers; or, if there is such a one, it is not likely that the police will discover him—in fact, the idea will not occur to them until they have exhausted all possibilities in connection with you three. Fourth, when they find you and question you, they will suspect you not only of knowledge of Scovil's murder, but also of some preposterous plot against Lord Clivers, since his name was on that paper.

"Fifth. When they question you, there will be three courses open to you. You may tell the truth, in which case your wild and extravagant tale will reinforce their suspicions and will be enough to convict you of almost anything, even murder. Or you may try to tone your tale down, tell only a little and improvise to fill in the gaps, whereupon they will catch you in lies and go after you harder than ever. Or you may assert your constitutional rights and refuse to talk at all; if you do that they will incarcerate you as material witnesses and hold you without bail. As you see, it is a dilemma with three horns and none of them attractive. As Miss Fox put it, you're in a fix. And any of the three courses will render you *hors de combat* for any further molestation of the Marquis of Clivers."

Hilda Lindquist's chin was way up in the air. Mike Walsh was leaning forward with his eyes on Wolfe narrower than ever. Clara Fox had stopped squeezing her hand and had her lips pressed tight. She opened them to say, "All right. We're game. Which do we do?"

"None." Wolfe sighed. "None of those. Confound it, I was born romantic and I shall never recover from it. But, as I have said, I expect to be paid. I hope I have made it clear that it will not do for the police to find you until we are ready for them to. Have I demonstrated that?"

The two women asked simultaneously, "Well?"

"Well . . . Archie, bring Saul."

I jumped from habit and not from enthusiasm. I was half sore. I didn't like it. I found Saul in the kitchen drinking port wine and telling Fred and Fritz stories, and led him to the office. He stood in front of Wolfe's desk. "Yes, sir."

Wolfe spoke, not to him. "Miss Lindquist, this is Mr. Saul Panzer. I would trust him further than might be thought credible. He is himself a bachelor, but has acquaintances who are married and possibly even friends, with the usual living quarters—an apartment or a house. Have you anything to say to him?"

But the Lindquist mind was slow. She didn't get it. Clara Fox asked Wolfe, "May I?"

"Please do."

She turned to Saul. "Miss Lindquist would like to be in seclusion for a while—a few days—she doesn't know how long. She thought you might know of a place . . . one of your friends . . ."

Saul nodded. "Certainly, Miss Lindquist." He turned to Wolfe. "Is there a warrant out?"

"No. Not yet."

"Shall I give the address to Archie?"

"By no means. If I need to communicate with Miss Lindquist I can do so through General Delivery. She can notify me on the telephone what branch."

"Shall we go out the back way onto Thirty-fourth Street?"

"I was about to suggest it. When you are free again, return here. Tonight." Wolfe moved his eyes. "Is there anything of value in your luggage at the hotel, Miss Lindquist?"

She was standing up. She shook her head. "Not much. No."

"Have you any money?"

"I have thirty-eight dollars and my ticket home."

"Good. Opulence. Good night, Miss Lindquist. Sleep well."

Clara Fox was up too. She went to the other woman and put her hands on her shoulders and kissed her on the mouth. "Good night, Hilda. It's rotten, but . . . keep your chin up."

Hilda Lindquist said in a loud voice, "Good night, everybody," and turned and followed Saul Panzer out of the room. In a few seconds I could hear their footsteps on the stairs leading down to the basement, where a door opened onto the court in the rear. We were all looking at Wolfe, who was opening a bottle of beer. I was thinking, the old lummox certainly fancies he's putting on a hot number, I suppose he'll send Miss Fox to board with his mother in Buda Pesth. It looked to me like he was stepping off over his head.

He looked at Mike Walsh. "Now, sir, your turn. I note your symptoms of disapproval, but we are doing the best we can. In the kitchen is a man named Fred Durkin, whom you have seen. Within his capacity, he is worthy of your trust and mine. I would suggest—"

"I don't want any Durkin." Walsh was on his feet again. "I don't want anything from you at all. I'll just be going."

"But Mr. Walsh." Wolfe wiggled a finger at him. "Believe me, it will not pay to be headstrong. I am not by nature an alarmist, but there are certain features of this affair—"

"So I notice." Walsh stepped up to the desk. "The features is what I don't like about it." He looked at Clara Fox, then at me, then at Wolfe, letting us know what the features were. "I may be past me prime, but I'm not in a box yet. What kind of a shenanigan would ye like to try on an old man, huh? I'm to go out and hide, am I? Do I get to ask a question or two?"

"That's three." Wolfe sighed. "Go ahead."

Walsh whirled on me. "You, Goodwin's your name? Was it you that answered the phone yesterday, the call that came for Harlan Scovil?"

"No." I grinned at him. "I wasn't here."

"Where was you?"

"At the office of the Seaboard Products Corporation, where Miss Fox works."

"Ha! Was you indeed. You wasn't here. I suppose it couldn't have been you that phoned here to Harlan."

"Sure it could have, but it wasn't. Listen, Mr. Walsh—"

"I've listened enough. I've been listening to this Clara Fox for a year and looking at her pretty face, and I had no reason to doubt her maybe, and this is what's come out of it, I've helped lead my old friend Harlan Scovil into an ambush to his death. My old friend Harlan." He stopped abruptly, and shut his lips tight, and looked around at us while a big fat tear suddenly popped out of each of his eyes and rolled on down, leaving a mark across his wrinkles. He went on, "I ate a meal with you. A meal and three drinks. Maybe I'd like to puke it up someday. Or maybe you're all square shooters, I don't know, but I know somebody ain't, and I'm going to find out who it is. What's this about them being after Miss Fox for stealing money? I can find out about that too. And if I want anything collected from this English Marquis nobleman, I can collect it myself. Good night to ye all." He turned and headed for the door.

Wolfe snapped, "Get him, Archie."

Remembering the gun on his hip, I went and folded myself around him and locked him. He let out a snarl and tried some twisting and unloosed a couple of kicks at my shins, but in four seconds he had sense enough to see it was no go. He quivered a little and then stood quiet, but I kept him tight. He said, "It's me now, is it?"

Wolfe spoke across the room at him. "You called me an idiot, Mr. Walsh. I return the compliment. What is worse, you are hot-headed. But you are an old man, so there is humanity's debt to you. You may go where you please, but I must warn you that every step you take may be a dangerous step. Furthermore, when you talk, every word may be dangerous not only to you but to Miss Fox and Miss Lindquist. I strongly advise you to adopt the precautions—"

"I'll do me own precautions."

"Mike!" Clara Fox came, her hand out. "Mike, you can't be thinking . . . what Mr. Wolfe says is right. Don't desert us now. Turn him loose, Mr. Goodwin. Shake hands, Mike."

He shook his head. "Did you see him grab me, and all I was doing was walking out on me own feet? I hate the damn detectives and always have, and what was he doing at your office? And if you're my enemy, Clara Fox, God help you, and if not then you can be my friend. Not now. When he turns me loose I'll be going."

Wolfe said, "Release him, Archie. Good night, Mr. Walsh."

I let my muscles go and stepped back. Mike Walsh put a hand up to feel his ribs, turned to look at me, and then to Wolfe. He said, "But I'm no idiot. Show me that back way."

Clara Fox begged him, "Don't go, Mike."

He didn't answer her. I started for the kitchen, and he followed me after stopping in the hall for his hat and coat. I told Fred to see him through the court and the fence and the passage leading to 34th Street, and switched on the basement light for them. I stood and watched them go down. I hadn't cared much for Wolfe's hot number anyhow, and now it looked like worse than a flop, with that wild Irishman in his old age going out to do his own precautions. But I hadn't argued about letting him go, because I knew that kind as well as Wolfe did and maybe better.

When I went back to the office Clara Fox was still standing up. She asked, "Did he really go?"

I nodded. "With bells on."

"Do you think he meant what he said?" She turned to Wolfe. "I don't think he meant it at all. He was just angry and frightened and sorry. I know how he felt. He felt that Harlan Scovil was killed because we started this business, and now he doesn't want to go away and hide. I don't either. I don't want to run away."

"Then it is lucky you won't have to." Wolfe emptied his glass, returned it to the tray, and slid the tray around to the other side of the pen block. That meant that he had decided he had had enough beer for the day, and therefore that he would probably open only one more bottle before going upstairs, provided he went fairly soon. He sighed. "You understand, Miss Fox, this is something unprecedented. It has been many years since any woman has slept under this roof. Not that I disapprove of them, except when they attempt to function as domestic animals. When they stick to the vocations for which they are best adapted, such as chicanery, sophistry, self-adornment, cajolery, mystification and incubation, they are sometimes splendid creatures. Anyhow . . . you will find our south room, directly above mine, quite comfortable. I may add that I am foolishly fond of good form, good color, and fine texture, and I have good taste in those matters. It is a pleasure to look at you. You have unusual beauty. I say that to inform you that while the idea of a woman sleeping in my house is theoretically insupportable, in this case I am willing to put up with it."

"Thank you. Then I'm to hide here?"

"You are. You must keep to your room, with the curtains drawn. Elaborate circumspection will be necessary and will be explained to you. Mr. Goodwin will attend to that. Should your stay be prolonged, it may be that you can join us in the dining room for meals; eating from a tray is an atrocious insult both to the food and the feeder; and in that case, luncheon is punctually at one and dinner at eight. But before we adjourn for the night there are one or two things I need still to know; for instance, where were you and Miss Lindquist and Mr. Walsh from five to six o'clock this evening?"

Clara Fox nodded. "I know. That's why you asked me if I had killed anybody, and I thought you were being eccentric. But of course you don't believe that. I've told you we were looking for Harlan Scovil."

"Let's get a schedule. Put it down, Archie. Mr. Goodwin informed me that you left the Seaboard office at a quarter past five."

She glanced at me. "Yes, about that. That was the time I was supposed to get Harlan Scovil at his hotel on Forty-fifth Street, and I didn't get there until nearly half past five. He wasn't there. I looked around on the street and went a block to another hotel, thinking possibly he had misunderstood me, and then went back again and he still wasn't there. They said he had been out all afternoon as far as they knew. Hilda was at a hotel on Thirtieth Street, and I had told Mike Walsh to be there in the lobby at a quarter to six, and I was to call there for them. Of course I was late, it was six o'clock when I got there, and we decided to try Harlan Scovil's hotel once more, but he wasn't there. We waited a few minutes and then came on without him, and got here at six-thirty." She stopped, and chewed on her lip. "He was dead . . . then. While we were there waiting for him. And I was planning . . . I thought . . ."

"Easy, Miss Fox. We can't resurrect. So you know nothing of Miss Lindquist's and Mr. Walsh's whereabouts between five and six. Easy, I beg you. Don't tell me again I'm an idiot or you'll have me believing it. I am merely filling in a picture. Or rather, a rough sketch. I think perhaps you should leave us here with it and go to bed. Remember, you are to keep to your room, both for your own safety and to preserve me from serious annoyance. Mr. Goodwin—"

"I know." She frowned at him and then at me. "I thought of that when you said I was to stay here. You mean what they call accessory after the fact—"

"Bosh." Wolfe straightened in his chair and his hand went forward by automatism, but there was no beer there. He sent a sharp glance at me to see if I noticed it, and sat back again. "I can't be an accessory after a fact that never existed. I am acting on the assumption that you are not criminally involved either in larceny or in murder. If you are, say so and get out. If you are not, go to bed. Fritz will show you your room." He pushed the button. "Well?"

"I'll go to bed." She brushed her hair back. "I don't think I'll sleep."

"I hope you will, even without appetite for it. At any rate, you won't walk the floor, for I shall be directly under you." The door opened, and Wolfe turned to it. "Fritz. Please show Miss Fox to the south room, and arrange towels and so on. In the morning, take her roses to her with breakfast, but have Theodore slice the stems first. And by the way, Miss Fox, you have nothing with you. The niceties of your toilet you will have to forego, but I believe we can furnish a sleeping garment. Mr. Goodwin owns some handsome silk pajamas which his sister sent him on his birthday, from Ohio. They are hideous, but handsome. I'm sure he won't mind. I presume, Fritz, you'll find them in the chest of drawers near the window. Unless . . . would you prefer to get them for Miss Fox yourself, Archie?"

I could have thrown my desk at him. He knew damn well what I thought of those pajamas. I was so sore I suppose it showed in my cheeks, because I saw Fritz pull in his lower lip with his teeth. I was slower on the come-back than usual, and I never did get to make one, for at that instant the doorbell rang, which was a piece of luck for Nero Wolfe. I got up and strode past them to the hall.

I was careless for two reasons. I was taking it for granted it was Saul Panzer, back from planting Hilda Lindquist in seclusion; and the cause of my taking something for granted when I shouldn't, since that's always a bad thing to do in our business, was that my mind was still engaged with Wolfe's vulgar attempt to be funny. Anyhow, the fact remains that I was careless. I whirled the lock and took off the bolt and pulled the door open.

They darned near toppled me off my pins with the edge of the door catching my shoulder. I saved myself from falling and the rest was reflex. There were two of them, and they were going right on past in a hurry. I sprang back and got in front and gave one of them a knee in the belly and used a stiff-arm on the other. He started to swing, but I didn't bother about it; I picked up the one that had stopped my knee and just used him for a whisk broom and depended on speed and my 180 pounds. The combination swept the hall out. We went through the door so fast that the first guy stumbled and fell down the stoop, and I dropped the one I had in my arms and turned and pulled the door shut and heard the lock click. Then I pushed the bell-button three times. The guy that had fallen down the stoop, the one who had tried to plug me, was on his feet again and coming up, with words.

"We're officers—"

"Shut up." I heard footsteps inside, and I called through the closed door. "Fritz? Tell Mr. Wolfe a couple of gentlemen have called and we're staying out on the porch for a talk. And hey! Those things are in the bottom drawer."

VIII

I SAID, "What do you mean, officers? Army or navy?"

He looked down at me. He was an inch taller than me to begin with, and he was stretching it. He made his voice hard enough to scare a schoolgirl right out of her socks. "Listen, bud. I've heard about you. How'd you like to take a good nap on some concrete?"

The other officer was back on his ankles too, but he was a short guy. He was built something like a whisk broom, at that. I undertook to throw oil on the troubled waters. Ordinarily I might have enjoyed a nice rough cussing-match, but I wanted to find out something and get back inside. I summoned a friendly grin.

"What the hell, how did I know you had badges? Okay, thanks, sergeant. All I knew was the door bumping me and a cyclone going by. Is that a way to inspire confidence?"

"All right, you know we've got badges now." The sergeant humped up a shoulder and let it drop, and then the other one. "Let us in. We want to see Nero Wolfe."

"I'm sorry, he's got a headache."

"We'll cure it for him. Listen. A friend of mine warned me about you once. He said the time would come when you would have to be taken down. Maybe that's the very thing I came here for. But so far it's a matter of law. Open that door or I'll open it myself. I want to see Mr. Wolfe on police business."

"There's no law about that. Unless you've got a warrant."

"You couldn't read it anyhow. Let us in."

I got impatient. "What's the use wasting time? You can't go in. The floor's just been scrubbed. Wolfe wouldn't see you anyhow, at this time of night. Tell me what you want like a gentleman and a cop, and I'll see if I can help you."

He glared at me. Then he put his hand inside to his breast pocket and pulled out a document, and I had a feeling in my knees like a steering wheel with a shimmy. If it was a search warrant the jig was up right there. He unfolded it and held it for me to look, and even in the dim light from the street lamp one glance was enough to start my heart off again. It was only a warrant to take into custody. I peered at it and saw among other things the name Ramsey Muir, and nodded.

The sergeant grunted, "Can you see the name? Clara Fox."

"Yeah, it's a nice name."

"We're going in after her. Open up."

I lifted the brows. "In here? You're crazy."

"All right, we're crazy. Open the door."

I shook my head, and got out a cigarette, and lit up. I said, "Listen, sergeant. There's no use wasting the night in repartee. You know damn well you've got no more right to go through that door than a cockroach unless you've got a search warrant. Ordinarily Mr. Wolfe is more than willing to cooperate with you guys; if you don't know that, ask Inspector Cramer. So am I. Hell, some of my best friends are cops. I'm not even sore because you tried to rush me and I got excited and thought you were mugs and pushed you. But it just happens that we don't want company of any kind at present."

He grunted and glared. "Is Clara Fox in there?"

"Now that's a swell question." I grinned at him. "Either she isn't, in which case I would say no, or she is and I don't want you to know it, in which case would I say yes? I might at that, if she was somewhere else and I didn't want you to go there to look for her."

"Is she in there?"

I just shook my head at him.

"You're harboring a fugitive from justice."

"I wouldn't dream of such a thing."

The short dick, the one I had swept the hall with, piped up in a tenor, "Take him down for resisting an officer."

I reproved him. "The sergeant knows better than that. He knows they wouldn't book me, or if they did I read about a man once that collected enough to retire on for false arrest."

The big one stood and stared into my frank eyes for half a minute, then turned and descended the stoop and looked up and down the street. I didn't know whether he expected to see the Russian Army or a place to buy a drink. He called up to his brother in arms, "Stay here, Steve. Cover that door. I'll go and phone a report and probably send someone to cover the rear. When that bird turns his back to go in the house give him a kick in the ass."

I waved at him, "Good night, sergeant," pushed the button three shorts, took my key from my pocket, unlocked the door, and went in. If that tenor had tickled me I'd have pulled his nose. I slid the bolt in place. Fritz was standing in the middle of the hall with my automatic in his hand. I said, "Watch out, that thing's loaded."

He was serious. "I know it is, Archie. I thought possibly you might need it."

"No, thanks. I bit their jugulars. It's a trick."

Fritz giggled and handed me the gun, and went to the kitchen. I strolled into the office. Clara Fox was gone, and I was reflecting that she might be looking at herself in the mirror with my silk pajamas on. I had tried them on once, but had never worn them. I had no more than got inside the office when the doorbell rang. As I returned to the entrance and opened the door, leaving the bolt and chain on, I wondered if it was the tenor calling me back to get my kick. But this time it was Saul Panzer. He stood there and let me see him. I asked him through the crack, "Did you find her?"

"No. I lost her. Lost the trail."

"You're a swell bird dog."

I opened up and let him in, and took him to the office. Wolfe was leaning back in his chair with his eyes closed. The tray had been moved back to its usual position, and there was a glass on it with fresh foam sticking to the sides, and two bottles. He was celebrating the hot number he was putting on.

I said, "Here's Saul."

"Good." The eyes stayed shut. "All right, Saul?"

"Yes, sir."

"Of course. Satisfactory. Can you sleep here?"

"Yes, sir. I stopped by and got a toothbrush."

"Indeed. Satisfactory. The north room, Archie, above yours. Tell Fred he is expected at eight in the morning, and send him home. If you are hungry, Saul, go to the kitchen; if not, take a book to the front room. There will be instructions shortly."

I went to the kitchen and pried Fred Durkin out of his chair and escorted him to the hall and let him out, having warned him not to stumble over any foreign objects that might be found on the stoop. But the dick had left the stoop and was propped against a fire plug down at the curb. He jerked himself up to take a stare at Fred, and I was hoping he'd be dumb enough to suspect it was Clara Fox with pants on, but that was really too much to expect. I barricaded again and returned to the office.

Saul had gone to the front room to curl up with a book. Wolfe stayed put behind his desk. I went to the kitchen and negotiated for a glass of milk, and then went back and got into my own swivel and started sipping. When a couple of minutes passed without any sign from Wolfe, I said indifferently, "That commotion in the hall a while ago was the Mayor and the Police Commissioner calling to give you the freedom of the city prison. I cut their throats and put them in the garbage can."

"One moment, Archie. Be quiet."

"Okay. I'll gargle my milk. It'll probably be my last chance for that innocent amusement before they toss us in the hoosegow. I remember you told me once that there is no moment in any man's life too empty to be dramatized. You seem to think that's an excuse for filling life up with—"

"Confound you." Wolfe sighed, and I saw his eyelids flicker. "Very well. Who was it in the hall?"

"Two city detectives, one a sergeant no less, with a warrant for the arrest of Clara Fox sworn to by Ramsey Muir. They tried to take us by storm, and I repulsed them single-handed and single-footed. Satisfactory?"

Wolfe shuddered. "I grant there are times when there is no leisure for finesse. Are they camping?"

"One's out there on a fire plug. The sergeant went to telephone. They're going to cover the back. It's a good thing Walsh and Hilda Lindquist got away. I don't suppose—"

The phone rang. I circled on the swivel and put down my milk and took it. "Hello, this is the office of Nero Wolfe." Someone asked me to wait. Then someone else: "Hello, Wolfe? Inspector Cramer."

I asked him to hold it and turned to Wolfe. "Cramer. Up at all hours of the night."

As Wolfe reached for the phone on his desk he tipped me a nod, and I kept my receiver and reached for a pencil and notebook.

Cramer was snappy and crisp, also he was surprised and his feelings were hurt. He had a sad tale. It seemed that Sergeant Heath, one of the best men in his division, in pursuance of his duty to make a lawful arrest, had attempted to call at the office of Nero Wolfe for a consultation and had been denied admittance. In fact, he had been forcibly ejected. What kind of cooperation was that?

Wolfe was surprised too, at this protest. At the time that his assistant, Mr. Goodwin, had hurled the intruders into the street single-handed, he had not known they were city employees; and when that fact was disclosed, their actions had already rendered their friendly intentions open to doubt. Wolfe was sorry if there had been a misunderstanding.

Cramer grunted. "Okay. There's no use trying to be slick about it. What's it going to get you, playing for time? I want that girl, and the sooner the better."

"Indeed." Wolfe was doing slow motion. "You want a girl?"

"You know I do. Goodwin saw the warrant."

"Yes, he told me he saw a warrant. Larceny, he said it was. But isn't this unusual, Mr. Cramer? Here it is nearly midnight, and you, an inspector, in a vindictive frenzy over a larceny—"

"I'm not in a frenzy. But I want that girl, and I know you've got her there. It's no use, Wolfe. Less than half an hour ago I got a phone call that Clara Fox was at that moment in your office."

"It costs only a nickel to make a phone call. Who was it?"

"That's my business. Anyhow, she's there. Let's talk turkey. If Heath goes back there now, can he get her? Yes or no."

"Mr. Cramer." Wolfe cleared his throat. "I shall talk turkey. First, Heath or anyone else coming here now will not be permitted to enter the house without a search warrant."

"How the hell can I get a search warrant at midnight?"

"I couldn't say. Second, Miss Clara Fox is my client, and, however ardently I may defend her interests, I do not expect to violate the law. Third, I will not for the present answer any question, no matter what its source, regarding her whereabouts."

"You won't. Do you call that cooperation?"

"By no means. I call it common sense. And there is no point in discussing it."

There was a long pause, then Cramer again: "Listen, Wolfe. This is more important than you think it is. Can you come down to my office right away?"

"Mr. Cramer!" Wolfe was aghast. "You know I cannot."

"You mean you won't. Forget it for once. I shouldn't leave here. I tell you this is important."

"I'm sorry, sir. As you know, I leave my house rarely, and only when impelled by exigent personal considerations. The last time I left it was in the taxicab driven by Dora Chapin, for the purpose of saving the life of my assistant, Mr. Goodwin."

Cramer cussed a while. "You won't come?"

"No."

"Can I come there?"

"I should think not, under the circumstances. As I said, you cannot enter without a search warrant."

"To hell with a search warrant. I've got to see you. I mean, come and talk with you."

"Just to talk? You are making no reservations?"

"No. This is straight. I'll be there in ten minutes."

"Very well." I saw the creases in Wolfe's cheeks unfolding. "I'll try to restrain Mr. Goodwin."

We hung up. Wolfe pushed the button for Fritz. I shut my notebook and tossed it to the back of the desk, and picked up the glass and took a sip of milk. Then, glancing at the clock and seeing it was midnight, I decided I had better reinforce my endurance and went to the cabinet and poured myself a modicum of bourbon. It felt favorable going down, so I took another modicum. Fritz had brought Wolfe some beer, and it was already flowing to its destiny.

I said, "Tell me where Mike Walsh is and I'll go and wring his neck. He must have gone to the first drug store and phoned headquarters. We should have had Fred tail him."

Wolfe shook his head. "You always dive into the nearest pool, Archie. Some day you'll hit a rock and break your neck."

"Yeah? What now? Wasn't it Walsh that phoned him?"

"I have no idea. I'm not ready to dive. Possibly Mr. Cramer will furnish us a sounding. Tell Saul to go to bed and come to my room for instructions at eight o'clock."

I went to the front room and gave Saul the program, and bade him good night, and went back to my desk again. There was a little white card lying there, fallen out of my notebook, where I had slipped it some hours before and forgotten about it. I picked it up and looked at it. *Francis Horrocks*.

I said, "I wonder how chummy Clara Fox got with that acquaintance she made. The young diplomat that sent her the roses. It was him that got her in to see his boss. Where do you suppose he fits in?"

"Fits in to what?"

So that was the way he felt. I waved a hand comprehensively. "Oh, life. You know, the mystery of the universe. The scheme of things."

"I'm sure I don't know. Ask him."

"Egad, I shall. I just thought I'd ask you first. Don't be so damn snooty. The fact is, I feel rotten. That Harlan Scovil that got killed was a good guy. You'd have liked him; he said no one could ever get to know a woman well enough to leave her around loose. Though I suppose you've changed your mind, now that there's a woman sleeping in your bed—"

"Nonsense. My bed—"

"You own all the beds in this house except mine, don't you? Certainly it's your bed. Is her door locked?"

"It is. I instructed her to open it only to Fritz's voice or yours."

"Okay. I'm apt to wander in there any time. Is there anything you want to tell me before Cramer gets here? Such as who shot Harlan Scovil and where that thirty grand is and what will happen when they pick Mike Walsh up and he tells them all about our convention this evening? Do you realize that Walsh was here when Saul took Hilda Lindquist away? Do you realize that Walsh may be in Cramer's office right now? Do you realize—"

"That will do, Archie. Definitely." Wolfe sat up and poured beer. "I realize up to my capacity. As I told Mr. Walsh, I am not an alarmist, but I certainly realize that Miss Fox is in more imminent danger than any previous client I can call to mind; if not danger of losing her life, then of having it irretrievably ruined. That is why I am accepting the hazard of concealing her here. As for the murder of Harlan Scovil, a finger of my mind points straight in one direction, but that is scarcely enough for my own satisfaction and totally insufficient for the safety of Miss Fox or the demands of legal retribution. We may learn something from Mr. Cramer, though I doubt it. There are certain steps to be taken without delay. Can Orrie Cather and Johnny Keems be here at eight in the morning?"

"I'll get them. I may have to pull Johnny off—"

"Do so. Have them here by eight if possible, and send them to my room." He sighed. "A riot for a levee, but there's no help for it. You will have to keep to the house. Before we retire certain arrangements regarding Miss Fox will need discussion. And by the way, the letter I dictated on behalf of our other client, Miss Lindquist, should be written and posted with a special-delivery stamp before the early-morning collection. Send Fritz out with it."

"Then I'd better type it now, before Cramer gets here."

"As you please."

I turned and got the typewriter up and opened my notebook, and rattled it off. I grinned as I wrote the "Dear sir," but the grin was bunk, because if Wolfe hadn't told me to be democratic I would have been up a stump and probably would have had to try something like "Dearest Marquis." From the article I had read the day before I knew where he was, Hotel Portland. Wolfe signed it, and I got Fritz and let him out the front door and waited there till he came back. The short dick was still out there.

I was back in the office but not yet on my sitter again, when the doorbell rang. I wasn't taking any chances, since Fred had gone home and Saul was upstairs asleep. I pulled the curtain away from the glass panel to get a view of the stoop, including corners, and when I saw Cramer was there alone I opened up. He stepped in and I shut the door and bolted it and then extended a paw for his hat and coat. And it wasn't so silly that I kept a good eye on him either, since I knew he had been enforcing the law for thirty years.

He mumbled, "Hello, son. Wolfe in the office?"

"Yeah. Walk in."

IX

WOLFE and the inspector exchanged greetings. Cramer sat down and got out a cigar and bit off the end, and held a match to it. Wolfe got a hand up and pinched his nostrils between a thumb and a forefinger to warn the membranes of the assault that was coming. I was in my chair with my notebook on my knee, not bothering to camouflage.

Cramer said, "You know, you're a slick son-of-a-gun. Do you know what I was trying to decide on my way over here?"

Wolfe shook his head. "I couldn't guess."

"I bet you couldn't. I decided it was a toss-up. Whether you've got that Fox woman here and you're playing for time or waiting for daylight to spring something, or whether you've sent her away for her health and you're kidding us to make us think she's here so we won't start nosing for her trail. For instance, I don't suppose it could have been this Goodwin here that phoned my office at half past eleven?"

"I shouldn't think so. Did you, Archie?"

"No, sir. On my honor I didn't."

"Okay." Cramer got smoke in his windpipe and coughed it out. "I know there's no use trying to play poker with you, Wolfe. I quit that years ago. I've come to lay some cards on the table and ask you to do the same. In fact, the Commissioner says we're not asking, we're demanding. We're taking no chances—"

"The Police Commissioner? Mr. Hombert?" Wolfe's brows were up.

"Right. He was in my office when I phoned you. I told you, this is more important than you think it is. You've stepped into something."

"You don't say so." Wolfe sighed. "I was sure to, sooner or later."

"Oh, I'm not trying to impress you. I've quit that too. I'm just telling you. As I told the Commissioner, you're tricky and you're hard to get ahead of, but I've never known you to slip in the mud. By and large, and of course making allowances, you've always been a good citizen."

"Thank you. Let us go on from there."

"Right." Cramer took a puff and knocked off ashes. "I said I'd show you some cards. First, there's the background, I'd better mention that. You know how it is nowadays, everybody's got it in for somebody else, and half of them have gone cuckoo. When a German ship lands here a bunch of Jews go and tear the flag off it and raise general hell. If a Wop professor that's been kicked out of Italy tries to give a lecture a gang of Fascists haul him down and beat him up. When you try your best to feed people that haven't got a job they turn Communist on you and start a riot. It's even got so that when a couple of bank presidents have lunch at the White House, the servants have to search the floor for banana peels that they may have put there for the President to slip on. Everyone has gone nuts."

Wolfe nodded. "Doubtless you are correct. I don't get around much. It sounds bewildering."

"It is. To get down to particulars, when any prominent foreigners come here, we have to watch our step. We don't want anything happening. For instance, you'd be surprised at the precautions we have to take when the German Ambassador comes up from Washington for a banquet. You might think there was a war on. As a matter of fact, there is! No one's ready for a scrap but everyone wants to hit first. Whoever lands at this port nowadays, you can be sure there's someone around that's got it in for him."

"It might be better if everybody stayed at home."

"Huh? Oh. That's their business. Anyway, that's the background. A couple of weeks ago a man called the Marquis of Clivers came here from England."

"I know. I've read about him."

"Then you know what he came for."

Wolfe nodded. "In a general way. A high diplomatic mission. To pass out slices of the Orient."

"Maybe. I'm not a politician, I'm a cop. I was when I pounded the pavement thirty years ago, and I still am. But the Marquis of Clivers seems to be as important as almost anybody. I understand we get the dope on that from the Department of State. When he landed here a couple of weeks ago we gave him protection, and saw him off to Washington. When he came back, eight days ago, we did the same."

"The same? Do you mean you have men with him constantly?"

Cramer shook his head. "Not constantly. All public appearances, and a sort of general eye out. We have special men. If we notice anything or hear of anything that makes us suspicious, we're on the job. That's what I'm coming to. At five-thirty-five this afternoon, just four blocks from here, a man was shot and killed. In his pocket he had a paper—"

Wolfe showed a palm. "I know all about that, Mr. Cramer. I know the man's name, I know he had left my office only a few minutes before he was killed, and I know that the name of the Marquis of Clivers was on the paper. The detective that was here, Mr. Foltz I believe his name was, showed it to me."

"Oh. He did. Well?"

"Well . . . I saw the names on the paper. My own was among them. But, as I explained to Mr. Foltz, I had not seen the man. He had arrived at our office, unexpected and unannounced, and Mr. Goodwin had—"

"Yeah." Cramer took his cigar from his mouth and hitched forward. "Look here, Wolfe. I don't want to get into a chinning match with you, you're better at it than I am, I admit it. I've talked with Foltz, I know what you told him. Here's my position: there's a man in this town representing a foreign government on important business, and I'm responsible both for his safety and his freedom from annoyance. A man is shot down on the street, and on a paper in his pocket we find the name of the Marquis of Clivers, and other names. Naturally I wouldn't mind knowing who killed Harlan Scovil, but finding that name there makes it a good deal more than just another homicide. What's the connection and what does it mean? The Commissioner says we've got to find out damned quick or it's possible we'll have a first-rate mess on our hands. It's already been bungled a little. Like a dumb flatfoot rookie, Captain Devore went to see the Marquis of Clivers this evening without first consulting headquarters."

"Indeed. Will you have some beer, Mr. Cramer?"

"No. The marquis just stared at Devore as if he was one of the lower animals, which he was, and said that possibly the dead man was an insurance salesman and the paper was a list of prospects. Later on the Commissioner himself telephoned the marquis, and by that time the marquis had remembered that a week ago today a woman by the name of Clara Fox had called on him with some kind of a wild tale, trying to get money, and he had had her put out. So there's a tie-up. It's some kind of a plot, no doubt about it, and since it's interesting enough so that someone took the trouble to bump off this Harlan Scovil, you couldn't call it tiddly-winks. Your name was on that paper. I know what you told Foltz. Okay. What I've got to do is find those other three, and I should have been in bed two hours ago. First let me ask you a plain straight question: What do you know about the connection between Clara Fox, Hilda Lindquist, Michael Walsh, and the Marquis of Clivers?"

Wolfe shook his head, slowly. "That won't do, Mr. Cramer."

"It'll do me. Will you answer it?" Cramer stuck his cigar in his mouth and tilted it up.

Wolfe shook his head again. "Certainly not. Permit me, please. Let us frame the question differently, like this: What have I been told regarding the relations between those four people which would either solve the problem of the murder of Harlan Scovil, or would threaten the personal safety of the Marquis of Clivers or subject him to undeserved or illegal annoyance? Will you accept that as your question?"

Cramer scowled at him. "Say it again."

Wolfe repeated it.

Cramer said, "Well . . . answer it."

"The answer is, nothing."

"Huh? Bellywash. I'm asking you, Wolfe—"

Wolfe's palm stopped him, and Wolfe's tone was snappy. "No more. I've finished with that. I admit your right to call on me, as a citizen enjoying the opportunities and privileges of the City of New York, not to hinder—even to some extent assist—your efforts to defend a distinguished foreign guest against jeopardy and improper molestation. Also your efforts to solve a murder. But here are two facts for you. First, it is possible that your two worthy enterprises will prove to be incompatible. Second, as far as I am concerned, for the present at least, that question and answer are final. You may have other questions that I may be disposed to reply to. Shall we try?"

Cramer, chewing his cigar, looked at him. "You know something, Wolfe? Someday you're going to fall off and get hurt."

"You said those very words to me, in this room, eight years ago."

"I wouldn't be surprised if I did." Cramer put his dead half-chewed cigar in the ash tray, took out a fresh one, and sat back. "Here's a question. What do you mean about incompatible? I suppose it was the Marquis of Clivers that pumped the lead in Harlan Scovil. There's a thought."

"I've already had it. It might very well have been. Has he an alibi?"

"I don't know. I guess the Commissioner forgot to ask him. You got any evidence?"

"No. No fragment." Wolfe wiggled a finger. "But I'll tell you this. It is important to me, also, that the murder of Harlan Scovil be solved. In the interest of a client. In fact, two."

"Oh. You've got clients."

"I have. I have told you that there are various questions I might answer if you cared to ask them. For instance, do you know who was sitting in your chair three hours ago? Clara Fox. And in that one? Hilda Lindquist. And in that? Michael Walsh. That, I believe, covers the list on that famous paper, except for the Marquis of Clivers. I am sorry to say he was absent."

Cramer had jerked himself forward. He leaned back again and observed, "You wouldn't kid me."

"I am perfectly serious."

Cramer stared at him. He scraped his teeth around on his upper lip, took a piece of tobacco from his tongue with his fingers, and kept on staring. Finally he said, "All right. What do I ask next?"

"Well . . . nothing about the subject of our conference, for that was private business. You might ask where Michael Walsh is now. I would have to reply, I have no idea. No idea whatever. Nor do I know where Miss Lindquist is. She left here about two hours ago. The commission I have undertaken for her is a purely civil affair, with no impingements on the criminal law. My other client is Clara Fox. In her case the criminal law is indeed concerned, but not the crime of murder. As I told you on the telephone, I will not for the present answer any question regarding her whereabouts."

"All right. Next?"

"Next you might perhaps permit me a question. You say that you want to see these people on account of the murder of Harlan Scovil, and in connection with your desire to protect the Marquis of Clivers. But the detectives you sent, whom Mr. Goodwin welcomed so oddly, had a warrant for her arrest on a charge of larceny. Do you wonder that I was, and am, a little skeptical of your good faith?"

"Well." Cramer looked at his cigar. "If you collected all the good faith in this room right now you might fill a teaspoon."

"Much more, sir, if you included mine." Wolfe opened his eyes at him. "Miss Fox is accused of stealing. How do you know, justly or unjustly? You thought she was in my house. Had you any reason to suppose that I would aid a person suspected of theft to escape a trial by law? No. If you thought she was here, could you not have telephoned me and arranged to take her into custody tomorrow morning, when I could have got her release on bail? Did you need to assault my privacy and insult my dignity by having your bullies burst in my door in order to carry off a sensitive and lovely young woman to a night in jail? For shame, sir! Pfui!" Wolfe poured himself a glass of beer.

Cramer shook his head slowly back and forth. "By God, you're a world-beater. I hand it to you. You know very well, Wolfe, I wasn't interested in any larceny. I wanted to talk with her about murder and about this damned marquis."

"Bah. After your talk, would she or would she not have been incarcerated?"

"I suppose she would. Hell, millions of innocent people have spent a night in jail, and sometimes much longer."

"The people I engage to keep out of it don't. If what you wanted was a talk, why the warrant? Why the violent and hostile onslaught?"

Cramer nodded. "That was a mistake. I admit it. I'll tell you the truth, the Commissioner was there demanding action. And the phone call came. I don't know who it was. He not only told me that Clara Fox was in your house, he also told me that the same Clara Fox was wanted for stealing money from the Seaboard Products Corporation. I got in touch with another department and learned that a warrant for her arrest had been executed late this afternoon. It was the Commissioner's idea to get the warrant and use it to send here and get her in a hurry."

I went on and got the signs for that down in my notebook, but my mind wasn't on that, it was on Mike Walsh. It was fairly plain that Wolfe had let one get by when he had permitted Walsh to walk out with no supervision, considering that New York is full not only of telephones, but also of subways and railroad trains and places to hide. And for the first time I put it down as a serious speculation whether Walsh could have had a reason to croak his dear old friend Harlan Scovil. Seeing Wolfe's lips moving slowly out and in, I suspected that the taste in his mouth was about the same as mine.

Cramer was saying, "Come on, Wolfe, forget it. You know what most Police Commissioners are like. They're not cops. They think all you have to do is flash a badge and strong men burst into tears. Be a sport and help me out once. I want to see this Fox woman. I'll take your word for Walsh and Lindquist and keep after them, but help me out on Clara Fox. If you've got her here, trot her out. If you haven't, tell me where to find her. If you've turned her loose too, which isn't a bad trick, show me her trail. She may be your client, but I'm not kidding when I say that the best thing you can do for her right now, and damn quick, is to let me see her. I don't care anything about any larceny—"

Wolfe interrupted. "She does. I do." He shook his head. "The larceny charge is of course in charge of the District Attorney's office; you haven't the power to affect it one way or another. I know that. As for the Marquis of Clivers, he is in no danger from Clara Fox that you need to protect him from. And as regards the murder of Harlan Scovil, she knows as little about that as I do. In fact, even less, since it is barely possible that I know who killed him."

Cramer looked at him. He puffed his cigar and kept on looking. At length he said, "Well. It's a case of murder. I'm in charge of the Homicide Squad. I'm listening."

"That's all. I volunteered that."

Cramer looked disgusted. "It can't be all. It's either too much or not enough. You've said enough to make you a material witness. You know what we can do with material witnesses if we want to."

"Yes, I know." Wolfe sighed. "But you can't very well lock me up, for then I wouldn't be free to unravel this tangle for my client—and for you. I said, barely possible." He sat up straight, abruptly. "Barely possible, sir! Confound all of you! You marquises that need protection, you hyenas of finance, you upholders of the power to persecute and defame! And don't mistake this outburst as a display of moral indignation; it is merely the practical protest of a man of business who finds his business interfered with by ignorance and stupidity. I expect to collect a fee from my client, Miss Fox. To do that I need to prosecute a claim for her, for a legal debt, I need to clear her from the false accusation of larceny, and I fear I need to discover who murdered Harlan Scovil. Those are legitimate needs, and I shall pursue them. If you want to protect your precious marquis, for God's sake do so! Surround him with a ring of iron and steel, or immerse him in antiseptic jelly! But don't annoy me when I'm trying to work! It is past one o'clock, and I must be up shortly after six, and Mr. Goodwin and I have things to do. I have every right to advise Miss Fox to avoid unfriendly molestation. If you want her, search for her. I have said that I will answer no question regarding her whereabouts, but I will tell you this much: if you undertake to invade these premises with a search warrant, you won't find her here."

Wolfe's half a glass of bear was flat, but he didn't mind that. He reached for it and swallowed it. Then he took the handkerchief from his breast pocket and wiped his lips. "Well, sir?"

Cramer put his cigar stub in the tray, rubbed the palms of his hands together for a while, pulled at the lobe of his ear, and stood up. He looked down at Wolfe.

"I like you, you know. You know damn well I do. But this thing is to some extent out of my hands. The Commissioner was talking on the telephone this evening with the Department of Justice. That's the kind of a layout it is. They might really send and get you. That's a friendly warning."

"Thank you, sir. You're going? Mr. Goodwin will let you out."

I did. I went to the hall and held his coat for him, and when I pulled the curtain aside to survey the stoop before opening the door he chuckled and slapped me on the back. That didn't make me want to kiss him. Naturally he knew when an apple was too high to reach without a ladder, and naturally there's no use letting a guy know you're going to sock him until you're ready to haul off. I saw his big car with a driver there at the curb, and there was a stranger on the sidewalk. Apparently the tenor had been relieved.

I went back to the office and sat down and yawned. Wolfe was leaning back with his eyes wide open, which meant he was sleepy. We looked at each other. I said, "So if he comes with a search warrant he won't find her here. That's encouraging. It's also encouraging that Mike Walsh is being such a big help. Also that you know who killed Harlan Scovil, like I know who put the salt in the ocean. Also that we're tied hand and foot with the Commissioner himself sore at us." I yawned. "I guess I'll prop myself up in bed tomorrow and read and knit."

"Not tomorrow, Archie. The day after, possibly. Your notebook."

I got it, and a pencil. Wolfe began.

"Miss Fox to breakfast with me in my room at seven o'clock. Delay would be dangerous. Do not forget the gong. You are not to leave the house. Saul, Fred, Orrie, and Keems are to be sent to my room immediately upon arrival, but singly. Arrange tonight for a long-distance connection with London at eight-thirty, Hitchcock's office. From Miss Fox, where does Walsh live and where is he employed as night watchman. As early as possible, call Morley of the District Attorney's office and I'll talk to him. Have Fritz bring me a copy of this when he wakes me at six-thirty. From Saul, complete information from Miss Lindquist regarding her father, his state of health, could he travel in an airplane, his address and telephone number in Nebraska. Phone Murger's—they open at eight-thirty—for copies of *Metropolitan Biographies*, all years available. Explain to Fritz and Theodore procedure regarding Miss Fox, as follows . . ."

He went on, in the drawling murmur that he habitually used when giving me a set-up. I was yawning, but I got it down. Some of it sounded like he was having hallucinations or else trying to make me think he knew things I didn't know. I quit yawning for grinning while he was explaining the procedure regarding Miss Fox.

He went to bed. After I finished the typing and giving a copy to Fritz and a few other chores, I went to the basement to take a look at the back door, and looked out the front to direct a Bronx cheer at the gumshoe on guard. Up the stairs, I continued to the third floor to take a look at the door of the south room, but I didn't try it to see if it was locked, thinking it might disturb her. Down again, in my room, I looked in the bottom drawer to see if Fritz had messed it up getting out the pajamas. It was all right. I hit the hay.

X

WHEN I leave my waking up in the morning to the vagaries of nature, it's a good deal like other acts of God—you can't tell much about it ahead of time. So Tuesday at six-thirty I staggered out of bed and fought my way across the room to turn off the electric alarm clock on the table. Then I proceeded to cleanse the form and the phiz and get the figure draped for the day. By that time the bright October sun had a band across the top fronts of the houses across the street, and I thought to myself it would be a pity to have to go to jail on such a fine day.

At seven-thirty I was in my corner in the kitchen, with Canadian bacon, pancakes, and wild-thyme honey which Wolfe got from Syria. And plenty of coffee. The wheels had already started to turn. Clara Fox, who had told Fritz she had slept like a log, was having breakfast with Wolfe in his room. Johnny Keems had arrived early, and he and Saul Panzer were in the dining room punishing pancakes. With the telephone I had pulled Dick Morley, of the District Attorney's office, out of bed at his home, and Wolfe had talked with him. It was Morley who would have lost his job, and maybe something more, but for Wolfe pulling him out of a hole in the Banister-Schurman business about three years before.

With my pancakes I went over the stories of Scovil's murder in the morning papers. They didn't play it up much, but the accounts were fairly complete. The tip-off was that he was a Chicago gangster, which gave me a grin, since he looked about as much like a gangster as a prima donna. The essentials were there, provided they were straight: no gun had been found. The car had been stolen from where some innocent perfume salesman had parked it on 29th Street. The closest eyewitness had been a man who had been walking along about thirty feet behind Harlan Scovil, and it was he who had got the license number before he dived for cover when the bullets started flying. In the dim light he hadn't got a good view of the man in the car, but he was sure it was a man, with his hat pulled down and a dark overcoat collar turned up, and he was sure he had been alone in the car. The car had speeded off across 31st Street and turned at the corner. No one had been found who had noticed it stopping on Ninth Avenue, where it had later been found. No fingerprints . . . and so forth and so forth.

I finished my second cup of coffee and got up and stretched and from then on I was as busy as a pickpocket on New Year's Eve. When Fred and Orrie came I let them in, and after they had got their instructions from Wolfe I distributed expense money to all four of them and let them out again. The siege was still on. There were two dicks out there now, one of them about the size of Charles Laughton before he heard beauty calling, and every time anyone passed in or out he got the kind of scrutiny you read about. I got the long-distance call through to London, and Wolfe talked from his room to Ethelbert Hitchcock, which I consider the all-time low for a name for a snoop, even in England. I phoned Murger's for the copies of *Metropolitan Biographies*, and they delivered them within a quarter of an hour and I took them up to the plant rooms, as Wolfe had said he would glance at them after nine o'clock. As I was going out I stopped where Theodore Horstmann was turning out some old Cattleyas trianae and growled at him, "You're going to get shot in the gizzard."

I swear to God he looked pale.

I phoned Henry H. Barber, the lawyer that we could count on for almost anything except fee-splitting, to make sure he would be available on a minute's notice all day, and to tell him that he was to consider himself retained, through us, by Miss Clara Fox, in two actions: a suit to collect a debt from the Marquis of Clivers, and a suit for damages through false arrest against Ramsey Muir. Likewise, in the first case, Miss Hilda Lindquist.

It looked as if I had a minute loose, so I mounted the two flights to the south room and knocked on the door, and called out my name. She said come in, and I entered.

She was in the armchair, with books and magazines on the table, but none of them was opened. Maybe she had slept like a log, but her eyes looked tired. She frowned at me.

I said, "You shouldn't sit so close to the window. If they wanted to bad enough they could see in here from that Thirty-fourth Street roof."

She glanced around. "I shouldn't think so, with those curtains."

"They're pretty thin. Let me move you back a little, anyhow." She got up, and I shoved the chair and table toward the bed. "I'm not usually nervous, but this is a stunt we're pulling."

She sat down again and looked up at me. "You don't like it, do you, Mr. Goodwin? I could see last night you didn't approve of it. Neither do I."

I grinned at her. "Bless your dear little heart, what difference does that make? Nero Wolfe is putting on a show and we're in the cast. Stick to the script, don't forget that."

"I don't call it a show." She was frowning again. "A man has been murdered and it was my fault. I don't like to hide, and I don't want to. I'd rather—"

I showed her both palms. "Forget it. You came to get Wolfe to help you, didn't you? All right, let him. He may be a nut, but you're lucky that he spotted the gleam of honesty in your eye or you'd be in one sweet mess this minute. You behave yourself. For instance, if that phone there on the stand is in any way a temptation . . ."

She shook her head. "If it is, I'll resist it."

"Well, there's no use leaving it here anyhow." I went and pulled the connection out of the plug and gathered the cord and instrument under my arm. "I learned about feminine impulses in school. There goes the office phone. Don't open the door and don't go close to the windows."

I beat it and went down two steps at a time. It was Dick Morley on the phone, with a tale. I offered to connect him with Wolfe in the plant rooms, but he said not to disturb him, he could give it to me. He had had a little trouble. The Clara Fox larceny charge was being handled by an Assistant District Attorney named Frisbie whom Morley knew only fairly well, and Frisbie hadn't seemed especially inclined to open up, but Morley had got some facts. A warrant for Clara Fox's arrest, and a search warrant for her apartment, had been issued late Monday afternoon. The apartment had not been searched because detectives under Frisbie's direction had gone first to the garage where she kept her car, and had found in it, wrapped in a newspaper under the back seat, a package of hundred dollar bills amounting to $30,000. The case was considered airtight. Frisbie's men no longer had the warrant for arrest because it had been turned over to Inspector Cramer at the request of the Police Commissioner.

I thanked Morley and hung up and went upstairs to the plant rooms and told Wolfe the sad story. He was in the tropical room trimming wilts. When I finished he said, "We were wrong, Archie. Not hyenas. Hyenas wait for a carcass. Get Mr. Perry on the phone, connect it here, and take it down."

I went back to the office. It wasn't so easy to get Perry. His secretary was reluctant, or he was, or they both were, but I finally managed to get him on and put him through to Wolfe. Then I began a fresh page of the notebook.

Perry said he was quite busy, he hoped Wolfe could make it brief. Wolfe said he hoped so too, that first he wished to learn if he had misunderstood Perry Monday afternoon. He had gathered that Perry had believed Miss Fox to be innocent, had been opposed to any precipitate action, and had desired a careful and complete investigation. Perry said that was correct.

Wolfe's tone got sharp. "But you did not know until after seven o'clock last evening that I was not going to investigate for you, and the warrant for Miss Fox's arrest was issued an hour earlier than that. You would not call that precipitate?"

Perry sounded flustered. "Well . . . precipitate . . . yes, it was. It was, yes. You see . . . you asked me yesterday if I am not the fount of justice in this organization. To a certain extent, yes. But there is always . . . well . . . the human element. I am not a czar, neither in fact nor by temperament. When you phoned me last evening you may have thought me irritable—as a matter of fact, I thought of calling you back to apologize. The truth is I was chagrined and deeply annoyed. I knew then that a warrant had been issued for the arrest at the instance of Mr. Muir. Surely you can appreciate my position. Mr. Muir is a high official of my corporation. When I learned later in the evening that the money had been found in Miss Fox's car, I was astounded . . . I couldn't believe it . . . but what could I do? I was amazed. . . ."

"Indeed." Wolfe still snapped. "You've got your money back. Do you intend to proceed with the prosecution?"

"You don't need to take that tone, Wolfe." Perry sharpened a little. "I told you there is the human element. I'm not a czar. Muir makes an issue of it. I'm being frank with you. I can't talk him off. Granted that I could kick the first vice-president out of the company if I wanted to, which is a good deal to grant, do you think I should? After all, he has the law—"

"Then you're with him on it?"

A pause. "No. No, I'm not. I . . . I have the strongest . . . sympathy for Clara—Miss Fox. I would like to see her get something . . . much more human than justice. For instance, if there is any difficulty about bail for her I would be glad to furnish it."

"Thank you. We'll manage bail. You asked me to be brief, Mr. Perry. First, I suggest that you arrange to have the charge against Miss Fox quashed immediately. Second, I wish to inform you of our intentions if that is not done. At ten o'clock tomorrow morning I shall have Miss Fox submit herself to arrest and shall have her at once released on bail. She will then start an action against Ramsey Muir and the Seaboard Products Corporation to recover one million dollars in damages for false arrest. We deal in millions here now. I think there is no question but that we shall have sufficient evidence to uphold our action. If they try her first, so much the better. She'll be acquitted."

"But how can . . . that's absurd . . . if you have evidence . . ."

"That's all, Mr. Perry. That's my brevity. Good-by."

I heard the click of Wolfe hanging up. Perry was sputtering, but I hung up too. I tossed the notebook away and got up and stuck my hands in my pockets and walked around. Perhaps I was muttering. I was thinking to myself, if Wolfe takes that pot with nothing but a dirty deuce he's a better man than he thinks he is, if that was possible. On the face of it, it certainly looked as if his crazy conceit had invaded the higher centers of his brain and stopped his mental processes completely; but there was one thing that made such a supposition unlikely, namely, that he was spending money. He had four expensive men riding around in taxis and he had got London on the phone as if it had been a delicatessen shop. It was a thousand to one he was going to get it back.

Still another expenditure was imminent, as I learned when the phone rang again. I sat down to get it, half hoping it was Perry calling back to offer a truce. But what I heard was Fred Durkin's low growl, and he sounded peeved.

"That you, Archie?"

"Right. What have you got?"

"Nothing. Less than that. Look here. I'm talking from the Forty-seventh Street Station."

"The . . . what? What for?"

"What the hell do you suppose for? I got arrested a little."

I made a face and took a breath. "Good for you," I said grimly. "That's a big help. Men like you are the backbone of the country. Go on."

His growl went plaintive. "Could I help it? They hopped me at the garage when I went there to ask questions. They say I committed something when I took that car last night. I think they're getting ready to send me somewhere, I suppose Centre Street. What the hell could I do, run and let him tag me? I wouldn't be phoning now if it hadn't happened that a friend of mine is on the desk here."

"Okay. If they take you to the DA's office keep your ears open and stick to the little you know. We'll get after it."

"You'd better. If I—hey! Will you phone the missis?"

I assured him he would see the missis as soon as she was expecting him, and hung up. I sat and scratched my nose a minute and then made for the stairs. It was looking as if being confined to the house wasn't going to deprive me of my exercise.

Wolfe was still in the tropical room. He kept on snipping stems and listened without looking around. I reported the development. He said, "These interruptions are abominable."

I said, "All right, let him rot in a dungeon."

Wolfe sighed. "Phone Mr. Barber. Can you pick Keems up? No, you can't. When you hear from him let me talk to him."

I went back down and got Barber's office and asked him to send someone out to make arrangements for Fred to sleep with his missis that night, and gave him the dope.

I had no idea when I might hear from Johnny Keems. They had all got their instructions direct from Wolfe, and as usual he was keeping my head clear of unnecessary obstructions. As I had let Orrie Cather out he had made some kind of a crack about being the only electrician in New York who understood directors' rooms, and of course I knew Saul Panzer had a contact on with Hilda Lindquist, but beyond that their programs were outside my circle. I guessed Fred had gone back to the garage to see if he could get a line on a plant, which made it appear that Wolfe didn't even have a dirty deuce, but of course he had talked with Clara Fox nearly an hour that morning, so that was all vague. But it did seem that Frisbie or someone around the District Attorney's office was busting with ardor over an ordinary larceny on which they already had the evidence, leaving a dick at the garage; but that was probably part of the net they were holding for Clara Fox. It might even have been one of Cramer's men.

I went on being a switchboard girl. A little before ten Saul Panzer called, and from upstairs Wolfe listened to him while I put down the details he had collected from Hilda Lindquist regarding her father in Nebraska. She thought that if riding in an airplane didn't kill him it would scare him to death. Apparently Saul had further instructions, for Wolfe told him to proceed. A little later Orrie phoned in, and what he reported to Wolfe gave me my first view of a new slant that hadn't occurred to me at all. Introducing himself to Sourface Vawter as an electrician, he had been admitted to the directors' room of the Seaboard Products Corporation, and had learned that besides the double door at the end of the corridor it had another door leading into the public hall. It had been locked but could be opened from the inside, and Orrie had himself gone out that way and around the hall to the elevators.

Wolfe told Orrie to wait and talked to me. "Don't type a note on that, Archie. Any that you do type, put them in the safe at once. Leave Orrie on with me and be sure the other line is open. A call I am expecting hasn't come. When Keems calls I'll talk to him, but I'll give Orrie Fred's assignment."

Taking the hint that he didn't want to burden my ears with Orrie's schedule, I hung up. I filed some notes in the safe and loaded Wolfe's pen and tested it, a chore that I hadn't been able to get around to before—absent-mindedly, because I was off on a new track. I had no idea what had started Wolfe in that direction. It had beautiful possibilities, no doubt of that, but a hundred-to-one shot in a big handicap is a beautiful possibility too, and how often would you collect on it? After taxing the brain a few minutes, this looked more like a million to one. I would probably have gone on to add more ciphers to that if I hadn't been interrupted by the doorbell. Of course I was still on that job too. I went to the hall and pulled the curtain to see through the glass panel, and got a surprise. It was the first time Wolfe's house had ever been taken for a church, but there wasn't any other explanation, for either that specimen on the stoop was scheduled for best man at a wedding or Emily Post had been fooling me for years.

The two dicks were down on the sidewalk, looking up at the best man as if it was too much of a problem for them. They had nothing on me. I opened the door and let it come three inches, leaving the chain on, and said in a well-bred tone, "Good morning."

He peered through at me. "I say, that crack is scarcely adequate. Really." He had a well-trained voice but a little squawky.

"I'm sorry. This is a bad neighborhood and we have to be careful. What can I do for you?"

He went on peering. "Is this the house of Mr. Nero Wolfe?"

"It is."

He hesitated, and turned to look down at the snoops on the sidewalk, who were staring up at him in the worst possible taste. Then he came closer and pushed his face up against the crack and said in a tone nearly down to a whisper, "From Lord Clivers. I wish to see Mr. Wolfe."

I took a second for consideration and then slid the bolt off and opened up. He walked in and I shut the door and shot the bolt again. When I turned he was standing there with his stick hung over his elbow, pulling his gloves off. He was six feet, spare but not skinny, about my age, fair-skinned with chilly blue eyes, and there was no question about his being dressed for it. I waved him ahead and followed him into the office, and he took his time getting his paraphernalia deposited on Wolfe's desk before he lowered himself into a chair. Meantime I let him know that Mr. Wolfe was engaged and would be until eleven o'clock, and that I was the confidential assistant and was at his service. He got seated and looked at me as if he would have to get around to admitting my right to exist before we could hope to make any headway.

But he spoke. "Mr. Goodwin? I see. Perhaps I got a bit ahead at the door. That is . . . I really should see Mr. Wolfe without delay."

I grinned at him. "You mean because you mentioned the Marquis of Clivers? That's okay. I wrote that letter. I know all about it. You can't see Mr. Wolfe before eleven. I can let him know you're here."

"If you will be so good. Do that. My name is Horrocks—Francis Horrocks."

I looked at him. So this was the geezer that bought roses with three-foot stems. I turned on the swivel and plugged in the plant room and pressed the button. In a minute Wolfe was on and I told him, "A man here to see you, Mr. Francis Horrocks. From the Marquis of Clivers. . . . Yeah, in the office. . . . Haven't asked him. . . . I told him, sure. . . . Okay."

I jerked the plugs and swiveled again. "Mr. Wolfe says he can see you at eleven o'clock, unless you'd care to try me. He suggests the latter."

"I should have liked to see Mr. Wolfe." The blue eyes were going over me. "Though I merely bring a message. First, though, I should—er—perhaps explain . . . I am here in a dual capacity. It's a bit confusing, but really quite all right. I am here, as it were, personally . . . and also semi-officially. Possibly I should first deliver my message from Lord Clivers."

"Okay. Shoot."

"I beg your pardon? Oh, quite. Lord Clivers would like to know if Mr. Wolfe could call at his hotel. An hour can be arranged—"

"I can save you breath on that. Mr. Wolfe never calls on anybody."

"No?" His brows went up. "He is not—that is, bedridden?"

"Nope, only house-ridden. He doesn't like it outdoors. He never has called on anybody and never will."

"You don't say." His forehead showed wrinkles. "Well. Lord Clivers wishes very much to see him. You say you wrote that letter?"

I nodded. "Yeah, I know all about it. I suppose Mr. Wolfe would be glad to talk with the marquis on the telephone—"

"He prefers not to discuss it on the telephone."

"Okay. I was going to add, or the marquis can come here. Of course the legal part of it is being handled by our attorney."

The young diplomat sat straight with his arms folded and looked at me. "You have engaged a solicitor?"

"Certainly. If it comes to a lawsuit, which we hope it won't, we don't want to waste any time. We understand the marquis will be in New York another week, so we'd have to be ready to serve him at once."

He nodded. "Just so. That's a bit candid." He bit his lip and cocked his head a little. "We appear to have reached a dead end. Your position seems quite clear. I shall report it, that's all I can do." He hitched his feet back and cleared his throat. "Now, if you don't mind, I assume my private capacity. I remarked that I am here personally. My name is Francis Horrocks."

"Yeah. Your personal name."

"Just so. And I would like to speak with Miss Fox. Miss Clara Fox."

I felt myself straightening out my face and hoped he didn't see me. I said, "I can't say I blame you. I've met Miss Fox. Go to it."

He frowned. "If you would be so good as to tell her I am here. It's quite all right. I know she's having a spot of seclusion, but it's quite all right. Really. You see, when she telephoned me this morning I insisted on knowing the address of her retreat. In fact, I pressed her on it. I confess she laid it on me not to come here to see her, but I made no commitment. Also, I didn't come to see her; I came semi-officially. What? Being here, I ask to see her, which is quite all right. What?"

My face was under control after the first shock. I said, "Sure it's quite all right. I mean, to ask. Seeing her is something else. You must have got the address wrong or maybe you were phoning in your sleep."

"Oh, no. Really." He folded his arms again. "See here, Mr. Goodwin, let's cut across. It's a fact, I actually must see Miss Fox. As a friend, you understand. For purely personal reasons. I'm quite determined about this."

"Okay. Find her. She left no address here."

He shook his head patiently. "It won't do, I assure you it won't. She telephoned me. Is she in distress? I don't know. I shall have to see her. If you will tell her—"

I stood up. "Sorry, Mr. Horrocks. Do you really have to go? I hope you find Miss Fox. Tell the Marquis of Clivers—"

He sat tight, shook his head again, and frowned. "Damn it all. I dislike this, really. I've never set eyes on you before. What? I've never seen this Mr. Wolfe. Could Miss Fox have been under duress when she was telephoning? You see the possibility, of course. Setting my mind at rest and all that. If you put me out, it will really be necessary for me to tell those policemen outside that Miss Fox telephoned me from this address at nine o'clock this morning. Also I should have to take the precaution of finding a telephone at once to repeat the information to your police headquarters. What?"

I stared down at him, and I admit he was too much for me. Whether he was deep and desperate or dumb and determined I didn't know. I said, "Wait here. Mr. Wolfe will have to know about you. Kindly stay in this room."

I left him there and went to the kitchen and told Fritz to stand in the hall, and if an Englishman emerged from the office, yodel. Then I bounced up two flights to the south room, called not too loud, and, when I heard the key turn, opened the door and entered. Clara Fox stood and brushed her hair back and looked at me half alarmed and half hopeful.

I said, "What time this morning did you phone that guy Francis Horrocks?"

She stared. It got her. She swallowed. "But I—he—he promised . . ."

"So you did phone him. Swell. You forgot to mention it when I asked you about it a while ago."

"But you didn't ask me if I *had* phoned."

"Oh, didn't I? Now that was careless." I threw up my hands. "To hell with it. Suppose you tell me what you phoned him about. I hope it wasn't a secret."

"No, it wasn't." She came a step to me. "Must you be so sarcastic? There was nothing . . . it was just personal."

"As for instance?"

"Why, it was really nothing. Of course, he sent those roses. Then . . . I had had an engagement to dine with him Monday evening, and when I made the appointment with Mr. Wolfe I had to cancel the one with Mr. Horrocks, and when he insisted I thought that three hours would be enough with Mr. Wolfe, so I told Mr. Horrocks I would go with him at ten o'clock to dance somewhere, and probably he went to the apartment and waited around there I don't know how long, and this morning I supposed he would keep phoning there and of course there would be no answer, and he couldn't get me at the office either, and besides, I hadn't thanked him for the roses—"

I put up a palm. "Take a breath. I see, romance. It'd be still more romantic if he came to visit you in jail. You're quite an adventuress, being as you are over ninety per cent nincompoop. I don't suppose you know that according to an article in yesterday's *Times* this Horrocks is the nephew of the Marquis of Clivers and next in line for the title."

"Oh, yes. He explained to me . . . that is . . . that's all right. I knew that. And Mr. Goodwin, I don't like—"

"We'll discuss your likes later. Here's something you don't know. Horrocks is downstairs in the office saying that he's got to see you or he'll run and get the police."

"What! He isn't."

"Yep. Somebody is, and from his looks I'm willing to admit it's Horrocks."

"But he shouldn't . . . he promised . . . send him away!"

"He won't go away. If I throw him out he'll yell for a cop. He thinks you're here under duress and need to be rescued—that's his story. You're a swell client, you are. With the chances Nero Wolfe's taking for you—all right. Anyhow, whether he's straight or not, there's no way out of it now. I'm going to bring him up here, and for God's sake make it snappy and let him go back to his uncle."

"But I—good heavens!" She brushed her hair back. "I don't want to see him. Not now. Tell him . . . of course I could . . . yes, that's it . . . I'll go down and just tell him—"

"You will not. Next you'll be wanting to go and walk around the block with him. You stay here."

Outside in the hall I hesitated, uncertain whether to go up and tell Wolfe of the party we were having, but decided there was no point in riling him. I went back down, tossing Fritz a nod as I passed by, and found the young diplomat sitting in the office with his arms still folded. He put his brows up at me. I told him to come on, and let him go first. Behind him on the stairs I noticed he had good springs in his legs, and at the top his air pump hadn't speeded up any. Keeping fit for dear old England and the bloody empire. I opened the door and bowed him in and followed him.

Clara Fox came across to him. He looked at her with a kind of sickening grin and put out his hand. She shook her head. "No. I won't shake hands with you. Aren't you ashamed of yourself? You promised me you wouldn't. Causing Mr. Goodwin all this trouble . . ."

"Now, really. I say." His voice was different from what it had been downstairs, sort of sweet and concentrated. Silly as hell. "After all, you know, it was fairly alarming . . . with you gone and all that . . . couldn't find a trace of you . . . and you look frightful, very bad in the eyes . . ."

"Thank you very much." All of a sudden she began to laugh. I hadn't heard her laugh before. It showed her teeth and put color in her cheeks. She laughed at him until if I had been him I'd have thought up some kind of a remark. Then she stuck out her hand. "All right, shake. Mr. Goodwin says you were going to rescue me. I warned you to let American girls alone—you see the sort of thing it leads to?"

With his big paw he was hanging onto her hand as if he had a lease on it. He was staring at her. "You know, they do, though. I mean the eyes. You're really quite all right? You couldn't expect me—"

I butted in because I had to. I had left the door open and the sound of the front doorbell came up plain. I glanced at Francis Horrocks and decided that if he really was a come-on I would at least have the pleasure of seeing how long he looked lying down, before he got out of that house, and I got brusque to Clara Fox. "Hold it. The door bell. I'm going to shut this door and go down to answer it, and it would be a good idea to make no sounds until I get back." The bell started ringing again. "Okay?"

Clara Fox nodded.

"Okay, Mr. Horrocks?"

"Certainly. Whatever Miss Fox says."

I beat it, closing the door behind me. Some smart guy was leaning on the button, for the bell kept on ringing as I went down the two flights. Fritz was standing in the hall, looking belligerent; he hated people that got impatient with the bell. I went to the door and pulled the curtain and looked out, and felt mercury running up my backbone. It was a quartet. Only four, and I recognized Lieutenant Rowcliff in front. It was him on the button. I hadn't had such a treat for a long while. I turned the lock and let the door come as far as the chain.

Rowcliff called through, "Well! We're not ants. Come on, open up."

I said, "Take it easy. I'm just the messenger boy."

"Yeah? Here's the message." He unfolded a paper he had in his hand. Having seen a search warrant before, I didn't need a magnifying glass. I looked through the crack at it. Rowcliff said, "What are you waiting for? Do you want me to count ten?"

XI

I SAID, "Hold your horses, lieutenant. If what you want is in here it can't get out, since I suppose you've got the rear and the roof covered. This isn't my house, it belongs to Nero Wolfe and he's upstairs. Wait a minute, I'll be right back."

I went up three steps at a time, paying no attention to Rowcliff yelling outside. I went in the south room; they were standing there. I said to Clara Fox, "They're here. Make it snappy. Take Horrocks with you, and if he's in on this I'll kill him."

Horrocks started, "Really—"

"Shut up! Go with Miss Fox. For God's sake—"

She might have made an adventuress at that; she was okay when it came to action. She darted to the table and grabbed her handbag and handkerchief, dashed back and got Horrocks by the hand, and pulled him through the door with her. I took a quick look around to make sure there were no lipsticks or powder puffs left behind, shoved the table toward the window where it looked more natural, and beat it. In the hall I stopped one second to shake myself. Noises of Rowcliff bellowing on the stoop floated up. Horrocks and Clara Fox had disappeared. I went down to the front door and slid the bolt and flung it open.

"Welcome," I grinned. "Mr. Wolfe says he wants the warrant for a souvenir."

They trooped in behind Rowcliff. He grunted. "Where's Wolfe?"

"Up with the plants. Until eleven o'clock. He told me to tell you this, that of course you have the legal right to search the entire premises, but that the city will pay for every nickel's worth of damage that's done if he has to go to City Hall himself to collect it."

"No! Don't scare me to death. Come on, boys. Where does that go to?"

"Front room." I pointed. "Office. Kitchen. Basement stairs. The rear door is down there, onto the court."

He turned, and then whirled to me again. "Look here, Goodwin. You've had your bluff called. Why not save time? Why don't you bring this Fox woman down here, or up here, and call it a trick? It'd save a lot of messing around."

I said, coldly, "Pish-tush. Which isn't for you, lieutenant; I know you've got orders. It's for Inspector Cramer, and you can take it to him. The horse laugh he'll get over this will be heard at Bath Beach. Does he think Nero Wolfe is simp enough to try to hide a woman under his bed? Go on and finish your button-button-who's-got-the-button and get the hell out of here."

He grunted and started off with his army toward the door of the basement stairs. I followed. I wanted to keep an eye on them anyway, on general principles, but, besides that, I had decided to ride him. Wolfe had told me to use my judgment, and I knew that was the best way to put a bird like Rowcliff in the frame of mind we wanted him in. So I was right behind them going down, and while they poked around all over the basement, pulling the curtains back from the shelves, opening trunks and looking into empty packing cartons, I exercised the tongue. Rowcliff tried to pass it back once or twice and then pretended not to hear me. I opened the door to the insulated bottle department, and kept jerking my head around at them as if I expected to catch them in a snatch at a quart of rye. They finished up down there by taking a look at the court out of the back door, and after I got the door locked again I followed them back up to the first floor.

Rowcliff stationed a man at the door to the basement stairs and then began at the kitchen and worked forward. I hung on his tail. I said, "Up here, now, you've got to take soundings. The place is lousy with trapdoors," and when he involuntarily looked down at his feet I turned loose a haw-haw. In the office I asked him, "Want me to open the safe? There's a piece of her in there. That's the way we worked it, cut her up and scattered her around." By the time we started for the second floor he was boiling and trying not to show it, and about ninety-seven per cent convinced. He left a man at the head of the stairs and tackled Wolfe's room. Fritz had come along to see that nothing got hurt, thinking maybe that my mind was on something else, for there was a lot of stuff in there. I'll admit they didn't get rough, though they were thorough. Wolfe's double mattress looked pretty thick under its black silk coverlet, and one of them wiggled under it to have a look. Rowcliff went around the rows of bookshelves taking measurements with his eyes for a concealed closet, and where the poker-dart board was hanging on a screen he pulled the screen around to look behind it. All the time I was making remarks as they occurred to me.

In my room, as Rowcliff was looking back of the clothes in the closet, I said, "Listen, I've got a suggestion. I'll put on an old mother hubbard I won once at a raffle and you take me to Cramer and tell him I'm Clara Fox. After this performance there's no question but what he's too damn dumb to know the difference."

He backed out of the closet, straightened up, and glared at me. He bellowed, "You shut your trap, see? Or I will take you somewhere, and it won't be to Cramer!"

I grinned at him. "That's childish, lieutenant. Make saps out of yourselves and then try to take it out on citizens. Oh, wait! Baby, wait till this gets out!"

He tramped to the hall and started up the next flight with his army behind. I'll admit I was a little squeamish as they entered the south room; it's hard for anyone to stay in a room ten hours and not leave a trace; but they weren't looking for traces, they were looking for a live woman. Anyway, she had followed Wolfe's instructions to the letter and it looked all right. That only took a couple of minutes, and the same for the north room, where Saul Panzer had slept. When they came out to the hall again I opened the door to the narrow stairs going up, and held it for them.

"Plant rooms fourth and last stop. And take it from me, if you knock over a bench of orchid pots you'll find more trouble here than you brought with you."

Rowcliff was licked. He wasn't saying so, and he was trying not to look it, but he was. He growled, "Wolfe up there?"

"He is."

"All right. Come along, Jack. You two wait here."

The three of us got to the top in single file and I called to him to push in. We entered and he saw the elevator standing there with the door gaping. He opened the door to the stairs and called down, "Hey, Al! Come up and give this elevator a go and look over the shaft!" Then he rejoined us.

Those plant rooms had been considered impressive by better men than Lieutenant Rowcliff—for example among many others, by Pierre Fracard, President of the Horticultural Society of France. I was in and out of them ten times a day and they impressed me, though I pretended to Theodore Horstmann that they didn't. Of course they were more startling in February than they were in October, but Wolfe and Horstmann had developed a technique of forcing that made them worth looking at no matter when it was. Inside the door of the first room, which had Odontoglossums, Oncidiums, and Miltonia hybrids, Rowcliff and the dick stopped short. The angle-iron staging gleamed in its silver paint, and on the concrete benches and shelves three thousand pots of orchids showed greens and blues and yellows and reds. It looked spotty to me, since I had seen it at the top of its glory, but it was nothing to sniff at.

I said, "Well, do you think you're at the flower show? You didn't pay to get in. Get a move on, huh?"

Rowcliff led the way. He didn't leave the center aisle. Once he stopped to stoop for a peek under a bench, and I let a laugh bust out and then choked it and said, "Excuse me, lieutenant, I know you have your duty to perform."

He went on with his shoulders up, but I knew the eager spirit of the chase had oozed down into his shoes.

In the next room, Cattleyas, Laelias, hybrids, and miscellaneous, Theodore Horstmann was over at one side pouring fertilizer on a row of Cymbidiums, which are terrestrials, and Rowcliff took a look at him but didn't say anything. The dick in between us stopped to bend down and stick his nose against a big lilac hybrid, and I told him, "Nope. If you smell anything sweet, it's me."

We went on through the tropical room, where it was hot with the sun shining and the lath screens already off, and continued to the potting room. It had enough free space to move around in, and it also had inhabitants. Francis Horrocks, still unsoiled, stood leaning with his back against an angle-iron, talking to Nero Wolfe, who was using the pressure spray. A couple of boards had been laid along the top of a long low wooden box which was filled with osmundine, and on the boards had been placed thirty-five or forty pots of Laeliocattleya lustre. Wolfe was spraying them with high pressure, and it was pretty wet around there.

Horrocks was saying, "It really seems a devilish lot of trouble. What? Of course, you know, it's perfectly proper for every chap . . ."

Rowcliff looked around. There were sphagnum, sand, charcoal, crock for drainage, stacks of hundreds of pots. Rowcliff moved forward, and Wolfe shut off the spray and turned to him.

"Do I know you, sir?"

I closed in. "Mr. Nero Wolfe, Lieutenant Rowcliff."

Wolfe inclined his head one inch. "How do you do." He looked toward the door, where the dick stood. "And your companion?"

He was using his aloof tone, and it was good. Rowcliff said, "One of my men. We're here on business."

"So I understand. If you don't mind, introduce him. I like to know the names of people who enter my house."

"Yeah? His name's Loedenkrantz."

"Indeed." Wolfe looked at him and inclined his head an inch again. "How do you do, sir."

The dick said without moving, "Pleased to meetcha."

Wolfe returned to Rowcliff. "And you are a lieutenant. Reward of merit? Incredible." His voice deepened and accelerated. "Will you take a message for me to Mr. Cramer? Tell him that Nero Wolfe pronounces him to be a prince of witlings and an unspeakable ass! Pfui!" He turned on the spray, directed it on the orchids, and addressed Francis Horrocks. "But my dear sir, since all life is trouble, the only thing is to achieve a position where we may select varieties . . ."

I said to Rowcliff, "There's a room there at the side, the gardener's. You don't want to miss that."

He went with me and looked in, and I hand it to him that he had enough face left to enter and look under the bed and open the closet door. He came out again, and he was done. But as he moved for the door he asked me, "How do you get out to the roof?"

"You don't. This covers all of it. Anyhow you've got it spotted. Haven't you? Don't tell me you overlooked that."

We were returning the way we had come, and I was behind them again. He didn't answer. Mr. Loedenkrantz didn't stop to smell an orchid. There was a grin inside of me trying to burst into flower, but I was warning it, Not yet, sweetheart, they're not out yet. We left the plant rooms and descended to the third floor, and Rowcliff said to the pair he had left there, "Fall in."

One began, "I thought I heard a noise—"

"Shut up."

I followed them down, on down. After all the diversion I had been furnishing I didn't think it advisable to go suddenly dumb, so I manufactured a couple of nifties during the descent. In the lower hall, before I unlocked the door, I squared off to Rowcliff and told him, "Listen. I've been free with the lip, but it was my day. We all have to take it sometimes, and hey-nonny-nonny. I'm aware it wasn't you that pulled this boner."

But, being a lieutenant, he was stern and unbending. "Much obliged for nothing. Open the door."

I did that, and they went. On the sidewalk they were joined by their brothers who had been left there. I shut the door, heard the lock snap, and put on the bolt. I turned and went to the office. I seldom took a drink before dark, but the idea of a shot of bourbon seemed pleasing, so I went to the cabinet and helped myself. It felt encouraging going down. In my opinion, there was very little chance that Rowcliff had enough eagerness left in him to try a turn-around, but I returned to the entrance and pulled the curtain and stood looking out for a minute. There was no one in sight that had the faintest resemblance to a city employee. So I mounted the stairs, clear to the plant rooms, and went through to the potting room. Wolfe and Horrocks were standing there, and Wolfe looked at me inquiringly.

I waved a hand. "Gone. Done."

Wolfe hung the spray tube on its hook and called, "Theodore!"

Horstmann came trotting. He and I together lifted the pots of Laeliocattleyas, which Wolfe had been spraying, from the boards, and put them on a bench. Then we removed the boards from the long box of osmundine; Horrocks took one. Wolfe said, "All right, Miss Fox."

The mossy fiber, dripping with water, raised itself up out of the box, fell all around us, and spattered our pants. We began picking off patches of it that were clinging to Clara Fox's soaked dress, and she brushed back her hair and blurted, "Thank God I wasn't born a mermaid!"

Horrocks put his fingers on the sleeve of her dress. "Absolutely saturated. Really, you know—"

He may have been straight, but he had no right to be in on it. I cut him off. "I know you'll have to be going. Fritz can attend to Miss Fox. If you don't mind?"

XII

AT TWELVE o'clock noon Wolfe and I sat in the office. Fred Durkin was out in the kitchen eating pork chops and pumpkin pie. He had made his appearance some twenty minutes before, with the pork chops in his pocket, for Fritz to cook, and a tale of injured innocence. One of Barber's staff had found him in a detention room down at headquarters, put there to weigh his sins after an hour of displaying his ignorance to Inspector Cramer. The lawyer had pried him loose without much trouble and sent him on his way, which of course was West 35th Street. Wolfe hadn't bothered to see him.

Up in the tropical room was the unusual sight of Clara Fox's dress and other items of apparel hanging on a string to dry out, and she was up in the south room sporting the dressing gown Wolfe had given me for Christmas four years before. I hadn't seen her, but Fritz had taken her the gown. It looked as if we'd have to get her out of the house pretty soon or I wouldn't have a thing to put on.

Francis Horrocks had departed, having accepted my hint without any whats. Nothing had been explained to him. Wolfe, of course, wasn't openly handing Clara Fox anything, but it was easy to see that she was one of the few women he would have been able to think up a reason for, from the way he talked about her. He told me that when she and Horrocks had come running into the potting room she had immediately stepped into the osmundine box, which had been all ready for her, and standing there she had fixed her eyes on Horrocks and said to him, "No questions, no remarks, and you do what Mr. Wolfe says. Understand." And Horrocks had stood and stared with his mouth open as she stretched herself out in the box and Horstmann had piled osmundine on her three inches deep while Wolfe got the spray ready. Then he had come to and helped with the boards and the pots.

In the office at noon, Wolfe was drinking beer and making random remarks as they occurred to him. He observed that since Inspector Cramer was sufficiently aroused to be willing to insult Nero Wolfe by having his house invaded with a search warrant, it was quite possible that he had also seen fit to proceed to other indefensible measures, such as tapping telephone wires, and that therefore we should take precautions. He stated that it had been a piece of outrageous stupidity on his part to let Mike Walsh go Monday evening before asking him a certain question, since he had then already formed a surmise which, if proven correct, would solve the problem completely. He said he was sorry that there was no telephone at the Lindquist prairie home in Nebraska, since it meant that the old gentleman would have to endure the rigors of a nine-mile trip to a village in order to talk over long distance; and he hoped that the connection with him would be made at one o'clock as arranged. He also hoped that Johnny Keems would be able to find Mike Walsh and escort him to the office without interference, fairly soon, since a few words with Walsh and a talk with Victor Lindquist should put him in a position where he could proceed with arrangements to clean up the whole affair. More beer. And so forth.

I let him rave on, thinking he might fill in a couple of gaps by accident, but he didn't.

The phone rang. I took it, and heard Keems' voice. I stopped him before he got started: "I can't hear you, Johnny. Don't talk so close."

"What?"

"I said, don't talk so close."

"Oh. Is this better?"

"Yeah."

"Well . . . I'm reporting progress backwards. I found the old lady in good health and took care of her for a couple of hours, and then she got hit by a brown taxi and they took her to the hospital."

"That's too bad. Hold the wire a minute." I covered the transmitter and turned to Wolfe. "Johnny found Mike Walsh and tailed him for two hours, and a dick picked him up and took him to headquarters."

"Picked up Johnny?"

"No. Walsh."

Wolfe frowned, and his lips went out and in, and again. He sighed. "The confounded meddlers. Call him in."

I told the phone, "Come on in, and hurry," and hung up.

Wolfe leaned back with his eyes shut, and I didn't bother him. It was a swell situation for a tantrum, and I didn't feel like a dressing-down. If his observations had been anything at all more than shooting off, this was a bad break, and it might lead to almost anything, since if Mike Walsh emptied the bag for Cramer there was no telling what might be thought necessary for protecting the Marquis of Clivers from a sinister plot. I didn't talk, but got out the plant records and pretended to go over them.

At a quarter to one the doorbell rang, and I went and admitted Johnny Keems. I was still acting as hall boy, because you never could tell about Cramer. Johnny, looking like a Princeton boy with his face washed, which was about the only thing I had against him, followed me to the office and dropped into a chair without an invitation. He demanded, "How did I come through on the code? Not so bad, huh?"

I grunted. "Perfectly marvelous. You're a wonder. Where did you find Walsh?"

He threw one leg over the other. "No trouble at all. Over on East Sixty-fourth Street, where he boards. Your instructions were not to approach him until I had a line or in case of emergency, so I found out by judicious inquiry that he was in there and then I stuck around. He came out at a quarter to ten and walked to Second Avenue and turned south. West on Fifty-eighth to Park. South on Park—"

Wolfe put in, "Skip the itinerary."

Johnny nodded. "We were about there anyhow. At Fifty-sixth Street he went into the Hotel Portland."

"Indeed."

"Yep. And he stayed there over an hour. He used the phone and then took an elevator, but I stayed in the lobby because the house dick knows me and he saw me and I knew he wouldn't stand for it. I knew Walsh might have got loose because there are two sets of elevators, but all I could do was stick, and at a quarter past eleven he came down and went out. He headed south and turned west on Fifty-fifth, and across Madison he went in at a door where it's boarded up for construction. That's the place you told me to try if I drew a blank at Sixty-fourth Street, the place where he works as a night watchman. I waited outside, thinking I might get stopped if I went in, and hoping he wouldn't use another exit. But he didn't. In less than ten minutes he came out again, but he wasn't alone any more. A snoop had him and was hanging onto him. They walked to Park and took a taxi, and I hopped one of my own and followed to Centre Street. They went in at the big doors, and I found a phone."

Wolfe, leaning back, shut his eyes. Johnny Keems straightened his necktie and looked satisfied with himself. I tossed my notebook to the back of the desk, with his report in it, and tried to think of some brief remark that would describe how I felt. The telephone rang.

I took it. A voice informed me that Inspector Cramer wished to speak to Mr. Goodwin, and I said to put him on and signaled to Wolfe to take his line.

The sturdy inspector spoke. "Goodwin? Inspector Cramer. How about doing me a favor?"

"Surest thing you know." I made it hearty. "I'm flattered."

"Yeah? It's an easy one. Jump in your wagon and come down to my office."

I shot a glance at Wolfe, who had his receiver to his ear, but he made no sign. I said, "Maybe I could, except for one thing. I'm needed here to inspect cards of admission at the door. Like search warrants, for instance. You have no idea how they pile in on us."

Cramer laughed. "All right, you can have that one. There'll be no search warrants while you're gone. I need you down here for something. Tell Wolfe you'll be back in an hour."

"Okay. Coming."

I hung up and turned to Wolfe. "Why not? It's better than sitting here crossing my fingers. Fred and Johnny are here, and together they're a fifth as good as me. Maybe he wants me to help him embroider Mike Walsh. I'd be glad to."

Wolfe nodded. "I like this. There's something about it I like. I may be wrong. Go, by all means."

I shook my pants legs down, put the notebook and plant record away in the drawers, and got going. Johnny came to bolt the door behind me.

I hadn't been on the sidewalk for nearly twenty hours, and it smelled good. I filled the chest, waved at Tony with a cart of coal across the street, and opened up my knees on the way to the garage. The roadster whinnied as I went up to it, and I circled down the ramp, scared the daylights out of a truck as I emerged, and headed downtown with my good humor coming in again at every pore. I doubt if anything could ever get me so low that it wouldn't perk me up to get out and enjoy nature, anywhere between the two rivers from the Battery to 110th Street, but preferably below 59th.

I parked at the triangle and went in and took an elevator. They sent me right in to Cramer's little inside room, but it was empty except for a clerk in uniform, and I sat down to wait. In a minute Cramer entered. I was thinking he might have the decency to act a little embarrassed, but he didn't; he was chewing a cigar and he appeared hearty. He didn't go to his desk, but stood there. I thought it wouldn't hurt to rub it in, so I asked him, "Have you found Clara Fox yet?"

He shook his head. "Nope. No Clara Fox. But we will. We've got Mike Walsh."

I lifted the brows. "You don't say. Congratulations. Where'd you find him?"

He frowned down at me. "I'm not going to try to bluff you, Goodwin. It's a waste of time. That's what I asked you to come down here for, this Mike Walsh. You and Wolfe have been cutting it pretty thin up there, but if you help me out on this we'll call it square. I want you to pick this Mike Walsh out for me. You won't have to appear, you can look through the panel."

"I don't get you. I thought you said you had him."

"Him hell." Cramer bit his cigar. "I've got eight of 'em."

"Oh." I grinned at him sympathetically. "Think of that, eight Mike Walshes! It's a good thing it wasn't Bill Smith or Abe Cohen."

"Will you pick him out?"

"I don't like to." I pulled a hesitation. "Why can't the boys grind it out themselves?"

"Well, they can't. We've got nothing at all to go on except that Harlan Scovil had his name on a piece of paper and he was at your place last night. We couldn't use a hose on all eight of them even if we were inclined that way. The last one was brought in less than an hour ago, and he's worse than any of the others. He's a night watchman and he's seventy if he's a day, and he says who he knows or doesn't know is none of our damn business, and I'm inclined to believe him. Look here, Goodwin. This Walsh isn't a client of Wolfe's. You don't owe him anything, and anyway we're not going to hurt him unless he needs it. Come on and take a look and tell me if we've got him."

I shook my head. "I'm sorry. It wouldn't go with the program. I'd like to, but I can't."

Cramer took his cigar from his mouth and pointed it at me. "Once more I'm asking you. Will you do it?"

I just shook my head.

He walked around the desk to his chair and sat down. He looked at me as if he regretted something. Finally he said, "It's too much, Goodwin. This time it's too much. I'm going to have to put it on to you and Wolfe both for obstructing justice. It's all set for a charge. Even if I hated to worse than I do, I've got upstairs to answer to."

He pushed a button on his desk. I said, "Go ahead. Then, pretty soon, go ahead and regret it for a year or two and maybe longer."

The door opened and a gumshoe came in. Cramer turned to him. "You'll have to turn 'em loose, Nick. Put shadows on all of them except the kid that goes to N. Y. U. and the radio singer. They're out. Take good men. If one of them gets lost you've got addresses to pick him up again. Any more they pick up, I'll see them after you've got a record down."

"Yes, sir. The one from Brooklyn, the McGrue Club guy, is raising hell."

"All right. Let him out. I'll phone McGrue later."

The gumshoe departed. Cramer tried to get his cigar lit. I said, "And as far as upstairs is concerned, to hell with the Commissioner. How does he know whether or not it's justice that Wolfe's obstructing? How about that cripple Paul Chapin and that bird Bowen? Did he obstruct justice that time? If you ask me, I think you had a nerve to ask me to come down here. Are we interfering with your legal right to look for these babies? You even looked for one of them under Wolfe's bed and under my bed. Do Wolfe and

I wear badges, and do we line up on the first and fifteenth for a city check? We do not."

Cramer puffed. "I ought to charge you."

I lifted the shoulders and let them drop. "Sure. You're just sore. That's one way cops and newspaper reporters are all alike, they can't bear to have anyone know anything they won't tell." I looked at my wrist watch and saw it was nearly two o'clock. "I'm hungry. Where do I eat, inside or out?"

Cramer said, "I don't give a damn if you never eat. Beat it."

I floated up and out, down the hall, down in the elevator, and back to the roadster. I looked around comprehensively, reflecting that within a radius of a few blocks eight Mike Walshes were scattering in all directions, six of them with tails, and that I would give at least two bits to know where one of them was headed for. But even if he had gone by my elbow that second I wouldn't have dared to take it up, since that would have spotted him for them, so I hopped in the roadster and swung north.

When I got back to the house Wolfe and Clara Fox were in the dining room, sitting with their coffee. They were so busy they only had time to toss me a nod, and I sat down at my end of the table and Fritz brought me a plate. She had on my dressing gown, with the sleeves rolled up, and a pair of Fritz's slippers with her ankles bare. Wolfe was reciting Hungarian poetry to her, a line at a time, and she was repeating it after him; and he was trying not to look pleased as she leaned forward with an ear cocked at him and her eyes on his lips, asking as if she were really interested, "Say it again, slower, please do."

The yellow dressing gown wasn't bad on her, at that, but I was hungry. I waded through a plate of minced lamb kidneys with green peppers, and a dish of endive, and as Fritz took the plate away and presented me with a hunk of pie I observed to the room, "If you've finished with your coffee and have any time to spare, you might like to hear a report."

Wolfe sighed. "I suppose so. But not here." He arose. "If Fritz could serve your coffee in the office? And you, Miss Fox . . . upstairs."

"Oh, my lord. Must I dig in again?"

"Of course. Until dinner time." He bowed, meaning that he inclined his head two inches, and went off.

Clara Fox got up and walked to my end. "I'll pour your coffee."

"All right. Black and two lumps."

She screwed up her face. "With all this grand cream here? Very well. You know, Mr. Goodwin, this house represents the most insolent denial of female rights the mind of man has ever conceived. No woman in it from top to bottom, but the routine is faultless, the food is perfect, and the sweeping and dusting are impeccable. I have never been a housewife, but I can't overlook this challenge. I'm going to marry Mr. Wolfe, and I know a girl that will be just the thing for you, and of course our friends will be in and out a good deal. This place needs some upsetting."

I looked at her. The hem of the yellow gown was trailing the floor. The throat of it was spreading open, and it was interesting to see where her shoulders came to and how the yellow made her hair look. I said, "You've already upset enough. Go upstairs and behave yourself. Wolfe has three wives and nineteen children in Turkey."

"I don't believe it. He has always hated women until he saw how nicely they pack in osmundine."

I grinned at her and got up. "Thanks for the coffee. I may be able to persuade Wolfe to let you come down for dinner."

I balanced my cup and saucer in one hand while I opened the door for her with the other, and then went to the office and got seated at my desk and started to sip. Wolfe had his middle drawer open and was counting bottle caps to see how much beer he had drunk since Sunday morning. Finally he closed it and grunted.

"I don't believe it for a moment. Bah. Statistics are notoriously unreliable. I had a very satisfactory talk with Mr. Lindquist over long distance, and I am more than ever anxious for a few words with Mr. Walsh. Did you see him?"

"No. I declined the invitation." I reported my session with Cramer in detail, mostly verbatim, which was the way he liked it.

Wolfe listened, and considered. "I see. Then Mr. Walsh is loose again."

"Yeah. Not only is he loose, but I don't see how we can approach him, since there's a tail on him. The minute we do they'll know it's him and grab him away from us."

"I suppose so." Wolfe sighed. "Of course it would not do to abolish the police. For nine-tenths of the prey that the law would devour they are the ideal hunters, which is as it should be. As for Walsh, it is essential that I see him . . . or that you do. Bring Keems."

I went to the front room, where Johnny was taking ten cents a game from Fred Durkin with a checkerboard, and shook him loose. He sat down next to the desk and Wolfe wiggled a finger at him.

"Johnny, this is important. I don't send Archie because he is needed here, and Saul is not available."

"Yes, sir. Shoot."

"The Michael Walsh whom you followed this morning has been released by the police because they don't know if he is the one they want. They have put a shadow on him, so it would be dangerous for you to pick him up even if you knew where to look. It is very important for Archie to get in touch with him. Since he is pretending to the police that he is not the man they seek, there is a strong probability that he will stick to the ordinary routine of his life; that is, that he will go to work this evening. But if he does that he will certainly be followed there and a detective will be covering the entrance all evening; therefore Archie could not enter that way to see him. I am covering all details so that you will know exactly what we want. Is it true that when a building project is boarded up, there is boarding where the construction adjoins the sidewalk but not on the other sides, where there are buildings? I would think so; at least it may be so sometimes. Very well, I wish to know by what means Archie can enter that building project at, say, seven o'clock this evening. Explore them all. I understand from Miss Fox, who was there last Thursday evening to talk with Mr. Walsh, that they have just started the steel framework.

"Miss Fox also tells me that Mr. Walsh goes to work at six o'clock. I want to know if he does so today. You can watch the entrance at that time, or you may perhaps have found another vantage point for observing him from inside. Use your judgment and your wit. Should you phone here, use code as far as possible. Be here by six-thirty with your report."

"Yes, sir." Johnny stood up. "If I have to sugar anybody around the other buildings in order to get through, I'll need some cash."

Wolfe nodded with some reserve. I got four fives from the safe and passed them over and Johnny tucked them in his vest. Then I took him to the hall and let him out.

I went back to my desk and fooled around with some things, made out a couple of checks, and ran over some invoices from Richardt. Wolfe was drinking beer and I was watching him out of the corner of my eye. I was keyed up, and I knew why I was; it was something about him. A hundred times I tried to decide just what it was that made it so plain to me when he had the feeling that he was closing in and was about ready for the blow-up. Once I would think that it was only that he sat differently in his chair, a little farther forward, and another time I would guess that it was the way he made movements, not quicker exactly but closer together, and still another time I would light on something else. I doubt if it was any of those. Maybe it was electric. There was more of a current turned on inside of him, and somehow I felt it. I felt it that day, as he filled his glass, and drained it and filled it again. And it made me uncomfortable, because I wasn't doing anything, and because there was always the danger that Wolfe would go off half cocked when he was keeping things to himself. So at length I offered an observation.

"And I just sit here? What's the idea, do you think those gorillas are coming back? I don't. They're not even watching the front. What was the matter with leaving Fred and Johnny here and letting me go to Fifty-fifth Street to do my own scouting? That might have been sensible, if you want me to see Mike Walsh by seven o'clock. All I'm suggesting is a little friendly chat.

I've heard you admit you've got lots of bad habits, but the worst one is the way you dig up odd facts out of phone calls and other sources when my back is turned and then expect me . . ." I waved a hand.

Wolfe said, "Nonsense. When have my expectations of you ventured beyond your capacity?"

"Never. How could they? But, for instance, if it's so important for me to see Mike Walsh it might be a good idea for me to know why, unless you want him wrapped up and brought here."

Wolfe shook his head. "Not that, I think. I'll inform you, Archie. In good time." He reached out and touched the button, then sighed and pushed the tray away. "As for my sending Johnny and letting you sit here, you may be needed. While you were out Mr. Muir telephoned to ask if he might call here at half past two. It is that now—"

"The devil he did. Muir?"

"Yes. Mr. Ramsey Muir. And as for my keeping you in ignorance of facts, you already interfere so persistently with my mental processes that I am disinclined to furnish you further grounds for speculation. In the present case you know the general situation as well as I do. Chiefly you lack patience, and my exercise of it infuriates you. If I know who killed Harlan Scovil—and since talking with Mr. Lindquist over long distance I think I do—why do I not act at once? Firstly because I require confirmation, and secondly because our primary interest in this case is not the solution of a murder but the collection of a debt. If I expect to get the confirmation I require from Mr. Walsh, why do I not get him at once, secure my confirmation, and let the police have him? Because the course they would probably take, after beating his story out of him, would make it difficult to collect from Lord Clivers, and would greatly complicate the matter of clearing Miss Fox of the larceny charge. We have three separate goals to reach, and since it will be necessary to arrive at all of them simultaneously—but there is the doorbell. Mr. Muir is three minutes late."

I went to the hall and took a look through the panel. Sure enough, it was Muir. I opened up and let him in. From the way he stepped over the door sill and snapped out that he wanted to see Wolfe, it was fairly plain that he was mad as hell. He had on a brown plaid topcoat cut by a tailor that was out of my class, but twenty-five years too young for him, and apparently he wasn't taking it off. I motioned him ahead of me into the office and introduced him, and allowed myself a polite grin when I saw that he wasn't shaking hands any more than Wolfe was. I pushed a chair around and he sat with his hat on his knees.

Wolfe said, "Your secretary, on the telephone, seemed not to know what you wished to see me about. My surmise was, your charge against Miss Clara Fox. You understand of course that I am representing Miss Fox."

"Yes. I understand that."

"Well, sir?"

The bones of Muir's face seemed to show, and his ears seemed to point forward, more than they had the day before. He kept his lips pressed together and his jaw was working from side to side as if all this emotion in his old age was nearly too much for him. I remembered how he had looked at Clara Fox the day before and thought it was remarkable that he could keep his digestion going with all the stew there must have been inside of him.

He said, "I have come here at the insistence of Mr. Perry." His voice trembled a little, and when he stopped his jaw slid around. "I want you to understand that I know she took that money. She is the only one who could have taken it. It was found in her car." He stopped a little to control his jaw. "Mr. Perry told me of your threat to sue for damages. The insinuation in it is contemptible. What kind of a blackguard are you, to protect a thief by hinting calumnies against men who . . . men above suspicion?"

He paused and compressed his lips. Wolfe murmured, "Well, go on. I don't answer questions containing two or more unsupported assumptions."

I don't think Muir heard him; he was only hearing himself and trying not to blow up. He said, "I'm here only for one reason, for the sake of the Seaboard Products Corporation. And not on account of your dirty threat either. That's not where the dirt is in the Seaboard Products Corporation that has got to be concealed." His voice trembled again. "It's the fact that the president of the corporation has to satisfy his personal sensual appetite by saving a common thief from what she deserves! That's why she can laugh at me! That's why she can stand behind your dirty threats! Because she knows what Perry wants, and she knows how—"

"Mr. Muir!" Wolfe snapped at him. "I wouldn't talk like that if I were you. It's so futile. Surely you didn't come here to persuade me that Mr. Perry has a sensual appetite."

Muir made a movement and his hat rolled from his knees to the floor, but he paid no attention to it. His movement was for the purpose of getting his hand into his inside breast pocket, from which he withdrew a square manila envelope. He looked in it and fingered around and took out a small photograph, glanced at it, and handed it to Wolfe. "There," he said, "look at that."

Wolfe did so, and passed it to me. It was a snapshot of Clara Fox and Anthony D. Perry seated in a convertible coupe with the top down. I laid it on the edge of the desk and Muir picked it up and returned it to the envelope. His jaw was moving. He said, "I have more than thirty of them. A dectective took them for me. Perry doesn't know I have them. I want to make it clear to you that she deserves . . . that she has a hold on him . . ."

Wolfe put up a hand. "I'm afraid I must interrupt you again, Mr. Muir. I don't like photographs of automobiles. You say that Mr. Perry insisted on your coming here. I'll have to insist on your telling me what for."

"But you understand—"

"No. I won't listen. I understand enough. Perhaps I had better put a question or two. Is it true that you have recovered all of the missing money?"

Muir glared at him. "You know we have. It was found under the back seat of her car."

"But if that was her car in the photograph, it has no back seat."

"She bought a new one in August. The photograph was taken in July. I suppose Perry bought it. Her salary is higher than any other woman in our organization."

"Splendid. But about the money. If you have it back, why are you determined to prosecute?"

"Why shouldn't we prosecute? Because she's guilty! She took it from my desk, knowing that Perry would protect her! With her body, with her flesh, with her surrender—"

"No, Mr. Muir." Wolfe's hand was up again. "Please. I put the question wrong, I shouldn't have asked why. I want to know, are you determined to prosecute?"

Muir clamped his lips. He opened them, and clamped them again. At last he spoke, "We were. I was."

"Was? Are you still?"

No reply. "Are you still, Mr. Muir?"

"I . . . no."

"Indeed." Wolfe's eyes narrowed. "You are prepared to withdraw the charge?"

"Yes . . . under certain circumstances."

"What circumstances?"

"I want to see her." Muir stopped because his voice was trembling again. "I have promised Perry that I will withdraw the charge provided I can see her, alone, and tell her myself." He sat up and his jaw tightened. "That . . . those are the circumstances."

Wolfe looked at him a moment and then leaned back. He sighed. "I think possibly that can be arranged. But you must first sign a statement exonerating her."

"Before I see her?"

"Yes."

"No. I see her first." Muir's lips worked. "I must see her and tell her myself. If I had already signed a statement, she wouldn't . . . no. I won't do that."

"But you can't see her first." Wolfe sounded patient. "There is a warrant in force against her, sworn to by you. I do not suspect you of treachery, I merely protect my client. You say that you have promised Mr. Perry that you will withdraw the charge. Do so. Mr. Goodwin will type the statement, you will sign it, and I will arrange a meeting with Miss Fox later in the day."

Muir was shaking his head. He muttered, "No. No . . . I won't." All at once he broke loose worse than he had in Perry's office the day before. He jumped up and banged his hand on the desk and leaned over at Wolfe. "I tell you I must see her! You damn blackguard, you've got her here! What for? What do you get out of it? What do you and Perry . . ."

I had a good notion to slap him one, but of course he was too old and too little. Wolfe, leaning back, opened his eyes to look at him and then closed them. Muir went on raving. I got out of my chair and told him to sit down, and he began yelling at me, something about how I had looked at her in Perry's office yesterday. That sounded as if he might really be going to have a fit, so I took a step and got hold of his shoulders with a fairly good grip and persuaded him into his chair, and he shut up as suddenly as he had started and pulled a handkerchief from his pocket and began wiping his face with his hand trembling.

As he did that and I stepped back, the doorbell rang. I wasn't sure about leaving Wolfe there alone with a maniac, but when I didn't move he lifted his brows at me, so I went to see who the customer was.

I looked through the panel. It was a rugged-looking guy well past middle age in a loose-hanging tweed suit, with a red face, straight eyebrows over tired gray eyes, and no lobe on his right ear. Even without the ear I would have recognized him from the *Times* picture. I opened the door and asked him what he wanted and he said in a wounded tone, "I'd like to see Mr. Nero Wolfe. Lord Clivers."

XIII

I NODDED. "Right. Hop the sill."

I proceeded to tax the brain. Before I go on to describe that, I'll make a confession. I had not till that moment seriously entertained the idea that the Marquis of Clivers had killed Harlan Scovil. And why not? Because like most other people, and maybe especially Americans, there was a sneaky feeling in me that men with noble titles didn't do things like that. Besides, this bird had just been to Washington and had lunch at the White House, which cinched it that he wasn't a murderer. As a matter of fact, I suspect that noblemen and people who eat lunch at the White House commit more than their share of murders compared to their numerical strength in the total population. Anyhow, looking at this one in the flesh, and reflecting that he carried a pistol and knew how to use one, and considering how well he was fixed in the way of motive, and realizing that since Harlan Scovil had been suspicious enough to make an advance call on Nero Wolfe he might easily have done the same on the Marquis of Clivers, I revised some of the opinions I had been forming. It looked wide open to me.

That flashed through my mind. Also, as I disposed of his hat and stick and gloves for him, I wondered if it might be well to arrange a little confrontation between Muir and the marquis, but I didn't like to decide that myself. So I escorted him to a seat in the front room, telling him Wolfe was engaged, and then returned to the hall and wrote on a piece of paper, "Old man Clivers," and went to the office and handed the paper to Wolfe.

Wolfe glanced at it, looked at me, and winked his right eye. I sat down. Muir was talking, much calmer but just as stubborn. They passed it back and forth for a couple of minutes without getting anywhere, until Wolfe said, "Futile, Mr. Muir. I won't do it. Tell Mr. Perry that I shall proceed with the program I announced to him this morning. That's final. I'll accept nothing less than complete and unconditional exoneration of my client. Good day, sir. I have a caller waiting."

Muir stood up. He wasn't trembling, and his jaw seemed to be back in place, but he looked about as friendly as Mussolini talking to the world. He didn't say anything. He shot me a mean glance and looked at Wolfe for half a minute without blinking, and then stooped to pick up his hat and straightened up and steered for the door. I followed and let him out, and stood on the stoop a second watching him start off down the sidewalk as if he had half a jag on. He was like the mule in the story that kept running into trees; he wasn't blind, he was just so mad he didn't give a damn.

I stood shaking my head more in anger than in pity, and then went back to the office and said to Wolfe, "I would say you hit bottom that time. He's staggering. If you called that foxy, what would you say if you saw a rat?"

Wolfe nodded faintly. I resumed, "I showed you that paper because I thought you might deem it advisable to let Clivers and Muir see each other. Unexpected like that, it might have been interesting. It's my social instinct."

"No doubt. But this is a detective bureau, not a fashionable salon. Nor a menagerie—since Mr. Muir is plainly a lecherous hyena. Bring Lord Clivers."

I went through the connecting door to the front room, and Clivers looked around, surprised at my entering from a new direction. He was jumpy. I pointed him ahead and he stopped on the threshold and glanced around before venturing in. Then he moved spryly enough and walked over to the desk. Wolfe took him in with his eyes half shut, and nodded.

"How do you do, sir." Wolfe indicated the chair Muir had just vacated. "Be seated."

Clivers did a slow-motion circle. He turned all the way around, encompassing with his eyes the bookshelves, the wall maps, the Holbein reproductions, more bookshelves, the three-foot globe on its stand, the engraving of Brillat-Savarin, more bookshelves, the picture of Sherlock Holmes above my desk. Then he sat down and looked at me with a frown and pointed a thumb at me.

"This young man," he said.

Wolfe said, "My confidential assistant, Mr. Goodwin. There would be no point in sending him out, for he would merely find a point of vantage we have prepared, and set down what he heard."

"The devil he would." Clivers laughed three short blasts, haw-haw-haw, and gave me up. He transferred the frown to Wolfe. "I received your letter about that horse. It's preposterous."

Wolfe nodded. "I agree with you. All debts are preposterous. They are the envious past clutching with its cold dead fingers the throat of the living present."

"Eh?" Clivers stared at him. "What kind of talk is that? Rot. What I mean to say is, two hundred thousand pounds for a horse. And uncollectible."

"Surely not." Wolfe sighed. He leaned forward to press the button for Fritz, and back again. "The best argument against you is your presence here. If it is uncollectible, why did you come? Will you have some beer?"

"What kind of beer?"

"American. Potable."

"I'll try it. I came because my nephew gave me to understand that if I wanted to see you I would have to come. I wanted to see you because I had to learn if you are a swindler or a dupe."

"My dear sir." Wolfe lifted his brows. "No other alternatives? Another glass and bottle, Fritz." He opened his and poured. "But you seem to be a direct man. Let's not get mired in irrelevancies. Frankly, I am relieved. I feared that you might even dispute the question of identity and create a lot of unnecessary trouble."

"Dispute identity?" Clivers glared. "Why the devil should I?"

"You shouldn't, but I thought you might. You were, forty years ago in Silver City, Nevada, known as George Rowley?"

"Certainly I was. Thanks, I'll pour it myself."

"Good." Wolfe drank, and wiped his lips. "I think we should get along. I am aware that Mr. Lindquist's claim against you has no legal standing on account of the expiration of time. The same is true of the claim of various others; besides, the paper you signed which originally validated it is not available. But it is a sound and demonstrable moral obligation, and I calculated that rather than have that fact shown in open court you would prefer to pay. It would be an unusual case and would arouse much public interest.

Not only are you a peer of England, you are in this country on an important and delicate diplomatic mission, and therefore such publicity would be especially undesirable. Would you not rather pay what you owe, or at least a fraction of it, than permit the publicity? I calculated that you would. Do you find the beer tolerable?"

Clivers put down his glass and licked his lips. "It'll do." He screwed up his mouth and looked at Wolfe. "By God, you know, you might mean that."

"Verily, sir."

"Yes, by God, you might. I'll tell you what I thought. I thought you were basing the claim on that horse with the pretense that it was additional to the obligation I assumed when I signed that paper. The horse wasn't mentioned in the paper. Not a bad idea, an excellent go at blackmail. It all sounds fantastic now, but it wasn't then. If I hadn't signed that paper and if it hadn't been for that horse I would have had a noose around my neck. Not so damn pleasant, eh? And of course that's what you're doing, claiming extra for the horse. But it's preposterous. Two hundred thousand pounds for a horse? I'll pay a thousand."

Wolfe shook his head. "I dislike haggling. Equally I dislike quibbling. The total claim is in question, and you know it. I represent not only Mr. and Miss Lindquist but also the daughter of Gilbert Fox, and indirectly Mr. Walsh; and I was to have represented Mr. Scovil, who was murdered last evening." He shook his head again. "No, Lord Clivers. In my letter I based the claim on the horse only because the paper you signed is not available. It is the total claim we are discussing, and, strictly speaking, that would mean half of your entire wealth. As I said, my clients are willing to accept a fraction."

Clivers had a new expression on his face. He no longer glared, but looked at Wolfe quietly intent. He said, "I see. So it's a serious game, is it? I would have paid a thousand for the horse, possibly even another thousand for the glass of beer. But you're on for a real haul by threatening to make all this public and compromise my position here. Go to hell." He got up.

Wolfe said patiently, "Permit me. It isn't a matter of a thousand or two for a horse. Precisely and morally, you owe these people half of your wealth. If they are willing—"

"Bah! I owe them nothing! You know damn well I've paid them."

Wolfe's eyes went nearly shut. "What's that? You've paid them?"

"Of course I have, and you know it. And I've got their receipt, and I've got the paper I signed." Clivers abruptly sat down again. "Look here. Your man is here, and I'm alone, so why not talk straight? I don't resent your being a crook, I've dealt with crooks before, and more pretentious ones than you. But cut out the pretense and get down to business. You have a good lever for blackmail, I admit it. But you might as well give up the idea of a big haul, because I won't submit to it. I'll pay three thousand pounds for a receipt from the Lindquists for that horse."

Wolfe's forefinger was tapping gently on the arm of his chair, which meant he was dodging meteors and comets. His eyes were mere slits. After a moment he said, "This is bad. It raises questions of credibility." He wiggled the finger. "Really bad, sir. How am I to know whether you really have paid? And if you have, how are you to know whether I was really ignorant of the fact and acting in good faith? Have you any suggestions?" He pushed the button. "I need some beer. Will you join me?"

"Yes. It's pretty good. Do you mean to say you didn't know I had paid?"

"I do. I do indeed. Though the possibility should certainly have occurred to me. I was too intent on the path under my feet." He stopped to open bottles, pushed one across to Clivers, and filled his glass. "You say you paid them. What *them*? When? How much? What with? They signed a receipt? Tell me about it."

Clivers, taking his time, emptied his glass and set it down. He licked his lips, screwed up his mouth, and looked at Wolfe, considering. Finally he shook his head. "I don't know about you. You're clever. Do you mean that if I show evidence of having paid, and their receipt, you will abandon this preposterous claim for the horse on payment of a thousand pounds?"

"Satisfactory evidence?" Wolfe nodded. "I'll abandon it for nothing."

"Oh, I'll pay a thousand. I understand the Lindquists are hard up. The evidence will be satisfactory, and you can see it tomorrow morning."

"I'd rather see it today."

"You can't. I haven't got it. It will arrive this evening on the *Berengaria*. My dispatch bag will reach me tonight, but I shall be engaged. Come to my hotel any time after nine in the morning."

"I don't go out. I am busy from nine to eleven. You can bring your evidence here any time after eleven."

"The devil I can." Clivers stared at him, and suddenly laughed his three blasts again. Haw-haw-haw. He turned it off. "You can come to my hotel. You don't look infirm."

Wolfe said patiently, "If you don't bring it here, or send it, I won't get to see it and I'll have to press the claim for the horse. And by the way, how does it happen to be coming on the *Berengaria*?"

"Because I sent for it. Monday of last week, eight days ago, a woman saw me. She got in to me through my nephew—it seems they had met socially. She represented herself as the daughter of Gil Fox and made demands. I wouldn't discuss it with her. I thought it was straight blackmail and I would freeze her out. She was too damned good-looking to be honest. But I thought it worthwhile to cable to London for these items from my private papers, in case of developments. They'll be here tonight."

"And this payment—when was it made?"

"Nineteen-six or seven. I don't know. I haven't looked at those papers for twenty years."

"To whom was the payment made?"

"I have the receipt signed by all of them."

"So you said. And you have the paper which you had signed. The man called Rubber Coleman had that paper. Did he get the money?"

Clivers opened his mouth and shut it again. Then he said, "I've answered enough questions. You'll see the check in the morning, signed by me, endorsed by the payee, and canceled paid." He looked at his empty glass. "I hadn't tried American lager before. It's pretty good."

Wolfe pressed the button. "Then why not anticipate it by a few hours? I'm not attempting a cross-examination, Lord Clivers. I merely want information. Was it Coleman?"

"Yes."

"How much did he get?"

"Two hundred and some odd thousand pounds. A million dollars. He came to me—July I think it was—about a year after I succeeded to the title. It must have been 1906. He made exorbitant demands. Much of my property was entail. He was unreasonable. We finally agreed on a million dollars. Of course I needed time to get that much cash together. He returned to the States and came back in a couple of months with a receipt signed by all of them. Besides, he was deputized in the original paper, which he surrendered. My solicitor wanted me to send over here and have the signatures verified, but Coleman said he had had difficulty in persuading them to agree to the amount and I was afraid to reopen the question. I paid him."

"Where is Coleman now?"

"I don't know. I've never seen him since, nor heard of him. I wasn't interested; it was a closed chapter. I'm not greatly interested now. If he swindled them and kept the money, they shouldn't have trusted him with their signatures." Clivers hesitated, then resumed, "It's a fact that when the Fox woman saw me a week ago I took it for blackmail, but when Harlan Scovil called to see me yesterday afternoon I had my doubts. Scovil was a square man, he was born square, and I didn't think even forty years could turn him into a blackmailer. When I learned from the police last evening that he had been killed, there was no longer any doubt about a stink in the wind, but I couldn't tell them what I didn't know, and what I did know was my own business."

"So Harlan Scovil saw you yesterday?" Wolfe rubbed his nose. "That's int—"

"He didn't see me. I was out. When I returned in the late afternoon I was told he had been there." Clivers drank his beer. "Then this morning your letter came and it looked like blackmail again. With a murder involved in it also, it appeared that publicity was inevitable if I consulted the official police. The only thing left was to deal with you. All you wanted was money, and I have a little of it left in spite of taxes and revolutions. I don't for a minute believe that you're prepared to drop it merely because I show evidence that I've paid. You want money. You present a front that shows you're not a damned piker." He pointed. "Look at that globe, the finest I ever saw, couldn't have cost less than a hundred pounds. Twice as big as the one in my library. I'll pay three thousand for Lindquist's receipt for that horse."

"Indeed." Wolfe sighed. "Back to three thousand again. I'm sorry, sir, that you persist in taking me for a horse trader. And I do want money. That globe was made by Gouchard and there aren't many like it." He suddenly straightened up. "By the way, was it Mr. Walsh who told you that the Lindquists are hard up?"

Clivers stared. "How the devil do you know that?" He looked around. "Is Walsh here?"

"No, he isn't here. I didn't know it, I asked. I was aware that Mr. Walsh had called at the Hotel Portland this morning, so you had a talk with him. You haven't been entirely frank, Lord Clivers. You knew when you came here that Mr. Walsh never got any of that money, possibly that he never signed the receipt."

"I knew he said he hadn't."

"Don't you believe him?"

"I don't believe anybody. I know damn well I'm a liar. I'm a diplomat." He did his three blasts again, haw-haw-haw. "Look here. You can forget about Walsh, I'll deal with him myself. I have to keep this thing clear, at least as long as I'm in this country. I'll deal with Walsh. Scovil is dead, God rest his soul. Let the police do what they can with that. As for the Lindquists, I'll pay them two thousand for the horse, and you would get a share of that. The Fox woman can look after herself; anyone as young and handsome as she is doesn't need any of my money. As far as I'm concerned, that clears it up. If you can find Coleman and put a twist on him, go ahead, but that would take doing. He was hard and tricky, and it's a safe bet he still is. You may see the documents tomorrow morning, but I won't bring them here and I won't send them. If you can't come, send your man to look at them. I'll see him, and we can arrange for the payment to the Lindquists and their receipt. Actually, a thousand pounds should be enough for a horse. Eh?"

Wolfe shook his head. He was leaning back again, with his fingers twined on his belly, and if you didn't know him you might have thought he was asleep. Clivers sat and frowned at him. I turned a new page of my notebook and wondered if we would have to garnishee Clara Fox's wages to collect our fee. Finally Wolfe's eyelids raised enough to permit the conjecture that he was conscious.

"It would have saved a lot of trouble," he murmured, "if they had hanged you in 1895. Isn't that so? As it stands, Lord Clivers, I wish to assure you again of my complete good faith in this matter, and I suggest that we postpone commitments until your evidence of payment has been examined. Tomorrow, then." He looked at me. "Confound you, Archie. I have you to thank for this acarpous entanglement."

It was a new one, but I got the idea. He meant that he had drawn his sword in defense of Clara Fox because I had told him that she was the ideal of my dreams. I suppose it was me that sat and recited Hungarian poetry to her.

XIV

WHEN Wolfe came down to the office from the plant rooms at six o'clock, Saul Panzer and Orrie Cather were there waiting for him. Fred Durkin, who had spent most of the afternoon in the kitchen with the cookie jar, had been sent home at five, after I had warned him to cross the street if he saw a cop.

Nothing much had happened, except that Anthony D. Perry had telephoned a little after Fred had left, to say that he would like to call at the office and see Wolfe at seven o'clock. Since I would be leaving about that time to sneak up on Mike Walsh, I asked him if he couldn't make it at six, but he said other engagements prevented. I tried a couple of leading questions on him, but he got brusque and said his business was with Nero Wolfe. I knew Saul would be around, or Johnny Keems, so I said okay for seven.

There had been no word from Johnny. The outstanding event of the afternoon had been the arrival of another enormous box of roses from the Horrocks person, and he had had the brass to have the delivery label addressed to me, with a card on the inside scribbled "Thanks Goodwin for forwarding," so now in addition to acting as hall boy and as a second-hand ladies' outfitter, apparently I was also expected to be a common carrier.

I had lost sixty cents. At a quarter to four, a few minutes after Clivers had gone, Wolfe had suggested that since I hadn't been out much a little exercise wouldn't hurt me any. He had made no comments on the news from Clivers, and I thought he might if I went along with him, but I told him I couldn't see it at two bits. He said, all right, a dime. So I mounted the stairs while he took the elevator and we met in his room. He took his coat and vest off, exhibiting about eighteen square feet of canary-yellow shirt, and chose the darts with yellow feathers, which were his favorites. The first hand he got an ace and two bull's eyes, making three aces. By four o'clock, time for him to go to the plant rooms, it had cost me sixty cents and I had got nothing out of it because he had been too concentrated on the game to talk.

I went on up to the south room and was in there nearly an hour. There were three reasons for it: first, Wolfe had instructed me to tell Clara Fox about the visits from Muir and Clivers; second, she was restless and needed a little discipline; and third, I had nothing else to do anyhow. She had her clothes on again. She said Fritz had given her an iron to press with, but her dress didn't look as if she had used it much. I told her I supposed an adventuress wouldn't be so hot at ironing. When I told her about Muir she just made a face and didn't seem disposed to furnish any remarks, but she was articulate about Clivers. She thought he was lying. She said that she understood he was considered one of the ablest of British diplomats, and it was to be expected he would use his talents for private business as well as public. I said that I hadn't observed anything particularly able about him except that he could empty a glass of beer as fast as Nero Wolfe; that while he might not be quite as big a sap as his nephew Francis Horrocks he seemed fairly primitive to me, even for a guy who had spent most of his life on a little island.

She said it was just a difference in superficial mannerisms, that she too had thought Horrocks a sap at first, that I would change my mind when I knew him better, and that after all traditions weren't necessarily silly just because they weren't American. I said I wasn't talking about traditions, I was talking about saps, and as far as I was concerned saps were out, regardless of race, nationality, or religion. It went on from there until she said she guessed she would go up and take advantage of Mr. Wolfe's invitation to look at the orchids, and I went down to send Fred home.

When Wolfe came down I was at my desk working on some sandwiches and milk, for I didn't know when I might get back from my trip uptown. I told him about the phone call from Perry. He went into the front room to get reports from Saul and Orrie, which made me sore as usual, but when he came back and settled into his chair and rang for beer I made no effort to stimulate him into any choice remarks about straining my powers of dissimulation, because he didn't give me a chance. Having sent Orrie home and Saul to the kitchen, he was ready for me, and he disclosed the nature of my mission with Mike Walsh. It wasn't precisely what I had expected, but I pretended it was by keeping nonchalant and casual. He drank beer and wiped his lips and told me, "I'm sorry, Archie, if this bores you."

I said, "Oh, I expect it. Just a matter of routine."

He winked at me, and I turned and picked up my milk to keep from grinning back at him, and the telephone rang.

It was Inspector Cramer. He asked for Wolfe and I passed the signal, and of course kept my own line. Cramer said, "What about this Clara Fox? Are you going to bring her down here, or tell me where to send for her?"

Wolfe murmured into the transmitter, "What is this, Mr. Cramer? A new tactic? I don't get it."

"Now listen, Wolfe!" Cramer sounded hurt and angry. "First you tell me you've got her hid because we tried to snatch her on a phony larceny charge. Now that that's out of the way, do you think you're going to pull—"

"What?" Wolfe stopped him. "The larceny charge out of the way?"

"Certainly. Don't pretend you didn't know it, since of course you did it, though I don't know how. You can put over the damnedest tricks."

"No doubt. But please tell me how you learned this."

"Frisbie over at the District Attorney's office. It seems that a fellow named Muir, a vice-president up at that Seaboard thing where she worked, is a friend of Frisbie's. He's the one that swore out the warrant. Now he's backed up, and it's all off, and I want to see this Miss Fox and hear her tell me that she never heard of Harlan Scovil, like all the Mike Walshes we got." Cramer became sarcastic. "Of course this is all news to you."

"It is indeed." Wolfe sent a glance at me, with a lifted brow. "Quite pleasant news. Let's see. I suspect it would be too difficult to persuade you that I know nothing of Miss Fox's whereabouts, so I shan't try. It is now six-thirty, and I shall have to make some inquiries. Where can I telephone you at eight?"

"Oh, for God's sake." Cramer sounded disgusted. "I wish I'd let the Commissioner pull you in, as he wanted to. I don't need to tell you why I hate to work against you, but have a heart. Send her down here, I won't bite her. I was going to a show tonight."

"I'm sorry, Mr. Cramer." Wolfe affected his sweet tone, which always made me want to kick him. "I must first verify your information about the larceny charge, and then I must get in touch with Miss Fox. You'll be there until eight o'clock."

Cramer grunted something profane, and we hung up.

"So." I tossed down my notebook. "Mr. Muir is yellow after all, and Mr. Perry is probably coming to find out how you knew he would be. Shake-up in the Seaboard Products Corporation. But where the devil is Johnny—ah, see that? All I have to do is pronounce his name and he rings the doorbell."

I went to the entrance and let him in. One look at his satisfied handsomeness was enough to show that he had been marvelous all over again. As a matter of fact, Johnny Keems unquestionably had an idea at the back of his head—and still has—that it would be a very fine thing for the detective business if he got my job. Which doesn't bother me a bit, because I know Wolfe would never be able to stand him. He puts slick stuff on his hair and he wears spats, and he would never get the knack of keeping Wolfe on the job by bawling him out properly. I know what I get paid high wages for, though I've never been able to decide whether Wolfe knows that I know.

I took Johnny to the office and he sat down and began pulling papers out of his pocket. He shuffled through them and announced, "I thought it would be better to make diagrams. Of course I could have furnished Archie with verbal descriptions, but along with my shorthand I've learned—"

Wolfe put in, "Is Mr. Walsh there now?"

Johnny nodded. "He came a few minutes before six. I was watching from the back of a restaurant that fronts on Fifty-sixth Street, because I knew he'd have a shadow and I didn't want to run a risk of being seen, a lot of those city detectives know me. By the way, there's only the one entrance to the boarding, on Fifty-fifth." He handed the papers across to Wolfe. "I dug up nine other ways to get in. Some of them you couldn't use, but with two of them, a restaurant and a pet shop that's open until nine, it's a cinch."

Instead of taking the papers, Wolfe nodded at me. "Give them to Archie. Is there anyone in there besides Mr. Walsh?"

"I don't think so. It's mostly steel men on the job now, and they quit at five. Of course it was dark when I left, and it isn't lit up much. There's a wooden shed at one side with a couple of tables and a phone and so on, and a man was standing there talking to Walsh, a foreman, but he looked as if he was ready to leave. The reason I was a little late, after I got out of there I went around to Fifty-fifth to see if there was a shadow on the job, and there was. I spotted him easy. He was standing there across the street, talking to a taxi driver."

"All right. Satisfactory. Go over the diagrams with Archie."

Johnny explained to me how good the diagrams were, and I had to agree with him. They were swell. Five of them I discarded, because four of them were shops that wouldn't be open and the other was the Orient Club, which wouldn't be easy to get into. Of the remaining four, one was the pet shop, one a movie theater with a fire alley, and two restaurants. After Johnny's detailed description of the relative advantages and disadvantages, I picked one of the restaurants for the first stab. It seemed like a lot of complicated organization work for getting ready to stop in and ask a guy a question, but considering what the question led to in Wolfe's mental arrangements it seemed likely that it might be worth the trouble. By the time we were through with Johnny's battle maps it lacked only a few minutes till seven, and I followed my custom of chucking things in the drawers, plugging the phone for all the house connections, and taking my automatic and giving it a look and sticking it in my pocket. I got up and pushed my chair in.

I asked Johnny, "Can you hang around for a couple of hours' overtime?"

"I can if I eat."

"Okay. You'll find Saul in the kitchen. There's a caller expected at seven and he'll tend to the door. Stick around. Mr. Wolfe may want you to exercise your shorthand."

Johnny strode out. I think he practiced striding. I started to follow, but turned to ask Wolfe, "Are you going to grab time by the forelock? Will there be a party when I get back?"

"I couldn't say." Wolfe's hand was resting on the desk; he was waiting for the door to close behind me, to ring for beer. "We'll await the confirmation."

"Shall I phone?"

"No. Bring it."

"Okay." I turned.

The telephone rang. From force of habit I wheeled again and stepped to my desk for it, though I saw that Wolfe had reached for his receiver. So we both heard it, a voice that sounded far away but thin and tense with excitement. "Nero Wolfe! Nero—"

I snapped, "Yes. Talking."

"I've got him! Come up here . . . Fifty-fifth Street . . . Mike Walsh this is . . . I've got him covered . . . come up—"

It was cut off by the sound of a shot in the receiver—a sound of an explosion so loud in my ear that it might have been a young cannon. Then there was nothing. I said "Hello, Walsh! Walsh!" a few times, but there was no answer.

I hung up and turned to Wolfe. "Well, by Godfrey. Did you hear anything?"

He nodded. "I did. And I don't understand it."

"Indeed. That's a record. What's the program, hop up there?"

Wolfe's eyes were shut, and his lips were moving out and in. He stayed that way a minute. I stood and watched him. Finally he said, "If Walsh shot someone, who was it? But if someone shot him, why now? Why not yesterday or a week ago? In any case, you might as well go and learn what happened. It may have been merely a steel girder crashing off its perch; there was enough noise."

"No. That was a gun."

"Very well. Find out. If you—ah! The doorbell. Indeed. You might attend to that first. Mr. Perry is punctual."

As I entered the hall Saul Panzer came out of the kitchen, and I sent him back. I turned on the stoop light and looked through the panel because it was getting to be a habit, and saw it was Perry. I opened the door and he stepped inside and put his hat and gloves on the stand.

I followed him into the office.

Wolfe said, "Good evening sir. I have reflected, Archie, that the less one meddles the less one becomes involved. You might have Saul phone the hospital that there has been an accident. Oh, no, Mr. Perry, nothing serious, thank you."

I went to the kitchen and told Saul Panzer: "Go to Allen's on Thirty-fourth Street and phone headquarters that you think you heard a shot inside the building construction on Fifty-fifth near Madison and they'd better investigate at once. If they want to know who you are, tell them King George. Make it snappy."

That was a nickel wasted, but I didn't know it then.

XV

PERRY glanced at me as I got into my chair and opened my notebook. He was saying, "I don't remember that anything ever irritated me more. I suppose I'm getting old. You mustn't think I bear any ill will; if you preferred to represent Miss Fox, that was your right. But you must admit I played your hand for you; so far as I know there wasn't the faintest shred of evidence with which you could have enforced your threat." He smiled. "You think, of course, that my personal—er—respect for Miss Fox influenced my attitude and caused me to bring pressure on Muir. I confess that had a great deal to do with it. She is a charming young lady and also an extremely competent employee."

Wolfe nodded. "And my client. Naturally, I was pleased to learn that the charge had been dropped."

"You say you heard it from the police? I hoped I was bringing the good news myself."

"I got it from Inspector Cramer." Wolfe had got his beer. He poured some, and resumed, "Mr. Cramer told me that he had been advised of it by a Mr. Frisbie, an Assistant District Attorney. It appears that Mr. Frisbie is a friend of Mr. Muir."

"Yes. I am acquainted with Frisbie. I know Skinner, the District Attorney, quite well." Perry coughed, watched Wolfe empty his glass, and resumed, "So I'm not the bearer of glad tidings. But," he smiled, "that wasn't the chief purpose of my call."

"Well, sir?"

"Well . . . I think you owe me something. Look at it this way. By threatening me with a procedure which would have meant most distasteful publicity for my corporation, you forced me to exert my authority and compel Muir to drop his charge. Muir isn't an employee; he is the highest officer of the corporation after myself and he owns a fair proportion of the stock. It wasn't easy." Perry leaned forward and got crisper. "I surrendered to you. Now I have a right to know what I surrendered to. The only possible interpretation of your threat was that Miss Fox had been framed, and you wouldn't have dared to make such a threat unless you had some sort of evidence for it." He sat back and finished softly, "I want to know what that evidence is."

"But, Mr. Perry." Wolfe wiggled a finger. "Miss Fox is my client. You're not."

"Ah." Perry smiled. "You want to be paid for it? I'll pay a reasonable amount."

"Whatever information I have gathered in the interest of Miss Fox is not for sale to others."

"Rubbish. It has served her well. She has no further use for it." He leaned forward again. "Look here, Wolfe. I don't need to try to explain Muir to you, you've talked with him. If he has got so bad that he tries to frame a girl out of senile chagrin and vindictiveness, don't you think I ought to know it? He is our senior vice-president. Wouldn't our stockholders think so?"

"I didn't know stockholders think." Wolfe sighed. "But to answer your first question: yes, sir, I do think you ought to know it. But you won't learn it from me. Let us not go on pawing the air, Mr. Perry. This is definite: I did have evidence to support my threat, but under no circumstances will you get from me any proof that you could use against Mr. Muir. So we won't discuss that. If there is any other topic . . ."

Perry insisted. He got frank. His opinion was that Muir was such an old goat that his active services were no longer of any value to the corporation. He wanted to deal fairly with Muir, but after all his first duty was to the organization and its stockholders. And so on. He had suspected from the first that there was something odd about the disappearance of that $30,000, and he reasserted his right to know what Wolfe had found out about it. Wolfe let him ramble on quite a while, but finally he sighed and sat up and got positive. Nothing doing.

Perry seemed determined to keep his temper. He sat and bit his lower lip and looked at me and back at Wolfe again.

Wolfe asked, "Was there anything else, sir?"

Perry hesitated. Then he nodded. "There was, yes. But I don't suppose . . . however . . . I want to see Miss Fox."

"Indeed." Wolfe's shoulders went up an inch and down again. "The demand for that young woman seems to be universal. Did you know the police are still looking for her? They want to ask her about a murder."

Perry's chin jerked up. "Murder? What murder?"

"Just a murder. A man on the street with five bullets in him. I would have supposed Frisbie had told you of it."

"No. Muir said Frisbie said something . . . I forget what . . . but this sounds serious. How can she possibly be connected with it? Who was killed?"

"A man named Harlan Scovil. Murder is often serious. But I think you needn't worry about Miss Fox; she really had nothing to do with it. You see, she is still my client. At present she is rather inaccessible, so if you could just tell me what you want to see her about . . ."

I saw a spot of color on Perry's temple, and it occurred to me that he was the fourth man I had that day seen badly affected in the emotions by either the presence or the name of Clara Fox. She wasn't a woman, she was an epidemic. But obviously Perry wasn't going to repeat Muir's performance. I watched the spot of color as it faded. At length he said to Wolfe quietly, "She is in this house. Isn't she?"

"The police searched this house today and didn't find her."

"But you know where she is?"

"Certainly." Wolfe frowned at him. "If you have a message for her, Mr. Goodwin will take it."

"Can you tell me when and where it will be possible to see her?"

"No. I'm sorry. Not at present. Tomorrow, perhaps . . ."

Perry arose from his chair. He stood and looked down at Wolfe, and all of a sudden smiled. "All right," he said. "I can't say that my call here has been very profitable, but I'm not complaining. Every man has a right to his own methods if he can get away with them. As you suggest, I'll wait till tomorrow; you may feel differently about it." He put out his hand.

Wolfe glanced at the outstretched hand, then opened his eyes to look directly at Perry's face. He shook his head. "No, sir. You are perfectly aware that in view of this . . . event, I am no friend of yours."

Perry's temple showed color again. But he didn't say anything. He turned and steered for the door. I lifted myself and followed him. He already had his hat and gloves by the time I got to the hall stand, and when I opened the door for him I saw that he had a car outside, one of the new Wethersill convertibles. I watched him climb in, and waited until he had glided off before I re-entered and slid the bolt to.

I stopped in the kitchen long enough to learn from Saul that he had phoned the message to headquarters but hadn't been able to convince them that he was King George and so had rung off.

In the office, Wolfe sat with his eyes closed and his lips moving. After sitting down and glancing over my notebook and putting it in the drawer, I observed aloud, "He's wise."

No reply, no acknowledgment. I added, "Which is more than you are." That met with the same lack of encouragement. I waited a courteous interval and resumed, "The poor old fellow would give anything in the world to forestall unpleasant publicity for the Seaboard Products Corporation. Just think what he has sacrificed! He has spent the best part of his life building up that business, and I'll bet his share of the profits is no more than a measly half a million a year. But what I want to know—"

"Shut up, Archie." Wolfe's eyes opened. "I can do without that now." He grimaced at his empty glass. "I am atrociously uncomfortable. It is sufficiently annoying to deal with inadequate information, which is what one usually has, but to sit thus while surmises, the mere ghosts of facts, tumble idiotically in my brain, is next to insupportable. It would have been better, perhaps, if you had gone to Fifty-fifth Street. With prudence. At any rate, we can try for Mr. Cramer. I told him I would telephone him by eight, and it lacks only ten minutes of that. I particularly resent this sort of disturbance at this time of day. I presume you know we are having guinea chicken *Braziliera*. See about Mr. Cramer."

That proved to be a job. Cramer's extension seemed to be permanently busy. After five or six tries I finally got it, and was told by someone that Cramer wasn't there. He had left shortly after seven o'clock, and it wasn't known where he was, and he had left no word about any expected message from Nero Wolfe. Wolfe received the information standing up, for Fritz had appeared to announce dinner. I reported Cramer's absence and added, "Why don't I go uptown now and see if something fell and broke? Or send Saul."

Wolfe shook his head. "No. The police are there, and if there is anything to hear we shall hear it later by reaching Mr. Cramer, without exposing ourselves." He moved to the door. "There is no necessity for Johnny to sit in the kitchen at a dollar and a half an hour. Send him home. Saul may remain. Bring Miss Fox."

I performed the errands.

At the dinner table, of course, business was out. Nothing was said to Clara Fox about the call for help from Mike Walsh or Perry's visit. In spite of the fact that she had a rose pinned on her, she was distinctly down in the mouth and wasn't making any effort in the way of peddling charm, but even so, appraising her coolly, I could see that she might be a real problem for any man who was at all impressionable. She had been in the plant rooms with Wolfe for an hour before six o'clock, and during dinner he went on with a conversation which they had apparently started then, about folk dances and that sort of junk. He even hummed a couple of tunes for her, after the guinea chicken had been disposed of, which caused me to take a firm hold on myself so as not to laugh the salad out of my mouth. At that, it was better than when he tried to whistle, for he did produce some kind of a noise.

With the coffee he told her that the larceny charge had been dropped. She opened her eyes and her mouth both. "No, really? Then I can go!" She stopped herself and put out a hand to touch his sleeve, and color came

to her cheeks. "Oh, I don't mean . . . that was terrible, wasn't it? But you
know how I feel, hiding . . ."

"Perfectly." Wolfe nodded. "But I'm afraid you must ask us to tolerate you
a little longer. You can't go yet."

"Why not?"

"Because, first, you might get killed. Indeed, it is quite possible, though I
confess not very likely. Second, there is a development that must still be
awaited. On that you must trust me. I know, since Archie told you of Lord
Clivers' statement that he has paid—"

I didn't hear the finish, because the doorbell rang and I wasn't inclined
to delay about answering it. I was already on pins and I would soon have
been on needles if something hadn't happened to open things up. I loped
down the hall.

It was only Johnny Keems, whom I had sent home over an hour before.
Wondering what for, I let him in. He said, "Have you seen it?"

I said, "No, I'm blind. Seen what?"

He pulled a newspaper from his pocket and stuck it at me. "I was going
to a movie on Broadway and they were yelling this extra, and I was nearby
so I thought it would be better to run over with it than to phone—"

I had looked at the headlines. I said, "Go to the office. No, go to the
kitchen. You're on the job, my lad. Satisfactory."

I went to the dining room and moved Wolfe's coffee cup to one side and
spread the paper in front of him. "Here," I said, "here's that development
you're awaiting." I stood and read it with him while Clara Fox sat and
looked at us.

MARQUIS ARRESTED!
BRITAIN'S ENVOY
FOUND STANDING OVER MURDERED MAN!
Gazette Reporter
Witnesses Unprecedented Drama!

At 7:05 this evening the Marquis of Clivers, special envoy of Great Britain to
this country, was found by a city detective, within the cluttered enclosure of a
building under construction on 55th Street, Manhattan, standing beside the body
of a dead man who had just been shot through the back of the head. The dead
man was Michael Walsh, night watchman. The detective was Purley Stebbins
of the Homicide Squad.

At 7:00 a *Gazette* reporter, walking down Madison Avenue, seeing a crowd
collected at 55th Street, stopped to investigate. Finding that it was only two cars
with shattered windshields and other minor damages from a collision, he strolled
on, turning into 55th. Not far from the corner he saw a man stepping off the
curb to cross the street. He recognized the man as Purley Stebbins, a city
detective, and was struck by something purposeful in his gait. He stopped, and

saw Stebbins push open the door of a board fence where a building is being constructed.

The reporter crossed the street likewise, through curiosity, and entered the enclosure after the detective. He ventured further, and saw Stebbins grasping by the arm a man elegantly attired in evening dress, while the man tried to pull away. Then the reporter saw something else: the body of a man on the ground.

Advancing close enough to see the face of the man in evening dress and recognizing him at once, the reporter was quick-witted enough to call sharply, "Lord Clivers!"

The man replied, "Who the devil are you?"

The detective, who was feeling the man for a weapon, instructed the reporter to telephone headquarters and get Inspector Cramer. The body was lying in such a position that the reporter had to step over it to get at the telephone on the wall of a wooden shed. Meanwhile Stebbins had blown his whistle and a few moments later a patrolman in uniform entered. Stebbins spoke to him, and the patrolman leaned over the body and exclaimed, "It's the night watchman, old Walsh!"

Having phoned police headquarters, the reporter approached Lord Clivers and asked him for a statement. He was brushed aside by Stebbins, who commanded him to leave. The reporter persisting, Stebbins instructed the patrolman to put him out, and the reporter was forcibly ejected.

The superintendent of the construction, reached on the telephone, said that the name of the night watchman was Michael Walsh. He knew of no possible connection between Walsh and a member of the British nobility.

No information could be obtained from the suite of Lord Clivers at the Hotel Portland.

At 7:30 Inspector Cramer and various members of the police force had arrived on the scene at 55th Street, but no one was permitted to enter the enclosure and no information was forthcoming.

There was a picture of Clivers, taken the preceding week on the steps of the White House.

I was raving. If only I had gone up there! I glared at Wolfe. "Be prudent! Don't expose ourselves! I could have been there in ten minutes after that phone call! Great God and Jehosaphat!"

I felt a yank at my sleeve and saw it was Clara Fox. "What is it? What—"

I took it out on her. I told her savagely, "Oh, nothing much. Just another of your playmates bumped off. You haven't got much of a team left. Mike Walsh shot and killed dead, Clivers standing there—"

"Mike Walsh . . . no!" She jumped up and her face went white. "No! Let me see . . ."

Wolfe had leaned back and closed his eyes, with his lips working. I reached for the paper and pushed it at her. "Sure, go ahead, hope you enjoy it." As she leaned over the paper I heard her breath go in. I said, "Of all the goddamn wonderful management—"

Wolfe cut in sharply, "Archie!"

I muttered, "Go to hell everybody," and sat down and bobbed my head from side to side in severe pain. The cockeyed thing had busted wide open and instead of going where I belonged I had sat and eaten guinea chicken Brazilisomething and listened to Wolfe hum folk tunes. Not only that, it had busted at the wrong place and Nero Wolfe had made a fool of himself. If I had gone I would have been there before Cramer or anyone else. . . .

Wolfe opened his eyes and said quietly, "Take Miss Fox upstairs and come to the office." He lifted himself from his chair.

So did Clara Fox. She arose with her face whiter than before and looked from one to the other of us. She announced, "I'm not going upstairs. I . . . I can't just stay here. I'm going . . . I'm going . . ."

"Yes." Wolfe lifted his brows at her. "Where?"

She burst out, "How do I know where? Don't you see I . . . I've got to do something?" She suddenly flopped back into her chair and clasped her hands and began to tremble. "Poor old Mike Walsh . . . why in the name of God . . . why did I ever . . ."

Wolfe stepped to her and put his hand on her shoulder. "Look here," he snapped. "Do you wonder I'd rather have ten thousand orchids than a woman in my house?"

She looked up at him, and shivered. "And it was you that let Mike Walsh go, when you knew—"

"I knew very little. Now I know even less. Archie, bring Saul."

"Johnny is here—"

"No. Saul."

I went to the kitchen and got him. Wolfe asked him, "How long will it take to get Hilda Lindquist here?"

Saul considered half an instant. "Fifty minutes if I phone. An hour and a half if I go after her."

"Good. Telephone. You had better tell her on the phone that Mike Walsh has been killed, since if she sees a *Gazette* on the way she might succumb also. Is there someone to bring her?"

"Yes, sir."

"Use the office phone. Tell her not to delay unnecessarily, but there is no great urgency. Wipe the spot of grease off the left side of your nose."

"Yes, sir," Saul went, pulling his handkerchief from his pocket.

Clara Fox said, in a much better tone, "I haven't succumbed." She brushed back her hair, but her hand was none too steady. "I didn't mean, when I said you let Mike Walsh go—"

"Of course not." Wolfe didn't relent any. "You weren't in a condition to mean anything. You still are not. Archie and I have one or two things to do. You can't leave this house, certainly not now. Will you go upstairs and wait till Miss Lindquist gets here? And don't be conceited enough to imagine yourself responsible for the death of Michael Walsh. Your meddlings have not entitled you to usurp the fatal dignity of Atropos; don't flatter yourself. Will you go upstairs and command patience?"

"Yes." She stood up. "But I want . . . if someone should telephone for me I want to talk."

Wolfe nodded. "You shall. Though I fancy Mr. Horrocks will be too occupied with this involvement of his chief for social impulses."

But it was Wolfe's off day; he was wrong again. A phone call from Horrocks, for Clara Fox, came within fifteen minutes. In the interim Wolfe and I had gone to the office and learned from Saul that he had talked to Hilda Lindquist and she was coming, and Wolfe had settled himself in his chair, disposed of a bottle of beer, and repudiated my advances. Horrocks didn't mention the predicament of his noble uncle; he just asked for Clara Fox, and I sent Saul up to tell her to take it in Wolfe's room, since there was no phone in hers. I should have listened in as a matter of business, but I didn't, and Wolfe didn't tell me to.

Finally Wolfe sighed and sat up. "Try for Mr. Cramer."

I did so. No result. They talked as if, for all they knew, Cramer might be up in Canada shooting moose.

Wolfe sighed again. "Archie. Have we ever encountered a greater jumble of nonsense?"

"No, sir. If only I had gone—"

"Don't say that again, or I'll send you upstairs with Miss Fox. Could that have ordered the chaos? The thing is completely ridiculous. It forces us to measures no less ridiculous. We shall have to investigate the movements of Mr. Muir since six o'clock this evening, to trust Mr. Cramer with at least a portion of our facts, to consider afresh the motivations and activities of Lord Clivers, to discover how a man can occupy two different spots of space at the same moment, and to make another long-distance call to Nebraska. I believe there is no small firearm that will shoot fifteen hundred miles, but we seem to be confronted with a determination and ingenuity capable of almost anything, and before we are through with this we may need Mr. Lindquist badly. Get that farm—the name is Donvaag?"

I nodded and got busy. At that time of night, going on ten o'clock, the lines were mostly free, and I had a connection with Plainview, Nebraska, in less than ten minutes. It was a person-to-person call and a good clear connection; Ed Donvaag's husky voice, from his farmhouse out on the western prairie, was in my ear as plain as Francis Horrocks' had been from the Hotel Portland. Wolfe took his line.

"Mr. Donvaag? This is Nero Wolfe. . . . That's it. You remember I talked to you this afternoon and you were good enough to go after Mr. Lindquist for a conversation with me. . . . Yes, sir. I have to ask another favor of you. Can you hear me well? Good. It will be necessary for you to go again to Mr. Lindquist tonight or the first thing tomorrow morning. Tell him there is reason to suspect that someone means him injury and may attempt it. . . . Yes. We don't know how. Tell him to be circumspect—to be careful. Does he eat candy? He might receive a box of poisoned candy in the mail. Even, possibly, a bomb. Anything. He might receive a telegram saying his daughter has died—with results expected from the shock to him. . . . No, indeed. His daughter is well and there is nothing to fear for her. . . . Well, this is a peculiar situation; doubtless you will hear all about it later. Tell him to be careful and to suspect anything at all unusual. . . . You can go at once? Good. You are a good neighbor, sir. Good night."

Wolfe rang off and pushed the button for beer. He sighed. "That desperate fool has a good deal to answer for. Another four dollars. Three? Oh, the night rate. Bring another, Fritz. Archie, give Saul the necessary facts regarding Mr. Muir and send him out. We want to know where he was from six to eight this evening."

I went to the kitchen and did that. Johnny Keems was helping Fritz with the dishes and Saul was in my breakfast corner with the remainder of the dish of ripe olives. He didn't write anything down; he never had to. He pointed his long nose at me and absorbed the dope, nodded, took a twenty for expenses, gathered up the last of the olives into a handful, and departed. I let him out.

Back in the office, I asked Wolfe if he wanted me to try for Cramer again. He shook his head. He was leaning back with his eyes closed, and the faint movement of his lips in and out informed me that he was in conference with himself. I sat down and put my feet on my desk. In a few minutes I got up again and went to the cabinet and poured myself a shot of bourbon, smelled it, and poured it back into the bottle. It wasn't whisky I wanted. I went to the kitchen and asked Johnny some more questions about the layout up at 55th Street, and drank a glass of milk.

It was ten o'clock when Hilda Lindquist arrived. There was a man with her, but when I told him Saul wasn't there he didn't come in. I told him Saul would fix it with him and he beat it. Hilda's square face and brown dress didn't look any the worse for wear during the twenty-four hours since she had gone off, but her eyes were solemn and determined. She said of course the thing was all off, since they had caught the Marquis of Clivers and he would be executed for murder, and her father would be disappointed because he was old and they would lose the farm, and would she be able to get her bag which she had left at the hotel, and she would like to start for home as soon as there was a train. I told her to drive in and park a while, there was still some fireworks left in the bag, but by the way she turned her eyes on me I saw that she might develop into a real problem, so I put her in the front room and asked her to wait a minute.

I ran up to the south room and said to Clara Fox, "Hilda Lindquist is downstairs and I'm going to send her up. She thinks the show is over and she has to go back home to her poor old dad with her sock empty, and by the look in her eye it will take more than British diplomacy to keep her off of the next train. Nero Wolfe is going to work this out. I don't know how and maybe he don't either this minute, but he'll do it. Nero Wolfe is probably even better than I think he is, and that's a mouthful. You wrote the music for this piece, and half your band has been killed, and it's up to you to keep the other half intact. Well?"

I had found her sitting in a chair with her lips compressed tight and her hands clenched. She looked at me. "All right. I will. Send her up here."

"She can sleep in here with you, or in the room in front on this floor. You know how to ring for Fritz."

"All right."

I went down and told Squareface that Clara Fox wanted to speak to her, and shooed her up, and heard them exchanging greetings in the upper hall.

There was nothing in the office but a gob of silence; Wolfe was still in conference. I would have tried some bulldozing if I had thought he was merely dreaming of stuffed quail or pickled pigs' feet, but his lips were moving a little so I knew he was working. I fooled around my desk, went over Johnny's diagrams again in connection with an idea that had occurred to me, checked over Horstmann's reports and entered them in the records, reread the *Gazette* scoop on the affair at 55th Street, and aggravated myself into such a condition of uselessness that finally, at eleven o'clock sharp, I exploded. "If this keeps up another ten minutes I'll get *Weltschmerz!*"

Wolfe opened his eyes. "Where in the name of heaven did you get that?"

I threw up my hands. He shut his eyes again.

The doorbell rang. I knew it couldn't be Johnny Keems with another extra, because he was in the kitchen with Fritz, since I hadn't been able to prod an instruction from Wolfe to send him home again. It was probably Saul Panzer with the dope on Muir. But it wasn't; I knew that when the bell started again as I entered the hall. It kept on ringing, so I leisurely pulled the curtain for a look through the panel, and when I saw there were four of them, another quartet, I switched on the stoop light to make a good survey. One of them, in evening dress, was leaning on the bell button. I recognized the whole bunch. I turned and beat it back to the office.

"Who the devil is ringing that bell?" Wolfe demanded. "Why don't you—"

I interrupted, grinning. "That's Police Commissioner Hombert. With him are Inspector Cramer, District Attorney Skinner, and my old friend Purley Stebbins of the Homicide Squad. Is it too late for company?"

"Indeed." Wolfe sat up and rubbed his nose. "Bring them in."

XVI

THEY entered as if they owned the place. I tipped Purley a wink as he passed me, but he was too impressed by his surroundings to reciprocate, and I didn't blame him, as I knew he might get either a swell promotion or the opposite out of this by the time it was over. From the threshold I saw a big black limousine down at the curb, and back of it two other police cars containing city fellers. Well, well, I thought to myself as I closed the door, this looks pretty damned ominous. Cramer had asked me if Wolfe was in the office and I had waved him on, and now I brought up the rear of the procession.

I moved chairs around. Cramer introduced Hombert and Skinner, but Skinner and Wolfe had already met. At Cramer's request I took Purley Stebbins to the kitchen and told him to play checkers with Johnny Keems. When I got back Hombert was shooting off his mouth about defiance of the law, and I got at my desk and ostentatiously opened my notebook. Cramer was looking more worried than I had ever seen him. District Attorney Skinner, already sunk in his chair as if he had been there all evening, had the wearied cynical expression of a man who had some drinks three hours ago and none since.

Hombert was practically yelling. ". . . and you're responsible for it! If you had turned those three people over to us last night this wouldn't have happened! Cramer tells me they were here in this office! Walsh was here! This afternoon we had him at headquarters and your man wouldn't point him out! You are directly and legally responsible for his death!" The Police Commissioner brought his fist down on the arm of his chair and glared. Cramer was looking at him and shaking his head faintly.

"This sudden onslaught is overwhelming," Wolfe murmured. "If I am legally responsible for Mr. Walsh's death, arrest me. But please don't shout at me—"

"All right! You've asked for it!" Hombert turned to the inspector. "Put him under arrest!"

Cramer said quietly, "Yes, sir. What charge?"

"Any charge! Material witness! We'll see whether he'll talk or not!"

Cramer stood up. Wolfe said, "Perhaps I should warn you, Mr. Hombert. If I am arrested, I shall do no talking whatever. And if I do no talking, you

have no possible chance of solving the problem you are confronted with."
He wiggled a finger. "I don't shout, but I never say anything I don't mean.
Proceed, Mr. Cramer."

Cramer stood still. Hombert looked at him, then looked grimly at Wolfe.
"You'll talk or you'll rot!"

"Then I shall certainly rot." Wolfe's finger moved again. "Let me make a
suggestion, Mr. Hombert. Why don't you go home and go to sleep and
leave this affair to be handled by Mr. Cramer, an experienced policeman,
and Mr. Skinner, an experienced lawyer? You probably have abilities of
some sort, but they are obviously inappropriate to the present emergency.
To talk of arresting me is childish. I have broken no law and I am a sufficiently respectable citizen not to be taken into custody merely for questioning. Confound it, sir, you can't go around losing your temper like this, it's
outrageous! You are entangled in a serious difficulty, I am the only man
alive who can possibly extricate you from it, and you come here and begin
yelling inane threats at me! Is that sort of conduct likely to appeal either to
my reason or my sympathy?"

Hombert glared at him, opened his mouth, closed it again, and looked at
Cramer. District Attorney Skinner snickered. Cramer said to Hombert,
"Didn't I tell you he was a nut? Let me handle him."

Wolfe nodded solemnly. "That's an idea, Mr. Cramer. You handle me."

Hombert, saying nothing, sat back and folded his arms and goggled.
Cramer looked at Wolfe. "So you know about Walsh."

Wolfe nodded. "From the *Gazette*. That was unfortunate, the reporter
happening on the scene."

"You're telling me," Cramer observed grimly. "Of course the marquis isn't
arrested. He can't be. Diplomatic immunity. Washington is raising hell because it got in the paper, as if there was any way in God's world of keeping
it out of that lousy sheet once that reporter got away from there." He waved
a disgusted hand. "That's that. The fact is, the Commissioner's right. You're
responsible. I told you yesterday how important this was. I told you it was
your duty as a citizen to help us protect the Marquis of Clivers."

Wolfe lifted his brows. "Aren't you a little confused, Mr. Cramer? Or am
I? I understood you wished to protect Lord Clivers from injury. Was it he
who was injured this evening?"

"Certainly it was," Hombert broke in. "This Walsh was blackmailing
him!"

Cramer said, "Let me. Huh?"

"Did Lord Clivers say that?" Wolfe asked.

"No." Cramer grunted. "He's not saying anything, except that he knew
Walsh a long time ago and went there to see him this evening by appointment and found him lying there dead. But we didn't come here to answer

questions for you, we came to find out what you know. We could have you pulled in, but decided it was quicker to come. It's time to spill it. What's it all about?"

"I suppose so." Wolfe sighed. "Frankly, I think you're wrong; I believe that while you may have information that will help me, I have none that will help you. But we'll get to that later. My connection with this affair arises from my engagement to press a civil claim on behalf of two clients, two young women. Also, to defend one of them from a trumped-up charge of larceny brought against her by an official of the Seaboard Products Corporation. Since I have succeeded in having the larceny charge withdrawn—"

District Attorney Skinner woke up. He croaked in his deep bass, "Don't talk so much. What has that got to do with it? Come to the point."

Wolfe said patiently, "Interruptions can only waste time, by forcing me to begin my sentences over again. Since I have succeeded in having the larceny charge withdrawn, and since they cannot possibly be suspected of complicity in the murder of Mr. Walsh, I am willing to produce my clients, with the understanding that if I send for them to come here they will be questioned here only and will not be taken from this house. I will not have—"

"The hell you won't!" Hombert was ready to boil again. "You can't dictate to us—"

But the authority of Wolfe's tone and the assurance of his manner had made enough impression so that his raised palm brought Hombert to a halt. "I'm not dictating," he snapped. "Confound it, let us get on or we shall be all night. I was about to say, I will not have the lives of my clients placed in possible jeopardy by releasing them from my own protection. Why should I? I can send for them and you can question them all you please—"

"All right, all right," Cramer agreed impatiently. "We won't take them, that's understood. How long will it take you to get them here?"

"One minute perhaps, if they are not in bed. Archie? If you please."

I arose, grinning at Cramer's stare, stepped over Skinner's feet, and went up and knocked at the door of the south room.

"Come in."

I entered. The two clients were sitting in chairs, looking as if they were too miserable to go to bed. I said, "Egad, you look cheerful. Come on, buck up! Wolfe wants you down in the office. There are some men down there that want to ask you some questions."

Clara Fox straightened up. "Ask us . . . now?" Hilda Lindquist tightened her lips and began to nod her head for I told you so.

"Certainly." I made it matter of fact. "They were bound to, sooner or later. Don't worry, I'll be right there, and tell them anything they want to know. There's three of them. The dressed-up one with the big mouth is

Police Commissioner Hombert, the one with the thin nose and ratty eyes is District Attorney Skinner, and the big guy who looks at you frank and friendly but may or may not mean it is Inspector Cramer."

"My God." Clara Fox brushed back her hair and stood up.

"All right," I grinned. "Let's go."

I opened the door, and followed them out and down.

The three visitors turned their heads to look at us as we entered the office. Skinner, seeing Clara Fox, got up first, then Hombert also made it to his feet and began shoving chairs around. I moved some up, while Wolfe pronounced names. He had rung for beer while I was gone, and got it poured. I saw there was no handkerchief in his pocket and went and got him one out of the drawer.

Cramer said, "So you're Clara Fox. Where were you this morning?"

She glanced at Wolfe. He nodded. She said, "I was here."

"Here in this house? All morning?"

"Yes, last night and all day."

Cramer handed Wolfe a glassy stare. "What did you do to Rowcliff, grease him?"

"No, sir." Wolfe shook his head. "Mr. Rowcliff did his best, but Miss Fox was not easily discoverable. I beg you to attach no blame to your men. It is necessary for you to know that three of us are prepared to state on oath that Miss Fox has been here constantly, to make it at once obvious that she is in no way involved in Mr. Walsh's death."

"I'll be damned. What about the other one?"

"Miss Lindquist came here at ten o'clock this evening. But she has been secluded in another part of the city. You may as well confine yourself to events previous to half past six yesterday. May I make a suggestion? Begin by asking Miss Fox to tell you the story which she recited to me at that hour yesterday, in the presence of Miss Lindquist and Mr. Walsh."

"Why . . . all right." Cramer looked at Clara Fox. "Go ahead."

She told the story. At first she was nervous and jerky, and I noticed that when she was inclined to stumble she glanced across at Wolfe as he leaned back, massive and motionless, with his fingers twined on his belly and his eyes nearly shut. She glanced at him and went ahead. They didn't interrupt her much with questions. She read the letter from her father, and when she finished and Cramer held out his hand for it, she glanced at Wolfe. Wolfe nodded, and she passed it over. Then she went on, with more detail even than she had told us. She spoke of her first letters with Harlan Scovil and Hilda Lindquist and her first meeting with Mike Walsh.

She got to the Marquis of Clivers and Walsh's recognition of him as he emerged from his hotel fifteen days back. From then on they were after her, not Cramer much, but Skinner and Hombert, and especially Skinner. He began to get slick, and of course what he was after was obvious. He asked her trick questions, such as where had her mother been keeping the letter from her father when she suddenly produced it on her deathbed. His way of being clever was to stay quiet and courteous and go back to one thing and then abruptly forward to another, and then after a little suddenly dart back again. Clara Fox was no longer nervous, and she didn't get mad. I remembered how the day before she had stood cool and sweet in front of Perry's desk. All at once Skinner began asking her about the larceny charge. She answered; but after a dozen questions on that Wolfe suddenly stirred, opened his eyes, and wiggled a finger at the District Attorney.

"Mr. Skinner. Permit me. You're wasting time. The larceny charge is indeed pertinent to the main issue, but there is very little chance that you'll ever discover why. The fact is that the line you have taken from the beginning is absurd."

"Thanks," Skinner said drily. "If, as you say, it is pertinent, why absurd?"

"Because," Wolfe retorted, "you're running around in circles. You have a fixed idea that you're an instrument of justice, being a prosecuting attorney, and that it is your duty to corner everyone you see. That idea is not only dangerous nonsense, in the present case it is directly contrary to your real interest. Why is this distinguished company"—Wolfe extended a finger and bent a wrist—"present in my house? Because thirty thousand dollars was mislaid and two men were murdered? Not at all. Because Lord Clivers has become unpleasantly involved, the fact has been made public, and you are seriously embarrassed. You have wasted thirty minutes trying to trap Miss Fox into a slip indicating that she and Mr. Walsh and Mr. Scovil and Miss Lindquist hatched a blackmailing plot against Lord Clivers; you have even hinted that the letter written by her father to her mother seventeen years ago, of which Mr. Cramer now has her typewritten copy in his pocket, was invented by her. Is it possible that you don't realize what your real predicament is?"

"Thanks," Skinner repeated, more drily still. "I'll get to you—"

"No doubt. But let me—no, confound it, I'm talking! Let me orient you a little. Here's your predicament. An eminent personage, an envoy of Great Britain, has been discovered alone with a murdered man and the fact has been made public. Even if you wanted to you can't keep him in custody because of his diplomatic immunity. Why not, then, to avoid a lot of official and international fuss, just forget it and let him go? Because you don't dare; if he really did kill Mr. Walsh you are going to have to ask his government to surrender him to you, and fight to get him if necessary, or the newspapers will howl you out of office. You are sitting on dynamite, and so is Mr. Hombert, and you know it. I can imagine with what distaste you contemplate being forced into an effort to convict the Marquis of Clivers of murder. I see the complications; and the devil of it is that at this moment you don't at all know whether he did it or not. His story that he went to see Mr. Walsh and found him already dead may quite possibly be true.

"So, since an attempt to put Lord Clivers on trial for murder, and convict him, would not only create an international stink but might be disastrous for you personally, what should be your first and immediate concern? It seems obvious. You should swiftly and rigorously explore the possibility that he is not guilty. Is there someone else who wanted Harlan Scovil and Michael Walsh to die, and if so, who, and where is he? I know of only six people living who might help you in pursuing that inquiry. One of them is the murderer, another is an old man on a farm in Nebraska, and the other four are in this room. And, questioning one of them, what do you do? You put on an exhibition of your cunning at cross-examination in an effort to infer that she has tried to blackmail Lord Clivers, though he has had various opportunities to make such an accusation and has not done so. Again, you aim the weapon of your cunning, not at your own ignorance, but directly at Miss Fox, when you pounce on the larceny charge, though that accusation has been dismissed by the man who made it.

"Bah!" Wolfe looked around at them. "Do you wonder, gentlemen, that I have not taken you into my confidence in this affair? Do you wonder that I have no intention of doing so even now?"

Cramer grunted, gazing at a cigar he had pulled out of his pocket five minutes before. Skinner, scratching his ear, screwed up his mouth and looked sidewise at Clara Fox. Hombert let out a "Ha!" and slapped the arm of his chair. "So that's your game! You're not going to talk, eh? By God, you will talk!"

"Oh, I'll talk." Wolfe sighed. "You may know everything you are entitled to know. You are already aware that Mr. Scovil was in this room yesterday afternoon and got killed shortly after leaving it. Mr. Goodwin talked with him and will repeat the conversation if you wish it. You may hear everything from Miss Fox and Miss Lindquist that I have heard; and from Miss Fox regarding Mr. Walsh. You may know of the claim which I have presented to Lord Clivers on behalf of Miss Lindquist and her father, which he has offered to settle. But there are certain things you may not know, at least not from me; for instance, the details of a long conversation which I had with Lord Clivers when he called here this afternoon. He can tell you—"

"What's that?" Skinner sat up, croaking. Hombert goggled. Cramer, who had finally got his cigar lit, jerked it up with his lip so that the ash fell to the rug. Skinner went on, "What are you trying to hand us? Clivers called on you today?"

Wolfe nodded. "He was here over an hour. Perhaps I shouldn't say today, since it is nearly one o'clock Wednesday morning. Yes, Lord Clivers called.

We drank eight bottles of beer, and he greatly admired that terrestrial globe you see there."

Without taking his cigar from his mouth, Cramer rumbled, "I'll be damned." Hombert still goggled. Skinner stared, and at length observed, "I've never heard of your being a plain liar, Wolfe, but you're dishing it up."

"Dishing it up?" Wolfe looked at me. "Does that mean lying, Archie?"

"Naw," I grinned, "it's just rhetoric."

"Indeed." Wolfe reached to push the button, and leaned back. "So you see, gentlemen, I not only have superior knowledge in this affair, I have it from a superior source. Lord Clivers gave me much interesting information, which of course I cannot consider myself free to reveal." He turned his eyes on the Police Commissioner. "I understand, Mr. Hombert, that Mr. Devore, Mr. Cramer, and you were all in communication with him, protecting him, following the death of Mr. Scovil. It's too bad he didn't see fit to take you into his confidence. Maybe he will do so now, if you approach him properly."

Hombert sputtered, "I don't believe this. We'll check up on this."

"Do so." Wolfe opened the bottle and filled his glass. "Will you have beer, gentlemen? No? Water? Whisky? Miss Fox? Miss Lindquist? You haven't asked Miss Lindquist anything. Must she sit here all night?"

Skinner said, "I could use a good stiff highball. Listen, Wolfe, are you telling this straight?"

"Of course I am. Fritz, serve what is required. Why would I be so foolish as to invent such a tale? Let me suggest that the ladies be permitted to retire."

"Well . . ." Skinner looked at Hombert. Hombert, tight-lipped, shrugged his shoulders. Skinner turned and asked abruptly, "Your name is Hilda Lindquist?"

Her strong square face looked a little startled at the suddenness of it, then was lifted by her chin. "Yes."

"You heard everything Clara Fox said. Do you agree with it?"

She stared. "What do you mean, agree with it?"

"I mean, as far as you know, is it true?"

"Certainly it's true."

"Where do you live?"

"Plainview, Nebraska. Near there."

"When did you get to New York?"

"Last Thursday. Thursday afternoon."

"All right. That's all. But understand, you're not to leave the city—"

Wolfe put in, "My clients will remain in this house until I have cleared up this matter."

"See that they do." Skinner grabbed his drink. "So you're going to clear it up. God bless you. If I had your nerve I'd own Manhattan Island." He drank.

The clients got up and went. I escorted them to the hall, and while I was out there the doorbell rang. It was Saul Panzer. I went to the kitchen with him and got his report, which didn't take long. Johnny Keems was there with his chair tipped back against the wall, half asleep, and Purley Stebbins was in a corner, reading a newspaper. I snared myself a glass of milk, took a couple of sips, and carried the rest to the office.

Hombert and Cramer had highballs and Fritz was arranging another one for Skinner. I said to Wolfe, "Saul's back. The subject left his office a few minutes before six and showed up at his apartment about a quarter after seven and dressed for dinner. Saul hasn't been able to trace him in between. Shall he keep after it tonight?"

"No. Send him home. Here at eight in the morning."

"Johnny too?"

"Yes. No, wait." Wolfe turned. "Mr. Cramer. Perhaps I can simplify something for you. I know how thorough you are. Doubtless you have discovered that there are various ways of getting into that place on Fifty-fifth Street, and I suppose you have had them all explored. You may even have learned that there was a man there this afternoon, investigating them."

Cramer was staring at him. "Now, somebody tell me, how did you know that? Yeah, we learned it, and we've got a good description, and there are twenty men looking for him . . ."

Wolfe nodded. "I thought I might save you some trouble. I should have mentioned it before. The man's out in the kitchen. He was up there for me."

Cramer went pop-eyed. "But good God! That was before Walsh was killed!" He put his drink down. "Now what kind of a—"

"We wanted to see Walsh, and knew you would have a man posted at the entrance. He was there to find a way. He left a few minutes after six and was here from six-thirty until eight o'clock. You may talk with him if you wish, but it will be a waste of time. My word for it."

Cramer looked at him, and then at me. He picked up his drink. "To hell with it."

Wolfe said, "Send Johnny home."

Cramer said, "And tell Stebbins to go out front and tell Rowcliff to cancel that alarm and call those men in."

I went to perform those errands, and after letting the trio out I left the door open a crack and told Purley to shut it when he came back in. The enemy was inside anyhow, so there was no point in maintaining the barricade.

Back in the office, Skinner and Hombert were bombarding Wolfe. It had got now to where it was funny. Clivers was the bird they had been busy protecting, and the one they were trying to get out of hanging a murder onto, and here they were begging Wolfe to spill what Clivers had disclosed to him over eight bottles of beer! I sat down and grinned at Cramer, and darned if he didn't have decency enough to wink back at me. I thought that called for another highball, and went and got it for him.

Skinner, with an open palm outstretched, was actually wheedling. "But, my God, can't we work together on it? I'll admit we went at it wrong, but how did we know Clivers was here this afternoon? He won't tell us a damn thing, and as far as I personally am concerned I'd like to kick his rump clear across the Atlantic Ocean. And I'll admit we can't coerce you into telling us this vital information you say you got from Clivers, but we can ask for it, and we do. You know who I am. I'm not a bad friend to have in this county, especially for a man in your business. What's Clivers to you, anyhow, why the devil should you cover him up?"

"This is bewildering," Wolfe murmured. "Last night Mr. Cramer told me I should help him to protect a distinguished foreign guest, and now you demand the opposite!"

"All right, have your fun," Skinner croaked. "But tell us this, at least. Did Clivers say anything to indicate that he had it ready for Mike Walsh?"

Wolfe's eyelids flickered, and after a moment he turned to me. "Your notebook, Archie. You will find a place where I asked Lord Clivers, 'Don't you believe him?' I was referring to Mr. Walsh. Please read Lord Clivers' reply."

I had the notebook and was thumbing it. I looked too far front, and flipped back. Finally I had it, and read it out, "Clivers: 'I don't believe anybody. I know damn well I'm a liar. I'm a diplomat. Look here. You can forget about Walsh. I'll deal with him myself. I have to keep this thing clear, at least as long as I'm in this country. I'll deal with Walsh. Scovil is dead, God rest his soul. Let the police do what they can with that. As for the Lindquists . . .'"

Wolfe stopped me with a finger. "That will do, Archie. Put the notebook away."

"He will not put it away!" Hombert was beating up the arm of his chair again. "With that in it? We want—"

He stopped to glare at Skinner, who had tapped a toe on his shin. Skinner was ready to melt with sweetness; his tone sounded like Romeo in the balcony scene. "Listen, Wolfe, play with us. Let us have that. Your man can type it, or he can dictate from his notes and I'll bring a man in to take it. Clivers is to sail for Europe Sunday. If we don't get this thing on ice there's going to be trouble."

Wolfe closed his eyes, and after a moment opened them again. They were all gazing at him, Cramer slowly chewing his cigar, Hombert holding in an explosion, Skinner looking innocent and friendly. Wolfe said, "Will you make a bargain with me, Mr. Skinner? Let me ask a few questions. Then, after considering the replies, I shall do what I can for you. I think it is more than likely you will find me helpful."

Skinner frowned. "What kind of questions?"

"You will hear them."

A pause. "All right. Shoot."

Wolfe turned abruptly to the inspector. "Mr. Cramer. You had a man following Mr. Walsh from the time you released him this afternoon, and that man was on post at the entrance of the boarding on Fifty-fifth Street. I'd like to know what it was that caused him to cross the street and enter the enclosure, as reported in the *Gazette*. Did he hear a shot?"

"No." Cramer took his cigar from his mouth. "The man's out in the kitchen. Do you want to hear it from him?"

"I merely want to hear it."

"Well, I can tell you. Stebbins was away from his post for a few minutes, he's admitted it. There was a taxi collision at the corner of Madison, and he had to go and look it over, which was bright of him. He says he was away only two minutes, but he may have been gone ten, you know how that is. Anyhow, he finally strolled back, on the south side of Fifty-fifth, and looking across at the entrance of the boarding he saw the door slowly opening, and the face of a man looked out and it wasn't Walsh. There were pedestrians going by, and the face went back in and the door closed. Stebbins got behind a parked car. In a minute the face looked out again, and there was a man walking by, and the face disappeared again. Stebbins thought it was time to investigate and crossed the street and went in, and it was just lousy luck that that damn newspaper cockroach happened to see him. It was Clivers all right, and Walsh's body was there on the ground—"

"I know." Wolfe sighed. "It was lying in front of the telephone. So Mr. Stebbins heard no shot."

"No. Of course, he was down at the corner and there was a lot of noise."

"To be sure. Was the weapon on Lord Clivers' person?"

"No." Cramer sounded savage. "That's one of the nice details. We can't find any gun, except one in Walsh's pocket that hadn't been fired. There's a squad of men still up there, combing it. Also there's about a thousand hollow steel shafts sticking up from the base construction, and it might have been dropped down one of those."

"So it might," Wolfe murmured. "Well . . . no shot heard, and no gun found." He looked around at them. "I can't help observing, gentlemen, that that news relieves me enormously. Moreover, I think you have a right to know that Mr. Goodwin and I heard the shot."

They stared at him. Skinner demanded, "You what? What the hell are you talking about?"

Wolfe turned to me. "Tell them, Archie."

I let them have my open countenance. "This evening," I said, and corrected it, "—last evening—Mr. Wolfe and I were in this office. At two minutes before seven o'clock the phone rang, and it happened that we both took off our receivers. A voice said, 'Nero Wolfe!' It sounded far off but very excited—it sounded—well, unnatural. I said, 'Yes, talking,' and the voice said, 'I've got him, come up here, Fifty-fifth Street, this is Mike Walsh, I've got him covered, come up.' The voice was cut off by the sound of an explosion, very loud, as if a gun had been shot close to the telephone. I called Walsh's name a few times, but there was no answer. We sent a phone call to police headquarters right away."

I looked around respectfully for approval. Skinner looked concentrated, Hombert looked about ready to bust, and Cramer looked disgusted. The inspector, I could see, didn't have far to go to get good and sore. He burst out at Wolfe, "What else have you got? First you tell me the man I've got the whole force looking for, thinking I've got a hot one, is one of your boy scouts acting as advance agent. Now you tell me that the phone call we're trying to trace about a shot being heard, and you can't trace a local call anyway with these damn dials, now you tell me you made that too." He stuck his cigar in his mouth and bit it nearly in two.

"But Mr. Cramer," Wolfe protested, "is it my fault if destiny likes this address? Did we not notify you at once? Did I not even restrain Mr. Goodwin from hastening to the scene, because I knew you would not want him to intrude?"

Cramer opened his mouth but was speechless. Skinner said, "You heard that shot on the phone at two minutes to seven. That checks. It was five after when Stebbins found Clivers there." He looked around sort of helpless, like a man who has picked up something he didn't want. "That seems to clinch it." He growled at Wolfe, "What makes you so relieved about not finding the gun and Stebbins not hearing the shot, if you heard it yourself?"

"In due time, Mr. Skinner." Wolfe's forefinger was gently tapping on the arm of his chair, and I wondered what he was impatient about. "If you don't mind, let me get on. The paper says that Mr. Stebbins felt Lord Clivers for a weapon. Did he find one?"

"No," Cramer grunted. "He got talkative enough to tell us that he always carries a pistol, but not with evening dress."

"But since Lord Clivers had not left the enclosure, and since no weapon can be found, how could he possibly have been the murderer?"

"We'll find it," Cramer asserted gloomily. "There's a million places in there to hide a gun, and we'll have to get into those shafts somehow. Or he might have thrown it over the fence. We'll find it. He did it, damn it. You've ruined the only outside leads I had."

Wolfe wagged his head at him. "Cheer up, Mr. Cramer. Tell me this, please. Since Mr. Stebbins followed Mr. Walsh all afternoon, I presume you know their itinerary. What was it?"

Skinner growled, "Don't start stalling, Wolfe. Let's get—"

"I'm not stalling, sir. An excellent word. Mr. Cramer?"

The inspector dropped his cigar in the tray. "Well, Walsh stopped at a lunch counter on Franklin near Broadway and ate. He kept looking around, but Stebbins thinks he didn't wise up. Then he took a surface car north and got off at Twenty-seventh Street and walked west. He went in the Seaboard Building and took the elevator and got off at the thirty-second floor and went into the executive offices of the Seaboard Products Corporation. Stebbins waited out in the hall. Walsh was in there nearly an hour. He took the elevator down again, and Stebbins didn't want to take the same one and nearly lost him. He walked east and went into a drug store and used a telephone in a booth. Then he took the subway and went to a boarding house in East Sixty-fourth Street, where he lived, and he left again a little after half past five and walked to his job at Fifty-fifth Street. He got there a little before six."

Wolfe had leaned back and closed his eyes. They all looked at him. Cramer got out another cigar and bit off the end and fingered his tongue for the shreds. Hombert demanded, "Well, are you asleep?"

Wolfe didn't move, but he spoke. "About that visit Mr. Walsh made at the Seaboard Products Corporation. Do you know whom he saw there?"

"No, how could I? Stebbins didn't go in. Even if there had been any reason—the office was closed by the time I got Stebbins's report. What difference does it make?"

"Not much." Wolfe's tone was mild, but to me, who knew it so well, there was a thrill in it. "No, not much. There are cases when a conjecture is almost as good as a fact—even, sometimes, better." Suddenly he opened his eyes, sat up, and got brisk. "That's all, gentlemen. It is past two o'clock, and Mr. Goodwin is yawning. You will hear from me tomorrow—today, rather."

Skinner shook his head wearily. "Oh, no no no. Honest to God, Wolfe, you're the worst I've ever seen for trying to put over fast ones. There's a lot to do yet. Could I have another highball?"

Wolfe sighed. "Must we start yapping again?" He wiggled a finger at the District Attorney. "I offered you a bargain, sir. I said if I could get replies to a few questions I would consider them and would then do what I could for you. Do you think I can consider them properly at this time of night? I assure you I cannot. I am not quibbling. I have gone much further than you gentlemen along the path to the solution of this puzzle, and I am confronted by one difficulty which must be solved before anything can be done. When it will be solved I cannot say. I may light on it ten minutes from now, while I am undressing for bed, or it may require extended investigation and labor. Confound it, do you realize it will be dawn in less than four hours? It was past three when I retired last night." He put his hands on the edge of his desk and pushed his chair back, rose to his feet, and pulled at the corners of his vest where a wide band of canary-yellow shirt puffed out. "Daylight will serve us better. No more tonight, short of the rack and the thumbscrew. You will hear from me."

Cramer got up too, saying to Hombert, "He's always like this. You might as well stick pins in a rhinoceros."

XVII

WHEN, about a quarter after nine Wednesday morning, I went up to the plant rooms with a message, I thought that Wolfe's genius had at last bubbled over and he had gone nuts for good. He was in the potting room, standing by the bench, with a piece of board about four inches wide and ten inches long in each hand. He paid no attention to me when I entered. He held his hands two feet apart and then swiftly brought them together, flat sides of the two pieces of board meeting with a loud clap. He did that several times. He shook his head and threw one of the boards down and began hitting things with the other one, the top of the bench, one of its legs and then another one, the seat of a chair, the palm of his hand, a pile of wrapping paper. He kept shaking his head. Finally, deciding to admit I was there, he tossed the board down and turned his eyes on me with ferocious hostility.

"Well, sir?" he demanded.

I said in a resigned tone, "Cramer phoned again. That's three times. He says that District Attorney Skinner got tight after he left here and is now at his office with a hangover, cutting off people's heads. As far as that's concerned, I've had four hours' sleep two nights in a row and I've got a headache. He says that the publisher of the *Gazette* told the Secretary of State to go to hell over long distance. He wants to know if we have seen the morning papers. He says that two men from Washington are in Hombert's office with copies of cables from London. He says that Hombert saw Clivers at his hotel half an hour ago and asked him about his visit to our office yesterday afternoon, and Clivers said it was a private matter and it will be a nice day if it don't rain. He says you have got to open up or he will open you. In addition to that, Miss Fox and Miss Lindquist are having a dogfight because their nerves are going back on them. In addition to that, Fritz is on the warpath because Saul and Johnny hang out in the kitchen too much and Johnny ate up some tambo shells he was going to put mushrooms into for lunch. In addition to that, I can't get you to tell me whether I am to go to the Hotel Portland to look at Clivers' documents which came on the *Berengaria*. In addition to that . . ."

I stopped for breath. Wolfe said, "You badger me. Those are all trivialities. Look at me." He picked up the board and threw it down again. "I am sacrificing my hours of pleasure in an effort to straighten out the only tangle that remains in this knot, and you harass me with these futilities. Did the Secretary of State go to hell? If so, tell the others to join him there."

"Yeah, sure. I'm telling you, they're all going to be around here again. I can't hold them off."

"Lock the door. Keep them out. I will not be hounded!"

He turned away, definitely. I threw up my hands and beat it. On my way downstairs I stopped a second at the door of the south room, and heard the voices of the two clients still at it. In the lower hall I listened at the kitchen door and perceived that Fritz was still shrill with fury. The place was a madhouse.

Wolfe had been impossible from the time I first went to his room around seven o'clock, because he hadn't taken his phone when I buzzed him, to report the first call from Cramer. I had never seen him so actively unfriendly, but I didn't really mind that, knowing he was only peeved at himself on account of his genius not working right. What got me on edge was first, I had a headache; second, Fritz and the clients had to unload their troubles on me; and third, I didn't like all the cussings from outsiders on the telephone. It had been going on for over two hours and it was keeping up.

After taking another aspirin and doing a few morning chores around the office, I sat down at my desk and got out the plant records and entered some items from Horstmann's reports of the day before, and went over some bills and so on. There were circulars and lists from both Richardt and Hoehn in the morning mail, also a couple of catalogues from England, and I glanced over them and laid them aside. There was a phone call from Harry Foster of the *Gazette*, who had found out somehow that we were supposed to know something, and I kidded him and backed him off. Then, a little after ten o'clock, the phone rang again, and the first thing I knew I was talking to the Marquis of Clivers himself. I had half a mind to get Wolfe on, but decided to take the message instead, and after I rang off I gathered up the catalogues and circulars and reports and slipped a rubber band around them and proceeded upstairs.

Wolfe was standing at one side of the third room, frowning at a row of seedling hybrids in their second year. He looked plenty forbidding, and

Horstmann, whom I had passed in the tropical room, had had the appearance of having been crushed to earth.

I sailed into the storm. I flipped the rubber band on my little bundle and said, "Here's those lists from Richardt and also some from Hoehn, and some catalogues from England. Do you want them or shall I leave them in the potting room? And Clivers just called on the telephone. He says those papers came, and if you want to go and look at them, or send me, okay. He didn't say anything about his little mix-up with the police last night, and of course I was too polite—"

I stopped because Wolfe wasn't listening. His lips had suddenly pushed out a full half inch, and he had glued his eyes on the bundle in my hand. He stood that way a long while and I shut my mouth and stared at him.

Finally he murmured, "That's it. Confound you, Archie, did you know it? Is that why you brought it here?"

I asked courteously, "Have you gone cuckoo?"

He ignored me. "But of course not. It's your fate again." He closed his eyes and sighed a deep sigh, and murmured, "Rubber Coleman. The Rubber Band. Of course." He opened his eyes and flashed them at me. "Saul is downstairs? Send him up at once."

"What about Clivers?"

He went imperious. "Wait in the office. Send Saul."

Knowing there was no use pursuing any inquiries, I hopped back down to the kitchen door and beckoned Saul out into the hall. He stuck his nose up at me and I told him, "Wolfe wants you upstairs. For God's sake watch your step, because he has just found the buried treasure and you know what to expect when he's like that. If he requests anything grotesque, consult me."

I went back to my desk, but of course plant records were out. I lit a cigarette, and took my pistol out of the drawer and looked it over and put it back again, and kicked over my wastebasket and let it lay.

There were steps on the stairs, and Saul's voice came from the door. "Let me out, Archie. I've got work to do."

"Let yourself out. What are you afraid of?"

I stuck my hands in my pockets and stretched out my legs and sat on my shoulder blades and scowled. Ten minutes after Saul had left the phone rang. I uttered a couple of expletives as I reached for it, thinking it was one of the pack with another howl, but Saul Panzer's voice was in my ear. "Archie? Connect me with Mr. Wolfe."

I thought, now that was quick work, and plugged and buzzed. Wolfe's voice sounded. "Nero Wolfe."

"Yes, sir. This is Saul. I'm ready."

"Good. Archie? You don't need to take this."

I hung up with a bang and a snort. My powers of dissimulation were being saved from strain again. But that kind of thing didn't really get me sore, for I knew perfectly well why Wolfe didn't always point out to me the hole he was getting ready to crawl through: he knew that half the time I'd be back at him with damn good proof that it couldn't be done, which would only have been a nuisance, since he intended to do it anyway. No guy who knows he's right because he's too conceited to be wrong can be expected to go into conference about it.

Five minutes after that phone call from Saul the fun began. I got a ring from Wolfe upstairs. "Try for Lord Clivers."

I got the Hotel Portland and got through to him, and Wolfe spoke. "Good morning, sir. I received your message . . . Yes, so I understand . . . No, he can't go . . . If you will be so good—one moment—a very important development has taken place, and I don't like to discuss details on the telephone. You may remember that on the phone yesterday afternoon Mr. Walsh spoke to you regarding a certain person whom he had just seen. . . . Yes, he is both dangerous and desperate; moreover, he is cornered, and there is only one course open to you that can possibly prevent the fullest and most distasteful publicity on the whole affair. . . . I know that, that's why I want you to come to my office at once. . . . No, sir, take my word for it, it won't do, I should have to expose him immediately and publicly. . . . Yes, sir. . . . Good. That's a sensible man. Be sure to bring those papers along. I'll expect you in fifteen minutes. . . ."

Clivers rang off, but Wolfe stayed on.

"Archie. Try for Mr. Muir."

I got the Seaboard Products Corporation, and Miss Barish, and then Muir, and buzzed Wolfe.

"Mr. Muir? Good morning, sir. This is Nero Wolfe. . . . One moment, sir, I beg you. I have learned, to my great discomfiture, that I did an act of injustice yesterday, and I wish to rectify it. . . . Yes, yes, quite so, I understand. . . . Yes, indeed. I prefer not to discuss it on the telephone, but I am sure you will find yourself as satisfied as you deserve to be if you will come to my office at half past eleven this morning, and bring Mr. Perry with you. . . . No, I'm sorry, I can't do that. Miss Fox will be here. . . . Yes, she is here now. . . . No, half past eleven, not before, and it will be necessary to have Mr. Perry present. . . . Oh, surely not, he has shown a most active interest. . . . Yes, it's only a short distance. . . ."

I heard Muir's click off, and said into my transmitter, "That will bring that old goat trotting up here without stopping either for Perry or his hat. Why didn't you—"

"Thanks, Archie. Try for Mr. Cramer."

I got headquarters, and Cramer's extension and his clerk. Then the inspector. Wolfe got on. "Good morning, Mr. Cramer . . . Yes, indeed, I received your messages, but I have been occupied to good purpose. . . . So I understand, but could I help that? Can you be at my office at half past eleven? I shall be ready for you at that time. . . . The fact is, I do not intend merely to give you information, I hope to deliver a finished case. . . . I can't help that either; do you think I have the Moerae running errands for me? . . . Certainly, if they wish to come, bring them, though I think it would be well if Mr. Hombert went back to diapers. . . . Yes, eleven-thirty. . . ."

Cramer was off. I said, "Shall I try for the Cabinet?"

"No, thanks." Wolfe was purring. "When Lord Clivers arrives, bring him up here at once."

XVIII

I LET Saul Panzer in when he came. There was no longer any reason why I shouldn't relinquish the job of answering the door, which normally belonged to Fritz, but it seemed tactful to give him time to cool off a little; and besides, if I left him to his own devices in the kitchen a while longer without interruption, there was a chance that he would bounce a stewpan on Johnny's bean, which would have done them both good.

So I let Saul in and parked him in the front room, and also, a little later, I opened up for the Marquis of Clivers. Whereupon I experienced a delightful surprise, for he had his nephew along. Apparently there was no wedding on today; Horrocks looked sturdy and wholesome in a sack suit that hung like a dream, and I got so interested looking at it that I almost forgot it was him inside of it. I suggested him toward the office and said to Clivers, "Mr. Wolfe would like to see you upstairs. Three flights. Climb, or elevator?"

He was looking concentrated and sour. He said climb, and I took him up to the plant rooms and showed him Wolfe and left him there.

When I got back down Horrocks was still standing in the hall.

"If you want to wait," I said, "there's a place in the office to hold the back of your lap. You know, chair."

"The back of my lap?" He stared, and by gum, he worked at it till he got it. "Oh, quite. Thanks awfully. But I . . . I say, you know, Miss Fox got quite a wetting. Didn't she?"

"Yeah, she was good and damp."

"And I suppose she is still here, what?"

It was merely a question of which would be less irritating, to let him go on and circle around it for a while, or cut the knot for him and hand him the pieces. Deciding for the latter, I said, "Wait here," and mounted the stairs again. They seemed to have quieted down in the south room.

I knocked and went in and told Clara Fox, "That young diplomat is down below and wants to see you and I'm going to send him up. Keep him in here. We're going to be busy in the office, and it gives me the spirit of seventy-six to look at him."

She made a dive for her vanity case, and I descended to the hall again and told Horrocks he knew the way.

It was ten after eleven. There was nothing for me to do but sit down and suck my finger. There was one thing I would have liked to remind Wolfe of before the party began, but I didn't myself know how important it was, and anyway I had no idea how he intended to stage it. There was even a chance that this was to be only a dress rehearsal, a preliminary, to see what a little panic would do, but that wouldn't be like him. The only hint he condescended to give me was to ring me on the house phone and tell me he would come down with Clivers after the others had arrived, and until then I was to say nothing of Clivers' presence. I went in to see if Saul was talking, but he wasn't, so I went back and sat down and felt my pulse.

The two contingents, official and Seaboard, showed up within three minutes of each other. I let them in. The official came first. I took them to the office, where I had chairs pulled up. Skinner looked bilious, Hombert harassed, and Cramer moderately grim. When they saw Wolfe wasn't in the office they started to get exasperated, but I silenced them with a few well-chosen phrases, and then the bell rang again and I went for the second batch.

Muir and Perry were together. Perry smiled a tight smile at me and told me good morning, but Muir wasn't having any amenities; I saw his hand tremble a little as he hung his hat up, and he could have gone from that right on into permanent palsy without any tears wasted as far as I was concerned. I nodded them ahead.

They stopped dead inside the office door, at sight of the trio already there. Muir looked astonished and furious; Perry seemed surprised, looking from one to the other, and then turned to me. "I thought . . . Wolfe said eleven-thirty, so I understood from Muir . . . if these gentlemen . . ."

"It's all right." I grinned at him. "Mr. Wolfe has arranged for a little conference. Have chairs. Do you know Mr. Hombert, the Police Commissioner? Inspector Cramer? Mr. Ramsey Muir. Mr. Anthony D. Perry."

I got to the house phone on my desk and buzzed the plant rooms. Wolfe answered, and I told him, "All here." The two bunches of eminent visitors were putting on a first-class exhibition of bad manners; neither had expected to see the other. Cramer looked around at them, slowly from one face to another, and then looked at me with a gleam in his eyes. Hombert was grumbling something to Perry. Skinner turned and croaked at me, "What kind of damn nonsense is this?" I just shook my head at him, and then I heard the creak of the elevator, and a moment later the door of the office opened and Wolfe entered with another visitor whom none of them had expected to see.

They approached. Wolfe stopped, and inclined his head. "Good morning, gentlemen. I believe some of you have met Lord Clivers. Not you, Mr. Perry? No. Mr. Muir. Mr. Skinner, our District Attorney. I want to thank all of you for being so punctual. . . ."

I was seeing a few things. First, Clivers stood staring directly at Perry, reminding me of how Harlan Scovil had stared at him two days before, and Clivers had thrust his right hand into the side pocket of his coat and didn't take it out. Second, Perry was staring back, and his temples were moving and his eyes were small and hard. Third, Inspector Cramer had put his weight forward in his chair and his feet back under him, but he was sitting too far away, the other side of Skinner, to get anywhere quick.

I swiveled and opened a drawer unostentatiously and got out my automatic and laid it on the desk at my elbow. Hombert was starting to bellyache. "I don't know, Wolfe, what kind of a high-handed procedure you think—"

Wolfe, who had moved around the desk and into his chair, put up a palm at him. "Please, Mr. Hombert. I think it is always advisable to take a short-cut when it is feasible. That's why I requested a favor of Lord Clivers." He looked at Clivers. "Be seated, sir. And tell us, have you ever met Mr. Perry before?"

Clivers, with his hand still in his pocket, lowered himself into his chair, which was between Hombert and me, without taking his eyes off Perry. "I have," he said gruffly. "By gad, you were right. He's Coleman. Rubber Coleman."

Perry just looked at him.

Wolfe asked softly, "What about it, Mr. Perry?"

You could see from Perry's chin that this teeth were clamped. His eyes went suddenly from Clivers to Wolfe and stayed there; then he looked at me, and I returned it. His shoulders started going up, slowly up, high, as he took in a long breath, and then slowly they started down again. When they touched bottom he looked at Wolfe again and said, "I'm not talking. Not just now. You go on."

Wolfe nodded. "I don't blame you, sir. It's a lot to give up, to surrender that old secret." He glanced around the circle. "You gentlemen may remember, from Miss Fox's story last night, that Rubber Coleman was the man who led that little band of rescuers forty years ago. That was Mr. Perry here. But you do not yet know that on account of that obligation Lord Clivers, in the year 1906, twenty-nine years ago, paid Coleman—Mr. Perry—the sum of one million dollars. Nor that this Coleman-Perry has never, to this day, distributed any of that sum as he agreed to do."

Cramer grunted and moved himself another inch forward. Skinner was sunk in his chair with his elbows on its arms and his fingertips placed neatly together, his narrowed eyes moving from Wolfe to Clivers to Perry and back again. Hombert was biting his lip and watching Clivers.

Muir suddenly squeaked, "What's all this about? What has this got to do—"

Wolfe snapped at him, "Shut up. You are here, sir, because that seemed the easiest way to bring Mr. Perry, and because I thought you should know the truth regarding your charge against Miss Fox. If you wish to leave, do so; if you stay, hold your tongue."

Clivers put in brusquely, "I didn't agree to this man's presence."

Wolfe nodded. "I think you may leave that to me. After all, Lord Clivers, it was you who originally started this, and if the hen has come home to roost and I am to pluck it for you, I must be permitted a voice in the method." He turned abruptly. "What about it, Mr. Perry? You've had a moment for reflection. You were Rubber Coleman, weren't you?"

"I'm not talking." Perry was gazing at him, and this time he didn't have to strain the words through his teeth. His lips compressed a little, his idea being that he was smiling. "Lord Clivers may quite possibly be mistaken." He tried the smile again. "It may even be that he will . . . will realize his mistake." He looked around. "You know me, Mr. Skinner. You too, Mr. Hombert. I am glad you are here. I have evidence to present to you that this man Wolfe is engaged in a malicious attempt to damage my reputation and that of my vice-president and the firm I direct. Mr. Muir will bear me out." He turned small hard eyes on Wolfe. "I'll give you rope. All you want. Go on."

Wolfe nodded admiringly. "Superlative." He leaned back and surveyed the group. "Gentlemen, I must ask you to listen, and bear with me. You will reach my conclusion only if I describe my progress toward it. I'll make it as brief as possible.

"It began some forty-five hours ago, when Mr. Perry called here and asked me to investigate a theft of thirty thousand dollars from the drawer of Mr. Muir's desk. Mr. Goodwin called at the Seaboard office and asked questions. He was there from four-forty-five until five-fifty-five, and for a period of thirty-five minutes, from five-twenty until five-fifty-five, he saw neither Mr. Perry nor Mr. Muir, because they had gone to a conference in the directors' room. The case seemed to have undesirable features, and we decided not to handle it. I find I shall need some beer."

He reached to push the button, and leaned back again. "You know of

Harlan Scovil's visit to this office Monday afternoon. Well, he saw Mr. Perry here. He not only saw him, he stared at him. You know of the phone call, at five-twenty-six, which summoned Mr. Scovil to his death. Monday night, in addition to these things, I also knew the story which Miss Fox had related to us in the presence of Mr. Walsh and Miss Lindquist; and when, having engaged myself in Miss Fox's interest, it became necessary to consider the murder of Harlan Scovil, I scanned the possibilities as they presented themselves at that moment.

"Assuming, until disproven, that Harlan Scovil's murder was connected with the Rubber Band affair, the first possibility was of course Lord Clivers himself, but Tuesday morning he was eliminated, when I learned that the murderer was alone in the automobile. An article in Sunday's *Times*, which Mr. Goodwin had kindly read to me, stated that Lord Clivers did not know how to drive a car, and on Tuesday, yesterday, I corroborated that through an agent in London, at the same time acquiring various bits of information regarding Lord Clivers. The second possibility was Michael Walsh. I had talked with him and formed a certain judgment of him, and no motive was apparent, but he remained a possibility. The same applied to Miss Lindquist. Miss Fox was definitely out of it, because I had upon consideration accepted her as a client."

Somebody burst out, "Ha!" Hombert ventured a comment, while Wolfe poured beer and gulped, but it went unheeded. Wolfe wiped his lips and went on.

"Among the known possibilities, the most promising one was Anthony D. Perry. On account of the phone call which took Mr. Scovil to the street to die, it was practically certain that his murderer had known he was in this office; and because, so far as I was aware, Mr. Perry was the only person who had known that, it seemed at least worth while to accept it as a conjecture. Through *Metropolitan Biographies* and also through inquiries by one of my men, I got at least negative support for the conjecture; and I got positive support by talking over long distance to Nebraska, with Miss Lindquist's father. He remembered with considerable accuracy the appearance of the face and figure of Rubber Coleman, and while of course there could be no real identification by a telephone talk after forty years, still it was support. I asked Mr. Lindquist, in fact, for descriptions of all the men concerned in that affair, thinking there might be some complication more involved than this most obvious one, but it was his description of Rubber Coleman which most nearly approximated that of Mr. Perry. The next step—"

"Wait a minute, Wolfe." Skinner's croak was imperative. "You can't do this. Not this way. If you've got a case, I'm the District Attorney. If you haven't—"

Perry cut in, "Let him alone! Let him hang himself."

Hombert muttered something to Cramer, and the inspector rumbled back. Clivers spoke up. "I'm concerned in this. Let Wolfe talk." He used a finger of his left hand to point at Perry because his right hand was still in his coat pocket. "That man is Rubber Coleman. Wolfe learned that, didn't he? What the devil have the rest of you done, except annoy me?"

Perry leveled his eyes at the marquis. "You're mistaken, Lord Clivers. You'll regret this."

Wolfe had taken advantage of the opportunity to finish his bottle and ring for another. Now he looked around. "You gentlemen may be curious why, if Mr. Perry is not Rubber Coleman, he does not express indignant wonderment at what I am talking about. Oh, he could explain that. Long ago, shortly after she entered Seaboard's employ, Miss Fox told him the story which you heard from her last night. He knows all about the Rubber Band, from her, and also about her efforts to find its surviving members. And by the way, as regards the identity—did Mr. Walsh telephone you around five o'clock yesterday afternoon, Lord Clivers, and tell you he had just found Rubber Coleman?"

Clivers nodded. "He did."

"Yes." Wolfe looked at Cramer. "As you informed me, immediately after leaving the Seaboard office, where he had gone on account of his unfortunate suspicions regarding Miss Fox and myself after Harlan Scovil had been killed, Mr. Walsh sought a telephone. There—as can doubtless be verified by inquiry, along with multitudinous other details—he had seen Mr. Perry. It is a pity he did not inform me, since in that case he would still be alive; but what he did do was to phone Lord Clivers, with whom he had had a talk in the morning. He had called at the Hotel Portland and Lord Clivers had considered it advisable to see him, had informed him of the payment which had been made to Rubber Coleman long before, and had declared his intention of giving him a respectable sum of money. Now, learning from Mr. Walsh over the telephone that he had found Rubber Coleman, Lord Clivers saw that immediate and purposeful action was required if publicity was to be avoided; and he told Mr. Walsh that around seven o'clock that evening, on his way to a dinner engagement, he would stop in at the place Mr. Walsh was working, which was a short distance from his hotel. I have been told these details within the last hour. Is that correct, sir?"

Clivers nodded. "It is."

Wolfe looked at Perry, but Perry's eyes were fixed on Clivers. Wolfe said, "So, for the identity, we have Mr. Lindquist's description, Mr. Walsh's phone call, and Lord Clivers' present recognition. Why, after forty years, Mr. Scovil and Mr. Walsh should have recognized Rubber Coleman is, I think, easily explicable. On account of the circumstances, their minds were at the moment filled with vivid memories of that old event, and alert with suspicion. They might have passed Mr. Perry a hundred times on the street without a second glance at him, but in the situations in which they saw him recollection jumped for them." He looked again at the Seaboard president, and again asked, "What about it now, Mr. Perry? Won't you give us that?"

Perry moved his eyes at him. He spoke smoothly. "I'm still not talking. I'm listening." He suddenly, spasmodically, jerked forward, and there was a stir around the circle. Cramer's bulk tensed in his chair. Skinner's hands dropped. Clivers stiffened. I got my hand to my desk, on the gun. I don't think Perry noticed any of it, for his gaze stayed on Wolfe, and he jerked back again and set his jaw. He said not quite so smoothly, "You go on."

Wolfe shook his head. "You're a stubborn man, Mr. Perry. However—as I started to say, the next step for me, yesterday afternoon, was to get in touch with Mr. Walsh, persuade him of my good faith, show him a photograph of Mr. Perry, and substantiate my conjecture. That became doubly important and urgent after Lord Clivers called here and I learned of the payment that had been made to Coleman in 1906. I considered the idea of asking Lord Clivers for a description of Coleman, and even possibly showing him Perry's photograph, but rejected it. I was at that moment by no means convinced of his devotion to scruple, and even had I been, I would not have cared to alarm him further by showing him the imminence of Coleman's discovery—and the lid blown off the pot. First I needed Mr. Walsh, so I sent a man to Fifty-fifth Street to reconnoiter.

"Of course, I had found out other things. For instance, one of my men had visited the directors' room of the Seaboard Products Corporation and learned that it has a second door, into the public hall, through which Mr. Perry might easily have departed at five-twenty or thereabouts Monday afternoon on some errand, and returned some thirty minutes later, without Mr. Goodwin's knowledge. Questions to his business associates who were present might elicit answers. For another instance, Miss Fox had breakfast with me yesterday morning—and I assure you, Mr. Skinner, I did not waste the time in foolish queries as to where her mother used to keep letters sixteen years ago.

"Combining information with conjecture, I get a fair picture of some of Mr. Perry's precautionary activities. In the spring of 1932 he saw an advertisement in a newspaper seeking knowledge of the whereabouts of Michael Walsh and Rubber Coleman. In a roundabout way he learned who had inserted it; and a month later Clara Fox was in the employ of the Seaboard Products Corporation. He could keep an eye on her, and did so. He cultivated her company, and earned a degree of her confidence. When she found Harlan Scovil, and later Hilda Lindquist, and still later Michael Walsh, he knew of it. He tried to convince her of the foolishness of her enterprise, but without success. Then suddenly, last Thursday, he learned she had found Lord Clivers, and he at once took measures to hamstring her. He may even then have considered murder and rejected it; at any rate, he decided that sending her to prison as a thief would completely discredit her and would be sufficient. He knew that her initiative was the only active force threatening him, and that with her removed there would be little danger. An opportunity was providentially at hand. Friday afternoon he himself took that thirty thousand dollars from Mr. Muir's desk, and sent Miss Fox into that room with a cablegram to be copied. I don't know—"

Muir had popped up out of his chair and was squealing, "By God, I believe it! By God if I don't! And all the time you were plotting against her! You dirty sneak, you dirty—"

Cramer, agile on his feet, had a hand on Muir's shoulder. "All right, all right, you just sit down and we'll all believe it. Come on, now." He eased him down, Muir chattering.

Perry said contemptuously, bitingly, "So that's you, Muir." He whirled, and there was a quality in his movement that made me touch my gun again. "Wolfe, all this you're inventing, you'll eat it." He added slowly, "And it will finish you."

Wolfe shook his head. "Oh no, sir, I assure you." He sighed. "To continue: I don't know how and when Mr. Perry concealed the money in Miss Fox's automobile, but one of my men has uncovered a possibility which the police can easily follow. At any rate, it is certain that he did. That is unimportant. Another thing that moved him to action was the fact that Clara Fox had told him that, having heard him speak favorably of the abilities of Nero Wolfe, she had decided to engage me in the Rubber Band enterprise. Apparently Mr. Perry did give my competence a high rating, for he took the trouble to come here himself to get me to act for the Seaboard Products Corporation, which would of course have prevented me from taking Miss Fox as a client.

"But he had an unpleasant surprise here. He was sitting in that chair, the one he is in now, when a man walked into the room and said, 'My name's Harlan Scovil.' And the man stared at Mr. Perry. We cannot know whether he definitely recognized him as Rubber Coleman or whether Mr. Perry merely suspected that he did. In any event, it was enough to convince Mr. Perry that something more drastic than a framed-up larceny charge was called for without delay; for obviously it would not do for any living person to have even the remotest suspicion that there was any connection between Anthony D. Perry, corporation president, bank director, multi-millionaire, and eminent citizen, and the Rubber Band. Lord Clivers tells me that forty years ago Rubber Coleman was headstrong, sharp of purpose, and quick on the trigger. Apparently he has retained those characteristics. He went to his office and at once phoned Mr. Goodwin to come there. At five-twenty he went to the directors' room. A moment later he excused himself to his associates, left by the door to the public hall, descended to the ground floor and telephoned Harlan Scovil, saying what we can only guess at but certainly arranging a rendezvous, went to the street and selected a parked automobile and took it, drove to where Scovil was approaching the rendezvous and shot him dead, abandoned the car on Ninth Avenue, and returned to the Seaboard Building and the directors' room. It was an action admirably quick-witted, direct and conclusive, with probably not one chance in a million of it's being discovered but for the fact that Miss Fox had happened to pick me to collect a fantastic debt for her."

Wolfe paused to open and pour beer. Skinner said, "I hope you've got something, Wolfe. I hope to heaven you've got something, because if you haven't . . ."

Wolfe drank, and put his glass down. "I know. I can see the open jaws of the waiting beasts." He thumbed at Perry. "This one here in front. But let him wait a little longer. Let us go on to last evening. That is quite simple. We are not concerned with the details of how Mr. Walsh got to see Mr. Perry at his office yesterday afternoon; it is enough to know that he did, since he phoned Lord Clivers that he had found Rubber Coleman. Well, there was only one thing for Mr. Perry to do, and he did it. Shortly after half past six o'clock he entered that building enclosure by one of the ways we know of—possibly he is a member of the Orient Club, another point for inquiry—crept up on old Mr. Walsh and shot him in the back of the head, probably muffling the sound of the shot by wrapping the gun in his overcoat or something else, moved the body to the vicinity of the telephone if it was not already there, left by the way he had come, and drove rapidly—"

"Wait a minute!" Cramer broke in, gruff. "How do you fit that? We know the exact time of that shot, two minutes to seven, when Walsh called you on the phone. And you heard the shot. We already know—"

"Please, Mr. Cramer." Wolfe was patient. "I'm not telling you what you already know; this, for you, is news. I was saying, Mr. Perry drove rapidly downtown and arrived at this office at exactly seven o'clock."

Hombert jerked up and snorted. Cramer stared at Wolfe, slowly shaking his head. Skinner, frowning, demanded, "Are you crazy, Wolfe? Yesterday you told us you heard the shot that killed Walsh, at six-fifty-eight. Now you say that Perry fired it, and then got to your office at seven o'clock." He snarled, "Well?"

"Precisely." Wolfe wiggled a finger at him. "Do you remember that last night I told you that I was confronted by a difficulty which had to be solved before anything could be done? That was it. You have just stated it. Archie, please tell Saul to go ahead."

I got up and went and opened the door to the front room. Saul Panzer was sitting there. I called to him, "Hey, Mr. Wolfe says to go ahead." Saul made for the hall and I heard him going out the front door.

Wolfe was saying, "It was ingenious and daring for Mr. Perry to arrange for Mr. Goodwin and me to furnish his alibi. But of course, strictly speaking, it was not an alibi he had in mind; it was a chronology of events which would exclude from my mind any possibility of his connection with Mr. Walsh's death. Such a connection was not supposed to occur to anyone, and above all not to me; for it is fairly certain that up to the time of his arrival here today Mr. Perry felt satisfactorily assured that no one had the faintest suspicion of his interest in this affair. There had been two chances against him: Harlan Scovil might have spoken to Mr. Goodwin between the time that Mr. Perry left here Monday afternoon and the time he phoned to summon Mr. Goodwin to his office; or Mr. Walsh might have communicated with me between five and six yesterday. But he thought not, for there was no indication of it from us; and he had proceeded to kill both of them as soon as he could reasonably manage it. So he arranged—"

Skinner growled, "Get on. He may not have had an alibi in mind, but he seems to have one. What about it?"

"As I say, sir, that was my difficulty. It will be resolved for you shortly. I thought it better—ah! Get it, Archie."

It was the phone. I swiveled and took it, and found myself exchanging greetings with Mr. Panzer. I told Wolfe, "Saul."

He nodded, and got brisk. "Give Mr. Skinner your chair. If you would please take that receiver, Mr. Skinner? I want you to hear something. And you, Mr. Cramer, take mine—here—the cord isn't long enough, I'm afraid you'll have to stand. Kindly keep the receiver fairly snug on your ear. Now, Mr. Skinner, speak into the transmitter, 'Ready.' That one word will be enough."

Skinner, at my phone, croaked, "Ready." The next development was funny. He gave a jump, and turned to glare at Wolfe, while Cramer, at Wolfe's phone, jerked a little too, and yelled into the transmitter, "Hey! Hey, you!"

Wolfe said, "Hang up, gentlemen, and be seated. Mr. Skinner, please! That demonstration was really necessary. What you heard was Saul Panzer in a telephone booth at the druggist's on the next corner. There, of course, the instrument is attached to the wall. What he did was this."

Wolfe reached into his pocket and took out a big rubber band. He removed the receiver from his French phone, looped the band over the transmitter end, stretched it out, and let it flip. He replaced the receiver.

"That's all," he announced. "That was the shot Mr. Goodwin and I heard over the telephone. The band must be three-quarters of an inch wide, and thick, as I learned from experiments this morning. On this instrument, of course, it is nothing; but on the transmitter of a pay-station phone, with the impact and jar and vibration simultaneous, the effect is startling. Didn't you find it so, Mr. Skinner?"

"I'll be damned," Cramer muttered. "I will be damned."

Skinner said, "It's amazing. I'd have sworn it was a gun."

"Yes." Wolfe's eyes, half shut, were on Perry. "I must congratulate you, sir. Not only efficient, but appropriate. Rubber Coleman. The Rubber Band. I fancy that was how the idea happened to occur to you. Most ingenious, and ludicrously simple. I wish you would tell us what old friend or employee you got to help you try it out, for surely you took that precaution. It would save Mr. Cramer a lot of trouble."

Wolfe was over one hurdle, anyway. He had Skinner and Hombert and Cramer with him, sewed up. When he had begun talking they had kept their eyes mostly on him, with only occasional glances at Perry; then, as he had uncovered one point after another, they had gradually looked more at Perry; and by now, while still listening to Wolfe, they weren't bothering to look at him much. Their gaze was on Perry, and stayed there, and, for that matter, so was mine and Muir's and Clivers'. Perry was obviously expecting too much of himself. He had waited too long for a convenient spot to open up with indignation or defiance or a counter-attack, and no doubt Wolfe's little act with the rubber band had been a complete surprise to him. He was by no means ready to break down and have a good cry, because he wasn't that kind of a dog, but you could see he was stretched too tight. Just as none of us could take our eyes off him, he couldn't take his off Wolfe. From where I sat I could see his temples moving, plain.

He didn't say anything.

Skinner's bass rumbled, "You've made up a good story, Wolfe. I've got a suggestion. How about leaving your man here to entertain Perry for a while and the rest of us go somewhere for a little talk? I need to ask some questions."

Wolfe shook his head. "Not at this moment, sir, if you please. Patience; my reasons will appear. First, is the chronology clear to all of you? At or about six-thirty-five Mr. Perry killed Mr. Walsh, leaving his body near the telephone, and immediately drove downtown, stopping, perhaps, at the same drug store where Saul Panzer just now demonstrated for us. I think that likely, for that store has a side entrance through which the phone booths can be approached with little exposure to observation. From there he phoned here, disguising his voice, and snapping his rubber band. Two minutes later he was at my door, having established the moment at which Michael Walsh was killed. There was of course the risk that by accident the body had been discovered in the twenty minutes which had elapsed, but it was slight, and in any event there was nothing to point to him. As it happened, he had great luck, for not only was the body not discovered prematurely, it was discovered at precisely the proper moment, and by Lord Clivers himself! I think it highly improbable that Mr. Perry knew that Lord Clivers was expected there at that hour, or indeed at all; that was coincidence. How he must have preened himself last evening—for we are all vainer of our luck than of our merits—when he learned the news! The happy smile of Providence! Isn't that so, Mr. Perry?"

Perry smiled into Wolfe's face—a thin tight smile, but he made a go of it. He said, "I'm still listening . . . but it strikes me you're about through. As Mr. Skinner says, you've made up a good story." He stopped, and his jaw worked a little, then he went on. "Of course you don't expect me to reply to it, but I'm going to, only not with words. You're in a plot to blackmail Lord Clivers, but that's his business. I'm going back to my office and get my lawyer, and I'm going to come down on you for slander and for conspiracy, and also your man Goodwin. I am also going to swear out a warrant against Clara Fox, and this time there'll be no nonsense about withdrawing it." He clamped his jaw, and loosened it again. "You're done, Wolfe. I'm telling you, you're done."

"Oh, no." Wolfe wiggled a finger at him. "You spoke too soon, sir. I am not done. Let me finish my slander and give you more basis for your action. I'm not boring you, am I? No."

Wolfe looked at the District Attorney. "I am aware, Mr. Skinner, that I have exasperated you, but in the end I think you will agree that my procedure was well advised. First, on account of the undesirable publicity in connection with Lord Clivers, and the fact that he is soon to sail for home, prompt action was essential. Second, there was the advantage of showing Mr. Perry all at once how many holes he will have to plug up, for he is bound to get frantic about it and make a fool of himself. He was really sanguine enough to expect to keep his connection with this completely concealed. His leaving the directors' room Monday afternoon and returning; his access to Clara Fox's car for concealing the money, which is now being investigated by one of my men, Orrie Cather; the visit to him by Michael Walsh; his entrance into, and exit from, the building enclosure last evening; his overcoat, perhaps, which he wrapped around his pistol; his entering the corner drug store to telephone; all these and a dozen other details are capable of inquiry; and, finding himself confronted by so many problems all requiring immediate attention, he is sure to put his foot in it."

Skinner grunted in disgust. "Do you mean to say you've given us all you've got? And now you're letting him know it?"

"But I've got all that's necessary." Wolfe sighed. "For, since we are all convinced that Mr. Perry did kill Harlan Scovil and Michael Walsh, it is of no consequence whether he can be legally convicted and executed."

Cramer muttered, "Uh-huh, you're nuts." Skinner and Hombert stared, speechless.

"Because," Wolfe went on, "he is rendered incapable of further mischief anyway; and even if you regard the criminal law as an instrument of barbarous vengeance, he is going to pay. What is it that he has been trying so desperately to preserve, with all his ruthless cunning? His position in society, his high repute among his fellow men, his nimbus as a master biped. Well, he will lose all that, which should be enough for any law." He extended his hand. "May I have those papers, Lord Clivers?"

Clivers reached to his breast pocket and pulled out an envelope, and I got it and handed it to Wolfe. Wolfe opened the flap and extracted some pieces of paper, and unfolded them, with the usual nicety of his fingers.

"I have here," he said, "a document dated Silver City, Nevada, June second, 1895, in which George Rowley agrees to make a certain future compensation for services rendered. It is signed by him, and attested by Michael Walsh and Rubber Coleman as witnesses. I also have another, same date, headed PLEDGE OF THE RUBBER BAND, containing an agreement signed by various persons. I also have one dated London, England, August eleventh, 1906, which is a receipt for two hundred thousand, seven hundred sixty-one pounds, signed by Rubber Coleman, Gilbert Fox, Harlan Scovil, Turtle-back, Victor Lindquist, and Michael Walsh. After the 'Turtle-back,' in parentheses, appears the name William Mollen. I also have a check for the same amount, dated September nineteenth, drawn to the order of James N. Coleman and endorsed by him for payment."

Wolfe looked around at them. "The point here is, gentlemen, that none of those men except Coleman ever saw that receipt. He forged the names of all the others." He whirled suddenly to Perry, and his voice was a whip. "Well, sir? Is that slander?"

Perry held himself. But his voice was squeezed in his throat. "It is. They signed it."

"Ha! They signed it? So at last we have it that you're Rubber Coleman?"

"Certainly I'm Coleman. They signed it, and they got their share."

"Oh, no." Wolfe pointed a finger at him and held it there. "You've made a bad mistake, sir; you didn't kill enough men. Victor Lindquist is still alive and in possession of all his faculties. I talked to him yesterday on the telephone, and I warned him against any tricks that might be tried. His testimony, with the corroboration we already have, will be ample for an English court. Slander? Pfui!" He turned to the others. "So you see, it isn't really so important to convict Mr. Perry of murder. He is now past sixty. I don't know the English penalty for forgery, but certainly he will be well over seventy when he emerges from jail, discredited, broken, a pitiable relic—"

Wolfe told me later that his idea was to work Perry into a state where he would then and there sign checks for Clara Fox and Victor Lindquist, and Walsh's and Scovil's heirs if any, for their share of the million dollars. I don't know. Anyhow, the checks didn't get signed, because dead men can't write even their names.

It happened like lightning, a bunch of reflexes. Perry jerked out a gun and turned it on Wolfe and pulled the trigger. Hombert yelled and Cramer jumped. I could never have got across in time to topple him, and anyway, as I say, it was reflex. I grabbed my gun and let him have it, but then Cramer was there and I quit. There was a lot of noise, Perry was down, sunk in his chair, and they were pawing him. I dived around the desk for Wolfe, who was sitting there looking surprised for once in his life, feeling with his right hand at his upper left arm.

Him protesting, I pulled his coat open and the sleeve off, and the spot of blood on the outside of the arm of the canary-yellow shirt looked better to me than any orchid. I stuck my finger in the hole the bullet had made and ripped the sleeve and took a look, and then grinned into the fat devil's face. "Just the meat, and not much of that. You don't use that arm much anyhow."

I heard Cramer behind me, "Dead as a doornail," and turned to see the major casualty. They had let it come on out of the chair and stretched it on the floor. The inspector was kneeling by it, and the others standing, and Clivers and Skinner were busy putting out a fire. Clivers was pulling and rubbing at the bottom front of one side of his coat, where the bullet and flame had gone through when he pulled the trigger with his hand still in his pocket, and Skinner was helping him. He must have plugged Perry one-tenth of a second before I did.

Cramer stood up. He said heavily, "One in the right shoulder, and one clear through him, through the heart. Well, he asked for it."

I said, "The shoulder was mine. I was high."

"Surely not, Archie." It was behind me, Wolfe murmuring. We looked at him; he was sopping blood off of his arm with his handkerchief. "Surely not. Do you want Lord Clivers' picture in the *Gazette* again? We must protect him. You can stand the responsibility of a justifiable homicide. You can—what do you call it, Mr. Cramer?—take the rap."

XIX

"FIVE thousand pounds," Clivers said. "To be paid at once, and to be returned to me if and when recovery is made from Coleman's estate. That's fair. I don't say it's generous. Who the devil can afford to be generous nowadays?"

Wolfe shook his head. "I see I'll have to get you on the wing. You dart like a hummingbird from two thousand to ten to seven to five. We'll take the ten, under the conditions you suggest."

Clara Fox put in, "I don't want anything. I've told you that. I won't take anything."

It was nearly three o'clock and we were all in the office. There had been six of us at lunch, which had meant another pick-me-up. Muir had gone, sped on his way by a pronouncement from Wolfe to the effect that he was a scabrous jackass, without having seen Clara Fox. Cramer and Hombert and Skinner had departed, after accepting Wolfe's suggestion for protecting the marquis from further publicity, and I had agreed to it. Doc Vollmer had come and fixed up Wolfe's arm and had gone again. What was left of Rubber Coleman–Anthony D. Perry had been taken away under Cramer's supervision, and the office floor looked bare because the big red and yellow rug where Perry had sat and where they had stretched him out was down in the basement, waiting for the cleaners to call. The bolt was back on the front door and I was acting as hall boy again, because reporters were still buzzing around the entrance like flies on the screen on a cloudy day.

Wolfe said, "You're still my client, Miss Fox. You are under no compulsion to take my advice, but it is my duty to offer it. First, take what belongs to you; your renunciation would not resurrect Mr. Scovil or Mr. Walsh, nor even Mr. Perry. Almost certainly, a large sum can be collected from Mr. Perry's estate. Second, remember that I have earned a fee and you will have to pay it. Third, abandon for good your career as an adventuress; you're much too soft-hearted for it."

Clara Fox glanced at Francis Horrocks, who was sitting there looking at her with that sickening sweet expression that you occasionally see in public and at the movies. It was a relief to see him glance at Wolfe and get his mind on something else for a brief moment. He blurted out, "I say, you know, if she doesn't want to take money from that chap's estate, she doesn't have to. It's her own affair, what? Now, if my uncle paid your fee . . . it's all the same . . ."

"Shut up, Francis." Clivers was impatient. "How the devil is it all the same? Let's get this settled. I've already missed one engagement and shall soon be late for another. Look here, seven thousand."

Hilda Lindquist said, "I'll take what I can get. It doesn't belong to me, it's my father's." Her square face wasn't exactly cheerful, but I wouldn't say she looked wretched. She leveled her eyes at Clivers. "If you had been halfway careful when you paid that money twenty-nine years ago, father would have got his share then, when mother was still alive and my brother hadn't died."

Clivers didn't bother with her. He looked at Wolfe. "Let's get on. Eight thousand."

"Come, come, sir." Wolfe wiggled a finger at him. "Make it dollars. Fifty thousand. The exchange favors you. There is a strong probability that you'll get it back when Perry's estate is settled; besides, it might be argued that you should pay my fee instead of Miss Fox. There is no telling how this might have turned out for you but for my intervention."

"Bah." Clivers snorted. "Even up there. I saved your life. I shot him."

"Oh, no. Read the newspapers. Mr. Goodwin shot him."

Clivers looked at me, and suddenly exploded with his three short blasts, haw-haw-haw. "So you did, eh? Goodwin's your name? Damned fine shooting!" He turned to Wolfe. "All right. Draw up a paper and send to my hotel, and you'll get a check." He got up from his chair, glancing down at the mess he had made of the front of his coat. "I'll have to go there now and change. A fine piece of cloth ruined. I'm sorry not to see more of your orchids. You, Francis! Come on."

Horrocks was murmuring something in a molasses tone to Clara Fox and she was taking it in and nodding at him. He finished, and got up. "Right-o." He moved across and stuck out his paw at Wolfe. "You know, I want to say, it was devilish clever, the way you watered Miss Fox yesterday morning and they never suspected. It was the face you put on that stumped them, what?"

"No doubt." Wolfe got his hand back again. "Since you gentlemen are sailing Saturday, I suppose we shan't see you again. *Bon voyage.*"

"Thanks," Clivers grunted. "At least for myself. My nephew isn't sailing. He has spent a fortune on cables and got himself transferred to the Washington embassy. He's going to carve out a career. He had better, because I'm damned if he'll get my title for another two decades. Come on, Francis."

I glanced at Clara Fox, and my dreams went short on ideals then and there. If I ever saw a woman look smug and self-satisfied . . .

XX

AT TWENTY minutes to four, with Wolfe and me alone in the office, the door opened and Fritz came marching in. Clamped under his left arm was the poker-dart board; in his right hand was the box of javelins. He put the box down on Wolfe's desk, crossed to the far wall and hung up the board, backed off and squinted at it, straightened it up, turned to Wolfe and did his little bow, and departed.

Wolfe emptied his glass of beer, arose from his chair, and began fingering the darts, sorting out the yellow ones.

He looked at me. "I suppose this is foolhardy," he murmured, "with this bullet wound, to start my blood pumping."

"Sure," I agreed. "You ought to be in bed. They may have to amputate."

"Indeed." He frowned at me. "Of course, you wouldn't know much about it. As far as my memory serves, you have never been shot by a high-caliber revolver at close range."

"The lord help me." I threw up my hands. "Is that going to be the tune? Are you actually going to have the nerve to brag about that little scratch? Now, if Hombert's foot hadn't jostled his chair and he had hit what he aimed at . . ."

"But he didn't." Wolfe moved to the fifteen-foot mark. He looked me over. "Archie. If you would care to join me at this . . ."

I shook my head positively. "Nothing doing. You'll keep beefing about your bullet wound, and anyway I can't afford it. You'll probably be luckier than ever."

He put a dignified stare on me. "A dime a game."

"No."

"A nickel."

"No. Not even for matches."

He stood silent, and after a minute of that heaved a deep sigh. "Your salary is raised ten dollars a week, beginning last Monday."

I lifted the brows. "Fifteen."

"Ten is enough."

I shook my head. "Fifteen."

He sighed again. "Confound you! All right. Fifteen."

I arose and went to the desk to get the red darts.

IN THE BEST FAMILIES

I

It was nothing out of the ordinary that Mrs. Barry Rackham had made the appointment with her finger pressed to her lips. That is by no means an unusual gesture for people who find themselves in a situation where the best thing they can think of is to make arrangements to see Nero Wolfe.

With Mrs. Barry Rackham the shushing finger was only figurative, since she made the date speaking to me on the phone. It was in her voice, low and jerky, and also in the way she kept telling me how confidential it was, even after I solemnly assured her that we rarely notified the press when someone requested an appointment on business. At the end she told me once more that she would have preferred to speak to Mr. Wolfe himself, and I hung up and decided it rated a discreet routine check on a prospective client, starting with Mr. Mitchell at the bank and Lon Cohen at the *Gazette*. On the main point of interest, could she and did she pay her bills, the news was favorable: she was worth a good four million and maybe five. Calling it four, and assuming that Wolfe's bill for services rendered would come to only half of it, that would be enough to pay my current salary—as Wolfe's secretary, trusted assistant and official gnat—for a hundred and sixty-seven years; and in addition to that, living as I did there in Wolfe's house, I also got food and shelter. So I was fixed for life if it turned out that she needed two million bucks' worth of detective work.

She might have at that, judging from the way she looked and acted at 11:05 the next morning, Friday, when the doorbell rang and I went to let her in. There was a man on the stoop with her, and after glancing quickly east and then west she brushed past him and darted inside, grabbed my sleeve, and told me in a loud whisper, "You're not Nero Wolfe!"

Instantly she released me, seized the elbow of her companion to hurry him across the sill, and whispered at him explosively, "Come in and shut the door!" You might have thought she was a duchess diving into a hock shop.

Not that she was my idea of a duchess physically. As I attended to the door and got the man's hat and topcoat hung on the rack, I took them in. She was a paradox—bony from the neck up and ample from the neck down.

On her chin and jawbone and cheekbone the skin was stretched tight, but alongside her mouth and nose were tangles of wrinkles.

As I helped her off with her fur coat I told her, "Look, Mrs. Rackham. You came to consult Nero Wolfe, huh?"

"Yes," she whispered. She nodded and said right out loud, "Of course."

"Then you ought to stop trembling if you can. It makes Mr. Wolfe uneasy when a woman trembles because he thinks she's going to be hysterical, and he might not listen to you. Take a deep breath and try to stop."

"You were trembling all the way down here in the car," the man said in a mild baritone.

"I was not!" she snapped. That settled, she turned to me. "This is my cousin, Calvin Leeds. He didn't want me to come here, but I brought him along anyhow. Where's Mr. Wolfe?"

I indicated the door to the office, went and opened it, and ushered them in.

I have never figured out Wolfe's grounds for deciding whether or not to get to his feet when a woman enters his office. If they're objective they're too complicated for me, and if they're subjective I wouldn't know where to start. This time he kept his seat behind his desk in the corner near a window, merely nodding and murmuring when I pronounced names. I thought for a second that Mrs. Rackham was standing gazing at him in reproach for his bad manners, but then I saw it was just surprised disbelief that he could be that big and fat. I'm so used to the quantity of him that I'm apt to forget how he must impress people seeing him for the first time.

He aimed a thumb at the red leather chair beyond the end of his desk and muttered at her, "Sit down, madam."

She went and sat. I then did likewise, at my own desk, not far from Wolfe's and at right angles to it. Calvin Leeds, the cousin, had sat twice, first on the couch toward the rear and then on a chair which I moved up for him. I would have guessed that both he and Mrs. Rackham had first seen the light about the same time as the twentieth century, but he could have been a little older. He had a lot of weather in his face with its tough-looking hide, his hair had been brown but was now more gray, and with his medium size and weight he looked and moved as if all his inside springs were still sound and lively. He had taken Wolfe in, and the surroundings too, and now his eyes were on his cousin.

Mrs. Rackham spoke to Wolfe. "You couldn't very well go around finding out things. Could you?"

"I don't know," he said politely. "I haven't tried for years, and I don't intend to. Others go around for me." He gestured at me. "Mr. Goodwin, of course, and others as required. You need someone to go around?"

"Yes." She paused. Her mouth worked. "I think I do. Provided it can be done safely—I mean, without anyone knowing about it." Her mouth worked some more. "I am bitterly ashamed—having at my age, for the first time in my life—having to go to a private detective with my personal affairs."

"Then you shouldn't have come," Leeds said mildly.

"Then you have come too soon," Wolfe told her.

"Too soon? Why?"

"You should have waited until it became so urgent or so intolerable that it would cause you no shame to ask for help, especially from one as expensive as me." He shook his head. "Too soon. Come back if and when you must."

"Hear that, Sarah?" Leeds asked, but not rubbing it in.

Ignoring him, she leaned forward and blurted at Wolfe, "No, I'm here now. I have to know! I have to know about my husband!"

Wolfe's head jerked around to me, to give me a look intended to scorch. But I met his eyes and told him emphatically, "No, sir. If it is, she fibbed. I told her we wouldn't touch divorce or separation evidence, and she said it wasn't."

He left me and demanded, "Do you want your husband followed?"

"I—I don't know. I don't think so—"

"Do you suspect him of infidelity?"

"No! I don't!"

Wolfe grunted, leaned back in his chair, squirmed to get comfortable, and muttered, "Tell me about it."

Mrs. Rackham's jaw started to quiver. She looked at Leeds. His brows went up, and he shook his head, not as a negative apparently, but merely leaving it to her. Wolfe let out a grunt. She moved her eyes to him and said plaintively, "I'm neurotic."

"I am not," Wolfe snapped, "a psychiatrist. I doubt if—"

She cut him off. "I've been neurotic as long as I can remember. I had no brother or sister and my mother died when I was three, and my father didn't enjoy my company because I was ugly. When he died—I was twenty then—I cried all during the funeral service, not because he was dead but because I knew he wouldn't have wanted me so close to him all that time —in the church and driving to the cemetery and there at the grave."

Her jaw started to quiver again, but she clamped it and got control. "I'm telling you this because it's no secret anyway, and I want you to understand why I must have help. I have never been sure exactly why my first husband married me, because he had money of his own and didn't really need mine, but it wasn't long until he hated looking at me just as my father had. So I—"

"That isn't true, Sarah," Calvin Leeds objected. "You imagined—"

"Bosh!" she quashed him. "I'm not that neurotic! So I got a divorce with his consent and gratitude, I think, though he was too polite to say so, and I hurried it through because I didn't want him to know I was pregnant. Soon after the divorce my son was born, and that made complications, but

I kept him—I kept him and he was mine until he went to war. He never
showed the slightest sign of feeling about my looks the way my father and
my husband had. He was never embarrassed about me. He liked being with
me. Didn't he, Calvin?"

"Of course he did," Leeds assured her, apparently meaning it.

She nodded and looked thoughtful, looking into space and seeing something not there. She jerked herself impatiently back to Wolfe. "I admit that
before he went away, to war, he got married, and he married a very beautiful girl. It is not true that I wished he had taken one who resembled me,
even a little bit, but naturally I couldn't help but see that he had gone to
the other extreme. Annabel is very beautiful. It made me proud for my son
to have her—it seemed to even my score with all the beautiful women I
had known and seen. She thinks I hate her, but that is not true. People as
neurotic as I am should not be judged by normal standards. Not that I
blame Annabel, for I know perfectly well that when the news came that
he had been killed in Germany her loss was greater than mine. He wasn't
mine any longer then, he was hers."

"Excuse me," Wolfe put in politely but firmly. "You wanted to consult
me about your husband. You say you're divorced?"

"Certainly not! I—" She caught herself up. "Oh. This is my second husband. I only wanted you to understand."

"I'll try. Let's have him now."

"Barry Rackham," she said, pronouncing the name as if she held the copy-
right on it, or at least a lease on subsidiary rights. "He played football at
Yale and then had a job in Wall Street until the war came. At the end of
the war he was a major, which wasn't very far to get in nearly four years. We
were married in 1946—three years and seven months ago. He is ten years
younger than I am."

Mrs. Barry Rackham paused, her eyes fixed on Wolfe's face as if chal-
lenging it for comment, but the challenge was declined. Wolfe merely
prodded her with a murmur.

"And?"

"I suppose," she said as if conceding a point, "there is no one in New
York who does not take it for granted that he married me simply for my
money. They all know more about it than I do, because I have never asked
him, and he is the only one that knows for sure. I know one thing: it does
not make him uncomfortable to look at me. I know that for sure because
I'm very sensitive about it, I'm neurotic about it, and I would know it the
first second he felt that way. Of course he knows what I look like, he knows
how ugly I am, he can't help that, but it doesn't annoy him a particle, not
even—"

She stopped and was blushing. Calvin Leeds coughed and shifted in his chair. Wolfe closed his eyes and after a moment opened them again. I didn't look away from her because when she blushed I began to feel a little uncomfortable myself, and I wanted to see if I could keep her from knowing it.

But she wasn't interested in me. "Anyway," she went on as the color began to leave, "I have kept things in my own hands. We live in my house, of course, town and country, and I pay everything, and there are the cars and so on, but I made no settlement and arranged no allowance for him. That didn't seem to me to be the way to handle it. When he needed cash for anything he asked for it and I gave it to him freely, without asking questions." She made a little gesture, a flip of a hand. "Not always, but nearly always. The second year it was more than the first, and the third year more again, and I felt he was getting unreasonable. Three times I gave him less than he asked for, quite a lot less, and once I refused altogether—I still asked no questions, but he told me why he needed it and tried to persuade me; he was very nice about it, and I refused. I felt that I must draw the line somewhere. Do you want to know the amounts?"

"Not urgently," Wolfe muttered.

"The last time, the time I refused, it was fifteen thousand dollars." She leaned forward. "And that *was* the last time. It was seven months ago, October second, and he has not asked for money since, not once! But he spends a great deal, more than formerly. For all sorts of things—just last week he gave a dinner, quite expensive, for thirty-eight men at the University Club. I have to know where he gets it. I decided that some time ago—two months ago—and I didn't know what to do. I didn't want to speak to my lawyer or banker about a thing like this, or in fact anybody, and I couldn't do it myself, so I asked my cousin, Calvin Leeds." She sent him a glance. "He said he would try to find out something, but he hasn't."

We looked at Leeds. He upturned a palm.

"Well," he said, half apology and half protest, "I'm no trained detective. I asked him straight, and he just laughed at me. You didn't want anyone else to get a hint of it, that you were curious about money he wasn't getting from you, so I was pretty limited in my asking around. I did my best, Sarah, you know I did."

"It seems to me," Wolfe told her, "that Mr. Leeds had one good idea—asking him. Have you tried that yourself?"

"Certainly. Long ago. He told me that an investment he had made was doing well."

"Maybe it was. Why not?"

"Not with my husband." She was positive. "I know how he is with money. It isn't in him to make an investment. Another thing: he is away more now. I don't know where he is as much as I used to. I don't mean weeks or even days, just an afternoon or evening—and several times he has had an appointment that he couldn't break when I wanted him to—"

Wolfe grunted, and she was at him. "I know! You think I feel that I've bought him and I own him! That's not it at all! All I really want is to be like a wife, just any wife—not beautiful and not ugly, not rich and not poor— just a wife! And hasn't a wife a right to know the source of her husband's income—isn't it her *duty* to know? If you had a wife wouldn't you *want* her to know?"

Wolfe made a face. "I can tell you, madam, what I *don't* want. I don't want this job. I think you're gulling me. You suspect that your husband is swindling you, either emotionally or financially, and you want me to catch him at it." He turned to me. "Archie. You'll have to change that formula. Hereafter, when a request comes for an appointment, do not say merely that we will not undertake to get divorce or separation evidence. Make it clear that we will not engage to expose a husband for a wife, or a wife for a husband, under any camouflage. May I ask what you are doing, Mrs. Rackham?"

She had opened her brown leather handbag and taken out a checkfold and a little gold fountain pen. Resting the checkfold on the bag, she was writing in it with the pen. Wolfe's question got no reply until she had finished writing, torn out the check, returned the fold and pen to the bag, and snapped the bag shut. Then she looked at him.

"I don't want you to expose my husband, Mr. Wolfe." She was holding the check with her thumb and fingertip. "God knows I don't! I just want to know. You're not ugly and afraid and neurotic like me, you're big and handsome and successful and not afraid of anything. When I knew I had to have help and my cousin couldn't do it, and I wouldn't go to anyone I knew, I went about it very carefully. I found out all about you, and no one knows I did, or at least why I did. If my husband is doing something that will hurt me that will be the end; but I don't want to expose him, I just have to know. You are the greatest detective on earth, and you're an honest man. I just want to pay you for finding out where and how my husband is getting money, that's all. You can't possibly say you won't do it. Not possibly!"

She left her chair and went to put the check on his desk in front of him. "It's for ten thousand dollars, but that doesn't mean I think that's enough. Whatever you say. But don't you dare say I want to expose him! My God— expose him?"

She had my sympathy up to a point, but what stuck out was her basic assumption that rich people can always get anything they want just by putting up the dough. That's enough to give an honest workingman, like a private detective for instance, a pain in three places. The assumption is of course sound in some cases, but what rich people are apt not to understand is that there are important exceptions.

This, however, was not one of them, and I hoped Wolfe would see that it wasn't. He did. He didn't want to, but the bank account had by no means fully recovered from the awful blow of March fifteenth, only three weeks back, and he knew it. He came forward in his chair for a glance at the check, caught my eye and saw how I felt about it, heaved a sigh, and spoke.

"Your notebook, Archie. Confound it."

II

THE following morning, Saturday, I was in the office typing the final report on a case which I will not identify by name because it was never allowed to get within a mile of a newspaper or a microphone. We were committed on Mrs. Rackham's job, since I had deposited her check Friday afternoon, but no move had been made yet, not even a phone call to any of the names she had given us, because it was Wolfe's idea that first of all we must have a look at him. With Wolfe's settled policy of never leaving his house on business, and with no plausible excuse for getting Barry Rackham to the office, I would have to do the looking, and that had been arranged for.

Mrs. Rackham had insisted that her husband must positively not know or even suspect that he was being investigated, and neither must anyone else, so the arrangements for the look were a little complicated. She vetoed my suggestion that I should be invited to join a small week-end gathering at her country home in Westchester, on the ground that someone would probably recognize the Archie Goodwin who worked for Nero Wolfe. It was Calvin Leeds who offered an amendment that was adopted. He had a little place of his own at the edge of her estate, where he raised dogs, called Hillside Kennels. A month ago one of his valuable dogs had been poisoned, and I was to go there Saturday afternoon as myself, a detective named Archie Goodwin, to investigate the poisoning. His cousin would invite him to her place, Birchvale, for dinner, and I would go along.

It was a quiet Saturday morning in the office, with Wolfe up in the plant rooms as usual from nine to eleven, and I finished typing the report of a certain case with no interruptions except a couple of phone calls which I handled myself, and one for which I had to give Wolfe a buzz—from somebody at Mummiani's on Fulton Street to say that they had just got eight pounds of fresh sausage from Bill Darst at Hackettstown, and Wolfe could have half of it. Since Wolfe regards Darst as the best sausage maker west of Cherbourg, he asked that it be sent immediately by messenger, and for heaven's sake not with dry ice.

When, at 11:01, the sound of Wolfe's elevator came, I got the big dictionary in front of me on my desk, opened to H, and was bent over it as he entered the office, crossed to his oversized custom-built chair, and sat. He didn't bite at once because his mind was elsewhere. Even before he rang for beer he asked, "Has the sausage come?"

Without looking up I told him no.

He pressed the button twice—the beer signal—leaned back, and frowned at me. I didn't see the frown, absorbed as I was in the dictionary, but it was in his tone of voice.

"What are you looking up?" he demanded.

"Oh, just a word," I said casually. "Checking up on our client. I thought she was illiterate, her calling you handsome—remember? But, by gum, it was merely an understatement. Here it is, absolutely kosher: 'Handsome: moderately large.' For an example it gives 'a handsome sum of money.' So she was dead right, you're a handsome detective, meaning a moderately large detective." I closed the dictionary and returned it to its place, remarking cheerfully, "Live and learn!"

It was a dud. Ordinarily that would have started him tossing phrases and adjectives, but he was occupied. Maybe he didn't even hear me. When Fritz came from the kitchen with the beer, Wolfe, taking from a drawer the gold bottle opener that a pleased client had given him, spoke.

"Fritz, good news. We're getting some of Mr. Darst's sausage—four pounds."

Fritz let his eyes gleam. "Ha! Today?"

"Any moment." Wolfe poured beer. "That raises the question of cloves again. What do you think?"

"I'm against it," Fritz said firmly.

Wolfe nodded. "I think I agree. I *think* I do. You may remember what Marko Vukcic said last year—and by the way, he must be invited for a taste of this. For Monday luncheon?"

"That would be possible," Fritz conceded, "but we have arranged for shad with roe—"

"Of course." Wolfe lifted his glass and drank, put it down empty, and used his handkerchief on his lips. That, he thought, was the only way for a man to scent a handkerchief. "We'll have Marko for the sausage at Monday dinner, followed by duck Mondor." He leaned forward and wiggled a finger. "Now about the shallots and fresh thyme: there's no use depending on Mr. Colson. We might get diddled again. Archie will have to go—"

At that point Archie had to go answer the doorbell, which I was glad to do. I fully appreciate, mostly anyhow, the results of Wolfe's and Fritz's pow-wows on grub when it arrives at the table, but the gab often strikes me as overdone. So I didn't mind the call to the hall and the front door. There I found a young man with a pug nose and a package, wearing a cap that said "Fleet Messenger Service." I signed the slip, shut the door, started back down the hall, and was met not only by Fritz but by Wolfe too, who can move well enough when there's something he thinks is worth moving for. He took the package from me and headed for the kitchen, followed by Fritz and me.

The small carton was sealed with tape. In the kitchen Wolfe put it on the long table, reached to the rack for a knife, cut the tape, and pulled the flaps up. My reflexes are quick, and the instant the hissing noise started I grabbed Wolfe's arm to haul him back, yelling at Fritz, "Watch out! Drop!"

Wolfe can move all right, considering what he has to move. He and I went through the open door into the hall before the explosion came, and Fritz came bounding after, pulling the door with him. We all kept going, along the short stretch of hall to the office door, and into the office. There we stopped dead. No explosion yet.

"It's still hissing," I said, and moved.

"Come back here!" Wolfe commanded.

"Be quiet," I commanded back, and dropped to my hands and knees and made it into the hall. There I stopped to sniff, crawled to within a yard of the crack under the kitchen door, and sniffed again.

I arose, returned to the office on my feet, and told them, "Gas. Tear gas, I think. The hissing has stopped."

Wolfe snorted.

"No sausage," Fritz said grimly.

"If it had been a trigger job on a grenade," I told him, "there would have been plenty of sausage. Not for us, of us. Now it's merely a damn nuisance. You'd better sit here and chat a while."

I marched to the hall and shut the door behind me, went and opened the front door wide, came back and stood at the kitchen door and took a full breath, opened the door, raced through and opened the back door into the courtyard, and ran back again to the front. Even there the air current was too gassy for comfort, so I moved out to the stoop. I had been there only a moment when I heard my name called.

"Archie!"

I turned. Wolfe's head with its big oblong face was protruding from a window of the front room.

"Yes, sir," I said brightly.

"Who brought that package?"

I told him Fleet Messenger Service.

When the breeze through the hall had cleared the air I returned to the kitchen and Fritz joined me. We gave the package a look and found it was quite simple: a metal cylinder with a valve, with a brass rod that had been adjusted so that when the package was opened so was the valve. There was still a strong smell, close up, and Fritz took it to the basement. I went to the office and found Wolfe behind his desk, busy at the phone.

I dropped into my chair and dabbed at my runny eyes with my handkerchief. When he hung up I asked, "Any luck?"

"I didn't expect any," he growled.

"Right. Shall I call a cop?"

"No."

I nodded. "The question was rhetorical." I dabbed at my eyes some more, and blew my nose. "Nero Wolfe does not call cops. Nero Wolfe opens his own packages of sausage and makes his own enemies bite the dust." I blew my nose again. "Nero Wolfe is a man who will go far if he opens one package too many. Nero Wolfe has never—"

"The question was not rhetorical," Wolfe said rudely. "That is not what rhetorical means."

"No? I asked it. I meant it to be rhetorical. Can you prove that I don't know what rhetorical means?" I blew my nose. "When you ask me a question, which God knows is often, do I assume—"

The phone rang. One of the million things I do to earn my salary is to answer it, so I did. And then a funny thing happened. There is absolutely no question that it was a shock to me to hear that voice, I know that, because I felt it in my stomach. But partly what makes a shock a shock is that it is unexpected, and I do not think the sound of that voice in my ear was unexpected. I think that Wolfe and I had been sitting there talking just to hear ourselves because we both expected, after what had happened, to hear that voice sooner or later—and probably sooner.

What it said was only, "May I speak to Mr. Wolfe, please?"

I felt it in my stomach, sharp and strong, but damned if I was going to let him know it. I said, but not cordially, "Oh, hello there. If I get you. Was your name Duncan once?"

"Yes. Mr. Wolfe, please."

"Hold the wire." I covered the transmitter and told Wolfe, "Whosis."

"Who?" he demanded.

"You know who from my face. Mr. X. Mr. Z. Him."

With his lips pressed tight, Wolfe reached for his phone. "This is Nero Wolfe."

"How do you do, Mr. Wolfe." I was staying on, and the hard, cold, precise voice sounded exactly as it had the four previous times I had heard it, over a period of three years. It pronounced all its syllables clearly and smoothly. "Do you know who I am?"

"Yes." Wolfe was curt. "What do you want?"

"I want to call your attention to my forbearance. That little package could have been something really destructive, but I preferred only to give you notice. As I told you about a year ago, it's a more interesting world with you in it."

"I find it so," Wolfe said dryly.

"No doubt. Besides, I haven't forgotten your brilliant exposure of the murderer of Louis Rony. It happened then that your interest ran with mine. But it doesn't now, with Mrs. Barry Rackham, and that won't do. Because of my regard for you, I don't want you to lose a fee. Return her money and withdraw, and two months from today I shall send you ten thousand dollars in cash. Twice previously you have disregarded similar requests from me, and circumstances saved you. I advise strongly against a repetition. You will have to understand—"

Wolfe took the phone from his ear and placed it on the cradle. Since the effect of that would be lost if my line stayed open, I did likewise, practically simultaneously.

"By God, we're off again," I began. "Of all the rotten—"

"Shut up," Wolfe growled.

I obeyed. He rested his elbows on his chair arms, interlaced his fingers in front of where he was roundest, and gazed at a corner of his desk blotter. I did not, as a matter of fact, have anything to say except that it was a lousy break, and that didn't need saying. Wolfe had once ordered me to forget that I had ever heard the name Arnold Zeck, but whether I called him Zeck or Whosis or X, he was still the man who, some ten months ago, had arranged for two guys with an SM and a tommy gun to open up on Wolfe's plant rooms from a roof across the street, thereby ruining ten thousand dollars' worth of glass and equipment and turning eight thousand valuable orchid plants into a good start on a compost heap. That had been intended just for a warning.

Now he was telling us to lay off of Barry Rackham. That probably meant that without turning a finger we had found the answer to Mrs. Rackham's question—where was her husband getting his pocket money? He had got inside the circle of Arnold Zeck's operations, about which Wolfe had once remarked that all of them were illegal and some of them were morally repulsive. And Zeck didn't want any snooping around one of his men. That was almost certainly the sketch, but whether it was or not, the fact remained that we had run smack into Zeck again, which was fully as bad as having a gob of Darst sausage turn into a cylinder of tear gas.

"He likes to time things right, damn him," I complained. "He likes to make things dramatic. He had someone within range of this house to see the package being delivered, and when I left the front door open and then went and stood on the stoop that showed that the package had been opened, and as soon as he got the word he phoned. Hell, he might even—"

I stopped because I saw that I was talking to myself. Wolfe wasn't hearing me. He still sat gazing at the corner of the blotter. I shut my trap and sat and gazed at him. It was a good five minutes before he spoke.

"Archie," he said, looking at me.

"Yes, sir."

"How many cases have we handled since last July?"

"All kinds? Everything? Oh, forty."

"I would have thought more. Very well, say forty. We crossed this man's path inadvertently two years ago, and again last year. He and I both deal with crime, and his net is spread wide, so that may be taken as a reasonable expectation for the future: once a year, or in one out of every forty cases that come to us, we will run into him. This episode will be repeated." He aimed a thumb at the phone. "That thing will ring, and that confounded voice will presume to dictate to us. If we obey the dictate we will be maintaining this office and our means of livelihood only by his sufferance. If we defy it we shall be constantly in a state of trepidant vigilance, and one or both of us will probably get killed. Well?"

I shook my head. "It couldn't be made plainer. I don't care much for either one."

"Neither do I."

"If you got killed I'd be out of a job, and if I got killed you might as well retire." I glanced at my wristwatch. "The hell of it is we haven't got a week to decide. It's twelve-twenty, and I'm expected at the Hillside Kennels at three o'clock, and I have to eat lunch and shave and change my clothes. That is, if I go. If I go?"

"Precisely." Wolfe sighed. "That's the point. Two years ago, in the Orchard case, I took to myself the responsibility of ignoring this man's threat. Last year, in the Kane case, I did the same. This time I don't want to and I won't. Basic policy is my affair, I know that, but I am not going to tell you that in order to earn your pay you must go up there today and look at Mr. Rackham. If you prefer, you may phone and postpone it, and we'll consider the matter at greater length."

I had my brows raised at him. "I'll be damned. Put it on me, huh?"

"Yes. My nerve is gone. If public servants and other respected citizens take orders from this man, why shouldn't I?"

"You damn faker," I said indulgently. "You know perfectly well that I would rather eat soap than have you think I would knuckle under to that son of a bitch, and I know that you would rather put horseradish on oysters than have me think you would. I might if you didn't know about it, and you might if I didn't know about it, but as it is we're stuck."

Wolfe sighed again, deeper. "I take it that you're going?"

"I am. But under one condition, that the trepidant vigilance begins as of now. That you call Fritz in, and Theodore down from the plant rooms, and tell them what we're up against, and the chain bolts are to be kept constantly on both doors, and you keep away from windows, and nothing and no one is to be allowed to enter when I'm not here."

"Good heavens," he objected sourly, "that's no way to live."

"You can't tell till you try it. In ten years you may like it fine." I buzzed the plant rooms on the house phone to get Theodore.

Wolfe sat scowling at me.

III

WHEN, swinging the car off Taconic State Parkway to hit Route 100, my dash clock said only 2:40, I decided to make a little detour. It would be only a couple of miles out of my way. So at Pines Bridge I turned right, instead of left across the bridge. It wouldn't serve my purpose to make for the entrance to the estate where EASTCREST was carved on the great stone pillar, since all I would see there was a driveway curving up through the woods, and I turned off a mile short of that to climb a bumpy road up a hill. At the top the road went straight for a stretch between meadows, and I eased the car off onto the grass, stopped, and took the binoculars and aimed them at the summit of the next hill, somewhat higher than the one I was on, where the roof and upper walls of a stone mansion showed above the trees. Now, in early April, with no leaves yet, and with the binoculars, I could see most of the mansion and even something of the surrounding grounds, and a couple of men moving about.

That was Eastcrest, the legal residence of the illegal Arnold Zeck—but of course there are many ways of being illegal. One is to drive through a red light. Another is to break laws by proxy only, for money only, get your cut so it can't be traced, and never try to buy a man too cheap. That was what Zeck had been doing for more than twenty years—and there was Eastcrest.

All I was after was to take a look, just case it from a hilltop. I had never seen Zeck, and as far as I knew Wolfe hadn't either. Now that we were headed at him for the third time, and this time it might be for keeps, I thought I should at least see his roof and count his chimneys. That was all. He had been too damn remote and mysterious. Now I knew he had four chimneys, and that the one on the south wing had two loose bricks.

I turned the car around and headed down the hill, and, if you care to believe it, I kept glancing in the mirror to see if something showed up behind. That was how far gone I was on Zeck. It was not healthy for my self-respect, it was bad for my nerves, and I was good and tired of it.

Mrs. Rackham's place, Birchvale, was only five miles from there, the other side of Mount Kisco, but I made a wrong turn and didn't arrive until a

quarter past three. The entrance to her estate was adequate but not impos-
ing. I went on by, and before I knew it there was a neat little sign on the
left:

HILLSIDE KENNELS
Doberman Pinschers

The gate opening was narrow and so was the drive, and I kept going on
past the house to a bare rectangle in the rear, not very well graveled, and
maneuvered into a corner close to a wooden building. As I climbed out a
voice came from somewhere, and then a ferocious wild beast leaped from
behind a bush and started for me like a streak of lightning. I froze except
for my right arm, which sent my hand to my shoulder holster automatically.

A female voice sounded sharp in command. "Back!"

The beast, ten paces from me, whirled on a dime, trotted swiftly to the
woman who had appeared at the edge of the rectangle, whirled again and
stood facing me, concentrating with all its might on looking beautiful and
dangerous. I could have plugged it with pleasure. I do not like dogs that
assume you're guilty until you prove you're innocent. I like democratic dogs.

A man had appeared beside the woman. They advanced.

She spoke. "Mr. Goodwin? Mr. Leeds had to go on an errand, but he'll be
back soon. I'm Annabel Frey." She came to me and offered a hand, and I
took it.

This was my first check on an item of information furnished us by Mrs.
Rackham, and I gave her an A for accuracy. She had said that her daughter-
in-law was very beautiful. Some might have been inclined to argue it, for
instance those who don't like eyes so far apart or those who prefer pink skin
to dark, but I'm not so finicky about details. The man stepped up, and she
pronounced his name, Hammond, and we shook. He was a stocky middle-
aged specimen in a bright blue shirt, a tan jacket, and gray slacks—a hell of a
combination. I was wearing a mixed tweed made by Fradick, with an off-
white shirt and a maroon tie.

"I'll sit in my car," I told them, "to wait for Mr. Leeds. With the livestock
around loose like that."

She laughed. "Duke isn't loose, he's with me. He wouldn't have touched
you. He would have stopped three paces off, springing distance, and waited
for me. Don't you like dogs?"

"It depends on the dog. You might as well ask if I like lemon pie. With a
dog who thinks of space between him and me only in terms of springing
distance, my attitude is strictly one of trepidant vigilance."

"My Lord." She blinked long lashes over dark blue eyes. "Do you always
talk like that?" The eyes went to Hammond. "Did you get that, Dana?"

"I quite agree with him," Hammond declared, "as you know. I'm not afraid to say so, either, because it shows the lengths I'll go to, to be with you. When you opened his kennel and he leaped out I could feel my hair standing up."

"I know," Annabel Frey said scornfully. "Duke knows too. I guess I'd better put him in." She left us, speaking to the dog, who abandoned his pose and trotted to her, and they disappeared around a corner of the building. There was a similarity in the movements of the two, muscular and sure and quick, but sort of nervous and dainty.

"Now we can relax," I told Hammond.

"I just can't help it," he said, irritated. "I'm not strong for dogs anyhow, and with these . . ." He shrugged. "I'd just as soon go for a walk with a tiger."

Soon Annabel rejoined us, with a crack about Hammond's hair. I suggested that if they had something to do I could wait for Leeds without any help, but she said no.

"We only came to see you," she stated impersonally. "That is, I did, and Mr. Hammond went to the length of coming along. Just to see you, even if you are Archie Goodwin, I wouldn't cross the street; but I want to watch you work. So many things fall short of the build-up, I want to see if a famous detective does. I'm skeptical already. You look younger than you should, and you dress too well, and if you really thought that dog might jump you, you should have done something to—where did that come from? Hey!"

Sometimes I fumble a little drawing from my armpit, but that time it had been slick and clean. I had the barrel pointed straight up. Hammond had made a noise and an involuntary backward jerk.

I grinned at her. "Showing off. Okay? Want to try it? Get him and send him out from behind that same bush, with orders to take me, and any amount up to two bits, even, that he won't reach me." I returned the gun to the holster. "Ready?"

She blinked. "You mean you *would*?"

Hammond giggled. He was a full-sized middle-aged man and he looked like a banker, and I want to be fair to him, but he giggled. "Look out, Annabel," he said warningly. "He might."

"Of course," I told her, "you would be in the line of fire, and I've never shot a fast-moving dog, so we would both be taking a risk. Only I don't like you being skeptical. Stick around and you'll see."

That was a mistake, caused by my temperament. It is natural and wholesome for a man of my age to enjoy association with a woman of her age, maid, wife, or widow, but I should have had sense enough to stop to realize what I was getting in for. She had said that she had come to watch me work, and there I was asking for it. As a result, I had to spend a solid hour pretending that I was hell bent to find out who had poisoned one of Leeds' dogs when I didn't care a hang. Not that I love dog-poisoners, but that wasn't what was on my mind.

When Calvin Leeds showed up, as he did soon in an old station wagon with its rear taken up with a big wire cage, the four of us made a tour of the kennels and the runs, with Leeds briefing me, and me asking questions and making notes, and then we went in the house and extended the inquiry to aspects such as the poison used, the method employed, the known suspects, and so on. It was a strain. I had to make it good, because that was what I was supposed to be there for, and also because Annabel was too good-looking to let her be skeptical about me. And the dog hadn't even died! He was alive and well. But I went to it as if it were the biggest case of the year for Nero Wolfe and me, and Leeds got a good fifty bucks' worth of detection for nothing. Of course nobody got detected, but I asked damn good questions.

After Annabel and Hammond left to return to Birchvale next door, I asked Leeds about Hammond, and sure enough he was a banker. He was a vice-president of the Metropolitan Trust Company, who handled affairs for Mrs. Rackham—had done so ever since the death of her first husband. When I remarked that Hammond seemed to have it in mind to handle Mrs. Rackham's daughter-in-law also, Leeds said he hadn't noticed. I asked who else would be there at dinner.

"You and me," Leeds said. He was sipping a highball, taking his time with it. We were in the little living room of his little house, about which there was nothing remarkable except the dozens of pictures of dogs on the walls. Moving around outside, there had been more spring to him than to lots of guys half his age; now he was sprawled on a couch, all loose. I was reminded of one of the dogs we had come upon during our tour, lying in the sun at the door of its kennel.

"You and me," he said, "and my cousin and her husband, and Mrs. Frey, whom you have met, and Hammond, and the statesman, that's seven—"

"Who's the statesman?"

"Oliver A. Pierce."

"I'm intimate with lots of statesmen, but I never heard of him."

"Don't let him know it." Leeds chuckled. "It's true that at thirty-four he has only got as far as state assemblyman, but the war made a gap for him the same as for other young men. Give him a chance. One will be enough."

"What is he, a friend of the family?"

"No, and that's one on him." He chuckled again. "When he was first seen here, last summer, he came as a guest of Mrs. Frey—that is, invited by her— but before long either she had seen enough of him or he had seen enough of her. Meanwhile, however, he had seen Lina Darrow, and he was caught anyhow."

"Who's Lina Darrow?"

"My cousin's secretary—by the way, she'll be at dinner too, that'll make eight. I don't know who invited him—my cousin perhaps—but it's Miss Darrow that gets him here, a busy statesman." Leeds snorted. "At his age he might know better."

"You don't think much of women, huh?"

"I don't think of them at all. Much or little." Leeds finished his drink. "Look at it. Which would you rather live with, those wonderful animals out there, or a woman?"

"A woman," I said firmly. "I haven't run across her yet, there are so many, but even if she does turn out to be a dog I hope to God it won't be one of yours. I want the kind I can let run loose." I waved a hand. "Forget it. You like 'em, you can have 'em. Mrs. Frey is a member of the household, is she?"

"Yes," he said shortly.

"Mrs. Rackham keeping her around as a souvenir of her dead son? Being neurotic about it?"

"I don't know. Ask her." Leeds straightened up and got to his feet. "You know, of course, that I didn't approve of her going to Nero Wolfe. I went with her only because she insisted on it. I don't see how any good can come of it, but I think harm might. I don't think you ought to be here, but you are, and we might as well go on over and drink their liquor instead of mine. I'll go and wash up."

He left me.

IV

HAVING been given by Leeds my choice of driving over—three minutes—or taking a trail through the woods, I voted for walking. The edge of the woods was only a hundred yards to the rear of the kennels. It had been a warm day for early April, but now, with the sun gone over the hill, the sharp air made me want to step it up, which was just as well because I had to, to keep up with Leeds. He walked as if he meant it. When I commented on the fact that we ran into no fence anywhere, neither in the woods nor in the clear, he said that his place was merely a little corner of Mrs. Rackham's property which she had let him build on some years ago.

The last stretch of our walk was along a curving gravel path that wound through lawns, shrubs, trees, and different-shaped patches of bare earth. Living in the country would be more convenient if they would repeal the law against paths that go straight from one place to another place. The bigger and showier the grounds are, the more the paths have to curve, and the main reason for having lots of bushes and things is to compel the paths to curve in order to get through the mess. Anyhow, Leeds and I finally got to the house, and entered without ringing or knocking, so apparently he was more or less a member of the household too.

All six of them were gathered in a room that was longer and wider than Leeds' whole house, with twenty rugs to slide on and at least forty different things to sit on, but it didn't seem as if they had worked up much gaiety, in spite of the full stock of the portable bar, because Leeds and I were greeted as though nothing so nice had happened in years. Leeds introduced me, since I wasn't supposed to have met Mrs. Rackham, and after I had been supplied with liquid Annabel Frey gave a lecture on how I worked. Then Oliver A. Pierce, the statesman, wanted me to demonstrate by grilling each of them as suspected dog poisoners. When I tried to beg off they insisted, so I obliged. I was only so-so.

Pierce was a smooth article. His manner was of course based on the law of nature regulating the attitude of an elected person toward everybody old enough to vote, but his timing and variations were so good that it was hard to recognize it, although he was only about my age. He was also about my size, with broad shoulders and a homely honest face, and a draw on his smile as swift as a flash bulb. I made a note to look up whether I lived in his assembly district. If he got the breaks the only question about him was how far and how soon.

If in addition to his own equipment and talents he acquired Lina Darrow as a partner, it would probably be farther and sooner. She was, I would have guessed, slightly younger than Annabel Frey—twenty-six maybe—and I never saw a finer pair of eyes. She was obviously underplaying them, or rather what was back of them. When I was questioning her she pretended I had her in a corner, while her eyes gave it away that she could have waltzed all around me if she wanted to. I didn't know whether she thought she was kidding somebody, or was just practicing, or had some serious reason for passing herself off as a flub.

Barry Rackham had me stumped and also annoyed. Either I was dumber than Nero Wolfe thought I was, and twice as dumb as I thought I was, or he was smarter than he looked. New York was full of him, and he was full of New York. Go into any Madison Avenue bar between five and six-thirty and there would be six or eight of him there: not quite young but miles from being old; masculine all over except the fingernails; some tired and some fresh and ready, depending on the current status; and all slightly puffy below the eyes. I knew him from A to Z, or thought I did, but I couldn't make up my mind whether he knew what I was there for, and that was the one concrete thing I had hoped to get done. If he knew, the question whether he was on Zeck's payroll was answered; if he didn't, that question was still open.

And I still hadn't been able to decide when, at the dinner table, we had finished the dessert and got up to go elsewhere for coffee. At first I had thought he couldn't possibly be wise, when I had him sized up for a dummy who had had the good luck to catch Mrs. Rackham's eye somewhere and then had happened to take the only line she would fall for, but further observation had made me reconsider. His handling of his wife had character in it; it wasn't just yes or no. At the dinner table he had an exchange with Pierce about rent control, and without seeming to try he got the statesman so tangled up he couldn't wiggle loose. Then he had a good laugh, took the other side of the argument, and made a monkey out of Dana Hammond.

I decided I'd better start all over.

On the way back to the living room for coffee, Lina Darrow joined me. "Why did you take it out on me?" she demanded.

I said I didn't know I had.

"Certainly you did. Trying to indict me for dog poisoning. You went after me much harder than you did the others." Her fingers were on the inside of my arm, lightly.

"Certainly," I conceded. "Nothing new to you, was it? A man going after you harder than the others?"

"Thanks. But I mean it. Of course you know I'm just a working girl."

"Sure. That's why I was tougher with you. That, and because I wondered why you were playing dumb."

The statesman Pierce broke us up then, as we entered the living room, and I didn't fight for her. We collected in the neighborhood of the fireplace for coffee, and there was a good deal of talk about nothing, and after a while somebody suggested television, and Barry Rackham went and turned it on. He and Annabel turned out lights. As the rest of us got settled in favorably placed seats, Mrs. Rackham left us. A little later, as I sat in the semi-darkness scowling at a cosmetic commercial, some obscure sense told me that danger was approaching and I jerked my head around. It was right there at my elbow: a Doberman pinscher, looking larger than normal in that light, staring intently past me at the screen.

Mrs. Rackham, just behind it, apparently misinterpreting my quick movement, spoke hastily and loudly above the noise of the broadcast. "Don't try to pat him!"

"I won't," I said emphatically.

"He'll behave," she assured me. "He loves television." She went on with him, farther forward. As they passed Calvin Leeds the affectionate pet halted for a brief sniff, and got a stroke on the head in response. No one else was honored.

Ninety minutes of video got us to half-past ten, and got us nothing else, especially me. I was still on the fence about Barry Rackham. Television is raising hell with the detective business. It used to be that a social evening at someone's house or apartment was a fine opportunity for picking up lines and angles, moving around, watching and talking and listening; but with a television session you might as well be home in bed. You can't see faces, and if someone does make a remark you can't hear it unless it's a scream, and you can't even start a private inquiry, such as finding out where a young widow stands now on skepticism. In a movie theater at least you can hold hands.

However, I did finally get what might have been a nibble. The screen had been turned off, and we had all got up to stretch, and Annabel had offered to drive Leeds and me home, and Leeds had told her that we would rather walk, when Barry Rackham moseyed over to me and said he hoped the television hadn't bored me too much. I said no, just enough.

"Think you'll get anywhere on your job for Leeds?" he asked, jiggling his highball glass to make the ice tinkle.

I lifted my shoulders and let them drop. "I don't know. A month's gone by."

He nodded. "That's what makes it hard to believe."

"Yeah, why?"

"That he would wait a month and then decide to blow himself to a fee for Nero Wolfe. Everybody knows that Wolfe comes high. I wouldn't have thought Leeds could afford it." Rackham smiled at me. "Driving back to-night?"

"No, I'm staying over."

"That's sensible. Night driving is dangerous, I think. The Sunday traffic won't be bad this time of year if you leave early." He touched my chest with a forefinger. "That's it, leave early." He moved off.

Annabel was yawning, and Dana Hammond was looking at her as if that was exactly what he had come to Birchvale for, to see her yawn. Lina Darrow was looking from Barry Rackham to me and back again, and pretending she wasn't looking anywhere with those eyes. The Doberman pinscher was standing tense, and Pierce, from a safe ten feet—one more than springing distance—was regarding it with an expression that gave me a more sympathetic feeling for him than I ever expected to have for a statesman.

Calvin Leeds and Mrs. Rackham were also looking at the dog, with a quite different expression.

"At least two pounds overweight," Leeds was saying. "You feed him too much."

Mrs. Rackham protested that she didn't.

"Then you don't run him enough."

"I know it," she admitted. "I will from now on, I'll be here more. I was busy today. I'll take him out now. It's a perfect night for a good walk—Barry, do you feel like walking?"

He didn't. He was nice about it, but he didn't. She broadened the invitation to take in the group, but there were no takers. She offered to walk Leeds and me home, but Leeds said she would go too slow, and he should have been in bed long ago since his rising time was six o'clock. He moved, and told me to come on if I was coming.

We said good night and left.

The outdoor air was sharper now. There were a few stars but no moon, and alone with no flashlight I would never have been able to keep that trail through the woods and might have made the Hillside Kennels clearing by dawn. For Leeds a flashlight would have been only a nuisance. He strode along at the same gait as in the daytime, and I stumbled at his heels, catching my toes on things, teetering on roots and pebbles, and once going clear down. I am not a deerstalker and don't want to be. As we approached the kennels Leeds called out, and the sound came of many movements, but not a bark. Who wants a dog, let alone thirty or forty, not even human enough to bark when you come home?

Leeds said that since the poisoning he always took a look around before going to bed, and I went on in the house and up to the little room where I had put my bag. I was sitting on the bed in pajamas, scratching the side of my neck and considering Barry Rackham's last-minute remarks, when Leeds entered downstairs and came up to ask if I was comfortable. I told him I soon would be, and he said good night and went down the short hall to his room.

I opened a window, turned out the light, and got into bed; but in three minutes I saw it wasn't working. My practice is to empty my head simultaneously with dropping it on the pillow. If something sticks and doesn't want to come out I'll give it up to three minutes but no more. Then I act. This time, of course, it was Barry Rackham that stuck. I had to decide that he knew what I was there for or that he didn't, or, as an alternative, decide definitely that I wouldn't try to decide until tomorrow. I got out of bed and went and sat on a chair.

It may have taken five minutes, or it could have been fifteen; I don't know. Anyhow it didn't accomplish anything except getting Rackham unstuck from my head for the night, for the best I could do was decide for postponement. If he had his guard up, so far I had not got past it. With that settled, I got under the covers again, took ten seconds to get into position on a strange mattress, and was off this time. . . .

Nearly, but not quite. A shutter or something began to squeak. Calling it a shutter jerked me back part way, because there were no shutters on the windows, so it couldn't be that. I was now enough awake to argue. The sound continued, at brief intervals. It not only wasn't a shutter, it wasn't a squeak. Then it was a baby whining; but it wasn't, because it came from the open window, and there were no babies out there. To hell with it. I turned over, putting my back to the window, but the sound still came, and I had been wrong. It was more of a whimper than a whine. Oh, nuts.

I rolled out of bed, switched on a light, went down the hall to Leeds' door, knocked on it, and opened it.

"Well?" he asked, full voice.

"Have you got a dog that whimpers at night?"

"Whimpers? No."

"Then shall I go see what it is? I hear it through my window."

"It's probably—turn on the light, will you?"

I found the wall switch and flipped it. His pajamas were green with thin white stripes. Giving me a look which implied that here was one more reason for disapproving of my being there, he padded past me into the hall and on into my room, me following. He stood a moment to listen, crossed and stuck his head out the window, pulled it in again, and this time went by me with no look at all and moving fast. I followed him downstairs and to the side door, where he pushed a light switch with one hand while he opened the door with the other, and stepped across the sill.

"By God," he said. "All right, Nobby, all right."

He squatted.

I take back none of my remarks about Doberman pinschers, but I admit that that was no time to expand on them, nor did I feel like it. The dog lay on its side on the slab of stone with its legs twitching, trying to lift its head enough to look at Leeds; and from its side that was up, toward the belly and midway between the front and hind legs, protruded the chased silver handle of a knife. The hair around was matted with blood.

The dog had stopped whimpering. Now suddenly it bared its teeth and snarled, but weakly.

"All right, Nobby," Leeds said. He had his palm against the side, forward, over the heart.

"He's about gone," he said.

I discovered that I was shivering, decided to stop, and did.

"Pull the knife out of him?" I suggested. "Maybe—"

"No. That would finish him. I think he's finished anyhow."

He was. The dog died as Leeds squatted there and I stood not permitting myself to shiver in the cold night breeze. I could see the slender muscular legs stretch tight and then go loose, and after another minute Leeds took his hand away and stood up.

"Will you please hold the door open?" he asked. "It's off plumb and swings shut."

I obliged, holding it wide and standing aside to let him through. With the dog's body in his arms, he crossed to a wooden bench at one side of the little square hall and put the burden down. Then he turned to me. "I'm going to put something on and go out and look around. Come or stay, suit yourself."

"I'll come. Is it one of your dogs? Or—"

He had started for the stairs, but halted. "No. Sarah's—my cousin's. He was there tonight, you saw him." His face twitched. "By God, look at him! Getting here with that knife in him! I gave him to her two years ago; he's been her dog for two years, but when it came to this it was me he came to. By God!"

He went for the stairs and up, and I followed. Over the years there have been several occasions when I needed to get some clothes on without delay, and I thought I was fast, but I was still in my room with a shoe to lace when Leeds' steps were in the hall again and he called in to me, "Wait downstairs. I'll be back in a minute."

I called that I was coming, but he didn't halt. By the time I got down to the little square hall he was gone, and the outside door was shut. I opened it and stepped out and yelled, "Hey, Leeds!"

His voice came from somewhere in the darkness. "I said wait!"

Even if he had decided not to bother with me there was no use trying to dash after him, with my handicap, so I settled for making my way around the corner of the house and across the graveled rectangle to where my car was parked. Getting the door unlocked, I climbed in and got the flashlight from the dash compartment. That put me, if not even with Leeds for a night out-doors in the country, at least a lot closer to him. Relocking the car door, I sent the beam of the flash around and then switched it off and went back to the side door of the house.

I could hear steps, faint, then louder, and soon Leeds appeared within the area of light from the hall's window. He wasn't alone. With him was a dog, a length ahead of him, on a leash. As they approached I courteously stepped aside, but the dog ignored me completely. Leeds opened the door and they entered the hall, and I joined them.

"Get in front of her," Leeds said, "a yard off, and stand still."

I obeyed, circling.

"See, Hebe."

For the first time the beast admitted I was there. She lifted her head at me, then stepped forward and smelled my pants legs, not in haste. When she had finished Leeds crossed to where the dead dog lay on the bench, made a sign, and Hebe went to him.

Leeds passed his fingertips along the dead dog's belly, touching lightly the smooth short hair. "Take it, Hebe."

She stretched her sinewy neck, sniffed along the course his fingertips had taken, backed up a step, and looked up at him.

"Don't be so damn sure," Leeds told her. He pointed a finger. "Take it again."

She did so, taking more time for it, and again looked up at him.

"I didn't know they were hounds," I remarked.

"They're everything they ought to be." I suppose Leeds made some signal, though I didn't see it, and the dog started toward the door, with her master at the other end of the leash. "They have excellent scent, and this one's extraordinary. She's Nobby's mother."

Outside, on the slab of stone where we had found Nobby, Leeds said, "Take it, Hebe," and when she made a low noise in her throat as she tightened the leash, he added, "Quiet, now. I'll do the talking."

She took him, with me at their heels, around the corner of the house to the graveled space, across that, along the wall of the main outbuilding, and to a corner of the enclosed run. There she stopped and lifted her head.

Leeds waited half a minute before he spoke. "Bah. Can't you tell dogs apart? Take it!"

I switched the flashlight on, got a reprimand, and switched it off. Hebe made her throat noise again, got her nose down, and started off. We crossed the meadow on the trail to the edge of the woods and kept going. The pace was steady but not fast; for me it was an easy stroll, nothing like the race Leeds had led me previously. Even with no leaves on the trees it was a lot darker there, but unless my sense of direction was completely cockeyed we were sticking to the trail I had been over twice before.

"We're heading straight for the house, aren't we?" I asked.

For reply I got only a grunt.

For the first two hundred yards or so after entering the woods it was a steady climb, not steep, and then a leveling off for another couple of hundred yards to the start of the easy long descent to the edge of the Birchvale manicured grounds. It was at about the middle of the level stretch that Hebe suddenly went crazy. She dashed abruptly to one side, off the trail, jerking Leeds so that he had to dance to keep his feet, then whirled and came back into him, with a high thin quavering noise not at all like what she had said before.

Leeds spoke to her sharply, but I don't know what he said. By then my eyes had got pretty well accommodated to the circumstances. However, I am not saying that there in the dark among the trees, at a distance of twenty feet, I recognized the blob on the ground. I do assert that at the instant I pressed the button of the flashlight, before the light came, I knew already that it was the body of Mrs. Barry Rackham.

This time I got no reprimand. Leeds was with me as I stepped off the trail and covered the twenty feet. She was lying on her side, as Nobby had been, but her neck was twisted so that her face was nearly upturned to the sky, and I thought for a second it was a broken neck until I saw the blood on the front of her white sweater. I stooped and got my fingers on her wrist. Leeds picked up a dead leaf, laid it on her mouth and nostrils, and asked me to kneel to help him keep the breeze away.

When we had gazed at the motionless leaf for twenty seconds he said, "She's dead."

"Yeah." I stood up. "Even if she weren't, she would be by the time we got her to the house. I'll go—"

"She is dead, isn't she?"

"Certainly. I'll—"

"By God." He got erect, coming up straight in one movement. "Nobby and now her. You stay here—" He took a quick step, but I caught his arm. He jerked loose, violently.

I said fast, "Take it easy." I got his arm again, and he was trembling. "You bust in there and there's no telling what you'll do. Stay here and I'll go—"

He pulled free and started off.

"Wait!" I commanded, and he halted. "But first get a doctor and call the police. Do that first. I'm going to your place. We left that knife in the dog, and someone might want it. Can't you put Hebe on guard here?"

He spoke, not to me but to Hebe. She came to him, a darting shadow, close to him. He leaned over to touch the shoulder of the body of Mrs. Barry Rackham and said, "Watch it, Hebe." The dog moved alongside the body, and Leeds, with nothing to say to me, went. He didn't leap or run, but he sure was gone. I called after him, "Phone the police before you kill anybody!" stepped to the trail, and headed for Hillside Kennels.

With the flashlight I had no trouble finding my way. This time, as I approached, the livestock barked plenty, and, hoping the kennel doors were all closed tight, I had my gun out as I passed the runs and the buildings. Nothing attacked me but noise, and that stopped when I had entered the house and closed the door. Apparently if an enemy once got inside it was then up to the master.

Nobby was still there on the bench, and the knife was still in him. With only a glance at him in passing, I made for the little living room, where I had previously seen a phone on a table, turned on a light, went to the phone, and got the operator and gave her a number. As I waited a look at my wristwatch showed me five minutes past midnight. I hoped Wolfe hadn't forgotten to plug in the line to his room when he went up to bed. He hadn't. After the ring signal had come five times I had his voice.

"Nero Wolfe speaking."

"Archie. Sorry to wake you up, but I need orders. We're minus a client. Mrs. Rackham. This is a quick guess, but it looks as if someone stabbed her with a knife and then stuck the knife in a dog. Anyhow, she's dead. I've just—"

"What is this?" It was almost a bellow. "Flummery?"

"No, sir. I've just come from where she's lying in the woods. Leeds and I found her. The dog's dead too, here on a bench. I don't—"

"Archie!"

"Yes, sir."

"This is insupportable. In the circumstances."

"Yes, sir, all of that."

"Is Mr. Rackham out of it?"

"Not as far as I know. I told you we just found her."

"Where are you?"

"At Leeds' place, alone. I'm here guarding the knife in the dog. Leeds went to Birchvale to get a doctor and the cops and maybe to kill somebody. I can't help it. I've got all the time in the world. How much do you want?"

"Anything that might help."

"Okay, but in case I get interrupted here's a question first. On two counts, because I'm here working for you and because I helped find the body, they're going to be damn curious. How much do I spill? There's no one on this line unless the operator's listening in."

A grunt and a pause. "On what I know now, everything about Mrs. Rackham's talk with me and the purpose of your trip there. About Mrs. Rackham and Mr. Leeds and what you have seen and heard there, everything. But you will of course confine yourself strictly to that."

"Nothing about sausage?"

"Absolutely nothing. The question is idiotic."

"Yeah, I just asked. Okay. Well, I got here and met dogs and people. Leeds' place is on a corner of Mrs. Rackham's property, and we walked through the woods for dinner at Birchvale. There were eight of us at dinner. . . ."

I'm fairly good with a billiard cue, and only Saul Panzer can beat me at tailing a man or woman in New York, but what I am best at is reporting a complicated event to Nero Wolfe. With, I figured, a probable maximum of ten minutes for it, I covered all the essentials in eight, leaving him two for questions. He had some, of course. But I think he had the picture well enough to sleep on when I saw the light of a car through the window, told him good-by, and hung up. I stepped from the living room into the little hall, opened the outside door, and was standing on the stone slab as a car with STATE POLICE painted on it came down the narrow drive and stopped. Two uniformed public servants piled out and made for me. I only hoped neither of them was my pet Westchester hate, Lieutenant Con Noonan, and had my hope granted. They were both rank-and-file.

One of them spoke. "Your name Goodwin?"

I conceded it. Dogs had started to bark.

"After finding a dead body you went off and came here to rest your feet?"

"I didn't find the body. A dog did. As for my feet, do you mind stepping inside?"

I held the door open, and they crossed the threshold. With a thumb I called their attention to Nobby, on the bench.

"That's another dog. It had just crawled here to die, there on the doorstep. It struck me that Mrs. Rackham might have been killed with that knife before it was used on the dog, and that you guys would be interested in the knife as is, before somebody took it to slice bread with, for instance. So when Leeds went to the house to phone I came here. I have no corns."

One of them had stepped to the bench to look down at Nobby. He asked, "Have you touched the knife?"

"No."

"Was Leeds here with you?"

"Yes."

"Did he touch the knife?"

"I don't think so. If he did I didn't see him."

The cop turned to his colleague. "We won't move it, not now. You'd better stick here. Right?"

"Right."

"You'll be getting word. Come along, Goodwin."

He marched to the door and opened it and let me pass through first. Outdoors he crossed to his car, got in behind the wheel, and told me, "Hop in."

I stood. "Where to?"

"Where I'm going."

"I'm sorry," I said regretfully, "but I like to know where. If it's White Plains or a barracks, I would need a different kind of invitation. Either that or physical help."

"Oh, you're a lawyer."

"No, but I know a lawyer."

"Congratulations." He leaned toward me and spoke through his nose. "Mr. Goodwin, I'm driving to Mrs. Rackham's house, Birchvale. Would you care to join me?"

"I'd love to, thanks so much," I said warmly, and climbed in.

V

THE rest of that night, more than six hours, from half-past midnight until well after sunrise, I might as well have been in bed asleep for all I got out of it. I learned only one thing, that the sun rises on April ninth at 5:39, and even that wasn't reliable because I didn't know whether it was a true horizon.

Lieutenant Con Noonan was at Birchvale, among others, but his style was cramped.

Even after the arrival of District Attorney Cleveland Archer himself, the atmosphere was not one of single-minded devotion to the service of justice. Not that they weren't all for justice, but they had to keep it in perspective, and that's not so easy when a prominent wealthy taxpayer like Mrs. Barry Rackham has been murdered and your brief list of suspects includes (a) her husband, now a widower, who may himself now be a prominent wealthy taxpayer, (b) an able young politician who has been elected to the state assembly, (c) the dead woman's daughter-in-law, who may possibly be more of a prominent wealthy taxpayer than the widower, and (d) a vice-president of a billion-dollar New York bank. They're all part of the perspective, though you wish to God they weren't so you could concentrate on the other three suspects: (e) the dead woman's cousin, a breeder of dogs which don't make friends, (f) her secretary, a mere employee, and (g) a private dick from New York whose tongue has needed bobbing for some time. With a setup like that you can't just take them all down to White Plains and tell the boys to start chipping and save the pieces.

Except for fifteen minutes alone with Con Noonan, I spent the first two hours in the big living room where we had looked at television, having for company the members of the family, the guests, five members of the domestic staff, and two or more officers of the law. It wasn't a bit jolly. Two of the female servants wept intermittently. Barry Rackham walked up and down, sitting occasionally and then starting up again, speaking to no one. Oliver Pierce and Lina Darrow sat on a couch conversing in undertones, spasmodically, with him doing most of the talking. Dana Hammond, the banker, was jumpy. Mostly he sat slumped, with his chin down and his eyes closed, but now and then he would arise slowly as if something hurt and go to say something to one of the others, usually Annabel or Leeds. Leeds had been getting a blaze started in the fireplace when I was ushered in, and it continued to be his chief concern. He got the fire so hot that Annabel moved away, to the other side of the room. She was the quietest of them, but from the way she kept her jaw clamped I guessed that it wasn't because she was the least moved.

One by one they were escorted from the room for a private talk and brought back again. It was when my turn came, not long after I had arrived, that I found Lieutenant Noonan was around. He was in a smaller room down the hall, seated at a table, looking harassed. No doubt life was hard for him—born with the instincts of a Hitler or Stalin in a country where people are determined to do their own voting. The dick who took me in motioned me to a chair across the table.

"You again," Noonan said.

I nodded. "That's exactly what I was thinking. I haven't seen you since the time I didn't run my car over Louis Rony."

I didn't expect him to wince, and he didn't. "You're here investigating that dog poisoning at Hillside Kennels."

I had no comment.

"Weren't you?" he snapped. "If you're answering questions."

"Oh, I beg your pardon. I didn't know it was a question. It sounded more like a statement."

"You are investigating the dog poisoning?"

"I started to. I spent an hour at it there with Leeds, before we came here to dinner."

"So he said. Make any progress?"

"Nothing remarkable. For one thing, I had kibitzers, which is no help. Mrs. Frey and Mr. Hammond."

"Did you all come over here together?"

"No. Leeds and I came about an hour after Mrs. Frey and Mr. Hammond left."

"Did you drive?"

"Walked. He walked and I ran."

"You ran? Why?"

"To keep up with him."

Noonan smiled. He has the meanest smile I know of except maybe Boris Karloff. "You get your comedy from the comics, don't you, Goodwin?"

"Yes, sir."

"Tell me about the dinner here and afterwards. Make it as funny as you can."

I took ten minutes for it, as much as I had had for Wolfe, but getting interrupted with questions. I stuck to facts and gave them to him straight. When we came to the end he went back and concentrated on whether all of them had heard Mrs. Rackham say she was going for a walk with the dog, as of course they had since she had issued a blanket invitation for company. Then I was sent back to the living room, and it was Lina Darrow's turn in the preliminaries. I wondered if she would play dumb with him as she had with me.

It was as empty a stretch of hours as I have ever spent. I might as well have been a housebroken dog; no one seemed to think I mattered, and I was not in a position to tell them how wrong they were. At one point I made a serious effort to get into a conversation, making the rounds and offering remarks, but got nowhere. Dana Hammond merely gave me a look, without opening his trap. Oliver Pierce didn't even look at me. Lina Darrow mumbled something and turned away. Calvin Leeds asked me what they had done with Nobby's remains, nodded and frowned at my answer, and went to put another log on the fire. Annabel Frey asked me if I wanted more coffee, and when I said yes apparently didn't hear me. Barry Rackham, whom I tackled at the far end of the room, was the most talkative. He wanted to know whether anyone had come from the District Attorney's office. I said I didn't know. He wanted to know the name of the cop in the other room who was asking questions, and I told him Lieutenant Con Noonan. That was my longest conversation, two whole questions and answers.

I did get in one piece of detection, somewhat later, when finally District Attorney Cleveland Archer made an appearance. As he came into the room and made himself known and everybody moved to approach him, I took a look at his shoes and saw that he had undoubtedly been in the woods to inspect the spot where Mrs. Rackham's body was found. Likewise Ben Dykes, the dean of the Westchester County dicks, who was with him. That made me feel slightly better. It would have been a shame to stick there the whole night without detecting a single damn thing.

After a few preliminary words to individuals Archer spoke to them collectively. "This is a terrible thing, an awful thing. It is established that Mrs. Rackham was stabbed to death out there in the woods—and the dog that was with her. We have the knife that was used, as you know—it has been shown to you—one of the steak knives that are kept in a drawer here in the dining room—they were used by you at dinner last evening. We have statements from all of you, but of course I'll have to talk further with you. I won't try to do that now. It's after three o'clock, and I'll come back in the morning. I want to ask whether any of you has anything to say to me now, anything that shouldn't wait until then." His eyes went over them. "Anyone?"

No sound and no movement from any quarter. They sure were a chatty bunch. They just stood and stared at him, including me. I would have liked to relieve the tension with a remark or question, but didn't want to remind him that I was present.

However, he didn't need a reminder. After all the others, including the servants, had cleared out, Leeds and I were moving toward the door when Ben Dykes's voice came. "Goodwin!"

Leeds kept going. I turned.

Dykes came to me. "We want to ask you something."

"Shoot."

District Attorney Archer joined us, saying, "In there with Noonan, Ben."

"Him and Noonan bring sparks," Dykes objected. "Remember last year at Sperling's?"

"I'll do the talking," Archer stated, and led the way to the hall and along to the smaller room where Noonan was still seated at the table, conferring with a colleague—the one who had brought me from Hillside Kennels. The colleague moved to stand against the wall. Noonan arose, but sat down again when Archer and Dykes and I had pulled chairs up.

Archer, slightly plumper than he had been a year ago, with his round red face saggy and careworn by the stress of an extremely bad night for him, put his forearms on the table and leaned at me.

"Goodwin," he said earnestly but not offensively, "I want to put something up to you."

"Suits me, Mr. Archer," I assured him. "I've never been ignored more."

"We've been busy. Lieutenant Noonan has of course reported what you told him. Frankly, I find it hard to believe. Almost impossible to believe. It is well known that Nero Wolfe refuses dozens of jobs every month, that he confines himself to cases that interest him, and that the easiest and quickest way to interest him is to offer him a large fee. Now I—"

"Not the only way," I objected.

"I didn't say it was. I know he has standards—even scruples. Now I can't believe that he found anything interesting in the poisoning of a dog—certainly not interesting enough for him to send you up here over a weekend. And I doubt very much if Calvin Leeds, from what I know of him, is in a position to offer Wolfe a fee that would attract him. His cousin, Mrs. Rackham, might have, but she did not have the reputation of throwing money around carelessly—rather the contrary. We're going to ask Wolfe about this, naturally, but I thought I might save time by putting it up to you. I appeal to you to cooperate with us in solving this dastardly and cowardly murder. As you know, I have a right to insist on it; knowing you and Wolfe as I do, I prefer to appeal to you as to a responsible citizen and a man who carries a license to work in this state as a private detective. I simply do not believe that you were sent up here merely to investigate the poisoning of a dog."

They were all glaring at me.

"I wasn't," I said mildly.

"Ha, you weren't!"

"Hell no. As you say, Mr. Wolfe wouldn't be interested."

"So you lied, you punk," Noonan gloated.

"Wrong, as usual." I grinned at him. "You didn't ask me what I was sent here for or even hint that you would like to know. You asked if I was investigating the dog poisoning, and I told you I spent an hour at it, which I did. You asked if I had made any progress, and I told you nothing remarkable. Then you wanted to know what I had seen and heard here, and I told you, in full. It was one of the bummest and dumbest jobs of questioning I have ever run across, but you may learn in time. The first—"

Noonan blurted, "Why, you goddam—"

"I'll handle it," Archer snapped at him. Back to me: "You might have supplied it, Goodwin."

"Not to him," I said firmly. "I tried supplying him once and he was displeased. Anyway, I doubt if he would have understood it."

"See if I can understand it."

"Yes, sir. Mrs. Rackham phoned Thursday afternoon and made an appointment to see Mr. Wolfe. She came yesterday morning—Friday—at eleven o'clock, and had Leeds with her. She said that it had been her custom, since marrying Rackham three years and seven months ago, to give him money for his personal use when he asked for it, but that he kept asking for bigger amounts, and she began giving him less than he asked for, and last October second he wanted fifteen grand, and she refused. Gave him zero. Since then, the past seven months, he had asked for none and got none, but in spite of that he had gone on spending plenty, and that was what was biting her. She hired Mr. Wolfe to find out where and how he was getting dough, and I was sent up here to look him over and possibly get hold of an idea. I needed an excuse for coming here, and the dog poisoning was better than average." I fluttered a hand. "That's all."

"You say Leeds was with her?" Noonan demanded.

"That's partly what I mean," I told Ben Dykes, "about Noonan's notion of how to ask questions. He must have heard me say she had Leeds along."

"Yeah," Dykes said dryly. "But don't be so damn cute. This is not exactly a picnic." He spoke to Noonan. "Leeds didn't make any mention of this?"

"He did not. Of course I didn't ask him."

Dykes stood up and asked Archer, "Hadn't I better send for him? He went home."

Archer nodded, and Dykes went. "Good God," Archer said with feeling, not to Noonan or me, so probably to the People of the State of New York. He sat biting his lip a while and then asked me, "Was that all Mrs. Rackham wanted?"

"That's all she asked for."

"Had she quarreled with her husband? Had he threatened her?"

"She didn't say so."

"Exactly what did she say?"

That took half an hour. For me it was simple, since all I had to use was my memory, in view of the instructions from Wolfe to give them everything but the sausage. Archer didn't know what my memory is capable of, so I didn't repeat any of Mrs. Rackham's speeches verbatim, though I could have, because he would have thought I was dressing it up. But when I was through he had it all.

Then I was permitted to stay for the session with Leeds, who had arrived early in my recital but had been held outside until I was done. At last I was one of the party, but too late to hear anything that I didn't already know. With Leeds, who was practically one of the family, they had to cover not only his visit with his cousin to Wolfe's office, but also the preliminaries to it, so he took another half-hour and more. He himself had no idea, he said, where Rackham had been getting money. He had learned nothing from the personal inquiry he had undertaken at his cousin's request. He had never heard, or heard of, any serious quarrel between his cousin and her husband. And so on. As for his failure to tell Noonan of the visit to Wolfe's office and the real reason for my presence at Birchvale, he merely said calmly that Noonan hadn't asked and he preferred to wait until he was asked.

District Attorney Archer finally called it a night, got up and stretched, rubbed his eyes with his fingertips, asked Dykes and Noonan some questions and issued some orders, and addressed me. "You're staying at Leeds' place?"

I said I hadn't stayed there much so far, but my bag was there.

"All right. I'll want you tomorrow—today."

I said of course and went out with Leeds. Ben Dykes offered to give us a lift, but we declined.

Together, without conversation, Leeds and I made for the head of the trail at the edge of the woods, giving the curving paths a miss. Dawn had come and was going; it was getting close to sunrise. The breeze was down and the birds were up, telling about it. The pace Leeds set, up the long easy slope and down the level stretch, was not quite up to his previous performances, which suited me fine. I was not in a racing mood, even to get to a bed.

Suddenly Leeds halted, and I came abreast of him. In the trail, thirty paces ahead, a man was getting up from his hands and knees to face us. He called, "Hold it! Who are you?"

We told him.

"Well," he said, "you'll have to keep off this section of trail. Go around. We're just starting on it. Bright and early!"

We asked how far, and he said about three hundred yards, to where a man had started at the other end. We stepped off the trail, to the right into the rough, and got slowed down, though the woods were fairly clean. After a couple of minutes of that I asked Leeds if he would know the spot, and he said he would.

Soon he stopped, and I joined him. I would have known it myself, with the help of a rope they had stretched from tree to tree, making a large semicircle. We went up to the rope and stood looking.

"Where's Hebe?" I asked.

"They had to come for me to get her. She's in Nobby's kennel. He won't be needing it. They took him away."

We agreed, without putting it in words, that there was nothing there we wanted, and resumed our way through the woods, keeping off the trail until we reached the scientist at the far end of the forbidden section, who not only challenged us but had to be persuaded that we weren't a pair of bloodthirsty liars. Finally he was bighearted enough to let us go on.

I was glad they had taken Nobby away, not caring much for another view of the little hall with that canine corpse on the bench. Otherwise the house was as before. Leeds had stopped at the kennels. I went up to my room and was peeling off the pants I had pulled on over my pajamas when I was startled by a sudden dazzling blaze at the window. I crossed to it and stuck my head out: it was the sun showing off, trying to scare somebody. I glanced at my wrist and saw 5:39, but as I said, maybe it wasn't a true horizon. Not lowering the window shade, I went and stretched out on the bed and yawned as far down as it could go.

The door downstairs opened and shut, and there were steps on the stairs. Leeds appeared at my open door, stepped inside, and said, "I'll have to be up and around in an hour, so I'll close your door."

I thanked him. He didn't move.

"My cousin paid Mr. Wolfe ten thousand dollars. What will he do now?"

"I don't know, I haven't asked him. Why?"

"It occurred to me that he might want to spend it, or part of it, in her interest. In case the police don't make any headway."

"He might," I agreed. "I'll suggest it to him."

He still stood, as if there was something else on his mind. There was, and he unloaded it.

"It happens in the best families," he stated distinctly and backed out, taking the door with him.

I closed my eyes but made no effort to empty my head. If I went to sleep there was no telling when I would wake up, and I intended to phone Wolfe at eight, fifteen minutes before the scheduled hour for Fritz to get to his room with his breakfast tray. Meanwhile I would think of something brilliant to do or to suggest. The trouble with that, I discovered after some poking around, was that I had no in. Nobody would speak to me except Leeds, and he was far from loquacious.

I have a way of realizing all of a sudden, as I suppose a lot of people do, that I made a decision some time back without knowing it. It happened that morning at 6:25. Looking at my watch and seeing that that was where it had got to, I was suddenly aware that I was staying awake, not so I could phone Wolfe at eight o'clock, but so I could beat it the hell out of there as soon as I was sure Leeds was asleep; and I was now as sure as I would ever be.

I got up and shed my pajamas and dressed, not trying to set a record but wasting no time, and, with my bag in one hand and my shoes in the other, tiptoed to the hall, down the stairs, and out to the stone slab. While it wasn't Calvin Leeds I was escaping from, I thought it desirable to get out of West-chester County before anyone knew I wasn't upstairs asleep. Not a chance. I was seated on the stone slab tying the lace of the second shoe when a dog barked, and that was a signal for all the others. I scrambled up, grabbed the bag, ran to the car and unlocked it and climbed in, started the engine, swung around the graveled space, and passed the house on my way out just as Leeds emerged through the side door. I stepped on the brake, stuck my head through the window, yelled at him, "Got an errand to do, see you later!" and rolled on through the gate and into the highway.

At that hour Sunday morning the roads were all mine, the bright new sun was at my left out of the way, and it would have been a pleasant drive if I had been in a mood to feel pleased. Which I wasn't. This was a totally different situation from the other two occasions when we had crossed Arnold Zeck's path and someone had got killed. Then the corpses had been Zeck's men, and Zeck, Wolfe, and the public interest had all been on the same side. This time Zeck's man, Barry Rackham, was the number one sus-pect, and Wolfe had either to return his dead client's ten grand, keep it without doing anything to earn it, or meet Zeck head on. Knowing Wolfe as I did, I hit eighty-five that morning rolling south on the Sawmill River Parkway.

The dash clock said 7:18 as I left the West Side Highway at 46th Street. I had to cross to Ninth Avenue to turn south. It was as empty as the country roads had been. Turning right on 35th, I went on across Tenth Avenue, on nearly to Eleventh, and pulled to the curb in front of Wolfe's old brown-stone house.

Even before I killed the engine I saw something that made me goggle —a sight that had never greeted me before in the thousands of times I had braked a car to a stop there.

The front door was standing wide open.

VI

MY HEART came up. I swallowed it down, jumped out, ran across the side-walk and up the seven steps to the stoop and on in. Fritz and Theodore were there in the hall, coming to me. Their faces were enough to make a guy's heart pop right out of his mouth.

"Airing the house?" I demanded.

"He's gone," Fritz said.

"Gone where?"

"I don't know. During the night. When I saw the door was open—"

"What's that in your hand?"

"He left them on the table in his room—for Theodore and me, and one for you—"

I snatched the pieces of paper from his trembling hand and looked at the one on top. The writing on it was Wolfe's.

Dear Fritz:

Marko Vukcic will want your services. He should pay you at least $2000 a month.

My best regards. . . .
Nero Wolfe

I looked at the next one.

Dear Theodore:

Mr. Hewitt will take the plants and will need your help with them. He should pay you around $200 weekly.

My regards. . . .
Nero Wolfe

I looked at the third one.

AG:

Do not look for me.

My very best regards and wishes. . . .

NW

I went through them again, watching each word, told Fritz and Theodore, "Come and sit down," went to the office, and sat at my desk. They moved chairs to face me.

"He's gone," Fritz said, trying to convince himself.

"So it seems," I said aggressively.

"You know where he is," Theodore told me accusingly. "It won't be easy to move some of the plants without damage. I don't like working on Long Island, not for two hundred dollars a week. When is he coming back?"

"Look, Theodore," I said, "I don't give a good goddam what you like or don't like. Mr. Wolfe has always pampered you because you're the best orchid nurse alive. This is as good a time as any to tell you that you remind me of sour milk. I do not know where Mr. Wolfe is nor if or when he's coming back. To you he sent his regards. To me he sent his very best regards and wishes. Now shut up."

I shifted to Fritz. "He thinks Marko Vukcic should pay you twice as much as he does. That's like him, huh? You can see I'm sore as hell, his doing it like this, but I'm not surprised. To show you how well I know him, this is what happened: not long after I phoned him last night he simply wrote these notes to us and walked out of the house, leaving the door open—you said you found it open—to show anyone who might be curious that there was no longer anyone or anything of any importance inside. You got up at your usual time, six-thirty, saw the open door, went up to his room, found his bed empty and the notes on the table. After going up to the plant rooms to call Theodore, you returned to his room, looked around, and discovered that he had taken nothing with him. Then you and Theodore stared at each other until I arrived. Have you anything to add to that?"

"I don't want to work on Long Island," Theodore stated.

Fritz only said, "Find him, Archie."

"He told me not to."

"Yes—but find him! Where will he sleep? What will he eat?"

I got up and went to the safe and opened it, and looked in the cash drawer, where we always kept a supply for emergency expenses. There should have been a little over four thousand bucks; there was a little over a thousand. I closed the safe door and twirled the knob, and told Fritz, "He'll sleep and eat. Was my report accurate?"

"Not quite. One of his bags is gone, and pajamas, toothbrush, razor, three shirts, and ten pairs of socks."

"Did he take a walking stick?"

"No. The old gray topcoat and the old gray hat."

"Were there any visitors?"

"No."

"Any phone calls besides mine?"

"I don't know about yours. His extension and mine were both plugged in, but you know I don't answer when you're out unless he tells me to. It rang only once, at eight minutes after twelve."

"Your clock's wrong. That was me. It was five after." I went and gave him a pat on the shoulder. "Okay. I hope you like your new job. How's chances for some breakfast?"

"But Archie! His breakfast . . ."

"I could eat that too. I drove forty miles on an empty stomach." I patted him again. "Look, Fritz. Right now I'm sore at him, damn sore. After some griddle cakes and broiled ham and eight or ten eggs in black butter and a quart of coffee, we'll see. I think I'll be even sorer than I am now, but we'll see. Is there any of his favorite honey left that you haven't been giving me lately? The thyme honey?"

"Yes—some. Four jars."

"Good. I'll finish off with that on a couple of hot cakes. Then we'll see how I feel."

"I would never have thought—" Fritz's voice had a quaver, and he stopped and started over again. "I would never have thought this could happen. What is it, Archie?" He was practically wailing. "What is it? His appetite has been good."

"We were going to repot some Miltonias today," Theodore said dismally.

I snorted. "Go ahead and pot 'em. He was no help anyhow. Beat it and let me alone. I've got to think. Also I'm hungry. Beat it!"

Theodore, mumbling, shuffled out. Fritz, following him, turned at the door. "That's it, Archie. Think. Think where he is while I get your breakfast."

He left me, and I sat down at my desk to do the thinking, but the cogs wouldn't catch. I was too mad to think. "Don't look for me." That was him to a T. He knew damn well that if I should ever come home to find he had vanished, the one activity that would make any sense at all would be to start looking for him, and here I was stopped cold at the take-off. Not that I had no notion at all. That was why I had left Leeds' place without notice and stepped it up to eighty-five getting back: I did have a notion. Two years had passed since Wolfe had told me, "Archie, you are to forget that you know that man's name. If ever, in the course of my business, I find that I am committed against him and must destroy him, I shall leave this house, find a place where I can work—and sleep and eat if there is time for it—and stay there until I have finished."

So that part was okay, but what about me? On another occasion, a year later, he had said to five members of a family named Sperling, in my presence, "In that event he will know it is a mortal encounter, and so will I, and I shall move to a base of operations which will be known only to Mr. Goodwin and perhaps two others." Okay. There was no argument with the mortal encounter or about the move. But I was the Mr. Goodwin referred to, and here I was staring at it—"Don't look for me." Where did that leave me? Certainly the two others he had had in mind were Saul Panzer and Marko Vukcic, and I didn't even dare to phone Saul and ask a couple of discreet questions; and besides, if he had let Saul in and left me out, to hell with him. And what was I supposed to say to people—for instance, people like the District Attorney of Westchester County?

That particular question got answered, partly at least, from an unexpected quarter. When I had finished with the griddle cakes, ham, eggs, thyme honey, and coffee, I went back to the office to see if I was ready to quit feeling and settle down to thinking, and was working at it when I became aware that I was sitting in Wolfe's chair behind his desk. That brought me up with a jerk. No one else, including me, ever sat in that chair, but there

I was. I didn't approve of it. It seemed to imply that Wolfe was through with that chair for good, and that was a hell of an attitude to take, no matter how sore I was. I opened a drawer of his desk to check its contents, pretending that was what I had sat there for, and was starting a careful survey when the doorbell rang.

Going to answer it, I took my time because I had done no thinking yet and therefore didn't know my lines. Seeing through the one-way glass panel in the front door that the man on the stoop was a civilian stranger, my first impulse was to let him ring until he got tired, but curiosity chased it away and I opened the door. He was just a citizen with big ears and an old topcoat, and he asked to see Mr. Nero Wolfe. I told him Mr. Wolfe wasn't available on Sundays, and I was his confidential assistant, and could I help. He thought maybe I could, took an envelope from a pocket, extracted a sheet of paper, and unfolded it.

"I'm from the *Gazette,*" he stated. "This copy for an ad we got in the mail this morning—we want to be sure it's authentic."

I took the paper and gave it a look. It was one of our large-sized letterheads, and the writing and printing on it were Wolfe's. At the top was written:

Display advertisement for Monday's *Gazette,* first section, two columns wide, depth as required. In thin type, not blatant. Send bill to above address.

Below the copy was printed by hand:

MR. NERO WOLFE

ANNOUNCES HIS RETIREMENT

FROM THE DETECTIVE BUSINESS

TODAY, APRIL 10, 1950

Mr. Wolfe will not hereafter be available. Inquiries from clients on unfinished matters may be made of Mr. Archie Goodwin. Inquiries from others than clients will not receive attention.

Beneath that was Wolfe's signature. It was authentic all right.

Having learned it by heart, I handed it back. "Yeah, that's okay. Sure. Give it a good spot."

"It's authentic?"

"Absolutely."

"Listen, I want to see him. Give me a break! Good spot hell; it's page one if I can get a story on it!"

"Don't you believe your own ads? It says that Mr. Wolfe will not hereafter be available." I had the door swung to a narrow gap. "I never saw you before, but Lon Cohen is an old friend of mine. He gets to work at noon, doesn't he?"

"Yes, but—"

"Tell him not to bother to phone about this. Mr. Wolfe is not available, and I'm reserved for clients, as the ad says. Watch your foot, here comes the door."

I shut it and put the chain bolt on. As I went back down the hall Fritz emerged from the kitchen and demanded, "Who was that?"

I eyed him. "You know damn well," I said, "that when Mr. Wolfe was here you would never have dreamed of asking who was that, either of him or of me. Don't dream of it now, anyway not when I'm in the humor I'm in at present."

"I only wanted—"

"Skip it. I advise you to steer clear of me until I've had a chance to think."

I went to the office and this time took my own chair. At least I had got some instructions from Wolfe, though his method of sending them was certainly roundabout. The ad meant, of course, that I wasn't to try to cover his absence; on the contrary. More important, it told me to lay off of the Rackham thing. I was to handle inquiries from clients on unfinished matters, but only from clients; and since Mrs. Rackham, being dead, couldn't inquire, that settled that. Another thing—apparently I still had my job, unlike Fritz and Theodore. But I couldn't sign checks, I couldn't—suddenly I remembered something. The fact that I hadn't thought of it before indicates the state I was in. I have told, in my account of another case of Wolfe's how, in anticipation of the possibility that some day a collision with Arnold Zeck would drive him into a foxhole, he had instructed me to put fifty thousand dollars in cash in a safe deposit box over in Jersey, and how I obeyed instructions. The idea was to have a source of supply for the foxhole; but anyway, there it was, fifty grand, in the box rented by me under the name I had selected for the purpose. I was sitting thinking how upset I must have been not to have thought of that before when the phone rang and I reached for it.

"Nero Wolfe's office, Archie Goodwin speaking."

I thought it proper to use that, the familiar routine, since according to Wolfe's ad he wouldn't retire until the next day.

"Archie?" A voice I knew sounded surprised. "Is that you, Archie?"

"Right. Hello, Marko. So early on Sunday?"

"But I thought you were away! I was going to give Fritz a message for you. From Nero."

Marko Vukcic, owner and operator of Rusterman's Restaurant, the only place where Wolfe really liked to eat except at home, was the only man in New York who called Wolfe by his first name. I told him I would be glad to take a message for myself.

"Not from Nero actually," he said. "From me. I must see you as soon as possible. Could you come here?"

I said I could. There was no need to ask where, since the only place he could ever be found was the restaurant premises, either on one of the two floors for the public, in the kitchen, or up in his private quarters.

I told Fritz I was going out and would be back when he saw me.

As I drove crosstown and up to 54th Street, I was around eighty per cent sure that within a few minutes I would be talking with Wolfe. For him it would be hard to beat that for a foxhole—the place that cooked and served the best food in America, with the living quarters of his best and oldest friend above it. Even after I had entered at the side door, as arranged, ascended the two flights of stairs, seen the look on Marko's face as he welcomed me, felt the tight clasp of his fingers as he took my hands in his, and heard his murmured "My friend, my poor young friend!"—even then I thought he was only preparing dramatically to lead me to Wolfe in an inner room.

But he wasn't. All he led me to was a chair by a window. He took another one, facing me, and sat with his palms on his knees, his head cocked a little to one side as usual.

"My friend Archie," he said sympathetically. "It is my part to tell you exactly certain things. But before I do that I wish to tell you a thing of my own. I wish to remind you that I have known Nero a much longer time than you have. We knew each other as boys in another country—much younger than you were that day many years ago when you first saw him and went to work for him. He is my old and dear friend, and I am his. So it was natural that he should come to me last night."

"Sure," I agreed. "Why not?"

"You must feel no pique. No *courroux.*"

"Okay. I'll fight it down. What time did he come?"

"At two o'clock in the night. He was here an hour, and then left. That I am to tell you, and these things. Do you want to write them down?"

"I can remember them if you can. Shoot."

Marko nodded. "I know of your great memory. Nero has often spoken of it." He shut his eyes and in a moment opened them again. "There are these five things. First, the plants. He telephoned Mr. Hewitt last night, and tomorrow Mr. Hewitt will arrange for the plants to be moved to his place, and also for Theodore to go there to work. Second—"

"Am I to list the plants? Do the records go too?"

"I don't know. I can say only what I was told to say. That's all about the plants. Perhaps Mr. Hewitt can tell you. Second, that is Fritz. He will work here, and I will pay him well. I will see him today and arrange the details. Of course he is unhappy?"

"He thinks Mr. Wolfe will starve to death."

"But naturally. If not that, something else. I have always thought it a folly for him to be a detective. Third—I am third. I have a power of attorney. Do you want to see it?"

"No, thanks, I'll take your word for it."

"It is in there locked up. Nero said it is legal, and he knows. I can sign checks for you. I can sign anything. I can do anything he could do."

"Within certain limits. You can't—" I waved a hand. "Forget it. Fourth?"

"Fourth is the house. I am to offer the house and its contents for sale. On that I have confidential instructions."

I goggled at him. "Sell the house *and* contents?"

"Yes. I have private instructions regarding price and terms."

"I don't believe it."

His shoulders went up and down. "I told Nero you would think I was lying."

"I don't think you're lying. I just don't believe it. Also the bed and other articles in my room are my property. Must I move them out today or can I wait until tomorrow?"

Marko made a noise that I think was meant for sympathy. "My poor young friend," he said apologetically, "there is no hurry at all. Selling a house is not like selling a lamb chop. You will, I suppose, continue to live there for the present."

"Did he say I should?"

"No. But why shouldn't you? That is my own thought, and it brings us to the fifth and last thing: the instructions Nero gave me for you."

"Oh, he did. That was thoughtful. Such as?"

"You are to act in the light of experience as guided by intelligence."

He stopped. I nodded. "That's a cinch, I always do. And specifically?"

"That's all. Those are your instructions." Marko upturned his palms. "That's all about everything."

"You call that instructions, do you?"

"I don't. He did." He leaned to me. "I told him, Archie, that his conduct was inexcusable. He was standing ready to leave, after telling me those five things and no more. Having no reply, he turned and went. Beyond that I know nothing, but nothing."

"Where he went? Where he is? No word for me at all?"

"Nothing. Only what I have told you."

"Hell, he's gone batty, like lots of geniuses," I declared, and got up to go.

VII

I DROVE around for two solid hours, mostly in the park. Now and then, for a change of scene, I left the park for a patrol of the avenues.

I hadn't been able to start thinking in the house, and it might work better on the move. Moreover, I didn't want any more just then of Fritz or Theodore, or in fact of anybody but me. So, in the light of experience and guided by intelligence, I drove around. Somewhere along the way I saw clearly what my trouble was: I was completely out of errands for the first time in years. How could I decide what to do when I had nothing to do? I now believe that the reason I never drove farther north than 110th Street, nor farther south than 14th Street during those two hours, was that I thought Wolfe was probably somewhere within those limits and I didn't want to leave them.

When I did leave them it wasn't voluntary. Rolling down Second Avenue in the Seventies, I had stopped for a red light abreast of a police car on my left. Just as the light was changing, the cop on my side stuck his head out and called, "Pull over to the curb."

Flattered at the attention as any motorist would be, not, I obeyed. The police car came alongside, and the cop got out and invented another new phrase. "Let me see your license."

I got it out and handed it to him, and he took a look.

"Yeah, I thought I recognized you." He handed the license back, walked around the front of my car to the other side, got in beside me, and suggested, "Let's go to the Nineteenth Precinct. Sixty-seventh east of Lexington."

"That's one idea," I admitted. "Or what's wrong with the Brooklyn Botanical Garden, especially on Easter? I'll toss you for it."

He was unmoved. "Come on, Goodwin, come on. I know you're a card, I've heard all about you. Let's go."

"Give me one reason, good or bad. If you don't mind?"

"I don't know the reason. All I know is the word that came an hour ago, to pick you up and take you in. Maybe you shouldn't have left the infant on the church steps on Easter Day."

"Of course not," I agreed. "We'll go get it."

I eased away from the curb into traffic, with the police car trailing behind. Our destination, the Nineteenth Precinct Station, was not new to me. That was where I had once spent most of a night, conversing with Lieutenant Rowcliff, the Con Noonan of the New York Police Department.

After escorting me in to the desk and telling the sergeant about it, my captor had a point to make. His name was not John F. O'Brien, it was John

R. O'Brien. He explained to the sergeant that he had to insist on it because last year one of his heroic acts had been credited to John F., and once was enough, and he damn well wanted credit for spotting a wanted man on the street. That attended to, he bade me a pleasant good-by and left. Meanwhile the sergeant was making a phone call. When he hung up he looked at me with a more active interest.

"Westchester wants you," he announced. "Leaving the scene of a crime and leaving jurisdiction. Want to drag it out?"

"It might be fun, but I doubt it. What happens if I don't?"

"There's a Westchester man downtown. He's on his way up here to take you."

I shook my head. "I'll fight like a cornered rat. I know fourteen lawyers all told. Ten to one he has no papers. This is one of those brotherly acts which I do not like. You're on a spot, Sergeant."

"Don't scare me to death. If he has no papers I'll send you downtown and let them handle it."

"Yeah," I admitted, "that would let you out. But we can make it simpler for both of us if you care to. Get the Westchester DA on the phone and let me talk to him. I'll even pay for the call."

At first he didn't like the idea and then he did. I think what changed his mind was the chance of picking up a piece of hot gossip on the murder of the month. He had to be persuaded, but when I told him the DA would be at the Rackham place and gave him the number, that settled it. He put the call in. However, he covered. When he got the number he made it clear that he merely wanted to offer the DA an opportunity to speak to Archie Goodwin if he wished to. He did. I circled the railing to get to the desk and took the phone.

"Mr. Archer?"

"Yes! This is—"

"Just a minute!" I said emphatically. "Whatever you were going to say this is, I double it. It's an outrage. It—"

"You were told to stay here, and you sneaked away! You left—"

"I was not told to stay there. You asked me if I was staying at Leeds' place, and I said my bag was there, and you said you would want me today, and I said of course. If I had stayed at Leeds' place I might have been permitted seven hours' sleep. I decided to do something else with seven hours, and they're not up yet. But you see fit to ring a bell on me. I'll do one of two things. I'll have a bite of lunch and then drive up there, unaccompanied, or I'll make it as hard as I possibly can for this man you sent to get me outside the city limits—whichever you prefer. Here he comes now."

"Here who comes?"

"Your man. Coming in the door. If you decide you want to see me today, tell him not to trail along behind me. It makes me self-conscious."

A silence. Then, "You were told not to leave the county."

"I was not. By no one."

"Neither you nor Wolfe was at home at eleven o'clock—or if you were you wouldn't see my man."

"I was in the Easter parade."

Another silence, longer. "What time will you be here? At Birchvale."

"I can make it by two o'clock."

"My man is there?"

"Yes."

"Let me talk to him."

That was satisfactory. I liked that all right, except for one thing. After the Westchester dick was finished on the phone and it was settled that I would roll my own, and the sergeant had generously said that the Police Department would contribute the phone call, I asked the dick if he understood that I didn't care to be tailed, and he replied that I needn't worry because he was going back to 35th Street to see Nero Wolfe. I didn't care much for that, but said nothing because I hadn't yet decided exactly what to say. So when I found a place on Lexington Avenue for a sandwich and a malted, I went first to a phone booth, called the house, and told Fritz to leave the chain bolt on, tell callers that Wolfe was out of the city and no more, and admit no one.

Being on the move did help. Having decided, while touring the park and avenues, what my immediate trouble was, I now, on my way to Birchvale, got the whole thing into focus. Considering the entire picture, including the detail of putting the house up for sale and the lack of even one little hint for me, let alone a blueprint, it was by no means a bet that Wolfe had merely dived into a foxhole. Look how free Marko had been with his poor-young-friending. It was not inconceivable that Wolfe had decided to chuck it for good. A hundred times and more, when things or people—frequently me—didn't suit him, he had told me about the house he owned in Egypt and how pleasant it would be to live there. I had always brushed it off. I now realized that a man who is eccentric enough to threaten to go and live in Egypt is eccentric enough to do it, especially when it gets to the point where he opens a package of sausage and has to run for his life.

Therefore I would be a dimwit to assume that this was merely time out to gather ammunition and make plans. Nor could I assume that it wasn't. I couldn't assume anything. Was he gone for good, or was he putting on a charade that would make all his other performances look like piker stuff in comparison? Presumably I was to answer that question, along with others, by the light of experience guided by intelligence, and I did not appreciate the compliment. If I was finally and permanently on my own, very well; I would make out. But apparently I was still drawing pay, so what? The result of my getting the whole picture into focus was that as I turned in at the entrance to Birchvale I was sorer than ever.

I was stopped at the entrance by one of Noonan's colleagues, there on guard, and was allowed to proceed up the curving drive only after I had shown him four documents. Parking in a space at the side of the house that was bordered by evergreens, I walked around to the front door and was admitted by a maid who looked pale and puffy. She didn't say anything, just held the door open, but a man was there too, one of the county boys whom I knew by sight but not by name. He said, "This way," and led me to the right, to the same small room I had seen before.

Ben Dykes, sitting there at the table with a stack of papers, grunted at me, "So you finally got here."

"I told Archer two o'clock. It's one-fifty-eight."

"Uh-huh. Sit down."

I sat. The door was standing open, but no sound of any kind came to my ears except the rustling of the papers Dykes was going through.

"Is the case solved?" I inquired courteously. "It's so damn quiet. In New York they make more noise. If you—"

I stopped because I was being answered. A typewriter started clicking somewhere. It was faint, from a distance, but unmistakably a typewriter, with a professional at it.

"I suppose Archer knows I'm here," I stated.

"Don't work up a lather," Dykes advised me without looking up.

I shrugged, stretched my legs and crossed my ankles, and tried to see what his papers were. I was too far away to get any words, but from various aspects I finally concluded that they were typewritten signed statements of the family, guests, and servants. Not being otherwise engaged at the moment, I would have been glad to help Dykes with them, but I doubted if it was worth the breath to make an offer. After the strain of trying to identify the papers, my eyes went shut, and for the first time I was aware how sleepy I was. I thought I had better open my eyes, and then decided it would show more strength of will if I kept awake with them shut. . . .

Someone was using my head for a cocktail shaker. Resenting it, I jerked away and made a gesture of protest with my fist closed, following up by opening my eyes and jumping to my feet. Backing away from me was a skinny guy with a long neck. He looked both startled and angry.

"Sorry," I told him. "I guess I dozed off a second."

"You dozed off forty minutes," Dykes declared. He was still at the table with the papers, and standing beside him was District Attorney Archer.

"That leaves me," I said, "still behind seven hours and more."

"We want a statement," Archer said impatiently.

"The sooner the better," I agreed, and pulled my chair up. Archer sat at the end of the table at my left, Dykes across from me, and the skinny guy, with a notebook and pen, at the other end.

"First," Archer said, "repeat what you told us last night about Mrs. Rackham's visit to Wolfe's office with Leeds."

"But," I objected, "that'll take half an hour, and you're busy. That's routine. I assure you it won't vary."

"Go ahead. I want to hear it, and I have questions."

I yawned thoroughly, rubbed my eyes with the heels of my palms, and started. At first it was fuzzy, but it flowed easy after a minute or two, and it would have been a pleasure to have them compare it with a record from the previous recital if there had been one.

Archer had some questions, and Dykes one or two. At the end Archer asked me, "Will you swear to that, Goodwin?"

"Sure, glad to. If you'll pay the notary fee."

"Go and type it, Cheney."

The skinny guy got up, with his notebook, and left. After the door was closed Archer spoke.

"You might as well know it, Goodwin; you've been contradicted. Mr. Rackham says you're lying about his wife's conversation with Wolfe."

"Yeah? How does he know? He wasn't there."

"He says that she couldn't possibly have said what you report because it wasn't true. He says that there was no question or misunderstanding about money between them. He also says that she told him that she suspected her financial affairs were being mishandled by Mr. Hammond of the Metropolitan Trust Company, and that she was going to consult Nero Wolfe about it."

"Well." I yawned. "That's interesting. Leeds is on my side. Who's on his?"

"No one so far."

"Have you tried it out on Leeds?"

"Yes. As you say, he's on your side. He has signed a statement. So has Mr. Rackham."

"What does Hammond say?"

"I haven't—" Archer paused, regarding me. "Perhaps I shouldn't have told you that. You will keep it to yourself. It's a delicate matter, to approach a responsible officer of a reputable bank on a thing like that."

"Right," I agreed. "It's also a delicate matter to call a millionaire a damn liar—that is, delicate for you. Not for me. I hereby call him a damn liar. I suppose he is a millionaire? Now?"

Archer and Dykes exchanged glances.

"Save it if you want to," I said understandingly. "Leeds will tell me. If he knows. Does he?"

"Yes. The will was read to the family today. I was present. There are a number of bequests to servants and distant relatives. Mrs. Frey gets this place and a million dollars. Leeds gets half a million. Lina Darrow gets two hundred thousand. The rest goes to Mr. Rackham."

"I see. Then he's a millionaire, so it's delicate. Even so, he's a damn liar and it's two to one. I'll sign that statement in triplicate if you want it. Beyond that what can I say?"

"I want to make it three to one." Archer leaned to me. "Listen, Goodwin. I have great respect for Nero Wolfe's talents. I have reason to, as you know. But I do not intend to let his whims interfere with the functions of my office. I want a statement from him supporting yours and Leeds', and I mean to have it without delay. I sent a man to get it. This morning at eleven o'clock he was told that Wolfe wasn't available and that you weren't there and your whereabouts were not known. That was when an alarm was spread for you. I had a phone call from my man an hour ago. He had gone back to Wolfe's house and had been told that Wolfe was out of the city, and that was all he could get."

Archer made a hand into a fist, resting on the table. "I won't stand for it, Goodwin. This is the toughest one I've had in my county since I took office, and I won't stand for it. Whatever else he is, he's a fat conceited peacock and it's time somebody called him. There's a phone you can use. Two hours from now, unless he's here and talking to me, there'll be a warrant for his arrest as a material witness. There's the phone."

"I doubt if you could paste material witness on him. He hasn't been anywhere near here."

"Nuts," Ben Dykes growled. "Don't be a sap. She takes troubles to him Friday and gets murdered Saturday."

I decided to take the plunge. The way I felt, it would have been a pleasure to let them go ahead with a warrant, but if I tried to stall I would need a very fancy excuse tomorrow when they saw the ad in the *Gazette*. So I thought what the hell, now is as good a time as any, and told them.

"I can't phone him because I don't know where he is."

"Ha ha," Dykes said. "Ha ha ha."

"Yes," I admitted, "it could be a gag. But it isn't. I don't know whether he's out of the city or not. All I know is that he left the house last night, while I was up here, and he hasn't come back—no, that isn't true. I also know that he called on a friend of his named Vukcic and arranged for his plants to be moved out and his cook to take another job. And he gave Vukcic a power of attorney. And he sent an ad to the *Gazette* announcing his retirement from the detective business."

Dykes did not ha-ha again. He merely sat and frowned at me. Archer, his lips puckered, had his eyes focused on me, but as if he was trying to see not me but through me. That went on for seconds, and I got uncomfortable. I can meet a pair of eyes all right, but not two pairs at once, one in front and one off to the left.

Finally Dykes turned his head to tell Archer, "This makes it nice."

Archer nodded, not taking his regard from me. "It's hard to believe, Goodwin."

"I'll say it is. For him to—"

"No, no. It's hard to believe that Wolfe and you would try anything as fantastic as this. Obviously he was absolutely compelled to. You phoned him from Leeds' place last night, as soon as you could get to a phone after Mrs. Rackham was murdered. That was—"

"Excuse me," I said firmly. "Not as soon as I could get to a phone after Mrs. Rackham was murdered. As soon as I could get to a phone after I found out she had been murdered."

"Very well. We're not in court." He was leaning at me. "That was shortly after midnight. What did you say to him?"

"I told him what had happened. I reported, as fully as I could in the time I had, everything from my arrival here up to then. If the operator listened in you can check with her. I asked if I should limit my talk with the cops to events here and leave the rest for him to tell, and he said no, I should withhold nothing, including all details of Mrs. Rackham's talk with him. That was all. As you know, I followed instructions."

"Jesus," Dykes said. "Son, it looks like your turn to sweat has come."

Archer ignored him. "And after telling you to withhold nothing from the police, Wolfe suddenly decides, in the middle of the night, that he has had enough of detective work, sends an ad to a newspaper announcing his retirement, calls on a friend to arrange for the care of his orchids—and what did he do then? I was so engrossed I may have missed something."

"I don't know what he did. He walked out. He disappeared."

I was aware, of course, of how it sounded. It was completely cuckoo. It was all rayon and a yard wide. I damn near made it even worse by telling them about the sausage and the tear gas, of course without letting on that we knew who had sent it, but realized in time how that would go over in the circumstances. That *would* have made a hit. But I had to say or do something, and decided to produce evidence, so I reached to my pocket for it.

"He left notes on the table in his bedroom," I said, "for Fritz and Theodore and me. Here's mine."

I handed it to Archer. He read it and passed it to Dykes. Dykes read it twice and returned it to Archer, who stuck it in his pocket.

"Jesus," Dykes said again, looking at me in a way I didn't like. "This is really something. I've always thought Nero Wolfe had a lot on the ball, and you too in a way, but this is about the worst I ever saw. Really." He turned to Archer. "It's plain what happened."

"It certainly is." Archer made a fist. "Goodwin, I don't ask you to tell me. I'll tell you. When you found Mrs. Rackham there dead, you and Leeds agreed on a tale about the visit to Nero Wolfe. Leeds came here to break the news. You went to his place to phone Wolfe and report, both the murder and the tale you and Leeds had agreed on—or maybe Wolfe knew that already, since you had pretended to investigate the dog poisoning. In any case, Wolfe knew something that he didn't dare to try to cover and that, equally, he didn't dare to reveal. What made it unbearably hot was the murder. So he arranged to disappear, and we haven't got him, and it may take a day or a week to find him. But we've got you."

The fist hit the table, not hard. "You know where Wolfe is. You know what he knows that he had to run away from. It is vital information required by me in my investigation of a murder. Surely you must see that your position is untenable, you can't possibly get away with it. Twenty Nero Wolfes couldn't bring you out of this with a whole skin. Even if he's cooking up one of his flashy surprises, even if he walks into my office tomorrow with the murderer and the evidence to convict him, I will not stand for this. There is no written record of what you said last night. I'll get the stenographer back in here and we'll tear up his notebook and what he has typed, and you can start from scratch."

"Better grab it, son," Dykes said, perfectly friendly. "Loyalty to your employer is a fine thing, but not when he's got a screw loose."

I yawned. "My God, I'm sleepy. I wouldn't mind this so much if I was helping out with a fix, good or bad, but it's a shame to get stuck with the truth. Ask me tomorrow, ask me all summer, I refuse to tell a lie. And I do not know where Mr. Wolfe is."

Archer stood up. "Get a material witness warrant and lock him up," he said, almost squeaking, and marched out.

VIII

THE jail at White Plains uses a gallon of strong disinfectant, diluting it, of course, every day including Sunday. I can back that statement up with two pieces of evidence: the word of the turnkey on the second-floor cell block, whose name is Wilkes, given to me personally, and my sense of smell, which is above average.

I had no opportunity to make a tour of inspection during the twenty hours

I was there, that Easter Sunday and the day following, but except for the smell I found nothing to write to the newspapers about, once you grant that society must protect itself against characters like me. My cell—or rather, our cell, since I had a mate—was as clean as they come. There was something about the blankets that made you keep them away from your chin, but that could have been just prejudice. The light was nothing wonderful, but good enough to read by for thirty days.

I didn't really get acquainted with my surroundings or my mate until Monday, I was so darned sleepy when they finally finished with me down below and showed me up to my room. They had been insistent but not ferocious. I had been allowed to phone Fritz that I wouldn't be home, which was a good thing, as there was no telling what he would have done with no word from me coming on top of Wolfe's fadeout, and also to try to call Nathaniel Parker, the only lawyer Wolfe has ever been willing to invite to dinner; but that was no go because he was away for the weekend. When at last I stretched out on the cot, I was dead to the world ten seconds after my head hit the pillow, consisting of my pants wrapped in my shirt.

It was the pants, or rather the coat and vest that went with them, that made my stay pleasanter than it might have been right from the start. I had had perhaps half as much sleep as I could have used when a hell of a noise banged at me and I lifted my head and opened my eyes. Across the cell on another cot, so far away that I would have had to stretch my arm its full length to touch him, was my cellmate—a broad-shouldered guy about my age, maybe a little older, with a mop of tousled black hair. He was sitting up, yawning.

"What's all the racket?" I asked. "Jail break?"

"Breakfast and check-up in ten minutes," he replied, getting his feet, with socks on, to the floor. "Stupid custom."

"Boneheads," I agreed, twisting up to sit on the edge of the cot.

Going to the chair where his wardrobe was, his eye fell on my chair, and he stepped to it for a look at the coat and vest. He fingered the lapel, looked inside at the lining, and inspected a buttonhole. Then, without comment, he returned to his side, two whole steps, and started to dress. I followed suit.

"Where do we wash?" I inquired.

"After breakfast," he replied, "if you insist."

A man in uniform appeared on the other side of the bars and used his hands, and the cell door swung open.

"Wait a minute, Wilkes," my mate told him, and then asked me, "You cleaned out?"

"Naturally. This is a modern jail."

"Would bacon and eggs suit you?"

"Just right."

"Toast white or rye?"

"White."

"Our tastes are similar. Make it two, Wilkes. Two of everything."

"As you say," the turnkey said distinctly, and went. My mate, getting his necktie under his shirt collar, told me, "They won't allow exceptions to the turnout and check-up, but you can pass up the garbage. We'll eat here in privacy."

"This," I said earnestly, "is the brotherhood of man. I would like this breakfast to be on me when I get my wallet back."

He waved it away. "Forget it."

The turnout and check-up, I discovered, were not to be taken as opportunities for conversation. There were around forty of us, all shapes and sizes, and on the whole we were frankly not a blue-ribbon outfit. The smell of the breakfast added to the disinfectant was enough to account for the expressions on the faces, not counting whatever it was that had got them there, and it was a relief to get back to my cozy cell with my mate.

We had our hands and faces washed, and he had his teeth brushed, when the breakfast came on a big clean aluminum tray. The eats were barely usable if you took Fritz's productions as a standard, but compared with the community meal which I had seen and smelled they were a handsome feast. My mate having ordered two of everything, there were two morning *Gazettes*, and before he even touched his orange juice he took his paper and, with no glance at the front page, turned to sports. Finishing his survey of the day's prospects, he drank some orange juice and inquired, "Are you interested in the rapidity of horses?"

"In a way." I added earnestly, "I like the way you talk. I enjoy being with cultured people."

He gave me a suspicious look, saw my honest candid countenance, and relaxed. "That's natural. Look at your clothes."

We were on the chairs, with the little wooden table between us. It was comfortable enough except that there was no room to prop up our morning papers. He flattened his out, still open at sports, on the end of the cot, and turned to it while disposing of a bite of food. I arranged mine, front page, on my knee. In the picture of Mrs. Rackham the poor woman looked homelier than she had actually been, which was a darned shame even though she wasn't alive to see it. Wolfe's name and mine both appeared in the subheads under the three-column spread about the murder. I glanced at the bottom, followed the instruction to turn to page four, and there saw more pictures. The one of Wolfe was only fair, making him look almost bloated, but the one of me was excellent. There was one of a Doberman pinscher standing at attention. It was captioned Hebe, which I doubted. The play in the text on Wolfe and me was on his sudden retirement from business and absence from the city, and on my presence at the scene of the murder and arrest as a material witness. There was also a report of an interview with Marko Vukcic, a *Gazette* exclusive, with Lon Cohen's by-line. I would have given at least ten to one that Lon had used my name in getting to Marko.

With the breakfast all down, including the coffee, which was pretty good, I was so interested in my reading that I didn't notice that my mate had finished with sports and proceeded to other current events. What got my attention was the feeling that I was being scrutinized, and sure enough I was. He was looking at me, and then at his page four, and back at me again.

I grinned at him. "Pretty good likeness, huh? But I don't think that's the right dog. I'm no expert, but Hebe isn't quite as slim as that."

He was regarding me with a new expression, not particularly matey. "So you're Nero Wolfe's little Archie."

"I was." I gestured. "Read the paper. Apparently I am now my own little Archie."

"So I bought a meal for a shamus."

"Not at all. Didn't I say it was on me when I get my wallet back?"

He shook his head. "I wouldn't have believed it. With them clothes? I supposed you had got snagged in the raid on the Covered Porch. It gets worse all the time, the dicks. Look at this, even here in the can I meet a guy with a suit of clothes like that, and he's a dick!"

"I am not a dick, strictly speaking." I was hurt. "I am a private eye. I said I liked the way you talk, but you're getting careless. I also noticed you were cultured, and that should have put me on my guard. Cultured people are not often found in the coop. But nowadays dicks are frequently cultured. They tossed me in here because they think I'm holding out on a murder, which I'm not, and the fact that it has been tried before doesn't mean they wouldn't try it again. Putting you in here with me wasn't so dumb, but you overplayed it, buying me a breakfast first pop. That started me wondering."

He was on his feet, glaring down at me. "Watch it, looselip. I'm going to clip you."

"What for?"

"You need a lesson. I'm a plant, am I?"

"Nuts. Who's insulted now?" I gestured. "You call me a name, I call you a name. I take it, you take it. Let's start over."

But he was too sensitive to make up as quick as all that. He undid his fist, glared at me some more, sidled between his chair and his cot, and got comfortable on the cot with his *Gazette*. With his head toward the corridor he was getting as good light as there was, and I followed his example, folding one of the blankets for a pillow and spreading my handkerchief on it. Two hours and ten minutes passed without a word from either cot. I happen to know because as I stretched out I glanced at my watch, wondering how soon I could reasonably expect Parker to show up with a crowbar to pry me loose, and it was twenty past nine; and, after giving that *Gazette* as good a play as a newspaper ever got, I had just looked at my watch for the twentieth time and seen 11:30 when he suddenly spoke.

"Look, Goodwin, what are you going to do now?"

I let the paper slide to the floor. "I don't know, take a nap, I guess."

"I don't mean now, this minute. Is anyone looking after you?"

"If he isn't he'd better be. A high-priced lawyer named Parker."

"Then what?"

"I'll go home and take a bath."

"Then what?"

"I'll brush my teeth and shave."

"Then what?"

I swiveled my head to glance at him. "You're pretty damn persistent. Where do you want us to get to?"

"Nowhere in particular." He stayed supine, and I noticed that in profile he looked a little like John L. Lewis, only a lot younger. He went on, "I was just thinking, with Nero Wolfe gone I suppose your job's gone. Can't I think?"

"Sure. If it doesn't hurt."

A brief silence. He spoke again. "I've heard about you a little. What kind of a guy are you?"

"Oh—I'm a thinker too, and I'm cultured. I got good marks in algebra. I sleep well. I'm honest and ambitious, with a good personality."

"You know your way around."

"In certain circles, yes. It would be hard to lose me within ten miles of Times Square unless I was blindfolded. What are the requirements of the position you are about to offer?"

He ignored that and took another angle. "My name is Christy—Max Christy. Ever hear of me?"

If I had it was vague, but I saw no point in hurting his feelings. "Max Christy?" I snorted. "Don't be silly."

"I thought you might have. I've only been around the big town a couple of years, and I don't toot a horn, but some people get talked about. How much has Wolfe been paying you?"

"That's asking," I objected mildly. "I wouldn't want it to get in the papers. I've been eating all right and I've got a government bond. Anything over—"

Footsteps in the corridor stopped at our door, and the turnkey's voice came. "Mr. Christy! They want you down in the office."

My mate stayed flat. "Come back in ten minutes, Wilkes," he called. "I'm busy."

I confirmed it. "We're in conference, Wilkes," I snapped.

"But I think it's your out."

"I suppose so. Come back in ten minutes."

Wilkes, mumbling something, went away. Christy resumed. "You were saying . . ."

"Yeah. That anything over fifty grand a year would find me a good listener."

"I'm being serious, Goodwin."

"So am I."

"You are not. You never got within a mile of fifty grand a year." His head was turned to face me now. "Anyway, it's not a question of so many grand a year—not in this business."

"In what business?"

"The business I'm in. What did I say my name is?"

"Max Christy."

"Then what more do you want? Take my being here now, for example. I got raked in at the Covered Porch yesterday by mistake, but I would have been loose in an hour if it hadn't been Sunday—and Easter too. Here it is" —he looked at his wrist—"not quite noon, and I'm walking out. There has never been an organization to compare with it. For a man like you there would be special jobs and special opportunities if you once got taken in. With your record, which is bad as far as I know it, that would take a while. You would have to show, and show good. Your idea about so many grand a year just isn't realistic, certainly not while you're being tried, but after that it would depend on you. If you've got it in you there's practically no limit. Another thing is income tax."

"Yeah, what about income tax?"

"You simply use your judgment. Say Wolfe paid you thirty grand a year, which he didn't, nothing like it, what did you have to say about income tax? Nothing. It was taken out before you got paid. You never even saw it. In this business you make your own decisions about it. You want to be fair, and you want to be in the clear, but you don't want to get gypped, and on that basis you use your judgment."

Christy raised his torso and sat on the edge of the cot. "You know, Goodwin, I'm just tossing this at you on the spur of the moment. I laid here reading about you, and I thought to myself, here's a man the right age and experience, not married, the right personality, he knows people, he knows lots of cops, he has been a private eye for years and so he would be open to anything that sounds good enough; he is just out of a job, he's got himself tangled in a hot homicide here in Westchester, and he may need help right now. That's what I was thinking, and I thought why not ask him? I can't guarantee anything, especially if you're headed for a murder rap, but if you need help now and then later on you would like a chance at something, I'm Max Christy and I could pass the word along. If you—"

He paused at the sound of footsteps. Wilkes's voice came from the door. "They want you down there, Mr. Christy. I told them you was busy personally, but they're sending up."

"All right, Wilkes. Coming." My mate stood up. "What about it, Goodwin?"

"I appreciate it," I said warmly. Wilkes, having unlocked the door, was standing there, and, using my judgment, I kept it discreet. "When I get out and look around a little I'll know better how things stand." I had got to my feet. "How do I get in touch with you?"

"Phone is best. Churchill five, three two three two. I'm not there much, but a message will reach me promptly. Better write it down."

"I'll remember it." I took his offered hand and we shook. "It's been a pleasure. Where can I mail a check for the breakfast?"

"Forget it. It was a privilege. Be seeing you, I hope." He strode out like an executive going to greet a welcome caller, Wilkes holding the door for him.

I sat down on the cot, thinking it was a hell of a note for a Max Christy to get sprung before an Archie Goodwin. What was keeping Parker? In jail a man gets impatient.

IX

IT WAS seven o'clock that evening, just getting dark, when I left the car at the curb on West 35th Street in front of Wolfe's house and climbed the seven steps to the stoop. Parker, armed with papers which stated, among other things, that my continued availability to the People of the State of New York was worth ten thousand dollars, had arrived at the jail shortly after two, and in another ten minutes I had been unleashed on society again, but District Attorney Archer had requested another session with me in the presence of my attorney, and Parker and I had obliged. It had dragged on and on, and was really a bore, because there was nothing for me to try to be witty about. Unlike some other occasions when I had been in conference with the law, there was nothing to stimulate me because all I had to do was tell the truth, and all of it—except the sausage part and the phone call from Arnold Zeck.

When they had finally called it a day and Parker and I were standing on the sidewalk in front of the courthouse, he asked me, "Am I to know where Wolfe is?"

"I doubt it. He told me not to look for him."

"I see."

His tone of voice irritated me. "Every word you heard me say in there," I asserted, "was the truth. I haven't the thinnest idea where he is or what he's doing."

He shrugged. "I'm not complaining. I only hope he hasn't tumbled in where it's too deep this time—and you too."

"Go to hell," I advised him, and marched off. I couldn't really blame the Westchester bunch, but Parker should have known me well enough to tell which side of my mouth I was talking out of. It's damn discouraging, when you do tell the truth, not to have it recognized.

Also discouraging was the welcome I got on entering Wolfe's house that evening. It was in the form of a note stuck in the corner of my desk blotter, unfolded.

Dear Archie—

I am sorry you are in jail and hope it will not last long. Mr. Vukcic has been to see me and I am leaving now to go to work for him $1500. There has been no word from Mr. Wolfe. God grant he is safe and well and I think you should find him no matter what he wrote. I threw out the jar of sardines and stopped the milk. My very best regards and wishes,

Fritz

1:35 PM

I was pleased to observe that he stuck to routine to the end, putting the time down. Also it was nice of him to end his note to me the same as Wolfe had ended his. Nevertheless, it was a discouraging welcome home after a night in the hoosegow. And there had been a period of more than five hours when any phone calls that might have come would not have been answered, something that had never happened before in all the years I had worked and lived there. Unless Theodore . . .

I beat it to the stairs and up the three flights, and entered the plant rooms. One step inside the first room, the warm one, I stopped and surveyed. It was more of a shock, somehow, than it had been a year ago when it had been used as a target for tommy guns from across the street. Then they had at least left a mess; now there was nothing but the benches and stands. It really got me for a minute. I moved on through: medium room, cool room, potting room, spray chamber, Theodore's room—all empty. Hewitt must have sent an army to clean all that out in one day, I thought, heading back downstairs.

In the kitchen was another longer note from Fritz, reporting phone calls that had come before he left and various minor matters. I opened the refrigerator and poked around, and settled for a jar of home-made paté, a hunk of Italian bread, Vermont cheese, and milk. As I sat working at it with an evening paper propped up before me, I kept listening for something—nothing in particular, just something. That had never been a noisy house, but I had never known it anything like that quiet. Almost no cars went by, and the few that did must have been coasting in neutral.

My meal finished and things put away, I wandered into the dining room, office, front room, down to the basement to Fritz's room, up one flight to Wolfe's room, up another to my room. As I undressed for my post-jail bath, I thought that the hell of it wasn't how I felt, but that I didn't know how to feel. If I had actually seen the last of Nero Wolfe, it was a damn sad day for me, there were no two ways about that, and if I got a lump in my throat and somebody walked in I would just as soon show him the lump as not. But what if it was Wolfe himself who walked in? That was the trouble. Damned if I was going to work up a fancy lump and then have him suddenly appear and start crabbing about something.

After I had bathed and shaved and got into clean pajamas, and answered a couple of phone calls from journalists, and moseyed down to the office and fooled around a while, someone did walk in. When I heard the front door open I made for the hall as if I had been expecting another package of sausage, and there was Fritz. He turned from closing the door, saw me, and beamed.

"Ah! Archie! You escaped?"

"I'm out on bail." He seemed to want to shake hands, and I was willing. "Thanks for your note. How's the new job?"

"Terrible. I'm played up. Mr. Wolfe?"

"I know nothing about Mr. Wolfe. I ate half a jar of paté."

He stopped beaming. "Mr. Vukcic is going to sell this house."

"He's going to offer it for sale, which is not the same thing."

"Perhaps not." He sighed. "I'm tired. Mr. Vukcic said there is no reason why I should not sleep here but I should ask you. It would be good for me— I am so used to that room . . ."

"Certainly. I'm used to mine too. I'm going to sleep here until further notice."

"Good." He started for the kitchen, stopped, and turned. "Are you going to look for him?"

"No!" Hearing myself shout, it seemed a relief and I did it again. "I am not!" I went to the stairs and started up. "Good night."

"Good night, Archie."

I was on the first landing when his voice came. "I'll get your breakfast! I don't have to leave until ten!"

"Swell!" I called back. "We'll never miss him!"

The next day, Tuesday, I had no time to raise a lump. There were dozens of phone calls, from newspapers, former clients, friends, and miscellaneous. One was from Calvin Leeds, asking me to go up there to see him, and I told him I had had enough of Westchester for a while. When he insisted, I agreed to receive him at the office at two o'clock. I took advantage of another call, from Lon Cohen at the *Gazette,* to ask about my recent cellmate, Max Christy. Lon asked why I wanted to know. Lon is a good guy, but no newspaperman on earth can answer the simplest question without asking you one first, and more if possible.

"Just curious," I told him. "I met him in jail over the weekend, and thought he was charming. I don't want a biography, just a line or two."

"For quotation?"

"No."

"Right. He's comparatively new to this section, but he's a fast mover. Not really big yet. As far as I know, the only thing he's close to right in town is a string of rooms for transients. He seems to be specializing on little weekend roundups in the suburbs."

"Just games, or women, or what?"

"Anything men risk money for. Or pay it for. I have heard that he is seen around sometimes with Brownie Costigan. How curious are you? Is it worth a steak? Or is it worth a phone number or address where I can reach Nero Wolfe?"

By that time I had abandoned the idea of selling anyone, even Lon Cohen, the idea that I ever told the truth, so I thanked him and hung up.

A couple of checks in the morning mail, one from a man who was paying in installments for having a blackmailer removed from his throat, were no problem, since there was a rubber stamp for endorsing them, but in order to pay three bills that came in I had to make a trip to 54th Street to see if the formalities about Marko's power of attorney had been attended to. They had, by Parker, and I was glad to see that Marko signed the checks on my say-so, without looking at the bills. If he had started auditing on me I swear to God I would have moved out and got a hotel room.

There were other chores, such as phoning Hewitt's place on Long Island to ask if the plants and Theodore had arrived safely, making arrangements with a phone-answering service, handling a report from Fred Durkin on a poison-letter job that was the main item of unfinished business, and so on, but I managed to have them all under control when two o'clock came and brought Calvin Leeds.

When I went to let him in and took him to the office, there was a problem. Should I sit at my desk or at Wolfe's? On the one hand, I was not Wolfe and had no intention of trying to be. On the other hand, when a pinch-hitter is called on he stands at the plate to bat, not off to one side. Also it would be interesting to see, from Wolfe's position, what the light was like on the face of a man sitting in the red leather chair. So again, this time intentionally, I sat behind Wolfe's desk.

"I came here to get an explanation," Leeds said, "and I'm going to get it."

He looked as if he could stand a dose of something—if not an explanation, then maybe castor oil. The hide of his face still looked tough and weathered, or rather as if it had been but someone had soaked it in something to make it stretch and get saggy. His eyes looked determined, but not clear and alert as before. No one would have guessed that he had just inherited half a million bucks, and not from a dearly beloved wife or sister but merely a cousin.

Something like a million times I had seen Wolfe, faced with a belligerent statement from a caller, lean back and close his eyes. I thought I might as well try it, and did so. But the springs which let the chair's back slant to the rear were carefully adjusted to the pressure of Wolfe's poundage, not mine, and I had to keep pushing to maintain the damn thing in the leaning position.

"A man who comes forty miles for an explanation," I said, with my eyes closed, "is entitled to one. What needs explaining?"

"Nero Wolfe's behavior does."

"That's nothing new." It was too much of a strain keeping the chair back in a leaning position, and I straightened up. "It often has. But that's not my department."

"I want to see him."

"So do I."

"You're a liar, Goodwin."

I shook my head, my lips tight. "You know," I said, "I have probably told as many lies as any man my age except psychos. But I have never been called a liar as frequently as in the past twenty-four hours, and I have never stuck so close to the truth. To hell with it. Mr. Wolfe has gone south to train with the Dodgers. He will play shortstop."

"That won't help any," Leeds said, patient but determined, "that kind of talk. If you don't like being called a liar, neither do I, and the difference is that I'm not. The District Attorney says I'm lying, because Nero Wolfe has suddenly disappeared, and he disappeared because he doesn't dare answer questions about my cousin Sarah's visit to him here, and that proves that your report of that visit is false, and since my report is the same as yours mine is false too. Now that sounds logical, but there's a flaw in it. The flaw is their assumption that his disappearance was connected with my cousin's visit. I knew it couldn't have been, because there was nothing about our talk that day that could possibly have had such a result. I have told them that, and they think I'm lying. As long as they think I'm lying, and you too, they'll have their minds on that and they won't find out who killed my cousin and why—and anyway, I don't want to be suspected of lying when I'm not, especially not in connection with the murder of my cousin."

Leeds paused for breath and went on, "There's only one way out that I can see, and that's for you to tell them the real reason for Wolfe's disappearance—or, better still, he ought to tell them himself. I want you to put this up to him. Even if his own safety is involved, he ought to manage somehow. If it was something about some client that made him disappear, in the interest of some client, then you can tell him from me that I saw him take a check from my cousin for ten thousand dollars and it seems to me he's under obligation to her as much as any other client, to protect her interests, and it surely isn't in her interest to have suspicion centered in the wrong place about who killed her—and killed her dog too." His jaw quivered a little, and he clamped it tight.

"Do you mean," I inquired, "that suspicion is centered on you? How come?"

"Not on me as—as a murderer, I don't suppose so, but on me as a liar, and you and Wolfe. Even though she left me a great deal of money—I'm not thinking about being arrested for murder."

"Who do you think ought to be?"

"I don't know." He gestured. "You're trying to change the subject. It's not a question of me and what I think, it's you and what you're going to do. From what I've heard of Wolfe, I doubt if it would help for you to tell him what I've said; I've got to see him and tell him myself. If he has really got to hide from somebody or something, do it however you want to. Blindfold me and put me face down in your car. I've got to see him. My cousin would have wanted me to, and he took her money."

I was half glad there for a moment that I did not know where Wolfe was. I had no admiration for Leeds' preference in pets, since I would put a woman ahead of a Doberman pinscher any day, and there was room for improvement in him in a few other respects, but I couldn't help but admit he had a point and was not being at all unreasonable. So if I had known where Wolfe was I would have had to harden my heart, and as it was all I had to harden was my voice. It struck me then, for the first time, that maybe I shouldn't be so sore at Wolfe after all.

Leeds hung on for another quarter of an hour, and I prolonged it a little myself by trying to get something out of him about the progress the cops had made, without success. He went away mad, still calling me a liar, which kept it unanimous. What he got from me was nothing. What I got from him was that Mrs. Rackham's funeral would be the next morning, Wednesday. Not a profitable way to spend most of an hour, for either of us.

I spent what was left of the afternoon looking into the matter of sausage. Within ten minutes after the package had been opened that day, Wolfe had phoned both Mummiani and the Fleet Messenger Service and got a blank as expected; but on the outside chance that I might at least get a bone for my curiosity to gnaw on I made a trip to Fulton Street and one uptown. At Mummiani's no one knew anything. Since Wolfe had been getting Darst's sausage from them for years, and in that time their personnel had come and gone, any number of outsiders could know about it. At the Fleet Messenger Service they were willing to help but couldn't. They remembered the package because Wolfe had phoned about it, but all I learned was that it had been left there by a youth who might have been playing hookey from the eighth grade, and I didn't even bother to listen to the description, such as it was.

Fed up with an empty house and the phone ringing and being called a liar, I put in a call myself from a drugstore booth, and made personal arrangements for dinner and a show.

Wednesday morning a visitor came that I let in. I had formed the habit, since returning from jail, of hearing the doorbell ring, going to the hall, observing through the one-way glass panel who it was out on the stoop, making a face, and returning to the office. If the bell kept ringing long enough to be a nuisance I flipped the switch that turned it off. This time, around eleven Wednesday morning, instead of making a face I went and opened the door and said, "Well, hello! Coming in?"

A chunky specimen about my height, with wrinkled pink skin and gray hair and sharp gray-blue eyes, grunted a greeting and stepped over the sill. I said it was cold for April, and he agreed. As I hung his topcoat on the rack I told myself that I must be more restrained. The fact that I was alone in the house was no reason to give Inspector Cramer of Manhattan Homicide the impression that I was glad to see him. Wolfe or no Wolfe, I could keep up appearances.

I let him lead the way to the office. This time I sat at my own desk. I was tempted to take Wolfe's chair again just to see how he would react, but it would have put me at a disadvantage, I was so used to dealing with him, in the red leather chair, from my own angle.

He eyed me. "So you're holding the fort," he growled.

"Not exactly," I objected. "I'm only the caretaker. Or maybe I'm going down with the ship. Not that those who have left are rats."

"Where's Wolfe?"

"I don't know. Next, you call me a liar. Then I say I have been, but not now. Then you—"

"Nuts. Where is he, Archie?"

That cleared the atmosphere. Over the years he had called me Goodwin fifty times to one Archie. He called me Archie only when he wanted something awful bad or when he had something wrapped up that Wolfe had given him and his humanity overcame him. So we were to be mellow.

"Listen," I said, friendly but firm. "That routine is all right for people like district attorneys and state cops and the representatives of the press, but you're above it. Either I don't know where he is, or I do know but I'm sitting on it. What's the difference? Next question."

He took a cigar from his pocket, inspected it, rubbed it between his palms, and inspected it again. "It must be quite a thing," he remarked, not growling. "That ad in the paper. The plants gone. Fritz and Theodore gone. Vukcic listing the house for sale. I'm going to miss it, I am, never dropping in to see him sitting there thinking he's smarter than God and all His angels. Quite a thing, it must be. What is it?"

I said slowly and wearily, "Either I don't know what it is, or I do know but—"

"What about the sausage that turned into tear gas? Any connection?"

I am always ready for Inspector Cramer, in the light of experience guided by intelligence, and therefore didn't bat an eye. I merely cocked my head a little, met his gaze, and considered the matter until I was satisfied. "I doubt if it was Fritz," I stated. "Mr. Wolfe has him too well trained. But in the excitement Sunday morning, Mr. Wolfe being gone, Fritz told Theodore, and you got it out of Theodore." I nodded. "That must be it."

"Did the tear gas scare him out of his skin? Or out of his house, which is the same thing. Was that it?"

"It might have, mightn't it? A coward like him?"

"No." Cramer put the cigar between his teeth, tilted up. "No, there are plenty of things about Wolfe I can and do object to, but he's not a coward. There might have been something about that tear gas that would have scared anybody. Was there?"

"As far as I know, it was just plain tear gas, nothing fancy." I decided to shove a little. "You know, it's nice to have you here any time, just for company, but aren't you spreading out some? Your job is homicide, and the tear gas didn't even make us sick, let alone kill us. Also your job is in the County of New York, and Mrs. Rackham died in Westchester. I enjoy talking with you, but have you got credentials?"

He made a noise that could have been a chuckle. "That's more like it," he said, not sarcastically. "You're beginning to sound natural. I'll tell you. I'm here at the request of Ben Dykes, who would give all his teeth and one ear to clear up the Rackham case ahead of the state boys. He thinks that Archer, the DA, may have swallowed the idea that you and Leeds are lying too deep, and he came to me as an expert on Nero Wolfe, which God knows I am. He laid it all out for me and wanted my opinion."

He shifted the cigar to a new angle. "The way it looked to me, there were three possibilities. First, the one that Archer has sold himself on, that you and Leeds are lying, and that what Mrs. Rackham really told Wolfe when she came here, together with her getting murdered the next day, somehow put Wolfe on a spot that was too hot for him, and he scooted, after fixing with you to cover as well as you could. I told Dykes I would rule that out, for various reasons—chiefly because neither you nor Wolfe would risk that much on a setup that depended on a stranger like Leeds sticking to a lie. Shall I analyze it more?"

"No, thanks, that'll do."

"I thought so. Next, the possibility that when you phoned Wolfe right after the body was found you told him something that gave him a line on the murderer, but it's tricky and he had to go outdoors to get his evidence, preparing to grandstand it for the front page. I told Dykes I would rule that out too. Wolfe is quite capable of a play like that, sure he is, but if that's all it amounted to, why move the plants out and put Fritz to work in a restaurant and list the house for sale? He's colorful, but not that colorful. Mrs. Rackham only paid him ten thousand, about what I make a year. Why should he spend it having his orchids carted around?"

Cramer shook his head. "Not for my money. That leaves the third possibility: that something really did scare him. That there was something about Mrs. Rackham's murder, or anyhow connected with it, that he knew he couldn't handle sitting there in that chair, but for some reason he had to handle it. So he scooted. As you say, you either don't know where he is or you know and won't tell—and that's no help either way. Now I've got a lot to say about this possibility. You got time to listen?"

"I've got all day, but Fritz isn't here to get our lunch."

"We'll go without." He clasped his hands behind his head and shifted his center of gravity. "You know, Archie, sometimes I'm not as far behind as you think I am."

"Also sometimes I don't think you're as far behind as you think I do."

"That's possible. Anyhow, I can add. I think he got word direct from Arnold Zeck. Did he?"

"Huh? Who's Arnold Zeck? Did you just make it up?"

I knew that was a mistake the instant it was out of my mouth. Then I had to try to keep it from showing on my face, the realization that I had fumbled it, but whether that was a success or not—and I couldn't very well look in a mirror to find out—it was too late.

Cramer looked pleased. "So you've been around all these years, a working detective, meeting the people you do, and you've never heard of Arnold Zeck. Either I've got to believe that, or I touched a tender spot."

"Sure I've heard of him. It just didn't click for a second."

"Oh, for God's sake. It's affecting you already, having Wolfe gone. That wasn't just a shot in the dark. One day two years ago I sat here in this chair. Wolfe sat there." He nodded at Wolfe's chair. "You were where you are now. A man named Orchard had been murdered, and so had a woman named Poole. In the course of our long talk Wolfe explained in detail how an ingenious and ruthless man could operate a blackmail scheme, good for at least a million a year, without sticking his neck out. Not only could; it was being done. Wolfe refused to name him, and since he wasn't behind the murders it was out of my territory, but a thing or two I heard and a couple of things that happened gave me a pretty clear idea. Not only me—it was whispered around: Arnold Zeck. You may perhaps remember it."

"I remember the Orchard case, certainly," I conceded. "I didn't hear the whispering."

"I did. You may also remember that a year later, last summer, Wolfe's plant rooms got shot up from a roof across the street."

"Yep. I was sitting right here and heard it."

"So I understand. Since no one was killed that never got to me officially, but naturally I heard things. Wolfe had started to investigate a man named Rony, and Rony's activities were the kind that might lead a first-class investigator like Wolfe in the direction of Arnold Zeck, maybe up close to Zeck, possibly even clear to him. I thought then that Wolfe had got warned off, by Zeck himself or someone near him, and he had disregarded it, and for a second warning they messed up his orchids. Then Rony got killed, and that was a break for Wolfe because it put him and Zeck on the same side."

"Gosh," I remarked, "it sounds awful complicated to me."

"I'll bet it does." Cramer moved the cigar—getting shorter now, although he never lit one—to the other side of his mouth. "All I'm doing is showing you that I'm not just hoping for a bite, and I don't want to string it out. It was a good guess that Wolfe had jostled up against Arnold Zeck in both the Orchard case and the Rony case, and now what happens? Not long after Mrs. Rackham calls on him and hires him to check on her husband's income, someone sends him a cylinder of tear gas—not a bomb to blow out his guts, which it could have been, just tear gas, so of course it was for a warning. And that night Mrs. Rackham gets murdered. You tell him about it on the phone, and when you get home he's gone."

Cramer took the cigar from his mouth and pointed it at me. "I'll tell you what I believe, Archie. I believe that if Wolfe had stayed and helped, the murderer of Mrs. Rackham would be locked up by now. I believe that he had reason to think that if he did that, helped to catch the murderer, he would have to spend the rest of his life trying to keep Arnold Zeck from getting him. I believe that he decided that the only way out was for him to get Zeck. How's that?"

"No comment," I said politely. "If you're right you're right, and if you're wrong I wouldn't want to hurt your feelings."

"Much obliged. But he did get a warning from Zeck—the tear gas."

"No comment."

"I wouldn't expect any. Now here's what I came for. I want you to give Wolfe a personal message from me, not as a police officer but as a friend. This is between you and me—and him. Zeck is out of his reach. He is out of anybody's reach. It's a goddam crime for an officer of the law to have to say a thing like that, even privately, but it's true. Here's a murder case, and thank God it's not mine. I'm not pointing at Ben Dykes or the DA up there, I'm not pointing at any person or persons, but if the setup is that Barry Rackham is tied in with one or more of Zeck's operations, and if Rackham killed his wife, I say he will never burn. I don't say at what point Zeck will get his hand in, or who or what he will use, but Rackham will never burn."

Cramer hurled his cigar at my wastebasket and missed it a foot. Since it wasn't lit I ignored it. "Hooray for justice," I cheered.

He snarled, but apparently not at me. "I want you to tell Wolfe that. Zeck is out of his reach. He can't get him."

"But," I objected, "granting that you've got it all straight, which I haven't, that's a hell of a message. Look at it from the other end. He is not out of Zeck's reach, not if he comes home. I know he doesn't go out much, but even if he never did people have to come in—and things, like packages of sausage. Not to mention that the damage they did to the plants and equipment last year came to thirty-eight thousand bucks. I get the idea that he is to lay off of Zeck, but that's only what he doesn't do. What does he do?"

Cramer nodded. "I know. That's it. He's so damn bullheaded. I want you to understand, Archie, why I came here. Wolfe is too cocky to live. He has enough brass and bluster to outfit a thousand sergeants. Sure, I know him; I ought to. I would love to bloody his nose for him, I've tried to often enough, and some day I will and enjoy it. But I would hate to see him break his neck on a deal like this where he hasn't got a chance. It's a good guess that in the past ten years there have been over a hundred homicides in this town that were connected in one way or another with one of the operations Arnold Zeck has a hand in. But not in a single case was there the remotest hope of tying Zeck up with it. We couldn't possibly have touched him."

"You're back where you started," I complained. "He can't be reached. So what?"

"So Wolfe should come back where he belongs, return what Mrs. Rackham paid him to her estate, let the Westchester people take care of the murder, which is their job anyhow, and go on as before. You can tell him I said that, but by God don't quote me around. I'm not responsible for a man like Zeck being out of reach."

"But you never strained a muscle stretching for him."

"Nuts. Facts are facts."

"Yeah, like sausage is tear gas." I stood up so as to look down my nose at him. "There are two reasons why your message will not get to Mr. Wolfe. First, he is to me as Zeck is to him. He's out of my reach. I don't know where he is."

"Oh, keep it up."

"I will. Second, I don't like the message. I admit that I have known Mr. Wolfe to discuss Arnold Zeck. I once heard him tell a whole family about him, only he was calling him X. He was describing the difficulties he would be in if he ever found himself tangled with X for a showdown, and he told them that he was acquainted, more or less, with some three thousand people living or working in New York, and there weren't more than five of them of whom he could say with certainty that they were in no way involved in X's activities. He said that none might be or that any might be. On another occasion I happened to be inquiring about Zeck of a newspaperman, and he had extravagant notions about Zeck's payroll. He mentioned, not by name, politicians, barflies, cops, chambermaids, lawyers, private ops, crooks of all types, including gunmen—maybe housewives, I forget. He did not specifically mention police inspectors."

"Just forgot, perhaps."

"I suppose so. Another thing, those five exceptions that Mr. Wolfe made out of his three thousand acquaintances, he didn't say who they were, but I was pretty sure I could name three of them. I thought probably one of the other two was you, but I could have been wrong. You have made a point of how you would hate to see him break his neck where he hasn't got a chance. You took the trouble to come here with a personal message but don't want to be quoted, which means that if I mention this conversation to anyone but Mr. Wolfe you'll call me a liar. And what's the message? That he should lay off of Zeck, that's what it amounts to. If in earning the fee Mrs. Rackham paid him he is liable to hurt somebody Zeck doesn't want hurt, he should return the fee. The way it looks from here, sending a message like that to the best and toughest detective on earth is exactly the kind of service Zeck would pay good money for. I wouldn't say—"

I didn't get to say what I wouldn't say. Cramer, out of his chair and coming, had a look on his face that I had never seen before. Time and again I had seen him mad at Wolfe, and me too, but never to the point where the pink left his cheeks completely and his eyes looked absolutely mean.

He swung with his right. I ducked. He came up from beneath with his left, and I stopped it with my forearm. He tried with the right again, and I jerked back, stepped aside, and dived around the corner of Wolfe's desk.

I spoke. "You couldn't hit me in a year and I'm not going to plug you.

I'm twenty years younger, and you're an inspector. If I'm wrong, some day I'll apologize. If I'm wrong."

He turned and marched out. I didn't go to the hall to help him on with his coat and open the door.

X

THREE weeks went by.

At first, that first night, I was thinking that word might come from Wolfe in the next hour. Then I started thinking it might come the next day. As the days kept creeping along they changed my whole attitude, and before the end of April I was thinking it might come next week. By the time May had passed, and most of June, and the calendar and the heat both said summer, I was beginning to think it might never come.

But first to finish with April. The Rackham case followed the routine of spectacular murders when they never quite get to the point of a first-degree charge against anyone. For a week, the front page by unanimous consent; then, for a week or ten days, the front page only by cooking up an angle; and then back to the minors. None of the papers happened to feel like using it to start a crusade in the name of justice, so it took a normal course. It did not roll over and die, not with that all-star cast, including Nobby and Hebe; even months later a really new development would have got a three-column spread; but the development didn't come.

I made three more trips, by official request, to White Plains, with no profit to anyone, including me. All I could do was repeat myself, and all they could do was think up new ways to ask the same questions. For mental exercise I tried to get a line on whether Cramer's notions about Arnold Zeck had been passed on to Archer and Ben Dykes, but if so they never let on.

All I knew was what I read in the papers, until one evening I ran into Sergeant Purley Stebbins at Jake's and bought him a lobster. From him I got two little unpublished items: two FBI men had been called in to settle an argument about the legibility of fingerprints on the crinkly silver handle of the knife, and had voted no; and at one point Barry Rackham had been held at White Plains for twenty straight hours while the battle raged over whether they had enough to charge him. The noes won that time too.

The passing days got very little help from me. I had decided not to start pawing the ground or rearing up until Wolfe had been gone a full month, which would be May ninth, and I caught up on a lot of personal things, including baseball games, which don't need to be itemized. Also, with Fred Durkin, I finished up the poison-pen case and other loose ends that Wolfe had left dangling—nothing important—drove out to Long Island to see if

Theodore and the plants had got settled in their new home, and put one of the cars, the big sedan, in dead storage.

One afternoon when I went to Rusterman's Restaurant to see Marko Vukcic he signed the checks I had brought, for telephone and electricity bills and my weekly salary, and then asked me what the bank balance was. I told him a little over twenty-nine thousand dollars, but I sort of regarded Mrs. Rackham's ten grand as being in escrow, so I would rather call it nineteen.

"Could you bring me a check for five thousand tomorrow? Drawn to cash."

"Glad to. But speaking as the bookkeeper, what do I charge it to?"

"Why—expense."

"Speaking as a man who may some day have to answer questions from an internal revenue snoop, whose expense and what kind?"

"Call it travel expense."

"Travel by whom and to where?"

Marko made some kind of a French noise, or foreign at least, indicating impatience, I think. "Listen, Archie, I have a power of attorney without limit. Bring me a check for five thousand dollars at your convenience. I am stealing it from my old friend Nero to spend on beautiful women or olive oil."

So I was not entirely correct when I said that I got no word at all from Wolfe during those weeks and months, but you must admit it was pretty vague. How far a man gets on five grand, and where he goes, depends on so many things.

When I returned to the office from a morning walk on the third day of May, a Wednesday, and called the phone-answering service as usual, I was told there had been three calls but only one message—to ring a Mount Kisco number and ask for Mrs. Frey. I considered the situation, told myself the thing to do was skip it, and decided that I must be hard of hearing when I became aware that I had dialed the operator and asked for the number. Then, after I had got it and spelled my name and waited a minute, Annabel Frey's voice was in my ear. At least the voice said it was her, but I wouldn't have recognized it. It was sort of tired and hopeless.

"You don't sound like you," I told her.

"I suppose not," she conceded. "It seems like a million years since you came that day and we watched you being a detective. You never found out who poisoned the dog, did you?"

"No, but don't hold it against me. I wasn't expected to. You may have heard that that was just a blind."

"Yes, of course. I don't suppose Nero Wolfe is back?"

"Nope."

"You're running his office for him?"

"Well, I wouldn't call it running. I'm here."

"I want to see you."

"Excuse me for staring, but do you mean on business?"

"Yes." A pause, then her voice got more energetic. "I want you to come up here and talk with us. I don't want to go on like this, and I'm not going to. When people look at me I can see it in their eyes—was it me that killed my mother-in-law?—or in some of them I can see it, and that makes me think it's there with all of them. It's been nearly a month now, and all the police are doing—but you read the papers. She left me this place and a lot of money, and I wish I could hire Nero Wolfe. You must know where he is."

"Sorry. I don't."

"Then I want to hire you. You're a good detective, aren't you?"

"Opinions vary. I rate myself close to the top, but you have to discount that for my bias."

"Could you come up here today? This evening?"

"I couldn't make it today." My brain was having some exercise for the first time in weeks. "Look, Mrs. Frey, I wouldn't be in a hurry about this. There's—"

"A hurry?" She sounded bitter. "It's been nearly a month!"

"I know, and that's why another few days won't matter. There's nothing fresh about it, to get stale. Why don't you do this, let me do a little looking around, just on my own, and then you'll hear from me. After that you can decide whether you want to hire me or not."

"I've already decided."

"I haven't. I don't want your dough if there's no chance of earning it."

Since her mind had been made up before she called me, she didn't like it my way but finally settled for it.

I discovered when I hung up that my mind was made up too. It had made itself up while I was talking to her. I couldn't go on like this forever, nothing but a damn caretaker with no telling from day to day how long it might last. Nor could I, while drawing pay as Wolfe's assistant, take a boat for Europe or run for Mayor of New York or buy an island and build up a harem, or any of the other things on my deferred list; and certainly, while taking his pay, I couldn't personally butt into a case that he had run away from.

But there was nothing to prevent me from taking advantage of the gratitude that was still felt, even after paying the fee, by certain former clients of ours, and I took up the phone again and got the president of one of the big realty outfits, and was glad to learn that I hadn't overestimated his gratitude. When I had explained my problem he said he would do all he could to help, starting right then.

So I spent the afternoon looking at offices in the midtown section. All I wanted was one little room with a light that worked, but the man that the realty president sent to go around with me was more particular than I was, and he turned his nose up at two or three that I would have bought. We finally got to one on Madison Avenue, tenth floor, in the forties, which he admitted might do. It wouldn't be vacated until the next day, but that didn't matter much because I still had to buy furniture. I was allowed to sign for it on a month-to-month basis.

The next couple of days I had to keep myself under control. I had never been aware of any secret longing to have my own agency, but I had to choke off an impulse to drop in at Macgruder's Thursday morning and blow a couple of thousand of my own jack on office equipment. Instead, I went to Second Avenue and found bargains. Having decided not to take anything from 35th Street, I made up a shopping list of about forty items, from ash trays to a Moorhead's Directory, and shot the works.

Late Saturday afternoon, with a package under my arm, I emerged from the elevator, went down the hall to the door of 1019, and backed off to give it a look.

ARCHIE GOODWIN
Private Detective

Not bad at all, I thought, unlocking the door and entering. I had considered having the painter put beneath it "By Appointment Only," to keep the crowd down, but decided to save the extra three bucks. I put my package on the desk, unwrapped it, and inspected my new letterheads and envelopes. The type of my name was a little too bold, maybe, but otherwise it was pretty neat. I uncovered the typewriter, a rebuilt Underwood that had set me back $62.75, inserted one of the letterheads, and wrote:

Dear Mrs. Frey:

If you still feel as you did when you phoned me on Wednesday, I would be glad to call on you to discuss the situation, with the understanding that I shall be representing no one but myself.

My new business address and phone number are above. Ring me or write if you wish me to come.

Sincerely,

AG:hs

I read it over and signed it. It looked businesslike, I thought, with the regulation initialing at the bottom, the "hs" being for "himself." When I left, after putting the stationery in a drawer and getting things in order for the rush of business on Monday morning, I dropped the envelope in the mail chute. I was doing it that way, instead of phoning her, for three reasons: if she had changed her mind she could just ignore it; I had a date, purely personal, for the weekend; and I had drawn myself a salary check, the last one, for that week. On my way home I made a detour to 54th Street, to tell Marko Vukcic what I had done, because I thought he should be the first to know.

He made it not only plain but emphatic that he disapproved. I told him, "Experience tells me that pants wear out quicker sitting down than moving around. Intelligence tells me that it's better to wait till you die to start to rot. I would appreciate it if you will convey that to him next time you write him or phone him."

"You know perfectly good, Archie, that—"

"Not perfectly good. Perfectly well."

"You know that I have said nothing, but nothing, that might make you think I can write him or phone him."

"You didn't need to. I know it's not your fault, but where does it leave me? Let me know any time you get a buyer for the house, and I'll move out."

I left him still wanting to argue.

I was not kidding myself that I had really cut loose, since I hadn't moved my bed out, but the way I figured it a caretaker who is drawing no pay has a right to a room; and besides, Fritz was still sleeping there and we were splitting on the groceries for breakfast, and I didn't want to insult either him or my stomach by breaking that up.

I shall now have to specify when I say office—or, better, I'll say office when I mean Wolfe's office, and when I mean my Madison Avenue suite I'll say 1019. Monday morning, arriving at 1019 a little after ten, I rang the phone-answering service and was told that there had been no calls, and then dug into the morning mail, which consisted of a folder from a window-cleaning outfit. After giving it full consideration, I typed notes on my new stationery to some personal friends, and an official letter to the City of New York giving notice of my change of address as a licensed detective. I was sitting trying to think who else I might write to when the phone rang—my first incoming call.

I picked it up and told the transmitter plainly, "Archie Goodwin's office."

"May I speak to Mr. Goodwin, please?"

"I'll see if he's in. Who is calling, please?"

"Mrs. Frey."

"Yes, he's in. This is me. You got my note?"

"It came this morning. I don't know what you mean about representing no one but yourself."

"I guess I didn't make it very clear. I only meant I wouldn't be acting as Nero Wolfe's assistant. I'm just myself now."

"Oh. Well—naturally, if you don't even know where he is. Can you come this evening?"

"To Birchvale?"

"Yes."

"What time?"

"Say eight-thirty."

"I'll be there."

You can't beat that, I thought to myself as I hung up, for the first incoming call to a new office—making a deal with a client who has just inherited a country estate and a million monetary units. Then, fearing that if it kept up like that I might get swamped, I closed the office for the day and headed for Sulka's to buy a tie.

XI

ON MY previous visit to Birchvale I had got the impression that Annabel Frey had her head on right side up, and her conduct that Monday evening strengthened it. For one thing, she had had sense enough not to gather that bunch around a dining table but invite them for half-past eight. With the kind of attitudes and emotions that were crisscrossing among those six people, an attempt to feed them at the same trough would have resulted in an acidosis epidemic.

In her first phone call, Wednesday, she had indicated that it was not a tête-à-tête she had in mind, so I was expecting to find company, probably the widower and the cousin, but to my surprise it was a full house. They were all there when I was shown into the big living room. Annabel Frey, as hostess there now, came to meet me and gave me her hand. The other five gave me nothing but dirty looks. I saw right off that my popularity index was way down, so I merely stood, gave them a cool collective greeting, and lifted a brow at my hostess.

"It's not you, Goodwin," the politician Pierce assured me, but in a raspy tone. "It's simply the strain of this unbearable situation. We haven't been all together like this since that terrible night." He glared at Annabel. "It was a mistake to get us here."

"Then why did you come?" Barry Rackham demanded, really nasty. "Because you were afraid not to, like the rest of us. We all hated to come, but we were all afraid to stay away. A bunch of cowards—except one, of course. You can't blame *that* one for coming."

"Nonsense," said Dana Hammond, the banker. The look he was giving Rackham was just the opposite of the kind of look a banker is supposed to give a millionaire. "It has nothing to do with cowardice. Not with me. By circumstances beyond my control I am forced into an association that is hateful to me."

"Have they," Lina Darrow asked him sweetly, "finished with the audit of your department?"

"They haven't finished anything," Calvin Leeds growled, and I didn't know he was aiming at her until he went on. "Not even with wondering what you see in Barry Rackham all of a sudden—if it is sudden."

Rackham was out of his chair, moving toward Leeds, snarling, "You can eat that, Cal, or—"

"Oh, stop it!" Annabel stepped to head Rackham off. She whirled, taking them in. "My God, isn't it bad enough without this?" She appealed to me. "I didn't know this was how it would be!" To Rackham, "Sit down, Barry!"

Rackham backed up and sat. Lina Darrow, who had been standing, went and stretched out on a couch, detaching herself. The others stayed put, with Annabel and me on our feet. I have had plenty of contacts with groups of people, all kinds, who have suddenly had a murder explode among them, but I don't think I have ever seen a bunch blown quite so high.

Annabel said, "I didn't want to have Mr. Goodwin come and discuss it just with me. I didn't want any of you to think—I mean, all I wanted was to find out, for all of us. I thought it would be best for all of us to be here."

"All of us?" Pierce asked pointedly. "Or all but one?"

"It was a mistake, Annabel," Hammond told her. "You can see it was."

"Exactly what," Rackham inquired, "was your idea in sending for Goodwin?"

"I want him to work for us. We can't let it go on this way, you all know we can't. I'll pay him, but he'll be working for all of us."

"All but one," Pierce insisted.

"Very well, all but one! As it is now, it isn't all but one, it's all of us!"

Lina Darrow sang out from the couch, "Is Mr. Goodwin giving a guarantee?"

I had taken a chair. Annabel dropped into one facing me and put it to me. "What about it? Can you do anything?"

"I can't give a guarantee," I told her.

"Of course not. Can you do anything?"

"I don't know. I don't know how it stands. Shall I try sketching it?"

"Yes."

"Stop me if I go wrong. It's true I was here when it happened, but that's no help except what I actually saw and heard. Does everyone know what I was here for?"

"Yes."

"Then they understand why I wasn't much interested in anyone but

Rackham. And you and Miss Darrow, of course, but that interest wasn't professional. It looks to me like a case that will probably never be solved by exhibits or testimony on facts. The cops have had plenty of good men on it, and if they had got anything usable on footprints or fingerprints, or getting the steak knife from the drawer, or alibis or timetables, or something like shoes that had been worn in the woods, someone would have been arrested long ago. And they've had it for a month, so no kind of routine would be any good now, and that's all most detective work amounts to. Motive is no help, with four of you inheriting piles from two hundred grand up, and the other two possibly counting on marrying one of the piles. Only I must say, in the atmosphere here tonight, courtship doesn't seem to be on the program."

"It isn't," Annabel asserted.

I glanced at Hammond and Pierce, but neither of them seemed to want the floor.

"So," I continued, "unless the cops have got a trap set that you don't know about, it's one of those things. You never can tell. It would be a waste of money to pay me to go over the ground the cops have covered—or any other detective except Nero Wolfe, and he's not around. There's only one way to use me, or anyhow only one way to start, and stand a chance of getting your money's worth, and that would be to give me a good eight or ten hours with each of you six people, each one separately. I have watched and listened to Nero Wolfe a good many years and I can now do a fair imitation. It might possibly turn out to be worth it to all of you—except one, as Mr. Pierce would say."

I flipped a hand. "That's the best suggestion I can offer. With nothing like a guarantee."

Annabel said, "No one would tell you everything you asked. I haven't myself, to the police."

"Sure. I understand that. That's part of it."

"You would be working for me—for us. It would be confidential."

"Things that weren't used would be confidential. Nothing that was evidence would be."

Annabel sat and regarded me. She had had her fingers twisted tight together, and now she loosened them and then they twisted again. "I want to ask you something, Mr. Goodwin. Do you think one of us killed Mrs. Rackham?"

"I do now. I don't know what I would think after I had worked at it."

"Do you think you know which one?"

"Nope. I'm impartial."

"All right. You can start with me." She turned her head. "Unless one of you would rather first?"

No one moved or spoke. Then Calvin Leeds: "Count me out, Annabel. Not with Goodwin. Let him tell us first where Nero Wolfe is and why."

"But Cal—you won't?"

"Not with him I won't."

"Dana?"

Hammond looked unhappy. He got up and went to her. "Annabel, this was a mistake. The whole idea was no good. What can Goodwin do that the police couldn't do? I doubt if you have any conception of how a private detective works."

"He can try. Will you help, Dana?"

"No. I hate to refuse, but I must."

"Oliver? Will you?"

"Well." The statesman was frowning, not at her, at me. "This seems to me to be a case of all or none. I don't see how anything could be accomplished—"

"Then you refuse me too?"

"Under the circumstances I have no other course."

"I see. You won't even give me a straight no. Barry?"

"Certainly not. Goodwin has lied to the police about my wife's visit to Wolfe. I wouldn't give him eight seconds, let alone eight hours."

Annabel left her chair and went toward the couch. "Lina, I guess it's up to the women. You and me. She was darned good to us, Lina—both of us. What about it?"

"Darling," Lina Darrow said. She sat up. "Darling Annabel. You know you don't like me."

"That isn't true," Annabel protested. "Just because—"

"Of course it's true. You thought I was trying to squeeze you out. You thought I was making a play for Barry merely because I was willing to admit he might be human, so wait and see. You thought I was trying to snatch Ollie from you, when as a matter of fact—"

"Lina, for God's sake," Pierce implored her.

Her fine dark eyes flashed at him. "She did, Ollie! When as a matter of fact she got bored with you, and I happened to be near." The eyes darted right to left, sweeping them. "And look at you now, all of you, and listen to you! You all think Barry killed her—all except one, you would say, Ollie. But you haven't got the guts to say so. And this Mr. Goodwin of yours, darling Annabel, have you told him that what you really want him for is to find some kind of proof that Barry did it? No, I suppose you're saving that for later."

Lina arose, in no hurry, and confronted Annabel from springing distance. "I thought it would be something like this," she said, and left us, detouring around Leeds' chair and heading for the door to the reception hall. Eyes followed her, but no one said anything; then, as she passed out of sight, Barry Rackham got up and, without a glance for any of us, including his hostess, tramped from the room.

The remaining three guests exchanged looks. Leeds and Pierce left their chairs.

"I'm sorry, Annabel," Leeds said gruffly. "But didn't I tell you about Goodwin?"

She didn't reply. She only stood and breathed. Leeds went, with not as much spring to his step as I had seen, and Pierce, mumbling a good night, followed. Dana Hammond went to Annabel, had a hand out to touch her arm, and then let it drop.

"My dear," he said, appealing to her, "it was no good. It couldn't be. If you had consulted me—"

"I'll remember next time, Dana. Good night."

"I want to talk with you, Annabel. I want to—"

"For God's sake, let me alone! Go!"

He backed up a step and scowled at me, as if I were to blame for everything. I lifted my right brow at him. It's one of my few outstanding talents, lifting one brow, and I save it for occasions when nothing else would quite serve the purpose.

He walked out of the room without another word.

Annabel dropped onto the nearest chair, put her elbows on her knees, and buried her face in her hands.

I stood looking down at her. "It was not," I told her sympathetically, "what I would call a success, but anyhow you tried. Not to try to make you feel better, but for future guidance, it might have been wiser, instead of calling a convention, to tackle them one at a time. And it was too bad you picked Leeds to sell first, since he has a grudge against me. But the truth is you were licked before you started. The shape their nerves are in, touching them with a feather wouldn't tickle them, it would give them a stroke. Thanks all the same for asking me."

I left her. By the time I got out to the parking space the cars of the other guests were gone. Rolling down the curving driveway, I was thinking that my first incoming phone call hadn't been so damned magnificent after all.

XII

ONE or two of my friends have tried to tell me that some of my experiences that summer are worth telling about, but even taking them at their word, I'm not going to drag it in here. However, it is true that after I ran an ad in the *Gazette* and word got around I soon quit keeping count of the incoming calls. All I'll do here is summarize it by months:

May. Woman with pet cat stolen. Got it back; fifty dollars and expenses. Guy who got rolled in a joint on Eighth Avenue and didn't want to call the cops. Found her and scared most of it out of her. Two Cs for me. Man who wanted his son pried loose from a blond sharpie. Shouldn't have tried it; fell on my nose; took a C above expenses anyhow. Restaurant with a dumb cashier with sticky fingers; took only one afternoon to hook her; client beefed about my request for sixty-five dollars but paid it.

June. Spent two full weeks handling a hot insurance case for Del Bascom and damn near got my skull cracked for good. Cleaned it up. Del had the nerve to offer me three Cs; demanded a grand and got it. My idea was to net more per week than I had been getting from Wolfe, not that I cared for the money, but as a matter of principle. Found a crooked bookie for a man from Meadville, Pa. A hundred and fifty dollars. Man wanted me to find his vanished wife, but it looked dim and he could pay only twenty bucks a day, so I passed it. Girl unjustly accused, she said, of giving secret business dope to a rival firm, and fired from her job, pestered me into tackling it. Proved she was right and got her job back, doing five hundred dollars' worth of work for a measly hundred and twenty, paid in installments. Her face wasn't much, but she had a nice voice and good legs. Got an offer of a job from the FBI, my ninth offer from various sources in six weeks, and turned it down.

July. Took a whirl at supervising ten men for a bunch of concessionaires at Coney Island; caught one of them taking a cut from doobey stands; he jumped me with a cooler and I broke his arm. Got tired of looking at a thousand acres of bare skin, mostly peeling, practically all nonseductive, and quit. Eight fifty for seventeen days. Had passed up at least two thousand worth of little chores. Screwball woman on Long Island had had jewelry stolen, uninsured, thought cops were in on it and stalling. Two things happened: I got some breaks, and I did a damn good piece of work. It took me into August. I got all the jewelry back, hung it on an interior decorator's assistant with proof, billed her for thirty-five hundred gross, and collected.

August. I had drawn no pay from Wolfe's checkbook since May sixth, I had not gone near my personal safe deposit box, and my personal bank balance had not only not sunk, it had lifted. I decided I had a vacation coming. The most I had ever been able to talk Wolfe out of was two weeks, and I thought I should double that at least. A friend of mine, whose name has appeared in print in connection with one of Wolfe's cases, had the idea that we should take a look at Norway, and her point of view seemed sound.

Slow but sure, I was working myself around to an attitude toward life without Nero Wolfe on a permanent basis. One thing that kept it slow was the fact that early in July Marko Vukcic had asked me to bring him another check for five grand drawn to cash. Since if you wanted to eat in his restaurant you had to reserve a table a day in advance, and then pay six bucks for one helping of guinea hen, I knew he wasn't using it himself, so who was? Another thing, the house hadn't been sold, and, doing a little snooping on my own account, I had learned that the asking price was a hundred and twenty thousand, which was plain silly. On the other hand, if Marko was getting money to Wolfe, that didn't prove that I was ever going to see him again, and there was no hurry about selling the house until the bank balance began to sag; and also there was Wolfe's safe deposit box. Visiting his safe deposit box was one item on the select list of purposes for which Wolfe had been willing to leave his house.

I did not really want to leave New York, especially to go as far as Norway. I had a feeling that I would about be passing Sandy Hook when word would come somehow, wire or phone or letter or messenger, to 35th Street or 1019, in a code that I would understand—if I was there to get it. And if it did come I wanted to be there, or I might be left out of the biggest charade Wolfe had ever staged. But it hadn't been days or weeks, it had been months, and my friend was pretty good at several things, including riding me about hanging on forever to the short end of the stick, so we had reservations on a ship that sailed August twenty-sixth.

Four days before that, August twenty-second, a Tuesday afternoon, I was sitting at my desk at 1019, to keep an appointment with a man who had phoned. I had told him I was soon leaving for a month's vacation, and he hadn't felt like giving a name, but I thought I recognized the voice and had agreed to see him. When he walked in on the dot, at 3:15, I was glad to know that my memory for voices was holding up. It was my old cellmate, Max Christy.

I got up and we shook. He put his panama on the desk and glanced around. His black mop was cut a little shorter than it had been in April, but the jungle of his eyebrows hadn't been touched, and his shoulders looked just as broad in gray tropical worsted. I invited him to sit and he did.

"I must apologize," I said, "for never settling for that breakfast. It was a life-saver."

He waved it away. "The pleasure was mine. How's it going?"

"Oh—no complaints. You?"

"I've been extremely busy." He got out a handkerchief and dabbed at his face and neck. "I certainly sweat. Sometimes I think it's stupid, this constant back and forth, push and shove."

"I hear you mentioned around."

"Yes, I suppose so. You never phoned me. Did you?"

"The number," I said, "is Churchill five, three two three two."

"But you never called it."

"No, sir," I admitted, "I didn't. One thing and another kept coming up, and then I didn't care much for your line about if I got taken in and my being given a trial. I am by no means a punk, and the ink on my license dried long ago. Here, look behind my ears."

He threw back his head and haw-hawed, then shut it off and told me soberly, "You got me wrong, Goodwin. I only meant we'd have to go slow on account of your record." He used the handkerchief on his forehead. "I certainly do sweat. Since then your name has been discussed a little, and I assure you, you are not regarded as a punk. We have noticed that you seem to have plenty of jobs since you opened this office, but so trivial for a man like you. Why did you turn down the offer from the Feds?"

"Oh, they keep such long hours."

He nodded. "And you don't like harness, do you?"

"I've never tried it and don't intend to."

"What have you got on hand now? Anything important?"

"Nothing whatever, important or otherwise. I told you on the phone, I'm taking a vacation. Sailing Saturday."

He regarded me disapprovingly. "You don't need a vacation. If anybody needs a vacation it's me, but I don't get one. I've got a job for you."

I shook my head. "Not right now. When I get back maybe."

"It won't wait till you get back. There's a man we want tailed and we're short of personnel, and he's tough. We had two good men on him, and he spotted both of them. You would need at least two helpers; three would be better. You use men you know, handle that yourself, and pay them and expenses out of the five hundred a day you'll get."

I whistled. "What's so hot about it?"

"Nothing. It's not hot."

"Then who's the subject, the Mayor?"

"I'm not naming him. Perhaps I don't even know. It's merely a straight tailing job, but it has to be watertight and no leaks. You can net three hundred a day easy."

"Not without a hint who he is or what he looks like." I waved it away. "Forget it. I'd like to oblige an old cellmate, but my vacation starts Saturday."

"Your vacation can wait. This can't. At ten o'clock tonight you'll be walking west on Sixty-seventh Street halfway between First and Second Avenues. A car will pick you up, with a man in it that wants to ask you some questions. If your answers suit him he'll tell you about the job—and it's your big chance, Goodwin. It's your chance for your first dip into the biggest river of fast dough that ever flowed."

"What the hell," I protested, "you're not offering me a job, you're just giving me a chance to apply for one I don't want."

It was perfectly true at that point, and it was still true ten minutes later, when Max Christy left, that I didn't want the job, but I did want to apply for it. It wasn't that I had a hunch that the man in the car who wanted to ask me some questions would be Arnold Zeck, but the way it had been staged gave me the notion that it was just barely possible; and the opportunity, slim as it was, was too good to miss. It would be interesting to have a chat with Zeck; besides, he might give me an excuse to take a poke at him and I might happen to inadvertently break his neck. So I told Christy that I would be walking on 67th Street at ten that evening as suggested. I had to break a date to do it, but even if the chance was only one in a million I wanted it.

To get that point settled and out of the way, the man who wanted to quiz me was not Arnold Zeck. It was not even a long black Cadillac; it was only a '48 Chevvy two-door sedan.

It was a hot August night, and as I walked along that block I was sweating a little myself, especially my left armpit under the holster. There was a solid string of parked cars at the curb, and when the Chevvy stopped and its door opened and my name was called, not loud, I had to squeeze between bumpers to get to it. As I climbed in and pulled the door shut the man in the front seat, behind the wheel, swiveled his head for a look at me and then, with no greeting, went back to his chauffeuring, and the car started forward.

My companion on the back seat muttered at me, "Maybe you ought to show me something."

I got out my display case and handed it to him with the license—detective, not driver's—uppermost. When we stopped for a light at Second Avenue he inspected it with the help of a street lamp, and returned it. I was already sorry I had wasted an evening. Not only was he not Zeck; he was no one I had ever seen or heard of, though I was fairly well acquainted, at least by sight, with the high brass in the circles that Max Christy moved in. This bird was a complete stranger. With more skin supplied for his face than was needed, it had taken up the slack in pleats and wrinkles, and that may have accounted for his sporting a pointed brown beard, since it must be hard to shave pleats.

As the car crossed the avenue and continued west, I told him, "I came to oblige Max Christy—if suggestions might help any. I'll only be around till Saturday."

He said, "My name's Roeder," and spelled it.

I thanked him for the confidence. He broadened it. "I'm from the West Coast, in case you wonder how I rate. I followed something here and found

238 FIVE OF A KIND

it was tied in with certain operations. I'd just as soon leave it to local talent
and go back home, but I'm hooked and I have to stick." Either he preferred
talking through his nose or that was the only way he knew. "Christy told
you we want a man tailed?"

"Yes. I explained that I'm not available."

"You have got to be available. There's too much involved." He was twisted
around to face me. "It'll be harder than ever now, because he's on guard. It's
been messed up. They say if anyone can do it you can, especially with the
help of a couple of men that Nero Wolfe used. You can get them, can't
you?"

"Yeah, I can get them, but I can't get me. I won't be here."

"You're here now. You can start tomorrow. As Christy told you, five Cs
a day. It's a straight tailing job, where you're working for a man named
Roeder from Los Angeles. The cops might not like it too well if you tied
in with a local like Wilts or Brownie Costigan, but what's wrong with me?
You never heard of me before. You're in business as a private detective. I
want to hire you, at a good price, to keep a tail on a man named Rackham
and report to me on his movements. That's all, a perfectly legitimate job."

We had crossed Park Avenue. The light was dim enough that I didn't
have to be concerned about my face showing a reaction to the name Rackham. The reaction inside me was my affair.

"How long would it last?" I inquired.

"I don't know. A day, a week, possibly two."

"What if something hot develops? A detective doesn't take a tailing job
sight unseen. You must have told me why you were curious about Rackham.
What did you tell me?"

Roeder smiled. I could just see the pleats tightening. "That I suspected
my business partner had come east to make a deal with him, freezing me
out."

"That could be all right if you'll fill it in. But why all the mystery? Why
didn't you come to my office instead of fixing it to pick me off the street at
night?"

"I don't want to show in the daytime. I don't want my partner to know I'm
here." Roeder smiled again. "Incidentally, that's quite true, that I don't want
to show in the daytime—not any more than I can help."

"That I believe. Skipping the comedy, there aren't many Rackhams.
There are none in the Manhattan phone book. Is this the Barry Rackham
whose wife got killed last spring?"

"Yes."

I grunted. "Quite a coincidence. I was there when she was murdered, and
now I'm offered the job of tailing him. If he gets murdered too that *would*
be a coincidence. I wouldn't like it. I had a hell of a time getting out from

under a bond as a material witness so I could take a vacation. If he got killed while I was on his tail—"

"Why should he?"

"I don't know. I didn't know why she should either. But it was Max Christy who arranged this date, and while he is not himself a marksman as far as I know, he moves in circles that like direct action." I waved a hand. "Forget it. If that's the kind of interest you've got in Rackham you wouldn't tell me anyhow. But another thing: Rackham knows me. It's twice as hard to tail a guy that knows you. Why hire a man that's handicapped to begin with? Why not—"

I held it because we had stopped for a red light, on Fifth Avenue in the Seventies, and our windows were open, and the open window of a car alongside was only arm's distance away.

When the light changed and we rolled again Roeder spoke. "I'll tell you, Goodwin, this thing's touchy. There'll be some people scattered around that are in on things together, and they trust each other up to a point. As long as their interests all run the same way they can trust each other pretty well. But when something comes up that might help some and hurt others, then it gets touchy. Then each man looks out for himself, or he decides where the strength is and lines up there. That's where I am, where the strength is. But I'm not trying to line you up; we wouldn't want to even if we could; how could we trust you? You're an outsider. All we want you for is an expert tailing job, and you report to me and me only. Where are you going, Bill?"

The driver half-turned his head to answer, "Here in the park it might be cooler."

"It's no cooler anywhere. I like straight streets. Get out again, will you?"

The driver said he would, in a hurt tone. Roeder returned to me. "There are three men named Panzer, Cather, and Durkin who worked for Nero Wolfe off and on. That right?"

I said it was.

"They'll work for you, won't they?"

I said I thought they would.

"Then you can use them, and you won't have to show much. I'm told they're exceptionally good men."

"Saul Panzer is the best man alive. Cather and Durkin are way above average."

"That's all you'll need. Now I want to ask you something, but first here's a remark. It's a bad thing to mislead a client, I'm sure you realize that, but in this case it would be worse than bad. I don't have to go into details, do I?"

"No, but you're going too fast. I haven't got a client."

"Oh, yes, you have." Roeder smiled. "Would I waste my time like this? You were there when Mrs. Rackham was killed, you phoned Nero Wolfe and in six hours he was gone, and you were held as a material witness. Now here I want to hire you to tail Rackham, and you don't know why. Can you say no? Impossible."

"It could be," I suggested, "that I've had all I want."

"Not you, from what I've heard. That's all right, not being able to let go is a good thing in a man, but it brings up this question I mentioned. You're on your own now apparently, but you were with Nero Wolfe a long time. You're still living in his house. Of course you're in touch with him—don't bother to deny it—but that's no concern of ours as long as he doesn't get in the way. Only on this job it has to be extra plain that you're working for the man who pays you. If you get facts about Rackham and peddle them elsewhere, to Nero Wolfe for example, you would be in a very bad situation. Perhaps you know how bad?"

"Sure, I know. If I were standing up my knees would give. Just for the record, I don't know where Mr. Wolfe is, I'm not in touch with him, and I'm in no frame of mind to peddle him anything. If I take this on, tailing Rackham, it will be chiefly because I've got my share of monkey in me. I doubt if Mr. Wolfe, wherever he is, would recognize the name Rackham if he heard it."

The brown pointed beard waggled as Roeder shook his head. "Don't overplay it, Goodwin."

"I'm not. I won't."

"You are still attached to Wolfe."

"Like hell I am."

"I couldn't pay you enough to tell me where he is—assuming you know."

"Maybe not," I conceded. "But not selling him is one thing, and carrying his picture around is another. I freely admit he had his good points, I have often mentioned them and appreciated them, but as the months go by one fact about him stands out clearer than anything else. He was a pain in the ass."

The driver's head jerked around for a darting glance at me. We had left the park and were back on Fifth Avenue, headed uptown in the Eighties. My remarks about Wolfe were merely casual, because my mind was on something else. Who was after Rackham and why? If it was Zeck, or someone in one of Zeck's lines of command, then something drastic had happened since the April day when Zeck had sent Wolfe a package of sausage and phoned him to let Rackham alone. If it wasn't Zeck, then Max Christy and this Roeder were lined up against Zeck, which made them about as safe to play with as an atomic stockpile. Either way, how could I resist it? Besides, I liked the logic of it. Nearly five months ago Mrs. Rackham had hired us to do a survey on her husband, and paid in advance, and we had let it slide. Now I could take up where we had left off. If Roeder and his colleagues, whoever they were, wanted to pay me for it, there was no use offending them by refusing.

So, rolling north on the avenue, Roeder and I agreed that we agreed in principle and got down to brass tacks. Since Rackham was on guard it couldn't be an around-the-clock operation with less than a dozen men, and I had three at the most. Or did I? Saul and Fred and Orrie might not be immediately available. There was no use discussing an operation until I found out if I had any operators. Having their phone numbers in my head, I suggested that we stop at a drugstore and use a booth, but Roeder didn't like that. He thought it would be better to go to my office and phone from there, and I had no objection, so he told the driver to go over to Madison and downtown.

At that hour, getting on toward eleven, Madison Avenue was wide open, and so was the curb in front of the office building. Roeder told the driver we would be an hour or more, and we left him parked there. In the brighter light of the elevator the pleats of Roeder's face were less noticeable, and he didn't look as old as I would have guessed him in the car, but I could see there was a little gray in his beard. He stood propped in a corner with his shoulders slumped and his eyes closed until the door opened for the tenth floor, and then came to and followed me down the hall to 1019. I unlocked the door and let us in, switched on the light, motioned him to a chair, sat at the desk, pulled the phone to me, and started dialing.

"Wait a minute," he said gruffly.

I put it back on the cradle, looked at him, got a straight clear view of his eyes for the first time, and felt a tingle in the small of my back. But I didn't know why.

"This must not be heard," he said. "I mean you and me. How sure are you?"

"You mean a mike?"

"Yes."

"Oh, pretty sure."

"Better take a look."

I left my chair and did so. The room being small and the walls mostly bare, it wasn't much of a job, and I made it thorough, even pulling the desk out to inspect behind it. As I straightened up from retrieving a pencil that had rolled off the desk when I pushed it back in place, he spoke to my back.

"I see you have my dictionary here."

Not through his nose. I whirled and went rigid, gaping at him. The eyes again—and now other items too, especially the forehead and ears. I had every right to stare, but I also had a right to my own opinion of the fitness of things. So while staring at him I got myself under control, and then circled the end of my desk, sat down and leaned back, and told him, "I knew you all—"

"Don't talk so loud."

"Very well. I knew you all the time, but with that damn driver there I had to—"

"Pfui. You hadn't the slightest inkling."

I shrugged. "That's one we'll never settle. As for the dictionary, it's the one from my room which you gave me for Christmas nineteen thirty-nine. How much do you weigh?"

"I've lost a hundred and seventeen pounds."

"Do you know what you look like?"

He made a face. With the pleats and whiskers, he didn't really have to make one, but of course it was an old habit which had probably been suppressed for months.

"Yes," he said, "I do. I look like a sixteenth-century prince of Savoy named Philibert." He flipped a hand impatiently. "This can wait, surely, until we're home again?"

"I should think so," I conceded. "What's the difference, another year or two? It won't be as much fun, though, because now I'll know what I'm waiting for. What I really enjoyed was the suspense. Were you dead or alive or what? A perfect picnic."

He grunted. "I expected this, of course. It is you, and since I decided long ago to put up with you, I even welcome it. But you, also long ago, decided to put up with me. Are we going to shake hands or not?"

I got up and went halfway. He got up and came halfway. As we shook, our eyes met, and I deliberately focused on his eyes, because otherwise I would have been shaking with a stranger, and one hell of a specimen to boot. We returned to our chairs.

As I sat down I told him courteously, "You'll have to excuse me if I shut my eyes or look away from time to time. It'll take a while to get adjusted."

XIII

"No OTHER course," Wolfe said, "was possible. I had accepted money from Mrs. Rackham and she had been murdered. I was committed in her interest, and therefore against Arnold Zeck, and I was no match for him. I had to ambush him. With me gone, how should you act? You should act as if I had disappeared and you knew nothing. Under what circumstances would you do that most convincingly? You are capable of dissimulation, but why try you so severely? Why not merely—"

"Skip it," I told him. "Save it for later. Where do we stand now, and what chance have we got? Any at all?"

"I think so, yes. If the purpose were merely to expose one or more of Zeck's operations, it could be done like that." He snapped his fingers. "But since he must himself be destroyed—all I can say is that I have reached the point where you can help. I have talked with him three times."

"Exactly who and what are you?"

"I come from Los Angeles. When I left here, on April ninth, I went to southern Texas, on the Gulf, and spent there the most painful month of my life—except one, long ago. At its end I was not recognizable." He shuddered. "I then went to Los Angeles, because a man of importance there considers himself more deeply in my debt even than he is. He is important but not reputable. The terms are not interchangeable."

"I never said they were."

"Through him I met people and I engaged in certain activities. In appearance I was monstrous, but in the circles I frequented my stubble was accepted as a masquerade, which indeed it was, and I displayed myself publicly as little as possible. With my two invaluable assets, my brains and my important debtor, and with a temporary abandonment of scruple, I made a substantial impression in the shortest possible time, especially with a device which I conceived for getting considerable sums of money from ten different people simultaneously, with a minimum of risk. Luck had a hand in it too, but without luck no man can keep himself alive, let alone prevail over an Arnold Zeck."

"So then Los Angeles was too hot for you."

"It was not. But I was ready to return east, both physically and psychologically, and knowing that inquiries sent to Los Angeles would get a satisfactory response. I arrived on July twelfth. You remember that I once spoke of Arnold Zeck, calling him X, to the Sperling family?"

"I do."

"And I described briefly the echelons of crime. First, the criminal himself —or gang. In the problem of disposal of the loot, or of protection against discovery and prosecution, he can seldom avoid dealing with others. He will need a fence, a lawyer, witnesses for an alibi, a channel to police or political influence—no matter what, he nearly always needs someone or something. He goes to one he knows, or knows about, one named A. A, finding a little difficulty, consults B. B may be able to handle it; if not, he takes it on to C. C is usually able to oblige, but when he isn't he communicates with D. Here we are getting close. D has access to Arnold Zeck, not only for the purpose described, but also in connection with one or more of the enterprises which Zeck controls."

Wolfe tapped his chest with a forefinger, a gesture I had never before seen him use, acquired evidently along with his pleats and whiskers. "I am a D, Archie."

"Congratulations."

"Thank you. Having earned them, I accept them. Look at me."

"Yeah, I am. Wait till Fritz sees you."

"If he ever does," Wolfe said grimly. "We have a chance, and that's all. If all we needed were evidence of Zeck's complicity in felonies, there would be no problem; I know where it is and I could get it. But his defenses are everywhere, making him next to invulnerable. It would be fatuous to suppose that he could ever be convicted, and even if he were, he would still be living, so that wouldn't help any. Now that I am committed against him, and he knows it, there are only two possible outcomes—"

"How does he know it?"

"He knows me. Knowing me, he knows that I intend to get the murderer of Mrs. Rackham. He intends to prevent me. Neither—"

"Wait a minute. Admitting he knows that about Nero Wolfe, what about you as Roeder? You say you're a D. Then you're on Zeck's payroll."

"Not on his payroll. I have been placed in charge of the operation here of the device which I conceived and used in Los Angeles. My handling of it has so impressed him that I am being trusted with other responsibilities."

"And Max Christy and that driver downstairs—they're Zeck men?"

"Yes—at a distance."

"Then how come salting Barry Rackham? Wasn't it Zeck money that Rackham was getting?"

Wolfe sighed. "Archie, if we had more time I would let you go on and on. I could shut my eyes and pretend I'm back home." He shook his head vigorously. "But we must get down to business. I said that driver is a Zeck man at a distance, but that is mere surmise. Being new and by no means firmly established in confidence, I am certainly being watched, and that driver might even report to Zeck himself. That was why I prolonged our talk in the car before suggesting that we come here. We shouldn't be more than an hour, so you'd better let me—"

He stopped as I grasped the knob and pulled the door open. I had tiptoed across to it as he talked. Seeing an empty hall in both directions, I closed the door and went back to my chair.

"I was only asking," I protested, "why the play on Rackham?"

"How long," Wolfe asked, "have you and I spent, there in the office, discussing some simple affair such as the forging of a check?"

"Oh, anywhere from four minutes to four hours."

"Then what should we take for this? By the way, you will resume drawing your pay check this week. How much have you taken from the safe deposit box in New Jersey?"

"Nothing. Not a cent."

"You should have. That was put there for the express purpose of financing this eventuality if it arose. You have been using your personal savings?"

"Only to buy these little items." I waved a hand. "Put it back long ago. I've been taking it easy, so my income from detective work has only been a little more than double what you were paying me."

"I don't believe it."

"I didn't expect you to, so I'll have an audit—" I stopped. "What the hell! My vacation!"

Wolfe grunted. "If we get Zeck you may have a month. If he gets me—" He grunted again. "He will, confound it, if we don't get to work. You asked about Rackham; yes, the source of his income, which his wife asked us to discover, was Zeck. He met him through Calvin Leeds."

I raised the brows. "Leeds?"

"Don't jump to conclusions. Leeds sold dogs to Zeck, two of them, to protect his house, and spent a week there, training them for their job. Zeck does not miss an opportunity. He used Rackham in one of his less offensive activities, gambling arrangements for people with too much money. Then when Rackham inherited more than half of his wife's wealth a new situation developed; it was already developing when I arrived six weeks ago. I managed to get informed about it. Of course I had to be extremely careful, new as I was, but on the other hand my being a newcomer was an advantage. In preparing a list of prospects for the device I had conceived, a man in Rackham's position was an eminently suitable candidate, and naturally I had to know all about him. That placed me favorably for starting, with the greatest caution, certain speculations and suspicions, and I got it to the point where it seemed desirable to put him under surveillance. Luckily I didn't have to introduce your name; your enlistment had previously been considered, on a suggestion by Max Christy. I was ready for you anyhow—I had gone as far as I could without you—and that made it easier. I wouldn't have dared to risk naming you myself, and was planning accordingly, but it's vastly better this way."

"Am I to proceed? Get Saul and Orrie and Fred? Tail Rackham?"

Wolfe looked at his wrist. His charade was certainly teaching him new tricks. In all my years with him he had never sported a watch, and here he was glancing at his wrist as if born to it. The way that wrist had been, normal, it would have required a custom-made strap.

"I told that man an hour or more," he said, "but we shouldn't be that long. A minim of cause for suspicion and I'm through. Nothing is too fantastic for them; they could even learn if we've been using the phone. Confound it, I must have hours with you."

"Ditch him and we'll meet somewhere."

"Impossible. No place would be safe—except one. There is only one circumstance under which any man is granted the right to an extended period of undisturbed privacy, either by deliberation or on impulse. We need a woman. You know all kinds."

"Not all kinds," I objected. "I do draw the line. What kind do we need?"

"Fairly young, attractive, a little wanton in appearance, utterly devoted to you and utterly trustworthy, and not a fool."

"My God, if I knew where to find one like that I'd have been married long ago. Also I would be bragging—"

"Archie," he snapped. "If after all your promiscuous philandering you can't produce a woman to those specifications, I've misjudged you. It's risky to trust anyone at all, but any other way would be still riskier."

I had my lips puckered. "Ruth Brady?"

"No. She's an operative, and known. Out of the question."

"There's one who might take this as a substitute for a trip to Norway, which is now out. I could ask her."

"What's her name?"

"You know. Lily Rowan."

He made a face. "She is rich, intemperate, and notorious."

"Nuts. She is well-heeled and playful. You remember the time she helped out with an upstate murderer. I have no further suggestions. Do I phone her?"

"Yes."

"And tell her what?"

He explained in some detail. When he had answered my three or four questions, and filed my objection by asking if I had something better to offer, I pulled the phone to me and dialed a number. No answer. I tried the Troubadour Room of the Churchill; she wasn't there. Next in order of priority was the Flamingo Club. That found her. Asked my name, I said to tell her it was Escamillo, though she hadn't called me that for quite a while.

After a wait her voice came. "Archie? Really?"

"I prefer Escamillo," I said firmly. "It's a question of security. How high are you?"

"Come and find out. I'm tired of the people I'm with, anyhow. Listen, I'll wander out and meet you in front and we'll go—"

"We will not. I'm working, and I'm on a spot, and I need help. You're just the type for it, and I pay a dollar an hour if you give satisfaction. I'm offering you a brand new thrill. You have never earned a nickel in your life, and here's your chance. What mood are you in?"

"I'm bored as the devil, but all I need is six dances with you and—"

"Not tonight, my colleen donn. Damn it, I'm working. Will you help?"

"When?"

"Now."

"Is it any fun?"

"So-so. Nothing to brag of."

"Are you coming here for me?"

"No. I'm going—you must get this straight. Now listen."

"That's exactly what I had in mind. I was just telling myself, Lily, my precious, if he starts talking you must listen, because he is very shy and sensitive and therefore—did you say something?"

"I said shut up. I'm at my office. A man is here with me. We'll leave as soon as I hang up. I'll go alone to your place and wait for you outside your door. The man—"

"You won't have to wait. I can make it—"

"Shut up, please. Your first hour has started, so this is on my time. The man with me has a car with a driver parked down in front. He will be driven to the Flamingo Club and stop at the curb, and you will be waiting there in front, and when he opens the door you will climb in, *not* waiting for him to get out like a gentleman, because he won't. You will not speak to the driver, who, when you're inside, will proceed to your address, where you and the man will find me waiting at your door."

"Unless I get in the wrong car, and—"

"I'm telling you. It's a dark gray forty-eight Chevvy two-door sedan, New York license OA six, seven, one, one, three. Got that?"

"Yes."

"I'll make it a dollar ten an hour. The man will call you Lily, and you will call him Pete. Joining him in the car and riding up to your place, you need not go to extremes, but it is important for the driver to get the idea that you are mighty glad to see Pete and that you are looking forward with pleasure to the next several hours with him. But—"

"Is it a reunion after a long absence?"

"I'll make it a dollar twenty an hour. I was about to say, you can leave it vague whether you last saw Pete a week ago or two months ago. You're just glad to be with him because you're so fond of him, but don't get thinking you're Paulette Goddard and ham it. Do it right. Pretend it's me. Which brings me to the crux. It's going to be an ordeal for you. Wait till you see Pete."

"What's the matter with him?"

"Everything. He's old enough to be your father and then some. He has whiskers, turning gray. His face is pleated. You will have to fight down the feeling that you're having a nightmare, and—"

"Archie! It's Nero Wolfe!"

Goddam a woman anyhow. There was absolutely no sense or reason for it. My brain buzzed.

"Sure," I said admiringly. "You do it with mirrors. If it was him, the way I feel about him, the first thing I would do would be to get him a date with you, huh? Okay, then don't call him Pete, call him Nero."

"Then who is it?"

"It's a man named Pete Roeder, and I've got to have a long talk with him that won't get in the papers."

"We could take him to Norway."

"Maybe. We have to discuss Norway. Give me a ring later in the week and tell me how you feel about this proposition."

"I'll be out on the sidewalk in ten minutes, less than that, waiting for my Pete."

"No public announcement."

"Certainly not."

"I'm very pleased with your work so far. We'll have to get you a social security number. I'll be waiting anxiously at your door."

I hung up and told Wolfe, "All set."

Out of his chair, he grunted. "You overdid it a little, perhaps? Nightmare, for instance?"

"Yes, sir," I agreed. "I get too enthusiastic."

I glared at him, and he glared back.

XIV

Since I do not intend to use up paper reporting the five-hour conference I had with Wolfe that night in Lily Rowan's living room, I could just as well go on to Wednesday morning, except for one thing. I have got to tell about their arrival at the door of Lily's penthouse apartment on East 63rd Street. Wolfe didn't speak and wouldn't look at me. Lily shook hands with me, a form of greeting we hadn't used for I don't know how long, then unlocked the door, and we entered. When her wrap and Wolfe's hat had been disposed of and we passed to the living room, she tossed her firecracker.

"Archie," she said, "I knew darned well that something would happen some day to make up for all the time I've wasted on you. I just felt it would."

I nodded. "Certainly. You'll show a profit on the night even if you feed us sandwiches, especially since Pete is a light eater. He's on a diet."

"Oh," she said, "I didn't mean money, and you can go the limit on sandwiches. I meant the distinction you've brought me. I'm the only woman in America who has necked with Nero Wolfe. Nightmare, my eye. He has a flair."

Wolfe, who had seated himself, cocked his head to frown at her—a first-rate performance.

I smiled at her. "I told Pete what you said on the phone, and he was flattered. Okay, woman of distinction."

She shook her head. "Turn loose, my brave fellow. I've got hold of it." She moved to Wolfe, looking down at him. "Don't be upset, Pete. I wouldn't have known you from Adam, no one would; that wasn't it. It's my hero here. Archie's an awful prude. He has been up against some tough ones, lots of them, and not once has he ever called on me to help. Never! A proud prude. Suddenly he calls me away from revelry—I might have been reveling for all he knew—to get into a car and be intimate with a stranger. There's only one person on earth he would do that for: you. So if I was pretty ardent in the car, I knew what I was doing. And don't worry about me—whatever you're up to, my lips are sealed. Anyway, to me you will always be Pete. The only woman in America who has necked with Nero Wolfe—my God, I'll treasure it forever. Now I'll go make some sandwiches. What kind of a diet are you on?"

Wolfe said through his teeth, "I care for nothing."

"That can't be. A peach? Grapes? A leaf of lettuce?"

"No!"

"A glass of water?"

"Yes!"

She left the room, leering at me as she went by. In a moment the sound of her movements in the kitchen came faintly.

I told Wolfe offensively, "It was you who said we needed a woman."

"It was you who selected her."

"You okayed her."

"It's done," he said bitterly. "So are we. She'll blab, of course."

"There's one hope," I suggested. "Marry her. She wouldn't betray her own husband. And apparently in that one short ride uptown with her—"

I stopped abruptly. The face as a whole was no longer his, but the eyes alone were enough to tell me when I had gone far enough.

"I'll tell you what I'll do," I offered. "I know her quite well. Two things that could conceivably happen: first, you might go to Zeck tomorrow and tell him who you are, and second, Lily might spill it either thoughtfully or thoughtlessly. I'll bet you ten bucks the first happens as soon as the second."

He growled. "She's a woman."

"All right, bet me."

The bet didn't get made. Not that Wolfe came to my point of view about Lily Rowan, but what could the poor son of a gun do? He couldn't even take to the bushes again and start all over. From that point on, though, up to the end, the strain was ten times worse for him than for me. It cramped his style some all that night, after Lily had gone off to bed and we talked in the living room until long after dawn. At six o'clock he went. Probably it

would then have been safe for me to go too, since if they were enough interested in him to have posted a sentry outside the building he would almost certainly leave when Roeder did, but probabilities weren't good enough
now, not after the picture Wolfe had given me and the program he had
drawn up, so I took a good two-hour nap before leaving for 35th Street and
a bath and breakfast.

At ten o'clock I was at 1019, starting at the phone to get hold of Saul and
Orrie and Fred.

I did not like it at all. The way Wolfe was getting set to play it, it looked
to me as if we had one chance in a thousand, and while that may be good
enough to go ahead on when what you're after is to nail a guy on a charge,
and if you muff it the worst you get is a new start under a handicap, it's a
little different when a muff means curtains. I had of course told Wolfe all I
knew, including Inspector Cramer's visit and advice, but that only made
him stubborner. With Zeck on Rackham's tail, through me, it seemed likely
that the murderer of Mrs. Rackham might get his proper voltage with
Zeck's blessing, and since that was all that Wolfe was committed to, why
not settle for it? For now anyway, and then take a good breath. As for commitments, I had one of my own. I had promised myself to see Norway before
I died.

So I didn't like it, and I either had to lump it or bow out. I tossed a coin:
heads I stick, tails I quit. It landed tails, but I had to veto it because I had
already talked to Orrie Cather and he was coming at noon, and I had left
messages for Fred Durkin and Saul Panzer. I tossed again, tails again. I
tossed once more and it was heads, which settled it. I had to stick.

The tailing of Barry Rackham was a classic, especially after the first week.
It was a shame to waste the talents of Saul Panzer on what was actually
a burlesque, but it was good to have him around anyhow. I briefed them
all together at 1019, Wednesday evening, with Saul perched on a corner of
the desk because there were only three chairs. Saul was undersized, incon-
spicuous all but his nose, and the best all-round man alive. Fred Durkin
was big and clumsy, with a big red face, with no Doberman pinscher in him
but plenty of bulldog. Orrie Cather was slender and muscular and handsome, just the man to mingle with the guests at a swell dinner party when
circumstances called for it. After I had explained the job, with details as
required, I supplied a little background.

"As far as you know," I told them, "I'm only doing this for practice. Your
only contact is me. There is no client."

"Jesus," Fred remarked, "a hundred bucks a day and more with expenses?
I guess you ought to pay in advance."

"Take it up with the NLRB," I said stiffly. "As an employer, I do not
invite familiarities from the help."

"Of course," Orrie stated with an understanding smile, "it's just a coincidence that this Rackham was with you once at the scene of a murder. When you got tossed in the coop."

"That's irrelevant. Let us stick to the point, gentlemen. I want to make it clear that I do not actually care a damn where Rackham goes or what he does or who he sees. You are to hang on and report in full, since that's the proper way to handle a dry run, but I don't want anyone to get hurt. If he turns on you and starts throwing rocks, dodge and run. If you lose him, as of course you will, don't bark your shins trying to hurdle."

"You ought to have workmen's compensation insurance," Fred advised. "Then we could be serious about it."

"Do you mean," Saul Panzer asked, "that the purpose is to get on his nerves?"

"No. Play it straight. I only mean it's not life and death—until further notice." I pushed my chair back and got up. "And now I wish to prove that being an employer hasn't changed me any. You may continue to call me Archie. You may come with me to Thirty-fifth Street, where we will find a poker deck, and Fritz will make five, and when we have finished I'll lend you carfare home."

For the record, I lost twelve dollars. Saul was the big winner. One hand, I had three nines and—but I'd better get on.

Rackham was living at the Churchill, in an air-conditioned suite in the tower. During the first week we compiled quite a biography of him. He never stuck his nose outside before one o'clock, and once not until four. His ports of call included two banks, a law office, nine bars, two clubs, a barber shop, seven other shops and stores, three restaurants, three theaters, two night spots, and miscellaneous. He usually ate lunch with a man or men, and dinner with a woman. Not the same woman; three different ones during the week. As described by my operatives, they were a credit to their sex, to the American way of life, and to the International Ladies' Garment Workers' Union.

I took on a little of it myself, but mostly I left it to the help. Not that I loafed. There were quite a few hours with Lily Rowan, off and on, both as a substitute for the trip to Norway, indefinitely postponed, and as a check on the soundness of the estimate of her I had given Wolfe. She caused me no qualms. Once when we were dancing she sighed for Pete, and once at her apartment she said she would love to help some more with my work, but when I tactfully made it plain that the detective business was not on our agenda she took it nicely and let it lay.

There were other things, including the reports on Rackham to be typed. Late every afternoon Max Christy called at my office to get the report of the day before, and he would sit and read it and ask questions. When he got critical, I would explain patiently that I couldn't very well post a man at the door of Rackham's suite to take pictures of all the comers and goers, and that we were scoring better than eighty per cent on all his hours outside, which was exceptional for New York tailing.

I had the advantage, of course, of having had the situation described to me by their Pete Roeder. They were worried a little about Westchester, but more about the city. Shortly after he had become a millionaire by way of a steak knife, whoever had used it, Rackham had got word to Zeck that he was no longer available for contacts. Brownie Costigan had got to Rackham, thinking to put the bee on him, and had been tossed out on his ear. The stink being raised in Washington on gambling and rackets, and the resulting enthusiasm in the office of the New York County District Attorney, had started an epidemic of jitters, and it was quite possible that if one of my typed reports had told of a visit by Rackham to the DA's office, or of one by an assistant DA to Rackham's suite, Rackham would have had a bad accident, like getting run over or falling into the river with lead in him. That was why Wolfe had given me careful and explicit instructions about what I should report and what I shouldn't.

I had no sight or sound of Wolfe. He was to let me know if and when there was something stirring, and I had been told how to reach him if I had to.

Meanwhile I had my schedule, and on the ninth day, a Friday, the first of September, it called for a move. Things looked right for it. Saul, on instructions, had let himself get spotted once, and Orrie twice, and Fred, without instructions, at least three times. I too had cooperated by letting myself be seen at the entrance of the Crooked Circle one night as Rackham emerged with companions. So Friday at five o'clock, when Saul phoned that the subject had entered the Romance Bar on 49th Street, I went for a walk, found Saul window-shopping, told him to go home to his wife and children, moseyed along to the Romance Bar entrance, and went on in.

Business was rushing, with as many as five at a table the size of a dishpan. Making no survey, I found a place at the long bar where two customers were carelessly leaving enough room for a guy to get an elbow through, and took the opening. After a while the bartender admitted I was there and let me buy a highball. I took a casual look around, saw Rackham at a table with a pair of males, turned my back that way, and got his range in the mirror.

I did not really expect a bite at the very first try; I thought it might take two or three exposures. But evidently he was ripe. I was in the middle of my second highball when my mirror view showed me the trio getting up and squeezing through the mob to the clear. I dropped my chin and looked at my thumb. They went on by, toward the door, and I turned to watch their manly backs. As soon as they were out I followed, and, on the side-walk, immediately turned right, thinking to reconnoiter from the shop entrance next door. But I was still two paces from it when there was a voice at my elbow.

"Here I am, Goodwin."

I turned to face him, looking mildly startled. "Oh, hello."

"What's the idea?" he demanded.

"Which one?" I asked politely. "There's so many around."

"There are indeed. You and three others that I know of. Who wants to know so much about me?"

"Search me." I was sympathetic. "Why, are you being harassed?"

Color had started to show in his face, and the muscles of his jaw were called upon. His right shoulder twitched.

"Not here on the street," I suggested. "A crowd will collect, especially after I react. See that man turning to look? You're standing like Jack Dempsey."

He relaxed a little. "I think I know," he said.

"Good for you. Then I'm not needed."

"I want to have a talk with you."

"Go ahead."

"Not here. At my place—the Churchill."

"I think I have a free hour next Tuesday."

"Now. We'll go there now."

I shrugged. "Not together. You lead the way, and I'll tag along."

He turned and marched. I gave him twenty paces and then followed. It takes the strain off of tailing a man to have a date with him, and since we had only a few blocks to go it would have been merely a pleasant little stroll if he hadn't been in such a hurry. I had to use my full stride to keep my distance. As we neared the Churchill I closed in a little, and when he entered an elevator I was there ready for the next one.

He had a corner suite at the setback, which gave him a terrace and also a soundbreak for the street noises. It was cool and quiet in his big sitting room, with light blue summer rugs and pretty pictures and light blue slip-covers on the furniture. While he adjusted venetian blinds I glanced around, and when he was through I told him, "Very nice. A good place for a heart-to-heart talk."

"What will you have to drink?"

"Nothing, thanks. I had my share at the bar, and anyway I don't drink with people I'm tailing."

I was in a comfortable chair, and he pulled a smaller one around to face me. "You've got your own office now," he stated.

I nodded. "Doing pretty well. Of course, summer's the slack season. After

Labor Day they'll start coming back and bringing their troubles along."

"You didn't take on that job for Mrs. Frey."

"How could I?" I upturned a palm. "No one would speak to me."

"You can't blame them." He got out a cigarette and lit it, and his hands were almost steady but not quite. "Look, Goodwin. There on the street I nearly lost my head for a second. You're merely doing what you're paid for."

"Right," I said approvingly. "People resent detectives more than they do doctors or plumbers, I don't see why. We're all trying to make it a better world."

"Certainly. Who are you working for?"

"Me."

"Who pays you to work for you?"

I shook my head. "Better start over. Show a gun or a steak knife or something. Even if I'm not hard to persuade, I must keep up appearances."

He licked his lips. Apparently that was his substitute for counting ten, but if so it didn't work, for he sprang up, towering over me, making fists. I moved nothing but my head, jerking it back to focus on his face.

"It's a bad angle," I assured him. "If you swing from up there I'll duck and hit your knees, and you'll lose your balance."

He held it a second, then his fists became hands, and he stooped to use one of them to recover the cigarette he had dropped on the rug. He sat down, took a drag, inhaled, and let it out.

"You talk too much, Goodwin."

"No," I disagreed, "not too much, but too frankly, maybe. Perhaps I shouldn't have mentioned a steak knife, but I was irritated. I might name my client if you stuck needles under my nails or showed me a dollar bill, but your being so damn casual annoyed me."

"I didn't kill my wife."

I smiled at him. "That's a straightforward categorical statement, and I appreciate it very much. What else didn't you do?"

He ignored it. "I know Annabel Frey thinks I did, and she would spend all the money my wife left her—well, say half of it—to prove it. I don't mind your taking her money, that's your business, but I hate to see her waste it, and I don't like having someone always behind me. There ought to be some way I can satisfy you and her that I didn't do it. Can't you figure one out? If it's arranged so you won't lose anything by it?"

"No," I said flatly.

"Why not? I said satisfy you."

"Because I'm getting irritated again. You don't care a damn what Mrs. Frey thinks. What's eating you is that you don't know who is curious enough about you to spend money on it, and you're trying to catch a fish without bait, which is unsportsmanlike. I'll bet you a finif you can't worm it out of me."

He sat regarding me half a minute, then got up and crossed to a portable bar over by the wall and began assembling a drink. He called to me, "Sure you won't have one?"

I declined with thanks. Soon he returned with a tall one, sat, took a couple of swallows, put the glass down, burped, and spoke. "A thousand dollars for the name."

"Just the name, cold?"

"Yes."

"It's a sale." I extended a hand. "Gimme."

"I like to get what I pay for, Goodwin."

"Absolutely. Guaranteed against defects."

He arose and left the room through a door toward the far end. I decided I was thirsty and went to the bar for a glass of soda and ice, and was back in my chair when he re-entered and came to me. I took his offering and counted it by flipping the edges: ten crackly new hundreds.

He picked up his glass, drank, and eyed me. "Well?"

"Arnold Zeck," I said.

He made a little squeaking noise, went stiff for a short count, and hurled the tall glass against the wall, where it smacked into the middle of the glass of a picture, which improved the effect both for the ear and for the eye.

XV

I ADMIT I was on my feet when it hit. He was so slapdash that there was no certainty about his target, and a well-thrown heavy glass can make a bruise.

"Now look what you've done," I said reproachfully, and sat down again. He glared at me a second, then went to the bar, and with slow precise movements of his hands mixed another long one. I was pleased to note that the proportion of whisky was the same as before. He returned to his chair and put the glass down without drinking.

"I thought so, by God," he said.

I merely nodded.

"Who hired you? Zeck himself?"

"Not in the contract," I objected firmly. "You bought the name, and you've got it."

"I'm in the market for more. I'll take it all."

I frowned at him. "Now I guess I'll have to do some talking. You comfortable?"

"No."

"Listen anyway. I'm taking Zeck's money and I'm crossing him. How do you know I won't cross you?"

"I don't. But I'll top him."

"That's the point exactly; you don't. Who is Zeck and who are you? You know the answer to that. You were taking his money too, up to five months ago, and you know for what. When your wife hired Nero Wolfe to take the lid off of you for a look, you yapped to Zeck and he took aim at Wolfe, and when your wife got it with that steak knife Wolfe took a powder, and for all I know he is now in Egypt, where he owns a house, talking it over with the Sphinx. It was Zeck and you, between you, that broke up our happy home on Thirty-fifth Street, and you can have three guesses how I feel about it. I may like it fine this way, with my own office and my time my own. I may figure to work close to Zeck and get in the big dough, which would mean I'm poison to you, or I may be loving a chance to stick one between Zeck's ribs and incidentally get a nice helping from your pile, or I may even be kidding both of you along with the loony idea of trying to earn the ten grand your wife paid Nero Wolfe. Zeck can guess and you can guess. Do I make myself clear?"

"I don't know. Are you just warning me not to trust you? Is that it?"

"Well, yes."

"Then save your breath. I've never trusted anybody since I started shaving. As for a nice helping from my pile, that depends. How do you earn it?"

I shrugged. "Maybe I don't want it. Guess. I got the impression that I have something you want."

"I think you have. Who hired you and what were you told to do?"

"I told you, Zeck."

"Zeck himself?"

"I would be risking my neck and you know it. Five grand now, and beyond that we can decide as we go along."

It was a mistake, though not fatal. He was surprised. I should have made it ten. He said, "I haven't got that much here."

"Tut. Send downstairs for it."

He hesitated a moment, regarding me, then got up and went to a phone on a side table. It occurred to me that it would be of no advantage for a clerk or assistant manager to see whose presence in Rackham's suite required the delivery of so much cash, so I asked where the bathroom was and went there. After a sufficient interval I returned, and the delivery had been made.

"I said I don't trust anybody," Rackham told me, handing me the engravings. "But I don't like to be gypped."

It was used bills this time, Cs and five-hundreds, which didn't seem up to the Churchill's standard of elegance. To show Rackham how vulgar it was not to trust people, I stowed it away without counting it.

"What do you want?" I asked, sitting. "Words and pictures?"

"I can ask questions, can't I?"

"Sure, that's included. I have not yet seen Zeck himself, but expect to. I was first approached by Max Christy. He—"

"That son of a bitch."

"Yeah? Of course you're prejudiced now. He was merely scouting. He didn't name Zeck and he didn't name you, but offered good pay for an expert tailing job. I was interested enough to make a date to get picked up on the street that night by a man in a car. He gave—"

"Not Zeck. He wouldn't show like that."

"I said I haven't seen Zeck. He gave me the layout. He said his name was Roeder—around fifty—"

"Roeder?" Rackham frowned.

"So he said. He spelled it—R-o-e-d-e-r. Around fifty, brown hair slicked back, face wrinkled and folded, sharp dark eyes, brown pointed beard with gray in it."

"I don't know him."

"He may be in a different department from the one you were in. He did name Zeck. He said—"

"He actually named Zeck?"

"Yes."

"To you? That's remarkable. Why?"

"I don't know, but I can guess. I had previously been tapped by Max Christy, some time ago, and I think they've got an idea that I may have it in me to work up to an executive job—now that Nero Wolfe is gone. And they figure I must know that Christy plays with Brownie Costigan, and that Costigan is close to the top, so why not mention Zeck to me to make it glamorous? Anyhow, Roeder did. He said that what they wanted was a tail on you. They wanted it good and tight. They offered extra good pay. I was to use as many men as necessary. I took the job, got the men, and we started a week ago yesterday. Christy comes to my office every day for the reports. You know what's been in them; you know where you've been and what you've done."

Rackham was still frowning. "That's all there is to it?"

"That's the job as I took it and as I've handled it."

"You weren't told why?"

"In a way I was. I gathered that they think you might be a bad influence on the District Attorney, and they want to be sure you don't start associating with him. If you do they would probably make a complaint. I suppose you know what their idea is of making a complaint."

The frown was going. "You say you gathered that?"

"I didn't put it right. I was told that in so many words."

"By Roeder?"

"Yes."

The frown was gone. "If this is straight, Goodwin, I've made a good buy."

"It's straight all right, but don't trust me. I warned you. Those are the facts, but you can have a guess without any additional charge if you want it."

"A guess about what?"

"About them and you. This guess is why I'm here. This guess is why I went into that bar so you would see me, and followed you out like a halfwit to give you a chance to flag me."

"Oh. So you staged this."

"Certainly. I wanted to tell you about this guess, and if you were in a mood to buy something first, why not?"

He looked aloof. "Let's have the guess."

"Well—" I considered. "It really is a guess, but with a background. Do you want the background first?"

"No, the guess."

"Right. That Zeck is getting set to frame you for the murder of your wife."

I think Rackham would have thrown another glass if he had happened to have it in his hand, possibly at me this time. His blood moved fast. The color came up in his neck and face, and he sort of swelled all over; then his jaw clamped.

"Go on," he mumbled.

"That's all the guess amounts to. Do you want the background?"

He didn't answer. I went on. "It won't cost you a cent. Take the way I was approached. If it's a plain tailing job with no frills, why all the folderol? Why couldn't Christy just put it to me? And why pay me double the market of the highest-priced agencies? Item. If Zeck has his friends at White Plains, which is far from incredible, and if the current furore is upsetting their stomachs, there's nothing they would appreciate more than having their toughest unsolved murder case wrapped up for them. Item. Hiring me is purely defensive, and Zeck and his staff don't function that way, especially not when the enemy is a former colleague and they've got a grudge."

I shook my head. "I can't see it with that background. But listen to this. Roeder came up to my office and stayed an hour, and do you know what he spent most of it doing? Asking me questions about the evening of April eighth! What has that got to do with my handling a tailing job? Nothing! Why should they be interested in April eighth at all? I think they brought me this job, at double pay, just to start a conversation with me and soften me up. It has already been hinted that Zeck might like to meet me. I think that to frame you for murder they've got to have first-hand dope from someone who was there, and I'm elected. I think they're probably sizing me up, to decide whether I'm qualified to be asked to remember something that happened that night which has slipped my mind up to now, at a nice juicy price."

I turned my palms up. "It's just a guess."

He still had nothing to say. His blood had apparently eased up a little. He was staring at my face, but I doubted if he was seeing it.

"If you care to know why I wanted you to hear it," I went on, "you can have that too. I have my weak spots, and one of them is my professional pride. It got a hard blow when Nero Wolfe scooted instead of staying to fight it out, with your wife's check for ten grand deposited barely in time to get through before she was croaked. If the ten grand is returned to her estate, who gets it? You. And it could be that you killed her. I prefer to leave it where it is and earn it. Among other things, she was killed while I was there, and I helped find the body. That's a fine goddam mess for a good detective, and I was thinking I was one."

He found his tongue. "I didn't kill her. I swear to you, Goodwin, I didn't kill her."

"Oh, skip it. Whether you did or didn't, not only do I not want to help frame you, I don't want anyone to frame anybody, not on this one. I've got a personal interest in it. I intend to earn that ten grand, and I don't want Zeck to bitch it up by getting you burned, even if you're the right one, on a fix. Therefore I wanted you to know about this. As I told you, I haven't got it spelled out, it's only a guess with background, and I admit it may be a bum one. What do you think? Am I hearing noises?"

Rackham picked up his drink, which hadn't been touched, took a little sip, about enough for a sparrow, and put it down again. He sat a while, licking his lips. "I don't get you," he said wistfully.

"Then forget it. You're all paid up. I've been known to guess wrong before."

"I don't mean that, I mean you. Why? What's your play?"

"I told you, professional pride. If that's too fancy for you, consider how I was getting boxed in, with Zeck on my right and you on my left. I wanted a window open. If you don't like that either, just cross me off as screwy. You don't trust me anyhow. I merely thought that if my guess is good, and if I get approached with an offer of a leading part, and maybe even asked to help with the script, and if I decided I would like to consult you about it, it would be nice if we'd already met and got a little acquainted." I flipped a hand. "If you don't get me, what the hell, I'm ahead six thousand bucks."

I stood up. "One way to settle it, you could phone Zeck and ask him.

That would be hard on me, but what can a double-crosser expect? So I'll trot along." I moved toward the door and was navigating a course through the scattered fragments of glass in the path when he decided to speak.

"Wait a minute," he said, still wistful. "You mentioned when you get approached."

"*If* I get approached."

"You will. That's the way they work. Whatever they offer, I'll top it. Come straight to me and I'll top it. I want to see you anyhow, every day—wait a minute. Come back and sit down. We can make a deal right now, for you to—"

"No," I said, kind but firm. "You're so damn scared it would be a temptation to bargain you out of your last pair of pants. Wait till you cool off a little and get some spunk back. Ring me any time. You understand, of course, we're still tailing you."

I left him.

Several times, walking downtown, I had to rein myself in. I would slow down to a normal gait, and in another block or so there I would be again, pounding along as fast as I could swing it, though all I had ahead was an open evening. I grinned at myself indulgently. I was excited, that was all. The game was on, I had pitched the first ball, and it had cut the inside corner above his knees. Not only that, it was a game with no rules. It was hard to believe that Rackham could possibly go to Zeck or any of his men with it, but if he did I was on a spot hot enough to fry an egg, and Wolfe was as good as gone. That was why I had tried to talk Wolfe out of it. But now that I had started it rolling and there was no more argument, I was merely so excited that I couldn't walk slow if you paid me.

I had had it in mind to drop in at Rusterman's Restaurant for dinner and say hello to Marko that evening, but now I didn't feel like sitting through all the motions, so I kept going to Eleventh Avenue, to Mart's Diner, and perched on a stool while I cleaned up a plate of beef stew, three ripe tomatoes sliced by me, and two pieces of blueberry pie. Even with a full stomach I was still excited. It must have shown, I suppose in my eyes, for Mart asked me what the glow was about, and though I had never had any tendency to discuss my business with him, I had to resist an impulse to remark casually that Wolfe and I had finally mixed it up with the most dangerous baby on two legs, one so tough that even Inspector Cramer had said he was out of reach.

I went home and sat in the office all evening, holding magazines open as if I were reading them. All I really did was listen for the phone or doorbell. When the phone rang at ten o'clock and it was only Fred Durkin wanting to know where Saul and the subject were, I was so rude that I hurt his feelings and had to apologize. I told him to cover the Churchill as usual, which was one of the factors that made it a burlesque, since that would have required four men at least. What I wanted to do so bad I could taste it was call the number Wolfe had given me, but that had been for emergency only. I looked emergency up in the dictionary, and got "an unforeseen combination of circumstances which calls for immediate action." Since this was just the opposite, a foreseen combination of circumstances which called for getting a good night's sleep, I didn't dial the number. I did get the good night's sleep.

Saturday morning at 1019 I had to pitch another ball, but not to the same batter. The typing of Friday's reports required only the customary summarizing of facts as far as Saul and Fred and Orrie were concerned, but my own share took time and thought. I had to account for the full time I had spent in Rackham's suite, since there was a double risk in it: the chance that I was being checked and had been seen entering and leaving, and the chance that Rackham had himself split a seam. So it was quite a literary effort and I spent three hours on it. That afternoon, when Max Christy called to get the report as usual, and sat to look it over, I had papers on my desk which kept me so busy that I wasn't even aware if he sent me a glance when he got to the middle of the second page, where my personal contribution began. I looked up only when he finally spoke.

"So you had a talk with him, huh?"

I nodded. "Have you read it?"

"Yes." Christy was scowling at me.

"He seemed so anxious that I thought it would be a shame not to oblige him. It's my tender heart."

"You took his money."

"Certainly. He was wild to spend it."

"You told him you're working for Mrs. Frey. What if he takes a notion to ask her?"

"He won't. If he does, who will know who to believe or what? I warned him about me. By the way, have I ever warned you?"

"Why did you play him?"

"It's all there in the report. He knew he had a tail, how could he help it, already on guard, after eight days of it? I thought I might as well chat with him and see what was on his mind. He could have said something interesting, and maybe he did, I don't know, because I don't know what you and your friends would call interesting. Anyway, there it is. As for his money, he practically stuffed it in my ear, and if I had refused to take it he would have lost all respect for me."

Christy put the report in his pocket, got up, rested his fingertips on the desk, and leaned over at me. "Goodwin," he asked, "do you know who you're dealing with?"

"Oh, for God's sake," I said impatiently. "Have I impressed you as the sort of boob who would jump off a building just to hear his spine crack? Yes, brother, I know who I'm dealing with, and I expect to live to ninety at least."

He straightened up. "Your chief trouble," he said, not offensively, "is that you think you've got a sense of humor. It confuses people, and you ought to get over it. Things strike you as funny. You thought it would be funny to have a talk with Rackham, and it may be all right this time, but some day something that you think is funny will blow your goddam head right off your shoulders."

Only after he had gone did it occur to me that that wouldn't prove it wasn't funny.

I had a date that Saturday evening with Lily Rowan, but decided to call it off. Evidently I wasn't tactful enough about it, for she took on. I calmed her down by promising to drown myself as soon as the present crisis was past, went home and got my dinner out of the refrigerator, and settled down in the office for another evening of not reading magazines. A little after nine the minutes were beginning to get too damn long entirely when the phone rang. It was Lily.

"All right," she said briskly, "come on up here."

"I told you—"

"I know, but now I'm telling you. I'm going to have company around eleven, and as I understand it you're supposed to get here first. Get started."

"Phooey. I'm flattered that you bothered to try it, but—"

"I wouldn't have dreamed of trying it. The company just phoned, and I'm following instructions. My God, are you conceited!"

"I'll be there in twenty minutes."

It took twenty-two, to her door. She was vindictive enough to insist that there were three television programs she wouldn't miss for anything, which was just as well, considering my disposition. I suppose I might have adjusted to it in time, say ten years, but I was so used to having Wolfe right at hand any minute of the day or night when difficulties were being met that this business of having to sit it out until word came, and then rushing up to a friend's penthouse and waiting another hour and a half, was too much of a strain.

He finally arrived. I must admit that when the bell rang Lily, having promised to behave like a lady, did so. She insisted on opening the door for him, but having got him into the living room, she excused herself and left us.

He sat. I stood and looked at him. Eleven days had passed since our reunion, and I hadn't properly remembered how grotesque he was. Except for the eyes, he was no one I had ever seen or cared to see.

"What's the matter?" I asked peevishly. "You look as if you hadn't slept for a week."

"I'm a little tired, that's all," he growled. "I have too much to watch, and I'm starving to death. So far as I know everything at my end is satisfactory. What about Miss Rowan?"

"She's all right. As you may remember, every week or so I used to send her a couple of orchids of a kind that couldn't be bought. I have told her that the custom may be resumed some day provided we get this difficulty ironed out, and that it depends on her. Women like to have things depend on them."

He grunted. "I don't like to have things depend on them." He sighed. "It can't be helped. I can only stay an hour. Bring me some of Miss Rowan's perfume."

I went and tapped on a door, got no answer, opened it and crossed a room to another door, tapped again, was told to enter, and did so. Lily was on a divan with a book. I told her what I wanted.

"Take the Houri de Perse," she advised. "Pete likes it. I had it on that night."

I got it from the dressing table, returned to the living room, aimed it at him from the proper distance, and squeezed the bulb. He shut his eyes and tightened his lips to a thin line.

"Now the other side," I said gently. "What's worth doing—"

But he opened his eyes, and their expression was enough. I put the sprayer on a table and went to a chair.

He looked at his wristwatch. "I read the report of your talk with Rackham. How did it go?"

"Fine. You might have thought he had rehearsed it with us."

"Tell me about it."

I obeyed. It felt good, giving him a communiqué again, and since it needed no apologies I enjoyed it. What I always tried for was to present it so that few or no questions were required, and though I was a little out of practice I did well enough.

When I was through he muttered, "Satisfactory. Confound this smell."

"It'll go away in time. Sixty dollars an ounce."

"Speaking of dollars, you didn't deposit what you took from Rackham?"

"No. It's in the safe."

"Leave it there for the present. It's Mrs. Rackham's money, and we may decide we've earned it. Heaven knows no imaginable sum could repay me for these months. I was thinking—"

He cut it off, tilted his head a little, and regarded me with eyes narrowed to slits.

"Well?" I said aggressively. "More bright ideas?"

"I was thinking, Archie. August is gone. The risk would be negligible. Get Mr. Haskins on the phone tomorrow and tell him to start a dozen chicks on blueberries. Uh—two dozen. You can tell him they are for gifts to your friends."

"No, sir."

"Yes. Tomorrow."

"I say no. He would know damn well who they were for. My God, is your stomach more important than your neck? Not to mention mine. You can't help it if you were born greedy, but you can try to control—"

"Archie." His voice was thin and cold with fury. "Nearly five months now. Look at me."

"Yes, sir." He had me. "You're right. I beg your pardon. But I am not going to phone Haskins. You just had a moment of weakness. Let's change the subject. Does Rackham's biting on the first try change the schedule any?"

"You could tell Mr. Haskins—"

"No."

He gave up. After sitting a while with his eyes closed, he sighed so deep it made him shudder, and then came back to black reality. Only a quarter of his hour was left, and we used it to review the situation and program. The strategy was unchanged. At midnight he arose.

"Please thank Miss Rowan for me?"

"Sure. She thinks you ought to call her Lily."

"You shouldn't leave on my heels."

"I won't. She's sore and wants to have a scene."

I went ahead to open the door for him. As I did so he asked, "What is this stuff called?"

"Houri de Perse."

"Great heavens," he muttered, and went.

XVI

HAVING my own office was giving me a new slant on some of the advantages of the setup I had long enjoyed at Wolfe's place. With a tailing job on, Sunday was like any other day, and I had to be at 1019 at the usual hour, both to type the report and to take calls from the man on the job in case he needed advice or help. It was no longer just burlesque, at least not for me. Even though Rackham knew we were on him, those were three good men, particularly Saul, and I stood a fair chance of being informed if he strayed anywhere out of bounds to keep an appointment. To some extent the tail now served a purpose: to warn me if the subject and the client made a contact, which was somewhat bassackwards but convenient for me.

After a leisurely Sunday dinner at Rusterman's Restaurant, where I couldn't make up my mind whether Marko Vukcic knew that I had my old job back, I returned to 1019 to find Max Christy waiting at the door. He seemed a little upset. I glanced at my wrist and told him he was early.

"This one-man business is no good," he complained. "You ought to have someone here. I tried to get you on the phone nearly two hours ago."

Unlocking the door and entering, I explained that I had dawdled over tournedos à la Béarnaise, which I thought would impress him. He didn't seem to hear me. When I unlocked a desk drawer to get the report, and handed it to him, he stuffed it in his pocket without glancing at it.

I raised the brows. "Don't you want to read it?"

"I'll read it in the car. You're coming along."

"Yeah? Where to?"

"Pete Roeder wants to see you."

"Well, here I am. As you say, this is a one-man business. I've got to stick here, damn it."

Christy was glaring at me under his brow thickets. "Listen, Goodwin, I'm supposed to have you somewhere at four o'clock, and it's five to three now. I waited for you nearly half an hour. Let's go. You can argue on the way."

I had done my arguing, double-quick, while he was speaking. To balk was out of the question. To stall and try to get an idea what the program really was would have been sappy. I got my keys out again, unlocked the bottom drawer, took off my jacket, got out the shoulder holster, slipped it on, and twisted my torso to reach for the buckle.

"What's that for, woodchucks?" Christy asked.

"Just force of habit. Once I forgot to wear it and a guy in an elevator stepped on my toe. I had to cut his throat. If we're in a hurry, come on."

We went. Down at the curb, as I had noticed on my way in, force of habit again, was a dark blue Olds sedan, a fifty, with a cheerful-looking young man with a wide mouth, no hat, behind the wheel. He gave me an interested look as Christy and I got in the back seat, but no words passed. The second the door slammed the engine started and the car went forward.

The Olds fifty is the only stock car that will top a hundred and ten, but we never reached half of that—up the West Side Highway, Saw Mill River, and Taconic State. The young man was a careful, competent, and considerate driver. There was not much conversation. When Christy took the report from his pocket and started reading it my first reaction was mild relief, on the ground that if I were about to die they wouldn't give a damn what my last words were, but on second thought it seemed reasonable that he might be looking for more evidence for the prosecution, and I left the matter open.

It was a fine sunny day, not too hot, and everything looked very attractive. I hoped I would see many more days like it, in either town or country, I didn't care which, though ordinarily I much prefer the city. But that day the country looked swell, and therefore I resented it when, as we were rolling along the Taconic State Parkway a few miles north of Hawthorne Circle, Christy suddenly commanded me, "Get down on the floor, face down."

"Have a heart," I protested. "I'm enjoying the scenery."

"I'll describe it to you. Shall we park for a talk?"

"How much time have we?"

"None to waste."

"Okay, pull your feet back."

The truth was, I was glad to oblige. Logic had stepped in. If that was intended for my last ride I wouldn't ever be traveling that road again, and in that case what difference did it make if I saw where we turned off and which direction we went? There must have been some chance that I would ride another day, and without a chaperon, or this stunt was pointless. So as I got myself into position, wriggling and adjusting to keep my face downward without an elbow or knee taking my weight, the worst I felt was undignified. I heard the driver saying something, in a soft quiet voice, and Christy answering him, but I didn't catch the words.

There was no law against looking at my watch. I had been playing hide and seek, with me it, a little more than sixteen minutes, with the car going now slower and now faster, now straight and now turning left and now right, when finally it slowed down to a full stop. I heard a strange voice and then Christy's, and the sound of a heavy door closing. I shifted my weight.

"Hold it," Christy snapped at me. He was still right above me. "We're a little early."

"I'm tired of breathing dust," I complained.

"It's better than not breathing at all," the strange voice said and laughed, not attractively.

"He's got a gun," Christy stated. "Left armpit."

"Why not? He's a licensed eye. We'll take care of it."

I looked at my watch, but it was too dark to see the hands, so of course we were in out of the sun. The driver had got out, shut the car door, and walked away, if I was any good at reading sounds. I heard voices indistinctly, not near me, and didn't get the words. My left leg, from the knee down, got bored and decided to go to sleep. I moved it.

"Hold it," Christy commanded.

"Nuts. Tape my eyes and let me get up and stretch."

"I said hold it."

I held it, for what I would put at another seven minutes. Then there were noises—a door opening, not loud, footsteps and voices, a door closing, again not loud, still steps and voices, a car's doors opening and shutting, an engine starting, a car moving, and in a minute the closing of the heavy door that had closed after we had stopped. Then the door which my head was touching opened.

"All right," a voice said. "Come on out."

It took acrobatics, but I made it. I was standing, slightly wobbly, on concrete, near a concrete wall of a room sixty feet square with no windows and not too many lights. My darting glance caught cars scattered around, seven or eight of them. It also caught four men: Christy, coming around the rear end of the Olds, and three serious-looking strangers, older than our driver, who wasn't there.

Without a word two of them put their hands on me. First they took the gun from my armpit and then went over me. The circumstances didn't seem favorable for an argument, so I simply stood at attention. It was a fast and expert job, with no waste motion and no intent to offend.

"It's all a matter of practice," I said courteously.

"Yeah," the taller one agreed, in a tenor that was almost a falsetto. "Follow me."

He moved to the wall, with me behind. The cars had been stopped short of the wall to leave an alley, and we went down it a few paces to a door where a man was standing. He opened the door for us—it was the one that made little noise—and we passed through into a small vestibule, also with no windows in its concrete walls. Across it, only three paces, steps down began, and we descended—fourteen shallow steps to a wide metal door. My conductor pushed a button in the metal jamb. I heard no sound within, but in a moment the door opened and a pasty-faced bird with a pointed chin was looking at us.

"Archie Goodwin," my conductor said.

"Step in."

I waited politely to be preceded, but my conductor moved aside, and the other one said impatiently, "Step in, Goodwin."

I crossed the sill, and the sentinel closed the door. I was in a room bigger than the vestibule above: bare concrete walls, well-lighted, with a table, three chairs, a water-cooler, and a rack of magazines and newspapers. A second sentinel, seated at the table, writing in a book like a ledger, sent me a sharp glance and then forgot me. The first one crossed to another big metal door directly opposite to the one I had entered by, and when he pulled it open I saw that it was a good five inches thick. He jerked his head and told me, "On in."

I stepped across and passed through, with him at my heels.

This was quite a chamber. The walls were paneled in a light gray wood with pink in it, from the tiled floor to the ceiling, and the rugs were the same light gray with pink borders. Light came from a concealed trough continuous around the ceiling. The six or seven chairs and the couch were covered in pinkish gray leather, and the same leather had been used for the frames of the pictures, a couple of big ones on each wall. All that, collected in my first swift survey, made a real impression.

"Archie Goodwin," the sentinel said.

The man at the desk said, "Sit down, Goodwin. All right, Schwartz," and the sentinel left us and closed the door.

I would have been surprised to find that Pete Roeder rated all this splash so soon after hitting this territory, and he didn't. The man at the desk was not Roeder. I had never seen this bozo, but no introduction was needed. Much as he disliked publicity, his picture had been in the paper a few times, as for instance the occasion of his presenting his yacht to the United States Coast Guard during the war. Also I had heard him described.

I had a good view of him at ten feet when I sat in one of the pinkish gray leather chairs near his desk. Actually there was nothing to him but his forehead and eyes. It wasn't a forehead, it was a dome, sloping up and up to the line of his faded thin hair. The eyes were the result of an error on the assembly line. They had been intended for a shark and someone got careless. They did not now look the same as shark eyes because Arnold Zeck's brain had been using them to see with for fifty years, and that had had an effect.

"I've spoken with you on the phone," he said.

I nodded. "When I was with Nero Wolfe. Three times altogether—no, I guess it was four."

"Four. Where is he? What has happened to him?"

"I'm not sure, but I suspect he's in Florida, training with an air hose, preparing to lay for you in your swimming pool and get you when you dive."

There was no flicker of response, of any kind, in the shark eyes. "I have been told of your habits of speech, Goodwin," he said. "I make no objection. I take men for what they are or not at all. It pleases me that, impressed as you must be by this meeting, you insist on being yourself. But it does waste time and words. Do you know where Wolfe is?"

"No."

"Have you a surmise?"

"Yeah, I just told you." I got irritated. "Say I tell you he's in Egypt, where he owns a house. I don't, but say I do. Then what? You send a punk to Cairo to drill him? Why? Why can't you let him alone? I know he had his faults —God knows how I stood them as long as I did—but he taught me a lot, and wherever he is he's my favorite fatty. Just because he happened to queer your deal with Rackham, you want to track him down. What will that get you, now that he's faded out?"

"I don't wish or intend to track him down."

"No? Then what made me so interesting? Your Max Christy and your bearded wonder offering me schoolboy jobs at triple pay. Get me sucked in, get me branded, and when the time comes use me to get at Wolfe so you can pay him. No." I shook my head. "I draw the line somewhere, and all of you together won't get me across that one."

I'm not up enough on fish to know whether sharks blink, but Zeck was showing me. He blinked perhaps one-tenth his share. He asked, "Why did you take the job?"

"Because it was Rackham. I'm interested in him. I was glad to know someone else was. I would like to have a hand in his future."

No blink. "You think you know, I suppose, the nature of my own interests and activities."

"I know what is said around. I know that a New York police inspector told me that you're out of reach."

"Name him."

"Cramer. Manhattan Homicide."

"Oh, him." Zeck made his first gesture: a forefinger straightened and curved again. "What was the occasion?"

"He wouldn't believe me when I said I didn't know where Wolfe was. He thought Wolfe and I were fixing to try to bring you down, and he was just telling me. I told him that maybe he would like to pull us off because he was personally interested, but that since Wolfe had scooted he was wasting it."

"That was injudicious, wasn't it?"

"All of that. I was in a bad humor."

Zeck blinked; I saw him. "I wanted to meet you, Goodwin. I've allowed some time for this because I want to look at you and hear you talk. Your idea of my interests and activities probably has some relation to the facts, and if so you may know that my chief problem is men. I could use ten times as many good men as I can find. I judge men partly by their record and partly by report, but mainly by my first-hand appraisal. You have disappointed me in one respect. Your conclusion that I want to use you to find Nero Wolfe is not intelligent. I do not pursue an opponent who has fled the field; it would not be profitable. If he reappears and gets in my path again, I'll crush him. I do want to suck you in, as you put it. I need good men now more than ever. Many people get money from me, indirectly, whom I never see and have no wish to see; but there must be some whom I do see and work through. You might be one. I would like to try. You must know one thing: if you once say yes it becomes impractical to change your mind. It can't be done."

"You said," I objected, "you would like to try. How about my liking to try?"

"I've answered that. It can't be done."

"It's already being done. I'm tailing Rackham for you. When he approached me I took it on myself to chat with him and report it. Did you like that or not? If not, I'm not your type. If so, let's go on with that until you know me better. Hell, we never saw each other before. You can let me know a day in advance when I'm to lose the right to change my mind, and we'll see. Regarding my notion that you want to use me to find Nero Wolfe, skip it. You couldn't anyway, since I don't know whether he went north, east, south, or west."

I had once remarked to Wolfe, when X (our name then for Zeck) had brought a phone call to a sudden end, that he was an abrupt bastard. He now abruptly turned the shark eyes from me, which was a relief, to reach for the switch on an intercom box on his desk, flip it, and speak to it. "Send Roeder in."

"Tell him to shave first," I suggested, thinking that if I had a reputation for a habit of speech I might as well live up to it. Zeck did not react. I was beginning to believe that he never had reacted to anything and never would. I turned my head enough for the newcomer to have my profile when he entered, not to postpone his pleasure at seeing me.

It was a short wait till the door opened and Roeder appeared. The sentinel did not come in. Roeder crossed to us, stepping flat on the rugs so as not to slide. His glance at me was fleeting and casual.

"Sit down," Zeck said. "You know Goodwin."

Roeder nodded and favored me with a look. Sitting, he told me, "Your reports haven't been worth what they cost."

It gave me a slight shock, but I don't think I let it show. I had forgotten that Roeder talked through his nose.

"Sorry," I said condescendingly. "I've been sticking to facts. If you want them dressed up, let me know what color you like."

"You've been losing him."

I flared up quietly. "I used to think," I said, "that Nero Wolfe expected too much. But even he had brains enough to know that hotels have more than one exit."

"You're being paid enough to cover the exits to the Yankee Stadium."

Zeck said, in his hard, cold, precise voice that never went up or down, "These are trivialities. I've had a talk with Goodwin, Roeder, and I sent for you because we got to Rackham. We have to decide how it is to be handled and what part Goodwin is to play. I want your opinion on the effect of Goodwin's telling Rackham that he is working for Mrs. Frey."

Roeder shrugged. "I think it's unimportant. Goodwin's main purpose now is to get Rackham scared. We've got to have him scared good before we can expect him to go along with us. If he killed his wife—"

"He did, of course. Unquestionably."

"Then he might be more afraid of Mrs. Frey than of you. We can see. If not, it will be simple for Goodwin to give him a new line." Roeder looked at me. "It's all open for you to Rackham now?"

"I guess so. He told me he wanted to see me every day, but that was day before yesterday. What are we scaring him for? To see him throw glasses?"

Zeck and Roeder exchanged glances. Zeck spoke to me. "I believe Roeder told you that he came here recently from the West Coast. He had a very successful operation there, a brilliant and profitable operation which he devised. It has some novel features and requires precise timing and expert handling. With one improvement it could be enormously profitable here in New York, and that one improvement is the cooperation of a wealthy and well-placed man. Rackham is ideal for it. We intend to use him. If you help materially in lining him up, as I think you can, your share of the net will be five per cent. The net is expected to exceed half a million, and should be double that."

I was frowning skeptically. "You mean if I help scare him into it."

"Yes."

"And help with the operation too?"

"No."

"What have I got to scare him with?"

"His sense of guilt first. He escaped arrest and trial for the murder of his wife only because the police couldn't get enough evidence for a case. He is under the constant threat of the discovery of additional evidence, which for a murderer is a severe strain. If he believes we have such evidence he will be open to persuasion."

"Have we got it?"

Zeck damn near smiled. "I shouldn't think it will be needed. If it is needed we'll have it."

"Then why drag him in on a complicated operation? He's worth what, three million? Ask him for half of it, or even a third."

"No. You have much to learn, Goodwin. People must not be deprived of hope. If we take a large share of Rackham's fortune he will be convinced that we intend to wring him dry. People must be allowed to feel that if our demands are met the outlook is not intolerable. A basic requirement for continued success in illicit enterprises is a sympathetic understanding of the limitations of the human nervous system. Getting Rackham's help in Roeder's operation will leave plenty of room for future requests."

I was keeping my frown. "Which I may or may not have a hand in. Don't think I'm playing hard to get, but this is quite a step to take. Using a threat of a murder rap to put the screws on a millionaire is a little too drastic without pretty good assurance that I get more than peanuts. You said five per cent of a probable half a million, but you're used to talking big figures. Could I have that filled in a little?"

Roeder reached for a battered old leather brief case which he had brought in with him and deposited on the floor. Getting it on his lap, he had it opened when Zeck asked him, "What are you after, the estimates?"

"Yes, if you want them."

"You may show them to him, but no names." Zeck turned to me. "I think you may do, Goodwin. You're brash, but that is a quality that may be made use of. You used it when you talked with Rackham. He must be led into this with tact or he may lose his head and force our hand, and all we want is his cooperation. His conviction for murder wouldn't help us any; quite the contrary. Properly handled, he should be of value to us for years."

The shark eyes left me. "What's your opinion of Goodwin, Roeder? Can you work with him?"

Roeder had closed the brief case and kept it on his lap. "I can try," he said, not enthusiastically. "The general level here is no higher than on the coast. But we can't get started until we know whether we have Rackham or not, and the approach through Goodwin does seem the best way. He's so damned cocky I don't know whether he'll take direction."

"Would you care to have my opinion of Roeder?" I inquired.

Zeck ignored it. "Goodwin," he said, "this is the most invulnerable organization on earth. There are good men in it, but it all comes to me. I am the organization. I have no prejudices and no emotions. You will get what you deserve. If you deserve well, there is no limit to the support you will get, and none to the reward. If you deserve ill, there is no limit to that either. You understand that?"

"Sure." His eyes were the hardest to meet in my memory. "Provided you understand that I don't like you."

"No one likes me. No one likes the authority of superior intellect. There was one man who matched me in intellect—the man you worked for, Nero Wolfe—but his will failed him. His vanity wouldn't let him yield, and he cleared out."

"He was a little handicapped," I protested, "by his respect for law."

"Every man is handicapped by his own weaknesses. If you communicate with him give him my regards. I have great admiration for him."

Zeck glanced at a clock on the wall and then at Roeder. "I'm keeping a caller waiting. Goodwin is under your direction, but he is on trial. Consult me as necessary within the routine."

He must have had floor buttons for foot-signaling, for he touched nothing with his hands, but the door opened and the sentinel appeared.

Zeck said, "Put Goodwin on the B list, Schwartz."

Roeder and I arose and headed for the door, him with his brief case under his arm.

Remembering how he had told me, tapping his chest, "I am a D, Archie," I would have given a lot if I could have tapped my own bosom and announced, "I am a B, Mr. Wolfe."

XVII

THERE was one chore Wolfe had given me which I haven't mentioned, because I didn't care to reveal the details—and still don't. But the time will come when you will want to know where the gun at the bottom of the brief case came from, so I may as well say now that you aren't going to know.

Since filing the number from a gun has been made obsolete by the progress of science, the process of getting one that can't be traced has got more complicated and requires a little specialized knowledge. One has to be acquainted with the right people. I am. But there is no reason why you should be, so I won't give their names and addresses. I couldn't quite meet Wolfe's specifications—the size and weight of a .22 and the punch of a .45—but I did pretty well: a Carson Snub Thirty, an ugly little devil, but straight and powerful. I tried it out one evening in the basement at 35th Street. When I was through I collected the bullets and dumped them in the river. We were taking enough chances without adding another, however slim.

The next evening after our conference with Zeck, a Monday, Wolfe and I collaborated on the false bottom for the brief case. We did the job at 1019. Since I was now a B and Roeder's lieutenant on his big operation, and he was supposed to keep in touch with me, there was no reason why he shouldn't come to 35th Street for an evening visit, but when I suggested it he compressed his lips and scowled at me with such ferocity that I quickly changed the subject. We made the false bottom out of an old piece of leather that I picked up at a shoe hospital, and it wasn't bad at all. Even if a sentinel removed all the papers for a close inspection, which wasn't likely with the status Roeder had reached, there was little chance of his suspecting the bottom; yet if you knew just where and how to pry you could have the Carson out before you could say Jackie Robinson.

However, something had happened before that: my second talk with Barry Rackham. When I got home late Sunday night the phone-answering service reported that he had been trying to reach me, both at 1019 and at the office, and I gave him a ring and made a date for Monday at three o'clock.

Usually I am on the dot for an appointment, but that day an errand took less time than I had allowed, and it was only twelve to three when I left the Churchill tower elevator at Rackham's floor and walked to his door. I was lifting my hand to push the button, when the door opened and I had to step back so a woman wouldn't walk into me. When she saw me she stopped, and we both stared. It was Lina Darrow. Her fine eyes were as fine as ever.

"Well, hello," I said appreciatively.

"You're early, Goodwin," Barry Rackham said. He was standing in the doorway.

Lina's expression was not appreciative. It didn't look like embarrassment, more like some kind of suspicion, though I had no notion what she could suspect me of so spontaneously.

"How are you?" she asked, and then, to make it perfectly clear that she didn't give a damn, went by me toward the elevator. Rackham moved aside, giving me enough space to enter, and I did so and kept going to the living room. In a moment the door closed, and in another moment he joined me.

"You're early," he repeated, not reproachfully.

He looked as if, during the seventy hours since I had last seen him, he had had at least seventy drinks. His face was mottled, his eyes were bloodshot, and his left cheek was twitching. Also his tie had a dot of egg yolk on it, and he needed a shave.

"A week ago Saturday," I said, "I think it was, one of my men described a girl you were out with, and it sounded like Miss Darrow, but I wasn't sure. I'm not leading up to something, I'm just gossiping."

He wasn't interested one way or the other. He asked what I would have to drink, and when I said nothing thank you he went to the bar and got himself a straight one, and then came and moved a chair around to sit facing me.

"Hell," I said, "you look even more scared than you did the other day. And according to my men, either you've started sneaking out side doors or you've become a homebody. Who said boo?"

Nothing I had to say interested him. "I said I wanted to see you every day," he stated. His voice was hoarse.

"I know, but I've been busy. Among other things, I spent an hour yesterday afternoon with Arnold Zeck."

That did interest him. "I think you're a goddam liar, Goodwin."

"Then I must have dreamed it. Driving into the garage, and being frisked, and the little vestibule, and fourteen steps down, and the two sentinels, and the soundproof door five inches thick, and the pinkish gray walls and chairs and rugs, and him sitting there drilling holes in things, including me, with his eyes, and—"

"When was this? Yesterday?"

"Yeah. I was driven up, but now I know how to get there myself. I haven't got the password yet, but wait."

With an unsteady hand he put his glass down on a little table. "I told you before, Goodwin, I did not kill my wife."

"Sure, that's out of the way."

"How did it happen? Your going to see him."

"He sent Max Christy for me."

"That son of a bitch." Suddenly his mottled face got redder and he yelled at me, "Well, go on! What did he say?"

"He said I may have a big career ahead of me."

"What did he say about me?"

I shook my head. "I'll tell you, Rackham. I think it's about time I let my better judgment in on this. I had never seen Zeck before, and he made quite an impression on me." I reached to my breast pocket. "Here's your six thousand dollars. I hate to let go of it, but—"

"Put that back in your pocket."

"No, really, I—"

"Put it back." He wasn't yelling now. "I don't blame you for being impressed by Zeck—God knows you're not the first. But you're wrong if you think he can't ever miss and I'm all done. There's one thing you ought to realize: I can't throw in my hand on this one; I've got to play it out, and I'm going to. You've got me hooked, because I can't play it without you since you were there that night. All right, name it. How much?"

I put the six grand on the little table. "My real worry," I said, "is not Zeck. He is nothing to sneer at and he does make a strong impression, but I have been impressed before and got over it. What called my better judgment in was the New York statutes relating to accessories to murder. Apparently Zeck has got evidence that will convict you. If you—"

"He has not. That's a lie."

"He seems to think he has. If you want to take dough from a murderer for helping him beat the rap you must be admitted to the bar, and I haven't been. So with my sincere regret at my inability to assist you in your difficulty, there's your dough."

"I'm not a murderer, Goodwin."

"I didn't mean an actual murderer. I meant a man against whom evidence has been produced in court to convince a jury. He and his accessory get it just the same."

Rackham's bloodshot eyes were straight and steady at me. "I'm not asking you to help me beat a rap. I'm asking you not to help frame me—and to help me keep Zeck from framing me."

"I know," I said sympathetically. "That's the way you tell it, but not him. I don't intend to get caught in a backwash. I came here chiefly to return your money and to tell you that it's got beyond the point where I name a figure and you pay it and then we're all hunky-dory, but I do have a suggestion to make if you care to hear it—strictly on my own."

Rackham started doing calisthenics. His hands, resting on his thighs, tightened into fists and then opened again, and repeated it several times. It made me impatient watching him, because it seemed so inadequate to the situation. By now the picture was pretty clear, and I thought that a guy who had had enough initiative to venture into the woods at night to stalk his wife, armed only with a steak knife, when she had her Doberman pinscher with her, should now, finding himself backed into a corner, respond with something more forceful than sitting there doing and undoing his fists.

He spoke. "Look, Goodwin, I'm not myself, I know damn well I'm not. It's been nearly five months now. The first week it wasn't so bad—there was the excitement, all of us suspected and being questioned; if they had arrested me then I wouldn't have skipped a pulse beat. I would have met it fair and square and fought it out. But as it stretched out it got tougher. I had broken off with Zeck without thinking it through—the way it looked then, I ought to get clean and keep clean, especially after the hearings in Washington, those first ones, and after the New York District Attorney took a hand. But what happened, every time the phone rang or the doorbell, it hit me in the stomach. It was murder. If they came and took me or sent for me and kept me, I could be damn sure it had been fixed so they thought it would stick. A man can stand that for a day or a week, or a month perhaps, but with me it went on and on, and by God, I've had about all I can take."

He had ended his calisthenics with the fists closed tight, the knobs of the knuckles the color of boils. "I made a mistake with Zeck," he said fretfully. "When I broke it off he sent for me and as good as told me that the only thing between me and the electric chair was his influence. I lost my temper. When I do that I can never remember what I said, but I don't think I actually told him that I had evidence of blackmailing against him personally. Anyhow, I said too much." He opened his fists and spread his fingers wide, his palms flat on his thighs. "Then this started, this stretching into months. Did you say you have a suggestion?"

"Yeah. And brother, you need one."

"What is it?"

"On my own, I said."

"What is it?"

"For you and Zeck to have a talk."

"What for? No matter what he said I couldn't trust him."

"Then you'd be meeting on even terms. Look straight at it. Could your wife trust you? Could your friends trust you—the ones you helped Zeck get at? Could I trust you? I warned you not to trust me, didn't I? There are only two ways for people to work together: when everybody trusts everyone or nobody trusts no one. When you mix them up it's a mess. You and Zeck ought to get along fine."

"Get along with Zeck?"

"Certainly." I turned a palm up. "Listen, you're in a hole. I never saw a man in a deeper one. You're even willing and eager to shell out to me, a double-crosser you can't trust, to give you a lift. You can't possibly expect to get out in the clear with no ropes tied to you—what the hell, who is? Your main worry is getting framed for murder, so your main object is to see that you don't. That ought to be a cinch. Zeck has a new man, a guy named Roeder, came here recently from the coast, who has started to line up an operation that's a beaut. I've been assigned to help on it, and I think I'm going to. It's as tight as a drum and as slick as a Doberman pinscher's coat. With the help of a man placed as you are, there would be absolutely nothing to it, without the slightest risk of any noise or a comeback."

"No. That's what got—"

"Wait a minute. As I said, this is on my own. I'm not going to tell you what Zeck said to me yesterday, but I advise you to take my suggestion. Let me arrange for you to see him. You don't have to take up where you left off, a lot of dirty little errands; you're a man of wealth now and can act accordingly. But also you're a man who is suspected by thirty million people of killing his wife, and that calls for concessions. Come with me to see Zeck, let him know you're willing to discuss things, and if he mentions Roeder's operation let him describe it and then decide what you want to do. I told you why I don't want to see you or anyone else framed for that murder, and I don't think Zeck will either if it looks as though you might be useful."

"I hate him," Rackham said hoarsely. "I'm afraid of him and I hate him!"

"I don't like him myself. I told him so. What about tomorrow? Say four o'clock tomorrow, call for you here at a quarter to three?"

"I don't—not tomorrow—"

"Get it over with! Would you rather keep on listening for the phone and the doorbell? Get it over with!"

He reached for his straight drink, which he hadn't touched, swallowed it at a gulp, shuddered all over, and wiped his mouth with the back of his hand.

"I'll ring you around noon to confirm it," I said, and stood up to go. He didn't come with me to the door, but under the circumstances I didn't hold it against him.

So that evening when Wolfe came to 1019 it appeared to be high time for getting the false bottom in the brief case ready, and we went on until midnight, discussing the program from every angle and trying to cover every contingency. It's always worth trying, though it can never be done, especially not with a layout as tricky as that one.

Then the next morning, Tuesday, a monkey wrench, thrown all the way from White Plains, flew into the machinery and stopped it. I had just finished breakfast, with Fritz, when the phone rang and I went to the office to get it. It was the Westchester DA's office.

The talk was brief. When I had hung up I sat a while, glaring at the phone, then with an exasperated finger dialed the Churchill's number. That talk was brief too. Finished with it, I held the button down for a moment and dialed another number.

There had been only two buzzes when a voice came through a nose to me. "Yes?"

"I'd like to speak to Mr. Roeder."

"Talking."

"This is Goodwin. I've just had a call from White Plains to come to the DA's office at once. I asked if I could count on keeping a two o'clock appointment and was told no. I phoned the Churchill and left a message that I had been called out of town for the day. I hope it can be tomorrow. I'll let you know as soon as I can."

Silence.

"Did you hear me?"

"Yes. Good luck, Goodwin."

The connection went.

XVIII

I HAD once sat and cooled my heels for three hours on one of the wooden benches in the big anteroom of the DA's office in the White Plains courthouse, but this time I didn't sit at all. I didn't even give my name. I entered and was crossing to the table in the fenced-off corner when a man with a limp intercepted me and said, "Come with me, Mr. Goodwin."

He took me down a long corridor, past rows of doors on either side, and into a room that I was acquainted with. I had been entertained there for an hour or so the evening of Sunday, April ninth. No one was in it. It had two big windows for the morning sun, and I sat and watched the dust dance. I was blowing at it, seeing what patterns I could make, when the door opened and Cleveland Archer, the DA himself, appeared, followed by Ben Dykes. I have never glanced at faces with a deeper interest. If they had looked pleased and cocky it would probably have meant that they had cracked the case, and in that event all our nifty plans for taking care of Arnold Zeck were up the flue and God help us.

I was so glad to see that they were far from cocky that I had to see to it that my face didn't beam. I responded to their curt greeting in kind, and when they arranged the seating with me across a table from them I said grumpily as I sat, "I hope this is going to get somebody something. I had a full day ahead, and now look at it."

Dykes grunted, not with sympathy and not with enmity, just a grunt. Archer opened a folder he had brought, selected from its contents some sheets of paper stapled in a corner, glanced at the top sheet, and gave me his eyes, which had swollen lids.

"This is that statement you made, Goodwin."

"About what? Oh, the Rackham case?"

"For God's sake," Dykes said gloomily, "forget to try to be cute just once. I've been up all night."

"It was so long ago," I said apologetically, "and I've been pretty busy."

Archer slid the statement across the table to me. "I think you had better read it over. I want to ask some questions about it."

I couldn't have asked for a better chance to get my mind arranged, but I didn't see that that would help matters any, since I hadn't the vaguest notion from which direction the blow was coming.

"May I save it for later?" I inquired. "If you get me up a tree and I need time out for study, I can pretend I want to check with what I said here." I tapped the statement with a forefinger.

"I would prefer that you read it."

"I don't need to, really. I know what I said and what I signed." I slid it back to him. "Test me on any part of it."

Archer closed the folder and rested his clasped hands on it. "I'm not as interested in what is in that statement as I am in what isn't in it. I think you ought to read it because I want to ask you what you left out—of the happenings of that day, Saturday, April eighth."

"I can answer that without reading it. I left nothing out that was connected with Mrs. Rackham."

"I want you to read what you said and signed and then repeat that statement."

"I don't need to read it. I left out nothing."

Archer and Dykes exchanged looks, and then Dykes spoke. "Look, Goodwin, we're not trying to sneak up on you. We've got something, that's all. Someone has loosened up. It looks like this is the day for it."

"Not for me." I was firm. "I loosened up long ago."

Archer told Dykes, "Bring her in." Dykes arose and left the room. Archer took the statement and returned it to the folder and pushed the folder to one side, then pressed the heels of his palms to his eyes and took a couple of deep breaths. The door opened and Dykes escorted Lina Darrow in. He pulled a chair up to the end of the table for her, to my left and Archer's right, so that the window was at her back. She looked as if she might have spent the night in jail, with red eyes and a general air of being pooped, but judging from the clamp she had on her jaw, she was darned determined about something. I got a glance from her but nothing more, not even a nod, as she took the chair Dykes pulled up.

"Miss Darrow," Archer told her, gently but firmly, "you understand that there is probably no chance of getting your story corroborated except through Mr. Goodwin. You haven't been brought in here to face him for the purpose of disconcerting or discrediting him, but merely so he can be informed first-hand." Archer turned to me. "Miss Darrow came to us last evening of her own accord. No pressure of any kind has been used with her. Is that correct, Miss Darrow? I wish you would confirm that to Mr. Goodwin."

"Yes." She lifted her eyes to me, and though they had obviously had a hard night, I still insist they were fine. She went on, "I came voluntarily. I came because—the way Barry Rackham treated me. He refused to marry me. He treated me very badly. Finally—yesterday it was too much."

Archer and Dykes were both gazing at her fixedly. Archer prodded her. "Go on, please, Miss Darrow. Tell him the main facts."

She was trying the clamp on her jaw to make sure it was working right. Satisfied, she released it. "Barry and I had been friendly, a little, before Mrs. Rackham's death. Nothing but just a little friendly. That's all it meant to me, or I thought it was, and I thought it was the same with him. That's how it was when we went to the country for the Easter weekend. She had told me we wouldn't do any work there, answer any mail or anything, but Saturday at noon she sent for me to come to her room. She was crying and was so distressed she could hardly talk."

Lina paused. She was keeping her eyes straight at mine. "I can rattle this off now, Mr. Goodwin. I've already told it now."

"That always makes it easier," I agreed. "Go right ahead."

She did. "Mrs. Rackham said she had to talk about it with someone, and she wanted to with her daughter-in-law, Mrs. Frey, but she just couldn't, so there was only me. She said she had gone to see Nero Wolfe the day before, to ask him to find out where her husband was getting money from, and he had agreed to do it. Mr. Wolfe had phoned her that evening, Friday evening, and told her that he had already partly succeeded. He had learned that her husband was connected with something that was criminal. He was helping somebody with things that were against the law, and he was getting well paid for it. Mr. Wolfe advised her to keep it to herself until he had more details. He said his assistant, Mr. Goodwin, would come up Saturday afternoon, and might have more to report then."

"And that Goodwin knew all about it?" Archer asked.

"Well, naturally she took that for granted. She didn't say that Mr. Wolfe told her in so many words that Mr. Goodwin knew all about it, but if he was his assistant and helping with it, naturally she would think so. Anyway that didn't seem to be important then, because she had told it all to her husband. They used the same bedroom at Birchvale, and she said that after they had gone to bed she simply couldn't help it. She didn't tell me their conversation, what they said to each other, but they had had a violent quarrel. She had told him they would have to separate, she was through with him, and she would have Mr. Wolfe go on with his investigation and get proof of what he had done. Mrs. Rackham had a very strong character, and she hated to be deceived. But the next day she wasn't sure she really meant it, that she really wanted to part from him. That was why she wanted to talk about it with someone. I think the reason she didn't want to talk with Mrs. Frey—"

"If you don't mind, Miss Darrow," Archer suggested gently, "just the facts now."

"Yes, of course." She sent him a glance and returned to me. "I told her I thought she was completely wrong. I said that if her husband had been untrue to her, or anything like that, that would be different, but after all he hadn't done wrong to her, only to other people and himself, and that she should try to help him instead of destroying him. At the very least, I said, she should wait until she knew all the details of what he had done. I think that was what she wanted to hear, but she didn't say so. She was very stubborn. Then, that afternoon, I did something that I will regret all my life. I went to Barry and told him she had told me about it, and said I was sure it would come out all right if he would meet her halfway—tell her the whole thing, tell her he was sorry, as he certainly should be—and no more foolishness in the future. And Barry said he loved me."

She weakened a little there for the first time. She dropped her eyes. I had been boring at her with as steady and sharp a gaze as I had in me, but up to that point she had met it full and fair.

"So then?" I asked.

Her eyes lifted and she marched on. "He said he didn't want it to come out all right because he loved me. Shall I try to tell you what I—how I felt!"

"Not now. Just what happened."

"Nothing happened then. That was in the middle of the afternoon. I didn't tell Barry I loved him—I didn't even know I loved him then. I got away from him. Later we gathered in the living room for cocktails, and you and Mr. Leeds came, and we played that game—you remember."

"Yep, I do."

"And dinner, and television afterward, and—"

"Excuse me. That is common knowledge. Skip to later, when the cops had come. Did you tell them all this?"

"No."

"Why not?"

"Because I didn't think it would be fair to Barry. I didn't think he had killed her, and I didn't know what criminal things he had helped with, and I thought it wouldn't be fair to tell that about him when all I knew was what Mrs. Rackham had told me." The fine eyes flashed for the first time. "Oh, I know the next part. Then why am I telling it now? Because I know more about him now—a great deal more! I don't know that he killed Mrs. Rackham, but I know he could have; he is cruel and selfish and unscrupulous— there is nothing he wouldn't do. I suppose you think I'm vindictive, and maybe I am, but it doesn't matter what you think about me as long as I'm telling the truth. What the criminal things were that he did, and whether he killed his wife—I don't know anything about it; that's your part."

"Not mine, sister. I'm not a cop."

She turned to the others. "Yours, then!"

This would have been a good moment for me to take time out to read my signed statement, since I could have used a few minutes for some good healthy thinking. Here was a situation that was new to me. About all that Barry Rackham's ticket to the electric chair needed was my endorsement, and I thought he had it coming to him. All I had to do was tell the truth. I could say that I had no knowledge whatever of the phone call Nero Wolfe was purported to have made to Mrs. Rackham, but that it was conceivable that he had made such a call without mentioning it to me, since he had often withheld information from me regarding his actions and intentions. You couldn't beat that for truth. In various occasions I had used all my wits to help pin it on a murderer, and here it would take no wit at all, merely tossing in a couple of facts.

But if I let it go at that, it was a cinch that before the sun went down Rackham would be locked up, and that would ruin everything. The program sunk, the months all wasted, the one chance gone, Zeck sailing on with the authority of his superior intellect, and Wolfe and me high and dry. My wits had a new job, and quick. I liked to think that they had done their share once or twice in getting a murderer corralled; now it was up to them to do more than their share in keeping a murderer running loose and free to keep appointments. Truth was not enough.

There was no time to draw a sketch and see how I liked it. All three of them were looking at me, and Archer was saying, "You can see, Goodwin, why I wanted you to read your statement and see if you left anything out."

"Yeah." I was regretful. "I can also see you holding your breath, and I don't blame you. If I now say that's right, I forgot, Wolfe did phone Mrs. Rackham that Friday evening and tell her that, you've got all you need and hallelujah. I would love to help out, but I like to stick to the truth as far as practical."

"The truth is all I'm asking for. Did you call on Rackham at his apartment yesterday afternoon?"

That punch had of course been telegraphed. "Yes," I said.

"What for?"

"On a job for a client. At first it was a tailing job, and then when Rackham spotted me my client thought I might learn something by chatting with him."

"Why is your client interested in Rackham?"

"He didn't say."

"Who's the client?"

I shook my head. "I don't think that would help you any. He's a man who came here recently from the West Coast, and I suspect he's connected with gambling or rackets or both, but my suspicions are no good at the bank. Let's table it for now."

"I want the name, Goodwin."

"And I want to protect my client within reason. You can't connect him up with the murder you're investigating. Go ahead and start the rigmarole. Charge me again as a material witness and I get released on bail. Meanwhile I'll be wanting my lawyer present and all that runaround. What will it get you in the long run?"

Ben Dykes said in a nasty voice, "We don't want to be arbitrary about it. We wouldn't expect you to name a client if you haven't got one. West Coast, huh?"

"Is Rackham your client?" Archer asked.

"No."

"Have you done any work for him?"

"No."

"Has he given you or paid you any money in the past week?"

That was enough and to spare. I was hooked good, and if the best I could do was flop around trying to wriggle off, the outlook was damn thin. "Oh," I said, "so that's it." I gave Lina Darrow an appreciative look and then transferred it to Archer. "This narrows it down. I've collected for withholding evidence against a murderer. That's bad, isn't it?"

No one answered. They just looked at me.

So I went on. "First, I hereby state that I have no money from Rackham, and that's all on that for now. Second, I'm a little handicapped because although I know what Miss Darrow has in her mind, I don't know how it got there. She's framing Rackham for murder, or trying to, but I'm not sure whether it's her own idea or whether she has been nudged. I would have to find out about that first before I could decide how I stand. I know you've got to give me the works, and that's all right, it's your job, you've got all day and all night for it, but you can take your pick. Either I clam up as of now, and

I mean clam, and you start prying at me, or first I am allowed to have a talk with Miss Darrow—with you here, of course. Then you can have the rest of the week with me. Well?"

"No," Archer said emphatically.

"Okay. May I borrow some adhesive tape?"

"We know everything Miss Darrow has to say."

"Sure you do. I want to catch up. I said with you here. You can always stop it if you get bored."

Archer looked at Dykes. I don't know whether he would have rather had Dykes nod his head or shake it, but he got neither. All Dykes did was concentrate.

"You gentlemen," I said, "want only one thing, to crack the case. It certainly won't help if I shut my trap and breathe through my nose. It certainly won't hurt if I converse with Miss Darrow in your presence."

"Let him," Lina said belligerently. "I knew he would deny it."

"What do you want to ask her?" Archer demanded.

"The best way to find that out is to listen." I turned to Lina. "When I saw you yesterday afternoon, coming out of his apartment, I thought something was stirring. It was rude the way you went right by me."

She met my gaze but had no comment.

"Was it yesterday," I asked, "that he treated you badly?"

"Not only yesterday," she said evenly. "But yesterday he refused definitely and finally to marry me."

"Is that so bad? I mean, a guy can't marry everyone."

"He had said he would—many times."

"But hadn't you been keeping your fingers crossed? After all, it was a kind of a special situation. He knew that you knew something that would get him arrested for murder if you spilled it—not to mention other criminal things, whatever they were. Didn't it occur to you that he might be kidding you along for security reasons?"

"Yes, I—yes, it did, but I didn't want to believe it. He said he loved me. He made love to me—and I wanted him for my husband." She decided that wasn't adequate and improved on it. "I wanted him so much!" she exclaimed.

"I'll bet you did." I tried not to sound sarcastic. "How do you feel about it now? Do you think he ever loved you?"

"No, I don't! I think he was heartless and cruel. I think he was afraid of me. He just wanted me not to tell what I knew. And I began to suspect—the way he acted—and yesterday I insisted that we must be married immediately, this week, and when I insisted he lost his temper and he was—he was hateful."

"I know he's got a temper. Was there any urgent reason for wanting to get married quick, like expecting a visitor from heaven, for instance a baby?"

She flushed and appealed to Archer. "Do I have to let him insult me?"

"I beg your pardon," I said stiffly, "but you seem to be pretty sensitive for a woman who was hell-bent to marry a murderer. Did—"

"I didn't know he was a murderer! I only knew if I told about what Mrs. Rackham told me and what he told me—I knew he would be suspected even more than he was."

"Uh-huh. When the blowup came yesterday, did you threaten to tell what you knew?"

"Yes."

I goggled at her. "You know, sister," I declared, "you should have spent more time thinking this through. You are unquestionably the bummest liar I have ever run across. I thought maybe—"

Dykes broke in. "She says Rackham probably figured he wasn't in much danger, so many months had passed."

"Yeah? That's partly what I mean. Whatever she says, what about Rackham? He's not boob enough to figure like that. He would know damn well that five months is nothing in the life of a murder. He has his choice between marrying this attractive specimen or having her run to you with the ink for his death warrant, and not only does he act heartless and cruel, he actually opens the door for her to go! This guy who had it in him to sneak into the woods at night with a knife to stab his wife to death *and* a fighting dog—he just opens the door for this poor pretty creature to tell the world about it! My God, you would buy that?"

"You can't tell about people," Archer said. "And she has details. Take the detail of the phone call Wolfe made to Mrs. Rackham and what he told her about her husband. Not even a good liar would have that detail, let alone a bum one."

"Nuts." I was disgusted. "No such phone call was made, and Mrs. Rackham never said it was. As for Rackham's having been in with crooks, either he wasn't and sister here invented it, in which case you'd better watch your step, or he was, and sister here got his tongue loosened enough for him to tell her about it. I'm perfectly willing to believe she is capable of that, however bum a liar she may be."

"You say Wolfe didn't make that call to Mrs. Rackham?"

"Yes."

"And he didn't learn that Rackham's income came from a connection with criminal activities?"

"My God, Mrs. Rackham didn't leave our office until after noon that Friday. And he called her that evening to tell her? When he hadn't moved a finger to start an inquiry, and I hadn't either? He was good, but not that good." I turned to Lina. "I thought maybe you had had a coach for this, possibly got in with some professionals yourself, but not now, the way you tell it. Obviously this is your own baby—I beg your pardon if you don't want babies mentioned—say your own script—and it is indeed a lulu. Framing a man for murder is no job for an amateur. Aside from the idea of Rackham's preferring a jury trial to you, which if I may get personal is plain loco, look at other features. If it had been the way you say, what would Wolfe and I have done after I phoned him that night and told him Mrs. Rackham had got it? Our only interest was the fee she had paid us. Why didn't we just hand it all to the cops? Another little feature, do you remember that gathering that evening? Did either Rackham or his wife act like people who were riding the kind of storm you describe? Don't ask me, I could be prejudiced; ask all the others."

I left her for Archer. "I could go on for an hour, but don't tell me you need it. I don't wonder you grabbed at it, it looked as if it might possibly be the break you had been hoping for, and besides, she had fixed it up with some trimmings that might be very juicy, like the crap about me working for Rackham. I have not and am not, and I have none of his dough. Must I punch more holes in it?"

Archer was studying me. "Is it your contention that Miss Darrow invented all this?"

"It is."

"Why?"

I shrugged. "I don't know. Do you want me to guess?"

"Yes."

"Well—my best one first. Have you noticed her eyes—the deep light in them? I think she's trying to take over for you. She liked Mrs. Rackham, and when she got left that two hundred grand it went to her head. She thought Rackham had killed her—I don't know whether it was a hunch or what—and when time passed and it looked as if he wasn't going to get tagged for it, she decided it was her duty or mission, or whatever word she uses for it, to step in. Having the two hundred grand, she could afford a hobby for a while. That was when she started to put the eyes on Rackham. I expect she thought she could get him into a state where he would dump it all out for her, and then she would not only know she was right but would also be able to complete her mission. But the months went by and he never dumped, and it probably got a little embarrassing, and she got fanatic about it, and she must even have got desperate, judging by the performance she finally ended up with. She decided Rackham was guilty, that part was all right, and the only thing lacking was evidence, so it was up to her to furnish it."

I leaned forward at her. "It's not enough to want to do a good deed, you damn fool. Wanting is fine, but you also need some slight idea of how to go about it. It didn't bother you that one by-product was making me out a cheap crook, did it? Many thanks sincerely yours."

She dropped her head into her hands to cover her face, and convulsions began.

They sat and looked at her. I looked at them. Archer was pulling jerkily at his lower lip. Dykes was shaking his head, his lips compressed.

"I suggest," I said modestly, raising my voice to carry over the noise Lina Darrow was making, "that when she quiets down it might pay to find out if Rackham has told her anything that might help. That item about his getting dough from gambling or rackets could be true, if they actually got intimate enough for him to tell her the story of his life."

They kept their eyes on her. She was crying away what had looked like a swell chance to wrap up a tough one, and I wouldn't have been surprised if they had burst into tears too. I pushed back my chair and stood up.

"If you get anything that I can be of any help on, give me a ring. I'll have a crowded afternoon, but word will reach me."

I walked out.

XIX

As I hit the sidewalk in front of the courthouse my watch said 11:17. It was sunny and warm, and people looked as if they felt pleased with the way things were going. I did not. In another few minutes they would have Lina Darrow talking again, and whether she gave it to them straight this time or tried her hand on a revised version, they might decide any minute that they wanted to talk with Barry Rackham, and that could lead to anything. The least it could lead to was delay, and my nerves were in no condition for it.

I dived across the street to a drugstore, found a booth, and dialed Roeder's number. No answer. I went to where my car was parked, got in, and headed for the parkway.

On my way back to Manhattan I stopped four times to find a phone and dial Roeder's number, and the fourth try, at 116th Street, I got him. I told him where I was. He asked what they had wanted at White Plains.

"Nothing much, just to ask some questions about a lead they had got. I'm going to the Churchill to fix it to go ahead with that date today."

"You can't. It has been postponed until tomorrow at the other end. Arrange it for tomorrow."

"Can't you switch it back to today at your end?"

"It would be difficult and therefore inadvisable."

I considered how to put it, in view of the fact that there was no telling who or how many might hear me. "There is a possibility," I said, "that the Churchill will have a vacant suite tomorrow. So my opinion is that it would be even more inadvisable to postpone it. I don't know, but I have an idea that it may be today or never."

A silence. Then, "How long will it take you to get to your office?"

"Fifteen minutes, maybe twenty."

"Go there and wait."

I returned to the car, drove to a parking lot on Third Avenue in the upper Forties, left the car there, and made steps to Madison Avenue and up to 1019. I sat down, stood at the window, sat down, and stood at the window. I wouldn't ring the phone-answering service because I wanted my line free, but after a few minutes I began thinking I better had, in case Roeder had tried for me before I arrived. The debate on that was getting hot when the ring came and I jumped for it.

It was Roeder. He asked me through his nose, "Have you phoned the Churchill?"

"No, I was waiting to hear from you."

"I hope you will have no trouble. It has been arranged for today at four o'clock."

I felt a tingle in my spine. My throat wanted to tighten, but I wouldn't let it. "I'll do my best. In my car?"

"No. I'll have a car. I'll stop in front of your office building precisely at two forty-five."

"It might be better to make it the Churchill."

"No. Your building. If you have to reach me I'll be here until two-thirty. I hope you won't have to."

"I do too."

I pressed the button down, held it for three breaths, and dialed the Churchill's number. It was only ten to one, so surely I would get him.

I did. As soon as he heard my name he started yapping about the message I had sent him, but I didn't want to try to fix it on the phone, so I merely said I had managed to call off the trip out of town and was coming to see him. He said he didn't want to see me. I said I didn't want to see him either, but we were both stuck with this and I would be there at one-thirty.

At a fountain service down on a side street I ate three corned-beef sandwiches and three glasses of milk without knowing how they tasted, burned my tongue on hot coffee, and then walked to the Churchill and took the elevator to the tower.

Rackham was eating lunch, and it was pitiful. Apparently he had done all right with a big glass of clam juice, since the glass was empty and I couldn't see where the contents had been thrown at anything, but all he did in my presence was peck at things—some wonderful broiled ham, hashed brown potatoes, an artichoke with anchovy sauce, and half a melon. He swallowed perhaps five bites altogether, while I sat at a distance with a magazine, not wanting to disturb his meal. When, arriving, I had told him that the appointment with Zeck was set for four o'clock, he had just glared at me with no comment. Now, as he sat staring at his coffee without lifting the cup, I got up and crossed to a chair near him and remarked that we would ride up to Westchester with Roeder.

I don't think I handled it very well, that talk with Barry Rackham, as he sat and let his coffee get cold and tried to pretend to himself that he still intended to eat the melon. It happened that he had already decided that his only way out was to come to some kind of an understanding with Arnold Zeck, but if he had been balky I doubt if I would have been able to manage it. I was so damned edgy that it was all I could do to sit still. It had been a long spring and summer, those five months, and here was the day that would give us the answer. So there are two reasons why I don't report in detail what Rackham and I said there that afternoon: first, I doubt if it affected the outcome any, one way or another; and second, I don't remember a word of it. Except that I finally said it was time to go, and he got himself a man-sized straight bourbon and poured it down.

We walked the few blocks to my building. As we waited at the curb I kept my eyes peeled for a Chevvy sedan, but apparently Roeder had been promoted, either that or the Chevvy wasn't used for important guests, for when a car nosed in to us it was a shiny black Cadillac. I got in front with the driver and Rackham joined Roeder in the rear. They didn't shake hands when I pronounced names. The driver was new to me—a stocky middle-aged number with black hair and squinty black eyes. He had nothing whatever to say to anyone, and for that matter neither did anybody else, all the way to our destination. Once on the Taconic State Parkway a car passed and cut in ahead of us so short that it damn near grazed our bumper, and the driver muttered something, and I went so far as to glance at him but ventured no words. Anyway, my mind was occupied.

Evidently Rackham had been there before with his eyes open, for there was no suggestion that he should take to the floor, and of course I was now a B. We left the parkway a couple of miles south of Millwood, to the right, followed a curving secondary road a while, turned onto another main route, soon left it for another secondary road, and after some more curves hit concrete again. The garage was at a four-corners a little out of Mount Kisco, and I never did know what the idea was of that roundabout way of getting there. In front it looked like any other garage, with gas-pumps and a graveled plaza, and cars and miscellaneous objects around, except that it seemed a little large for its location. Two men were there in front, one dressed like a mechanic and the other in a summer suit, even a necktie, and they exchanged nods with our driver as we headed in.

The big room we drove into was normal too, like a thousand others anywhere, but a variation was coming. Our car rolled across, past pillars, to the far end, and stopped just in front of a big closed door, and our driver stuck his head out, but said nothing. Nothing happened for thirty seconds; then the big door slowly opened, rising; the driver pulled his head in, and the car went forward. As we cleared the entrance the door started back down, and by the time we had eased across to a stop the door was shut again, and our reception committee was right there—two on one side and one on the other. I had seen two of them before, but one was a stranger. The stranger was in shirt sleeves, with his gun in a belt holster.

Stepping out, I announced, "I've got that same gun under my armpit."

"Okay, Goodwin," the tenor said. "We'll take care of it."

They did. I may have been a B, but there was no discernible difference between inspection of a B and of an unknown. In fact, it seemed to me that they were slightly more thorough than they had been on Sunday, which may have been because there were three of us. They did us one at a time, with me first, then Rackham, then Roeder. With Roeder they were a little more superficial. They went over him, but not so enthusiastically, and all they did with the brief case was open it and glance inside and let Roeder himself shut it again.

One change from Sunday was that two of them, not one, accompanied us to the door in the rear wall, and through, across the vestibule, and down the fourteen steps to the first metal door. The sentinel who opened and let us in was the same pasty-faced bird with a pointed chin—Schwartz. This time the other sentinel did not stay at the table with his book work. He was right there with Schwartz, and interested in the callers, especially Rackham.

"We're a little early," Roeder said, "but they sent us on in."

"That's all right," Schwartz rumbled. "He's ahead of schedule today. One didn't come."

He went to the big metal door at the other end, pulled it open, and jerked his head. "On in."

Entering, Roeder took the lead, then Rackham, then me. Schwartz brought up the rear. He came in three paces and stood. Arnold Zeck, from behind his desk, told him, in the cold precise tone that he used for everything, "All right, Schwartz."

Schwartz left us. As the door closed I hoped to heaven it was as soundproof as it was supposed to be.

Zeck spoke. "The last time you were here, Rackham, you lost control of yourself and you know what happened."

Rackham did not reply. He stood with his hands behind him like a man ready to begin a speech, but his trap stayed shut, and from the expression of his face it was a good guess that his hands, out of sight, were making a tight knot.

"Sit down," Zeck told him.

Since the seating was an important item of the staging, I had stepped up ahead after we entered and made for the chair farthest front, a little to the left of Zeck's desk and about even with it, and Roeder had taken the one nearest me, to my right. That left, for Rackham, of the chairs near the desk, the one on the other side, and he went to it. He was about twelve feet from Zeck, Roeder about the same, and I was slightly closer.

Zeck asked Roeder, "Have you had a talk?"

Roeder shook his head. "Since Mr. Rackham had never met me before, I thought it might be better for you to explain the proposal to him. Naturally he will want to know exactly how it is to be handled before deciding whether to help with it." He reached to get his brief case from the floor, put it on his lap, and opened it.

"I think," Zeck said, "that you should describe the operation, since you conceived it and will manage it. But you were right to wait." He turned to Rackham. "You remember our last talk some time ago."

Rackham said nothing.

"You remember it?" Zeck demanded. He made it a demand by the faintest possible sharpening of his tone.

"I remember it," Rackham stated, not much above a whisper.

"You know the position you took. Ordinarily that course is not permitted to any man who has been given a place in my organization, and I made an exception of you only because the death of your wife had changed your circumstances. I thought it better to await an opportunity to take advantage of that change, and now it has come—through Roeder here. We want your help and we are prepared to insist on getting it. How do you feel about it?"

"I don't know." Rackham licked his lips. "I'd have to know more about what you want."

Zeck nodded. "But first your attitude. You will need to recognize the existence of mutual interests—yours and mine."

Rackham said nothing.

"Well?" The faint sharpening.

"Damn it, of course I recognize them!"

"Good. Go ahead, Roeder."

Roeder had got some papers from his brief case. One of them fluttered away from him, and I left my chair to retrieve it for him. I believe he did that on purpose. I believe he knew that now that the moment had come every nerve and muscle in me was on a hair trigger, and he was giving me an excuse to loosen them up.

"As I understand it," he said, "we're going to give Rackham a cut, and before I tell him about it I wish you'd take a look at this revised list of percentages. Yours is of course fixed, and I don't like to reduce mine unless it's absolutely unavoidable . . ."

He had a sheet of paper in his hand. With his brief case on his lap, and loose papers, it was awkward for him to get up, so I obliged. I reached, and he handed me the paper, and I had to leave my chair to get it to Zeck. On my way I took a glance at the paper because I thought it was in character to do that, and if I ever needed my character to stay put for another four seconds I did right then. When I extended my hand to Zeck I released the paper an instant too soon and it started to drop. I grabbed at it and missed, and that made me take another step and bend over, which put me in exactly the right position to take him away from there before he could possibly get a toe on one of the buttons under his desk.

Not wanting to knock his chair over, I used my left knee to push him back, chair and all, my right knee to land on his thighs and keep him there, and my hands for his throat. There was only one thing in my mind at that precise instant, the instant I had him away from the desk, and that was the fear that I would break his neck. Since I was in front of him I had to make absolutely sure, not only that he didn't yap, but also that he was too uncomfortable to try things like jabbing his thumbs in my eyes, but God knows I didn't want to overdo it, and bones and tendons are by no means all alike. What will be merely an inconvenience for one man will finish another one for good.

His mouth was open wide and his shark eyes were popping. With my knee on him he couldn't kick, and his arms were just flopping around. And Roeder was there by me, with a wadded handkerchief in one hand and a piece of cord in the other. As soon as he had the handkerchief stuffed tight in the open mouth he moved to the rear of the chair, taking Zeck's right hand with him, and reached around for the left hand. It tried to elude him, and I increased the pressure of my fingers a little, and then he got it.

"Hurry up," I growled, "or I'll kill him sure as hell."

It took him a year. It took him forever. But finally he straightened up, came around to take another look at the handkerchief and poke it in a little tighter, backed up, and muttered, "All right, Archie."

When I took my hands away my fingers ached like the devil, but that was nerves, not muscles. I leaned over to get my ear an inch away from his nose; there was no question about his breathing.

"His pulse is all right," Roeder said, not through his nose.

"You're crazy," Rackham said hoarsely. "Good God! You're crazy!"

He was out of his chair, standing there in front of it, trembling all over. Roeder's hand went to his side pocket for the Carson Snub Thirty, which he had got from the brief case along with the piece of cord. I took it and aimed it at Rackham.

"Sit down," I said, "and stay."

He sank down into the chair. I moved to the end of the desk so as to have him in a corner of my eye while looking at Zeck. Roeder, at my left elbow, spoke rapidly but distinctly.

"Mr. Zeck," he said, "you told me on the telephone two years ago that you had great admiration for me. I hope that what has just happened here has increased it. I'm Nero Wolfe, of course. There are many things it would give me satisfaction to say to you, and perhaps I shall some day, but not now. It is true that if one of your men suddenly opened the door Mr. Goodwin would kill you first, but I'm afraid you'd have company. So I'll get on. Having by your admission matched you in intellect, it's a question of will, and mine has not failed me, as you thought. Confound it, I wish you could speak."

The expression of Zeck's eyes, no longer popping, indicated that Wolfe had nothing on him there.

"Here's the situation," Wolfe went on. "During the two months I've been here in this outlandish guise I have collected enough evidence to get you charged on thirty counts under Federal law. I assure you that the evidence is sound and sufficient, and is in the hands of a man whom you cannot stop or deflect. You'll have to take my word for it that if that evidence is produced and used you are done for, and that it will be immediately produced and used if anything untoward happens to Mr. Goodwin or me. I fancy you will take my word since you admit that I match you in intellect, and to climax these five frightful months with such a bluff as this, if it were one, would be witless. However, if you think I'm bluffing there's no point in going on. If you think I'm bluffing, please shake your head no, meaning you don't believe me."

No shake.

"If you think I have the evidence as described, please nod your head." No nod.

"I warn you," Wolfe said sharply, "that Mr. Goodwin and I are both ready for anything whatever."

Zeck nodded. Nothing violent, but a nod.

"You assume my possession of the evidence?"

Zeck nodded again.

"Good. Then we can bargain. While I have great respect for the Federal laws, I am under no obligation to catch violators of them. Without compunction I can leave that to others. But I am under an obligation to a certain individual which I feel strongly and which I must discharge. Mrs. Rackham paid me a large sum to serve her interest, and the next day she was murdered. It was clearly my duty to expose her murderer—not only my duty to her but to my own self-respect—and I have failed. With an obligation of that nature I have never accepted failure and do not intend to. Mr. Goodwin, working in my behalf, has been a party to that failure, and he too will not accept it."

Zeck nodded again, or I thought he did, probably to signify approval of our high moral standards.

"So we can bargain," Wolfe told him. "You said day before yesterday that you have evidence, or can easily get it, that will convict Rackham of the murder of his wife. Was that true?"

Zeck nodded. The shark eyes were intent on Wolfe.

"Very well. I believe you because I know what you are capable of. I offer a trade. I'll trade you the evidence I have collected against you for the evidence that will convict Rackham. Will you make the trade?"

Zeck nodded.

"It will have to be more or less on my terms. I can be trusted; you cannot. You will have to deliver first. But I realize that the details of anything as vital as this is to you cannot be settled without discussion, and it must be discussed and settled now. We are going to release your hands and take that handkerchief from your mouth, but before we do so, one more warning. You are to stay where you are until we're finished. If you move toward the floor signals under your desk, or try to summon your men in any other manner, you will die before anyone else does. Also, of course, there is the evidence that exists against you. You understand the situation?"

Zeck nodded.

"Are you ready to discuss the matter?"

Zeck nodded.

"Release him, Archie," Wolfe snapped.

Needing two hands to untie the cord, I put the Carson Snub Thirty down on the polished top of Zeck's desk. I would have given a year's pay for a glance at Rackham, to see what the chances were, but that might have ruined it. So I put the gun there, stepped around to the rear of Zeck's chair, knelt, and started untying the knot. My heart was pounding my ribs like a sledgehammer.

So I didn't see it happen; I could only hear it. I did see one thing there behind Zeck's chair: a sudden convulsive jerk of his arms, which must have been his reaction to the sight of Rackham jumping for the gun I had left on the desk. More even than a sight of Rackham, to see if he was rising to it, I wanted a sight of Wolfe, to see if he was keeping his promise to duck for cover the instant Rackham started for the gun, but I couldn't afford it.

My one desperate job now was to get that cord off of Zeck's wrists in time, and while Wolfe had used the trick knot we had practiced with, he had made it damn tight. I barely had it free and was unwinding the cord from the wrists when the sound of the shot came, followed immediately by another.

As I got the cord off and jammed it in my pocket, Zeck's torso slumped sideways and then forward. Flat on the floor, I slewed around, saw Zeck's contorted face right above my eyes, pulled the handkerchief out of his mouth and stuffed it in my pocket with the cord, slid forward under the desk, and reached for one of the signal buttons.

I didn't know, and don't know yet, whether the noise of the shots had got through the soundproof door or whether it was my push on the button that brought them. I didn't hear the door open, but the next shots I heard were a fusillade that came from no Carson, so I came back out from under the desk and on up to my feet. Schwartz and his buddy were standing just inside the door, one with two guns and one with one. Rackham was stretched out on the floor, flat on his face. Wolfe was standing at the end of the desk, facing the door, scowling as I had never seen him scowl before.

"The dirty bastard," I said bitterly, and I admit my voice might have trembled even if I hadn't told it to.

"Reach up," Schwartz said, advancing.

Neither Wolfe nor I moved a muscle. But Wolfe spoke. "What for?" He was even bitterer than me, and contemptuous. "They let him in armed, not us."

"Watch 'em, Harry," Schwartz said, and came forward and on around behind the desk where I was. Ignoring me, he bent over Zeck's collapsed body, spent half a minute with it, and then straightened and turned.

"He's gone," he said.

Harry, from near the door, squealed incredulously. "He's gone?"

"He's gone," Schwartz said.

Harry wheeled, pushed the door open, and was gone too.

Schwartz stared after him three seconds, not more than that, then jumped as if I had pinched him, made for the door, and on through.

I went and took a look at Rackham, found he was even deader than Zeck, and turned to Wolfe. "Okay, that's enough. Come on."

"No." He was grim. "It will be safer when they've all skedaddled. Phone the police."

"From here?"

"Yes."

I went to Zeck's desk and pulled one of the phones to me.

"Wait." I had never heard him so grim. "First get Marko's number. I want to speak to Fritz."

"Now? For God's sake, *now?*"

"Yes. Now. A man has a right to have his satisfactions match his pains. I wish to use Mr. Zeck's phone to tell Fritz to go home and get dinner ready."

I dialed the operator.

XX

THREE days later, Friday afternoon, I said to Wolfe, "Anyway, it's all over now, isn't it?"

"No, confound it," he said peevishly. "I still have to earn that fee."

It was six o'clock, and he had come down from the plant rooms with some more pointed remarks about the treatment the plants had got at Hewitt's place. The remarks were completely uncalled for. Considering the two journeys they had taken, out to Long Island and then back again, the plants were in splendid shape, especially those hard to handle like the Miltonias and Phalaenopsis. Wolfe was merely trying to sell the idea, at least to himself, that the orchids had missed him.

Fritz might have been a mother whose lost little boy has been brought home after wandering in the desert for days, living on cactus pulp and lizards' tails. Wolfe had gained not an ounce less than ten pounds in seventy-two hours, in spite of all the activity of getting resettled, and at the rate he was going he would be back to normal long before Thanksgiving. The pleats in his face were already showing a tendency to spread out, and of course the beard was gone, and the slick had been shampooed out of his hair. I had tried to persuade him to stay in training, but he wouldn't even bother to put up an argument. He just spent more time than ever with Fritz, arranging about meals.

He had not got home for dinner Tuesday evening after all, in spite of the satisfaction he had got by putting in a call to Fritz on Zeck's phone. We were now cleaned up with Westchester, but it had not been simple. The death of Arnold Zeck had of course started a chain reaction that went both deep and wide, and naturally there had been an earnest desire to make goats out of Wolfe and me, but they didn't have a damn thing on us, and when word came from somewhere that Wolfe, during his association with Zeck, might have collected some facts that could be embarrassing to people who shouldn't be embarrassed, the attitude toward us changed for the better right away.

As for the scene that ended with the death of Zeck and Rackham, we were clean as a whistle. The papers in Roeder's brief case, which of course the cops took, proved nothing on anybody. By the time the cops arrived there had been no one on the premises but Wolfe and me and the two corpses. A hot search was on, especially for Schwartz and Harry, but so far no take. No elaborate lying was required; our basic story was that Wolfe, in his disguise as Roeder, had got in with Zeck in order to solve the murder of Mrs. Rackham, and the climax had come that afternoon when Zeck had put the screws on Rackham by saying that he had evidence that would convict him for killing his wife, and Rackham had pulled a gun, smuggled somehow past the sentinels, and had shot Zeck, and Schwartz and Harry had rushed in and drilled Rackham. It was surprising and gratifying to note how much of it was strictly true.

So by Friday afternoon we were cleaned up with Westchester, as I thought, and therefore it was a minor shock when Wolfe said, "No, confound it, I still have to earn that fee."

I was opening my mouth to ask him how come, when the phone rang. I got it. It was Annabel Frey. She wanted to speak to Wolfe. I told him so. He frowned and reached for his phone, and I stayed on.

"Yes, Mrs. Frey? This is Nero Wolfe."

"I want to ask you a favor, Mr. Wolfe. That is, I expect to pay for it of course, but still it's a favor. Could you and Mr. Goodwin come up here this evening? To my home, Birchvale?"

"I'm sorry, Mrs. Frey, but it's out of the question. I transact business only in my office. I never leave it."

That was a little thick, I thought, from a guy who had just spent five months the way he had. And if she read newspapers she knew all about it—or anyhow some.

"I'm sorry," she said, "because we must see you. Mr. Archer is here, the District Attorney, and I'm calling at his suggestion. We have a problem—two problems, really."

"By 'we' do you mean you and Mr. Archer?"

"No, I mean all of us—all of us who inherited property from Mrs. Rackham, and all of us who were here the night she was killed. Our problem is about evidence that her husband killed her. Mr. Archer says he has none, none that is conclusive—and perhaps you know what people are saying, and the newspapers. That's what we want to consult you about—the evidence."

"Well." A pause. "I'm trying to get a little rest after a long period of overexertion. But—very well. Who is there?"

"We all are. We met to discuss this. You'll come? Wonderful! If you—"

"I didn't say I'll come. All five of you are there?"

"Yes—and Mr. Archer—"

"Be at my office, all of you, at nine o'clock this evening. Including Mr. Archer."

"But I don't know if he will—"

"I think he will. Tell him I'll be ready then to produce the evidence."

"Oh, you will? Then you can tell me now—"

"Not on the phone, Mrs. Frey. I'll be expecting you at nine."

When we had hung up I lifted the brows at him. "So that's what you meant about earning that fee? Maybe?"

He grunted, irritated that he had to interrupt his convalescence for a job of work, sat a moment, reached for a bottle of the beer Fritz had brought, grunted again, this time with satisfaction, and poured a glass with plenty of foam.

I got up to go to the kitchen, to tell Fritz we were having company and that refreshments might be required.

XXI

I WAS mildly interested when the six guests arrived—a little early, five to nine—in such minor issues as the present state of relations between Annabel Frey and the banker, Dana Hammond, and between Lina Darrow and the statesman, Oliver Pierce, and whether Calvin Leeds would see fit to apologize for his unjust suspicions about Wolfe and me.

To take the last first, Leeds was all out of apologies. The spring was in his step all right, but not in his manners. First to enter the office, he plumped himself down in the red leather chair, but I figured that Archer rated it ex officio and asked him to move, which he did without grace. As for the others, there was too much atmosphere to get any clear idea. They were all on speaking terms, but the problem that brought them there was in the front of their minds, so much so that no one was interested in the array of liquids and accessories that Fritz and I had arranged on the table over by the big globe. Annabel was in the most comfortable of the yellow chairs, to Archer's left; then, working toward me at my desk, Leeds and Lina Darrow; and Hammond and Pierce closest to me.

Wolfe's eyes swept the arc.

"This," he said, "is a little awkward for me. I have met none of you before except Mr. Leeds. I must be sure I have you straight." His eyes went along the line again. "I think I have. Now if you'll tell me what you want—you, Mrs. Frey, it was you who phoned me."

Annabel looked at the DA. "Shouldn't you, Mr. Archer?"

He shook his head. "No, you tell him."

She concentrated, at Wolfe. "Well, as I said, there are two problems. One is that it seems to be supposed that Barry Rackham killed his wife, but it hasn't been proven, and now that he is dead how can it be proven so that everyone will know it and the rest of us will be entirely free of any suspicion? Mr. Archer says there is no official suspicion of us, but that isn't enough."

"It is gratifying, though," Wolfe murmured.

"Yes, but it isn't gratifying to have some of the people who say they are your friends looking at you as they do." Annabel was earnest about it. "Then the second problem is this. The law will not allow a man who commits a murder to profit by it. If Barry Rackham killed his wife he can't inherit property from her, no matter what her will said. But it has to be legally proven that he killed her, and unless that is done her will stands, and what she left to him will go to his heirs."

She made a gesture. "It isn't that we want it—the rest of us. It can go to the state or to charity—we don't care. But we think it's wrong and a shame for it to go to his people, whoever will inherit from him. It's not only immoral, it's illegal. It can't be stopped by convicting him of murder, because he's dead and can't be tried. My lawyer and Mr. Archer both say we can bring action and get it before a court, but then we'll have to have evidence that he killed her, and Mr. Archer says he hasn't been able to get it from you, and he hasn't got it. But surely you can get it, or anyhow you can try. You see, that would solve both problems, to have a court rule that his heirs can't inherit because he murdered her."

"You have stated it admirably," Archer declared.

"We don't want any of it," Lina blurted.

"My interest," Pierce put in, "is only to have the truth fully and universally known and acknowledged."

"That," Wolfe said, "will take more than me. I am by no means up to that. And not only my capacities, but the circumstances themselves, restrict me to a much more modest ambition. I can get you one of the things you want, removal of all suspicion from the innocent, but the other, having Mrs. Rackham's bequest to her husband set aside, is beyond me."

They all frowned at him, in their various fashions. Hammond, the banker, protested, "That doesn't seem to make sense. What accomplishes one accomplishes the other. If you prove that Rackham killed his wife—"

"But I can't prove that." Wolfe shook his head. "I'm sorry, but it can't be done. It is true that Rackham deserved to die, and as a murderer. He killed a woman here in New York three years ago, a woman named Delia Montrose—one of Mr. Cramer's unsolved cases; Rackham ran his car over her. That was how Zeck originally got a noose on Rackham, by threatening to expose him for the murder he did commit. As you know, Mr. Archer, I penetrated some distance—not very far, but far enough—into Zeck's confidence, and I learned a good deal about his methods. I doubt if he ever had conclusive evidence that Rackham had killed Delia Montrose, but Rackham, conscious of his guilt, hadn't the spine to demand a showdown. Murderers seldom have. Then Rackham got a spine, suddenly and fortuitously, by becoming a millionaire; he thought then he could fight it; he defied Zeck; and Zeck, taking his time, retorted by threatening to expose Rackham for the murder of his wife. The threat was dangerous and effective even without authentic evidence to support it; there could of course be no authentic evidence that Rackham killed his wife, because he didn't."

They all froze, still wearing the frowns. Knowing Wolfe as I did, I had suspected that was coming, so I was taking them all in to get the impact, but there wasn't much to choose. After the first shock they all began to make noises, then words came, and then, as the full beauty of it hit them, the words petered out.

All but Archer's. "You have signed a statement," he told Wolfe, "to the effect that Zeck told Rackham he could produce evidence that would convict him of murder, and that Rackham thereupon shot Zeck. Now you say, in contradiction—"

"There is no contradiction," Wolfe declared. "The fact of Rackham's innocence would have been no defense against evidence manufactured by Zeck, and Rackham knew it. Innocent as he was—of this murder, that is—he knew what Zeck was capable of."

"You have said that you think Rackham killed his wife, but that you have no proof."

"I have not," Wolfe snapped. "Read your transcripts."

"I shall. And you now say that you think Rackham did not kill his wife?"

"Not that I think he didn't. I know he didn't, because I know who did." Wolfe flipped a hand. "I've known that from the beginning. That night in April, when Mr. Goodwin phoned me that Mrs. Rackham had been murdered, I knew who had murdered her. But I also knew that the interests of Arnold Zeck were involved and I dared not move openly. So I—but you know all about that." Wolfe turned to me. "Archie. Precautions may not be required, but you might as well take them."

I opened a desk drawer and got out the Grisson .38. My favorite Colt, taken from me in Zeck's garage antechamber, was gone forever. After a glance at the cylinder I dropped the Grisson in my side pocket and as I did so lifted my head to the audience. As if they had all been on one circuit, the six pairs of eyes left me and went to Wolfe.

"I don't like this," Archer said in a tight voice. "I am here officially, and I don't like it. I want to speak to you privately."

Wolfe shook his head. "It's much better this way, Mr. Archer, believe me. We're not in your county, and you're free to leave if it gets too much for you, but—"

"I don't want to leave. I want a talk with you. If you knew, that night, who had killed Mrs. Rackham, I intend to—"

"It is," Wolfe said cuttingly, "of no importance what you intend. You have had five months to implement your intentions, and where are you? I admit that up to three days ago I had one big advantage over you, but not since then—not since I told you of the package I got with a cylinder of tear gas in it, and of the phone call from Mr. Zeck. That brought you even with me. It was after noon on a Friday that Mrs. Rackham left here after hiring me. It was the next morning, Saturday, that I received that package and the phone call from Zeck. How had he learned about it? Apparently he even knew the amount of the check she had given me. How? From whom?"

I was not really itching to shoot anybody. So I got up and unobtrusively moved around back of them, to the rear of the chair that was occupied by Calvin Leeds. Wolfe was proceeding.

"It was not inconceivable that Mrs. Rackham had told someone else about it, her daughter-in-law or her secretary, or even her husband, but it was most unlikely, in view of her insistence on secrecy. She said she had confided in no one except her cousin, Calvin Leeds." Wolfe's head jerked right and he snapped, "That's correct, Mr. Leeds?"

Being back of Leeds, I couldn't see his face, but there was no difficulty about hearing him, since he spoke much too loud.

"Certainly," he said. "Up to then—before she came to see you—certainly."

"Good," Wolfe said approvingly. "You're already drawing up your lines of defense. You'll need them."

"What you're doing," Leeds said, still too loud, "if I understand you— you're intimating that I told Zeck about my cousin's coming here and hiring you. You're intimating that in front of witnesses."

"That's right," Wolfe agreed. "But it's not vital to me; I mention it chiefly to explain why I suspected you of duplicity, and of being involved in some way with Arnold Zeck even before Mr. Goodwin left here that day to go up there. It draws attention to you, no doubt of that; but it is not primary evidence that you murdered your cousin. The proof that it was you who killed her was given to me on the phone that night by Mr. Goodwin."

There were stirrings and little noises. Leeds ignored them.

"So," he said, not so loud now, "you're actually accusing me before witnesses of murdering my cousin?"

"I'm accusing you of that, yes, sir, but also I'm accusing you of something much worse than that." Wolfe spat it at him. "I'm accusing you of deliberately and ruthlessly, to protect yourself from the consequences of your murder of your cousin for the money you would inherit from her, thrusting that knife into the belly of a dog that loved you and trusted you!"

Leeds started up, but hadn't got far when my hands were on his shoulders, and with plenty of pressure. He let down. I moved my hands to the back of his chair.

Wolfe's voice was cold and cutting. "No one could have done that but you, Mr. Leeds. In the woods at night, that trained dog would not have gone far from its mistress. Someone else might possibly have killed the dog first and then her, but it wasn't done that way, because the knife was left in the dog. And if someone else, permitted to get close to her, had succeeded in killing her with a sudden savage thrust and then defended himself against the dog's attack, it is not believable that he could have stopped so ferocious a beast by burying the knife in its side without himself getting a single tooth-mark on him. You know those dogs; you wouldn't believe it; neither will I.

"No, Mr. Leeds, it could have been only you. When Mr. Goodwin went on to your house and you stayed out at the kennels, you joined your cousin on her walk in the woods. I doubt if the dog would have permitted even you to stab her to death in its presence; I don't know; but you didn't have to. You sent the dog away momentarily, and, when the knife had done its work on your cousin, you withdrew it, stood there in the dark with the knife in your hand, and called the dog to come. It came, and despite the smell of fresh blood, it behaved itself because it loved and trusted you. You could have spared it; you could have taken it home with you; but no. That would have put you in danger. It had to die for you, and by your hand."

Wolfe took a breath. "To this point I know I am right; now conjecture enters. You stabbed the dog, of course, burying the blade in its belly, but did you leave the knife there intentionally, to prevent a gush of blood on you, or did the animal convulsively leap from you at the feel of the prick, jerking the knife from your grasp? However that may be, all you could do was make for home, losing no time, for you must show yourself to Mr. Goodwin as soon as possible. So you did that. You said good night and went to bed. I don't think you slept; you may even have heard the dog's whimpering outside the door, after it had dragged itself there; but maybe not, since it was beneath Mr. Goodwin's window, not yours. You pretended sleep, of course, when he came for you."

Leeds was keeping his head up, but I could see his hands gripping his legs just above the knees.

"You used that dog," Wolfe went on, his voice as icy as Arnold Zeck's had ever been, "even after it died. You were remorseless to your dead friend. To impress Mr. Goodwin, you were overcome with emotion at the thought that, though you had given the dog to your cousin two years ago, it had come to your doorstep to die. It had not come to your doorstep to die, Mr. Leeds, and you knew it; it had come there to try to get at you. It wanted to sink its teeth in you just once. I say you knew it, because when you squatted beside the dog and put your hand on it, it snarled. It would not have snarled if it had felt your hand as the soothing and sympathetic touch of a trusted friend in its last agony; indeed not; it snarled because it knew you, at the end, to be unworthy of its love and trust, and it scorned and hated you. That snarl alone is enough to convict you. Do you remember that snarl, Mr. Leeds? Will you ever forget it? Your old friend Nobby, his last words for you—"

Leeds' head went forward, dropping, and his hands came up to cover his face.

He made no sound, and no one else did either. The silence darted around us and into us, coming out from Leeds. Then Lina Darrow took in a breath with a sighing, sobbing sound, and Annabel got up and went to her.

"Take him, Mr. Archer," Wolfe said grimly. "I'm through with him, and it's about time."

XXII

I'M SITTING at a window overlooking a fiord, typing this on a new portable I bought for the trip. In here it's pleasant. It's late in the season for outdoors in Norway, but if you run hard to keep your blood going you can stand it.

I got a letter yesterday which read as follows:

Dear Archie:

The chickens came from Mr. Haskins Friday, four of them, and they were satisfactory. Marko came to dinner. He misses Fritz, he says. I have given Fritz a raise.

Mr. Cramer dropped in for a talk one day last week. He made some rather pointed comments about you, but on the whole behaved himself tolerably.

I am writing this longhand because I do not like the way the man sent by the agency types.

Vanda peetersiana has a raceme 29 in. long. Its longest last year was 22 in. We have found three snails in the warm room. I thought of mailing them to Mr. Hewitt but didn't.

Mr. Leeds hanged himself in the jail at White Plains yesterday and was dead when discovered. That of course cancels your promise to Mr. Archer to return in time for the trial, but I trust you will not use it as an excuse to prolong your stay.

We have received your letters and they were most welcome. I have received an offer of $315 for the furniture in your office but am insisting on $350. Fritz says he has written you. I am beginning to feel more like myself.

My best regards,
NW

I let Lily read it. "Darn him anyhow," she said. "No message, not a mention of me. My Pete! Huh. Fickle Fatty."

"You'd be the last," I told her, "that he'd ever send a message to. You're the only woman that ever got close enough to him, at least in my time, to make him smell of perfume."

THREE DOORS TO DEATH

FOREWORD

LOOKING over the scripts of these accounts of three of Nero Wolfe's cases, it struck me that they might give a stranger a wrong impression of him, so I thought it wouldn't hurt to put in this foreword for those who haven't met him before. In only one of these three cases did he get paid—I mean paid money—for working on it, and that might give someone a woolly idea which could develop into a nuisance. I want to make it clear that Wolfe does not solve murders just for the hell of it. He does it to make a living, which includes me, since he can't live the way he likes to without signing my pay check each and every Friday afternoon. Also please note that in the other two cases he did get something: in one, the satisfaction of doing a favor for an old and dear friend, and in the other, a fill-in for Theodore.

With that warning, I like the idea of putting these three cases together because they make a kind of complicated pattern of pairs. In two of them Wolfe got no fee. In two of them he had to forge a document to get a crack started. In two of them the homicide was strictly a family affair. In two of them I became acquainted with a young female, not the same one, who might have sent my pulse up a beat if she hadn't been quite so close to a murder. So I think they'll be a little more interesting, in a bunch like this, provided they don't start people phoning in to ask me to ask Wolfe to solve murders as a gift. I'm just telling you.

ARCHIE GOODWIN

MAN ALIVE

I

SHE said, in her nicely managed voice that was a pleasure to listen to, "Daumery and Nieder."

I asked her politely, "Will you spell it, please?"

I meant the Daumery, since I already had the Nieder down in my notebook, her name being, so she had said, Cynthia Nieder.

Her lovely bright blue eyes changed expression to show that she suspected me of kidding her—as if I had asked her to spell Shakespeare or Charlie Chaplin. But I was so obviously innocent that the eyes changed again and she smiled.

She spelled Daumery and added, "Four ninety-six Seventh Avenue. That's what we get for being so cocky about how famous we are—we get asked how to spell it. What if someone asked you how to spell Nero Wolfe?"

"Try it," I suggested, smiling back at her. I extended a hand. "Put your fingers on my pulse and ask me. But don't ask me how to spell Archie Goodwin, which is me. That would hurt."

Wolfe grunted peevishly and readjusted a few hundred of his pounds in his built-to-order high-test chair behind his desk. "You made," he told our visitor, "an appointment to see me. I supposed you needed a detective. If so tell me what for, without encouraging Mr. Goodwin to start caterwauling. It takes very little to set him off."

I let it go by, though I am much more particular than his insult implied. I felt like indulging him because he had just bought a new Cadillac sedan, which meant that I, Archie Goodwin, had a new car, because, of the four men who lived in Nero Wolfe's brownstone house on West 35th Street not far from the river, I was the only one who drove. Wolfe himself, who suspected all machinery with moving parts of being in a plot to get him, rarely left the house for any reason whatever, and never—well, hardly ever—on business. He stayed in his office, on the ground floor of the house, and used his brain if and when I could pester him into it. Fritz Brenner, chef and supervisor of household comforts, knew how to drive but pretended he didn't, and had no license. Theodore Horstmann, curator of the orchids in the plant rooms on the roof, thought walking was good for people and was still, at his age, trying to prove it.

That left me. In addition to being chief assistant detective, bookkeeper and stenographer, the flea in the elephant's ear, and balance wheel, I was also chauffeur and errand boy. Therefore the new car was, in effect, mine, and I thought I ought to show my appreciation by letting him call me a tom-cat at least once. Another thing, the car had cost plenty, and we hadn't been offered an acceptable job for over a week. We could use a fee. This blue-eyed female treat looked as if she wasn't short on cash, and if I riled Wolfe about a little thing like a personal insult he might react by broadening out and insulting her too, and she might go somewhere else to shop.

So all I did was grin understandingly at Cynthia Nieder, brandish my pen over my notebook, and clear my throat.

II

"DAUMERY and Nieder," Cynthia said, "is as good a name as there is on Seventh Avenue, including Fifty-seventh Street, but of course if you're not in the garment trade and know nothing about it—I imagine your wives would know the name all right."

Wolfe shuddered.

"No wife," I stated. "Neither of us. That's why we caterwaul."

"Well, if you had one she would know about Daumery and Nieder. We make top-quality coats, suits, and dresses, and we confine our line, even here in New York. The business was started twenty years ago by two men, Jean Daumery and Paul Nieder—my Uncle Paul—my father's brother. It's—"

"Excuse me," Wolfe put in. "Will it save time to tell you that I don't do industrial surveillance?"

"No, that's not it," she said, waving it away. "I know you don't. It's about him, my uncle. Uncle Paul."

She frowned, and was looking at the window beyond Wolfe's desk as if she were seeing something. Then her shoulders lifted and dropped again, and she went back to Wolfe.

"You need some background," she told him. "At least I think it would be better. Daumery was the business head of the firm, the organizer and manager and salesman, and Uncle Paul was the designer, the creator. If it hadn't been for him Daumery wouldn't have had anything to manage and sell. They owned it together—a fifty-fifty partnership. It was my uncle's half that I inherited when my uncle killed himself—anyway, that's how it was announced, that he committed suicide—a little over a year ago."

That gave me two thoughts: one, that I had been right about her having the price of a fee; and two, that we were probably in for another job of translating a suicide into a murder.

"I suppose I should tell about me," Cynthia was saying. "I was born and brought up out West, in Oregon. My father and mother died when I was fourteen, and Uncle Paul sent for me, and I came to New York and lived with him. He wasn't married. We didn't get along very well together, I guess because we were so much alike, because I'm creative too; but it wasn't really so bad, we just fought all the time. And when it came down to it he let me have my way. He was determined about my going to college, but I knew I was creative and it would be a waste of time. We fought about it every day, and finally he said if I didn't go to college I would have to earn my living, and then what do you think he did? He gave me a job modeling for Daumery and Nieder at top salary! That's what he was like! Actually he was wonderful. He gave me the run of the place too, to catch on about designing, but of course he wouldn't have done that if he hadn't known I had unusual talent."

"What kind of talent?" Wolfe asked skeptically.

"As a clothes designer, of course," she said, as if that were the only talent worth mentioning. "I was only eighteen—that was three years ago—and completely without training, and for two years I only modeled and caught onto things, but I had a few little chances to show what I could do. I was surprised that my uncle was willing to help me along, because most established designers are so jealous; but he did. Then he went West on a vacation, and then the word came that he had killed himself. Maybe I ought to tell you why I wasn't surprised that he had killed himself."

"Maybe," Wolfe conceded.

"Because I knew how unhappy he was. Helen Daumery had died. A horse she was riding had gone crazy and thrown her off on some stones and killed her. She was Daumery's wife—the wife of my uncle's partner—and my uncle was in love with her. She had been one of their models—she was much younger than Daumery—and I think she was the only woman Uncle Paul ever loved—anyhow he certainly loved her. She didn't love him because she didn't love anybody but herself, but I think she probably gave him the cherry out of her cocktail just because she enjoyed having him like that when no other woman could get him. She would."

I didn't put it in my notes that Miss Nieder had disapproved of Mrs. Daumery, but I could have, and signed it.

"Helen's death broke my uncle up completely," Cynthia went on. "I never saw anything like it. I was still living in his apartment. He didn't say a word to me for three days—not a single word—nor to anyone else, and he didn't leave the apartment day or night—right in the middle of getting ready for the showings of the fall line—and then he said he was going away for a rest, and he went. Four days later the news came that he had committed suicide, and under the circumstances it didn't occur to me to question it."

When she paused Wolfe inquired, "Do you question it now?"

"I certainly do," she said emphatically. "I wasn't surprised, either, at the way he did it. He was always keyed up and dramatic, about everything. He was by far the best designer in New York, and he was the best showman, too. So you would expect him to do something startling about killing himself, no matter how unhappy he was. He took all his clothes off and jumped into a geyser in Yellowstone Park."

Wolfe let out a mild grunt. I gave her an admiring eye for her calm voice and manner in dishing out a fact like that, but of course it was a year old for her.

"Under the surface of that geyser," she said, "down below, the pressure in the pipe from above keeps the temperature far above the boiling point, according to an article about it I read in a newspaper."

"That seems conclusive," Wolfe murmured. "Why do you now question it?"

"Because he didn't die. Because he's not dead. I saw him last week, here in New York, alive."

III

I FELT myself relaxing. It had seemed that we were about to be tagged for the chore of ripping the false face off of a murder disguised as a suicide, and at the smell of murder I always go tight all over. In the detective business that's the center ring in the big tent. The headline MAN DEAD gets the eye good, but Cynthia Nieder had scrapped that and changed it to MAN ALIVE, which was quite a comedown. Another thought had struck me: that if Uncle Paul was alive her inheriting half the business was out the window and her ability to pay a good exorbitant fee was open to question. My attitude toward her personally remained intact; she rated high priority on looks, voice, and other observable factors. But professionally I was compelled to grade her way down in the little routine items.

So I relaxed and tossed my notebook on my desk, which is so placed that a half-turn of my swivel chair puts me facing Wolfe, and with another half-turn I am confronting the red leather chair beyond the end of his desk where a lone visitor is usually seated. Some visitors clash with it, but Cynthia, in a deep-toned yellow dress, maybe silk, a jacket in brown and yellow checks, flaring open, and a little brown affair slanting on her head, looked fine. Having learned one or two little things about women's clothes from Lily Rowan and other reliable sources, I decided that if Cynthia had designed that outfit Wolfe should eat his skepticism about her talent.

She was talking, telling about the man alive.

"It was last Tuesday," she said, "a week ago tomorrow, June third. We were showing our fall line to the press. We don't show in hotels because we don't have to, since our showroom seats over two hundred comfortably. For a press showing we don't let anyone in without a ticket because if we did the place would be mobbed. I was modeling a blue and black ensemble of lightweight Bishop twill when I saw him. He was in the fifth row, between Agnes Pemberton of *Vogue* and Mrs. Gumpert of the *Herald Tribune*. If you asked me how I recognized him I couldn't tell you, but I simply knew it was him, there wasn't the slightest doubt—"

"Why shouldn't you recognize him?" Wolfe demanded.

"Because he had a beard, and he wore glasses, and his hair was slick and parted on the left side. That sounds like a freak, but Uncle Paul would know better than to look freaky. The beard was trimmed, and somehow it didn't make him conspicuous. It was lucky I didn't completely recognize him when I first saw him, or I would probably have stood and gawked at him. Later in the dressing room Polly Zarella asked Bernard—that's Bernard Daumery, Jean's nephew—who was the man that was growing his own wool, and Bernard said he didn't know, probably from the *Daily Worker*. Of course we know most of the guests at a press showing, but not all of them. When I modeled another number—a full-back calf-covering coat in tapestry tones of Kleinsell ratiné—I took him in without being obvious about it, and all of a sudden I knew who it was—I didn't guess, I *knew*. It staggered me so that I had to get off quick, quicker than I should have, and in the dressing room it was all I could do to keep them from seeing me tremble. I wanted to run out and speak to him, but I couldn't because it would have ruined the show. I had four more numbers to model—one of them was our headliner, a tailored dress and jacket in black with white stripes, with slightly bouffant sleeves and a double hemline—and I had to go on to the end. When it was over I hurried out front and he was gone."

"Indeed," Wolfe muttered.

"Yes. I went outside, to the elevators, but he was gone."

"You haven't seen him since?"

"No. Just that one time."

"Did anyone else recognize him?"

"I don't think so. I'm sure they didn't, or there would have been a noise. A dead man come back to life?"

Wolfe nodded. "Many of those present had known him?"

"Certainly, nearly all of them. He was famous, as famous as you are."

Wolfe skipped that one. "How sure are you it was he?"

"I'm absolutely positive. There simply isn't any argument about it."

"Did you find out who he was supposed to be?"

She shook her head. "I couldn't find out a thing about him. I didn't want to ask questions of too many people, but no one could tell me anything." She hesitated. "I must admit the ticket thing is handled pretty loosely. The tickets aren't just scattered around, but anyone who knows the ropes wouldn't have much trouble getting one, and my uncle certainly knows the ropes."

"Whom have you told about this?"

"No one. Not a soul. I've been trying to decide what to do."

"You might," Wolfe suggested, "just erase it. You say you inherited a half-interest in that"—he grimaced—"that business from your uncle?"

"Yes."

"Anything else? Property, securities, money in the bank?"

"No. He had no property, except the furniture in his apartment, and the lawyer said there were no securities or bank accounts."

"Hunh," Wolfe said. "Those are portable. But you have half of that business. Is it solvent?"

Cynthia smiled. "As Polly Zarella puts it, we grossed over two million last year with a swelled-up profit."

"Then why not erase it, if your uncle likes his beard and his hair slicked? If you corner him and make him shave and wash his hair, and make him take his old label, you'll have no share of the swelled-up profits. He will. I would charge moderately for this interview."

"No." She shook her head emphatically. "I have to know what's going on, and I have to know where I stand. I—" She stopped and bit her lip. Apparently she had been keeping emotions, whatever they might be, under control, and they were trying to break loose. When she was ready for speech again all she said was, "I'm upset."

"Then you should reserve decision." Wolfe was being very patient with her. "Never decide anything while you're upset." He wiggled a finger. "And in spite of your dogmatism you may be wrong. True, you might have recognized him when others didn't, since you lived with him and knew him intimately, but others knew him intimately too. One especially—his business partner, Mr. Daumery—for twenty years, you say. Was he there that day and did he see the man with the beard?"

Cynthia's eyes had widened. "Oh," she exclaimed, "didn't I—I thought I had mentioned that! Of course Bernard Daumery, the nephew, was there —I know I mentioned him—but Jean Daumery, my uncle's partner, he's dead!"

Wolfe's eyes opened to more than a slit for the first time. "The devil he is. Jumped in a geyser?"

"No, in an accident. He was drowned. He was fishing and fell from the boat."

"Where was this?"

"In Florida. Off the west coast."

"When?"

"It was—let's see, today is June ninth—a little over six weeks ago."

"Who was on the boat with him?"

"Bernard, his nephew."

"Anyone else?"

"No."

"And the nephew inherited that half?"

"Yes, but—" She frowned. Her hand fluttered. She had a habit of making gestures which were graceful and a pleasure to look at. "But that's all right."

"Why is it all right?"

"That's a silly question," she said with spirit. "I merely mean that if there had been any question of anything wrong the Florida people would have attended to it."

"Perhaps," Wolfe conceded grumpily. "Only it's quite a list. Mrs. Daumery thrown from a horse onto stones and killed. Mr. Nieder propelled into a geyser and boiled. Mr. Daumery hurtled into an ocean and drowned. It's not my affair, thank heaven, but if it were I should want better testimony than that of what you call the Florida people." He got brusque. "About your uncle, what do you want me for?"

She knew the answer to that one. "I want you to find him, and I want to see him."

"Very well. It may take time and it will be expensive. A retainer of two thousand dollars?"

She didn't blink. "Of course," she agreed, speaking as a millionaire. "I'll mail you a check today. I suppose it's understood that this is extremely confidential, as I said at the beginning, and no reports are to be phoned to me, and written reports are not to be mailed but handed to me personally. One thing I was going to suggest."

She directed her clear blue eyes at me, and back at Wolfe.

"I'll be glad," she said, "to tell you all I know about his former associates, but I doubt if that will help. He had no relatives but me, and no really close friends that I know of. The only person he ever loved was Helen Daumery—unless he had some affection for me; I guess maybe he did. But he loved designing, his work, and he loved that business. I think he came there last Tuesday because he simply couldn't stay away. I don't believe he knew I recognized him, so why wouldn't he come back? If he does, it will probably be today, because this afternoon we have our big show of the fall line for buyers. That's why I came to see you this morning. He wouldn't

even need a ticket, and I have a feeling he'll be there. I know you do everything in your office and practically never go out, but couldn't Mr. Goodwin
come? He could sit near the front, and I could arrange to give him a signal
if I see my uncle—only he would have to be extremely careful not to spoil
the show in any way—"

Wolfe was nodding at her. "Excellent," he declared.

IV

At 2:55 that Monday afternoon in June I entered the building at 496 Seventh Avenue and took an elevator to the twelfth floor.

Since that was only a ten-minute walk from Wolfe's place my choice
would have been to hoof it, but Wolfe was proceeding to spend chunks of
the two grand even before he got it. He had called in Saul Panzer, the best
free-lance operative on earth, and Saul and I went together in a taxi driven
by our old pal Herb Aronson, whom we often used. Saul and Herb stayed
at the curb in the cab, with the flag down. It had developed that Cynthia
didn't want Uncle Paul's whiskers yanked off in any public spot, and therefore he would have to be tailed. Tailing in New York, if you really mean it,
being no one-man job, we were setting it up right, with me on foot and
Saul on wheels.

Cynthia had filled in a few gaps before leaving our office. She had inherited her uncle's half of the business under a will he had left, but was not
yet in legal possession because of the law's attitude about dead people who
leave no remains. There had been no serious doubt of his being pressure-
cooked in the geyser, though no one had actually seen him jump in, since
his clothes had been found at the geyser's rim, and the farewell letters in
the pocket of the coat, one to his lawyer and one to his niece, had unquestionably been in his handwriting. But the law was chewing its cud. Apparently Jean Daumery, up to the moment he had fallen off the boat and
got drowned, had done likewise, and, in the six weeks since his death, his
nephew Bernard had carried on with the chewing. That was the impression
I got from a couple of Cynthia's remarks about her current status at Daumery and Nieder's. She was still modeling, and most of the designing was
being done by a guy named Ward Roper, whose name she pronounced
with a good imitation of the inflection Winston Churchill used in pronouncing Mussolini.

She had got in another dig or two at Helen Daumery, replying to Wolfe's
casual questions. It was possible, she said, that Jean Daumery had known
what was going on between his wife and his business partner, but it was
doubtful because Helen had been an extremely slick article. And when

Wolfe inquired about Helen's death and Cynthia told him that it happened on a country lane where Helen and her husband were out for a Sunday morning ride on their own horses, and the husband was the only eyewitness, she added that whoever or whatever was in charge of accidents might as well get the credit for that one, and that anyway Jean Daumery was dead too.

So it still looked as if we were fresh out of murders as far as Cynthia was concerned. To get any attention from Wolfe a murder must be attached to a client with money to spend and a reason for spending it. Cynthia didn't fit. As for her uncle, he wasn't dead. As for Helen Daumery, Cynthia wasn't interested a nickel's worth. As for Jean Daumery, Cynthia was stringing along with the Florida people who had decided there was nothing wrong.

Therefore there was no tingle in me as I got off the elevator at the twelfth floor.

Double doors were standing open, with a few human beings gathered there. As I approached, a bulky female who had been in my elevator swept past me and was going on through, but a man sidestepped to cut her off and asked politely, "What is your firm, please?"

The woman glared at him. "Coats and suits for Driscoll's Emporium, Tulsa."

The man shook his head. "Sorry, there's no place for you." His face suddenly lit up with a cordial smile, and I thought unexpected grace was about to drop on her until I saw that the smile was for another one from my elevator, a skinny dame with big ears.

"Good afternoon, Miss Dixon," the smiler said, serving it with sugar. "Mr. Roper was asking about you just a minute ago."

Miss Dixon nodded indifferently and went on in. I maneuvered around Driscoll's Emporium, who was looking enraged but impotent, and murmured at the man in a refined voice.

"My name is Goodwin, British Fabrics Association. Miss Cynthia Nieder invited me. Shall I wait while you check with her?"

He looked me over and I took it without flinching, wearing, as I was, a tropical worsted tailored by Breslow and a shirt and tie that were fully worthy. "It isn't necessary," he finally conceded and motioned me through.

The room was so nearly packed that it took a couple of minutes to find an empty seat far enough front to be sure of catching Cynthia's signal, which was to be brushing her hair back on the right side with her left hand. I saw no point in pretending I wasn't there, and before sitting down I turned in a slow complete circle, giving the audience the eye as if I were looking for a friend. There were close to two hundred of them, and I was surprised to see that nearly a third of them were men, though Cynthia had explained that they would be not only buyers from all over the country, but also merchandise executives, department heads, presidents, vice-presidents, fashion writers, fabrics people, and miscellaneous.

I saw no one with whiskers.

Also before sitting I picked up, from the chair, a pad of paper and a pencil. The pad consisted of sheets with DAUMERY AND NIEDER and the address neatly printed in an upper corner. I was supposed, as I soon learned from watching my neighbors, to use it for making notes about the numbers I wanted to buy. On my right was a plump gray-haired specimen with sweat below her ear, and on my left was a handsome woman with an extremely good mouth, fairly young but not quite young enough. Neither had given me more than an indifferent glance.

The room was high-ceilinged, and the wood-paneled walls were pretty well covered with drawings and photographs. Aside from that, and us on our chairs, there was nothing but a large raised platform, in the open space between the front row of seats and the wall beyond. That wall had two doors, twenty feet apart. I had been seated only a minute or two when the door on the left opened and a woman emerged. She was old enough to be my mother but wasn't. My mother wouldn't use that much lipstick in a year, and her shoulders would never get that much padding no matter what high fashion said.

The woman stood a moment, looking us over, turned to signal to someone through the open door, closed the door, and went to a chair near the end of the front row that had evidently been held for her. She was no sooner seated than the door opened again and out came the girl that I was waiting to marry. I put my teeth together to keep from whistling. I got the impression that she was the girl they were all waiting to marry, seeing how concentrated and alert everyone became the second she appeared, and then I realized what this meant to the buyers. For them it was the make or break. It meant their jobs. They had just so many thousands to spend, on so many numbers, and it was up to them to pick the winners or else.

Anyone could have picked the girl with one eye shut, but they weren't picking girls. She stepped up on the platform, came to the front edge, walking in a highly trained manner, extended her arms to the sides, full out, and said in a clear and friendly voice, "Six-forty-two." Six-forty-two was a dress and coat, looking like wool and I suppose it was, sort of confused about colors like a maple tree in October. She gave it the works. She walked to the right and then to the left, threw her arms around to show that the seams would hold even if you got in a fight or wore it picking apples, and turned around to let us see the back. She said "Six-forty-two" four times altogether, at appropriate intervals, distinctly and amiably, with just the faintest suggestion in her voice and manner that she wouldn't dream of letting that out except to the few people she was very fond of; and when she took the coat off and draped it over her arm and lifted her chin to smile at the back row, there was some clapping of hands.

She left by the other door, the one on the right, and immediately the one on the left opened and out came the girl I was waiting to marry, only this was a blonde, and she had on a gray fur evening wrap lined in bright red, and what she said was "Three-eighty and Four-nineteen." The 380, I gathered from neighbors' mutterings, was the wrap, and the 419 was the simple red evening gown that was disclosed when she ditched the wrap. It was fairly simple in front at the top, just covering essentials, but at the back it got even simpler by simply not starting until it hit the waistline. The woman on my right whispered to the one on her other side, "The hell of that is I've got a customer that would love it but I wouldn't dare let her buy it."

To clear up one point, they had there that afternoon six of the girls I was waiting to marry, if you count Cynthia Nieder, and I don't see why you shouldn't. Each of them made around a dozen appearances, some more, some less, and as for picking and choosing, if the buyers were as far up a stump as I was by the time it was over the only way they could possibly handle it was to send in an order for one of each.

As I explained to Wolfe in the office that evening, after I had reported a blank and we were conversing, "Imagine it! After the weddings I will of course have to take a good-sized apartment between Fifth and Madison in the Sixties. On a pleasant autumn evening I'll be sitting in the living room reading the newspaper. I'll toss the paper aside and clap my hands, and in will come Isabel. She will have on a calf-exposing kitchen apron with a double hemline and will be carrying a plate of ham sandwiches and a pitcher of milk. She will say seductively, 'Two-ninety-three,' make interesting motions and gestures without spilling a drop, put the plate and pitcher on a table at my elbow, and go. In will come Francine. She will be wearing slim-silhouette pajamas with padded shoulders and a back-flaring hipline. She'll walk and wave and whirl, say 'Nine-thirty-one' four times, and light me a cigarette and dance out. Enter Delia. She'll be dressed in a high-styled bra of hand-made lace with a billowing sweep to the—"

"Pfui," Wolfe said curtly. "Enter another, naked, carrying a basket full of bills, your checkbook, and a pen."

He has a personal slant on women.

Back to the show. It lasted over two hours, and for some of the numbers the applause was unrestrained, and it looked to me as if the Daumery and Nieder profits were likely to go on swelling up. Cynthia, in my opinion, was the star, and others seemed to agree with me. The numbers she modeled got much more applause than the rest of the line, and I admit I furnished my share, which was as it should be since I was her guest. Remarks from my neighbor on the right, who was evidently in the know, informed me that Cynthia's numbers had all been designed by herself, whereas the others were the work of Ward Roper, who had been Paul Nieder's assistant and was merely a good imitator and adapter.

In the office that evening I explained that to Wolfe, too, partly because I knew it would bore and irritate him, and partly because I wanted to demonstrate that I hadn't been asleep although my report of results had had no bodice at all and a very short skirt.

A breath and a half had done it. "I got in by following Cynthia's instructions, found a seat in the fifth row, and sat down after doing a survey of the two hundred customers and seeing no whiskers. Miss Nieder made fourteen appearances and did not signal me. When she came out front after the show she was immediately encircled by people, and I beat it, again following instructions, went down to the sidewalk, told Saul nothing doing, and handed Herb Aronson a ten-dollar bill."

Wolfe grunted. "What next?"

"That requires thought, which is your department. We can't sick the cops on him because the client doesn't want that. We can buy a gross of combs and comb the city. Or we can try again at their next show for buyers, which, as you know, will be Thursday morning at ten. Or you may remember what the client said about her uncle's private file."

Wolfe poohed. "She doesn't even know whether it exists. She thinks Jean Daumery took it and locked it up, and that the nephew, Bernard Daumery, is hanging onto it. She thinks she may possibly be able to find it."

"Okay, you admit she thinks, so why not you? You're merely objecting, not thinking. Think."

That was before dinner. If he did put his brain in motion there were no visible or audible results. After dinner, back in the office again, he started reading a book. That disgusted me, because after all we had a case, and for the sake of appearances I started in on a blow-by-blow account of the Daumery and Nieder show. The least I could do was to make it hard for him to read. I went on for over an hour, covering the ground, and then branched out into commentary.

"Imagine it!" I said. "After the weddings I will of course have to take a good-sized apartment . . ."

I've already told about that.

The next morning, Tuesday, he was still shirking. When we have a job on he usually has breakfast instructions for me before he goes up to the plant rooms for his nine-to-eleven session with Theodore and the orchids, but that day there wasn't a peep out of him, and when he came down to the office at eleven o'clock he got himself comfortable in his chair behind his desk, rang for Fritz to bring beer—two short buzzes—and picked up his book. Even when I showed him the check from Cynthia which had come in the morning mail, two thousand smackers, he merely nodded indifferently. I snorted at him and strode to the hall and out the front door, on my way to the bank to make a deposit. When I got back he was on his second bottle of beer and and deep in his book. Apparently his idea was to go on reading until Thursday's show for buyers.

For one o'clock lunch in the dining room, which was across the hall from the office, Fritz served us with chicken livers and tomato halves fried in oil and trimmed with chopped peppers and parsley, followed by rice cakes and honey. I took it easy on the livers because of my attitude toward Fritz's rice cakes. I was on my fifth cake, or maybe sixth, when the doorbell rang. During meals Fritz always answers the door, on account of Wolfe's feeling that the main objection to atom bombs is that they may interrupt people eating. Through the open door from the dining room to the hall I saw Fritz pass on his way to the front, and a moment later his voice came, trying to persuade someone to wait in the office until Wolfe had finished lunch. There was no other voice, but there were steps, and then our visitor was marching in on us—a man about Wolfe's age, heavy-set, muscular, red-faced, and obviously aggressive.

It was our chum Inspector Cramer, head of Homicide. He advanced to the table before he stopped and spoke to Wolfe.

"Hello. Sorry to break in on your meal."

"Good morning," Wolfe said courteously. For him it was always morning until he had finished his lunch coffee. "If you haven't had lunch we can offer you—"

"No, thanks, I'm busy and in a hurry. A woman named Cynthia Nieder came to see you yesterday."

Wolfe put a piece of rice cake in his mouth. I had a flash of a thought: Good God, the client's dead.

"Well?" Cramer demanded.

"Well what?" Wolfe snapped. "You stated a fact. I'm eating lunch."

"Fine. It's a fact. What did she want?"

"You know my habits and customs, Mr. Cramer." Wolfe was controlling himself. "I never talk business at a meal. I invited you to join us and you declined. If you will wait in the office—"

Cramer slapped a palm on the table, rattling things. My guess was that Wolfe would throw the coffee pot, since it was the heaviest thing handy, but I couldn't stay for it because along with the sound of Cramer's slap the doorbell rang again, and I thought I'd better not leave this one to Fritz. I got up and went, and through the one-way glass panel in the front door I saw an object that relieved me. The client was still alive and apparently unhurt. She was standing there on the stoop.

I pulled the door open, put my finger on my lips, muttered at her, "Keep your mouth shut," and with one eye took in the police car parked at the curb, seven steps down from the stoop. The man seated behind the wheel, a squad dick with whom I was acquainted, was looking up at us with an expression of interest. I waved at him, signaled Cynthia to enter, shut the door, and elbowed her into the front room, which faces the street and adjoins the office.

She looked scared, untended, haggard, and determined.

"The point is," I told her, "that a police inspector named Cramer is in the dining room asking about you. Do you want to see him?"

"Oh." She gazed at me as if she were trying to remember who I was. "I've already seen him." She looked around, saw a chair, got to it, and sat. "They've been—asking me—questions for hours—"

"Why, what happened?"

"My uncle—" Her head went forward and she covered her face with her hands. In a moment she looked up at me and said, "I want to see Nero Wolfe," and then covered her face with her hands again.

It might, I figured, take minutes to nurse her to the point of forming sentences. So I told her, "Stay here and sit tight. The walls are soundproofed, but keep quiet anyhow."

When I rejoined them in the dining room the coffee pot was still on the table unthrown, but the battle was on. Wolfe was out of his chair, erect, rigid with rage.

"No, sir," he was saying in his iciest tone, "I have not finished my gobbling now, as you put it. I would have eaten two more cakes, and I have not had my coffee. You broke in, and you're here. If you were not an officer of the law Mr. Goodwin would knock you unconscious and drag you out."

He moved. He stamped to the door, across the hall, and into the office. I was right behind him. By the time Cramer was there, seated in the red leather chair, Wolfe was seated too, behind his desk, breathing at double speed, with his mouth closed tight.

"Forget it," Cramer rasped, trying to make up.

Wolfe was silent.

"All I want," Cramer said, "is to find out why Cynthia Nieder came to see you. You have a right to ask why I want to know, and I would have told you if you hadn't lost your temper just because I arrived while you were stuffing it in. There's been a murder."

Wolfe said nothing.

"Last night," Cramer went on. "Time limits, eight P.M. and midnight. At the place of business of Daumery and Nieder on the twelfth floor of Four-ninety-six Seventh Avenue. Cynthia Nieder was there last night between nine and nine-thirty, she admits that; and nobody else as far as we know now. She says she went to get some drawings, but that's got holes in it. The body was found this morning, lying in the middle of the floor in the office. He had been hit in the back of the head with a hardwood pole, one of those used to raise and lower windows, and the end of the pole with the brass hook on it had been jabbed into his face a dozen times or more—like spearing a fish."

Wolfe had his eyes closed. I was considering that after all Cramer was the head of Homicide and he was paid for handling murders, and he always tried hard and deserved a little encouragement, so I asked in a friendly manner, "Who was it?"

"Nobody knows," he said sarcastically and without returning the friendliness. "A complete stranger to all the world, and nothing on him to tell." He paused, and then suddenly barked at me, "*You* describe him!"

"Nuts. Who was it?"

"It was a medium-sized man around forty, with a brown beard and slick brown hair parted on the left side, with glasses that were just plain glass. Can you name him?"

I thought it extremely interesting that Cramer's description consisted of the three items that Cynthia had specified. It showed what a well-planned disguise could do.

V

WOLFE remained silent.

"Sorry," I said. "Never met him."

Cramer left me for Wolfe. "Under the circumstances," he argued, still sarcastic, "you may concede that I have a right to ask what she came to you for. It was only after she tried two lies on us about how she spent yesterday morning that we finally got it out of her that she came here. She didn't want us to know, she was dead against it, and she wouldn't tell what she came for. Add to that the fact that whenever you are remotely connected with anyone who is remotely connected with a murder you always know everything, and there's no question about my needing to know what you were consulted about. I came to ask you myself because I know what you're like."

Wolfe broke his vow. He spoke. "Is Miss Nieder under arrest?"

The phone rang before Cramer could answer. I took it, a voice asked to speak to Inspector Cramer, and Cramer came to my desk and talked. Or rather, he listened. About all he used was grunts, but at one point he said "Here?" with an inflection that started my mind going, and simple logic carried it on to a conclusion.

So as Cramer hung up I pushed in ahead of him to tell Wolfe. "An-swering your question, she is not under arrest. They turned her loose because they didn't have enough to back up anything stiffer than material witness, and they put a tail on her, and the tail phoned in that she came here, and the call Cramer just got was a relay of the tail's report. She's in the front room. I put her there because I know how you are about having your meals interrupted. Shall I bring her in?"

Cramer returned to the red leather chair, sat, and said to someone, "You snippy little bastard." I ignored it, knowing it couldn't be for me, since I am just under six feet and weigh a hundred and eighty and therefore could not be called little.

Cramer went at Wolfe. "So the minute we let her go she comes here. That has some bearing on my wanting to know what she was after yesterday, huh?"

Wolfe spoke to me. "Archie. You say Miss Nieder is in the front room?"

"Yes, sir."

"It was she who rang the bell while Mr. Cramer was trying to knock my luncheon dishes off the table?"

"Yes, sir."

"What did she say?"

"Nothing, except that she wanted to see you. She has spent hours with cops and her tongue's tired."

"Bring her in here."

Cramer started offering objections, but I didn't hear him. I went and opened the connecting door to the front room, which was as soundproof as the wall, and said respectfully for all to hear, "Inspector Cramer is here asking about you. Will you come in, please?"

She stood up, hesitated, stiffened herself, and then walked to me and on through. I placed one of the yellow chairs for her, facing Wolfe, closer to my position than to Cramer's. She nodded at me, sat, gave Cramer a straight full look, transferred it to Wolfe, and swallowed.

Wolfe was frowning at her and his eyes were slits. "Miss Nieder," he said gruffly, "I am working for you and you have paid me a retainer. Is that correct?"

She nodded, decided to wire it for sound, and said, "Yes, certainly."

"Then first some advice. The police could have held you as a material witness and you would have had to get bail. Instead, they let you go to give you an illusion of freedom, and they are following you around. Should you at any time want to go somewhere without their knowledge, there's nothing difficult about it. Mr. Goodwin is an expert on that and can tell you what to do."

Cramer was unimpressed. He had got out a cigar and was rolling it between his palms. I never understood why he did that, since you roll a cigar to make it draw better, and he never lit one but only chewed it.

"I understand," Wolfe continued, "that Mr. Cramer and his men have dragged it out of you that you came here yesterday, but that you have refused to tell them what for. Is that correct?"

"Yes."

"Good. I think that was sensible. You are suspected of murder, but that puts you under no compulsion to disclose all the little secrets you have locked up. We all have them, and we don't surrender them if we can help it. But my position in this is quite different from yours. It is true you have hired me, but I am not an attorney-at-law, and therefore what you said to me was not a privileged communication. In my business I need to have the good will, or at least the tolerance, of the police, in order to keep my license to work as a detective. I cannot afford to be intransigent with a police inspector. Besides, I respect and admire Mr. Cramer and would like to help him. I tell you all this so that you will not misunderstand what I am about to do."

Cynthia opened her mouth, but Wolfe pushed a palm at her, and no words came. He turned to Cramer.

"Since your army has had several hours to poke into corners, you have learned, I suppose, that Mr. Goodwin went to that place yesterday and sat through a show."

"Yeah, I know about that."

"You didn't mention it."

"I hadn't come to it."

"Your reserves?" Wolfe smiled, as mean a smile as I had ever seen. "Well. You heard what I just told Miss Nieder. She came yesterday morning to consult me about her uncle."

"Yeah? What uncle?"

"Mr. Paul Nieder. He is dead. Miss Nieder inherited half of that business from him. Back files of newspapers will tell you that he committed suicide a little over a year ago by jumping into a geyser in Yellowstone Park. Miss Nieder told me about that and many other things—the present status of the business, her own position in it, the deaths of her uncle's former partner and his wife, and so on. I don't remember everything she said, and I don't intend to try. Anyhow it was a *mélange* of facts which your men can easily collect elsewhere. The only thing I can furnish that might help you is the conclusion I formed. I concluded that Miss Nieder had herself pushed her uncle into the geyser, murdered him, and had become fearful of exposure, and had come to me with the fantastic notion of having me get her out of it."

"Why you—" Cynthia was sputtering. "You—"

"Shut up," Wolfe snapped at her. He turned. "Archie. Wasn't that the impression you got?"

"Precisely," I declared.

Cynthia had done fine, I thought, by shutting up as instructed, but I would have risked a wink at her, or at least a helpful glance, if Cramer's eyes hadn't been so comprehensive.

"Thanks for the conclusion," Cramer growled. "Did she tell you that? That she had killed her uncle?"

"Oh, no. No, indeed."

"Exactly what did she want you to do?"

Wolfe smiled the same smile. "That's why I came to that conclusion. She left it very vague about what I was to do. I couldn't possibly tell you."

"Try telling me what you told Goodwin to do when you sent him up there."

Wolfe frowned and called on me. "Do you remember, Archie?"

"Sure I remember." I was eager to help. "You told me to keep a sharp lookout and report everything that happened." I beamed at Cramer. "Talk about the dancers of Bali! Did you ever sit and watch six beautiful girls prancing—"

"You're a goddam liar," he rasped at Wolfe.

Wolfe's chin went up an eighth of an inch. "Mr. Cramer," he said coldly, "I'm tired of this. Mr. Goodwin can't throw you out of here once you're in, but we can leave you here and go upstairs, and you know the limits of your license as well as I do."

He pushed back his chair and was on his feet. "You say I'm lying. Prove it. But for less provocation than you have given me by your uncivilized conduct in my dining room, I would lie all day and all night. Regarding this murder of a bearded stranger, where do I fit, or Mr. Goodwin? Pah. Connect us if you can! Should you be rash enough to constrain us as material witnesses, we would teach you something of the art of lying, and we wouldn't squeeze out on bail; we would dislocate your nose with a habeas corpus ad subjiciendum."

His eyes moved. "Come, Miss Nieder. Come, Archie."

He headed for the door to the hall, detouring around the red leather chair, and I followed him, gathering Cynthia by the elbow as I went by. I presumed we were bound for the plant rooms, which were three flights up, and as we entered the hall I was wondering whether all three of us could crowd into Wolfe's personal elevator without losing dignity. But that problem didn't have to be solved. I was opening my mouth to tell Wolfe that Cynthia and I would use the stairs when here came Cramer striding by. Without a glance at us or a word he went to the front door, opened it, crossed the sill to the stoop, and banged the door shut.

I stepped to the door and put the chain bolt in its slot. Any city employee arriving with papers would have only a two-inch crack to hand the papers through.

Wolfe led us back to the office, motioned us to our chairs, sat at his desk, and demanded of Cynthia, "Did you kill that man?"

She met his eyes and gulped. Then her head went down, her hands went up, her shoulders started to shake, and sounds began to come.

VI

THAT was terrible. The only thing that shakes Wolfe as profoundly as having a meal rudely interrupted is a bawling woman. His reaction to the first is rage, to the second panic.

I tried to reassure him. "She'll be all right. She just has to—"

"Stop her," he muttered desperately.

I crossed to her, yanked her hands away, using muscle, pulled her face up, and kissed her hard and good on the lips. She jerked her face aside, shoved at me, and protested, "What the hell!"

That sounded better, and I turned to Wolfe and told him reproachfully, "You can't blame her. I doubt if it's fear or despair or anything normal like that. It's probably hunger. I'll bet she hasn't had a bite since breakfast."

"Good heavens." His eyes popped wide open. "Is that true, Miss Nieder? Haven't you had lunch?"

She shook her head. "They kept me there—and then I had to see you—"

Wolfe was pushing the button. Since it was only five steps from the office to the kitchen door, in seconds Fritz was there.

"Sandwiches and beer at once," Wolfe told him. "Beer, Miss Nieder?"

"I don't have to eat."

"Nonsense. Beer? Claret? Milk? Brandy?"

"Scotch and water. I could use that."

Which of course halted progress for a good twenty minutes. It wasn't only his own meals that Wolfe insisted on safeguarding from extraneous matters. When Fritz brought the tray Cynthia wasn't reluctant about the Scotch, but she needed urging on the sandwiches and got it from both of us. After a taste of the homemade pâté no further urging was required. To make her feel that she could take her time Wolfe conversed with me about the plant germination records. Not about Cramer. His feelings about Cramer were much too warm and too recent. When she was through I put the tray on the table by the big globe, leaving her a glass full of her mixture, and then resumed my seat at my desk.

Wolfe was regarding her warily. "Do you feel better?"

"Much better, yes. I guess I was pretty empty."

"Good." Wolfe leaned back and sighed. "Now. You came to me as soon as the police let you go. Does that mean that you want my help in this new circumstance?"

"It certainly does. I want—"

"Excuse me. We'll go faster if I lead, and Mr. Cramer is quite capable of sending men here with warrants. Let's compress it. There are two points on which I must be satisfied before we can proceed. First, whether you killed that man. An attorney may properly work for a murderer, but I'm not an attorney, and anyway I don't like money from murderers. Did you kill him?"

"No. I want to—"

"Just the no will do if it's the truth. Is it?"

"Yes. It's no."

"I'm inclined to accept it, for reasons mostly not communicable. Some are. For instance, if you had been unable to eat that pâté—" Wolfe cut himself off and sent his eyes at me. "Archie. Did Miss Nieder kill that man?"

I looked at her, my lips puckered, and her gaze met mine. I must admit that she looked pretty ragged, not at all the same person as the one who had modeled, just twenty-four hours before, a dancing dress of Swiss eyelet organdy with ruffled shoulders. She had sure been through something, but not necessarily a murder.

I shook my head and told Wolfe, "No, sir. No guarantee with sanctions, but I vote no. My reasons are like yours, but I might mention that I strongly doubt if I would have had the impulse to make her stop crying by kissing her thoroughly if she had jabbed a window pole into a man's face more than a dozen times. No."

Wolfe nodded. "Then that's settled. She didn't, unless we get cornered by facts, and in that case we'll deserve it. The other point, Miss Nieder, is this: Was the man you saw up there a week ago today your uncle, and was it he who was killed last night?"

A "yes" popped out of her. She added, "It was Uncle Paul. I saw him. I went—"

"Don't dash ahead. We'll get to that. Since I'm assuming your good faith, tentatively at least, I am not suggesting that what you told me yesterday was flummery. I grant that you thought it was your uncle you saw a week ago today, and I accepted it then, but now it's too flimsy for me. You'll have to give me something better if you've got it. What was it that convinced you it was your uncle?"

"I *knew* it was," Cynthia declared. "Maybe if I tried I could tell you how I knew, but I don't have to because now I do know so I could prove it. I've been trying to tell you. You remember what I said about my uncle's private file—that I thought Jean Daumery had taken it and that Bernard has it now.

I went there last night to look for it, and saw that—that dead man there on the floor. You can imagine—"

She stopped and made a gesture.

"Yes, I can imagine," Wolfe agreed. "Go ahead."

"I made myself go close to look at him—his face was dreadful but he had the beard and the slick hair. I wanted to do something but I didn't have nerve enough, and I had to sit down to pull myself together. Now they say I was in there fifteen minutes, but I wouldn't think it took me that long to get up my nerve, but maybe it did, and then I went and pulled up the right leg of his trousers and pulled his sock down. He had two little scars about four inches above the ankle, and I knew those scars—that's where my uncle got bit by a dog once. I looked at them close. I had to sit down again—" She stopped, with her mouth open. "Oh! That's why it was fifteen minutes! I had forgotten all about that, sitting down again—"

"Then you left? What did you do?"

"I went home to my apartment and phoned Mr. Demarest. I hadn't—"

"Who's Mr. Demarest?"

"He's a lawyer. He was a friend of Uncle Paul's, and he's the executor. I hadn't told him about seeing my uncle last week because after all I had no proof, and I wanted to find my uncle and talk with him first, so I decided to get you to find him for me. But when I got home I thought the only thing to do was to phone Mr. Demarest, so I did, but he had gone out—"

"Confound it," Wolfe grumbled, "why didn't you phone me?"

"Well—" Cynthia looked harassed. "I didn't know you, did I? Well enough for that? How could I tell what you would believe and what you wouldn't?"

"Indeed," Wolfe said sarcastically. "So you decided to keep it from me, running the risk that I might glance at a newspaper. What is the lawyer doing? Reading up?"

She shook her head. "I didn't get him. I phoned again at eleven-thirty, thinking he would be home by then, but he wasn't, and the state I was in it didn't even occur to me to leave word for him to call. Intending to phone again at midnight, I lay down on the couch to wait, and then—it may be hard to believe but I went to sleep and didn't wake up until nearly seven o'clock. I thought it over and decided not to tell Mr. Demarest or anybody else. During a show season there are lots of people going up and down in those elevators in that building after hours, and I thought they wouldn't remember about me, and my name wasn't in the book because they know me so well and they're not strict about it. That was dumb, wasn't it?"

Wolfe acquiesced with a restrained groan.

She finished the story. "Of course I had to go to work as if nothing had happened. It wasn't easy, but I did, and the place was full of people, police and detectives, when I got there. I had only been there a few minutes when they took me to a fitting room to ask questions, and like a fool I told them I hadn't been there last night when they already knew about it."

Cynthia fluttered a hand. "When they were through with me I phoned Mr. Demarest's office and he was out at lunch. So I came here."

VII

WOLFE heaved a sigh that filled his whole interior. "Well." He opened his eyes and half closed them again. "You said you want my help in this new circumstance. What do you want me to do? Keep you from being convicted of murder?"

"Convicted?" Cynthia goggled at him. "Of murdering my uncle?" Her chin hinges began to give. "I wouldn't—"

"Lay off," I growled at Wolfe, "unless you want to make me kiss her again. She's not a crybaby, but your direct approach is really something. Use synonyms."

"She's not hungry again, is she?" he demanded peevishly. But he eased it. "Miss Nieder. If you're on the defense and intend to stay there, get a lawyer. I'm no good for that. If you want your uncle's murderer caught, whoever it is, and doubt whether the police are up to it, get me. Which do you want, a lawyer or me?"

"I want you," she said, her chin okay.

Wolfe nodded in approval of her sound judgment. "Then we know what we're doing." He glanced at the wall clock. "In twenty minutes I must go up to my orchids. I spend two hours with them every afternoon, from four to six. The most urgent question is this: Who knows that the murdered man was Paul Nieder? Who besides you?"

"Nobody," she declared.

"As far as you know, no one has said or done anything to indicate knowledge or suspicion of his identity?"

"No. They all say they never saw him before, and they have no idea how he got there or who he is. Of course—the way his face was—you wouldn't expect—"

"I suppose not. But we'll assume that whoever killed him knew who he was killing; we'd be donkeys if we didn't. Also we'll assume that he thinks no one else knows. That gives us an advantage. Are you sure you have given no one a hint of your recognition of your uncle last week?"

"Yes, I'm positive."

"Then we have that advantage too. But consider this: if that body is buried without official identification as your uncle, your possession of your inheritance may be further delayed. Also this: you cannot claim the body and give it appropriate burial. Also this: if the police are told who the murdered man was they may be able to do a better job."

"Would they believe—would they keep it secret until they caught him?"

"They might, but I doubt it. Possibly they would fancy the theory that you had killed him in order to hold onto half of that business, and if so your associates up there would be asked to confirm the identification. Certainly Mr. Demarest would be. That's one reason why I shall not tell the police. Another one is that I wouldn't tell Mr. Cramer anything whatever, after his behavior today. But you can do as you please. Do you want to tell them?"

"No."

"Then don't. Now." Wolfe glanced at the clock. "Do you think you know who killed your uncle?"

Cynthia looked startled. "Why no, of course not!"

"You have no idea at all?"

"No!"

"How many people work there?"

"Right now, about two hundred."

"Pfui." Wolfe scowled. "Can any of them get in after hours?"

"No, not unless they have a key—or are let in by someone who has a key. Up to the time of the press showing, even up to yesterday, the first buyers' show, there were people there every evening in the rush of getting the line ready, but most times there's no one there after hours. That's why I picked last night to go to look for that file."

"There was no one working there last night?"

"No, not a soul."

"Who has keys?"

"Let's see." She concentrated. "I have one. Bernard Daumery. . . . Polly Zarella. . . . Ward Roper. That's—oh no, Mr. Demarest has one. As my uncle's executor he is in legal control of the half-interest."

"Who opens up in the morning and locks up at night?"

"Polly Zarella. She has been doing that for years, since before I came there."

"So there are just five keys?"

"Yes, that's all."

"Pah. I can't depend on you. I myself know of two you haven't mentioned. Didn't your uncle have one? He probably let himself in with it last night. And didn't Jean Daumery have one?"

"I was telling about the ones that are there now," Cynthia said with a touch of indignation. "I suppose Uncle Paul had one, of course. I don't know about Jean Daumery's, but if he had it in his clothes that day fishing it's at the bottom of the ocean, and if he didn't have it I suppose Bernard has it now."

Wolfe nodded. "Then we know of four people with keys besides you. Miss Zarella, Mr. Daumery, Mr. Roper, Mr. Demarest. Can you have them here this evening at half-past eight?"

Cynthia gawked. "You mean—here?"

"At this office."

"But good lord." She was flabbergasted. "I can't just order them around! What can I say? I can't say I want them to help find out who killed my uncle because they don't know it was my uncle! You must consider they're much older than I am—all but Bernard—and they think I'm just a fresh kid. Even Bernard is seven years older. After all, I'm only twenty-one—that is, I will be—my God!"

She looked horror-struck, as if someone had poked a window pole at her.

"What now?" Wolfe demanded.

"Tomorrow's my birthday! I'll be twenty-one tomorrow!"

"Yes?" Wolfe said politely.

"Happy birthday!" she cried.

"Not this one," Wolfe stated.

"Look out," I warned him. "That's one of a girl's biggest dates."

He pushed his chair back hastily, arose, and looked at me.

"Archie. I would like to see those people this evening. Six o'clock would do, but I prefer eight-thirty, after dinner. Go up there with Miss Nieder. She is under suspicion of murder, and has engaged me, and can reasonably expect their co-operation. She is in fact half-owner of that business, and one of them is her partner, one is her lawyer, and the other two are her employees. What better do you want?"

He made for the door, on his way to the elevator.

VIII

ONE of my little notions—that I had already exchanged words with Bernard Daumery—turned out to be wrong. Evidently it is not a Seventh Avenue custom for half-owners to act as doortenders at buyers' shows. At least, contrary to my surmise, it had not been Bernard Daumery who on Monday afternoon had barred Driscoll's Emporium and had given me a head-to-foot survey before letting me in. I never saw that number again.

Business as usual is one of the few things that the Police Department makes allowances for in handling a homicide. The wheels of commerce must not be stalled unless it is unavoidable. So at the Daumery and Nieder premises eight hours after the discovery of the body, a pug-nosed dick hovering inside near the entrance was the only visible hint that this was the scene of the crime. The city scientists had done all they could and got all that was gettable and had departed. As Cynthia and I entered, the dick recognized me and wanted to know how come, and I told him amiably that I was working for Nero Wolfe and Mr. Wolfe was working for Miss Nieder, pausing just long enough not to seem boorish. I wasn't worried about Cramer. He knew damn well that if he took drastic steps Wolfe would perform exactly as outlined, and that he had been a plain jackass not to wait until Wolfe had downed the other two rice cakes and had some coffee. If the case got really messy and made him desperate he might explode something, but not today or tomorrow.

Cynthia and I were sitting in Bernard Daumery's office, waiting for him to finish with some customers in the showroom. It had been his uncle Jean's room, and was large, light, and airy, with good rugs and furniture, and the walls even more covered with drawings and photographs than in the showroom. We had decided to start with Bernard.

"The trouble with him," Cynthia was telling me with a frown, "is that he can't bear to decide anything. Especially if it's important, you might think he had to wait to see what the stars say or maybe a crystal ball. Then when he does make up his mind he's as stubborn as a mule. The way I do when I want him to agree about something, I act as if it wasn't very important—"

The door came open and a man was there. He shut the door and approached her.

"I'm sorry, Cynthia, it was Miss Dougherty of Bullock's-Wilshire, and Brackett was with her. She thinks you're better than ever, and she's lost her head completely over those three—Oh! Who—?"

"Mr. Goodwin of Nero Wolfe's office," Cynthia told him. "Mr. Daumery, Mr. Goodwin."

I got up to offer a hand and he took it.

"Nero Wolfe the detective?" he asked.

I told him yes. His exuberance about Miss Dougherty of Bullock's-Wilshire evaporated without a trace. He sent Cynthia a look, shook his head, though not apparently at her, went to a chair, not the one at his desk, and sat. Cynthia's statistics had informed me that he was four years younger than me, and I might as well concede them to him. On account of the intimate way he had beamed at Cynthia on entering, naturally I looked upon him as a rival, but to be perfectly fair to him he was built like a man, he knew where to get clothes and how to wear them, and he was not actually ugly.

Now the exuberance was gone. "This godawful mess," he glummed. "Where does Nero Wolfe come in?"

"I went to see him," Cynthia said. "I've hired him."

"What for? To do what?"

"Well—I need somebody, don't I? After the way the police acted with me? When they know I came here last night and apparently no one else did?"

"But that's absolutely idiotic! Why shouldn't you come here?"

"All right, I should. But I think they came within an inch of arresting me."

"Then you need a lawyer. Where's Demarest? Did he send you to Nero Wolfe?"

Cynthia shook her head. "I haven't seen him, but I'm going to as soon as—"

"Damn it, you should have seen him first!"

"I'm not taking your time," Cynthia declared, "to ask you what I should have done. I'll tend to that, thank you. I want to ask you to do something."

I thought she was making a bad start and needed help. "May I join in?" I inquired pleasantly.

Bernard scowled at me. "This thing is absolutely crazy," he complained. "What we ought to do is ignore it! Simply ignore it!"

"Yeah," I agreed, "that would be innocent and brave, but it might get complicated. If one of you gets charged with murder and locked up it would take a master ignorer—"

"Good God, why should we? How could we? Why would any of us kill a man we never saw or heard of before? The thing for the police to do is find out how he ever got in here—that's their problem."

"I completely agree," I assured him heartily. "The trouble is you've got a logical mind and some cops haven't. So the fact remains that one of you, especially one of you that has a key to this place, is apt to get arrested for murder, and right now the odds strongly favor Miss Nieder because they know she used her key last night. Getting convicted is something else, but she would rather not even be arrested right in the middle of the showings of the fall line. May I go on a minute?"

"We're busy as the devil," Bernard muttered.

"I'll be brief. Miss Nieder has hired Mr. Wolfe. She will consult her lawyer, Demarest, within the hour. But meanwhile—"

The door swung open and a man entered. He too shut the door behind him, half turning to close it gently, and then spoke as he advanced.

"Good afternoon, Cynthia. Good afternoon, Bernard. What on earth is going on here?" He saw me. "Who are you, sir, an officer of the law? So am I, in a way. My name is Demarest—Henry R. Demarest, Counselor." He was coming to me to shake on it, and I stood up and obliged.

"Goodwin, Archie," I said, "assistant to Nero Wolfe, private detective."

"Oho!" His brows went up. "Nero Wolfe, eh?" he turned to the others and I had his broad back and the pudgy behind of his neck. "What is all this? A dead man found on the premises and I have to learn it from a policeman asking me about my key? May I ask why I was not informed?"

"We were busy," Bernard said gruffly. "And not with business. The whole police force was here."

"I tried to phone you last night," Cynthia said, "but you weren't at home, and today you were out at lunch, and I have arranged with Nero Wolfe to keep me from being convicted of murder, and Mr. Goodwin came here with me. I was nearly arrested because I came here last night and stayed fifteen minutes."

Demarest nodded. He had deposited his hat on Bernard's desk and his fanny on Bernard's chair the other side of the desk, which seemed a little arbitrary. He nodded again at Cynthia.

"I know. A friend at the District Attorney's office has given me the particulars. But my dear child, you should have called on me at once. I should have been beside you! You went to Nero Wolfe instead? Why?"

He irritated me. Also Cynthia sent me a glance which I interpreted to mean that hired help are supposed to earn their pay, so I horned in.

"Maybe I can answer that, Mr. Demarest. In fact that's what I was about to do when you entered. You know how it stands now, do you?"

"I know how it stood thirty minutes ago."

"Then you're up with us. I was explaining to Mr. Daumery that Miss Nieder would prefer not to be arrested. Primarily that's what sent her to Mr. Wolfe. I was going on to explain what she can expect of Mr. Wolfe. She won't have to pay him for an all-out job. On a case like this that would mean checking on everybody who entered or left the building last evening after hours, which would be quite a chore itself, considering how careless elevator men get. Things like that are much better left to the police, and a lot of similar jobs, for instance the fingerprint roundup, the laboratory angles, checking alibis, and so on. Naturally the five people who have keys to this place are special cases. Their alibis will get it good, and they'll be tailed day and night, and all the rest of it. We'll let the city pay for all that, not Miss Nieder. That's what Mr. Wolfe won't do."

"It doesn't leave much, does it?" Demarest inquired.

"Enough to keep him occupied. Apparently you've heard of him, Mr. Demarest, so you probably know he goes about it his way. That's what he's doing now, and that's why I'm here. He sent me to arrange a little meeting at his office tonight. Miss Nieder, Miss Zarella, Mr. Daumery, Mr. Roper, and you. You are the five who have keys. Half-past eight would suit him fine if it would suit you. Refreshments served."

Bernard and Demarest made noises. The one from Bernard was an impatient grunt, but the one from Demarest sounded more like a chuckle.

"We're summoned," the lawyer said.

I grinned at him. "I wouldn't dream of putting it that way."

"No, but we are." He chuckled again. "We who have keys. I offer a comment. You said that Wolfe's primary function, as Miss Nieder sees it, is to prevent her arrest. Obviously he intends to perform it by getting someone else arrested—and tried and convicted. That may prove to be a difficult and expensive undertaking, and possibly quite unnecessary. I would engage, with the situation as it is now, to get the same result with one-tenth the effort and at one-tenth the expense. It's only fair to her, isn't it, to give her that alternative?"

He turned. "It's your money, Cynthia. What about it? Do you want to pay Wolfe to do it his way?"

For a second I thought she was weakening. But she was only deciding how to put it.

"Yes, I do," she declared firmly. "I never had a detective working for me before, and if you can't hire a detective when you're suspected of murder when can you hire one?"

Demarest nodded. "I thought so," he said in a satisfied tone. "Just what I thought. Did you say eight-thirty, Goodwin?"

"That would be best. Mr. Wolfe works better when he isn't looking forward to a meal. You'll come?"

"Certainly I'll come. To save energy. I like to economize on energy, and it will take less to attend that meeting than it would to argue Miss Nieder out of it." He smiled at her. "My dear child! I want a private talk with you."

"Maybe it can wait a few minutes?" I suggested. "Until I finish arranging this? How about it, Mr. Daumery? You'll be with us?"

Bernard was sunk in gloom or something—anyhow, he was sunk. He was hunched in his chair, his eyes going from Cynthia to Demarest to me to Cynthia.

"Okay?" I prodded him.

"I don't know," he muttered. "I'll think it over."

Cynthia emitted a little snort.

Demarest regarded Bernard with exasperation. "As usual. You'll think it over. What is there to think about?"

"There's this business to think about," Bernard declared. "It's bad enough already, with a murdered man found here in the office. We would practically be admitting our connection with it, wouldn't we, the five of us going to discuss it with a detective?"

"I've hired the detective personally," Cynthia snapped.

"I know you have, Cynthia." His tone implied that he was imploring her to make allowances for the air spaces in his skull. "But damn it, we have to consider the business, don't we? It may be inadvisable. I don't know."

"How long would you need to think?" I asked pleasantly. "It's five o'clock now, so there isn't a lot of time. Say an hour and a half? By six-thirty?"

"I suppose so." He sounded uncertain. He looked around at us as if he were a woodchuck in a hole and we were terriers digging to get him. "I'll let you know. Where'll you be?"

"That depends," I replied for us. "There are two more to invite—Miss Zarella and Mr. Roper. It might help if you would get them in here. Would that require thinking over too?"

Demarest chuckled. Cynthia sent me a warning glance, to caution me against aggravating him.

Bernard retorted with spirit. "You do your thinking and I'll do mine." He got up and went to his desk. "Would you mind using another chair, Mr. Demarest?"

Demarest moved out. Bernard sat down and picked up the phone transmitter, and told it, "Please ask Mr. Roper and Miss Zarella to come in here."

IX

THEY entered together.

I had seen Polly Zarella before. It was she who, the preceding afternoon, had emerged from the door on the left and given the signal that started the show. She still resembled my mother only in point of age. Her lipstick supply was holding out, and so was her shoulder padding, though she had on a different dress. Seeing her on the street, I would have tagged her for a totally different role from the one she filled—Cynthia having informed me that she was a scissors-and-needle wizard, in charge of all Daumery and Nieder production, and a highly important person.

After I had been introduced Bernard invited them to sit. Then he said, "I'm sorry to take your time, but this day is all shot to hell anyhow. Mr. Goodwin wants to ask you something."

They aimed their eyes at me. I grinned at them engagingly.

"You're busy and I'll cut it short. More trouble and fuss, all on account of a dead man. The cops are making it hot for Miss Nieder because she was here last night and said she wasn't when they first brought it up. Now she's in a fix, and she has hired my boss, Nero Wolfe, to get her out. Mr. Wolfe would like to have a talk with five people, the five who carry keys to this place—the five who are here now. He sent me to ask if you will come to his office this evening at half-past eight. Miss Nieder will of course be there. Mr. Demarest is coming. Mr. Daumery is thinking it over and will let us know later. It will be in the interest of justice, it will help to clear up this muddle and let you get back to work, and it will be a favor to Miss Nieder. Will you come?"

"No," Polly Zarella said emphatically.

"No?" I inquired courteously.

"No," she repeated. "I losed much time today. I will be here all evening with cutters cutting."

"This is pretty important, Miss Zarella."

"I do not think so." She said "zink." "He was here, he is gone, and we forget it. I told that to the policemen and I tell it to you. Miss Nieder is not dangered. If she was dangered I would fight it off with these hands" —she lifted them as claws—"because she is the best designer in America or Europe or the world. But she is not. No."

She got up and started for the door. Cynthia, darting to her feet, intercepted her and caught her by the arm.

"I think you ought to wait," I said, "for Mr. Roper's vote. Mr. Roper?"

Ward Roper cleared his throat. "It doesn't seem to me," he offered, in the sort of greasy voice that makes me want to take up strangling, "that this is exactly the proper step to take, under the circumstances."

Seeing that Polly's exit was halted, I was looking at Roper. Getting along toward fifty, by no means too old to strangle, he was slender, elegant, and groomed to a queen's taste if you let him pick the queen. His voice fitted him to a T.

"What's wrong with it?" I asked him.

He cocked his head to one side to contemplate me. "Almost everything, I would say. I understand and sympathize with Mr. Daumery's desire to think it over. It assumes that we, the five of us, are involved in this matter, which is ridiculous. One may indeed be involved, deeply involved, but not the other four. Not the rest of us."

"What the hell are you getting at?" Bernard demanded with heat.

"Nothing, Bernard. Nothing specific. Just a comment expressing my reaction."

Plainly it was no time for diplomacy. I arose and stepped to a spot nearer Cynthia, where I could face them all without neck-twisting.

"This is a joke," I declared offensively, "and if you ask me, a rotten one." I focused on Bernard. "Have you got around to your thinking, Mr. Daumery? Made up your mind?"

"Certainly not!" He resented it. "Who do you think you are?"

"Just at present I'm Miss Nieder's hired man." My eyes went around. "You're acting, all but Demarest, like a bunch of halfwits! Who do I think I am? Who do you think Miss Nieder is, some little girl asking you to please be nice and help her out? You damn fools, she owns half of this outfit!" I looked at Bernard. "Who are you? You're her business partner, fifty-fifty, and what couldn't she do to you if she felt like it! So you say you'll think it over! Nuts!" I looked at Polly and Roper. "And what are you? You're her employees, her hired help. She owns half of this firm that you work for. And through me she makes a sensible and reasonable request, and listen to you! As for you, Roper, I hear that you're a good imitator and adapter. I understand that you, Miss Zarella, are as good as they come at producing the goods. But you're not indispensable—neither or both of you. In this affair Mr. Wolfe and I are acting for Miss Nieder. Speaking as her representative, I hereby instruct you to report at the office of Nero Wolfe, Nine-twenty-four West Thirty-fifth Street, at half-past eight this evening."

I wheeled and got Cynthia's eye. "You confirm that, Miss Nieder?"

Her yes was creaky. There was a tadpole in her throat, and she got rid of it and repeated, "Yes. I confirm it."

"Good for you." I turned. "You'll be there, Miss Zarella?"

Polly was staring at me with what seemed to be wide-eyed admiration, but I could be wrong. "But certainly," she said, fully as emphatically as she had previously said no. "If it is so exciting as you make it I will be there with bells on."

"Fine. You, Mr. Roper?"

Roper was chewing his lip. No doubt it was hard for a man of his eminence to swallow a threat of being fired.

"The way you put it," he told me, with a strong suggestion of a tremble in his greasy voice, "I hardly know what to say. It is true, of course, that at some future time Miss Nieder will probably own a half-interest in this business, in the success of which I have had some part for the past fourteen years. That is, she will if she is—available."

"What do you mean, available?"

"Isn't it obvious?" He spread out his hands. "Of course your job is to get her out of it, so you can't be expected to take an objective attitude. But the police are usually right about these things, and you know what they think." The grease suddenly got acutely bitter. "So I merely ask, what if she's not available? As for your—"

What stopped him was movement by Bernard. Cynthia's partner had left his chair and taken four healthy strides to the one occupied by Roper. Roper, startled, got erect in a hurry, nearly knocking his chair over.

"I warned you last night, Ward," Bernard said as if he meant it. "I told you to watch your nasty tongue." His hands were fists. "Apologize to Cynthia, and do it quick."

"Apologize? But what did I—"

Bernard slapped him hard. I couldn't help approving of my rival's good taste in making it a slap, certainly better than my strangling idea, and to spend a solid punch on him would have been flattering him. The first slap teetered Roper's head to the left, and a second one, harder if anything, sent it the other way.

A thought struck me. "Don't fire him!" I called. "Miss Nieder doesn't want him fired! She wants him there tonight!"

"He'll be there," Bernard said grimly, without turning. He had backed up a step to glare at Roper. "You'll be there, Ward, understand?"

That sounded swell, so I crowded my luck. "You will too, Mr. Daumery, won't you?"

What the hell, it was a cinch, with him ordering Roper to come. But he turned around to tell me, "I'll decide later. I'll let you know. I'll phone you. Your number's in the book?"

Demarest chuckled.

X

I LIKE to keep my word, and having on the spur of the moment promised refreshments, they were there. On the table near the big globe were tree-ripened olives, mahallebi, three bowls of nuts, and a comprehensive array of liquids ranging from Wolfe's best brandy down to beer. Each of the guests had a little table at his elbow. At a quarter to nine, when the last arrival had been ushered in, Bernard Daumery and Ward Roper had nothing on their tables but their napkins, Cynthia had Scotch and water, Demarest a Tom Collins, and Polly Zarella a glass and a bottle of Tokaji Essencia. Bernard had phoned around seven o'clock that we could expect him.

If the cops were tailing all of them, as they almost certainly were, I thought there must be quite a convention outside on 35th Street.

I had completed, before dinner, an extra fancy job of reporting. Wolfe had wanted all the details of my party-arranging mission at Daumery and Nieder's, both the libretto and the full score, and I had to get it all in and still leave time for questions before Fritz announced dinner, knowing as I did that if we were late to the table and had to hurry Wolfe would be in a bad humor all evening. In my opinion there would be plenty of bad humor to go around without Wolfe contributing a share, which was another reason for keeping my promise on the refreshments.

Since the staging had been left to me I had placed Cynthia in the red leather chair because I liked her there. Polly Zarella had insisted on having the chair nearest to mine, which might have been just her maternal instinct. On her right was Demarest, and then Roper and Bernard. That seemed a good arrangement, since if Bernard took it into his head to do some more slapping he wouldn't have far to go.

"Thank you for coming," Wolfe said formally.

"We had to," Demarest stated. "Your man Goodwin dragooned us."

"Not you, I understand, Mr. Demarest."

"Oh yes, me too. Only I saw the compulsion a little ahead of the others."

Wolfe shrugged. "Anyway, you're here." His eyes swept the arc. "I believe that Mr. Goodwin has explained to you that, guided by inclination and temperament and compelled by circumstances, my field of investigation in a case like this is severely limited. Fingerprints, documentation, minute and exhaustive inquiry, having people followed around—those are not for me. If this murderer can be identified and exposed by such activities as a thorough examination of all entrances and exits of people at that building last evening, which is possible but by no means assured, the police will do the job. They're fairly good at it. I haven't the patience. But I think we might start by clearing up one point: how you spent your time last evening from eight o'clock to midnight. I take it you have told the police, so I hope you will have no objection to telling me in my capacity as Miss Nieder's servant."

Wolfe's eyes fastened on Demarest. "Will you begin, sir?"

The lawyer was smiling. "If your man had asked that question this afternoon it might have simplified matters. I didn't mention it because I saw Miss Nieder wanted us here."

"It's been mentioned now."

"And now I'll simplify it. You want it all, of course. Yesterday afternoon there was a showing of the Daumery and Nieder fall line to buyers. You know about that, since your man was there. It brought a situation to a climax. For two years now—it began even before Paul Nieder's death—Mr. Roper here has been getting increasingly jealous of Miss Nieder's talent as a creative designer. The reactions to this new line have made it evident that she is vastly superior to him—entirely out of his class. What happened at the buyers' show yesterday enraged him. He wanted to quit. Daumery and Nieder still need him and can use him; his services are valuable within the limits of his abilities. It was desirable to calm him down. Mr. Daumery thought it proper to inform me of the matter and ask my help, since I legally represent a half-share in the firm. Last evening, Tuesday, Mr. Daumery, Miss Zarella, and Mr. Roper dined with me in a restaurant and then we all went to Mr. Daumery's apartment to continue our discussion. Mr. Roper wanted a new contract. My wife was with us. We were together continuously, all five of us, from half-past seven to well after midnight."

Demarest smiled. "It does simplify things, doesn't it?"

It simplified me all right. The best my head could do was let in a wild idea about the four of them taking turns with the window pole, presumably with Mrs. Demarest along to keep count of the jabs. That little speech by that lawyer was one of the few things that made me let my mouth hang open in public.

"It does indeed," Wolfe agreed without a quiver. His eyes moved. "You verify that, Mr. Daumery? All of it as told?"

"I do," Bernard said.

"Do you, Miss Zarella?"

"Oh, yes!"

"Do you, Mr. Roper?"

"I do not," Roper declared, his grease oozing bitterness. "To say that Miss Nieder is vastly my superior is absolutely absurd. I have in my possession three books of clippings from *Women's Wear Daily, Vogue, Harper's Bazaar, Glamour—*"

"No doubt," Wolfe conceded. "We'll allow your exception to that part. Do you verify Mr. Demarest's account of what happened last evening?"

"No. There wasn't the slightest necessity of 'calming me down,' as he put it. I merely wanted—"

"Confound it, were you four people together, with Mrs. Demarest, from seven-thirty till after midnight?"

"Yes, we were."

Wolfe grunted. In a moment he grunted again and turned to me.

"Archie. Miss Nieder's glass is empty. So is Mr. Demarest's. See to it, please."

He leaned back, shut his eyes, and began making little circles on the arm of his chair with the tip of his forefinger. He was flummoxed good, his nose pushed right in level with his face.

I performed as host. Since Demarest's requirement was another Tom Collins it took a little time, but Polly Zarella took none at all since she had shown herself capable of pouring the Tokay herself. Apparently the statement about Cynthia's superiority, out loud for people to hear, had made Roper thirsty, for this time he accepted my offer and chose B & B. In between, glances at Wolfe showed that he was working, and working hard, for his lips were pushing out and then pulling in, out and in, out and in. . . .

I finished the replenishing and resumed my seat.

Wolfe half opened his eyes.

"So," he said conversationally, as if he were merely starting a new paragraph with the continuity intact, "naturally the police are specially interested in Miss Nieder, since she alone, of those who have keys, is vulnerable. By the way, Mr. Daumery, how did it happen that Miss Nieder wasn't invited to that conference? Isn't she a half-owner?"

"I represented her interest," Demarest stated.

"But before long she'll probably be representing herself. Shouldn't she be consulted on important matters?"

Bernard spoke. "Damn it, isn't it obvious? If she had been there we couldn't have handled Roper at all. He can't bear the sight of her."

"I deny—" Roper began, but Wolfe cut him off.

"Even so, isn't it true that Miss Nieder has been deliberately and consistently ignored in the management of the business?"

"Yes," Polly said, nodding emphatically.

The three men said no simultaneously, and all were going on to elaborate, but again Wolfe took it away.

"This will finish sooner if you let me dominate it. I am not implying that Miss Nieder is unappreciated. You all admit her designing talent, all but Mr. Roper, and just this afternoon one of you was quick and eager to resent an aspersion on her. I mean, Mr. Daumery, your assaulting Mr. Roper only because he hinted that Miss Nieder might have killed a man. Your business needs him, and surely you were risking losing him. You leaped hotheaded to Miss Nieder's defense. It isn't easy to reconcile that with your reluctance to come here this evening at her request."

"I wasn't reluctant. I had to think it over, that's all."

"You often have to think things over, don't you?"

Bernard resented it. "What's it to you if I do?"

"It's a great deal to me," Wolfe declared. "I have engaged to prevent Miss Nieder's arrest for murder, and I suspect that your habit of thinking things over is going to show me how to do it, and I intend to learn if I'm right."

His gaze shifted. "Mr. Demarest. How long have you known Mr. Daumery?"

"Six years. Ever since he graduated from college and started to work in his uncle's business."

"You've known him intimately?"

"Yes and no. I was an intimate friend of Paul Nieder, the partner of Bernard's uncle."

"Please give me a considered answer to this: has he always had to think things over? Have you noticed any change in him in that respect, at any time?"

Demarest smiled. "I don't have to consider it. He was always a very decisive young man, even aggressive, until he became the active head of the business after his uncle's death some six weeks ago. But that was only natural, wasn't it? A man of his age suddenly taking on so great a responsibility?"

"Perhaps. Miss Zarella, do you agree with what Mr. Demarest has said?"

"Oh, yes!" Polly was emphatic as usual. "Bernard has been so different!"

"And do you, Miss Nieder?"

Cynthia was frowning. "Well, I suppose people might have got that impression—"

"Nonsense," Wolfe bit her off. "You're hedging. Mr. Daumery was ardent in resenting a suspicion that you had committed a murder, but you don't have to reciprocate for him. His alibi is impregnable. Was there a change in Mr. Daumery, as stated, about six weeks ago?"

"Yes, there was, but Mr. Demarest has explained why."

"He thinks he has. Now we're getting somewhere." Wolfe's eyes darted at Bernard. "Mr. Daumery, I wish to ask you some questions as Miss Nieder's agent. They may strike you as irrelevant or even impertinent, but if they are not actually offensive will you answer them?"

Bernard had the look of a man who suspects that someone is sneaking up behind him but for reasons of his own doesn't want to turn and see. "I probably will," he said. "What are the questions?"

"Thank you," Wolfe said graciously. "Are your parents alive?"

"Yes."

"Where are they?"

"In Los Angeles. My father is a professor in the university there."

"Is either of them conversant with your business affairs?"

"Not especially. In a vague general way."

"Have you brothers or sisters?"

"Two younger sisters. In college."

"Have you any other relatives that you see or correspond with frequently?"

Bernard looked at Cynthia. "Do you want me to go on with this autobiography?"

"She has no opinion in the matter," Wolfe said curtly, "because she doesn't know what I'm after. You may or may not have guessed. But can you object that my questions are offensive?"

"No, they're only silly."

"Then humor me—or humor Miss Nieder through me. Any other relatives that you see or correspond with frequently?"

"None whatever."

"I'm about through. I won't name any names, because the only ones I know are already eliminated. For help in making important decisions, manifestly it is not Mr. Demarest you turn to, since he has had to rationalize the change he has noticed in you. Nor Miss Zarella nor Mr. Roper, since their attitude toward Mr. Goodwin's invitation to come here this evening had no effect on yours. I'll have to put it in general terms: is there a banker, or lawyer, or friend, or any other person or persons, on whose judgment you frequently rely for guidance in your business? Anyone at all?"

"No special person. I discuss things with people, naturally—including Mr. Demarest—"

"Ha! Not Mr. Demarest. He has noticed a change in you. This is your last chance, Mr. Daumery, to drag somebody in."

"I don't have to drag anybody in. I'm of sound mind and body and over twenty-one."

"I know you are, and of a decisive and aggressive temperament, and that's why I'm making progress." Wolfe wiggled a finger at him. "One last question. Yesterday Miss Nieder suggested, frivolously I thought, that you might find counsel in the stars or a crystal ball. Do you?"

Bernard croaked at Cynthia, "Where the hell did you get that idea?"

"I said she was being frivolous," Wolfe told him. "Do you? Or tea leaves or a fortune-teller?"

"No!"

Wolfe nodded. "That's all, Mr. Daumery. Thank you again. That satisfies me."

He took them all in. "You have a right to know, I think, who it was that was killed in the Daumery and Nieder office last evening. It was Mr. Paul Nieder, the former partner in the business."

XI

EVERYBODY stared at him. If I had had a pin handy I would have tried dropping it.

"What did you say?" Demarest demanded.

"By my mother's milk," Polly Zarella cried, springing to her feet, "it was! It was Paul! When they made me look at him I saw he had Paul's hands, Paul's wonderful artist hands, only I knew it couldn't be!" At Wolfe's desk, glaring at him ferociously, she drummed on the desk with her fists. "How?" she demanded. "Tell me how!"

I had to get up and help out or she might have climbed over the desk and drummed on Wolfe's belly, which would have stopped the party. The others were reacting too, but not as spectacularly as Polly. My firmness in getting her back in her chair had a quieting effect on them too, and Wolfe's words could come through.

"You'll want to know all about it, of course, and eventually you will, but right now I have a job to do. Since, as I say, Mr. Nieder was killed last night, it follows that he didn't kill himself over a year ago. He only pretended to. A week ago today Miss Nieder saw him in your showroom, disguised with a beard and glasses and slick parted hair. She recognized him, but he departed before she could speak to him. When she entered that office last evening the body was there on the floor, and she confirmed the identification by recognizing scars on his leg. Further particulars must wait. The point is that this time he was killed indeed, and I think I know who killed him."

His eyes went straight at Bernard.

"Where is he, Mr. Daumery?"

Bernard was not himself. He was trying hard to be but couldn't make it. He was meeting Wolfe's hard gaze with a fascinated stare, as if he were entering the last stage of being hypnotized.

"Where is he?" Wolfe insisted.

The best Bernard could do was a "Who?" that didn't sound like him at all.

Wolfe slowly shook his head. "I'm not putting anything on," he said dryly. "When Mr. Goodwin told me what happened this afternoon this possibility occurred to me, along with many others, but up to half an hour ago, when I got my head battered in by being told that you four people spent last evening together, I had no idea of where my target was. Then, after a little consideration, I decided to explore, and now I know. Your face tells me. Don't reproach yourself. The attack was unexpected and swift and everything was against you."

Wolfe extended a hand with the palm up. "Even if I didn't know, but still only guessed, that would be enough. I would merely give it to the police as a suspicion deserving inquiry, and with their trained noses and their ten thousand men how long do you think it would take them to find him? Another fact that may weigh with you: he is a murderer. Even so, you are a free agent in every respect but one; you will not be permitted to leave this room until either you have told me where he is or I have given the police time to start on his trail and cover my door."

Demarest chuckled. "Unlawful restraint with witnesses," he commented.

Wolfe ignored it and gave the screw another turn on Bernard. "Where is he, Mr. Daumery? You can't take time to think it over, to consult him on this one. Where is he?"

"This is awful," Bernard said hoarsely. "This is an awful thing."

"He can't do this!" came suddenly from the red leather chair. Cynthia's concentrated gaze at Bernard was full of a kind and degree of sympathy that I had hoped never to see her spend on a rival. "He can't threaten you and keep you here! It's unlawful!" Her head jerked to Wolfe and she snapped at him, "You stop it now!"

"It's too late, my dear child," Demarest told her. "You hired him—and I must admit you're getting your money's worth." His head turned. "You'd better tell him, Bernard. It may be hard, but the other way's harder."

"Where is he, Mr. Daumery?" Wolfe repeated.

Bernard's chin lifted a little. "If you're right," he said, still hoarse, "and God knows I hope you're not, it's up to him. The address is Eight-sixteen East Ninetieth Street. I want to phone him."

"No," Wolfe said curtly. "You will be unlawfully restrained if you try. What is it, an apartment building?"

"Yes."

"Elevator?"

"Yes."

"What floor?"

"The tenth. Apartment Ten C. I rented it for him."

"Is he there now?"

"Yes. I was to phone him there when I left here. I said I would go to see him, but he said I might be followed and I had better phone from a booth."

"What is the name?"

"Dickson. George Dickson."

"That's his name?"

"Yes."

"Thank you. Satisfactory. Archie."

"Yes, sir?"

"Give Fritz a revolver and send him in. I don't know how some of these minds might work. Then get Mr. Dickson and bring him here. Eight-one-six East—"

"Yeah, I heard it."

"Don't alarm him any more than you have to. Don't tell him we know who got killed last night. I don't want you killed, and I don't want a suicide."

"Don't worry," Demarest volunteered, "about *him* committing suicide. What I'm wondering is how you expect to prove anything about a murder. You've admitted that half an hour ago you didn't even know he existed. He's tough and he's anything but a fool."

I was at a drawer of my desk, getting out two guns and loading them— one for Fritz and one for me. So I was still there to hear Ward Roper's contribution.

"That explains it," Roper said, the bitterness all gone, replaced by a tone of pleased discovery. "If Paul was alive up to last night, he designed those things himself and got them to us through Cynthia! Certainly! That explains it!"

I didn't stay for the slapping, if any.

"There's no hurry," Wolfe told me as I was leaving. "I have things to do before you get back."

XII

For transportation I had my pick of the new Cadillac, the subway, or a taxi. It might not be convenient to have my hands occupied with a steering wheel, and escorting a murderer on a subway without handcuffs is a damn nuisance, so I chose the taxi. The driver of the one I flagged on Tenth Avenue had satisfactory reactions to my license card and my discreet outline of the situation, and I elected him.

Eight-sixteen East Ninetieth Street was neither a dump nor a castle of luxury—just one of the big clean hives. Leaving the taxi waiting at the curb, I entered, walked across the lobby as if I were in my own home, entered the elevator, and mumbled casually, "Ten, please."

The man moved no muscle but his jaw. "Who do you want to see?"

"Dickson."

"I'll have to phone up. What's your name?"

"Tell him it's a message from Mr. Bernard Daumery."

The man moved. I followed him out of the elevator and around a corner to the switchboard, and watched him plug in and flip a switch. In a moment he was speaking into the transmitter, and in another moment he turned to me.

"He says for me to bring the message up."

"Tell him my name is Goodwin and I was told to give it to him personally."

Apparently Dickson didn't have to think things over. At least there was no extended discussion. The man pulled out the plug, told me to come ahead, and led me back to the elevator. He took me to the tenth floor and thumbed me to the left, and I went to the end of the hall, to the door marked 10C. The door was ajar, to a crack big enough to stick a peanut in, and as my finger was aiming for the pushbutton a voice came through.

"You have a message from Mr. Daumery?"

"Yes, sir, for George Dickson."

"I'm Dickson. Hand it through to me."

"I can't. It's verbal."

"Then say it. What is it?"

"I'll have to see you first. You were described to me. Mr. Daumery is in a little trouble."

For a couple of seconds nothing happened, then the door opened wide enough to admit ten bags of peanuts abreast. Since he had certainly had his hoof placed to keep it from opening, I evened up by promptly placing mine to keep it from shutting. The light was nothing wonderful, but good enough to see that he was a husky middle-aged specimen with a wide mouth, dark-colored deepset eyes, and a full share of chin.

"What kind of trouble?" he snapped.

"He'll have to tell you about it," I said apologetically. "I'm just a messenger. All I can tell you is that I was instructed to ask you to come to him."

"Why didn't he phone me?"

"A phone isn't available to him right now."

"Where is he?"

"At Nero Wolfe's office on West Thirty-fifth Street."

"Who else is there?"

"Several people. Mr. Wolfe, of course, and men named Demarest and Roper, and women named Zarella and Nieder—that's all."

The dark eyes had got darker. "I think you're lying. I don't think Mr. Daumery sent for me at all. I think this is a put-up job and you can get out of here and stay out."

"Okay, brother." I kept the foot in place. "Where did I get your name and address, from a mailing list? You knew Mr. Daumery was at Nero Wolfe's, since he phoned you around seven o'clock to ask your advice about going, and he told you who else was invited, so what's wrong with that? Why do you think he can't use a phone, because he don't speak English? Even if it were a put-up job as you say, I don't quite see what you can do except to come along and unput it, unless you'd rather do it here. They've got the impression that your help is badly needed. My understanding was that if I didn't get there with you by eleven o'clock they would all pile into a taxi, including Mr. Daumery, and come here to see you. So if you turn me down all I can do is push on inside and wait with you till they arrive. If you try to bounce me, we'll see. If you call on that skinny elevator pilot for help, we'll still see. If you summon cops, I'll try my hardest to wiggle out of it by explaining the situation to them. That seems to cover it, don't you think? I've got a taxi waiting out front."

From the look in his eye I thought it likely that he was destined to take a poke at me, or even make a dash for some tool, say a window pole, to work with. There was certainly no part of me he liked. But, as Demarest had said, he was anything but a fool. Most men would have needed a good ten minutes alone in a quiet corner to get the right answer to the problem this bird suddenly found himself confronted with. Not Mr. Dickson. It took him a scant thirty seconds, during which he stood with his eyes on me but his brain doing hurdles, high jumps, and fancy dives.

He wheeled and opened a door, got a hat from a shelf and put it on, emerged to the hall as I backed out, pulled the door shut, marched to the elevator, and pushed the button.

By the time we had descended to the sidewalk, climbed into the taxi, been driven to Wolfe's address, mounted the stoop and entered, and proceeded to the office, he had not uttered another word. Neither had I. I am not the kind that shoves in where he isn't wanted.

XIII

WE WERE back again to the headline we had started with: MAN ALIVE. This time, however, I did not regard it as a letdown. I took it for granted that by the time I got back everyone there would know who was coming with me, even if one or two of them hadn't caught on before I left. I thought it would be interesting to see how they would welcome, under those difficult circumstances, their former employer and associate on his return from a watery grave, but he took charge of the script himself as he entered the office. He strode across to face Bernard and glare down at him. Bernard scrambled to his feet.

Dickson asked, his tone cold and biting, "What the hell's the matter with you? Can't you handle anything at all?"

"Not this I can't," Bernard said, and he was by no means whimpering. "This man Wolfe is one for you to handle, and I only hope to God you can!"

Without moving his shoulders, Dickson pivoted his head to take them in. "Well, I'm back," he announced. "I would have been back soon anyway, but this bright nephew of mine has hurried it up a little. Ward, you're looking like a window display in a fire sale. Still putting up with them, Polly? Now you'll have to put up with me again. Cynthia, I hear you're on the way to lead the whole pack." His head pivoted some more. "Where's Henry? I thought he was here."

I was asking that question myself. Neither Wolfe nor Demarest was in sight. I had turned to ask Fritz where they were, but he had left the room as soon as I appeared. And not only were those two missing, but what was fully as surprising, there had been two additions to the party. Inspector Cramer and my favorite sergeant, Purley Stebbins, were seated side by side on the couch over in the far corner.

I dodged my way through the welcomers, some sitting and some standing, and asked Cramer respectfully, "Where's Mr. Wolfe?"

"Somewhere with a lawyer," Cramer growled, "making up charades. Who's that you brought in?"

"George Dickson, so I'm told. I suppose Mr. Wolfe phoned you to come and get a murderer?"

"He did."

"Your face is dirty, Purley."

"Go to hell."

"I was just starting. Excuse me."

I began to dodge my way back to the hall door, thinking that I had better find my employer and inform him that I had delivered as usual, but I was only halfway there when he and Demarest appeared, coming in to us. After one swift glance at the assembly, the lawyer sidled off along the wall to a remote chair over by the bookshelves, evidently not being in a welcoming mood. Wolfe headed for his desk, but in the middle of the room found himself blocked. George Dickson was there, facing him.

"Nero Wolfe?" Dickson put out a hand. "I'm Jean Daumery. This is a real pleasure!"

Wolfe stood motionless. The room was suddenly quiet, painfully quiet, and all eyes were going in one direction, at the two men.

"How do you do, Mr. Daumery," Wolfe said dryly, stepped around him, and walked to his chair. Except for the sound of that movement the quiet held. Jean Daumery let his hand fall, which is about all you can do with a rejected hand unless you want to double it into a fist and use it another way. After solving the hand problem, Jean turned a half-circle to face Wolfe's desk and spoke in a different tone.

"I was told that my nephew sent for me. He didn't. You got me here by a trick. What do you want?"

"Sit down, sir," Wolfe said. "This may take all night."

"Not all of my night. What do you want?"

"Sit down and I'll tell you. I want to present some facts, offer my explanation of them, and get your opinion. There's a chair there beside your nephew."

To a man trying to grab the offensive and hold it, it's a comedown to accept an invitation to be seated. But the alternative, to go on standing in a room full of sitters, is just as awkward, unless you intend to walk out soon, and Jean couldn't know what he intended until he learned what he was up against. He took the chair next to Bernard.

"What facts?" he asked.

"I said," Wolfe told him, "that this may take all night, but that doesn't mean that I want it to. I'll make it as short as possible." He reached to his breast pocket and pulled out folded sheets of paper. "Instead of telling you what this says I'll read it to you." He glanced around. "I suppose you all know, or most of you, that tomorrow will be Miss Nieder's twenty-first birthday."

"Oh, yes!" Polly Zarella said emphatically.

Wolfe glared at her. He couldn't stand emphatic women. "I persuaded Mr. Demarest," he said, "to anticipate the delivery date of this paper by a few hours. It was intended, as you will see, only for Miss Nieder, but, as

Mr. Cramer would tell you if you asked him, evidence in a case of murder has no respect for confidences."

He unfolded the paper. "This," he said, "is a holograph. It is written on two sheets of plain bond paper, and is dated at the top Yellowstone Park, May sixteenth, Nineteen forty-six. It starts, 'My dearest Cynthia,' and goes on:

"I'll send this to Henry, sealed, and tell him not to open it and to give it to you on your twenty-first birthday. That will be June eleventh next year. How I would love to be with you that day! Well, perhaps I will. If I'm not, I think by that time you will know your way around enough to decide for yourself how to look at this. You ought to know about it, but I don't want you to right now."

Wolfe looked up. "This is not paragraphed. Evidently Mr. Nieder didn't believe in paragraphs." He returned to the paper:

"You are going to get the news that I have killed myself and a farewell note from me. I know that will affect you, because we are fond of each other in spite of all our differences, but it won't break your heart. I'm not going to kill myself. I hope and expect to be with you again and with the work I love. I'm writing this to explain what I'm doing. I think you know that I loved Helen. You didn't like her, and that's one thing I have against you, because she gave me the only warm happiness I have ever known outside of my work. She understood what I—but I don't want to make this too long. I only want you to know what happened. Jean found out about us and killed her. Just how he did it I don't know, but out alone with her on the horses it would have been easy for a man like him, with his will power and cleverness. He intended to kill me too, and he still intends to, and as you know, Jean always does everything he intends to do. That's why I wouldn't leave the apartment those three days and nights, and that's why I came away. I don't suppose I am very brave, at least not physically brave, and of course you know that Jean has always overwhelmed me. I was in complete terror of him after he killed Helen, and I still am. He will not forget and he will never leave anything undone. I'm surprised that he hasn't followed me out here, and perhaps he has, but he loves his part of that business nearly as much as I love mine, and the fall line is being assembled, and I think he'll wait until I get back. I tore myself away only to save my life. Only I'm not coming back, not now. When he gets the news he'll think I'm dead. I can't stay away forever, I know that. I'll see what happens. He might die himself. People do die. But I'm trying to study what I know of his character. I know him pretty well. I think it is possible that if he thinks of me as dead for a long time, perhaps two or three years or even only one year, and then I suddenly return to join him in that business again and do for it what no one else can do, his mind may work in such a way that he will not feel he has to carry out his intention of killing me. That's one of the possibilities. Anyhow I'll see what happens. I know I can't stay away forever. It may be that somehow I'll be back with you and my work before your twenty-first birthday comes, and if so I'll get this from Henry and you will never see it. But I'll send it to him because if I never do get back I want you to know the truth of this. I'm going to tell you in my farewell note that I am depending on you to keep that business at the top because you have a fine talent, a very fine talent that I'm proud of, and that will be the only part of my farewell note that will not be a fake. I mean every word of that. I am very fond of you and proud of you. Your Uncle Paul."

Wolfe folded the sheets and returned them to his pocket, and looked up. "It is a capital U in Uncle," he announced.

Polly Zarella and Cynthia both had tears in their eyes.

Polly jumped to her feet, brushing the tears away without bothering about a handkerchief, and faced Jean Daumery with her eyes blazing. "I quit!" she shrieked. "I give you two weeks' notice before people! You said I'll have to put up with you but I won't! There will be a new business, Zarella and Nieder, and Cynthia and I will show you! You and Ward Roper to compete with us? Phut!"

Her spitting at him seemed to be unintentional, merely coming out with the phut.

"Confound it, madam, sit down," Wolfe grumbled.

Polly darted to Cynthia and was apparently going to begin arrangements for the new partnership then and there, but the sound of Jean Daumery's voice sidetracked her.

"I see," Jean said calmly. He had tightened up. "You got me down here to accuse me of murdering my wife, with that hysterical letter from Paul Nieder to back it up. This is absolutely fantastic!"

Wolfe nodded. "It would be," he agreed, "so that's not what I'm doing. I don't waste time on fantasy. I read that letter only for background. To get down to our real business: when and where did you last see Mr. Nieder?"

Jean shook his head. "From fantasy to fact? *Our* business? When and where I did this or that is certainly my business, but not yours. You were going to tell *me* facts."

"You won't answer that?"

"Certainly not, why should I? I don't owe you any answers to anything."

"You're entirely correct," Wolfe conceded, "but not very intelligent. I suppose you know that those two gentlemen on the couch are Police Inspector Cramer and Sergeant Stebbins. Their presence does not mean that I asked that question with the voice of authority, but surely it makes it obvious that if you don't answer me you will be given an opportunity to answer them. Suit yourself. I'll try again. When and where did you last see Mr. Paul Nieder?"

Once more Jean proved himself capable of a swift and sensible decision. "I don't know the exact date," he said, "but it was early in May last year, at our place of business, just before he left for a vacation."

"Aha," Wolfe murmured in a pleased tone, "that's more like it. Now, Mr. Daumery, here are a few of the facts I promised. Mr. Nieder did not kill himself a year ago May; you heard that letter I read. He was seen, alive, here in New York, last week, by his niece, disguised with a beard, slick hair parted on the left side, and glasses. He was seen again this morning, by many people, only this time he was dead. The manner of his death—"

"So that's what you had!" Inspector Cramer was no longer on the couch but right among us—or at least among Wolfe, at his desk, barking at him. "By God, this time you've asked for it!"

"Pfui," Wolfe said peevishly. "I've got Mr. Daumery here for you, haven't I? Do you want to take it over now? Are you ready to? Or shall I give him some more facts?"

Cramer's eyes left Wolfe for a look around. When they hit Cynthia they must have had a message for her, for she left her seat and walked to one over near Demarest. Cramer went and sat in the red leather chair, which put him in the center of things with a full-face view of Jean Daumery. Purley Stebbins had moved too, quietly pulling up a chair to Jean's rear about arm's length off.

"Let's hear your facts," Cramer growled.

Wolfe's gaze was back at Jean. "I was about to say," he resumed, "that the manner of that man's death—no one but his niece knew it was Mr. Nieder—made it necessary to call in the police. They did what they were supposed to do, and naturally they concentrated on the most important point: who was he? As you see, Mr. Daumery, Mr. Cramer resents not being told by the only people who knew—Miss Nieder, Mr. Goodwin, and me—but that's really foolish of him. For if he had known who the dead man was he would probably, and reasonably, have focused on the most likely culprit, Miss Nieder, who was known to have been on the spot and who had the excellent motive of wanting to keep her inheritance of a half-share in the business. As it stood, it was vital for the police to identify the corpse. I don't know, Mr. Daumery, whether you are aware of the stupendous resources of the New York police in attacking a problem like that. You may be sure that they employed all of them in trying to trace that man with a beard and slick hair parted on the left side and glasses. That's one of the facts I ask you to consider. Is it likely that they failed entirely? Is it likely that they found no one, anywhere, who had seen such a man? I am anxious to be quite fair with you. Is it not likely, for instance, that if the bearded man had been seen recently, on the street or in some other public place, talking with another man—say a man whose description tallies well with yours—that the police have learned of it and can produce a witness or witnesses to identify the second man?"

Wolfe raised a finger, and suddenly bent it to aim straight at Jean. "I am fairly warning you. It is nothing against you that you told me you last saw Paul Nieder over a year ago. Nobody likes to be involved in disagreeable matters. But now be careful. If, after what I have just said, you persist in lying, you can't blame us if we surmise—look at his face, Mr. Cramer! Do you see his face?"

Wolfe let the silence work, and the pairs of eyes all fixed on Jean's face, with his finger still nailing the target, for a full five seconds, and then suddenly snapped, like the snap of a whip.

"When and where did you last see Paul Nieder, Mr. Daumery?"

It was devilish. No man could have stood up under it completely whole. What was Jean going to do about his face? What was he going to say?

He said nothing.

Wolfe leaned back and let his eyes open to more than slits. "It offers," he said like a lecturer, "a remarkable field for speculation. What, for instance, made you suspect that his suicide was a fake? Possibly you were as well acquainted with his character as he was with yours, and you knew it was extremely improbable that he could jump into a geyser with no clothes on. Indeed, there are few men who could. In any case, he was right about you; you did not forget or abandon your intention. It would have been dangerous to hire someone to find him, and if you undertook it yourself it might have taken years. You decided to coax him out. You went to Florida on a fishing trip with your nephew, and you arranged with him to stage a drowning for you. Another speculation: how much did you tell him? Did you have to let him in—"

"No!"

It was Bernard. He was out of his chair, but not to confront his uncle or to bear down on Wolfe. He had turned to where Cynthia's new position had put her in his rear, and his explosion was for her.

"Get this straight, Cynthia!" he told her. "I'm not trying any scuttle or any sneak, and whatever he has done that's up to him with no pushes from me, but this is my part and you've got to have it straight!" He wheeled to his uncle. "You told me that someone had it in for you and your life was in danger. You said nothing about Paul Nieder, and of course I thought he was dead. You said that your supposed death would force this person to take certain steps and that the situation would soon be changed so that you could reappear. For all I know, that's how it really was. I don't know." He turned back to Cynthia. "I don't know anything, except that I'm damned if I'm going to have you listen to insinuations that I'm mixed up in this."

"Shut up and sit down," his uncle told him.

Bernard wheeled again. Wolfe nodded at him. "Thank you, sir, for relieving us of that speculation. There are plenty left." He looked at Jean. "For example, at that encounter with your disguised former partner, wherever it was and however it came about, did you two arrange to meet Tuesday evening at your place of business to discuss matters and reach an understanding? It must have been an interesting meeting, with him thinking you dead and you supposedly thinking him dead. Did you persuade him that you hadn't killed your wife? And why didn't you kill him somewhere else? Was it bravado, to leave him there, with his mutilated face, on the floor of his own office, or were you afraid to postpone it even for an hour, for fear he would disclose himself to Miss Nieder or Mr. Demarest, and so increase your risk? And why on earth did you jab that thing at him more than a dozen times? Were you hysterical? Surely you didn't think it necessary to prevent his being identified, with everyone thinking him dead long ago."

"It was a wolf tearing a carcass into pieces," Polly Zarella declared emphatically.

"Perhaps." Wolfe's shoulders went up a quarter of an inch and down again. "You can have him, Mr. Cramer. I'm through with him."

Cramer was scowling. "I could use some more facts."

"Bah." Wolfe resented it. "What more do you want? You saw his face; you are seeing it now, with all the time he's had to arrange it. I phoned you that he would be here for you, and there he is. I've done my part and you can do yours. He got into that building last night and out again, and was not invisible. That's really all you need."

Cramer arose. Purley Stebbins was already up.

"One thing I need," said Cramer, stepping to the desk, "is that letter Nieder wrote." He extended a hand. "There in your breast pocket."

Wolfe shook his head. "I'll keep that—or rather, I'll destroy it. It's mine."

"Like hell it is!"

"Certainly it is. It's in my handwriting. I wrote it while Archie was going for him—with Mr. Demarest's help. You won't need it. Just take him out of here and get to work."

XIV

FOR my own satisfaction I have got to add that that was one time Wolfe outsmarted himself. Not far from the top of the list of the things he abhors is being a witness at a trial, and ordinarily he takes good care to handle things so that he won't get a subpoena. But only last week I had the pleasure of sitting in the courtroom and watching him—and listening to him—in the witness chair. The District Attorney wasn't any too sure of his case, and on this one Wolfe couldn't shake him loose. It was a good thing for Cynthia that Wolfe didn't know that would happen at the time we sent her a bill, or she might have had to hock her half of the business to pay it. Wolfe got sore about it all over again just yesterday morning, when the paper informed him that the jury had stayed out only two hours and forty minutes before bringing in a first-degree verdict. That proved, he claimed, that his testimony hadn't been needed.

The owners of Daumery and Nieder tell me that not only will I be welcome at any of their shows, front row seat, but also that any number I want to pick will be sent with their compliments to any name and address I choose. I thought Cynthia understood me better than that. Women just don't give a damn. I suppose in a month or so she'll be lightheartedly sending me an invitation to the wedding.

OMIT FLOWERS

I

IN MY opinion it was one of Nero Wolfe's neatest jobs, and he never got a nickel for it.

He might or might not have taken it on merely as a favor to his old friend Marko Vukcic, who was one of the only three people who called him by his first name, but there were other factors. Rusterman's Restaurant was the one place besides home where Wolfe really enjoyed eating, and Marko owned it and ran it, and he put the bee on Wolfe in one of the small private rooms at Rusterman's as the cheese cart was being wheeled in to us at the end of a specially designed dinner. Furthermore, the man in trouble had at one time been a cook.

"I admit," Marko said, reaching to give me another hunk of Cremona Gorgonzola, "that he forfeited all claim to professional respect many years ago. But in my youth I worked under him at Mondor's in Paris, and at the age of thirty he was the best sauce man in France. He had genius, and he had a generous heart. I owe him much. I would choke on this cheese if I sat on my hands while he gets convicted of a murder he did not commit." Marko gestured with the long thin knife. "But who am I? A Boniface. Whereas you are a great detective, and my friend. I appeal to you to save him." Marko pointed the knife at me. "And, naturally, to Archie—also, I hope, my friend."

I nodded with much feeling, having his food and wine all through me. "Absolutely," I agreed, "but don't waste any butter on me. All I do is carry things."

"Ha," Marko said skeptically. "I know how deep you go, my friend. As for the money that will be required, I shall of course furnish it."

Wolfe grunted, drawing our eyes to him. His big face, which never looked big on account of the great expanse of the rest of him, was cheerful and a little flushed, as always after a good meal, but the annoyance that had brought forth the grunt showed in his eyes. They were on our host.

"Pfui." He grunted again. "Is this right, Marko? No. If you want to hire me and pay me, I do business in my office, not at your table. If you want to draw on friendship, why mention money? Do you owe this man—what's his name?"

"Pompa. Virgil Pompa."

"Do you owe him enough to warrant a draft on my affection?"

"Yes." Marko was slightly annoyed too. "Damn it, didn't I say so?"

"Then I have no choice. Come to my office tomorrow at eleven and tell me about it."

"That won't do," Marko declared. "He's in jail, charged with murder. I had a devil of a time getting to him this afternoon, with a lawyer. Danger is breathing down his neck and he's nearly dead of fear. He is sixty-eight years old."

"Good heavens." Wolfe sighed. "Confound it, there were things I wanted to talk about. And what if he killed that man? From the newspaper accounts it seems credible. Why are you so sure he didn't?"

"Because I saw him and heard him this afternoon. Virgil Pompa could conceivably kill a man, of course. And having killed, he certainly would have sense enough to lie to policemen and lawyers. But he could not look me in the eye and say what he said the way he said it. I know him well." Marko crossed his chest with the knife as if it had been a sword. "I swear to you, Nero, he did not kill. Is that enough?"

"Yes." Wolfe pushed his plate. "Give me some more cheese and tell me about it."

"Le Bondon?"

"All five, please. I haven't decided yet which to favor."

II

AT HALF-PAST eight the following morning, Wednesday, Wolfe was so furious he got some coffee in his windpipe. This was up in his bedroom, where he always eats breakfast on a tray brought by Fritz. Who got him sore was a butler—at least, the male voice on the phone was a butler's if I ever heard one. First the voice asked him to spell his name, and then, after keeping him waiting too long, told him that Mrs. Whitten did not care to speak with any newspapermen. After that double insult I was surprised he even remembered there was coffee left in his cup, and it was only natural he should swallow the wrong way.

Also we were up a stump, since if we were going to make a start at honoring Marko's draft on Wolfe's affection we certainly would have to get in touch with Mrs. Whitten or some member of the family.

It was strictly a family affair, as we had got it from the newspapers and from Marko's account of what Virgil Pompa had told him. Six months ago Mrs. Floyd Whitten had been not Mrs. Whitten but Mrs. H. R. Landy, a widow, and sole owner of AMBROSIA. You have certainly seen an AMBROSIA unless you're a hermit, and have probably eaten in one or more. The only ones I have ever patronized are AMBROSIA 19, on Grand Central Parkway near Forest Hills, Long Island; AMBROSIA 26, on Route 7 south of Danbury; and AMBROSIA 47, on Route 202 at Flemington, New Jersey. Altogether, in twelve states, either ninety-four thousand people or ninety-four million, I forget which, eat at an AMBROSIA every day.

H. R. Landy created it and built it up to AMBROSIA 109, died of overwork, and left everything to his wife. He also left her two sons and two daughters. Jerome, thirty-three, was a partner in a New York real estate firm. Mortimer, thirty-one, sort of fiddled around with radio packages and show business, and only the Internal Revenue Bureau, if anyone, knew how he was making out. Eve, twenty-seven, was Mrs. Daniel Bahr, having married the newspaper columnist whose output appeared in three times as many states as AMBROSIA had got to. Phoebe, twenty-four, had graduated from Vassar and then pitched in to help mama run AMBROSIA.

But most of the running of AMBROSIA had been up to Virgil Pompa, after Landy's death. Years ago Landy had coaxed him away from high cuisine by talking money, thereby causing him, as Marko had put it, to forfeit all claim to professional respect. But he had gained other kinds of respect and had got to be Landy's trusted field captain and second in command. When Landy died Pompa had almost automatically taken over, but it had soon begun to get a little difficult. The widow had started to get ideas, one especially, that son Mortimer should take the wheel. However, that experiment had lasted only two months, coming to an abrupt end when Mortimer had bought eight carloads of black-market lamb which proved to have worms or something. Then for a while the widow had merely been irritating, and Pompa had decided to carry on until his seventieth birthday. It became even easier for him when Mrs. Landy married a man named Floyd Whitten, for she took her new husband on a three months' trip in South America, and when they returned to New York she was so interested in him that she went to the AMBROSIA headquarters in the Empire State Building only one or two mornings a week. Phoebe, the younger daughter, had been on the job, but had been inclined to listen to reason—that is, to Pompa.

Suddenly, a month ago, Mrs. Whitten had told Pompa that he was old enough to retire, and that they would start immediately to train her husband to take over the direction of the business.

This dope on Floyd Whitten is partly from the papers, but mostly from Pompa via Marko. For a year before Landy's death Whitten had been in charge of public relations for AMBROSIA, and had kept on after Landy died, but when he married the boss, and came back from the long trip with his bride, he didn't resume at the office. Either he wanted to spend his time with her, or she wanted to spend hers with him, or both. Whitten (this from Pompa) was a smoothie who knew how to work his tongue. He was too selfish and conceited to get married, though he had long enjoyed intimate relations with a Miss Julie Alving, a woman about his age who earned her living by buying toys for Meadows' department store. It appeared that the facts about Whitten which had outraged Pompa most were, first, he had married a woman a dozen years his senior, second, he had coolly and completely discarded Julie Alving when he married his boss, and third, he had kept extra shirts in his office at AMBROSIA so he could change every day after lunch. It was acknowledged and established that any draft by Whitten on Pompa's affection would have been returned with the notation *Insufficient Funds*.

So the situation had stood the evening of Monday, July fifth—twenty-four hours before Marko had appealed to Wolfe to save Pompa from a murder conviction. That Monday had of course been a holiday, but Mrs. Whitten, proceeding with characteristic slapdash energy to get her husband trained for top man in AMBROSIA, had arranged a meeting for eight-thirty that evening at her house in the East Seventies between Fifth and Madison. She and Whitten would drive in from their country place near Katonah, which had been named AMBROSIA 1000 by the late Mr. Landy, though the public was neither admitted nor fed there, and Pompa would join them for a training session.

Pompa had done so, arriving at the Landy (then nominally Whitten) town house in a taxi precisely at half-past eight, and having with him a large leather case full of knives, forks, and spoons, but mostly knives. One of the tabloids had had a grand time with that prop, presenting the statistics that the case had contained a total of 126 knives, with blades all the way from 1½ inches in length to 28 inches, and speculating on the probability of any man being so thorough and comprehensive in providing himself with a murder weapon. The reason for Pompa's toting the leather case was silly but simple. Mrs. Whitten, having decided that her husband was to be It in AMBROSIA, had made a list of over a hundred items to be embraced in his training, and they had reached Item 43, which was Buying of Cutlery.

Pompa pushed the bell button several times without result. That didn't surprise him, since he knew that the servants were at AMBROSIA 1000 for the summer, and there was no telling how much the heavy holiday traffic might delay Mr. and Mrs. Whitten, driving in from the country. He had waited on the stoop only a few minutes when they drove up, in a long low special body job with Whitten at the wheel, parked at the curb, and joined him. Whitten used a key on the door and they entered.

The house, which Pompa knew well, had four stories. The first floor had a reception hall, a large living room to the right, and a dining room in the rear. The stairs were at the left of the reception hall. The trio had mounted directly to the second floor, where the front room had been used by H. R. Landy as an office-at-home and was now similarly used by Mrs. Whitten. They got down to business at once, and Pompa opened the leather case and took knives out. Whitten graciously pretended to be interested, though his real attitude was that it was foolish to waste time on Item 43, since cutlery buying was a minor detail which should be left to a subordinate. But Mrs. Whitten was quite serious about it, and therefore they stuck for nearly an hour to the contents of the leather case before Whitten managed to get onto the subject he was really hot about: unit managers.

There were four managers whom Whitten wanted to fire immediately, and one that he wanted to transfer to headquarters in New York. Within five minutes he had got sarcastic and personal, and Pompa was yelling at the top of his voice. Pompa, according to Marko, had always been a yeller and always would be. When Mrs. Whitten, intervening, lined up on her husband's side, it was too much. Pompa yelled that he was done, finished, and through for good, and tramped out and down the stairs. Mrs. Whitten came after him, caught him in the reception hall, and pulled him into the living room. She appealed to him, but he stood pat. She made him sit down, and practically sat on him, and insisted. She was keenly aware, she said, that no one, not even her Floyd, was capable of directing successfully the complex and far-flung AMBROSIA enterprise without long and thorough preparation. Her attempt to put her son Mortimer in charge had taught her a lesson. One more year was all she asked of Pompa. She knew he owed no loyalty to her, and certainly not to Floyd, but what about the dead H. R. Landy and AMBROSIA itself? Would he desert the magnificent structure he had helped to build? As for the immediate point at issue, she would promise that Floyd should have no authority regarding unit managers for at least six months. Pompa, weakening, stated that Floyd was not even to mention managers. Mrs. Whitten agreed, kissed Pompa on the cheek, took his hand, and led him out of the room and across the reception hall to the stairs. They had been in the living room with the door closed, by Pompa's best guess, about half an hour.

As they started to mount the stairs they heard a noise, a crash of something falling, from the dining room.

Mrs. Whitten said something like "My God." Pompa strode to the door to the dining room and threw it open. It was dark in there, but there was enough light from the hall, through the door he had opened, to see that there were people. He stepped to the wall switch and flipped it. By then Mrs. Whitten was in the doorway, and they both stood and gaped. There were indeed people, five of them, now all on their feet: the two Landy sons, Jerome and Mortimer; the two Landy daughters, Eve and Phoebe;

and the son-in-law, Eve's husband, Daniel Bahr. As for the noise that had betrayed them, there was an overturned floor lamp.

Pompa, having supposed that these sons and daughters of AMBROSIA wealth were miles away on Independence Day weekends, continued to gape. So, for a moment, did Mrs. Whitten. Then, in a voice shaking either with anger or something else, she asked Pompa to go and wait for her in the living room. He left, closing the dining-room door behind him, and stood outside and listened.

The voices he heard were mostly those of Jerome, Eve, Daniel Bahr, and Mrs. Whitten. It was Bahr, the son-in-law—the only one, according to Pompa, not in awe of Mother—who told her what the conclave was for. They had gathered thus secretly and urgently to consider and discuss the matter of Floyd Whitten. Did the intention to train him to become the operating head of AMBROSIA mean that he would get control, and eventually ownership, of the source of the family fortune? If so, could anything be done, and what? He, Bahr, had come because Eve asked him to. For his part, he was glad that Mr. and Mrs. Whitten had unexpectedly arrived on the scene, and that an accidental noise had betrayed their presence; they had been sitting in scared silence, as darkness came, for nearly two hours, afraid even to sneak away because of the upstairs windows overlooking the street, talking only in low whispers, which was preposterous conduct for civilized adults. The way to handle such matters was open discussion, not furtive scheming. The thing to do now was to get Whitten down there with them and talk it out—or fight it out, if it had to be a fight.

The others talked some too, but Bahr, the professional word user, had more to use. Pompa had been surprised at Mrs. Whitten. He had supposed she would start slashing and mow them down, reminding them that AMBROSIA belonged exclusively to her, a fact she frequently found occasion to refer to, but apparently the shock of finding them there in privy powwow, ganging up on her Floyd, had cramped her style. She had not exactly wailed, but had come close to it, and had reproached them bitterly for ever dreaming that she could forget or ignore their right to a proper share in the proceeds of their father's work. For that a couple of them apologized. Finally Bahr took over again, insisting that they should bring Whitten down and reach a complete understanding. There were murmurs of agreement with him, and when Mrs. Whitten seemed about to vote yes too, Pompa decided it was time for him to move. He walked out the front door and went home.

That was all we had from Pompa. He wasn't there when Mrs. Whitten and her son Jerome and Daniel Bahr went upstairs together to get Whitten, and found him hunched over on the table with a knife in him from the back. It was one of the pointed slicing knives, with an eight-inch blade.

III

WEDNESDAY morning, as I said, in Wolfe's bedroom, when he started to save old Virgil Pompa by getting Mrs. Whitten on the phone before he finished breakfast, instead of getting Mrs. Whitten he got coffee in his windpipe. He coughed explosively, gasped, and went on coughing.

"You shouldn't try to drink when you're mad," I told him. "Peristalsis is closely connected with the emotions. Anyhow, I think it was only a butler. Naturally she has brought the hired help in from the country. Do you care whether a butler has heard of you? I don't."

With the panic finally out of his windpipe, Wolfe took off his yellow silk pajama top, revealing enough hide to make shoes for four platoons, tossed it on the bed, and frowned at me.

"I have to see those people. Preferably all of them, but certainly Mrs. Whitten. Apparently they squirm if she grunts. Find out about her."

So that was what I spent the day at.

The Homicide Bureau was of course a good bet, and, deciding a phone call would be too casual, I did a few morning chores in the office and then went to 20th Street. Inspector Cramer wasn't available, but I got to Sergeant Purley Stebbins. I was handicapped because my one good piece of bait couldn't be used. It was a fair guess that Mrs. Whitten and the Landy children had given the cops a distorted view of the reason for the secret gathering in the dining room and the two-hour silent sit in the dark—possibly even a fancy lie. If so, it would have helped to be able to give Purley the lowdown on it, but I couldn't. Pompa, when first questioned by the city employees, had stated that when Mrs. Whitten had asked him to go to the living room and wait there for her, he had done so, and had left when he got tired of waiting. The damn fool hadn't wanted to admit he had eavesdropped, and now he was stuck with it. If he tried to change it, or if Wolfe and I tried to change it for him, it would merely make his eye blacker than ever and no one would believe him.

Therefore the best I could do with Purley was to tell him Wolfe had been hired to spring Pompa, and of course that went over big. He was so sure they had Pompa for good that after a couple of supercilious snorts he got bighearted and conversed a little. It seemed that the secret meeting of scions in the dining room had been to discuss a scrape Mortimer had got into—a threatened paternity suit—which mamma mustn't know about. So for me they were a bunch of barefaced liars, since Wolfe had decided to take Pompa for gospel. Purley had lots of fun kidding me, sure as he was that for once Wolfe had got roped in for a sour one. I took it, and also took all I could get on Mrs. Whitten and other details. The Homicide and DA line was that while waiting for Mrs. Whitten in the living room Pompa had got bored and, instead of just killing time, had trotted upstairs and killed Whitten, who was about to toss him out of his job.

Altogether I saw eight or nine people that day, building up an inventory on Mrs. Whitten and her offspring, and bought a drink for nobody, since there was no client's expense account. They were a couple of radio men, a realtor who had once paid Wolfe a fee, a gossip peddler, and others, naturally including my friend Lon Cohen of the *Gazette*. During the afternoon Lon was tied up on some hot item, and I got to him so late that I made it back to West 35th Street barely in time for dinner. Marko Vukcic was there when I arrived.

After a meal fully as good as the one Marko had fed us the evening before, the three of us went across the hall to the office. Wolfe got himself arranged in the chair behind his desk, the only chair on earth he really loves; Marko sat on the red leather one; and I stood and had a good stretch.

"Television?" Wolfe inquired politely.

"In the name of God," Marko protested. "Pompa will die soon, perhaps tonight."

"What of?"

"Fear, rage, mortification. He is old."

"Nonsense. He will live to get his eye back, if for nothing else." Wolfe shook his head. "As you said yesterday, Marko, you're a Boniface, not a detective. Don't crack a whip at me. What have you got, Archie?"

"No news." I pulled my chair away from my desk and sat. "Are we still swallowing Pompa whole?"

"Yes."

"Then they're all lying about what they were there for, except Daniel Bahr, Eve's husband, who merely says it was a family matter which he prefers not to discuss. They say they met to consider a jam Mortimer is in with a female by the name of—"

"No matter. Mrs. Whitten?"

"She's in on the lie, of course. Probably she clucked them into it. During Landy's life he was absolutely the rooster, and she merely came along with the flock, but when he died she took command and kept it. She is of the flock, by the flock, and for the flock, or at least she was until Whitten got his hooks in. Since her marriage she has unquestionably been for Whitten, though there has been no sign that she intended to swear off clucking—at least there wasn't until a month ago, when she installed Whitten in the big corner office that had been Landy's. Pompa never moved into it. She is fifty-four, fairly bright, watches her figure, and looks as healthy as she is."

"Have you seen her?"

"How could I? She wouldn't even talk to you on the phone."

"The son, Mortimer. Is he really in a scrape? Does he urgently need money?"

"Sure, I suppose so, like lots of other people, but this girl trouble is apparently nothing desperate, only enough of a mess so they could drag it in. About people urgently needing money, who knows? Maybe they all do. Jerome owns part of a real estate business, but he's a big spender. Mortimer could owe a million. Eve and her husband might be betting on horse races, if you want to be trite. Phoebe may want to finance a big deal in narcotics, though that would be pretty precocious at twenty-four. There are plenty—"

"Archie. Quit talking. Report."

I did so. It filled an hour and went on into the second, my display of all the little scraps I had collected, while Wolfe leaned back with his eyes closed and Marko obviously got more and more irritated. When the question period was finished too Marko exploded.

"Sacred Father above! If I prepared a meal like this my patrons would all starve to death! Pompa will die not of fear but of old age!"

Wolfe made allowances. "My friend," he said patiently, "when you are preparing a meal the cutlet or loin does not use all possible resource, cunning, resolution, and malice to evade your grasp. But a murderer does. Assuming that Mr. Pompa is innocent, as I do on your assurance, manifestly one of those six people is behind a shield that cannot be removed by a finger's flick. They may even be in concert, if one of them went upstairs and dealt with Mr. Whitten while Mrs. Whitten and Mr. Pompa were in the living room. But before I can move I must start." Wolfe looked at the clock on the wall, which said ten past ten, and then at me. "Archie."

"Yes, sir."

"Get them down here. As many of them as possible."

"Yeah. During the week?"

"Tonight. Now."

I gawked at him. "You don't mean it."

"The devil I don't." He was positively serious. "You probably can't do it, but you can try. Confound it, look at Marko! At least you can bring the younger daughter. A woman that age likes to be with you no matter where you go, heaven knows why."

"It's my glass eye and wooden leg." I stood up. "This is Wednesday. Hold your breath until Saturday." I crossed to the door, and asked over my shoulder, "Have you any suggestions?"

"None. The circumstances may offer one."

IV

SINCE there would be no parking problem in the East Seventies at that hour, I decided to take my own wheels and went around the corner to the garage for the car.

On the way uptown I went over it. I was quite aware that Wolfe didn't really expect me to deliver, not even Phoebe. He merely wanted to get Marko off his neck, and sending me out to pass a miracle was his first and most natural notion, and also the least trouble for him. He knew it would make me sore, so the first thing I decided was not to be sore. When, stopping for a light on Fifth Avenue in the Forties, I caught myself muttering, "The fat lazy bum," I saw that wasn't working very good and took a fresh hold.

I parked a few yards west of the house I wanted to get into, on the same side of the street, just back of a dark gray sedan with an MD plate alongside the license. Sitting there with my eyes on the house entrance, which was the sort of granite portal to be expected in that upper-bracket neighborhood, I tried going over it again. I could get the door to open just by pushing the bell button. I could get inside by the momentum of 180 pounds. There were even simple stratagems that would probably get me to Mrs. Whitten. But what about from there on? With the house right there in front of me I got ambitious. It would be nice to make a delivery that Wolfe didn't expect. The notion of playing it straight, saying that we had been engaged by Pompa and would like to have a conversation with the family, had been rejected before I had got to 42nd Street. I had other notions, some risky, some screwy, and some clever, but nothing that seemed to fit all the requirements. When I looked at my wrist watch and saw 10:40 I decided I had better settle for one and shoot it, did so, and climbed out to the sidewalk. As I swung the car door shut, I saw a man emerging from the entrance I was bound for. The light wasn't very bright there, but there was plenty to see that it wasn't either of the sons or the son-in-law. He was past middle age, and he was carrying the kind of black case that means doctor anywhere. He crossed the sidewalk to the gray sedan with an MD plate on it, got in, and rolled away. Naturally, with my training and habits, I automatically noted the license number and filed it.

I walked to the portal, entered the vestibule, and pushed the button. In a moment the door opened enough to show me a baldheaded guy in conventional black, with a big pointed nose, and to show me to him.

"My name is Archie Goodwin," I informed him, "and I would like to see Mrs. Whitten."

He said authoritatively, "No newspapermen are being admitted," and started to close the door. My foot stopped it after a couple of inches.

"You have newspapermen on the brain," I told him courteously but firmly. "I happen to be a detective." I got my card case from my pocket. "Like this." I pulled my license card, with photograph and thumbprint, from under the cellophane and handed it to him, and he inspected it.

"This does not indicate," he asserted, "that you are a member of the police force."

"I didn't say I was. I merely—"

"What's the trouble, Borly?" a voice came from behind him. He turned, and the pressure of my foot made the door swing in more. Since an open door is universally regarded as an invitation to enter, I crossed the threshold.

"There's no trouble, Mr. Landy," I said cheerfully. "The butler was just doing his duty." As I spoke two other men came in sight from a door to the right, which made it four to one. I was going on. "My name's Goodwin, and I work for Nero Wolfe, and I want to see Mrs. Whitten."

"The hell you do. On out." With a gesture he indicated the door he wished me to use. "I said out!"

He took a step toward me. I was mildly confused because I hadn't expected to have to deal with a whole quartet immediately on entering. Of course it was no trick to spot them, from their pictures in the papers and descriptions. The one outing me, which he might possibly have done since he was a little bigger, up to heavyweight specifications, with a big red face having eyes too far apart, was Mortimer. The one with dark hair slicked back, wirier and smaller and smarter looking, was his elder brother Jerome. The middle-sized one, who looked like a washed-out high school teacher, was their brother-in-law, the famous columnist who was more widespread than AMBROSIA, Daniel Bahr.

"You can," I admitted, "put me out, but if you wait half a minute you can still put me out. I have come to see Mrs. Whitten on behalf of Miss Julie Alving. It would be only fair to let Mrs. Whitten herself decide whether she wants to see someone who wishes to speak for Miss Alving. If you—"

"Beat it." He took another step. "You're damn right we can put you out—"

"Take it easy, Mort." Jerome was approaching, in no haste or alarm. He saw the license card in the butler's hand, took it and glanced at it, and handed it to me. "My mother's upstairs asleep. I'm Jerome Landy. Tell me what you want to say for Miss Alving and I'll see that it gets attention."

"She's asleep?"

"Yes."

"Who's sick?"

"Sick?"

"Yeah. Ill."

"I don't know. Not me. Why?"

"I just saw a doctor leave here carrying his case, and of course if he gave her sleeping pills and then stopped for a chat with you, naturally she would be asleep now. It's the way a detective's mind works, that's all." I grinned at him. "Unless she's not the patient. One of your sisters maybe? Anyhow, I have nothing to say for Miss Alving except direct to Mrs. Whitten. I don't know whether she would agree that it's urgent and strictly personal, and there's no way of deciding but to ask her. By tomorrow it might be too late. I don't know about that either."

"Ask him," suggested Daniel Bahr, who had joined us, "whether it's a request for money. If it is an attempt at a shakedown there is only one possible answer."

"If that was it," I said, "our blackmail department would be handling it, and I've been promoted from that. That's as far as I can go except to Mrs. Whitten."

"Wait here," Jerome instructed me, and made for the stairs.

I stood in quiet dignity, but allowed my eyes to move. This, of course, was the reception hall, with the stairs at the left, the door to the living room on the right, and at the far end the door to the dining room, where the secret meeting of sons and daughters had been held. The hall was large and high-ceilinged and not overfurnished, except maybe a pink marble thing against the wall beyond the living-room door. It had a bare look because there was nothing but a couple of straw mats on the floor, but since it was July that was understandable. The only action while Jerome was gone was Mortimer's dismissing the butler, who disappeared through the door to the dining room.

It wasn't too long before Jerome came halfway down the stairs and called to me.

"Up here, Goodwin."

I mounted to join him. On the landing above he turned to face me.

"You'll keep it brief. I'm telling you. Is that understood?"

"Sure."

"My mother's in bed but not asleep. The doctor didn't give her sleeping pills because she doesn't need them. Her heart isn't as good as it might be, and what happened here night before last, and these two days—I tried to persuade her not to see you, but she takes a lot of persuading. You'll make it brief?"

"Sure."

I followed him up to the third floor, which seemed a bad location for a woman with a weak heart, and into a room at the front. Inside I halted. Within range there was not one woman, but three. The one standing over by the bed, dark and small like Jerome, was Eve. The one who had been doing something at a bureau and turned as we entered was Phoebe, the child who, according to my day's collection of scraps, most resembled her father. My quick glance at her gave me the impression that Father could have asked for no nicer compliment. Jerome was pronouncing my name, and I advanced to the bedside. As I did so there were steps to my rear and I swiveled my neck enough to get a glimpse of Mortimer and Daniel Bahr entering. That made it complete—all the six that Wolfe wanted to see!

But not for long. A voice of authority came from the bed.

"You children get out!"

"But mother—"

They all protested. From the way she insisted, not with any vehemence, it was obvious that she took obedience for granted, and she got it, though for a moment I thought Phoebe, who was said to resemble her father, might stick it. But she too went, the last one out, and closed the door after her as instructed.

"Well?" Mrs. Whitten demanded. She took in a long breath, with a long loud sigh. "What about Miss Alving?"

She was lying flat on her back with a thin blue silk coverlet nearly up to her throat, and against the blue pillow her face was so pale that I might not have recognized her from the pictures and descriptions. That made her look older, of course, and then her hair was in no condition for public display. But the snap and fire were in her eyes, as specified, and the firm pointed chin was even exaggerated at that angle.

"What about her?" she repeated impatiently.

"Excuse me," I apologized. "I was wondering if I should bother you after all—right now. You look sick."

"I'm not sick. It's only—my heart." She took a long sighing breath. "What would you expect? What about Miss Alving?"

I could and would have done better if my mind had been on it, but it wasn't. I couldn't even remember which tack I had decided to take, because an interesting idea had not only entered my head but evicted all the previous tenants. But I couldn't just turn on my heel and blow, so I spoke.

"I don't want to be crude, Mrs. Whitten, but you understand that while you have your personal situation and problems, other people have theirs. At least you will grant that the death of Floyd Whitten means more to Miss Alving than it does to people who never knew him, though they're all reading about it and talking about it. The idea was for Nero Wolfe to have a little talk with you regarding certain aspects of the situation which are of special interest to Miss Alving."

"I owe Miss Alving nothing." Mrs. Whitten had raised her head from the pillow, aiming her eyes at me, but now she let it fall back, and again she sighed, taking in all the air she could get. "It is no secret that my husband knew her once, but their—it was ended when he got married. That is no secret either."

"I know that," I agreed. "But I couldn't discuss things even if I knew about them. I'm just a messenger boy. My job was to arrange for Mr. Wolfe to talk with you, and it looks as if I'll have to pass it up for now, since he never leaves his house to see anyone on business, and you can't very well be expected to leave yours if your doctor has put you to bed." I grinned down at her. "That's why I apologized for bothering you. Maybe tomorrow or next day?" I backed away. "I'll phone you, or Mr. Wolfe will."

Her head had come up again. "You're going to tell me," she said in a tone that could not have been called a cluck, "exactly why Miss Alving sent you here to annoy me."

"I can't," I told her from the door. "Because I don't know. And I promised your son I'd make it brief." I turned the knob and pulled. "You'll be hearing from us."

Two daughters and a son were out on the landing. "Okay," I told them cheerfully, got by, and started down. Bahr and Mortimer were in the reception hall, and I nodded as I breezed past, opened the door for myself, and was out.

Since what I wanted was the nearest phone booth, I turned left, toward Madison, and one block down, at the corner, entered a drug store.

Routine would have been to call Wolfe and get his opinion of my interesting idea, but he had sicked me onto them with nothing to go by but his snooty remark that circumstances might offer suggestions, so I went right past him. I could have got what I wanted from 20th Street, but if I got a break and my hunch grew feathers I didn't want the Homicide boys in on it, so the number I dialed was that of the *Gazette* office. Lon Cohen was always there until midnight, so I soon had him.

"I'm looking," I told him, "for a good doctor to pierce my ears for earrings, and I think I've found one. Call me at this number"—I gave it to him—"and tell me who New York license UMX four three three one seven belongs to."

He had me repeat it, which shouldn't have been necessary with a veteran newspaperman. I hung up and did my waiting outside the booth, since the temperature inside was well over a hundred. The phone rang in five minutes, exactly par for that routine item of research, and a voice—not Lon's, for he was a busy man at that time of night—gave me a name and address: Frederick M. Cutler, M.D., with an office on East 65th and a residence on Park Avenue.

It was ten blocks away, so I went for the car and drove it, parked on the avenue a polite distance from the canopy with the number on it, and went in. The lobby was all it should have been in that locality, and the night man took exactly the right attitude toward a complete stranger. On my way I had decided what would be exactly the right attitude for me.

"Dr. Frederick M. Cutler," I said. "Please phone up."

"Name?"

"Tell him a private detective named Goodwin has an important question to ask him about the patient he was visiting forty minutes ago."

I thought that would do. If that got me to him my hunch would already have an attractive fuzz on its bare pink skin. So when, after finishing at the phone, he crossed to the elevator with me and told his colleague I was to be conveyed to 12C, my heart had accelerated a good ten per cent.

At 12C I was admitted by the man I had seen leaving the Whitten house with his black case. Here, with a better view of him, I could note such details as the gray in his hair, his impatient gray-blue eyes, and the sag at the corners of his wide full mouth. Also I could see, through an arch, men and women at a couple of card tables in the large room beyond.

"Come this way, please," my victim said gruffly, and I followed him down a hall and through a door. This was a small room, its walls solid with books, and a couch, a desk, and three chairs, leaving no space at all. He closed the door, confronted me, and was even gruffer.

"What do you want?"

The poor guy had already given me at least half of what I wanted, but of course he would have had to be very nifty on the draw not to.

"My name," I said, "is Archie Goodwin, and I work for Nero Wolfe."

"So that's who you are. What do you want?"

"I was sent to see Mrs. Floyd Whitten, and while I was parking my car in front I saw you leaving her house. Naturally I recognized you, since you are pretty well known." I thought he might as well have a lump of sugar. "I went in and had a little talk with Mrs. Whitten up in her bedroom. Her son said, and she said, that the trouble was her heart. But then how come? There is a widespread opinion that she is in splendid health and always has been. At her age she plays tennis. She walks up two flights to her bedroom. People who know her admire her healthy complexion. But when I saw her, there in bed, she was as pale as a corpse, in fact she was pale *like* a corpse, and she kept taking long sighing breaths. I'm not a doctor, but I happen to know that those two symptoms—that kind of pallor and that kind of breathing—go with a considerable loss of blood, say over a pint. She didn't have a cardiac hemorrhage, did she?"

Cutler's jaw was working. "The condition of my patient is none of your business. But Mrs. Whitten has had an extremely severe shock."

"Yeah, I know she has. But the business I'm in, I have seen quite a few people under the shock of the sudden death of someone they loved, and

I've seen a slew of reactions, and this one is brand new. The pallor possibly, but combined with those long frequent sighs?" I shook my head. "I will not settle for that. Besides, why did you let me come up after the kind of message I sent, if it's just shock? Why did you let me in and herd me back here so private? At this point I think you ought to either toss me out or invite me to sit down."

He did neither. He glared.

"Lookit," I said, perfectly friendly. "Do some supposing. Suppose you were called there and found her with a wound and a lot of blood gone. You did what was needed, and when she asked you to keep it quiet you decided to humor her and ignore your legal obligation to make a report to the authorities in such cases. Ordinarily that would be nothing for a special broadcast; doctors do it every day. But this is far from ordinary. Her husband was murdered, stabbed to death. A man named Pompa has been charged with it, but he's not convicted yet. Suppose one of the five people hid in the dining room killed Whitten? They could have, easily, while Pompa and Mrs. Whitten were in the living room—a whole half-hour. Those five people are in Mrs. Whitten's house with her now, and two of them live there. Suppose the motive for killing Whitten is good for her too, and one of them tried it, and maybe tonight or tomorrow makes another try and this time it works? How would you feel about clamming up on the first try? How would others feel when it came out, as it would?"

"You're crazy," Cutler growled. "They're her sons and daughters!"

"Oh, for God's sake," I growled back at him. "And you a doctor who sees inside people? The parents who have been killed by sons and daughters would fill a hundred cemeteries. I'm not crazy, but I'm good and scared. I guess I scare easier than you. I say that woman has lost blood, and you're not denying it, so one of two things has to happen. Either you give me the lowdown confidentially, and it will have to sound right, or I suggest to the cops that they send a doctor to have a look at her. Then if my supposes all come true I won't have to feel that I helped to kill her. How you will feel is your affair."

"The police have no right to invade a citizen's privacy in that manner."

"You'd be surprised. In a house where a murder was committed, and she was there and so were they?"

"Your suppositions are contrary to the facts."

"Fine. That's what I'm after, the facts. Let me have a look at them. If they appeal to us, Mr. Wolfe and I can ignore obligations as easy as you."

He sat down, rested his elbows on the arms of the chair with his hands dangling, and thoroughly inspected a corner of a rug. I inspected him. He stood up again, said, "I'll be back shortly," and started for the door.

"Hold it," I snapped. "This is your place and I can't keep you from going to another room to phone, but if you do, any facts you furnish will need a lot of checking. It all comes down to which you like better, giving it to me straight or having a police doctor go over your patient."

"I ought to kick you the hell out of here," he said grimly.

I shook my head. "Not now. If you had taken that attitude when that message was phoned up to you I would have had to think again, but now it's too late." I gestured at the desk. "Use that phone, if all you want is to tell Mrs. Whitten that a skunk named Goodwin has got you by the tail and you've got to break your promise to keep it quiet." I took a step and held his eye with mine. "You see, brother, when I said I was scared I meant it. Sons and daughters phooey. If Pompa is innocent, and he is, there's a murderer in that house, and an animal that has killed can kill again, and often does. What is going on there right now? I'd like to know, and I'm getting tired of talking to you. And what's more, something's biting you too or you wouldn't have let me up here."

Cutler went and sat down again, and I sat on the edge of the couch, facing him. I waited.

"It couldn't be," he declared.

"What couldn't be?"

"Something biting me."

"Something bit Mrs. Whitten. Or was it a bite or a bullet or what?"

"It was a cut." His voice was weary and precise, not gruff at all. "Her son Jerome phoned me at a quarter to ten, and I went at once. She was upstairs on the bed and things were bloody. They had towels against her, pressing the wound together. There was a cut on her left side, five inches long and deep enough to expose the eighth rib, and a shallow cut on her left arm above the elbow, two inches long. The cuts had been made with a sharp blade. Twelve sutures were required in the side wound, and four in the arm. The loss of blood had been substantial, but not serious enough to call for more than iron and liver, which I prescribed. That was all. I left."

"How did she get cut?"

"I was proceeding to tell you. She said she had gone in the late afternoon to a conference in her business office, made urgent by the death of her husband and the arrest of Pompa. It had lasted longer than expected. Riding back uptown, she had dismissed her chauffeur, sent him home in a taxi, and had driven herself around the park for a while. Then she drove to her house. As she got out of her car someone seized her from behind, and she thought she was being kidnaped. She gouged with her elbows and kicked, and suddenly her assailant released her and darted away. She crossed the sidewalk to her door, rang, and was admitted by Borly, the butler. Only after she was inside did she learn that she had been stabbed, or cut. The sons and daughters were there, and they phoned me and got her upstairs. They also, directed by her, cleaned up; indoors and out. The butler washed the sidewalk with a hose. He was doing that when I arrived. Mrs. Whitten explained to me that the haste in cleaning up was on account of her desire to have no hullabaloo, as she put it. Under the circumstances the episode would naturally have been greatly—uh, magnified. She asked me to do her the favor of exercising professional discretion, and I saw no sufficient reason to refuse. I shall explain to her that your threat to have a police doctor see her left me no choice."

He turned up his palms. "Those are the facts."

I nodded. "As you got them. Who was it that jumped her?"

"She doesn't know."

"Man or woman?"

"She doesn't know. She was attacked from behind, and it was after dark. When her assailant dashed off, by the time she got straightened and turned he—or she—was the other side of a parked car. Anyway, she was frightened, and her concern was safety."

"She didn't see him before he jumped her? As she drove up?"

"No. He could have been concealed behind the parked car."

"Were there no passers-by?"

"None. No one appeared."

"Did she scream?"

"I didn't ask her." He was getting irritated. "I didn't subject her to an inquisition, you know. She had been hurt and needed attention, and I gave it to her."

"Sure." I stood up. "I won't say much obliged because I squeezed it out. I accept your facts—that is, what you were told—but I ought to warn you that you may get a phone call from Nero Wolfe. I can find my way out."

He stood up. "I think you used the word 'confidential.' May I tell Mrs. Whitten that she need not expect a visit from a police doctor?"

"I'll do my best. I mean it. But if I were you I wouldn't give her any more quick promises. They're apt not to stick."

I reached for the doorknob, but he was ahead of me and opened it. He took me back down the hall and let me out, and even told me good night. The elevator man kept slanted eyes on me, evidently having been told of the vulgar message I had sent up to a tenant, so I told him that his starting lever needed oil, which it did. Outside I climbed in the car and rolled downtown a little faster than I was supposed to. The clock on the dash said ten minutes to midnight.

When I'm not in the house, especially at night, the front door is always chain bolted, so I had to ring for Fritz to let me in. I went along with him to the kitchen, got a glass and a pitcher of milk, took them to the office, and announced, "Home again, and I brought no company. But I've got a tool I think you can pry Pompa loose with, if you want to play it that way. I need some milk on my stomach. My nerves are doubling in brass."

"What is it?" Marko demanded, out of his chair at me. "What did you—"

"Let him alone," Wolfe muttered, "until he has swallowed something. He's hungry."

V

"IF you don't tell the police about this at once, I will," Marko said emphatically. He hit the chair arm with his fist. "This is magnificent! It is a masterpiece of wit!"

I had finished my report, along with the pitcher of milk, and Wolfe had asked questions, such as whether I had seen any bloodstains, inside or out, which the cleaners had overlooked. I hadn't. Wolfe was leaning back in his chair with his eyes closed, and Marko was pacing back and forth. I was smirking, but not visibly.

"They must release him at once!" Marko exclaimed. "Tell them now! Phone! If you don't—"

"Shut up," Wolfe said rudely.

"He's using his brain," I informed Marko, "and you're breaking the rules. Yell at me if you want to, but not at him. It's not as simple as it looks. If we pass it to the cops it's out of our hands, and if they're stubborn and still like the idea of Pompa where are we? We couldn't get through to that bunch again with anything less than a Sherman tank. If we don't tell the cops but keep it for our private use, and we monkey around until whoever used a knife on Mrs. Whitten uses it again only more to the point, the immediate question would be how high the judge would set our bail."

"Including me?" Marko demanded.

"Certainly including you. You especially, because you started the conspiracy to spring Pompa."

Marko stopped pacing to frown at me. "But you make it impossible. We can't tell the police, and we can't not tell the police. Is this what I called a masterpiece?"

"Sure, and you were right. It was so slick that I'm going to ask for a raise. Because there's a loophole, namely we don't have to monkey around. We can keep going the way I started. We've got a club to use on Mrs. Whitten, which means all of them, and if she hadn't just been sliced and had her side sewed up we could phone her that we want her down here within the hour, along with the family. As it is, I guess that's out. The alternative is for Mr. Wolfe and me to get in the car, which is out at the curb, and go there—now."

I ignored a little grunt from Wolfe's direction.

"It has been years," I told Marko, "since I tried to get him to break his rule never to go anywhere outside this house on business, and I wouldn't waste breath on it now. But this has nothing to do with business. You're not a client, and Pompa isn't, and he has told you that he wouldn't take your money. This is for love, a favor to an old friend, which makes it entirely different. No question of rule-breaking is involved."

Marko was gazing at me. "You mean go to Mrs. Whitten's home?"

"Certainly. Why not?"

"Would they let you in?"

"You're damn right they would, if that doctor has phoned her, and it's ten to one he did."

"Would it accomplish anything?"

"The least it would accomplish would be that there wouldn't be a second murder as long as we were there. Beyond that—circumstances might offer suggestions. I might add, not being a candidate for president, that when I went there alone it accomplished a little something."

Marko wheeled to Wolfe with his arms extended. "Nero, you must go! At once! You must!"

Wolfe's eyes came half open, slowly. "Pfui," he said scornfully.

"But it is the only thing! Let me tell you what Archie—"

"I heard him." The open eyes saw an unfinished glass of beer, and he picked it up and drank. He looked at me. "There was a flaw. You assume that if we withhold this information from the police, and Mrs. Whitten gets killed, we'll be in a pickle. Why? Technically it is not murder evidence; it has no necessary connection with a committed crime. Legally we are clear. Morally we are also clear. What if we accept and credit Mrs. Whitten's explanation as she gives it? Then there is no menace to her from the members of her family."

"You mean you buy it?" I demanded. "That she couldn't even tell whether it was a man or a woman?"

"Why not?"

I got up, threw up my hands, and sat down again.

"But this is not logical," Marko protested earnestly. "Your questions indicated that you thought she had lied to the doctor. I don't see why—"

"Nuts," I said in disgust. "He knows damn well she lied. If he liked to bet he would give you odds that it was one of the family that cut her up, either in the house or out, and she knows who it was and so do the rest of them. I know him better than you do, Marko. If he did leave his damn house and ride at night through the dangerous streets, when he got there he would have to work like a dog, put all he's got into it, to nail the one that has it coming. If instead of that he goes to bed and sleeps well, something may happen to simplify matters. That's all there is to it."

"Is that true, Nero?" Marko demanded.

"It contains truth," Wolfe conceded big-heartedly. "So does this. Patently Mrs. Whitten is in danger. Anyone who cuts a five-inch gash in the territory of the eighth rib may be presumed to have maleficent intentions, and probably pertinacity to boot. But though Archie is normally humane, his exasperation does not come from a benevolent passion to prevent further injury to Mrs. Whitten. She is much too old for him to feel that way. It comes from his childish resentment that his coup, which was unquestionably brilliant, will not be immediately followed up as he would like it to be. That is understandable, but I see no reason—"

The doorbell rang. I got up and went for it. I might have left it to Fritz, but I was glad of an excuse to walk out on Wolfe's objectionable remarks. The panel in our entrance door is one-way glass, permitting us to see out but not the outsider to see in, and on my way down the hall I flipped the switch for the stoop light to get a look.

One glance was enough, but I took a step for another one before turning, marching back to the office, and telling Wolfe, "You may remember that you instructed me to get six people down here—as many of them as possible, you said. They're here. Out on the stoop. Shall I tell them you're sleepy?"

"All of them?"

"Yes, sir."

Wolfe threw his head back and laughed. He did that about once a year. When it had tapered off to a chuckle he spoke.

"Marko, will you leave by way of the front room? Through that door. Your presence might embarrass them. Bring them in, Archie."

I went back out, pulled the door wide open, and greeted them.

"Hello there! Come on in."

"You goddam rat," Mortimer snarled at me through his teeth.

VI

THE two sons were supporting their mother, one on either side, and continued to do so along the hall and on into the office. She was wearing a tan summer outfit, dotted with brown, which I would have assumed to be silk if I had not heard tell that in certain shops you can part with three centuries for a little number in rayon. Eve was in white, with yellow buttons, and Phoebe was in what I would call calico, two shades of blue. My impulse to smile at her of course had to be choked.

Thinking it might prevent an outburst, or at least postpone it, I formally pronounced their names for Wolfe and then saw that their chairs were arranged the way he liked it when we had a crowd, so that he wouldn't have to work his neck too much to take them all in. Jerome and Mortimer, declining my offer of the big couch for Mom, got her comfortable in the red leather chair, but it was Phoebe who took the chair next to her. Mortimer stayed on his feet. The others sat.

Wolfe's eyes swept the arc. "You all look mad," he said inoffensively.

"If you think that's witty," Eve snapped.

"Not at all," he assured her. "I was merely acknowledging an atmosphere." His eyes moved to Mrs. Whitten. "Do you want me to talk, madam? You came here, and you might like to tell me why."

"Your lousy punk," Mortimer blurted, "might like to step outside and ask me why!"

"Mortimer!" Mrs. Whitten turned to him. "Sit down."

He hesitated, opened his trap and shut it again, moved, and sat, next to Phoebe. A fine brother she picked.

"You will please remember," Mrs. Whitten told the flock, "that I am to do the talking. I wanted to come alone, but you talked me out of it, and now you will please keep silent. Including you, Dan," she added to the son-in-law. She returned to Wolfe. "I was getting my breath. The exertion was—not too much, but enough." She was still using sighs to get oxygen, and she was even paler than when I had seen her in bed.

"I can wait," Wolfe said placidly. "Would you like some brandy?"

"No, thank you." She breathed long and deep. "I don't take alcohol, even as medicine, though all my children do. Their father permitted it. I apologize for my son calling your associate, Mr. Goodwin, a lousy punk. Do you wish an apology from him?"

"Certainly not. He wouldn't mean it."

"I suppose not. Do you share Mr. Goodwin's opinions?"

"Often. Not always, heaven knows."

"He told Dr. Cutler that Virgil Pompa did not kill my husband, that he is innocent. Do you believe that too?"

"Yes."

"Why?"

Wolfe regarded her. "It seems to me," he suggested, "that you're going a long way round, and it's an hour past midnight, you need rest and quiet, and and I have myself a great many questions to ask—all of you. What you most urgently want to know is whether I intend to tell the police about the assault that was made on you, and if not, what do I intend. That's right, isn't it?"

"It isn't only a matter of intention," Daniel Bahr said like a lecturer. "It may well be asked, by what right do you—"

"Dan, what did I tell you?" came at him from his mother-in-law.

"Hold it, chum," Mortimer growled. "We're just tassels."

"Goodness knows," Mrs. Whitten told Wolfe, "I didn't get up and dress and come down here just to have an argument. My children all love to argue, just like their father, but I don't. About my being assaulted, it was silly for me to ask my doctor not to report it, but I thought I simply couldn't stand more talks with policemen." She took a long breath. "That would have been better than this, but how could I know an extremely intelligent young man was going to come to see me on behalf of Miss Alving? He said he didn't know why she sent him, but that you did. What does she want—money? I don't owe her anything. Then he told my doctor that Virgil Pompa is innocent. Why did he tell my doctor that? Maybe he can prove Pompa is innocent—I don't know, maybe he can. If he can, that police inspector is the man to tell, not my doctor. So I thought there were several things you might tell me about."

"We agreed with her," Jerome said quietly.

"I see." Wolfe pursed his lips. His eyes took them in and settled on Mrs. Whitten. "Three things, apparently. First, Miss Alving. That is a private matter and should be tête-à-tête, so we'll postpone it. Second, the innocence of Mr. Pompa. My reasons for assuming it would convince neither the police nor you, so we won't waste time on them. Third, the assault on you with a knife. We might get somewhere discussing that."

"One thing I didn't tell Dr. Cutler," Mrs. Whitten offered. "I didn't notice it until after he had gone. My bag was stolen. The person who stabbed me must have taken it and run with it."

"Good heavens." Wolfe's eyes widened at her. "You're only making it worse, and it was bad enough already. It was a mistake to say you didn't know whether it was a man or a woman, but this is pure poppycock. A bag snatcher who carries a naked knife and uses it on your torso as he snatches? Bah!"

"She probably dropped it," Eve explained.

"And no one noticed its absence for an hour?" Wolfe shook his head. "No, this makes it worse. I offer an alternative. Either you, all of you, will discuss with me what happened up there Monday evening, and give me responsive answers to questions, or I put a case to Inspector Cramer."

"What case?" Bahr demanded.

"I'll give Mr. Cramer both the facts and my inferences. I'll tell him of Mrs. Whitten's injuries, and why her explanation of them is unacceptable. I'll say that the use of a deadly weapon on her, soon after the fatal use of a similar weapon on her husband, is highly suggestive and demands the fullest inquiry; that if the same person made both attacks, which is at least a permissible conjecture, it could not have been Mr. Pompa, since he is locked up; that if the same person made both attacks it must have been one of you five here present, since only you and Mr. Pompa had an opportunity to kill Mr. Whitten; that—"

"Why, you bastard!" Mortimer blurted.

"Keep quiet, Mort," Phoebe muttered at him.

"—that," Wolfe continued, "this conjecture gets strong support from Mrs. Whitten's untenable explanation of her injuries." Wolfe upturned a palm. "That's the kernel of it." He spoke to Mrs. Whitten. "Why would you make up a story, good or bad? To conceal the identity of your assailant. Why would you want to protect one who had used a deadly weapon on you? Because it was one of these five people, a member of your family. But it must have been one of these five people who, if Mr. Pompa is innocent, killed Mr. Whitten. It fits neatly. It deserves inquiry; I propose to inquire; and if you won't let me, then it will have to be the police."

"This was inherent in the situation," Bahr announced, as if that took the sting out of it.

"You're accusing one of us of murder," Jerome Landy told Wolfe.

"Not one, Mr. Landy. All of you. I'm not prepared yet to particularize."

"That's serious. Very serious."

"It is indeed."

"If you expect us to answer questions we have a right to have a lawyer present."

"No. You have no right at all, except to get up and leave. I am not speaking for the people of the State of New York; I am merely a private detective who has you cornered. There are two ways out, and you are free to choose. But before you do so it is only fair to warn you that I have concealed weapons. I'll show you one. I do not surmise that all of you lied to the police; I know it. You said that your clandestine meeting was for a discussion of a difficulty your brother Mortimer had encountered."

"It was," Jerome asserted.

"No, it wasn't. Mr. Bahr told Mrs. Whitten that you had gathered to consider the problem posed by her new husband. What was indicated for the future by putting him at the head of the family business? Was he to be permitted to take it over and own it? If so, what about the Landy children? Mrs. Whitten, shocked by this concerted onset, did not counterattack as might have been expected. She did not even remind you that the business belonged to her. She reproached you for assuming that she was capable of violating your rights as your father's children. During the talk Mr. Bahr twice suggested that the proper course was to have Mr. Whitten join you, and have it out. The second time he made the suggestion it was approved by all of you, including the one who knew it was futile because Mr. Whitten was dead. So, as I say, you all lied to the police."

"I didn't," Bahr declared. "I only said it was a family matter which I could not discuss."

"You see?" Wolfe snapped at them. "Thank you, Mr. Bahr. That might not be corroboration for a jury, but it is for me. Now." He aimed his eyes at Eve. "I'll start with you, Mrs. Bahr. There's no point in sequestering you, since there has been ample time to arrange for concord. During the time you five were in the dining room Monday evening, who left the room and when?"

VII

BUT Mrs. Whitten delayed the question period another ten minutes by entering a demurrer. She had a point all right, but it seemed foolish for her to press it then. Of course it was obvious that one of two things was true: either Pompa had made a sucker of Marko, or Wolfe had boiled it down to the plain question of how to break through the family interference and get the one with the ball. If Mrs. Whitten saw him coming, as she certainly did, and if she was determined to protect the flock even if one of them had killed her Floyd and taken a whack at her, her best bet was just to sit on it and not budge. But she wanted to do it her way, so she called Wolfe on the detail of lying to the cops.

Her point was that he couldn't possibly have learned anything about what happened Monday evening except from Pompa, and what would he expect from a man under arrest for murder? Jerome also had a point. Even if they had lied about the object of the meeting, which wasn't so, that was no proof, not even an indication, that one of them had killed Whitten. Would any group of people, having found Whitten dead upstairs, have admitted that they had met secretly to find ways and means of keeping him from getting what belonged to them? Though completely innocent, they would be fools so to complicate a simple situation—simple, because Pompa was obviously guilty, not only to them but to the police.

Wolfe let them make their points.

The questions and answers went on for two hours. It seemed to me like an awful waste of time and breath, since no matter what was fact and what was fancy, they were certainly all glued together on it and the glue had had two days to dry. The first interruption in the dining room Monday evening had been when Pompa had rung the doorbell. They hadn't known who it was, and had merely sat tight, supposing the bell ringer would depart. But in a few minutes had come the sound of the front door opening, and through the closed door of the dining room they could recognize voices in the reception hall and hear feet mounting the stairs. From there on they had talked in whispers and more about their immediate predicament than the object of the meeting. There were fierce arguments. Bahr had advocated ascending to the second floor in a body and going to the mat on it, but no one had supported him. Mortimer and Eve had wanted them to sneak out and go to the Bahr apartment, but were voted down on account of the risk of being seen from the upstairs windows. They spent the last hour sitting in the dark, hissing at one another, and Jerome had joined the Mortimer-and-Eve faction, making it a majority, when steps were heard descending the stairs, then, soon, other steps coming down fast, and Mrs. Whitten calling to Pompa. The voices were loud enough for them to hear words. After a door had closed and the voices were gone, a cautious reconnoiter by Phoebe had informed them that Pompa and Mrs. Whitten were in the living room. That had settled the argument about sneaking out, and the next event on the program, some half an hour later, had been the upsetting of a floor lamp by a careless movement in the dark by Bahr.

On the crucial question the glue held everywhere. Who had left the room after Pompa and Mrs. Whitten had entered the living room? Only Phoebe, for reconnaissance, and never for more than half a minute at a time. It didn't leave much elbow room for genius, not even Wolfe's. It was all well enough to remind them that it had been pitch dark, and to keep digging at where this one or that one had been, and what was Bahr doing when he upset the lamp, but if they were unanimous that they knew beyond doubt that no one had left the room except Phoebe for her brief excursions, what were you going to do, even if you knew in your bones that what they were really unanimous on was a resolution not to let one of them get tagged for murder? If what they had to be solid on had been some intricate series of events with a tricky time table, it might have been cracked open, but all they had to do was keep repeating that no one left the room during that half an hour except Phoebe, and that she wasn't out for more than thirty seconds at a time.

It was exactly the same for that evening, Wednesday, as it was for Monday. No fancy getup was required. They simply stated that they had all been in the house together for nearly an hour when the bell had rung and the butler had answered it, and Mrs. Whitten had staggered in with blood all over her. Again there was no place to start a wedge. Jerome, in his quiet subdued manner, offered to help by going to bring the butler, but Wolfe declined without thanks.

Wolfe glanced at the clock on the wall; it was a quarter to three. He tightened his lips and moved his eyes along the arc.

"Well. I am merely flattening my nose, to no purpose. We can't go on all night, ladies and gentlemen. You'd better go home and go to bed." He looked at Mrs. Whitten. "Except you, madam. You will of course sleep here. We have a spare room with a comfortable—"

There were protests in five voices, of various tones and tenors. Mortimer was of course the loudest, with Eve a close second. Wolfe shut his eyes while the storm blew, and then opened them.

"What do you think?" he demanded peevishly. "Am I a dunce? In a murder case it sometimes happens that a detective, stopped at a dead end, simply withdraws to wait upon a further event that may start a new path. That may be allowable, but not when the expected event is another murder. Not for me. A desire or intention to harm Mrs. Whitten may be in none of your minds, but I'm not going to risk it. She would be dead now if that blade had gone five inches in instead of across. I am willing, for the time being, to pursue this inquiry myself without recourse to the police or the District Attorney, but only with that condition: Mrs. Whitten stays under my roof until I am satisfied on certain points. She can leave at any moment if she regards the police as less obnoxious than me."

"If you ask me, they are," Eve snapped.

"This is blackmail and actionable," Bahr declared.

"Okay, she goes home and you call the goddam cops," was Mort's contribution.

"If she stays," Phoebe said firmly, "I stay."

Mrs. Whitten found use for a long deep sigh for about the thousandth time. Twice during the session I had been sure she was going to faint. But there was plenty of life in her eyes as she met Wolfe's gaze. "You said you would speak to me privately about Miss Alving."

"Yes, madam, I did."

"Then you could do that in the morning. I'm afraid I couldn't listen now —I'm pretty tired." Her hands, on her lap, tightened into fists and then relaxed. She turned to her younger daughter. "Phoebe, you'll have to go home and get things for us." She went back to Wolfe. "Your spare room—will it do for two?"

"Admirably. There are twin beds."

"Then my daughter Phoebe will be with me. I don't think you need to fear for my safety—I'm sure she won't kill me in my sleep. Tomorrow afternoon, if I'm still here, you will have to excuse me. My husband's funeral will be at four o'clock."

"Mother," Jerome said quietly, "let me take you home."

She didn't use breath to answer him, but asked Wolfe, "Will I have to walk upstairs?"

"No indeed," Wolfe said, as if that made everything fine and dandy. "You may use my elevator."

VIII

THE fact is we have two spare rooms. Wolfe's room is at the rear of the house on the second floor, which he uses because its windows face south, and there is another bedroom on that floor in front, unoccupied. On the third floor my room is the one at the front, on the street, and there is another spare at the rear which we call the South Room. We put Mrs. Whitten and Phoebe there because it is large, and has better furniture and rugs, its own bathroom, and twin beds. I had told them where I could be found in case of fire.

I heard a noise. That put it up to me to decide whether I was awake or asleep, and I went to work on it. But I didn't feel like working and was going to let it slide when there was another noise.

"Mr. Goodwin."

Recognizing the name, I opened my eyes. An attractive young woman in a blue summer negligee, with hair the color of maple sirup, was standing at the foot of my bed. There was plenty of daylight from the windows to get details.

"I didn't knock," she said, "because I didn't want to disturb anyone."

"You've disturbed me," I asserted, swinging my legs around and sitting on the bed's edge. "What for?"

"I'm hungry."

I looked at my wrist. "My God, it'll be time for breakfast in three hours, and Fritz will bring it up to you. You don't look on the brink of starvation." She didn't. She looked all right.

"I can't sleep and I'm hungry."

"Then eat. The kitchen is on the same—" I stopped, having got enough awake to remember that (a) she was a guest and (b) I was a detective. I slipped my feet into my sandals, arose, told her, "Come on," and headed for the door. Halfway down the first flight I thought of a dressing gown, but it was too hot anyway.

Down in the kitchen I opened the door of the refrigerator and asked her, "Any special longing?"

"No, just food. Bread and meat and milk would be nice."

We got out an assortment: salami, half a Georgia ham, pâté, cheese, cucumber rings, Italian bread, and milk. She volunteered to slice some ham, and was very nifty at it. Now that she had broken my sleep I saw no reason to let her monopolize things, so I joined in. I took the stool and let her have the chair. I had happened to notice before that she had good teeth, and now I also noticed that they knew how to deal with bread and meat. She chewed as if she meant it, but with no offense.

We made conversation. "When I heard my name and opened my eyes and saw you," I told her, "I supposed it was one of two things. Either you had been drawn to my room as a moth to a candle, or you wanted to tell me something. When you said you were hungry it was a comedown. However —" I waved a hand, and on the way back it snared a slice of salami.

"I don't think there's much moth in me," she said. "And you're not so hot as a candle, with your hair like that and in those wrinkled pajamas. But I do want to tell you something. The hunger was just an opening."

"My pajamas always get wrinkled by the middle of the week no matter how careful I am. What's on your mind?"

She finished with a bite of cheese. Then she drank some milk. Then she arranged for her eyes to meet mine.

"We're more apt to do some good if you'll tell *me* something. What makes you think Pompa didn't kill Floyd Whitten?"

That got me wide awake and I hastily shifted things around inside my head. Up to then the emphasis had been on this interesting, informal, early-morning, intimate association with a really pretty specimen, but she had made it quite different. Having never seen H. R. Landy, I didn't know how much she looked like her father, but her manner and tone as she asked that question, and the look in her fine young eyes, had sure come straight from the man who had built up a ten-million-dollar business.

I grinned at her. "That's a swell way to repay me for getting up to feed you. If we have any evidence it's Mr. Wolfe's, not mine, so ask him. If we haven't any you wouldn't be interested."

"I might be. Try me."

"I wouldn't dream of boring you. More milk?"

"Then I'll bore you. I know Pompa pretty well. I have been with him a lot the past two years, working with him—I suppose you know that. He's an awful old tyrant in some ways, and he certainly is pig-headed, but I like him. I don't believe he would have killed Floyd Whitten for the only motive he had, and I know darned well he wouldn't have killed him by stabbing him in the back."

I frowned. "What kind of a dodge is this? You're out of my reach. Have you told that to the cops?"

"Of course not. I haven't told it to you, either, in case they ask me, and anyhow it's just my opinion. But that's what I think, and you see what it means. If Pompa didn't do it then one of us did, and I know we didn't. Or take it the way you're looking at it, that that's a lie, that we're all lying together—even so, there's no way on earth of proving we're lying, so it goes back on Pompa and he'll have to suffer for it. But I've told you what I think about him, and so I wonder if he has told the police all the details, and if they believe him. I would like to help him if I can—I mean it. Has he told about the front door being open?"

"I don't know. What front door, up at your house?"

She nodded. "As we told you, I left the room several times during that half-hour, to make sure Mother and Pompa were still in the living room. And each time, all the time, the front door wasn't closed. It was standing a little open. I supposed that when Mother came down to keep Pompa from going, he had already opened the front door to leave when she stopped him, and they neglected to close it when they went into the living room. That must have been it, because I had looked out there before, before Mother and Pompa came down, and so had Eve and Jerome, and the front door had been closed up to then."

I was letting the tingles inside of me enjoy themselves, and staying dead-pan. "That's very interesting," I granted. "You've told about this, have you?"

"No, I haven't mentioned it. I don't know—I just didn't mention it. It didn't occur to me until this evening, from the questions Mr. Wolfe asked, how important it was. Of course the door being open meant that any time during that half-hour someone could have gone in and upstairs, and killed Floyd, and out again. So I wonder if Pompa has told about it. He must know it, since he must have opened the door himself and not closed it. I thought maybe he had told about it and they hadn't believed him. But they would have to believe him if I said I saw the door open too. Wouldn't they?"

"It would help," I conceded. "And of course it would split it wide open. It would be a beautiful out, not only for Pompa, but for everybody. Two are much better than one, and three would be simply splendid. Do you suppose there's any chance that your mother remembers about the open door too?"

Her eyes left mine, and she covered up fairly well by reaching for the milk bottle and pouring herself a third of a glass. I didn't mark it against her, for she was too young to be expected to meet any and all contingencies.

"I sure was hungry and thirsty," she said, retrieving. "I don't know about Mother. I didn't ask her about it because she was completely all in. But when I tell her I saw it, and she puts her mind on it, I'm practically certain she'll remember about the door being open. She's very observant and she has a good memory. I don't think there's any question about her remembering it. That would clear up everything, wouldn't it?"

"It would at least scatter the clouds all over the sky," I conceded. "What would be even sweeter would be if the first couple of times you ventured forth you noticed the door was open, and the last time you saw it had been closed. That would be really jolly. You probably have a good memory too, so why don't you try it on that?"

But she wasn't having any fancy touches from comparative strangers. Nope, she remembered it quite clearly, the door had been open all the time. Furthermore, she remembered going to close it herself, when her mother and brother and Dan Bahr had gone upstairs to get Floyd Whitten. I didn't think it would be polite to urge her, and while we were cleaning up and putting things back in the refrigerator I told her that it was darned white of her to come out with it like that, and this was a real break for Pompa, and I would give Wolfe the good news just as soon as he was awake. We went back up the two flights together, and in the upper hall I took her offered hand and got a fine firm clasp and a friendly smile. Then I went back to bed and was sound asleep before I knew it.

My eyes opened again without any order from me. Naturally that was irritating, and I wondered why I couldn't sleep. Seeing it was broad daylight, I glanced at my wrist. It was a quarter past nine. I jumped out and leaped for the bathroom, set a record dressing, ran down to the kitchen, and asked Fritz if Wolfe was awake. Yes, he had breakfasted at eight-fifteen as usual and was up in the plant rooms. There had just been word from the South Room, on the house phone, from the guests, and Fritz was getting their trays ready. On account of my snack at dawn I wasn't starving, so I had my orange juice and some toast and coffee, and then went, three steps at a time, up to the roof.

Wolfe was in the intermediate room inspecting some two-year Miltonia roezelis. The brief glance he gave me was as sour as expected, since he hates being interrupted up there.

I apologized without groveling. "I'm sorry I overslept, but it was Phoebe's fault. She has a nerve. She came to my room, and damned if she didn't complain about my wrinkled pajamas."

He dehydrated me with a look. "If true, boorish. If false, inane."

"Just adjectives. She came because she was hungry, and I took her down and fed her. But what she really wanted was to peddle a lie. Would you care to buy a good lie? It's a beaut."

"Describe it."

"She offers to trade an out for Pompa for an out for the dining-room gang. During that crucial half-hour, each time she sallied to the reception hall she noticed that the front door was part way open. Mama will corroborate. But Pompa will have to say that when he started to beat it he got as far as the front door and had opened it when Mom caught up with him, and neither of them closed it before they went into the living room. Which is that, boorish or inane?"

Wolfe finished inspecting a plant, returned it to the bench, and turned to inspect me. He seemed to have a notion there was something wrong with my necktie, as there may well have been since I had set a record.

"What inspired you to use Miss Alving's name to get in to Mrs. Whitten?" he demanded.

"Hell, I had to use something. Knowing how women are apt to feel about their husbands' former sweethearts, I thought that was as good as anything and probably better."

"Was that all?"

"Yep. Why, did I spill salt?"

"No. On the contrary. Do you know where Miss Alving can be found?"

I nodded. "She's the toy buyer at Meadow's. But you certainly have changed the subject. What about that Grade A lie, do we want it at the price? Phoebe will be after me as soon as she gets through breakfast."

"We'll see. That can wait. How do you know it's a lie? Come in the potting room where we can sit down. I have some instructions."

IX

NEVER to find yourself in a situation where you have to enter a big department store is one of the minor reasons for not getting married. I guess it would also be a reason for not being a detective. Anyway, Meadow's is unquestionably a big department store, and that Thursday morning I had to enter it in the practice of my profession. The toy department is on the fourth floor, I suppose to give the kids more fun on the escalators. By the time I got there the sweat on my back was starting to freeze in the conditioned air, and I had to resist an impulse to go up another flight and buy a topcoat.

The salesperson I approached said she thought Miss Alving was busy and would I wait. I found an empty chair over by the scooters. I thought contact with the chair's back might melt the ice on mine, but it was plastic, so I sat straight. After a while a woman came hurrying to me, and I arose.

"Miss Julie Alving?"

"Yes, I'm Miss Alving."

When Marko had told us about Floyd Whitten's former love whom he had ditched when he married the boss, I had made a casual mental comment that there was something droll about a man living in sin with a toy buyer, but one look at Julie Alving showed me that such casual comments can be silly. She was forty and looked it, and she was not an eyestopper in any obvious way, but everything about her, the way she walked, the way she stood, her eyes and mouth and whole face, seemed to be saying, without trying or intending to, that if you had happened to be hers, and she yours, life would be full of pleasant and interesting surprises. It wasn't anything personal, it was just her. I was so impressed, in spite of her age, that I was smiling at her before I knew it.

I spoke. "My name's Archie Goodwin, Miss Alving, and I work for Nero Wolfe. You may have heard of him? The detective?"

"Yes, I've heard of him." Her voice was a little thin.

"He would like to see you. He would appreciate it very much if you can get away for an hour and come to his office with me. He has something to say to you on behalf of Mrs. Floyd Whitten."

I thought for a second she was going to topple. The way her head jerked up and then came down again as all her muscles sagged, it was as if I had landed an uppercut. My hand even started to reach, to be there if the muscles really quit, but she stayed upright.

"Mrs.—Mrs. Whitten?" she stammered.

I nodded. "You used to know her husband. Here, sit down."

She ignored that. "What does she want?"

"I don't know, but Mr. Wolfe does. She came to see him last night and they talked. He said to tell you it's important and urgent, and he has to see you this morning."

"But I—I'm here at work."

"Yeah, I know. I work too and know how it is. I told him you might not be able to make it until after the store closes, but he said that wouldn't do."

"What did Mrs. Whitten talk to him about?"

I shook my head. "You'll have to ask him."

She got her teeth on her lower lip, kept them there a while, said, "Wait here, please," and left me. She passed behind a counter and disappeared through a partition opening. I sat down. When my watch showed me that I had waited twenty-two minutes I began to wonder if I was being imposed on, but no, she returned.

She came to me and said, "I'll leave right away. What's the address?"

I told her we might as well go together, and when she objected that she must go out by the employees' entrance I hurdled that by arranging for us to meet outside. My instructions were to bring her, and I'm great for instructions. My guesses on the role Wolfe was casting her for were nothing but guesses, and they contradicted one another, but if by any chance he had her down for top billing I didn't want to be responsible for her not showing up. So I was really pleased to see her when she reached the meeting place on the sidewalk not more than a minute after I did.

On the way down in the taxi she sat with a tight two-handed grip on her bag, and had no comments or questions. That suited me, since I hadn't the faintest idea what she was heading into and therefore would have been able to make no contribution except grunts.

Since I had been instructed not to tell her that Mrs. Whitten and Phoebe were our house guests, I wouldn't have been surprised to see them both there in the office when I entered with Julie Alving, but Wolfe was alone, in his chair behind his desk, with a newspaper. He put the paper down, got to his feet, and bowed, which was quite a tribute, either to Julie or the part she was supposed to take. I've seen him react to a woman's entrance in that office with nothing but a ferocious scowl. So I participated by giving Miss Alving the red leather chair.

She sat, still clutching her bag, and gazed at him. Wolfe told me to get my notebook and I did so. A man getting a notebook and pen ready sometimes makes quite an effect.

Wolfe returned her gaze. "I suppose Mr. Goodwin told you that I wanted to speak with you about Mrs. Whitten."

She nodded. "Yes, that's what he said—no, he said on behalf of Mrs. Whitten."

Wolfe waved it away with a finger. "He may have used that phrase. He likes it. In any case, I'll come straight to the point. I think I can arrange it so that Mrs. Whitten will not prosecute, if you'll help me."

"Prosecute?" She was only so-so at faking surprise. "Prosecute who?"

"You, Miss Alving. Have you no notion of what charge Mrs. Whitten can lay against you?"

"Certainly not. There isn't any."

"When did you last see her?"

"I never have seen her—that is, I've never met her."

"When did you last see her?"

"I don't know—a long while—months ago. I only saw her two or three times—never to speak to."

"That was months ago?"

"Yes."

"Do you owe her anything?"

"No."

"Does she owe you anything?"

"No."

"Have you ever had anything to do with her—anything at all?"

"No."

"Have you any reason to expect or fear anything from her, good or bad?"

"No."

"Then will you please tell me why, when Mr. Goodwin told you I wanted to speak with you on behalf of Mrs. Whitten, you left your work immediately and came here with him?"

Julie looked at him, and then at me as if it was up to me to answer that one. Seeing that I was no nearer ready with something adequate than she was, she went back to Wolfe.

"Why wouldn't I?" she demanded. "After what has happened, wouldn't I want to know what she wanted?"

Wolfe nodded approvingly. "That was much the best you could do, and you did it. But it's not good enough. If you maintain this attitude, Miss Alving, I'm afraid I'm out of it, and you'll have others to deal with. I would advise you to reconsider. I think you're wrong to assume that they will believe you, and not Mrs. Whitten, when she tells them that you attacked her with a knife and your target was her heart."

"I didn't!" Julie cried. That was only so-so too.

"Nonsense. Of course you did. I can understand your reluctance, since nothing has been published about it, and for all you know Mrs. Whitten may be at the point of death. But she isn't. Your blade didn't get beyond the rib, and twelve stitches were all that was necessary to make her capable of riding here to my office. Except for a little loss of blood she's as good as ever. She hasn't even reported it to the police, not wishing to give the public another mouthful to chew on—a mortal assault on her by the former friend of her murdered husband. So the limit of a charge against you would be assault with intent to kill."

Wolfe waved that aside as if it were a mere peccadillo. "And if you'll be frank with me and answer some questions, I undertake to arrange that Mrs. Whitten will not prosecute. If you had achieved your purpose, if she were dead, that would be different and I wouldn't be so foolish as to expect frankness from you. I wouldn't ask you to confess a murder, Miss Alving."

She was doing her best and I admired her for it. But the trouble was that she had to decide on her line right there facing us, and having to make up your mind with Nero Wolfe's eyes, open an eighth of an inch, on you, is no situation for an amateur.

However, she wasn't made of jelly. "When did this—when and where was Mrs. Whitten attacked?"

"I'll refresh your memory," Wolfe said patiently, "if you want it that way. A quarter to ten last evening, in front of her house, as she got out of her car."

"It wasn't in the papers. I should think a thing like that would be in the papers."

"Only if the papers heard of it, and they didn't. Naturally you searched for it. I've told you why Mrs. Whitten didn't report it."

Julie was still making up her mind. "It seems to me you're expecting a good deal—I mean, even if I did it, and I didn't. If I had, the way it looks to me, I wouldn't know whether you were trying to get me to confess to a murder or not. I wouldn't know whether she were dead, or had just lost some blood as you said. Would I?"

She had him there. He sat and gazed at her a long moment, grunted, and turned to me.

"Archie. Bring that witness down here. Only the one. If the other one is importunate, remind her that I said our talk about Miss Alving must be tête-à-tête."

X

PHOEBE wasn't importunate. When I entered the South Room on the third floor she was talking on the phone, that extension having been plugged in for an outside line, and her mother was sitting in a chair by the window with a newspaper on her lap. She arose at once, with no need for assistance, when I said Wolfe was ready for their private talk, and Phoebe, having finished on the phone, had no comment on that, but she wanted to know what I had for her. I told her she would be hearing from me shortly, or more probably from Wolfe, and escorted Mrs. Whitten to the elevator, which I never used except when I was convoying casualties, and out at the lower hall and into the office.

I kept right at her elbow because I didn't want to miss the expression on Julie Alving's face when she saw her. It was first just plain surprise and then a mixture in which the only ingredient I could positively label was just plain hate. As for Mrs. Whitten, I had only her profile from a corner of my eye, but she stopped dead and went as stiff as a steel beam.

Wolfe spoke. "This is my witness, Miss Alving. I believe you ladies haven't met. Mrs. Whitten, Miss Alving."

Mrs. Whitten moved, and for a second I thought she was turning to march out, but she was merely reaching for a hold on my sleeve. I took her arm and herded her left oblique. Being wounded, she rated the red leather chair, but it seemed inadvisable to ask Julie to move, so I took the witness to a yellow one with arms, not as roomy but just as comfortable. When she was in it I resumed my post at my desk with notebook and pen.

"I'm sorry," Wolfe said, "if it makes a queasy atmosphere, you two here together, but Miss Alving left me no alternative." He focused on Mrs. Whitten. "I was having a little trouble with Miss Alving. I wanted her to talk about certain aspects of the assault she made on you last evening, but she wouldn't have it—and I don't blame her—because she didn't know how badly you were hurt. There was only one way to handle it—let her see for herself."

I had to hand it to him. He not only wasn't taking too big a risk, he was taking none at all, since they weren't on speaking terms.

"How did you find out it was her?" Mrs. Whitten demanded. Her voice was harsh and high-pitched.

"Oh, that was simple. I'll tell you presently. But first we should understand one another. I appreciate your reason for not wanting it bruited, and sympathize with it, but here in private there should be candor. You positively recognized her?"

"Certainly I did."

"Beyond possibility of doubt?"

"Certainly. I saw her face when I got turned and that was when she tore loose and ran. And she spoke to me."

"What did she say?"

"I'm not sure of the words, but it was something like 'I'll kill you too.' That's what I thought it was, but later I thought it must be wrong because I thought Pompa had killed my husband and I didn't realize she could have done it. But now that my daughter remembers about the open door, and I remember it too, I see that must have been it—what she said."

"That's a lie!" Julie blurted, not at Mrs. Whitten, since she wasn't speaking to her, but at Wolfe. She was fully as pale as Mrs. Whitten had been the evening before, but not like a corpse, anything but. She was blurting on. "I didn't say that! I said 'You killed him and I'll kill you!' And I wish I had—oh, I wish I had!"

"You came close to it," Wolfe growled. He let his eyes come halfway open, now that he had them. "I should explain to both of you that I've merely been trying to get started. Please forget each other, as far as possible, and listen to me. If we're going to work this out together you need to know how I got where I am now."

The doorbell rang. Under the circumstances it was up to Fritz, but on the other hand we didn't want any trivial interruptions just then, so I scooted for the hall, closing the office door as I went. One glance through the glass panel showed that my point was well taken. Inspector Cramer was there. He was alone, so I didn't bother with the chain bolt but put my foot where it would keep the door to a six-inch crack. I spoke through the crack to his big broad shoulders and his round, red, but by no means flabby face.

"Good morning. What have I done now?"

"We sent a man," he snapped, "to see Mrs. Whitten about something, and he was told she's here. What's Wolfe up to? I want to see her."

"I never know what he's up to, but I'll go ask him. He'll want to know how it stands. Is there a warrant for her?"

"Hell no. A warrant for what?"

"I merely asked. Kindly withdraw your toe."

I banged the door shut, went to the office, and told Wolfe, "The man about the chair. The one with a gash in it. He learned more or less accidentally that it's here, and that made him curious, and he wants to talk.

He has no signed paper and no idea of getting one. Shall I tell him you're busy?"

I was sure he would say yes, but he didn't. Instead, he decoded it. "Is it Mr. Cramer?"

"Yes, sir." He knew darned well it was, since I had started years ago calling Cramer that.

"He wants to speak with Mrs. Whitten?"

"One of his men did, probably about some trifle, and found out she was here. What he really wants is to see if you're getting up a charade."

"He's barely in time. If he engages to let me proceed without interruption until I've finished, admit him."

"I don't like it. He's got Pompa."

"He won't have him long. We're waiting for you. I want a record of this."

I didn't like it at all, but when Wolfe has broken into a gallop what I like has about the weight of an undersized feather from a chicken's neck.

I returned to the front and opened to a crack again and told the inspector, "Mrs. Whitten is in the office with him, chatting. So is Miss Julie Alving, toy buyer at Meadow's, who was formerly on good terms with the late Whitten. You may have heard of her."

"Yeah, I have. What the hell is he trying to pull?"

"You name it. I'm just the stenographer. You have a choice. Being an inspector, you can go somewhere for lunch and then take in a ball game, or you can give me your sacred word of honor that you'll absolutely keep your mouth shut until and unless Wolfe hands you the torch. If you choose the latter you're welcome, and you can have a chair to sit on. After all, you have no ticket even for standing room, since neither of those females is under a charge."

"I'm a police officer. I'm not going to tie myself—"

"Don't haggle. You know damn well where you stand. I'm needed in there to take notes. Well?"

"I'm coming in."

"Under the terms as I stated?"

"Yes."

"Strictly clam?"

"Yes."

"Okay. Otherwise you'd better bring a bulldozer if you ever want in again." I swung the door open.

Wolfe greeted him curtly and left it to me to introduce him to the ladies. It wasn't surprising that he hadn't met Mrs. Whitten, since his men had settled on Pompa as a cinch after a few hours' investigation and therefore there had been no occasion for their superior officer to annoy the widow. He acknowledged the introductions with stingy nods, gave Wolfe a swift keen glance that would have liked to go on through his hide to the interior, and indicated that he intended to keep his vow by taking a chair well out of it, to the rear and right of Mrs. Whitten.

Wolfe spoke to him. "Let's put it this way, Mr. Cramer. You're here merely as a caller waiting to see me."

"That will do," Cramer growled.

"Good. Then I'll proceed. I was just starting to explain to these ladies the manner and extent of my progress in an investigation I'm on."

"Go ahead."

From there on Wolfe ignored Cramer completely. He looked at Julie and Mrs. Whitten. "What persuaded me," he said conversationally, "of Mr. Pompa's innocence, and who engaged me to prove it, are details of no importance. Neither is it important why, when Mr. Goodwin wanted to contrive an entree to Mrs. Whitten, he hit on the stratagem of saying he wished to speak with her on behalf of Miss Alving."

Julie made a sound.

"Oh, it was a lie," he told her. "We use a great many of them in this business, sometimes calculated with great care, sometimes quite at random. This one was extremely effective. It got Mr. Goodwin admitted to Mrs. Whitten at once, though she was in bed with a gash in her side, having just narrowly escaped from an attempt on her life."

Cramer let out a growl, no doubt involuntary, and stood up. Wolfe ignored him and went on to his female audience.

"That, of course, is news to Mr. Cramer, and there will be more for him, but since he's merely waiting to see me I'll finish with you ladies. The success—"

"You not only lie," Mrs. Whitten said harshly, "you break your promise. You promised that if we answered your questions you wouldn't report the attack on me to the police."

"No," Wolfe said curtly. "I do not break promises. It was implied, not explicit, and it was without term, and assuredly not for eternity. Certainly I could not be expected to keep that information to myself if and when it became necessary evidence for the disclosure of a murderer. It has now become necessary."

"It has?" She wasn't so harsh.

"Yes."

"Then—go on."

He did. "The success of Mr. Goodwin's device for getting to Mrs. Whitten was highly suggestive. True, her husband had been intimate with Miss Alving at one time, but he had discarded her before his marriage. Then why should the name of Miss Alving get quick entry to Mrs. Whitten at such a moment? There had to be a good reason, but I could only guess. Among my guesses was the possibility that the assault on Mrs. Whitten had been made by Miss Alving, but that's all it was at the time, one of a string of guesses. However, when Mr. Goodwin reported that detail to me we already had a good deal more. He had, in a keen and rapid stroke, discovered why Mrs. Whitten had been put to bed by a doctor, and, on account of her determination not to let it be known, had provided us with a powerful instrument to use on her. It was indeed powerful. It got her out of bed after midnight and brought her down here to see me, accompanied by her family."

"When, last night?" Cramer demanded.

Wolfe glared at him. "Sir, you are committed. Later you'll get all you want. Now I'm working."

"Who told you he discarded me?" Julie asked. I thought her voice sounded much like Mrs. Whitten's, and then I realized that it wasn't the voices that were similar, it was the emotions. It was hate.

"The source was Mr. Pompa," Wolfe told her. "If the word was unfortunate and offends you, I am sorry. It may not fit the occasion at all. To go on. Last evening, looking at those people and hearing them, I concluded that none of them was capable of trying to kill their mother. I couldn't exclude the possibility, but I could tentatively reject it, and I did. But that brought Miss Alving in again. Mrs. Whitten claimed that not only could she not identify her assailant, she didn't even know whether it was a man or a woman. That was absurd. It was of course intrinsically improbable, but it was made absurd by the question, if she had no idea who the attacker was why was she going to such lengths to keep the incident from disclosure? Even leaving her bed to come to see me in the dead of night? Therefore she knew who had attacked her, and desperately wanted no one else to know. I excluded her children, as I have said, whom she might have shielded through love or pride, and I knew of no one else in that category. But not only love rides with pride; hate also does. There was Miss Alving again."

Wolfe shook his head. "Miss Alving was still only a guess, though now a much more likely one. It was worth having a try at her. The device Mr. Goodwin had used on Mrs. Whitten got an encore. He went to see Miss Alving and told her that I wished to speak with her on behalf of Mrs. Whitten. It worked beautifully. For a department buyer in a great department store to leave her post in the middle of the morning on her private affairs is by no means routine or casual, but Miss Alving did that. She came here at once with Mr. Goodwin. My guess was now good enough to put to the test, and Miss Alving's reaction removed all doubt, though she did her best. Mr. Goodwin brought Mrs. Whitten down, and that made the situation impossible for both of you. You have both admitted that the attack on Mrs. Whitten was made by Miss Alving. That is true, Miss Alving?"

"Yes." Julie tried to swallow. "I wish I had killed her."

"A very silly wish. It is true, Mrs. Whitten?"

"Yes." Mrs. Whitten's expression was not a wishing one. "I didn't want it to be known because I knew—I knew my husband wouldn't. I hadn't thought of the open door, and so I didn't realize that she had killed him. She had waited for six long months, waited and hoped, hoping to get him back." Mrs. Whitten's eyes left Wolfe, and they were hot with hate and accusation as they fixed on Julie. "But you couldn't! He was mine, and you couldn't have him! So you killed him!"

"That's a lie," Julie said, deadly quiet and low. "It's a lie and you know it. I did have him. He was mine all the time, and you knew it. You found it out."

Wolfe pounced. "What's that?" he snapped. "She found it out?"

"Yes."

"Look at me, Miss Alving. Let her go. Look at me. You are in no danger; there was no open door. When did she find it out?"

Julie's head had slowly turned to face him. "A month ago."

"How do you know?"

"He wrote me that he didn't dare to come—where we met—because she had learned about it. He was afraid, terribly afraid of her. I knew he was a coward. Don't ever fall in love with a coward."

"I'll guard against it. Have you got the letter?"

She nodded. The pallor was gone and her face was flushed, but her voice was quiet and dull. "I have all of them. He wrote eleven letters in that month, but I never saw him again. He kept saying he would come soon, and he would as soon as he could, but he was a coward."

"Did he tell you how she learned about it?"

"Yes, it was in the first letter."

"And when he died, and you knew she had killed him, you thought you would avenge him yourself, was that it?"

"Yes. What else could I do?"

"You might—but no matter. You loved him?"

"I do love him."

"Did he love you?"

"Yes—oh, yes!"

"Better than he loved his wife?"

"He hated her. He despised her. He laughed at her."

Mrs. Whitten made a choking noise and was out of her chair. But I, rather expecting a little something, was on my feet too, and in front of her. She started to stretch a hand to me and then sat down again. Thinking it remotely possible that she had a cutlery sample in her bag, I stood by.

Wolfe spoke to her. "I should tell you, madam, that I've had you in mind from the first. When you discovered your family secretly gathered in the dining room you were not yourself. Instead of upbraiding and bullying them, which would have been in character, you appealed to them. What better explanation could there be of that reversal in form than that you knew your husband was upstairs dead, you having killed him with one swift stab in the back as you passed behind him, leaving to go down after Mr. Pompa? Your shrewd and careful plan to have it laid to Pompa was badly disarranged by the awful discovery that your sons and daughters were there too; no wonder you were upset. Your plan was not only shrewd and careful, but long and deep, for when, a month ago, you learned of your husband's infidelity, what did you do? Drive him out with a blast of fury and contempt? No. Understand him and forgive him and try to win him all for you? No. You displayed the blooming and ripening of your affection and trust for him by announcing that he was to be put in control of the family business. That made it certain, you thought, that when you chose your moment and he died, you would be above suspicion. And indeed you were, but you had bad luck. It was ruthless, but wise, to arrange for the police to have a victim at hand, but you had the misfortune to select for that role a man who was once a good cook—indeed, a great one."

Wolfe jerked his head up. "Mr. Cramer, you are no longer committed. I don't know how you handle a case like this. You have a man in jail charged with murder, but the murderer is here. How do you proceed?"

"I need things," Cramer rasped. He was flabbergasted and trying not to show it. "I need those letters. What's that about an open door? I need—"

"You'll get all of it. I mean what happens immediately? What about Mrs. Whitten?"

"That's no problem. There are two men in my car out front. If her wound didn't keep her from riding down here last night it won't keep her from riding downtown now."

"Good." Wolfe turned to Julie. "I was under an obligation to you. I told you that I thought I could arrange it so that Mrs. Whitten would not prosecute, if you would help me. You have unquestionably helped me. You have done your part. Do you agree that I have done mine?"

I don't think she heard a word of it. She was looking at him but not seeing him. "There was a notice in yesterday's paper," she said, "that his funeral would be today at four o'clock, and it said omit flowers. Omit flowers!" She seemed to be trying to smile, and suddenly her head dropped into her hands and she shook with sobs.

XI

I stood facing the door of the South Room, in the hall on the third floor, with my hand raised. Wolfe, positively refusing to do it himself, had left it to me. I knocked. A voice told me to come in, and I entered.

Phoebe tossed a magazine onto the table and left the chair. "You certainly took long enough. Where's Mother?"

"That's what I came to tell you."

Her face changed and she took a step and demanded, "Where is she?"

"Don't push. First I apologize. When you pulled that gag about the front door being open I thought you knew that one of you in the dining room had killed Whitten, and possibly even you had been involved in it, and you thought maybe Mr. Wolfe was getting warm and you wanted to fix an out. Now I know how it was. You couldn't believe Pompa had done it, and you knew none of you had, so it was your mother. So it was her you wanted the out for. Therefore it seems to me I should apologize, and I do."

"I don't want your apology. Where is my mother?"

"She is either at Police Headquarters or the District Attorney's office, depending on where they took her. I don't know. She is, or soon will be, charged with murder. Mr. Wolfe did most of it of course, but I had a hand in it. For that I don't apologize. You know damn well she's a malicious and dangerous woman—look at her framing Pompa—and while I appreciate the fact that she's your mother, she is not mine. So much for her. You are another matter. What do you want me to do? Anything?"

"No."

She hadn't batted an eyelash, nor turned pale, nor let a lip quiver, but the expression of her eyes was plenty.

"What I mean," I told her, "I got you down here, and you're here alone now, and I would like to do anything at all that will help. Phone somebody, drive you somewhere, get a taxi, send your things to you later—"

"No."

"Okay. Fritz will let you out downstairs. I'll be in the office typing, in case."

That was the last chat I had with her for a long time, until day before yesterday, a month after her mother was sentenced by Judge Wilkinson. Day before yesterday, Tuesday afternoon, she phoned to say she had changed her mind about accepting my apology, and would I care to drive her up to Connecticut and eat dinner with her at AMBROSIA 26? Even if I hadn't had another date I would have passed. An AMBROSIA may be perfectly okay as a source of income, but with the crowd and the noise it is no place to make any progress in human relations.

DOOR TO DEATH

I

NERO WOLFE took a long stretching step to clear a puddle of water at the edge of the graveled driveway, barely reached the grass of the lawn with his left foot, slipped, teetered, pawed wildly at the air, and got his sixth of a ton of flesh and bone balanced again without having actually sprawled.

"Just like Ray Bolger," I said admiringly.

He scowled at me savagely, which made me feel at home though we were far from home. More than an hour of that raw and wet December morning had been spent by me driving up to northern Westchester, with him in the rear seat on account of his silly theory that when the inevitable crash comes he'll lose less blood and have fewer bones broken, and there we were at our destination in the environs of the village of Katonah, trespassers on the estate of one Joseph G. Pitcairn. I say trespassers because, instead of wheeling up to the front of the big old stone mansion and crossing the terrace to the door like gentlemen, I had, under orders, branched off onto the service drive, circled to the rear of the house, and stopped the car at the gravel's edge in the neighborhood of the garage. The reason for that maneuver was that, far from being there to see Mr. Pitcairn, we were there to steal something from him.

"That was a fine recovery," I told Wolfe approvingly. "You're not used to this rough cross-country going."

Before he could thank me for the compliment a man in greasy coveralls emerged from the garage and came for us. It didn't seem likely, in view of the greasy coveralls, that he was what we had come to steal, but Wolfe's need was desperate and he was taking no chances, so he wiped the scowl off and spoke to the man in hearty friendliness.

"Good morning, sir."

The man nodded. "Looking for someone?"

"Yes, Mr. Andrew Krasicki. Are you him?"

"I am not. My name's Imbrie, Neil Imbrie, butler and chauffeur and handyman. You look like some kind of a salesman. Insurance?"

Butlers were entirely different, I decided, when you came at them by the back way. When Wolfe, showing no resentment at the accusation, whatever he felt, told him it wasn't insurance but something personal and agreeable, he took us to the far end of the garage, which had doors for five cars, and pointed out a path which wound off into shrubbery.

"That goes to his cottage, way the other side of the tennis court. In the summer you can't see it from here on account of the leaves, but now you can a little. He's down there taking a nap because he was up last night fumigating. Often I'm up late driving, but it don't mean I get a nap. The next time around I'm going to be a gardener."

Wolfe thanked him and made for the path, with me for rearguard. It had just about made up its mind to stop raining, but everything was soaking wet, and after we got into the shrubbery we had to duck whenever a bare twig stretched out low to avoid making our own private rain. For me, young and limber and in good trim, that was nothing, but for Wolfe, with his three hundred pounds, which is an understatement, especially with his heavy tweed overcoat and hat and cane, it was asking a lot. The shrubbery quit at the other side of the tennis court, and we entered a grove of evergreens, then an open space, and there was the cottage.

Wolfe knocked on the door, and it opened, and facing us was a blond athlete not much older than me, with big bright blue eyes and his whole face ready to laugh. I never completely understand why a girl looks in any other direction when I am present, but I wouldn't have given it a moment's thought if this specimen had been in sight. Wolfe told him good morning and asked if he was Mr. Andrew Krasicki.

"That's my name." He made a little bow. "And may I—by God, it's Nero Wolfe! Aren't you Nero Wolfe?"

"Yes," Wolfe confessed modestly. "May I come in for a little talk, Mr. Krasicki? I wrote you a letter but got no reply, and yesterday on the telephone you—"

The blond prince interrupted. "It's all right," he declared. "All settled!"

"Indeed. What is?"

"I've decided to accept. I've just written you a letter."

"When can you come?"

"Any time you say. Tomorrow. I've got a good assistant and he can take over here."

Wolfe did not whoop with glee. Instead, he compressed his lips and breathed deep through his nose. In a moment he spoke. "Confound it, may I come in? I want to sit down."

II

WOLFE's reaction was perfectly natural. True, he had just got wonderful news, but also he had just learned that if he had stayed home he would have got it just the same in tomorrow morning's mail, and that was hard to take standing up. He hates going outdoors and rarely does, and he would rather trust himself in a room alone with three or four mortal enemies than in a piece of machinery on wheels.

But he had been driven to the wall. Four people live in the old brownstone house on West 35th Street. First, him. Second, me, assistant everything from detective to doorbell answerer. Third, Fritz Brenner, cook and house manager. And fourth, Theodore Horstmann, tender and defender of the ten thousand orchids in the plant rooms on the roof. But that was the trouble: there was no longer a fourth. A telegram had come from Illinois that Theodore's mother was critically ill and he must come at once, and he had taken the first train. Wolfe, instead of spending a pleasant four hours a day in the plant rooms pretending he was hard at it, had had to dig in and work like a dog. Fritz and I could help some, but we weren't experts. Appeals were broadcast in every direction, especially after word came from Theodore that he couldn't tell whether he would be back in six days or six months, and there were candidates for the job, but no one that Wolfe would trust with his rare and precious hybrids. He had already heard of this Andrew Krasicki, who had successfully crossed an Odontoglossum cirrhosum with an O. nobile veitchianum, and when he learned from Lewis Hewitt that Krasicki had worked for him for three years and was as good as they come, that settled it. He had to have Krasicki. He had written him; no answer. He had phoned, and had been brushed off. He had phoned again, and got no further. So, that wet December morning, tired and peevish and desperate, he had sent me to the garage for the car, and when I rolled up in front of the house there he was on the sidewalk, in his hat and overcoat and cane, grim and resolute, ready to do or die. Stanley making for Livingstone in the African jungle was nothing compared to Wolfe making for Krasicki in Westchester.

And here was Krasicki saying he had already written he would come! It was an awful anticlimax.

"I want to sit down," Wolfe repeated firmly.

But he didn't get to, not yet. Krasicki said sure, go on in and make himself at home, but he had just been starting for the greenhouse when we arrived and he would have to go. I put in to remark that maybe we'd better get back to town, to our own greenhouse, and start the day's work. That reminded Wolfe that I was there, and he gave Krasicki and me each other's names, and we shook hands. Then Krasicki said he had a Phalaenopsis Aphrodite in flower we might like to see.

Wolfe grunted. "Species? I have eight."

"Oh, no." It was easy to tell from Krasicki's tone of horticultural snobbery, by no means new to me, that he really belonged. "Not species and not dayana. Sanderiana. Nineteen sprays."

"Good heavens," Wolfe said enviously. "I must see it."

So we neither went in and sat down nor went back to our car, which was just as well, since in either case we would have been minus a replacement for Theodore. Krasicki led the way along the path by which we had come, but as we approached the house and outbuildings he took a fork to the left which skirted shrubs and perennial borders, now mostly bare but all neat. As we passed a young man in a rainbow shirt who was scattering peat moss on a border, he said, "You owe me a dime, Andy. No snow," and Krasicki grinned and told him, "See my lawyer, Gus."

The greenhouse, on the south side of the house, had been hidden from our view as we had driven in. Approaching it even on this surly December day, it stole the show from the mansion. With stone base walls to match the house, and curving glass, it was certainly high, wide, and handsome. At its outer extremity it ended in a one-story stone building with a slate roof, and the path Krasicki took led to that, and around to its door. The whole end wall was covered with ivy, and the door was fancy, stained oak slabs decorated with black iron, and on it was hanging a big framed placard, with red lettering so big you could read it from twenty paces:

DANGER
DO NOT ENTER
DOOR TO DEATH

I muttered something about a cheerful welcome. Wolfe cocked an eye at the sign and asked, "Cyanogas G?"

Krasicki, lifting the sign from its hook and putting a key in the hole, shook his head. "Ciphogene. That's all right; the vents have been open for several hours. This sign's a little poetic, but it was here when I came. I understand Mrs. Pitcairn painted it herself."

Inside with them, I took a good sniff of the air. Ciphogene is the fumigant Wolfe uses in his plant rooms, and I knew how deadly it was, but there was only a faint trace to my nose, so I went on breathing. The inside of the stone building was the storage and workroom, and right away Wolfe started looking things over.

Andy Krasicki said politely but briskly, "If you'll excuse me, I'm always behind a morning after fumigating . . ."

Wolfe, on his good behavior, followed him through the door into the greenhouse, and I went along.

"This is the cool room," Krasicki told us. "Next is the warm room, and then, the one adjoining the house, the medium. I have to get some vents closed and put the automatic on."

It was quite a show, no question about that, but I was so used to Wolfe's arrangement, practically all orchids, that it seemed pretty messy. When we proceeded to the warm room there was a sight I really enjoyed: Wolfe's face as he gazed at the P. Aphrodite sanderiana with its nineteen sprays. The admiration and the envy together made his eyes gleam as I had seldom seen them. As for the flower, it was new to me, and it was something special—rose, brown, purple, and yellow. The rose suffused the petals, and the brown, purple, and yellow were on the labellum.

"Is it yours?" Wolfe demanded.

Andy shrugged. "Mr. Pitcairn owns it."

"I don't care a hang who owns it. Who grew it?"

"I did. From a seed."

Wolfe grunted. "Mr. Krasicki, I'd like to shake your hand."

Andy permitted him to do so and then moved along to proceed through the door into the medium room, presumably to close more vents. After Wolfe had spent a few more minutes coveting the Phalaenopsis, we followed. This was another mess, everything from violet geraniums to a thing in a tub with eight million little white flowers, labeled Serissa foetida. I smelled it, got nothing, crushed one of the flowers with my fingers and smelled that, and then had no trouble understanding the foetida. My fingers had it good, so I went out to the sink in the workroom and washed with soap.

I got back to the medium room in time to hear Andy telling Wolfe that he had a curiosity he might like to see. "Of course," Andy said, "you know Tibouchina semidecandra, sometimes listed as Pleroma macanthrum or Pleroma grandiflora."

"Certainly," Wolfe assented.

I bet he had never heard of it before. Andy went on. "Well, I've got a two-year plant here that I raised from a cutting, less than two feet high, and a branch has sported. The leaves are nearly round, not ovate, foveolate, and the petioles—wait till I show you—it's resting now out of light—"

He had stepped to where a strip of green canvas hung from the whole length of a bench section, covering the space from the waist-high bench to the ground, and, squatting, he lifted the canvas by its free bottom edge and stuck his head and shoulders under the bench. Then he didn't move. For too many seconds he didn't move at all. Then he came back out, bumping his head on the concrete bench, straightened up to his full height, and stood as rigid as if he had been made of concrete himself, facing us, all his color gone and his eyes shut.

When he heard me move his eyes opened, and when he saw me reaching for the canvas he whispered to me, "Don't look. No. Yes, you'd better look."

I lifted the canvas and looked. After I had kept my head and shoulders under the bench about as long as Andy had, I backed out, not bumping my head, and told Wolfe, "It's a dead woman."

"She looks dead," Andy whispered.

"Yeah," I agreed, "she *is* dead. Dead and cooled off."

"Confound it," Wolfe growled.

III

I WILL make an admission. A private detective is not a sworn officer of the law, like a lawyer, but he operates under a license which imposes a code on him. And in my pocket was the card which put Archie Goodwin under the code. But as I stood there, glancing from Wolfe to Andy Krasicki, what was in the front of my mind was not the next and proper step according to the code, but merely the thought that it was one hell of a note if Nero Wolfe couldn't even take a little drive to Westchester to try to lasso an orchid tender without a corpse butting in to gum the works. I didn't know then that Wolfe's need for an orchid tender was responsible for the corpse being there that day, and that what I took for coincidence was cause and effect.

Andy stayed rigid. Wolfe moved toward the canvas, and I said, "You can't bend over that far."

But he tried to, and, finding I was right, got down on his knees and lifted the canvas. I squatted beside him. There wasn't much light, but enough, considering what met the eye. Whatever had killed her had done things to her face, but it had probably been all right for looks. She had fine light brown hair, and nice hands, and was wearing a blue patterned rayon dress. She lay stretched out on her back, with her eyes open and also her mouth open. There was nothing visible under there with her except an overturned eight-inch flower pot with a plant in it which had a branch broken nearly off. Wolfe withdrew and got erect, and I followed suit. Evidently Andy hadn't moved.

"She's dead," he said, this time out loud.

Wolfe nodded. "And your plant is mutilated. The branch that sported is broken."

"What? Plant?"

"Your Tibouchina."

Andy frowned, shook his head as if to see if it rattled, squatted by the canvas again, and lifted it. His head and shoulders disappeared. I violated the code, and so did Wolfe, by not warning him not to touch things. When he reappeared he had not only touched, he had snitched evidence. In his hand was the broken branch of the Tibouchina. With his middle finger he raked a furrow in the bench soil, put the lower stem of the branch in it, replaced the soil over the stem, and pressed the soil down.

"Did you kill her?" Wolfe snapped at him.

In one way it was a good question and in another way a bad one. It jolted Andy out of his trance, which was okay, but it also made him want to plug Wolfe. He came fast and determined, but the space between the benches was narrow and I was in between. As for plugging me, I had arms too. He stopped close against me, chest to chest, with pressure.

"That won't help you any," Wolfe said bitterly. "You were going to start to work for me tomorrow. Now what? Can I leave you here with this? No. You'd be in jail before I got home. That question you didn't like, you'll be answering it many times before the day ends."

"Good God." Andy fell back.

"Certainly. You might as well start with me. Did you kill her?"

"No. Good God, no!"

"Who is she?"

"She's—it's Dini. Dini Lauer. Mrs. Pitcairn's nurse. We were going to be married. Yesterday, just yesterday, she said she would marry me. And I'm standing here." Andy raised his hands, with all the fingers spread, and shook them. "I stand here! What am I going to do?"

"Hold it, brother," I told him.

"You're going to come with me," Wolfe said, squeezing past me. "I saw a telephone in the workroom, but we'll talk a little before we use it. Archie, stay here."

"I'll stay here," Andy said. The trance look was gone from his eyes and he was fully conscious again, but his color hadn't returned and there were drops of sweat on his forehead. He repeated it. "I'll stay here."

It took two good minutes to get him to let me have the honor. Finally he shoved off, with Wolfe behind, and after they had left that room I could see them, through the glass partitions, crossing the warm and cool rooms and opening the door to the workroom. They closed it behind them, and I was alone, but of course you're never really alone in a greenhouse. Not only do you have the plants and flowers for company, but also the glass walls give you the whole outdoors. Anyone within seeing distance, in three directions, was really with me, and that led me to my first conclusion: that Dini Lauer, alive or dead, had not been rolled behind that canvas between the hours of seven in the morning and five in the afternoon. The question, alive or dead, made me want a second conclusion, and again I squatted to lift the canvas in search of it. When, some four years previously, the ciphogene tank had been installed in Wolfe's plant rooms to replace cyanogas and Nico-Fume, I had read the literature, which had included a description of what you would look like if you got careless, and a second thorough inspection of Dini's face and throat brought me my second conclusion: she had been alive when she was rolled or pushed under the bench. It was the ciphogene that did it. Since it seemed improbable that she had consciously and obligingly crawled under the bench and lain still, I went on to look and feel for a bump or broken skin, but found neither.

As I got upright again a noise came, knuckles on wood, and then a man's voice, raised to carry through the wood.

"Andy!" It raised some more. "Andy!"

The wood belonged to a large door at the end of the room, the end where the greenhouse was attached to the mansion. The benches stopped some twenty feet short of that end, leaving room for an open space where there was a floor mat flanked by tubs and jars of oversized plants. The pounding came again, louder, and the voice, also louder. I stepped to the door and observed three details: that it opened away from me, presumably into the house, that it was fastened with a heavy brass bolt on my side, and that all its edges, where it met the frame and sill, were sealed with wide bands of tape.

The voice and knuckles were authoritative. No good could come of an attempt to converse through the bolted door, me with the voice of a stranger. If I merely kept still, the result would probably be an invasion at the other end of the greenhouse, via the workroom, and I knew how Wolfe hated to be interrupted when he was having a talk. And I preferred not to let company enter, under the circumstances.

So I slid the bolt back, pushed the door open enough to let myself through, shut it by backing against it, and kept my back there.

The voice demanded, "Who the hell are you?"

It was Joseph G. Pitcairn, and I was in, not a hall or vestibule, but the enormous living room of his house. He was not famous enough to be automatically known, but when we had started, by mail, to try to steal a gardener from him, I had made a few inquiries and, in addition to learning that he was an amateur golfer, a third-generation coupon clipper, and a loafer, I had got a description. The nose alone was enough, with its list to starboard, the result, I had been told, of an accidental back stroke from someone's Number Four iron.

"Where's Andy?" he demanded, without giving me time to tell him who the hell I was.

"My name—" I began.

"Is Miss Lauer in there?" he demanded.

My function, of course, was to gain time for Wolfe. I let him have a re-fined third-generation grin in exchange for his vulgar glare, and said quietly, "Make it an even dozen and I'll start answering."

"A dozen what?"

"Questions. Or I'll trade you. Have you ever heard of Nero Wolfe?"

"Certainly. What about him? He grows orchids."

"That's one way of putting it. As he says, the point is not who owns them but who grows them. In his case, Theodore Horstmann was in the plant rooms twelve hours a day, sometimes more, but he had to leave because his mother took sick. That was a week ago yesterday. After floundering around, Mr. Wolfe decided to take Andy Krasicki away from you. You must remember that he—"

It wasn't Joseph G. who made me break off. He and I were not alone. Standing back of him were a young man and young woman; off to one side was a woman not so young but still not beyond any reasonable deadline, in a maid's uniform; and at my right was Neil Imbrie, still in his coveralls. It was the young woman who stopped my flow by suddenly advancing and chopping at me.

"Quit stalling and get away from that door. Something's happened and I'm going in there!" She grabbed my sleeve to use force.

The young man called to her without moving, "Watch it, Sibby! It must be Archie Goodwin and he'd just as soon hit a woman as—"

"Be quiet, Donald!" Joseph G. ordered him. "Sybil, may I suggest a little decent restraint?" His cold gray eyes came back to me. "Your name is Archie Goodwin and you work for Nero Wolfe?"

"That's right."

"You say you came to see Krasicki?"

I nodded. "To get him away from you." I rubbed that in hoping to get a nice long argument started, but he didn't bite.

"Does that excuse your bursting into my house and barricading a door?"

"No," I conceded. "Andy invited me into the greenhouse, and I was stand-ing there when I heard you knocking and calling him. He was busy with Mr. Wolfe, and I saw the door was bolted, and I thought it must be you and you certainly had a right to have the door of your own greenhouse opened, so I opened it. As for the barricading, that's where we get to the point. I admit I'm not acting normal. Assuming that the reason is somehow connected with this Miss Lauer, whom I have never met, naturally I would like to know why you asked me if Miss Lauer is in there. Why did you?"

Joseph G. took one long stride, which was all he needed to reach me. "Get away," he said, meaning it.

I shook my head, keeping my grin refined, and opened my mouth to speak just as he reached for me. I had already decided that it wouldn't be tactful to let the cold war get hot, especially since he had Donald and Neil Imbrie in reserve, and that as a last resort I would release some facts, but it didn't get that far. As my muscles tightened in reflex to the touch of his hand, the sound of a car's engine came from outdoors. From where Imbrie stood he had to move only two steps to get a view through a window, and he did so, staring out. Then he turned to his employer.

"State police, Mr. Pitcairn," he said. "Two cars."

Evidently Wolfe's talk with Andy had been short and sour, since he hadn't waited long to do something that he never resorts to if he can help it: calling the cops.

IV

FIVE hours later, at three o'clock in the afternoon, seated in the one decent chair in the workroom of the greenhouse, Nero Wolfe was making a last frantic despairing try.

"The charge," he urged, "can be anything you choose to make it, short of first degree murder. The bail can be any amount and it will be furnished. The risk will be minimal, and in the end you'll thank me for it, when I've got the facts and you've got to take them."

Three men shook their heads with finality.

One said, "Better give up and get yourself a gardener that's not a killer." That was Ben Dykes, head of the county detectives.

Another said nastily, "If it was me you'd be wanting bail yourself as a material witness." That was Lieutenant Con Noonan of the State Police. He had been a stinker from the start, and it was only after the arrival of the DA, who had good reason to remember the Fashalt case, that Wolfe and I had been accepted as human.

The third said, "No use, Wolfe. Of course any facts you get will be welcome." That was Cleveland Archer, District Attorney of Westchester County. Any common murder he would have left to the help, but not one that a Joseph G. Pitcairn was connected with, no matter how. He went on, "What can the charge be but first degree murder? That doesn't mean the file is closed and I'm ready for trial. Tomorrow's another day, and there are a couple of points that need some attention and they'll get it, but it looks as if he's guilty."

The five of us were alone at last. Wolfe was in the best chair available, I was perched on a corner of a potting bench, and the other three were standing. The corpse had left long ago in a basket, the army of official scientists had finished and gone, ten thousand questions had been asked and answered by everyone on the premises, the statements had been signed, and

Andy Krasicki had departed for White Plains in a back seat, handcuffed to a dick. The law had made a quick clean job of it.

And Wolfe, having had nothing to eat since breakfast but four sandwiches and three cups of coffee, was even more desperate than when he had sent me for the car that dark December morning. Andy had been his, and he had lost him.

The case against him was fair to middling. There was general agreement that he had been jelly for Dini Lauer since he had first sighted her, two months back, when she had arrived to take care of Mrs. Pitcairn, who had tumbled down some steps and hurt her back. That had been testified to even by Gus Treble, the young man in the rainbow shirt, Andy's assistant, who was obviously all for Andy. Gus said that Dini had given Andy the fanciest runaround he had ever seen, which wasn't too bright of Gus if he had his sympathy on straight.

To the question why should Andy want to get rid of Dini the very day she consented to marry him, the answer was, who says she consented? Only Andy. No one else had heard tell of it, and he himself had announced the good news only to Wolfe and me. Then had he fumigated her to death merely because he couldn't have her? That was probably one of the points which the DA thought needed attention. For a judge and jury some Grade A jealousy would have helped. That was a little ticklish, and naturally the DA wanted a night to sleep on it. Who had been the third point of the jealous triangle? Of those present, Neil Imbrie didn't look the part, Gus Treble didn't act it, and Pitcairn and son were not the sort of people a DA will take a poke at if he can help it. So he couldn't be blamed for wanting to take a look around. Besides, he had asked them all questions, plenty, and to the point, without getting a lead.

Noonan and Dykes had got all their personal timetables early in the game, but when the quickie report on the p.m. had come from White Plains, telling about the morphine, the DA had had another try at them. The laboratory reported that there was morphine present but not enough to kill, and that it could safely be assumed that Dini had died of ciphogene poisoning. The morphine answered one question—how had she been made unconscious enough to stay put under the bench until the ciphogene would take over? —but it raised another one. Was the law going to have to prove that Andy had bought morphine? But that had been a cinch. They had it covered in a matter of minutes. Vera Imbrie, the cook, Neil's wife, whom I had seen in the background in uniform when I invaded the living room, was troubled with facial neuralgia and kept a box of morphine pellets in a cupboard in the kitchen. She hadn't had to use them for nearly a month, and now the box was gone. Andy, along with everyone else, had known about them and where she kept them. It gave the law a good excuse to search the whole house, and a dozen or so spent an hour at it, but found no morphine and no box. Andy's cottage had of course already been frisked, but they had another go at that too.

So the DA checked over their personal timetables with them, but found nothing new. Of course Andy's was featured. According to him, at a tête-à-tête in the greenhouse late in the afternoon Dini had at last surrendered and had agreed not only to marry him sometime soon, but also, since he wanted to accept the offer from Nero Wolfe, to quit the Pitcairn job and get one in New York. She had asked him to keep it quiet until she had broken the news to Mrs. Pitcairn. That had been around five o'clock, and he had next seen her some four hours later, a little after nine, when he had been in the greenhouse on his evening round and she had entered through the door that connected with the living room. They had looked at flowers and talked, and then had gone to sit in the workroom and talk some more, and to drink beer, which Dini had brought from the kitchen. At eleven o'clock she had said good night and left via the door to the living room, and that was the last he had seen of her. That's how he told it.

He too had left, by the outside door, and gone to his cottage and written the letter to Wolfe, deciding not to go to bed because, first, he was so excited with so much happiness, and second, he would have to be up at three anyway. He had worked at propagation records and got his things in order ready to pack. At three o'clock he had gone to the greenhouse and had been joined there by Gus Treble, who was to get his last lesson in the routine of preparation for fumigation. After an hour's work, including bolting and taping the door to the living room, and opening the ciphogene master valve in the workroom for eight minutes and closing it again, and locking the outside door and putting up the DOOR TO DEATH sign, Gus had gone home and Andy had returned to the cottage. Again he admitted he had not gone to bed. At seven o'clock he had gone to the greenhouse and opened the vents with outside controls, returned to the cottage, finally felt tired, and slept. At eight-thirty he awoke, ate a quick breakfast and drank coffee, and was ready to leave for the day's work when there was a knock on the door and he opened it to find Nero Wolfe and me.

The timetables of the others, as furnished by them, were less complicated. Gus Treble had spent the evening with a girl at Bedford Hills and stayed late, until it was time to leave for his three o'clock date with Andy at the greenhouse. Neil and Vera Imbrie had gone up to their room a little before ten, listened to the radio for half an hour, and gone to bed and to sleep. Joseph G. Pitcairn had left immediately after dinner for a meeting of the Executive Committee of the Northern Westchester Taxpayers' Association, at somebody's house in North Salem, and had returned shortly before midnight and gone to bed. Donald, after dining with his father and Dini Lauer, had gone to his room to write. Asked what he had written, he said fiction. He hadn't been asked to produce it. Sybil had eaten upstairs with her mother, who was by now able to stand up and even walk around a little but wasn't venturing downstairs for meals. After eating, she had read aloud to her mother for a couple of hours and helped her with going to bed, and had then gone to her own room for the night.

None of them had seen Dini since shortly after dinner. Asked if it wasn't unusual for Dini not to make an evening visit to the patient she was caring for, they all said no, and Sybil explained that she was quite capable of turning down her mother's bed for her. Asked if they knew about Mrs. Imbrie's morphine pellets and where the box was kept, they all said certainly. They all admitted that no known fact excluded the possibility that one of them, sometime between eleven and three, had got Dini to drink a glass of beer with enough morphine in it to put her out, and, after the morphine took, had carried her to the greenhouse and rolled her under the bench, but the implication didn't seem to quicken anyone's pulse except Vera Imbrie's. She was silly enough to assert that she hadn't known Andy was going to fumigate that night, but took it back when reminded that everyone else admitted that the word of warning had been given to all as usual. The cops didn't hold it against her, and I concede that I didn't either.

Nor were there any contradictions about the morning. The house stirred late and breakfast was free-lance. Sybil had had hers upstairs with her mother. They hadn't missed Dini and started looking for her until after nine o'clock, and their inquiries had resulted in the gathering in the living room and Pitcairn's knocking on the door to the greenhouse and yelling for Andy.

It was all perfectly neat. No visible finger pointed anywhere except at Andy.

"Someone's lying," Wolfe insisted doggedly.

The law wanted to know, "Who? What about?"

"How do I know?" He was plenty exasperated. "That's your job! Find out!"

"Find out yourself," Lieutenant Noonan sneered.

Wolfe had put questions, such as, if Andy wanted to kill, why did he pick the one spot and method that would point inevitably to him? Of course their answer was that he had picked that spot and method because he figured that no jury would believe that he had been fool enough to do so, but that was probably another point which the DA thought needed attention. I had to admit, strictly to myself, that none of Wolfe's questions was unanswerable. His main point, the real basis of his argument, was a little special. Other points, he contended, made Andy's guilt doubtful; this one proved his innocence. The law assumed, and so did he, Wolfe, that the flower pot under the bench was overturned when Dini Lauer, drugged but alive, was rolled under. It was inconceivable that Andy Krasicki, not pressed for time, had done that. Firstly, he would have moved the pot out of harm's way; secondly, if in his excitement he had failed to do that and had overturned the pot he would certainly have righted it, and, seeing that the precious branch, the one that had sported, was broken, he would have retrieved it. For such a plant man as Andy Krasicki righting the pot and saving the branch would have been automatic actions, and nothing could have prevented them. He had in fact performed them under even more trying circumstances than those the law assumed, when still stunned from the shock of the discovery of the body.

"Shock hell," Noonan snorted. "When he put it there himself? I've heard tell of your fancies, Wolfe. If this is a sample, I'll take strawberry."

By that time I was no longer in a frame of mind to judge Wolfe's points objectively. What I wanted was to get my thumbs in a proper position behind Noonan's ears and bear down, and, since that wasn't practical, I was ready to break my back helping to spring Andy as a substitute. Incidentally, I had cottoned to Andy, who had handled himself throughout like a two-handed man. He had used one of them, the one not fastened to the dick, to shake hands again with Wolfe just before they led him out to the vehicle.

"All right," he had said, "I'll leave it to you. I don't give a damn about me, not now, but the bastard that did it . . ."

Wolfe had nodded. "Only hours, I hope. You may sleep at my house tonight."

But that was too optimistic. As aforesaid, at three o'clock they were done and ready to go, and Noonan took a parting crack at Wolfe.

"If it was me you'd be wanting bail yourself as a material witness."

I may get a chance to put thumbs on him yet some day.

V

AFTER they had left I remarked to Wolfe, "In addition to everything else, here's a pleasant thought. Not only do you have no Andy, not only do you have to get back home and start watering ten thousand plants, but at a given moment, maybe in a month or maybe sooner, you'll get a subpoena to go to White Plains and sit on the witness stand." I shrugged. "Well, if it's snowy and sleety and icy, we can put on chains and stand a fair chance of getting through."

"Shut up," he growled. "I'm trying to think." His eyes were closed.

I perched on the bench. After some minutes he growled again, "I can't. Confound this chair."

"Yeah. The only one I know of that meets the requirements is fifty miles away. By the way, whose guests are we, now that he who invited us in here has been stuck in the coop?"

I got an answer of a kind, though not from Wolfe. The door to the warm room opened, and Joseph G. was with us. His daughter Sybil was with him. By that time I was well acquainted with his listed nose, and with her darting green eyes and pointed chin.

He stopped in the middle of the room and inquired frostily, "Were you waiting for someone?"

Wolfe opened his eyes halfway and regarded him glumly. "Yes," he said. "Yes? Who?"

"Anyone. You. Anyone."

"He's eccentric," Sybil explained. "He's being eccentric."

"Be quiet, Sybil," Father ordered her, without removing his eyes from Wolfe. "Before Lieutenant Noonan left he told me he would leave a man at the entrance to my grounds to keep people from entering. He thought we might be annoyed by newspapermen or curious and morbid strangers. But there will be no trouble about leaving. The man has orders not to prevent anyone's departure."

"That's sensible," Wolfe approved. "Mr. Noonan is to be commended." He heaved a deep sigh. "So you're ordering me off the place. That's sensible too, from your standpoint." He didn't move.

Pitcairn was frowning. "It's neither sensible nor not sensible. It's merely appropriate. You had to stay, of course, as long as you were needed—but now you're not needed. Now that this miserable and sordid episode is finished, I must request—"

"No," Wolfe snapped. "No indeed."

"No what?"

"The episode is not finished. I didn't mean Mr. Noonan is to be commended by me, only by you. He was, in fact, an ass to leave the people on your premises free to go as they please, since one of them is a murderer. None of you should be allowed to take a single step unobserved and unrecorded. As for—"

Sybil burst out laughing. The sound was a little startling, and it seemed to startle her as much as it did her audience, for she suddenly clapped her hand to her mouth to choke it off.

"There you are," Wolfe told her, "you're hysterical." His eyes darted back to Pitcairn. "Why is your daughter hysterical?"

"I am not hysterical," she denied scornfully. "Anyone would laugh. It wasn't only melodramatic, it was corny." She shook her head, held high. "I'm disappointed in you, Nero. I thought you were better than that."

I think what finally made him take the plunge was her calling him Nero. Up to then he had been torn. It's true that his telling Andy he hoped it would be only a matter of hours had been a commitment of a sort, and God knows he needed Andy, and the law trampling over him had made bruises, especially Lieutenant Noonan, but up to that point his desire to get back home had kept him from actually making the dive. I knew him well, and I had seen the signs. But this disdainful female stranger calling him Nero was too much, and he took off.

He came up out of the chair and was erect. "I am not comfortable," he told Joseph G. stiffly, "sitting here in your house with you standing. Mr. Krasicki has engaged me to get him cleared and I intend to do it. It would be foolhardy to assume that you would welcome a thorn for the sake of such abstractions as justice or truth, since that would make you a rarity almost unknown, but you have a right to be asked. May I stay here, with Mr. Goodwin, and talk with you and your family and servants, until I am either satisfied that Mr. Krasicki is guilty or am equipped to satisfy others that he isn't?"

Sybil, though still scornful, nodded approvingly. "That's more like it," she declared. "That rolled."

"You may not," Pitcairn said, controlling himself. "If the officers of the law are satisfied, it is no concern of mine that you are not." He put his hand in his side coat pocket. "I've been patient and I'm not going to put up with any more of this. You know where your car is."

His hand left the pocket, and damned if there wasn't a gun in it. It was a Colt .38, old but in good condition.

"Let me see your license," I said sternly.

"Pfui." Wolfe lifted his shoulders a millimeter and let them down. "Very well, sir, then I'll have to manage." He put his hand into his own side pocket, and I thought my God, he's going to shoot it out with him, but when the hand reappeared all it held was a key. "This," he said, "is the key to Mr. Krasicki's cottage, which he gave me so I could enter to collect his belongings—whatever is left of them after the illegal visitations of the police. Mr. Goodwin and I are going there, unaccompanied. When we return to our car we shall await you or your agent to inspect our baggage. Have you any comment?"

"I—" Pitcairn hesitated, frowning, then he said, "No."

"Good." Wolfe turned and went to a table for his coat, hat, and cane. "Come, Archie." He marched.

As we reached the door Sybil's voice came at our backs. "If you find the box of morphine don't tell anybody."

Outdoors I held Wolfe's coat for him and got mine on. The whole day had been dark, but now it was getting darker, though a cold wind was herding the clouds down to the horizon and on over. When we reached the rear of the house I swung left for a detour to the car to get a flashlight, and caught up with Wolfe on the path. No ducking was necessary now, as the twigs had dried. We passed the tennis court and entered the grove of evergreens, where it was already night.

I glanced at my wrist. "Four o'clock," I announced cheerily to Wolfe, who was ahead. "If we were home, and Theodore was still there, or Andy had come, you would be just going up to the plant rooms to poke around."

He didn't even tell me to shut up. He was way beyond that.

It was dark enough in the cottage to need lights, and I turned them on. Wolfe glanced around, spotted a chair nearly big enough, took off his hat and coat, and sat, while I started a tour. The dicks had left it neat. This medium-sized room wasn't bad, though the rugs and furniture had seen better days. To the right was a bedroom and to the left another one, and in the rear was a bathroom and a kitchen.

I took only a superficial look and then returned to Wolfe and told him, "Nothing sticks out. Shall I pack?"

"What for?" he asked forlorn.

"Shall I see if they missed something important?"

He only grunted. Not feeling like sitting and looking at him, I began a retake. A desk and a filing cabinet yielded nothing but horticultural details and some uninteresting personal items, and the rest of the room nothing at all. The bedroom at the left was even blanker. The one at the right was the one Andy had used, and I went over it good, but if it contained anything that could be used to flatten Lieutenant Noonan's nose I failed to find it. The same for the bathroom. And ditto for the kitchen, except that at the rear of a shelf, behind some packages of prunes and cereals, I dug up a little cardboard box. There was no morphine in it, and there was no reason to suppose there ever had been, and I reported its contents to Wolfe merely to get conversation started.

"Keys," I said, jiggling the box, "and one of them is tagged d-u-p period g-r-n-h-s period, which probably means duplicate to the greenhouse. It would come in handy if we want to sneak in some night and swipe that Phalaenopsis."

No comment. I put the keys in my pocket and sat down.

Pretty soon I spoke. "I'd like to make it plain," I said distinctly, "that I don't like the way you're acting. Many times, sitting in the office, you have said to me, 'Archie, go get Whosis and Whosat and bring them here.' Usually, I have delivered. But if you now tell me to drive you home, and, upon arriving, tell me to go get the Pitcairns and Imbries and Gus Treble, which is what I suspect you of, save it. I wouldn't even bother to answer, not after the way you've bitched it up just because a pretty girl called you by your first name."

"She isn't pretty," he growled.

"Nuts. Certainly she's pretty, though I don't like her any better than you do. I just wanted to make sure that you understand what the situation will be if we go home."

He studied me. After a while he nodded, with his lips compressed, as if in final acceptance of an ugly fact.

"There's a phone," he said. "Get Fritz."

"Yeah, I saw it, but what if it's connected with the house?"

"Try it."

I went to the desk and did so, dialing the operator, and, with no audible interference, got her, gave the number, and heard Fritz's voice in my ear. Wolfe got up and came across and took it away from me.

"Fritz? We have been delayed. No, I'm all right. I don't know. The delay is indefinite. No, confound it, he's in jail. I can't tell now but you'll hear from me again well before dinnertime. How are the plants? I see. No, that's all right, that won't hurt them. I see. No no no, not those on the north! Not a one! Certainly I did, but . . ."

I quit listening, not that I was callous, but because my attention was drawn elsewhere. Turning away, for no special reason, a window was in my line of vision, and through it, outdoors near the pane, I saw a branch of a shrub bob up and down and then wiggle to a stop. I am no woodsman, but it didn't seem reasonable that wind could make a leafless branch perform like that, so I turned to face Wolfe again, listened for another minute, and then sauntered across the room and into the kitchen. I switched off the light there, carefully and silently eased the back door open, slipped outside, and pulled the door to.

It was all black, but after I had stood half a minute I could see a little. I slipped my hand inside my vest to my shoulder holster, but brought it out again empty; it was just an automatic check. I saw now that I was standing on a concrete slab only a shallow step above the ground. Stepping off it to the left, I started, slow motion, for the corner of the house. The damn wind was so noisy that my ears weren't much help. Just as I reached the corner a moving object came from nowhere and bumped me. I grabbed for it, but it, instead of grabbing, swung a fist. The fist was hard when it met the side of my neck, and that got me sore. I sidestepped, whirled, and aimed one for the object's kidney, but there wasn't enough light for precision and I missed by a mile, nearly cracking a knuckle on his hip. He came at me with a looping swing that left him as open as a house with a wall gone, I ducked, and he went on by and then turned to try again. When he turned I saw who it was: Andy's assistant, Gus Treble.

I stepped back, keeping a guard up for defense only.

"Lookit," I said, "I'd just as soon go on if you really want to, but why do you want to? It's more fun when I know what it's for."

"You double-crossing sonofabitch," he said, not panting.

"Okay, but it's still vague. Who did I cross? Pitcairn? The daughter? Who?"

"You made him think you were with him and then you helped get him framed."

"Oh. You think we crossed Andy?"

"I know damn well you did."

"Listen, brother." I let my guard down. "You know what you are? You're the answer to a prayer. You're what I wanted for Christmas. You're dead wrong, but you're wonderful. Come in and have a talk with Nero Wolfe."

"I wouldn't talk with that crook."

"You were looking at him through a window. What for?"

"I wanted to see what you were up to."

"That's easy. You should have asked. We were up to absolutely nothing. We were sunk up to our ears. We were phut. We were and are crazy for Andy. We wanted to take him home with us and pamper him, and they wouldn't let us."

"That's a goddam lie."

"Very well. Then you ought to come in and tell Mr. Wolfe to his face that he's a double-crosser, a crook, and a liar. You don't often get such a chance. Unless you're afraid. What are you afraid of?"

"Nothing," he said, and wheeled and marched to the kitchen door, opened it, and went in. I was right behind.

Wolfe's voice boomed from the other room. "Archie! Where the devil—"

We were with him. He had finished with the phone. He shot a glance at Gus and then at me.

"Where did you get him?"

I waved a hand. "Oh, out there. I've started deliveries."

VI

IT TOOK a good ten minutes to convince Gus Treble that we were playing it straight, and though Wolfe used a lot of his very best words and tones, it wasn't words that put it over, it was logic. The major premise was that Wolfe wanted Andy in his plant rooms, quick. The minor was that Andy couldn't be simultaneously in Wolfe's plant rooms and in the coop at White Plains, or in the death house at Sing Sing. Gus didn't have to have the conclusion written out for him, but even so it took ten minutes. The last two were consumed by my recital, verbatim, of the conversation with Joseph G. and Sybil just before leaving the greenhouse.

Gus was seated at the desk, turned to face Wolfe, and I was straddling a straight-backed chair.

"Last July," Gus said, "that Noonan beat up a friend of mine, for nothing."

Wolfe nodded. "There you are. A typical uniformed blackguard. I take it, Mr. Treble, that you share my opinion that Mr. Krasicki didn't kill that woman. And I heard you tell those men that you didn't, so I won't pester you about it. But though you answered freely and fully all questions concerning yourself, you were manifestly more circumspect regarding others. I understand that. You have a job here and your words were being recorded. But it won't do for me. I want to get Mr. Krasicki out of jail, and I can do so only by furnishing a replacement for him. If you want to help you can, but not unless you forget your job, discard prudence, and tell me all you know about these people. Well, sir?"

Gus was scowling, which made him look old enough to vote. In the artificial light he looked paler than he had outdoors in the morning, and his rainbow shirt looked brighter.

"It's a good job," he muttered, "and I love it."

"Yes," Wolfe agreed sympathetically, "Mr. Krasicki told me you were competent, intelligent, and exceptionally talented."

"He did?"

"Yes, sir. He did."

"Goddam it." Gus's scowl got blacker. "What do you want to know?"

"About these people. First, Miss Lauer. I gathered that you were not yourself attracted by her."

"Me? Not that baby. You heard what I told them. She was out for a sucker."

"You mean out for money?"

"No, not money. I don't think so. Hell, you know the kind. She liked to see males react, she got a kick out of it. She liked to see females react too. Even Neil Imbrie, old enough to be her father, you should have seen her giving him the idea when his wife was there. Not that she was raw; she could put it in a flash and then cover. And what she could do with her voice! Sometimes I myself had to walk off. Anyhow I've got a girl at Bedford Hills."

"Wasn't Mr. Krasicki aware of all this?"

"Andy?" Gus leaned forward. "Listen. That was one of those things. From the first day he glimpsed her and heard her speak, he got drowned. He didn't even float, he just laid there on the bottom. And him no fool, anything but, but it hit him so quick and hard he never got a chance to analyze. Once I undertook to try a couple of words, very careful, and the look he gave me! It was pathetic." Gus shook his head. "I don't know. If I had known he had talked her into marrying him I might have fumigated her myself, just as a favor to him."

"Yes," Wolfe agreed, "that would have been an adequate motive. So much for you. You mentioned Mr. Imbrie. What about him? Assume that Miss Lauer also gave him the idea when his wife was *not* there, that he reacted like a male, as you put it, that developments convinced him that he was in heaven, that she told him last evening of her intention to go away and marry Mr. Krasicki, and that he decided she must die. Are those assumptions permissible?"

"I wouldn't know. They're not mine, they're yours."

"Come come," Wolfe snapped. "I'm not Mr. Noonan, thank God. Prudence will get us nowhere. Has Mr. Imbrie got that in him?"

"He might, sure, if she hooked him deep enough."

"Have you any facts that contradict the assumptions?"

"No."

"Then we'll keep them. You understand, of course, that there are no alibis. There were four hours for it: from eleven o'clock, when Miss Lauer said good night to Mr. Krasicki and left him, to three o'clock, when you and Mr. Krasicki entered the greenhouse to fumigate. Everyone was in bed, and in separate rooms except for Mr. and Mrs. Imbrie. Their alibi is mutual, but also marital and therefore worthless. His motive we have assumed. Hers is of course implicit in the situation as you describe it, and besides, women do not require motives that are comprehensible by any intellectual process."

"You said it," Gus acquiesced feelingly. "They roll their own."

I wondered what the girl at Bedford Hills had done now. Wolfe went on.

"Let's finish with the women. What about Miss Pitcairn?"

"Well—" Gus opened his mouth wide to give his lips a stretch, touched the upper one with the tip of his tongue, and closed up again. "I guess I don't understand her. I feel as if I hate her, but I don't really know why, so maybe I don't understand her."

"Perhaps I can help?"

"I doubt it. She puts up a hell of a front, but one day last summer I came on her in the grove crying her eyes out. I think it's a complex, only she must have more than one. She had a big row with her father one day on the terrace, when I was working there in the shrubs and they knew it—it was a couple of weeks after Mrs. Pitcairn's accident and he was letting the registered nurse go and sending for a practical nurse which turned out later to be this Dini Lauer—and Miss Pitcairn was raising the roof because she thought she ought to look after her mother herself. She screamed fit to be tied, until the nurse called down from an upstairs window to please be quiet. Another thing, she not only seems to hate men, she says right out that she does. Maybe that's why I feel I hate her, just to balance it up."

Wolfe made a face. "Does she often have hysterics?"

"I wouldn't say often, but of course I'm hardly ever in the house." Gus shook his head. "I guess I don't understand her."

"I doubt if it's worth an effort. Don't try. What I'd like to get from you, if you have it, is not understanding but a fact. I need a scandalous fact about Miss Pitcairn. Have you got one?"

Gus looked bewildered. "You mean about her and Dini?"

"Her and anyone or anything. The worse the better. Is she a kleptomaniac or a drug addict? Does she gamble or seduce other women's husbands or cheat at cards?"

"Not that I know of." Gus took a minute to concentrate. "She fights a lot. Will that help?"

"I doubt it. With what weapons?"

"I don't mean weapons; she just fights—with family, friends, anyone. She always knows best. She fights a lot with her brother. As far as he's concerned, it's a good thing somebody knows best, because God knows he don't."

"Why, does he have complexes too?"

Gus snorted. "He sure has got something. The family says he's sensitive—that's what they tell each other, and their friends, and him. Hell, so am I sensitive, but I don't go around talking it up. He has a mood every hour on the hour, daily including Sundays and holidays. He never does a damn thing, even pick flowers. He's a four-college man—he got booted out of Yale, then Williams, then Cornell, and then something out in Ohio."

"What for?" Wolfe demanded. "That might help."

"No idea."

"Confound it," Wolfe complained, "have you no curiosity? A good damning fact about the son might be even more useful than one about the daughter. Haven't you got one?"

Gus concentrated again, and when a minute passed without any sign of contact on his face, Wolfe insisted, "Could his expulsion from those colleges have been on account of trouble with women?"

"Him?" Gus snorted again. "If he went to a nudist camp and they lined the men up on one side and the women on the other, he wouldn't know which was which. With clothes on I suppose he can tell. Not that he's dumb, I doubt if he's a bit dumb, but his mind is somewhere else. You asked if he has complexes—"

There was a knock at the door. I went and opened it and took a look, and said, "Come in."

Donald Pitcairn entered.

I had surveyed him before, but now I had more to go on and I checked. He didn't look particularly sensitive, though of course I didn't know which mood he had on. He had about the same weight and volume as me, but it's no self flattery to say that he didn't carry them the same. He needed tuning. He had dark deep-set eyes, and his face wouldn't have been bad at all if he had felt better about it.

"Oh, you here, Gus?" he asked, which wasn't too bright.

"Yeah, I'm here," Gus replied, getting that settled.

Donald, blinking in the light, turned to Wolfe. His idea was to make it curt. "We wondered why it took so long to pack Andy's things. That's what you said you wanted to do, but it doesn't look as if you're doing it."

"We were interrupted," Wolfe told him.

"I see you were. Don't you think it would be a good idea to go ahead and pack and get started?"

"I do, yes. We'll get at it shortly. I'm glad you came, Mr. Pitcairn, because it provides an opportunity for a little chat. Of course you are under—"

"I don't feel like chatting," Donald said apologetically, and turned and left.

The door closed behind him and we heard his steps across the porch.

"See?" Gus demanded. "That's him to a T. Papa told him to come and chase you out, and did you hear him?"

"Yes, I heard him. With sensitive people you never know." Wolfe sighed. "We'd better get on, since I want to get back to the house before Mr. Pitcairn decides to come at us himself. What about him? Not what he's like, I've seen him and spoken with him, but the record—what you know of it. I got the impression this afternoon that he does not share his son's confusion about the sexes. He can tell a woman from a man?"

"I'll say he can." Gus laughed shortly. "With his eyes shut. From a mile off."

"You say that as if you could prove it."

Gus had his mouth open to go on, but he shut it. He cocked an eye at Wolfe, tossed me a glance, and regarded Wolfe again.

"Oh," he said. "Now you want me to prove things."

"Not at all. I don't even insist on facts. I'll take surmises—anything you have."

Gus was considering, rubbing the tips of his thumbs with his forefingers and scowling again. Finally he made a brusque gesture. "To hell with it," he decided. "I was sore at you for crossing Andy, and you don't owe him anything, and here look at me. There's other jobs. He choked a girl once."

"Mr. Pitcairn did?"

"Yes."

"Choked her to death?"

"Oh, no, just choked her. Her name's Florence Hefferan. Her folks used to live in a shack over on Greasy Hill, but now they've got a nice house and thirty acres down in the valley. I don't think it was Florence that used the pliers on him, or if she did her old man made her. I know for a fact it took twenty-one thousand dollars to get that thirty acres, and also Florence was by no means broke when she beat it to New York. If it didn't come from Pitcairn, then where? There are two versions about the choking. One is that he was nuts about her and he was jealous because he thought the baby she was going to have wasn't his—that's what Florence told her best friend, who is a friend of mine. The other is that he was sore because he was being forced to deliver some real dough—that came from Florence too, later, after she had gone to New York, I guess because she thought it sounded better. Anyhow I know he choked her enough to leave marks because I saw them."

"Well." Wolfe was looking as pleased as if someone had just presented him with thirty acres of orchids. "When did this happen?"

"About two years ago."

"Do you know where Miss Hefferan is now?"

"Sure, I can get her address in New York."

"Good." Wolfe wiggled a finger. "I said I wouldn't insist on proof, and I won't, but how much of this is fact and how much gossip?"

"No gossip at all. It's straight fact."

"Has any of it ever been published? For instance, in a newspaper reporting a proceeding in a court?"

Gus shook his head. "It wasn't in a court. How would it get in a court when he paid forty or fifty thousand to keep it out?"

"Just so, but I wanted to be sure. Were these facts generally known and discussed in the neighborhood?"

"Well—not known, no." Gus gestured. "Of course there was some talk, but only two or three really knew what happened, and I happened to be one of them because of my friend being Florence's best friend. And I didn't help start any talking. I've never opened my trap about it until now, and I told you only to help Andy, but damned if I see how it's going to."

"I do," Wolfe said emphatically. "Has Mr. Pitcairn been helpful in any other real estate deals?"

"Not that I know of. He must have lost his head that time. But it's more a question of a guy's general approach, and I've seen him performing with house guests here. What I can say for sure is that his son didn't catch it from him. I don't know why—when a man starts turning gray why don't he realize the whistle has blowed and concentrate on something else? Take you, you show some gray. I'll bet you don't dash around crowing and flapping your arms."

I tittered without meaning to. Wolfe gave me a withering glance and then returned to Gus.

"No, Mr. Treble, I don't. But while your general observations are interesting and sound, they won't help me any. I can use only specific items. I need scandal, all I can get. More about Mr. Pitcairn, I hope?"

But apparently Gus had shot his main wad. He had a further collection of details pertaining to Joseph G., and he was now more than willing to turn the bag up and shake it, but it didn't seem to me to advance Pitcairn's promotion to the grade of murder suspect. For one thing, there wasn't even a morsel about him and Dini Lauer, though, as Gus pointed out, he was an outside man and therefore knew little of what went on in the house.

Finally Wolfe waved Pitcairn aside and asked, "What about his wife? I haven't heard her mentioned more than twice all day. What's she like?"

"She's all right," Gus said shortly. "Forget her."

"Why, is she above reproach?"

"She's a nice woman. She's all right."

"Was her accident really an accident?"

"Certainly it was. She was alone, going down the stone steps into the rose garden, and she took a tumble, that was all."

"How much is she hurt?"

"I guess it was pretty bad, but it's getting better now, so she can sit in a chair and walk a little. Andy's been going up to her room every day for orders—only she don't give orders. She discusses things."

Wolfe nodded. "I can see you like her, but even so there's a question. What valid evidence have you that she is incapable of carrying an object weighing a hundred and ten pounds down a flight of stairs and into the greenhouse?"

"Oh, skip it," Gus said scornfully. "Hell, she broke her back!"

"Very well," Wolfe conceded. "But you should consider that whoever drugged Miss Lauer and carried her through the house was under a pressure that demanded superhuman effort. I advise you never to try your hand at detective work. At least you can tell me where Mrs. Pitcairn's room—no." He wiggled a finger. "Is there paper in that desk? And a pencil?"

"Sure."

"Please sketch me a plan of the house—ground plans of both floors. I heard it described this afternoon, but I want to be sure I have it right. Just roughly, but identify all the rooms."

Gus obliged. He got a pad and pencil from a drawer and set to work. The pencil moved fast. In no time he had two sheets torn from the pad and crossed over to hand them to Wolfe, and told him, "I didn't show the back stairs leading up to the room where Mr. and Mrs. Imbrie sleep, but the little passage upstairs goes there too."

Wolfe glanced at the sheets, folded them, and stuck them in his pocket. "Thank you, sir," he said graciously. "You have been—"

What stopped him was the sound of heavy steps on the porch. I got up to go and open the door, not waiting for a knock, but there was no knock. Instead, there was the noise of a key inserted and turned, the door swung open, and a pair entered.

It was Lieutenant Noonan and one of the rank and file.

"Who the hell," he demanded, "do you think you are?"

VII

Gus was on his feet. I whirled and stood. Wolfe spoke from his chair.

"Of course, Mr. Noonan, if that was a rhetorical—"

"Can it. I know damn well who you are. You're a Broadway slickie that thinks you can come up to Westchester and tell us the rules. Get going! Come on. Move out."

"I have Mr. Pitcairn's permission—"

"You have like hell. He just phoned me. And you're taking nothing from this cottage. You may have them buffaloed down in New York, and even the DA and the county boys, but I'm different. Do you want to go without help?"

Wolfe put his hands on the arms of his chair, got his bulk lifted, said, "Come, Archie," got his hat and coat and cane, and made for the door. There he turned, said grimly, "I hope to see you again, Mr. Treble," and was saved the awkwardness of reaching for the knob by my being there to open for him. Outside I got the flashlight from my hip pocket, switched it on, and led the way.

As we navigated the path for the fourth time there were seven or eight things I would have liked to say, but I swallowed them. Noonan and his bud were at our heels and, since Wolfe had evidently decided that we were outmatched, there was nothing for me to do but take it. When, after we were beyond the grove of evergreens, I swung the light up for a glance at the tennis court, there was a deep growl from Wolfe behind, so from there on I kept the light on the path.

We crunched across the gravel to where we had left the car. As I opened the rear door for Wolfe to get in, Noonan, right at my elbow, spoke.

"I'm being generous. I could phone the DA and get an okay to take you in as material witnesses, but you see I'm not. Our car's in front. Stop at the entrance until we're behind. We're going to follow until you're out of the county, and we won't need you back here again tonight or any other time. Got it?"

No reply. I banged the door, opened the front one, slid in behind the wheel, and pushed the starter.

"Got it?" he barked.

"Yes," Wolfe said.

They strode off and we rolled forward. When we reached the entrance to the Pitcairn grounds and stopped, the accomplice Noonan had stationed there flashed a light at us but said nothing.

I told Wolfe over my shoulder, "I'll turn right and go north. It's only ten miles to Brewster, and that's in Putnam County. He only said to leave the county, he didn't say which way."

"Turn left and go to New York."

"But—"

"Don't argue."

So when their lights showed behind I rolled on into the highway and turned left. When we had covered a couple of miles Wolfe spoke again.

"Don't try to be witty. No side roads, no sudden changes of pace, and no speeding. It would be foolhardy. That man is an irresponsible maniac and capable of anything."

I had no comment because I had to agree. We were flat on our faces. So I took the best route to Hawthorne Circle and there, with the enemy right behind, swung into the Sawmill River Parkway. The dashboard clock said a quarter to seven. My biggest trouble was that I couldn't see Wolfe's face. If he was holding on and working, fine. If he was merely nervous and tense against the terrific extra hazards of driving after dark, maybe okay. But if he had settled for getting back home and that was all, I should be talking fast and I wanted to. I couldn't tell. I had never realized how much I depended on the sight of his big creased face.

We made the first traffic light in eleven minutes from Hawthorne Circle, which was par. It was green and we sailed through. Four minutes farther on, at the second light, we were stopped by red, and Noonan's car practically bumped our behind. Off again, we climbed the hills over Yonkers, wound down into the valley and the stretch approaching the toll gates, parted with a dime, and in another mile were passing the sign that announces New York City.

I kept to the right and slowed down a little. If he once got inside his house I knew of no tool that could pry him loose again, but we were now only twenty-five minutes away and from where I sat it looked hopeless.

However, I slowed to thirty and spoke. "We've left Westchester, and Noonan is gone. They turned off back there. That's as far as my orders go. Next?"

"Where are we?"

"Riverdale."

"How soon will we get home?"

But there I fooled you. That's what I was sure he would say, but he didn't. What he said was, "How can we get off of this race course?"

"Easy. That's what the steering wheel's for."

"Then leave it and find a telephone."

I never heard anything like it. At the next opening I left the highway, followed the side drive a couple of blocks and turned right, and rolled up a hill and then down. I was a stranger in the Riverdale section, but anybody can find a drugstore anywhere, and soon I pulled up at the curb in front of one.

I asked if he was going in to phone and he said no, I was. I turned in the seat to get a look at him.

"I don't know, Archie," he said, "whether you have ever seen me when my mind was completely dominated by a single purpose."

"Sure I have. I've rarely seen you any other way. The purpose has always been to keep comfortable."

"It isn't now. It is—never mind. A purpose is something to achieve, not talk about. Get Saul if possible. Fred or Orrie would do, but I'd rather have Saul. Tell him to come at once and meet us—where can we meet?"

"Around here?"

"Yes. Between here and White Plains."

"He's to have a car?"

"Yes."

"The Covered Porch near Scarsdale would do."

"Tell him that. Phone Fritz that we are still delayed and ask him how things are. That's all."

I got out, but even at a risk I wanted to have it understood, so I poked my head in and asked, "What about dinner? Fritz will want to know."

"Tell him we won't be there. I've already faced that. My purpose is enough to keep me from going home, but I wouldn't trust it to get me out again if I once got in."

Evidently he knew himself nearly as well as I knew him. I entered the drugstore and found the booth.

I got Fritz first. He thought I was kidding him, and then, when I made it plain that I was serious, he suspected me of concealing a calamity. He simply couldn't believe that Wolfe was a free man and sound of mind and body, and yet wasn't coming home to dinner. It looked for a while as if I would have to go and bring Wolfe to the phone, but I finally convinced him, and then went after Saul.

As Wolfe had said, Fred or Orrie would do, but Saul Panzer was worth ten of them or nearly anyone else, and I had a feeling that we were going to need the best we could get for whatever act Wolfe was preparing to put on to achieve his dominant purpose. So when I learned that Saul wasn't home but was expected sometime, I gave his wife the number and told her I would wait for a call. It was so long before it came that when I went back out to the car I expected Wolfe to make some pointed remarks, but all he did was grunt. The purpose sure was dominant. I told him that from Saul's home in Brooklyn it would take him a good hour and a quarter to drive to the rendezvous, whereas we could make it easy in thirty minutes. Did he have any use for the extra time? No, he said, we would go and wait, so I got the car moving and headed for the parkway.

When, a little before nine o'clock, Saul Panzer joined us at the Covered Porch, we were at a table in a rear corner, as far as we could get from the band. Wolfe had cleaned up two dozen large oysters, tried a plate of clam chowder and swallowed five spoonfuls of it, disposed of a slice of rare roast beef with no vegetables, and was starting to work on a pile of zwieback and a dish of grape jelly. He hadn't made a single crack about the grub.

By the time Wolfe had finished the zwieback and jelly and had coffee Saul had made a good start on a veal cutlet. Wolfe said he would wait until Saul was through, but Saul said no, go ahead, he liked to hear things while he ate. Wolfe proceeded. First he described the past, enough of it to give Saul the picture, and then gave us a detailed outline of the future as he saw it. It took quite a while, for he had to brief us on all foreseeable contingencies. One of them was the possibility that the key tagged "Dup Grnhs" which was in my pocket wouldn't fit. Another prop was the sketch made by Gus Treble of the ground plans of the mansion. Saul transferred it to his head, but Wolfe told him to keep the sketch. Still another prop was a sheet of plain white paper, donated on request by the management of the Covered Porch, on which Wolfe wrote a couple of paragraphs with my fountain pen. That too was for Saul, and he put it in his pocket.

It sounded to me as if the whole conception was absolutely full of fleas, but I let it pass. If Wolfe was man enough to stay away from dinner at his own table, damned if I was going to heckle just because it looked as if we stood a very fine chance of joining Andy in jail before midnight. The only item I pressed him on was the gun play.

"On that," I told him, "I want it A, B, C. When you're in the cell next to mine, on a five-year ticket, I won't have you keep booming at me that I bollixed it up with the gun. Do I shoot at all and if so when?"

"I don't know," he said patiently. "There are too many eventualities. Use your judgment."

"What if someone makes a dash for a phone?"

"Head him off. Stop him. Hit him."

"What if someone starts to scream?"

"Make her stop."

I gave up. I like to have him depend on me, but I only have two hands and I can't be two places at once.

The arrangement was that Saul was to follow us in his car because it would be useful for a preliminary approach. It was after ten when we rolled out of the parking lot of the Covered Porch and turned north. When I pulled off the road at a wide place, in the enemy country, the dashboard clock said twelve minutes to eleven, and it had started to snow a little. Saul's car had stopped behind us.

I turned off the lights, got out and went back, and told him, "Half a mile on, maybe a little more, at the left. You can't miss the big stone pillars."

He swung his car back into the road and was off. I returned to our car and climbed in, and turned to face the rear because I thought a little cheerful conversation was called for, but Wolfe wouldn't cooperate, and I well knew why. He was holding his breath until he learned whether Saul would bring good news or bad. Would we be able to drive right in and make ourselves at home? Or . . . ?

The news wasn't long in coming, and it was bad. Saul's car came back, turned around, and parked close behind us, and Saul came to us with snow-flakes whirling around him and announced, "He's still there."

"What happened?" Wolfe demanded peevishly.

"I turned in at the entrance, snappy, and he flashed a light at me and yelled. I told him I was a newspaperman from New York, and he said then I'd better get back where I belonged quick because it was snowing. I tried a little persuasion to stay in character, but he was in a bad humor. So I backed out."

"Confound it." Wolfe was grim. "I have no rubbers."

VIII

BEFORE we got to the Pitcairn greenhouse Wolfe fell down twice, I fell four times, and Saul once. My better score, a clear majority, was because I was in the lead.

Naturally we couldn't show a light, and while the snow was a help in one way, in another it made it harder, since enough of it had fallen to cover the ground and therefore you couldn't see ups and downs. For walking in the dark without making much noise levelness is a big advantage, and there was none of it around there at all, at least not on the route we took.

It had to be all by guess. We left the road and took to the jungle a good three hundred yards short of the entrance, to give the guy in bad humor a wide miss. Almost right away we were mountain climbing, and I slipped on a stone someone had waxed and went down, grabbing for a tree and missing.

"Look out, a stone," I whispered.

"Shut up," Wolfe hissed.

Just when I had got used to the slope up, the terrain suddenly went haywire and began to wiggle, bobbing up and down. After a stretch of that it went level, but just as it did so the big trees quit and I was stopped by a thicket which I might possibly have pushed through but Wolfe never could, so I had to detour. The thicket forced me around to the rim of a steep decline, though I didn't know it until my feet told me three times. It was at the foot of that decline that we struck the brook. I realized what the dark streak was only when I was on its sloping edge, sliding in, and I leaped like a tiger, barely reaching the far bank and going to my knees as I landed, which I didn't count as a fall. As I got upright I was wondering how in God's name we would get Wolfe across, but then I saw he was already coming, wading it, trying to hold the skirt of his coat up with one hand and poking his cane ahead of him with the other.

I have admitted I'm no woodsman, and I sure proved it that dark night. I suppose I didn't subtract enough for the curves of the driveway. I had it figured that we would emerge into the open about even with the house, on the side where the greenhouse was. But after we had negotiated a few more mountains, and a dozen more twigs had stuck me in the eye, and I had had all my tumbles, and Wolfe had rolled down a cliff to a stop at Saul's feet, and I was wishing the evergreens weren't so damn thick so I could see the lights of the house, I suddenly realized we had hit a path, and after I had turned left on it and gone thirty steps its course seemed familiar. When we reached the edge of the evergreens and saw the house lights there was no question about it: it was the path we knew.

From there on the going was easy and, since the snow was coming thicker, no belly crawling seemed called for as we neared the house. When we reached the spot where the path branched to the left, toward the south of the house, I turned and asked Wolfe, "Okay?"

"Shut up and go on," he growled.

I did so. We reached the greenhouse at its outer end. I took the key from my pocket and inserted it, and it worked like an angel. I carefully pushed the door open, and we entered, and I got the door shut with no noise. So far so good. We were in the workroom. But was it dark!

According to plan, we took off our snow-covered coats and dropped them on the floor, and our hats. I didn't know until later that Wolfe hung onto his cane, probably to use on people who screamed or dashed for a phone. I led the way again, with Wolfe against my back and Saul against his, through into the cool room, but it wasn't cool, it was hot. It was ticklish going down the alley between the benches, and I learned something new: that with all lights out in a glass house on a snowy night the glass is absolutely black.

We made it without displacing any horticulture, and on through the warm room, which was even hotter, into the medium room. When I judged that we were about in the middle of it I went even slower, stopping every couple of feet to feel at the bottom of the bench on my left. Soon I felt the beginning of the canvas, and got hold of Wolfe's hand and guided him to it. He followed me on a little, and then together we pulled the canvas up and Saul crawled under and stretched out where the body of Dini Lauer had been. Unable to see him, I felt him to make sure he was under before I let the canvas fall. Then Wolfe and I moved on to the open space beyond the end of the benches.

By now it was sure enough that there was no one in the dark greenhouse, and whispers would have been perfectly safe, but there was nothing to say. I took my gun from the holster and dropped it in my side pocket, and moved to the door that opened into the living room, with Wolfe beside me. It was a well-fitted door, but there was a tiny thread of light along the bottom. Now our meanest question would be answered: was the door locked on the inside? I heard the sound of voices beyond the thick door, and that helped. With a firm grasp on the knob, I turned it at about the speed of the minute hand on a clock, and when it came to a stop I pushed slow and easy. It wasn't locked.

"Here we go," I muttered to Wolfe, and flung the door open and stepped in.

The first swift glance showed me we were lucky. All three of them were there in the living room—Joseph G., daughter, and son—and that was a real break. Another break was the way their reflexes took the sight of the gun in my hand. One or more might easily have let out a yell, but no, all three were stunned into silence. Sybil was propped against cushions on a divan with a highball glass in her hand. Donald was on a nearby chair, also with a drink. Papa was on his feet, and he was the only one who had moved, whirling to face us as he heard the door open.

"Everybody hold it," I told them quick, "and no one gets hurt."

The noise from Joseph G. sounded like the beginning of an outraged giggle. Sybil put hers in words.

"Don't you dare shoot! You wouldn't dare shoot!"

Wolfe was moving past me, approaching them, but I extended my left arm to stop him. Shooting was the last thing I wanted, by me or anyone else, since a yell might or might not have been heard by the law out at the entrance but a shot almost certainly would. I stepped across to Joseph G., poked the gun against him, rubbed his pockets, and went to Donald and repeated. I would just as soon have given Sybil's blue dinner dress a rub, but it would have been hard to justify it.

"Okay," I told Wolfe.

"This is a criminal act," Pitcairn stated. The words were virile enough, but his voice squeaked.

Wolfe, who had approached him, shook his head. "I don't think so," he said conversationally. "We had a key. I admit that Mr. Goodwin's flourishing a gun complicates matters, but anyway, all I want is a talk with you people. I asked for it this afternoon and was refused. Now I intend to have it."

"You won't get it." Pitcairn's eyes went to his son. "Donald, go to the front door and call that officer."

"I'm still flourishing the gun," I said, doing so. "I can use it either to slap with or shoot with, and if I didn't intend to when necessary I wouldn't have it."

"More corn," Sybil said scornfully. She hadn't moved from her comfortable position against the cushions. "Do you actually expect us to sit here and converse with you at the point of a gun?"

"No," Wolfe told her. "The gun is childish, of course. That was merely a formality. I expect you to converse with me for reasons which it will take a few minutes to explain. May I sit down?"

Father, daughter, and son said "No" simultaneously.

Wolfe went to a wide upholstered number and sat. "I must overrule you," he said, "because this is an emergency. I had to wade your confounded brook." He bent over and unlaced a shoe and pulled it off, did likewise with the other one, took off his socks, pulled his wet trousers up nearly to his knees, and then leaned to the right to get hold of the corner of a small rug.

"I'm afraid I've dripped a little," he apologized, wrapping the rug around his feet and calves.

"Wonderful," Sybil said appreciatively. "You think we won't drive you out into the snow barefooted."

"Then he's wrong," Pitcairn said furiously. His squeak was all gone.

"I'll get him a drink," Donald offered, moving.

"No," I said firmly, also moving. "You'll stay right here." I still had the formality in my right hand.

"I think, Archie," Wolfe told me, "you can put that thing in your pocket. We'll soon know whether we stay or go." He glanced around at them, ending with Joseph G. "Here are your alternatives. Either we remain here until we are ready to leave, and are allowed a free hand for our inquiry into the murder of Miss Lauer on these premises, or I go, return to my office in New York—"

"No, you don't," Pitcairn contradicted. He remained standing even after his guest was seated. "You go to jail."

Wolfe nodded. "If you insist, certainly. But that will merely postpone my return to my office until I get bail, which won't take long. Once there, I act. I announce that I am convinced of Mr. Krasicki's innocence and that I intend to get him freed by finding and exposing the culprit. There are at least three papers that will consider that newsworthy and will want to help. All the inmates of this house will become legitimate objects of inquiry and public report. Anything in their past that could conceivably have a bearing on their guilt or innocence will be of interest and printable."

"Aha," Sybil said disdainfully, still reclining.

"The devil of it," Wolfe went on, ignoring her, "is that everyone has a past. Take this case. Take the question of Mr. Hefferan's purchase of a home and acres surrounding it, only a few miles from here. I'm sure you remember the name—Hefferan. Where did he get the money? Where did a certain member of his family go to, and why? The newspapers will want all the facts they can get, all the more since their employees are not permitted to enter these grounds. I shall be glad to cooperate, and I have had some experience at investigation."

Joseph G. had advanced a step and then stiffened. Sybil had left the cushions to sit up straight.

"Such facts," Wolfe went on, "would of course never properly get to a jury trying a man for the murder of Miss Lauer, but they would be of valid concern to the unofficial explorers of probabilities, and the public would like to know about them. They would like to know whether Miss Florence Hefferan still feels any discomfort from the severe choking she got, and whether the marks have entirely disappeared from her throat. They would want to see pictures of her in newspapers, the more the better. They would—"

"You filthy fat louse!" Sybil cried.

Wolfe shook his head at her. "Not I, Miss Pitcairn. This is the inexorable miasma of murder."

"By God," Pitcairn said harshly. He was shaking with fury and trying not to. "I wish I had shot you there today. I wish I had."

"But you didn't," Wolfe said curtly, "and here I am. You will have no secrets left, none of you. If Miss Hefferan has run through the money you paid her and needs more, there will be generous bidders for the story of her life in installments. You see the possibilities. There will even be interest in such details as your daughter's incorrigible talent for picking quarrels, and your son's nomadic collegiate career. Did he leave Yale and Williams and Cornell because the curriculum didn't suit him, or because—"

Without the slightest warning Donald abruptly changed moods. After bouncing up to offer to get Wolfe a drink he had returned to his chair and seemed to be put, but now he came out of it fast and made for Wolfe. I had to step some to head him off. He came against me, recoiled, and started a right for the neighborhood of my jaw. The quicker it was settled the better, so instead of trying anything fancy I knocked his fist down with my left, and with my right slammed the gun flat against his kidney good and hard. He wobbled, then bent, and doubled up to sit on the floor. I disregarded him to face the others, not at all sure of their limitations.

"Stop!" a voice came from somewhere. "Stop it!"

Their eyes left the casualty to turn to the voice. A woman had come from behind some drapes at the side of a wide arch at the far end of the room, and was approaching with slow careful steps. Sybil let out a cry and rushed to her. Joseph G. went too. They got to the newcomer and each took an arm, both talking at once, one scolding and the other remonstrating. They wanted to know how she got downstairs. They wanted to turn her around, but nothing doing. She kept coming, them with her, until she was only a step away from her son, who was still sitting on the floor. She looked down at him and then turned to me.

"How much did you hurt him?"

"Not much," I told her. "He'll be a little sore for a day or two."

Donald lifted his face to speak. "I'm all right, Mom. But did you hear what—"

"Yes, I heard everything."

"You come back upstairs," Joseph G. commanded her.

She paid no attention to him. She was no great treat to look at—short and fairly plump, with a plain round face, standing with her shoulders pulled back, probably on account of her injured back—but there was something to her, especially to her voice, which seemed to come from deeper than her throat.

"I've been standing too long," she said.

Sybil started to guide her to the divan, but she said no, she preferred a chair, and let herself be helped to one and to sit, after it had been moved so that she would be facing Wolfe.

Donald, who had managed to get himself back on his feet, went and patted her on the shoulder and told her, "I'm all right, Mom."

She paid no attention to him either. She was gazing straight at Wolfe.

"You're Nero Wolfe," she told him.

"Yes," he acknowledged. "And you're Mrs. Pitcairn?"

"Yes. Of course I've heard of you, Mr. Wolfe, since you are extremely famous. Under different circumstances I would be quite excited about meeting you. I was behind those curtains, listening, and heard all that you said. I quite agree with you, though certainly you know a great deal more about murder investigations than I do. I can see what we have ahead of us, all of us, if a ruthless and thorough inquiry is started, and naturally I'd like to prevent it if I possibly can. I have money of my own, aside from my husband's fortune, and I think we should have someone to protect us from the sort of thing you described, and certainly no one is better qualified than you. I would like to pay you fifty thousand dollars to do that for us. Half would be paid—"

"Belle, I warn you—" Joseph G. blurted, and stopped.

"Well?" she asked him calmly, and when she had waited for him a moment and he was silent, she went on to Wolfe.

"Certainly it would be foolish to pretend that it wouldn't be well worth it to us. As you say, everyone has a past, and it is our misfortune that this terrible crime in our house has made us, again as you say, legitimate objects of inquiry. Half of the fifty thousand will be paid immediately, and the other half when—well, that can be agreed upon."

This, I thought, is more like it. We now have our pick of going to jail or taking fifty grand.

Wolfe was frowning at her. "But," he objected, "I thought you said that you heard all I said."

"I did."

"Then you missed the point. The only reason I'm here is that I'm convinced that Mr. Krasicki did not kill Miss Lauer, and how the devil can I protect him and you people too? No; I'm sorry, madam; it's true that I came here to blackmail you, but not for money. I've stated my price: permission to remain here, with Mr. Goodwin, and so make my inquiry privately instead of returning to my office and starting the hullabaloo you heard me describe. For as brief a period as possible; I don't want to stay away from home longer than I have to. I shall expect nothing unreasonable of any of you, but I can't very well inquire unless I am to get answers—as I say, within reason."

"A dirty incorruptible blackmailer," Sybil said bitterly.

"You said a brief period," Donald told Wolfe. "Until tomorrow noon."

"No." Wolfe was firm. "I can't set an hour. But I don't want to prolong it any more than you do."

"If necessary," Mrs. Pitcairn persisted, "I think I could make it more than I said. Much more. I can say definitely that it will be double that." She was as stubborn as a woman, and she sure was willing to dig into her capital.

"No, madam. I told Mr. Goodwin this evening that my mind was dominated by a single purpose, and it is. I did not go home to dinner. I fought my way through a snowstorm, at night, over strange and difficult terrain. I entered by force, supported by Mr. Goodwin's gun. Now I'm going to stay until I'm through, or—you know the alternative."

Mrs. Pitcairn looked at her husband and son and daughter. "I tried," she said quietly.

Joseph G. sat down for the first time and fastened his eyes on Wolfe's face. "Inquire," he said harshly.

"Good." Wolfe heaved a deep sigh. "Please get Mr. and Mrs. Imbrie. I'll need all of you."

IX

FOR the last several minutes, since it had become evident that we were going to be invited to spend the night, I had had a new worry. The plan was that as soon as possible after we had got the halter on them Wolfe would get them all into the kitchen, to show him where Mrs. Imbrie had kept her box of morphine pills, and it seemed to me that the appearance of Mrs. Pitcairn had turned that from a chore into a real problem. How could he expect a woman with a bum back to get up from a chair and go to the kitchen with him just to point to a spot on a shelf, when three other people were available, all perfectly capable of pointing?

Or rather, five other people, when Mr. and Mrs. Imbrie had come. She was in a kind of dressing gown instead of her uniform, but he had got into his butler's outfit, and I decided I liked him better in his greasy coveralls. They both looked scared and sleepy, and not a bit enthusiastic. As soon as they were with us Wolfe said he wanted to see where Mrs. Imbrie had kept the box of morphine, and that he would like all of them to come along. His tone indicated that he fully expected to be able to tell from the expressions on their faces which one had snitched the morphine to dope Dini Lauer.

The way they responded showed that my psychology needed overhauling and I shouldn't have worried. Guilty or innocent, granted that the guilty one was present, obviously they thought this was a cinch and what a relief it wasn't starting any tougher. There wasn't even any protest about Mrs. Pitcairn exerting herself, except a question from Sybil.

As they started off, Wolfe in his bare feet, he paused to speak to me.

"Archie, will you put my socks near a radiator to dry? You can wring them out in the greenhouse."

So I was left behind. I picked up the socks, and as soon as they were out of the room I darted into the greenhouse, leaving the door open, wrung out the socks with one quick twist over the soil of the bench, stooped to lift the canvas, and muttered, "You awake, Saul?"

"Nuts," he hissed.

"Okay, come on. Mrs. Pitcairn is with us. Don't stop to shut the door after you."

I returned to the living room, crossed to the open door by which the others had left, stood with my back to the voices I could hear in the distance, and watched Saul enter, cross to another door at the far end, which led to the reception hall, and disappear. Then I went and hung the socks on the frame of a magazine rack near a radiator grille, and beat it to the kitchen.

They were gathered around an open cupboard door. After exchanging glances with me Wolfe brought that phase of the investigation to a speedy end and suggested a return to the living room. On the way there Sybil insisted that her mother should go back upstairs, but didn't get far. Mrs. Pitcairn was sticking, and I privately approved. Not only did it leave Saul an open field, but it guaranteed him what he needed most—time. Even if they had wanted to adjourn until morning Wolfe could probably have held them, but it was better this way.

"Now," Wolfe said, when he had got settled in the chair of his choice again with the rug around his feet, "look at it like this. If the police were not completely satisfied with Mr. Krasicki they would be here asking you questions, and you wouldn't like it but you couldn't help it. You are compelled to suffer my inquisition for quite a different reason from the one that would operate in the case of the police, but the result is the same. I ask you questions you don't like, and you answer them as you think best. The police always expect a large percentage of the answers to be lies and evasions, and so do I, but that's my lookout. Any fool could solve the most difficult of cases if everyone told the truth. Mr. Imbrie, did you ever hold Miss Lauer in your arms?"

Imbrie, with no hesitation and in a voice unnecessarily loud, said, "Yes!"

"You did? When?"

"Once in this room, because I thought she wanted me to, and she knew my wife was watching us and I didn't. So I thought I would try it."

"That's a lie!" Vera Imbrie said indignantly.

So the first crack out of the box he had one of them calling another a liar.

Neil spoke sternly to his wife. "I'm telling you, Vera, the only thing to do is tell it straight. When the cops left I thought it was all over, but I know about this man and he's tough. We're not going to do any monkeying about murder. How do I know who else saw me? I'm not going to tell him no, I never went near that girl, and then have someone else say they saw me."

"That's the spirit," Sybil said sarcastically. "We'll all confess everything. You lead the way, Neil."

But within three minutes Neil was lying, saying that his wife hadn't minded a bit catching him trying to make a pass at Dini Lauer. He maintained that she had just passed it off as a good joke.

It went on for over two hours, until my wristwatch said five minutes to

three, and I'm not saying it was dull because it was interesting to watch
Wolfe bouncing the ball, first against one and then another, and it was
equally interesting to see them handling the returns. But though it wasn't
dull it certainly didn't seem to me that it was getting us anywhere, particularly when Wolfe was specializing in horticulture. He spent about a third
of the time finding out how they felt about plants and flowers, and actually
got into an argument with Joseph G. about hairy begonias. It was obvious
what he had in mind, but no matter what they said it wasn't worth a damn
as evidence, and I suspected him of merely passing the time waiting for
Saul, and hoping against hope as the minutes dragged by.

Aside from horticulture he concentrated mainly on the character and
characteristics of Dini Lauer. He tried over and over again to get them
started on a free-for-all discussion of her, but they refused to oblige, even
Neil Imbrie. He couldn't even get a plain unqualified statement that Sybil
would have preferred to take care of her mother herself, their position apparently being that if they gave him an inch he'd want a mile. He certainly
didn't get the inch.

As I glanced at my watch at five to three Wolfe pronounced my name.

"Archie. Are my socks dry?"

I went and felt them and told him just about, and he asked me to bring
them to him. As he was pulling the first one on Mrs. Pitcairn spoke.

"Don't bother with the wet shoes, since you're going to sleep here. Vera,
there's a pair of slippers—"

"No, thank you," Wolfe said energetically. He got the other sock on and
picked up a shoe. "Thank heaven I get them big enough." He got his toes
in, tugged and pushed, finally got the shoe on and tied the lace, and
straightened up to rest. In a moment he tackled the second shoe. By the
time he got it on the silence was as heavy as if the ceiling had come down
to rest on our heads.

Pitcairn undertook to lift it. "It's nearly morning," he rasped. "We're going
to bed. This has become a ridiculous farce."

Wolfe sighed from all the exertion. "It has been a farce from the beginning," he declared. He looked around at them. "But I didn't make it a farce,
you did. My position is clear, logical, and invulnerable. The circumstances
of Miss Lauer's death—the use of Mrs. Imbrie's morphine, the preknowledge
of the fumigation, and others—made it unarguable that she was killed by a
familiar of these premises. Convinced with good reason, as I was and am,
that Mr. Krasicki didn't do it, it followed that one of you did. There we
were and there we are. I had no notion who it was; I forced my way in here
to find out; and I'm going to stay until I do—or until you expel me and face
the alternative I have described. I am your dangerous and implacable enemy. I have had you together; now I'll take you one by one; and I'll start

with Mrs. Pitcairn. It will soon be dawn. Do you want to take a nap first, madam?"

Mrs. Pitcairn was actually trying to smile. "I'm afraid," she said in a firm full voice, "that I made a mistake when I offered to pay you to protect us from publicity. I'm afraid it made a bad impression on you. If you misunderstood—*who is that?*"

It was Saul Panzer, entering from behind the drapes where she had previously concealed herself for eavesdropping. He was right on the dot, since the arrangement had been for him to walk on at three o'clock unless he got a signal.

Most of us could get our eyes on him without turning, but Wolfe, in his chair with a high wide back, had to lean over and screw his head around. While he was doing that Donald was rising to his feet, and Joseph G. and Imbrie were both moving. I moved faster. When I had passed them I whirled and snapped, "Take it easy. He came with us and he don't bite."

They started ejaculating and demanding. Wolfe ignored them and asked Saul, "Did you find anything?"

"Yes, sir."

"Useful?"

"I think so, yes, sir." Saul extended a hand with a piece of folded paper in it.

Wolfe took it and commanded me, "Archie, your gun."

I already had it out. It wasn't desirable to have them anywhere near Wolfe while he examined Saul's find. I poked the barrel against Joseph G. and told him, "More formality. Back up."

He was still ejaculating but he went back, and the others with him, and I turned sideways enough to have all in view. Wolfe had unfolded the sheet of paper and was reading it. Saul was at his right hand, and he too was displaying a gun.

Wolfe looked up. "I should explain," he said, "how this happened. This is Mr. Saul Panzer, who works for me. When you went to the kitchen with me he entered from the greenhouse, went upstairs, and began to search. I was not satisfied that the police had been sufficiently thorough." He fluttered the paper. "This proves me right. Where did you find it, Saul?"

"I found it," Saul said distinctly, "under the mattress on the bed in the room of Mr. and Mrs. Imbrie."

Vera and Neil both made noises, and Neil came forward to where my arm stopped him.

"Take it easy," I advised him. "He didn't say who put it there, he just said where he found it."

"What is it?" Mrs. Pitcairn inquired, her voice not quite as firm.

"I'll read it," Wolfe told her. "As you see, it's a sheet of paper. The writing is in ink, and I would judge the hand to be feminine. It is dated December sixth, yesterday—no, since it's past midnight, the day before yesterday. It says:

"Dear Mr. Pitcairn:

"I suppose now I will never call you Joe, as you wanted me to. I am quite willing to put my request in writing, and I only hope you will put your answer in writing too. As I told you, I think your gift to me should be twenty thousand dollars. You have been so very sweet, but I have been sweet too, and I really think I deserve that much.

"Since I have decided to leave here and get married I don't think you should expect me to wait more than a day or two for the gift. I'll expect you in my room tonight at the usual time, and I hope you'll agree how reasonable I am."

Wolfe looked up. "It's signed 'Dini,'" he stated. "Of course it can be authenti—"

"I never saw it!" Vera Imbrie cried. "I never—"

But her lines got stolen. For my part, I didn't even give her a glance. Their faces had all been something to see while Wolfe had read, as might have been expected, but by the time he had reached the third sentence it was plain that Donald was in for something special in the way of moods. First his face froze, then it came loose and his mouth opened, and then the blood rushed up and it was purple. He was a quick-change artist if I ever saw one, and, as I say, I had no glance to spare for Vera Imbrie when she cried out. Then Donald took over.

"So that's why you wouldn't let me marry her!" he screamed, and jumped at his father.

I had the gun, sure, but that was for us, not for them if and when their ranks broke. The women were helpless, and Neil Imbrie would have had to be bigger and faster than he was to stop that cyclone.

Donald toppled his father to his knees more by bodily impact than by his swinging fists, kicked him down the rest of the way, and bent over him screaming, "You thought I was no man! But I was with her! I loved her! For the first time—I loved her! And you wouldn't let me and she was going away and now I know! By God, if I could kill her I can kill you too! I can! I can!"

It looked as if he might try to prove it, so I went and grabbed him, and Saul came to help.

"Oh, my son," Mrs. Pitcairn moaned.

Wolfe looked at her and growled, "Mr. Krasicki is a woman's son too, madam." I didn't think he had it in him.

X

At six o'clock the next afternoon but one I was at my desk in the office, catching up on neglected details, when I heard the sound of Wolfe's elevator descending from the plant rooms, and a moment later he entered, got himself comfortable in his chair back of his desk, rang for beer, leaned back, and sighed with deep satisfaction.

"How's Andy making out?" I asked.

"Considering the blow he got, marvelously."

I put papers in a drawer and swiveled to face him.

"I was just thinking," I said, not offensively, "that if it hadn't been for you Dini Lauer might still be alive and giving males ideas. Ben Dykes told me an hour ago on the phone that Donald has admitted, along with other things, that her telling him she was leaving and going to get married was what put him into a mood to murder. If you hadn't offered Andy a job he wanted to take he might not have got keyed up enough to talk her into marrying him—or anyhow saying she would. So in a way you might say you killed her."

"*You* might," Wolfe conceded, taking the cap from one of the bottles of beer Fritz had brought.

"By the way," I went on, "Dykes said that ape Noonan is still trying to get the DA to charge you for destroying evidence. Burning that letter you wrote to Pitcairn, signing Dini's name."

"Bah." He was pouring and watching the foam. "It wasn't evidence. No one even saw what was on it. It could have been blank. I merely read it to them—ostensibly."

"Yeah, I know. Anyhow the DA is in no position to charge you with anything, let alone destroying evidence. Not only has Donald told it and signed it, how she was his first and only romance, how his parents threatened to cross him off the list if he married her, how he begged her not to marry Andy and she laughed at him, how he got her to split a bottle of midnight beer with him and put morphine in hers, and even how he lugged her into the greenhouse to make it nice for Andy—not only that, but Vera Imbrie has contributed details of some contacts between Donald and Dini which she saw."

Wolfe put down the empty glass and got out his handkerchief to wipe his lips. "That of course will help," he said complacently.

I grunted. "Help is no word for it. Would it do any good to ask you exactly what the hell you would have done if they had all simply sneered when you read that letter?"

"Not much." He poured more beer. "I knew one of them was toeing a thin and precarious line, and probably more than one. I thought a good hard jolt would totter him or her, no matter who it was, and possibly others. That was why I had Saul find it in the Imbries' room; they had to be jolted too. If all of them had simply sneered, it would at least have eliminated Mr. Pitcairn and his son, and I would have proceeded from there. That would have been a measurable advance, since up to that point a finger pointed nowhere and I had eliminated no one but Andy, who—"

He stopped abruptly, pushed his chair back, arose, muttered, "Good heavens, I forgot to tell Andy about those Miltonia seedlings," and marched out.

I got up and went to the kitchen to chin with Fritz.